*Never before has the world seen his equal,*
*never again his like.*

# THE PENDRAGON

"For twenty years I, Bedivere, have kept the flame of Arthur's memory burning among his own people, in the hills and lonely places, in outlaw camps and roadside resthouses, in farmhouse kitchens and turf huts of the Hill People, with my harp's singing. Celidon the Merlin told me long ago that the fire in the heart of a nation can burn for a thousand years, if its harpers guard the spark.

"There are facts—yes. And there is memory's secret flame, and that is another matter. Back of it all, far away and clear, so clear now, like the reflection of bare branches in a windless lake, there is the truth of things as they actually happened, the truth that only those who were there can know, the reflection that will fade when darkness comes and be lost in the minds of the dead . . ."

*THUS BEGINS THE TRUE LIFE AND HISTORY OF ARTHUR, KING OF BRITAIN.*

## A Note About the Author

Catherine Christian has worked at different times as a journalist, magazine editor, museum curator and farmer, and during World War II served as organizing secretary to the Girl Guide Refugee Service. She is also the author of a number of adventure stories for children and several historical novels. She now lives in Devon and devotes her time to writing and gardening.

# The Pendragon

## Catherine Christian

WARNER BOOKS

A Warner Communications Company

This Warner Books Edition is published by arrangement with
Alfred A. Knopf, 201 East 50th Street, New York, N.Y.

*Cover art by Tom Hall*

Warner Books, Inc., 75 Rockefeller Plaza, New York, N.Y. 10019

A Warner Communications Company

Printed in the United States of America

First Printing: December, 1980

10 9 8 7 6 5 4 3 2 1

*Time was. Time is. Time shall be.*

# ACKNOWLEDGMENTS

I would like to thank all the people who, by encouragement, advice and criticism, have helped to make this book. My special thanks to Laurence Bendit, who first challenged me to write it; Moir and Angus Gordon, Alison Harvey, Allien Scott-Elliot and Elizabeth Bartlett, who shared the struggle of its writing; and Phyllis Jones, who typed the manuscript against formidable odds.

I would particularly like to put on record my gratitude to the staff of Totnes and Buckfastleigh branches of Devon County Library, who, with unfailing patience, courtesy and ingenuity over the years have traced and obtained for me so many rare and obscure books of reference.

*C. C.*

# Contents

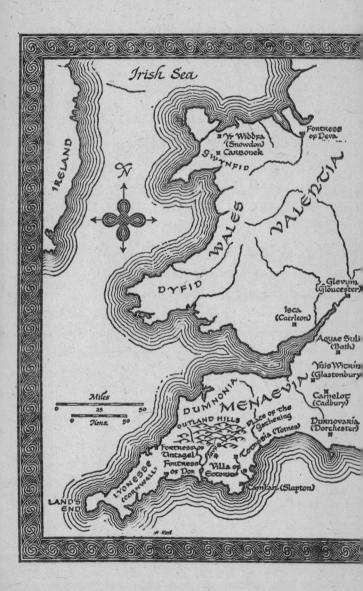

# The
# Pendragon

# I
# AUBADE

# Chapter One

It is twenty years since my lord Arthur, the king—the Pendragon—was carried to his secret resting place on this Island in the marshes.

Now I, the last, as I was once the first, of his Companions, lie in a quiet cell, and hear the white monks chant their Christmas midnight mass, and I know that I shall not again feel the world turn from the solstice of winter on towards the spring.

Snow lies deep on the sill, blue-shadowed in the moonlight, marked by the tiny tracks of the birds for whom Father Paulinus shakes out crumbs: the same snow that finally drove me from the roads I have been travelling for so long, to die like an old dog, close by my master's grave.

Paulinus is a good boy; an honest boy. He warned me fairly from the first that he was Saxon-born. I did not need to be told, for his accent grates on the ear. At a guess, listening to them singing tonight, half the brothers here share the same blood. Their abbot, who once, so long ago it seems another life, was Griffin, my freckled page, makes no distinction. He tells me, smiling (and the smile at least I remember), that Christ, like the emperors, is content to accept auxiliaries in his legions. What with wars and sickness and emigration, there are not many of the true Celtic blood left in these lowlands of Britain now.

When my wits are not wandering and I have voice

enough to dictate, Paulinus writes down what I can remember of the Matter of Britain. His kin burned our records when they sacked Camelot. I think he would like to make amends for that burning. Now they are conquerors and have no more need to fear him, the Saxons respect Arthur as a hero. They even, I believe, sing his story in their barbarous glee music, round the fires of evening.

So Paulinus, Saxon industrious, sits at the foot of my bed, with his inkhorn and his parchment, scratching swiftly, very anxious lest I die too soon, before his record is complete.

"Facts! All you need remember are the *facts,* my lord Bedivere. Don't tire yourself. All we need to record are the facts."

Facts? What are facts? A centurion's report. The sort of report Theodoric the Goth taught me to make half a century ago and half a world away.

For twenty years I, Bedivere, have kept the flame of Arthur's memory burning among his own people, in the hills and lonely places, in outlaw camps and roadside resthouses, in farmhouse kitchens and turf huts of the Hill People, with my harp's singing. Celidon the Merlin taught me long ago that the fire in the heart of a nation can burn for a thousand years, if its harpers guard the spark.

There are facts—yes. And there is memory's secret flame, and that is another matter. Back of it all, far away and clear, so clear now, like the reflection of bare branches in a windless lake, there is the truth of things as they actually happened, the truth that only those who were there can know, the reflection that will fade when darkness comes and be lost in the minds of the dead.

For Paulinus, I suppose, the Matter of Britain should begin with the "facts" of Arthur's birth—and these I cannot tell him. An oath is an oath, and my oath binds me still.

For the harper, the story should start with one great chord, swept right across the strings, to catch men's hearts and hold them, rapt and breathless, waiting for marvels.

But for me, Bedivere, the picture that comes to mind, clearer now than when I was a part of it, sharper and more vivid, like the reflection of color in still lake water, is of three children, wild as winter gulls, and an old, shabby Colonial homestead, deep in the Dumnonian country.

It began the day Vivian dared Arturus and me to put frogs in Father Gregorius' bed while he slept. It was spring, and they were very little frogs, new-turned from tadpoles, delighted with their own ability to jump.

Father Gregorius was very old and simple and a little soft in the head. He had lived as a hermit in our woods until one bad winter the charcoal burners found him half dead from exposure and hauled him up to the homestead for doctoring. My uncle, Ectorius, who never turned away a stray dog or a starving kitten, kept him around the place after that. Officially all Rome had been declared Christian in the Emperor Constantine's day, a hundred years or more before. My uncle always preserved the conventions. Being by choice a philosopher and by military training a Raven of Mithras, it suited him to turn over the instruction of children and slaves in the state religion to Gregorius. The task gave the old hermit a recognizable niche in the household and kept him occupied until the evenings. Then he regularly played chess (surprisingly well, I believe) with my uncle. Evenings must have been long for a widower in that remote fortress-farm in the west country.

Gregorius had a horror of frogs and Vivian knew it. She knew most of the idiosyncrasies of the people round us in those days; she was very observant. Also, she had strong likes and dislikes and Father Gregorius' lessons bored her unutterably. Why frogs affected the old fellow as they did is a mystery. Having lived by choice for years in a peculiarly noisome little cave, he should have been inured to slimy things. But the rumpus he raised when he woke to find his bed full of what he declared to be "devilkins" brought all the household running.

Arturus and I got nine strokes each with the lictor's

rod kept in Uncle's library for our benefit. He believed in Roman discipline when he remembered (or, as on that occasion, was forcibly reminded of) our existence. Three strokes were for discourteous behavior to a servant, and six for disturbing him at his work on the History of the Wars of Britain. Afterwards we were shut into separate rooms to commit to memory a very long passage of Virgil. He made it clear that supper was to be our next meal. As we had missed breakfast in the uproar I considered this was excessive. When, near noon, we were released from bondage, my main desire was for vengeance.

"It was all Vivian's fault. Everything always is," I said, kicking a stone through the gap in the palisade for which Arturus and I were heading. "If only she didn't have ideas!"

"She can't help it." Arturus stopped in his tracks to consider the matter. "They come to some people. The worst of it is, they always seem such good ideas at the time!"

He was smiling thoughtfully—being, as always, strictly fair. I had to look up a little to meet his eyes. Although we were the same age, almost to a day, he might have been a year the elder. Already he topped me by half a head, with the fine bone structure of a thoroughbred colt, and hair the color of ripe barley, with glints in it the red-gold of a last year's beech leaf.

Reluctantly, I smiled back at him. He made me ashamed to sulk.

"We'd better find her. She's probably miserable. Don't be hard on her, Verus," he said. He was always ready to forgive before I was, unless something had roused him into one of his passionate rages.

We started off again towards the gap. A voice behind us shouted irritably:

"Where are you two going now?"

We turned. My cousin Caius had come out of the byre, and was hurrying after us with his quick, uneven stride. My heart sank. Arturus and I exchanged glances.

"Only going to look for Vivian," I muttered defensively.

"Have you permission? Have you done your punishment?" he wanted to know. He was a tall, too-thin youth, with a careworn, anxious expression, part of the grown-up world to which, at twelve years old, we were still in bondage.

"Yes. All of it," I assured him.

"Well, I suppose you may as well find her. You'll know where to look. She's run off somewhere, and I can't spare Olwen from the weaving all day hunting for her. The old fool's been rushing around like a hen with its head cut off all the morning. The trouble you three make! Why can't you behave? I was only one year older than you when I was an armor-bearer in Ambrosius' army. You aren't children any more."

".No, Cai," Arturus said, agreeing seriously.

"I wish *I* could be an armor-bearer next year!" I said. "I wish both of us could be."

Cai stared at me, still scowling a little. Suddenly his ugly, worried face broke into a smile.

"It's what you both need—discipline," he grumbled. "Get away now from under everyone's feet and behave yourselves. See you are all three clean and presentable for the evening meal. I needn't, for once, remind you to be punctual for it, I imagine!" He turned away with a short bark of laughter.

Poor Caius! He can't have been twenty at that time. To us he seemed middle-aged. The whole weight of the household had lain on his shoulders since his army career ended at seventeen, with an arrow through his ankle that pinned him to his horse, and brought the horse down to roll on him. He had come home, virtually crippled, from that battle. His two older brothers died in it. Now he was my uncle's only surviving child, and Uncle himself had withdrawn more and more into his books, broken by ill-health and trouble. It was the sort of story you might have duplicated, with minor variations, in half the poverty-stricken old Colonial families in Britain. Years after, I realized just how lonely and bitter his youth had been when he said to me, smiling crookedly, "I used to dream at nights of mouths—all the mouths of men and beasts that had got to be fed!"

I was a man by then, and he mocked me when he

saw there were tears in my eyes. It was no wonder that
he seemed to us children an unreasonable, nagging task-
master, out of whose way we kept whenever possible.
Those of us who are of the Aurelian line, descended direct
from Maximus the Emperor, are born to the army. We
expect something better of life than the drudging cares of
a small-farm bailiff. There were few slaves left to work
with him and no money to buy more. Our land was steep
and stony, with the forest always encroaching on the
plough. He would work all day in the fields like a common laborer at hay-time and harvest, and come in at
night grimly in pain with that ankle of his. The army
surgeon had set it badly, expecting him to die from his
other injuries anyway, and to the end of his days, it was
too misshapen for him to wear a war-boot. His heart then,
and always, was with the army; and the frustrations he
suffered left their mark on him for the rest of his life. Had
my mother lived, life would have been easier for all of us.
But she had died when I was six, in one of the plague
years. I could just remember her, bustling and capable,
very unlike her brother, my uncle. My father, one of
Ambrosius' legionary prefects, had been killed the year I
was born.

　　The conditions of our life seemed normal to us
children. There had been forty years of war, following on
the time of the Great Troubles, and all Britain was poor.
One lived off the land or starved. Cai was not the only
one who slept with the spectre of famine at his shoulder.
Every winter folk died from hunger. It was nothing unusual to find the skeleton-thin corpse of some Outlander
in our woods in spring, though my uncle gave away more
than could be spared each year to beggars. He had,
ingrained in him, that true patrician *gravitas* which feels
responsibility for poorer folk, and he was, besides, essen-
tially kind; he must have been, I realized even then, to
shoulder the burden of three orphan children—and I the
only one with claim of kinship on him. Arturus and
Vivian were children of Celtic war comrades who had
fallen in the last great Pict invasion from the north.

　　A child accepts the world he finds. We three never

questioned the conditions of our life in the fortress-farm that we, like the native Celts, called the "Dunn." Bare feet and patched woollen tunics, rough country food and few companions were no hardship. All that distinguished us from the children of the peasants and fishermen was the discipline of cleanliness and manners imposed by our Colonial standing; that, and the fact we had to do lessons, which they did not. Those were the things we counted hardships and escaped from, day-long, when we could, into the freedom of forest and river strand, and the close-knit fellowship of our own small, private world.

Once free of Cai, but reminded by his parting mockery of the barren hours that stretched to suppertime, I said, dolefully:

"I'm so *hungry!*"

Arturus nodded, his expression purposeful.

"We can't exist until supper. Get on down to the Telling Floor. Vivian will be there. I shall go up to Caw's hut and get us food. He can't be punished for giving it to us. In the kitchen, they would be afraid to."

I looked at him with admiration. He always found the way out of a difficulty, where Vivian wept and I was prepared to endure stolidly. Caw the Hunter was our friend and he belonged to Arturus. He had come with him, as his personal slave, when he was only a baby, new-born, and given to my mother to suckle with me. Caw wore the iron slave ring, but proudly, counting himself apart from the field slaves, and he and his fat wife adored Arturus.

Now, without waiting for my answer, Arturus shot away, running with his quick, leggy stride, back among the buildings, towards the track that led up into the forest.

I padded obediently off through the dust the dead thorn bushes sweep smooth each day, when they are drawn back to let the cattle out, feeling it, warm and soft with spring, between my bare toes; then ran across the cropped grass of the home pasture, down into the rustle of last year's leaves under the great beech trees. I wondered if I should find Vivian at the Telling Floor, but I guessed I should. She and Arturus could generally sense

where to look for one another. The link between them
was very strong.

The half-timbered buildings of the Dunn, clustered
around with clay-and-wattle huts for the slaves, stood
high on a good, defensible outcrop of rock. Below, in the
water meadows, were the ruins of the villa that some
ancestor of ours had built when the Peace of Rome still
held Britain secure. Fifty years back, Saxon pirates had
come raiding up the tidal river that flows through our
land, down from the Outland hills past the little port of
Totnesia and away to the open sea.

"What a place to build a great house—anyone could
have seen it could not be defended!" Arturus said of the
villa scornfully.

The country folk whispered of torture and murder
that the pirates had inflicted and of ghosts that wailed
and gibbered in the dark. That had not prevented them
from thieving the villa's good dressed stones for building,
and its pillars for gate posts, over the years. Now only a
few crumbling walls and grass-grown hummocks of rub-
ble remained, about one wide pavement of patterned
black and white, which we kept cleared for use. The
sacks of tribute corn were put out there each harvest for
the Totnesia barges to collect, and in spring the women
stretched blankets to bleach there on washdays. It had got
the name of Telling Floor because the grain sacks were
checked there before loading.

It was a pleasant place. The sun was warm, under
the shelter of the hill, and young ash saplings had grown
up around it, screening it from the towing path. With the
beech woods heavy above it, it was a very private place.
We three had taken it for our own, for it had the advantage of being out of sight and call of the Dunn and,
except at bleaching time and harvest, no one disturbed us
in our games there.

I saw Vivian before she saw me. Caw the Hunter
had taught us how to walk silently. She was kneeling,
peering into a little broken fountain, where clear water
still trickled into a moss-greened marble basin shaped like
a shell. She was a thin slip of a child then, who might, by

her looks, have been two years the youngest of us three. As she knelt, her straight dark hair swung forward. I could not see if she had been crying. In justice I felt she should have been.

I picked up a pebble and threw it, carefully aimed to splash into the pool. She whipped round on me, her small pointed face angry as a startled cat's.

"Now you've broken it!" she spat at me.

"Broken what? I haven't broken anything," I said, defensive on principle.

"The reflection," she said.

Curious, I went and knelt beside her.

"What were you looking at?" I wanted to know.

"Me," she said.

The water lipped the shell's rim and steadied. I leaned over and my own face looked back at me—a boy's face, blunt-featured and smudgy, hair the color of reed thatch springing to an untidy cockscomb above wide-set, surprised grey eyes.

"Is that how *I* look?" I asked, intrigued.

Her face reflected beside mine, frowning.

"Yes. But it doesn't matter for you. I ought to be beautiful, because I'm a girl. Princesses should be beautiful. I'm not."

"Well, you aren't a princess, either," I said reasonably.

She gave me a sidelong glance.

"Olwen says I am. But it's a secret. Uncle would have her beaten if he knew she'd told me. She says I am of the oldest royal blood in Britain."

"Slaves' talk," I said, not impressed. "She's probably lying to get you to do something she wants. Anyway, Celtic titles don't count. Cai says High Princes are as thick as blackberries in the Clans."

She scowled. "They *do* count. We were here before the Romans, so our royal blood is older than the emperor's. I mean to be all Celt from now on. You must call me by my proper name, Ygern, and I shall call you Bedivere, and Arturus, Arthur."

"Uncle wouldn't like that. You know those are the

names only the slaves and fisherfolk use, because they speak the Celtic still." I was annoyed and remembered suddenly I had the right to be. "You and your frogs!" I reminded her gruffly. "Look what that's led to; *and* you ran off and left us. Coward!"

Her face turned tragic.

"I couldn't help it. They all shouted and you know I can't bear that. It wasn't the beating I was afraid of, truly. I'd rather have been beaten. Oh, Verus, did it hurt very badly?" Tears sparkled under her lashes and began to slip down her face. She turned her shoulder to me, and scrubbed her hand impatiently across her eyes. She always hated us to see her cry.

Relenting, I said:

"It wasn't bad. The Virgil was worse. The words wouldn't stick in my mind. Arturus was ready long before I was."

"Where is he?" she asked. "Is he—angry, Verus?"

"No. He said you weren't to be miserable. He's gone to Caw's to get us food. Look! Here he comes."

He was running down the hill, his hair flying, his eyes bright with laughter.

"Caw wasn't there. Maeva gave me this—bread, cheese and apples. She wanted to cook meat for us, but I wouldn't wait. Too much of today has been wasted."

He sat down, cross-legged by the fountain, emptying a flat loaf, a goat's cheese and withered russet apples onto the grass from the cloth they had been wrapped in.

"Come on—eat!" he commanded, breaking the loaf into three.

"Not for me," Vivian muttered.

"Why not? There's enough. We always share." Arturus looked at her keenly.

She rubbed a tear that had trickled down the side of her nose with a grubby finger, leaving a smear of earth instead.

"I didn't share the beating," she whispered. That, from Vivian, was an apology. Even I accepted it. Arturus divided the food and pushed hers across to her, saying simply:

"Eat!"

At this she obeyed him. (We always did.) She bit into a hunk of bread and sighed, admitting:

"I am hungry!"

Arturus looked at her kindly.

"You are a fool—sometimes," he said. "This morning was a mistake." He munched for a moment, reflectively. Then his face lit up. "It was almost worth it. Will you ever forget how Gregorius hopped, with all the frogs hopping round him?"

We began to laugh. Soon we could not stop laughing, but rolled about on the grass like puppies, punishment forgotten. Ahead of us, under the blue sky and the racing clouds, the long free afternoon stretched to infinity, full of beckoning promise.

We had climbed trees and explored the muddy rock pools of low tide. We had taken one of the battered coracles moored to the riverbank and paddled it perilously across to the far shore and back. To crown the day, we had gone swimming for the first time that year, gasping and spluttering, naked as fishes in the ice-cold water that comes down from the high hills. As we dressed again, the sun was setting and the shadows of the ash saplings stretched long across the Telling Floor.

"Ponies on the towing path!" Arturus warned sharply. He was half in, half out of his tunic and stood motionless, head up, listening.

"Two, I think." Vivian, already dressed, tossed back her wet hair and ran to look. Over her shoulder she called back softly:

"It's Celidonius, Celidonius and Gobo."

I was glad. Celidonius was a harper and I loved harp music.

Arturus scrambled into his tunic and I fastened my belt as we ran to join her.

"If only Cai lets him play in hall—not only in the kitchen!" I murmured.

Cai mistrusted wandering native harpers. They had a reputation for inflaming nationalist feeling among the

Clans. He had not much ear for music and a great respect
for convention. No decent Colonial family, according to
him, invited a native harper into the hall. Luckily, my
uncle was more tolerant. He sometimes made an exception for Celidonius and would even have him into his
library after supper, alone, to consult with him, so he
said, about the Wars of Britain, for harpers know the
history of their own people.

We ran along the towing path to meet the riders and
the leading one drew rein. We clustered round him and
Vivian began stroking the strong, wise-eyed white mule
he was riding.

"Greetings, children! Shall I be welcome at the Dunn
tonight?" he asked.

"A harper is always welcome!" Arturus told him. He
liked Celidonius' songs as much as I did.

I said nothing, keeping in the background as I generally did, but staring curiously.

Celidonius was an odd-looking man, I thought. Thin,
not very tall and desperately shabby, with a face it was
hard to remember because he could twist it into so many
expressions. Nothing about him ever fitted into a tidy
pattern. His threadbare cloak and tunic, greenish-black
with exposure to all weathers, his battered horseman's
boots split in the creases, the harness of his mule, mended
with rope, put him on a level with the poorest folk I
knew. But the harp slung behind him was a good one,
cased in soft leather that was worked in scrolls and
twisted designs of colored needlework. It even had a little
hawk, of silver and enamels, on the pillar, that stood up
through the casing and seemed to look over his shoulder.
Not a poor man's harp. With his dark, thin hair, already
receding a little to show a high, rounded forehead, small,
forked beard, sharp nose and long beautiful hands, there
was something of the bird about him, himself. He had
eyes like a sparrowhawk's, I thought, golden-brown eyes,
with a dark rim to the iris, and heavy, hooded lids.

He was only a travelling harper. Yet he behaved and
he spoke, always, to everyone, as though he were their
equal. It puzzled me. I'd heard Caius say of him that he
needed putting in his place. But what *was* his place?

He chatted pleasantly to us for a few minutes, answering Vivian's questions, but watching Arturus while he talked. Behind him his servant, Gobo, a hideous little dwarf from the Outlands, squatted on his shaggy pony like a toad on a stone, half hidden behind a big untidy saddlebag, with only his greasy red cap showing.

Suddenly Arturus glanced at the sky. The sun was nearing the top of the hill beyond the river.

"It's almost suppertime. We must go! Ride on, Celidonius," he commanded.

Celidonius laughed and gave him a mocking salute.

"I obey!" he cried. "An invitation to supper I will always obey!" and he started the mule into a sharp trot.

"Up the short way, and in by the kitchens. We can be in time—but hurry!" Arthur gave us, too, our orders. As we shot into the woods, I reminded him:

"We've been swimming. No need to wash!" and he nodded.

"We can make it. Just," he said, urgently.

We pelted through the cattle-gap and dodged between the round huts of the slave quarters, scattering hens and naked toddlers as we went. Supper was important to us that evening and if we were late we should get none. We knew that.

Gobo was leading away the pony and the mule, and the harper was crossing the empty cobbled yard of the kitchen premises as we came out into it. He walked lightly and quickly; a bird's walk. As he went he glanced about him as a bird does, also. Then a strange thing happened, and instinctively we three paused.

Caw the Hunter, who feared no man and respected few, except my uncle and Arturus, came out of the black yawn of the open kitchen door. At sight of Celidonius his lined, leathery face lit up in a great smile of welcome. He began to say something, but Celidonius made him a sign—not a gesture of ordinary greeting, but something that reminded me of a priest giving a blessing. Caw's face changed and he hurried forward. Celidonius spoke to him quickly and softly, in the Celtic tongue, at the same time sweeping back his tattered cloak, so that, for a moment, I

saw a gleam of gold and bright color. Caw shaded his
eyes with his clenched fist—a sign of greatest respect
among the Celtic Clansmen—and went down on one
knee, saying, as he did so, a sentence in the Old Tongue
in a deep, rumbling voice. Then he rose quickly, took the
harper by the arm and, glancing around the courtyard,
drew him into one of the nearby storerooms, closing the
door behind him.

We had paused in the shadow of the entrance arch.
They had not seen us. We looked at each other, questioningly.

We were all three bi-lingual—speaking Latin and
Celtic equally fluently. But only Vivian, whose nurse
Olwen was an Outlander, understood the Old Tongue,
and only a few words of it, at that.

"What did Caw say to him?" Arturus asked, puzzled.

She frowned.

"He said—'You are the'—it sounded like 'the Merlin.' I never heard that word before."

Arturus looked troubled.

"It was odd, wasn't it?" he said slowly.

"Oh, come *on*," I urged. "Remember supper!"

We fled into the house.


The horn that announced the evening meal had not
sounded, by the time, in clean tunics and wearing our
only pairs of sandals, we were ready. Everything was
strangely quiet.

"Perhaps we were too late and missed hearing it," I
said, unhappily, sniffing the good cooking smells that
drifted down the corridor that led from our sleeping cells
to the inner courtyard.

"If it hasn't, Uncle will still be playing chess," Arturus reminded us.

We went along to the veranda of the courtyard and
peered out into it cautiously.

Our Dunn had been built on the Roman pattern, in a
square, and single-storied, with all the main rooms opening onto a stone-flagged inner court. Facing them were

the stables, and to right and left, the smith's forge, the weaving shed, the granary and forage store. It was neat and compact and solid, and probably much smaller than a child's memory of it. The veranda that sheltered the main rooms was supported on roughly trimmed tree trunks, up which the creepers my mother had planted still grew luxuriantly.

Outside the door of my uncle's library were stone benches and a table. He liked to sit there reading on warm days and there, on fine evenings, he and old Gregorius played their games of chess.

He was sitting there that evening, with the chessboard, a game half-finished, on the table before him. Father Gregorius' cloak of undyed wool lay across the empty bench he usually occupied, half-trailing on the ground, as though he had risen in a hurry.

Dusk filled the courtyard and it was very quiet there. Only the ponies stamped and clinked their tether rings in the stable, and on the uneven line of its thatch Vivian's white doves cooed sleepily, settling to roost. Behind the stables the afterglow of sunset filled the sky; one of those sunsets that come in the west country after the rains. Right up to the zenith it reflected on a dapple of little clouds that brooded above the Dunn like tall wings.

Before my uncle, facing him across the unfinished game, stood Celidonius, a dark figure, whose shadow fell across the chessboard and seemed to reach out towards the man who sat behind it, tense and wary.

We three stood very still, daunted by something we sensed rather than saw, instinctively uneasy, and drawing close to each other, as cattle bunch before thunder.

Celidonius, speaking Latin, but with the faint lisping lilt the Celts always give to it, said softly:

"The time has come, Sir Ector. I am here to remind you of your oath. It will be the twelfth new moon of May, remember. I must have the boy."

Although he used the slaves' name for my uncle, he spoke with dignity, an equal to an equal. His voice was light and cold, with a faint inflection in it that held a hint, almost, of mockery.

My uncle said nothing. He looked frail and tired, his face pale with a strange gleam on it that emphasized the fine, sharply carved profile, the hollows under the cheekbones, and the high, thinker's forehead. Only his hand moved, outstretched on the table, opening and closing on the ivory king he held. At last he said:

"You would keep me to that oath? After twelve years, with Britain as Britain is today?"

Celidonius said gently, almost pityingly:

"An oath is an oath. You gave Uther your word, and he a dying man. Have you forgotten in twelve short years?"

Suddenly my uncle slammed the king down on the board and stood up.

"No, Celidonius! He's too young. A child still. You must wait another two years, at least. Wait until, even by your custom, he is old enough for Warrior Making."

Celidonius shook his head.

"The Clans will not wait. Blaize, the Master, has told them this Spring Sowing the stars demand a King Choosing. From the first we knew and Uther knew that it would be when he was twelve years old. No one, not our Master Blaize himself, can say to a star 'Delay your rising.' I must have the boy, Sir Ector."

"When?" my uncle asked. "How soon?"

"Tomorrow. At daybreak."

"Impossible!" My uncle slumped back into his chair as though strength had deserted him. "Be reasonable, man. His clothes—his escort—it will take me a month to get a message to Ambrosius and even then he may not be able to spare me men enough for a guard. I've no one here, except perhaps Caw and his sons, who could serve as escort. The rest are too old—peasants, or slaves I would not care to trust. You know that."

"I know it, Ectorius Aurelianus. We do not need a Roman guard. The boy will ride alone with me, except for Caw and Caw's sons. They have the Right of Gathering, and their going will account for his absence. He has been out hunting with them before now."

"Never alone—nor for so long. What shall I say when he does not return?"

"He will return. At the next new moon after May I will bring him back—*this* time."

"And after that?"

Celidonius shrugged.

"Three things are always uncertain: the way the wind will blow, where a seed will fall—and the hour of a man's destiny. When the Spring Sowing is over we must wait on events—five years, six—perhaps longer. Britain owes you a great debt already. You must keep the trust of him for us still, between his King Choosing and his King Making, for Britain's sake and for the love you bore to Uther."

Uncle Ectorius sighed deeply. His shoulders drooped and his head bent forward. He looked old and sad and defeated.

"This is a matter for you and your people. I cannot interfere. I have no right." Suddenly he looked up at Celidonius. "Is it true, the rumor I have heard, that since the death of Emrys, you are the Merlin of Britain?"

Celidonius bowed in assent.

"I am that, Ectorius Aurelianus, and may the Light that was in him shine again through me, in these dark days. But remember, when I sing in hall tonight, I am still only a wandering harper. The secret must be kept closer than ever, from now on. Do not you be forgetting that."

"I am not likely to forget." My uncle's voice sounded harsh. "Do not sing too long. After supper I must speak to the boy."

"With permission, *I* will speak to him," Celidonius said, with quiet authority. "Let you call him into your room here, and I will come to you as soon as I can be sure none will see my coming. I may not sing long, but I will sing well for you tonight, Sir Ector. We of Britain honor a man who keeps his oath."

He turned on his heel and was gone, seeming to fade instantly into the shadows.

My uncle got up heavily, went into his library and closed the door.

A little cold wind blew across the courtyard, rustling dead leaves that still clung to the creepers on the veranda.

Somewhere, away down by the river, an owl hooted.
Behind the uneven line of the stable thatch the afterglow
had died. Tall wings of cloud brooded over the Dunn,
grey now as the feathers of a stooping buzzard.

# Chapter Two

Firelight flickers on the white walls of the hut where I lie. As the days lengthen, the cold strengthens, and the good brothers do not grudge their labor to pile my brazier high with oak logs. Through the night, every hour or so one of them comes in quietly to mend my fire. They think I sleep, but my mind is far away, and wide awake. I am looking through the eyes of a twelve-year-old boy at other flames—at a fire that burns, deep in the forest. Round it trees lean from a darkness that is full of small sounds and rustlings. I am tired, and elated, and, though I will not admit it, even to myself, I am homesick. Was it only yesterday we put frogs in Father Gregorius' bed, went swimming, met Celidonius on the river path? Surely it must be years ago! All life has changed since then. I am a long day's journey away from the life I have always known—and I am glad that Caw the Hunter and his tall sons, Amil, Rianon and Gerwent, are close at hand. If a wolf or a wild boar were to come out of the black night under the trees, they would know what to do. Arturus has asked for me to go with him, and that is a shining and marvellous thought, warmer than the glow of the firelight, brighter than the flames that dance and blur as my eyelids droop with sleep. But I will not sleep, because I want to hear everything that Celidonius has to tell us. My curiosity is as avid as the beak of a nestling bird. I shake myself wide awake and ask:

"Where are we going, Celidonius—and what for, and why do we have to go there?"

It had been late, the evening before, when my uncle sent for me to his library. He was sitting in his usual chair—the cross-legged one with lions' heads on the arms. Across the hearth from him, like an honored guest, sat Celidonius. Between them, his back to the hearth, his head up, his eyes brilliant and defiant in a face so white I thought he might be going to be sick soon, stood Arturus.

"Verus, you have to make a decision," my uncle said, and his voice was tight and reluctant. I thought he must be angry with me still because of the frogs. "Arturus starts tomorrow on a journey. He will travel with Celidonius, attended by Caw and Caw's sons. He says he wishes you to make this journey with him. Do you want to go, or not?"

I looked at my uncle's closed face, at Celidonius, who was smiling a little as though the question amused him, then at Arturus, who gave me no sign.

I felt as if I had stepped accidentally off the riverbank, where the water is deepest and closes over one's head before one can strike out and begin to swim. But one thing was clear in my mind. Where Arturus went, I went. All our lives that had been the way of things. That thought brought me to the surface. I said:

"Yes!" and then, stammering a little, because so many questions were rushing in on me, and instinct warned me not to ask any of them, "That is—if you will let me go, sir. We—we always do things together, Arturus and I."

My uncle flinched, as though something hurt him. But he was often in pain, I knew, and that night he looked very ill.

He said, briefly, glancing at Celidonius:

"That settles it, then?"

The color came flooding back into Arturus' face and he too turned to Celidonius, all alight with eagerness.

"What must we do? When do we start?"

Celidonius laughed.

"Gently!" he said. "There is still *my* permission to give. Bedivere, can you keep a secret?"

I stared at him. *His* permission? A harper's permission? But he looked—different. The black robe he was wearing now was of fine cloth, and very clean. On his breast hung a jewel in the shape of a six-pointed star. It was of real gold, bright with colored enamels. On his right hand, where it lay along the arm of the chair, a great amethyst ring caught the light.

"Can you?" he pressed me and meeting those strange eyes, I felt uncomfortably that he saw into my mind. It was no use to lie.

"Except from Vivian," I said. "And Arturus, of course."

He laughed again, and glanced across at my uncle.

"Their stars bind them, those three. It will always be like this," he said, and for the second time that night, I thought there was a note of pity in his voice. Then he turned back to me.

"Arthur must go for a time to his own people, Bedivere. You are his milk-brother and, as such, his Clansmen will accept you. But what you see and hear and learn will be his secret and theirs. Ygern may share it with you, for she, too, is of the blood. But no one else. Do you understand?"

I was far from understanding and he must have known it. But I nodded, dumbly.

"Very well. I will take you, since Arthur wishes it. Caw will see to the clothes you must wear, and call you at dawn. We should be away from here before the world is stirring."

I looked again, questioningly, at Uncle Ectorius. I had never taken orders before from anyone but him.

He gave me a thin-lipped smile (his pain must be bad, I thought):

"Obey Celidonius as you would obey me on this journey, Verus. And Verus—remember the things I have taught you. Do not forget you come of the Aurelianii, and mind your manners, boy," he said. His voice was stern, but very weary.

Beside the fire in the forest, Celidonius ran his fingers
over the strings of his harp. It sounded like a trill of
ghostly laughter.

"Three questions, eh Bedivere? *Where? What?
Why?*" he mocked me.

"You *said* you would tell us this evening. You promised," Arturus reminded him.

All day we had ridden by lonely hidden tracks, deep
in the forest, Caw and his sons padding tirelessly on foot
beside us, with their easy, hunters' lope. All day Celidonius had parried our seething curiosity, telling us we should
attend only to the journey. Now the slaves were busy at a
little distance off, about their own cookfire, and we had
been well fed on hunters' stew. Celidonius smiled at
me.

"Very well. Where we go is a long journey, to Ynis
Witrin. What for? To make a Dragon. Why? Because it is
appointed by destiny and a man must fulfill his fate."

"Harpers' talk!" I said, crossly. "Please don't laugh
at us! Please explain."

His face in the firelight went suddenly grave and
very kind.

"It is time I did. Come close, both of you. Now
listen, and I will tell you a true story, not a harper's tale.
Long and long ago, at the beginning of time, wise men
came from over the sea, from the Lands of the Sunrise, to
this island."

"Before we Romans conquered it?" I asked.

"Before Rome was built. They taught the people of
the land how to plough, and when to sow crops, how to
increase their cattle and flocks, and, more important by
far, how to live well and honestly together. Because they
were the Knowers, folk revered and obeyed them. They
were the teachers of kings, the judges in all disputes, the
link between men and the gods."

"Which gods?" I asked. (There are so many!)

"That is a question we will discuss some other
time," Celidonius told me smoothly. "These Wise Ones
ruled the island for many generations. On the mainland
their wisdom was known and kings sent sons here to be
taught and trained. Princes who completed their educa-

tion were given a distinguishing title. They were called 'Dragons.' "

"Why? Why Dragons?" I asked.

"Because a dragon, though a beast, has wings and can mount into the sky. Man also is part beast, no better than wolf or sheep, unless he grows the wings of the spirit, to rise above himself, into the light of true understanding.

"Times changed. Invaders came, and wars, and conquests. Disputes arose, even among the Wise Ones themselves. These islands became divided into Clans and Clan Territories. The Romans came and because the Clans were divided, Rome conquered and ruled—ruled well, in its own way, for close on four hundred years. Then, as you know, the time of the Troubles began. Rome ceased, for a while at any rate, to be able to defend the island. So, once more, the Clans after their custom rallied under a chosen Chieftain—their Great Dragon—the Pendragon." Celidonius paused, and again he touched his harp, this time to one deep, solemn chord. His eyes on the fire, he said softly: "The last of those was Uther Pendragon, High King of Dumnonia, chosen for his great strength, his courage and his cunning in war. Ten years ago he died in battle. But he left an heir—a two-year-old boy, his only son, who, because of the dangers of the time, has been hidden away in a secret place, until at twelve years old, he should be ready to receive the initiation of a Dragon Prince."

"Twelve years old?" Arturus said, breathlessly. "That's the same age as Bedivere and me. Oh, Celidonius, is it to *his* Dragon Making we are going?"

Again Celidonius struck that one deep chord. Then he turned and looked at Arturus—a long, strange, searching look.

"It is, Arthur, son of Uther Pendragon," he said, and his voice vibrated, deep and solemn as the harp strings.

Arthur sprang up and stood staring at him.

"Me? *Me?*" he said, his voice breaking. "You mean? —You mean?—Celidonius, *what* do you mean?"

"I mean that you, child, are the High Prince of

Dumnonia, only son of Uther the Pendragon, appointed by him on his deathbed as his heir, to follow him in due time as war leader of the Clans of Britain," Celidonius said quietly.

"But—but I can't be!" Arturus' face flushed painfully. "Uncle Ectorius—I asked him—he would only say my father was his battle comrade. I think, the way he spoke, that I must be baseborn in some way—my mother a slave, perhaps."

Celidonius shook his head, one eyebrow raised in mockery that was kind.

"Your mother is of royal blood and more than royal blood. But your father had many enemies, Arthur, and so have you. The year of your birth, Uther was beset on all sides, and foresaw his end might be near. Ectorius was, indeed, his trusted battle comrade, and the last place warring Clans would look for Uther's son to be hidden was in a Colonial household. That was why I carried you, a new-born babe, from your father's Fortress of Tintagel to the home where you have been fostered ever since. Only Caw, who came with us, shared the secret. But the Dunn of Ectorius lies deep in your own Clan country and we let it be known in the Clan that you were of the blood and must be well guarded. Until today you were too young to keep your own secret. Now you must learn to guard it as the Clan has guarded you."

Slender and tense, Arturus stood silent in the firelight. It gleamed on his bright hair and caught the soft heather purples and greens of the Celtic tunic and trews he wore. Almost in a whisper, saying the words over to himself as one does to make a thing come true, he repeated:

*"Son of Uther Pendragon!"*

I knew what they meant to him. Caw, who had always been our friend, had told us stories often enough of that last hero king who had led Britain's resistance against the onrush of a great Pictish invasion; the king who, dying of the wasting sickness, had had himself lifted from his litter into the saddle so that he could lead the last, desperate stand of an army outnumbered five to one. I thought: "Arturus was always *our* leader in everything.

This is truly a harper's tale—only better, because it is
true!" Then I saw that, like a greyhound, he was trembling all over. Celidonius saw it too. He said, in an
altogether different voice, kindly and matter-of-fact:

"Come—sit down. So—close to the fire, where you
can share my cloak. These spring nights are chilly, and I
have still much to tell you about this journey of ours.
First, child, remember one thing. On earth every man
plays a part and that part is appointed to him by the gods
before he is born. In one incarnation a slave, in another a
king, in another a merchant or a seaman, or a common
soldier. In each part, as he plays it well or ill, he learns
something that he needs to know, until all good and all
evil have been experienced and the soul can distinguish
for itself between the two, and so grow towards the
perfection that is man's final goal. A king is not greater
than a slave, for both are men; and it is of equal importance to the play that they should act their part, so that
the play itself should mirror truth. Do you understand?"

Arturus nodded.

"I think so, yes."

"So you need not be afraid—and you need not feel
puffed up with pride, either. King's son or slave's son, it is
the same thing—only the part of a king is hardest, because how he chooses to live affects the lives of his
people, and the shape of the play for them. In the Holy
Island, when you are made a Dragon, you will begin to
learn how to play the part of a king. It is for that reason
we have set out upon this journey."

Men say of Celidonius the Merlin that he was a magician.
Most of my life I have been a soldier, and it has not been
my trade to understand magic. But as I knew him, and
most of all in those years of our childhood, I can say this
for certain, he had a subtle understanding of men and
nature that went deeper than that of any other man I
have ever known.

I have marvelled often, looking back, how wisely he
handled Arthur—me too, for that matter—on that first
forest journey. He made himself into that most perfect
companion of any child—the man who answers every

question; and ours flowed endlessly from dawn to dusk. There seemed nothing he did not know about the green forest world, through which we were riding in fine spring weather. The private, hidden lives of birds and beasts, the names, the uses of every plant and tree, the courses of the stars in the dark night sky, the fragile strength of a fallen feather, the secret jewel hidden in the heart of a shiny pebble—he could name and explain, it seemed to us, the very fabric of the world. He had skills, too, which enchanted us. He knew the trick which brings fire out of dead wood with a whirling stick—and how to fashion elder stems to make a range of little pipes that played true music. He could render himself more invisible than Caw the Hunter in country that hardly promised cover for a cat; and could turn himself with only such properties as a charred stick, an old cloak, a handful of crushed leaf juice, a tall staff, into a completely different person: a henwife, a charcoal burner, an outlaw, an old, and very holy, hermit. He always knew what roots and berries one might safely eat, the way to snare a coney or pheasant for the pot, and which pool the trout lay in, that could, with practice, be tickled and landed. Often, afterwards, on campaign, I found myself warm, dry and fed in country where other men shivered and starved, because I called to mind the Merlin's "magic." Sometimes, when folk spoke in hushed tones of his power to escape danger by vanishing into thin air, or puzzled by what spell he had gathered news out of the very camp of the enemy, I had to turn aside to hide a smile. I thought I could guess—though in that craft I never learned to equal him. The secret of disguise is a gift one must be born with, for it lies in voice and gesture and long, patient study of how all manner of people think and move and feel. One must put on the whole man—not only a borrowed garment. He said the Roman in me hindered me from that. Arthur could do it and the skill served him well most times.

Threading the many questions with which we badgered him day-long, as we rode, were some that had to do with matters other than the new scenes through which we passed.

It was quite early in the journey that, feeling heady

with spring and inclined to dare my elders, I voiced a
query that had been burning in my mind from the start. I
asked him:

"What does it mean, to be a Merlin, Celidon?" (We
called him by the Celtic version of his name, as he used
ours.)

Arthur made a quick gesture, warning me against
the question, but I chose, deliberately, not to see.

Celidon seemed unmoved.

"It is a title," he said calmly. "A title of honor.
Among the Bards of Britain the Merlin is the one who
has been acclaimed the greatest, Bedivere."

I dared again.

"Does it mean you are a Druid, Celidon? Cai says
you are."

Arthur said sharply:

"Bedivere!" and frowned across at me. I guessed it
was unmannerly, but I did not care. I wanted so much to
know.

Celidon said, smiling:

"Let him ask, Arthur. He is your milk-brother, and
as such there are things he had better understand. Yes,
Bedivere. I am of the Old Faith. The Merlin stands third
in rank of the Chief Druids of Britain, after Blaize, the
present Arch-Druid, and the Chief Priestess, whom men
call The Lady of the Lake."

"But Druids are *bad*," I said, feeling my heart hammer so that my voice came out shrill and uneven. "At
least—Cai says they are—*and* my uncle," I added, defensively.

Celidon's eyebrows rose.

"Since Ectorius permits you to ride with me, I think,
perhaps, you are mistaken somewhere. You heard him
give me my title, did you not? He and I have known each
other since before you were born, remember. As to Cai's
opinion"—he laughed. "What does he say of our order,
Bedivere?"

I felt myself blushing.

"He says Druids incite rebellions." I stammered.
"That they are a pro- pro-"

" 'Proscribed' is the word you have forgotten." Celidon mocked sotfly. "Yes—we are a proscribed religion. That is true. So were the Christians until the days of Constantine, and for the same reasons. But let that pass. What else?"

"You—you burn people alive in wicker cages to please your gods and you eat babies!" I blurted out, suddenly defiant.

"Now where did he get that idea, do you suppose?" Celidon sounded interested.

"It's history. The Emperor Julius wrote it in his book on the Wars of Gaul. Really he did. I've read it," I said triumphantly. Then, catching Arthur's eye, I had to admit, "At least, it was Uncle who read it as a lesson, really. He makes us learn all about wars: Alexander's; Julius the Caesar's; all of them. There was another lesson, about wars in Britain, too—when a queen of the Iceni rebelled once, and *that* was because the Druids told her to. Our general, Suetonius Paulinus, marched right across Britain and burned a great Druid stronghold."

Celidon's face darkened for a moment, then he said, very quietly:

"Bedivere, tell me something. If you were a man and the Saxons invaded and conquered Britain, and you lived on, under their rule, would *you* submit tamely, accept their gods, forget and let your children forget, all you have been taught of Rome's greatness?"

"*No!*" I said, so violently that my pony started.

"Neither did we," he said, and paused so long, I thought that was all the answer he meant to give.

"But Caesar wrote . . ." I said, still trying to argue the point.

"He said, in fact, that he had been *told* certain things. He never pretends he saw those things done." Celidon smiled. "Listen, boy. Three things no man can rule: a babe's crying; a woman's tongue; and the rumor that runs in the market place. Blood sacrifice of prisoners has no part in the Old Faith and I give you my solemn oath that I have never tasted boiled baby in my life. The Old Faith, as I have told you, is concerned with wisdom and knowledge—with understanding the universe and man's true place in it, not with propitiation of ancient gods or murder of the innocent. There *are* men—evil men, without comprehension—who do such things, and have always done them down the centuries, giving themselves over to the powers of darkness. They may call themselves Wise Ones. Through many lives to come they will learn, the hard way, to distinguish how mistaken they have been."

"The Black Druids? Caw told me about them," Arthur said thoughtfully.

Celidon made a quick sign with his hand in the air, warding off evil.

"The common folk speak of them by that name, I believe," he said. "Now, come—all this talk of eating babies has made my stomach queasy. It needs light, nourishing food for supper tonight. There is a stream. Let us go and see if you two can get me a fat brown trout by tickling. We have wasted enough of a fine day in idle talk of matters too solemn for my liking!"

In the late afternoon of the eighth day—the first that had threatened, though it had not brought, rain—we broke clear of the forest on an open upland ridge. Below lay a plain, stretching into hazy distance; marsh country, laced with dikes and winding streams that merged into a pattern of wide lakes, with little, hilly islands rising out of them. Celidon turned to us, and pointed across the marshes.

"Yonder lies Ynis Witrin, the Apple Island. It is a most holy and most secret place—the holiest place in all Britain. Prince Arthur rides there by right, to his Dragon Making. By custom, one free-born attendant may ride with him. Young Roman Verus, do you choose to put aside your Colonial rank, you, who claim descent from Maximus, and, remembering only that you are foster brother to the Pendragon's son, Bedivere, his milk-brother, attend him now? Or will you stay here with Caw until we return? The choice is yours."

"Where Arthur goes, I go," I said. I said it with defiance. Surely he knew, without asking, what my choice would be?

"Very well. Close in behind me. We must ride single file for the way is narrow and, in some places, dangerous.

From now on, I want no questions and no idle chatter, understand? Speak only if there is vital need to speak."

We glanced at each other, Arthur and I. Celidon's manner had changed. He was no longer our friend the harper. Both of us recognized it was the Merlin who spoke.

We reined our ponies in behind his white mule, letting them pick their own way down the steep, rocky pathway to the plain.

Riding close behind Arthur, I was not happy. Something in the way Celidon had looked and spoken, something in the country around us, made my skin prickle, and the hairs rise on the back of my neck. The afternoon was darkening early, under a grey lid of cloud. Ahead, the land stretched to meet the horizon. A flat land, striped and speckled like the scales of a snake, with the shine of sluggish waterways and stagnant pools, interspersed with mudflats and the sharp, acid green of bog. Far down in the west a red ember of sunset smoldered and was reflected here and there, turning the water it touched to the color of blood. An empty land. A silent land, where the wind in the reeds had a stealthy sound, and the ripple of water beside the narrow, raised causeways by which we travelled sounded a secret whispered behind the hand.

Riding last, where no one saw me, I made the sign of the horns, that wards off ill luck, and then, to be on the safe side, the sign of the Cross, also. Uncle Ectorius had done his best to educate us in his own tradition of cultured skepticism and made it clear that a Colonial gentleman should extend only contemptuous tolerance to the superstitions of the common people. But I had heard tales in plenty of spells and enchantments, of spooks and ghosts and spirits from the slaves (old Olwen was a mine of them and so was Caw's wife, Maeva).

"Where Arthur goes, I go!" I repeated to myself jerkily, and took comfort in the straightness of his back, the sturdy set of his shoulders and the alert, interested cock of his head. In all our life together, I had never known him afraid.

Ahead of us, the largest of the green islands grew steadily clearer, sailing like a galley on a wide sheet of

lake water. It was long and narrow, rising at one end to a
sharp green hill, that, from the flats, looked to me a
mountain. The causeway wound about and about, dou-
bling on itself, to avoid the bog, making the distance seem
greater than it was. The last light had faded to the dusk
Caw called "dog and wolf" when we rode out at last over
thin, hard turf, to the shingle of the lake's edge. A
wooden jetty ran down into the water, with a row of
hitching posts beside it.

"Leave your ponies here. They will be cared for,"
Celidon said briefly.

He dismounted and tied his mule's rein to a post.
Then he went down to the lake's edge and uttered a
strange, discordant cry, far-carrying and harsh, like the
call of some great waterbird. The echo of it came back
across the water, eerie and lonesome. I shivered and
glanced at Arthur. He was leaning against his pony's
flank, gazing across at the Island. I went and stood beside
him.

"Where you go, I go," I muttered.

His hand, rough and warm and reassuring, closed
over mine, but he said nothing. The ponies pricked their
ears and stamped restlessly. Arthur let go my hand and
pointed.

"Look. A boat," he said. His voice was tense.

A dark shape had detached itself from the Island
and was moving towards us. At first it seemed a shadow
among shadows, but gradually it took shape—a barge,
rowed by long sweeps.

Celidon turned his head and said:

"Come!"

We joined him as the barge reached the jetty, and
followed him down into it. There were only two rowers—
big, shock-haired men, naked to the waist, who put fist to
forehead in silent greeting, as Celidon spoke to them in a
language I did not recognize. Green fire dripped from the
oar blades and broke in ripples round the prow, sliding
back alongside in trails of green flame. Ahead stretched
the dark water, and rising from it, darker still, the loom
of the Island, with its great hill cutting the lesser blackness of the sky.

As we drew nearer, I saw, close down by the shore, a strange, silvery iridescence—not torchlight, not candle-light, a purer, whiter light—something that looked like moonlight. But there was no moon. I shivered again, gripping the wet thwarts on each side of me until my hands hurt. The silence was like a cloak of dark velvet covering us, fold on fold. Only the oars splashed and the green fire dripped and on the shore we were approaching the silver light grew clearer. A little spark of it seemed to break away and bob towards us.

"A will-o'-the-wisp!" I thought. Then, quite sudden-ly, the rowers shipped their oars, and the barge slid alongside another, higher jetty. The silver spark moved downwards, and I saw above me, lit by it, a boy's face, looking down at us—a dark, vivid face, the eyes alert and eager—reflecting the flame of the small cresset lamp he held.

"My Lord the Merlin? The Lady expects you," came a low greeting, in the Celtic, that held an accent I had not heard before.

Celidon answered softly:

"Lead. We follow." Then, over his shoulder, as he started up weed-slippery steps, he said to us again: "Come!"

Arthur went first and I was close behind him. As my foot left the barge's gunnel, I felt it move, and the oars dipped again, as it slid away out onto the lake. I felt short turf under my feet. For a moment Celidon paused for us to come up one on each side of him. I felt his hand press my shoulder and, bending down, he whispered:

"When I bid you, kneel, Bedivere, and remain kneel-ing until you are given a further order."

I nodded. I dared not speak.

Ahead of us, the boy walked steadily forward, carry-ing the lamp and leading us uphill towards the moonlight glow, that shone, I saw presently, from an open-sided shrine, such as folk set up in the old days to wayside gods. It stood on solid pillars of stone, raised by a flight of shallow steps, and housed an altar, where incense curled up from a glow of charcoal. It was brilliantly lit by more cressets of silver hanging from the roof. To one side of the altar there stood what I took at first to be a silver statue of the goddess or nymph to whom the shrine belonged.

At the foot of the steps the boy stopped and, moving aside, knelt. I felt Celidon's hand press my shoulder, and needed no spoken order, for the awe of the place was on me, but went down on my knees. He took Arthur by the hand and they went up the steps together. As they mounted, the image by the altar moved forward to meet them, and I saw that the goddess of the place had come alive.

The Merlin's voice, deep and strong, rang out:

"The years of waiting time are ended. I, Merlin the Messenger, bring the Chosen One to his Dragon Making. I bring you, Lady, the true son of the Traveller at the Ford, Arthur, heir of Uther Pendragon, the child the stars foretold. Receive him, safe out of my hand, for, from now on, he passes into your keeping."

I had known few women, then, and none of striking beauty. As I gazed up into the light it seemed to me that I must truly be looking at a being from another world— that Uncle Ectorius had been wrong when he taught us the gods existed only in men's minds. She was tall, slender, clothed in a robe white and shining as the spray of a waterfall, with cloudy silver hair caught back with a jewelled circlet from a face that seemed to have no age, pale and serene and intent—a face strange to me, yet, in some way, known and familiar as that of my nearest kin. The keeper of the shrine advanced and laid both hands on Arthur's shoulders. Looking over his head, directly at Celidon, she said:

"At your hands we receive him, Merlin the Messenger." Then she looked down at Arthur, and I saw him, his head up, meet that long, searching glance, unflinchingly. Her face changed, trembled into a sudden smile that transformed it from that of an other-world, enchanted image into a tender and loving woman.

"Welcome, my son," she said and, bending, kissed him on the forehead. Then, laying her arm about his

shoulders, turned with him towards the altar, and spoke
some words—a prayer I thought it must be—in a language I could not understand.

Her voice had a quality I have never heard in any
other woman's. It was clear and vibrant, not deep, but
with some note of hidden music in it, like the falling,
secret song of an Outland stream in the long June twi-
lights, or the distant murmur of waves rippling on a
moonlit shore.

When the prayer—if it was a prayer—was ended,
she took Arthur by the hand, and led him round the altar,
and with him passed out of sight. Celidon came quickly
and purposefully down the steps and spoke to the boy,
who had risen from his knees.

"You know your orders, Lancelot. From now on,
Bedivere here is in your charge."

He came across to me.

"Where Arthur goes now, you cannot go. But this
lad will tell you what you must do. Obey him as you
would obey me. It is understood?"

I had got up from my knees, bewildered and unhappy.

"But . . ." I began.

He touched me lightly on the shoulder, his face
stern, but his eyes kind.

"Do not be afraid. Arthur is safe here among his
own people. You help him now by doing only exactly as
Lancelot tells you. Understood?"

I nodded, and the next moment I was standing alone
before the lit and empty shrine, looking into the dark,
smiling face of a stranger, about my own age, who was
staring at me with friendly curiosity.

"No need to look so bewildered," he said, briskly. "I
know who you are—Bedivere, the milk-brother of the
High Prince. I am Lancelot, Prince of Armorica. Wait
while I put out the lamps. Then we will go to the Boys'
House and eat. Bors, my cousin, will have saved supper
for us. You must be hungry after your journey."

I could not find any words to answer him. After the
magic and the awe of the past hour this matter-of-fact
talk of supper seemed blasphemous. But while I watched

him go up to the shrine and deftly, neatly, extinguish each of the hanging lamps there, I realized that shamefully I was, in fact, hollow with a boy's sudden hunger.

"Doesn't he know *anything?*" Bors asked Lancelot gruffly, speaking across me, as one speaks across the head of a small child. I did not resent the question. I liked Bors. He was square and kind, a plain and dependable sort of person, who gave one a reassuring sense of ordinary life going on in spite of puzzling, magical happenings. I liked Lancelot, too, but there was a quizzical, foreign gaiety about him that made me not quite sure he was not secretly laughing at me. Now, there was definitely amusement in his voice as he said:

"How should he know? Everything here is as strange to him as it would be to us in a Roman household. What is it that puzzles you now, Bedivere?"

We were sitting, huddled together in a little grassy hollow, watching, across the water, lights winding up and up the mountain on the Holy Island, and hearing fitfully on the night wind the sound of solemn chanting. Overhead the sky had cleared to a great inverted bowl of darkest blue, prickled with stars, and above the mountain's blunt peak sailed the slim crescent of the new moon of May.

Lancelot pulled me nearer to him, spreading the great black cloak we were sharing further over my way.

"It's getting colder. No wonder. It must be almost midnight," he said, glancing up at the swinging outline of the Bear that had moved a long way since we had first settled in our vantage point. "Now—tell! What makes you afraid?"

"I'm *not* afraid," I said. "But—I wish I understood what everything *means.* Why did we have to come away, over the water, to this other Island? Why couldn't we stay and *see* what happened—over there?"

"Because it is a holy mystery. No one may see the hidden mysteries, Bedivere, until their own time comes to be initiated. Surely that must be true in all religions? Isn't it true in yours?"

"I don't know," I said.

"What *is* your religion?" Bors asked bluntly.

I was at a loss. I'd never thought about religion much.

"I don't know," I said again, and Bors grunted with a sort of despairing impatience. Defensively, I suggested, "My uncle says all religions are superstition. But one has to be a Christian now because it is an order of the emperor."

"Our Grand Master, Blaize, teaches that all religions are one, and all are holy." Lancelot was staring out across the lake. I could just see the outline of his lifted head in the starlight. "Religion is the pattern behind the universe, he says."

Bors said, still a little impatiently:

"Ours is the oldest in the world. Our Wise Men are trained for twenty years before they become Priests. But they teach us to respect all the others. Your Christian white brothers have lived down *there*—by the harbor," he pointed to the lower end of the Island, farthest from the mountain, "ever since the Christ God died and they had to take refuge far from his country. They are good men. I like them. Only they do not have mysteries, perhaps."

"They have their own," Lancelot corrected him. "Remember—they share the Mystery of the Cup with us, Bors, at Spring Sowing."

"*Why* must things be mysteries?" I asked, rebelliously.

Lancelot turned his head and looked at me. I could not see his face, but his voice sounded abrupt and impatient, suddenly.

"Because they are part of—of the pattern. Like tides, and seasons and the march of the stars. Things have to happen when they are ready to happen, at the right time; not all in chaos. *We* aren't ready for our Dragon Making—yet. The Chosen One is. It—it's like growing up. A child has to *grow* into a warrior. Oh, I can't explain! Ask the Merlin."

"Don't *you* know what they are doing to Arthur over there?" I asked, suspiciously.

"Making him free of Air and Water, Earth and Fire.

Ah!" Lancelot sprang up, throwing back the cloak and pulling me up with a sudden tug at my hand. "Look—there goes the Fire! The ceremony is complete. *Hail to the Dragon! Hail to the Dragon!*"

"*Hail to the Dragon!*" Boys' voices were echoing from all along the hillside on each side of us, as, across the water, on the blunt tip of the mountain, a red spark grew and spread into a great, flaming beacon and, faint and strange and exciting, there came the echo of horns blown and voices raised in a deep, triumphant chant.

For a few moments, Bors and Lancelot capered beside me like mad things and, catching the infection of their excitement, I capered and shouted, too. Then suddenly, Lancelot stood still, turned, and gripped both my hands.

"It doesn't matter that you don't understand. It's *happened*. Everything's all right, Bedivere," he said and, to my embarrassment, flung his arms round me and kissed me on both cheeks.

Bors said, gruff and practical:

"That's over, then. Best get down to the guest hut, Lancelot. Remember what the Merlin said."

Lancelot nodded.

"Yes. Before the other boys start coming in from watching. If they see *him* now, they'll start asking questions."

They took my hands and hurried me away, over the low hill behind us, and down to a cluster of huts that lay beyond.

Lancelot explained, a little breathlessly:

"The others of the school here come from many Clans, and some—a few—might not understand *you* having been allowed to land on these islands because you are Roman-born. They are—old-fashioned—some of them, who have not been here long. The Merlin wanted no trouble, so he said we should slip away quietly. You will sleep alone with us in the guest hut, and before dawn I am to rouse you and see you are ferried back to meet him on the mainland—him and the High Prince." He added, suddenly and charmingly, "We wish you could stay with us longer, Bedivere, but, who knows? Maybe the High Prince will serve his term of training here later. If so, they just might let you come too. Then you would understand everything. I hope that will happen. We should like it very much, Bors and I, to have you for our friend!"

# Chapter Three

Celidon, Arthur and I left the lake country of Ynis Witrin in the dawn next day, and were back in deep forest by noon. There was an altogether different and more urgent atmosphere to our journey from then on. Later, when I came to know the land about there well, I understood why Celidon plunged us immediately into the all but impenetrable trackways of uncleared woodlands. Had we ridden by the nearest route to the destination he had in mind, we must have passed across a tract of long-settled Colonial country. Those who rode to a Gathering in those days avoided, when possible, drawing attention to their passing.

Our journey took on a strict discipline of haste. Once we had rejoined Caw and his sons and the dwarf Gobo, we moved like a military patrol in enemy territory, commanded by a strict and alert officer, who insisted constantly on speed and silence. Alert, wary, watchful, Celidon's whole face and manner changed, so that we were aware, instinctively, of danger; and the sheer hardship of the going kept boys of our age, hardy though we were, at the full stretch of endurance. Later, when we were grown men and, in war, penetrated similar shaggy wilderness, we found it taxed our strength, for the uncleared forests of Britain go back, time out of mind, and the narrow tracks that the Little People have made are meant for small, bare feet, and not for the passage of horsemen. Hunters like Caw can follow their bewildering pattern, always darkened by the green gloom of the close-growing trees, winding about and about to avoid impenetrable scrub, barred by vast thickets of holly, made dangerous by overgrowth of bramble, strong as hempen rope, and slippery with rotten wood and fallen leaves. There are tracts, besides, of swamp and bog; and deep rivers, where fords are hard to find. Always there is the green gloom, and the smell of rotting vegetation and—when it rains— the steady drip off the trees long after the rain has passed. That week it rained most of the time.

We pressed on, single file, day after day, for fifteen days, with Caw and his sons clearing the path ahead for us whenever the ponies could not pass. There was no time for talk, and at night we were too dog-weary for it.

The first day, I watched Arthur sidelong, looking for any sign on him of the Island's enchantment, wondering if he would be changed in some fashion. His expression warned me to ask no questions. He looked pale and his eyes were very bright, but his face had a closed look I recognized, the mouth firm, the chin up, a little frown between the brows. In that mood, one waited for him to speak first, if one did not want a snub. The only new thing that was visible about him was a great coiled ring he wore on his right arm. It was of heavy, red gold, and shaped like a snake, with jewelled eyes. It was too big for his brown, boy's arm, and every now and then it slipped down to his wrist and he pushed it quickly back into place as he rode ahead of me.

I was not happy. I had never known loneliness before, so I did not recognize the heaviness of it, but blamed the dark forest, and wished, through a mist of discomfort and weariness, that we were riding back to-wards home, and not, as it seemed to me, half across a world away from it.

Quite suddenly, early one morning, the weather changed and the country changed, and the nightmare was over. We were riding across open moorland, in bright sunshine and a racing wind, towards rolling hills, and the whole feeling of life was miraculously different. We still rode too fast for talk, until, about noon, we were among the foothills, and Celidon drew rein under a little rowan tree, covered with tossing white bloom, and smiled at us, his face the face of the friend we had known at first.

"So!" he said, "That's the worst of the way safely over! Caw, you've guided us well. Am I right, two more days should bring us to the Place of Gathering?"

Grinning, Caw touched fist to forehead:

"If the gods will it, master."

"Then we can afford to rest and eat. Come, boys, off your ponies and down here into the hollow out of the wind. Ah, but it's good to feel the warmth of the sun again!"

As we slid to the ground, and Caw's sons led our ponies away, Arthur stretched his arms over his head, standing suddenly up on tiptoe, as though he wanted to fly.

"The sun!" he shouted. "The sun at last!"

His whole face had come alive. He looked, I thought, as though he had just woken up out of a deep sleep. Suddenly he dived at me, catching me round the waist in a running tackle.

"Come on. Wrestle!" he challenged.

We scuffled happily, until he tripped me and we rolled together in the short, dry heather. Then, breathless and laughing, he pulled me up, and ran me over to drop down in the warm hollow at the Merlin's feet. His arm ring had slipped down to his wrist again. He pushed it back carefully, then looked up at the Merlin: a quick, shy glance.

"I shall grow to it—soon," he said challengingly.

"You will grow to it. Your father was a big man, though, and it will take some years yet." Celidon's smile answered his. He was our friend again—not the stern, anxious guardian who had driven us so hard through the dark forest. "Meanwhile . . ." He paused, and called, "Gobo, come here."

The dwarf waddled across from the saddlebag he had been helping Caw to unload, and pulled off his greasy red cap.

"Master?" he queried.

"You know this country. How far are we from the village of Lob the Cunning?"

Gobo turned around, as a dog will, sniffing for a scent. Then pointed up into the hills to the right.

"One hour, maybe two hours. That way, it lies."

"He's still working?"

Gobo's toad face split into a grin.

"Lob's working. Makes a good thing. Making a King Sword," he said.

Celidon's eyebrows shot up.

"Is he, by the old gods! Now what, I wonder, put that into his head?"

Gobo puffed out his cheeks.

"Lob very old, very wise. He know things before they happen. Little People of the Hills always know."

"They do, indeed," Celidon said softly. Then, suddenly frowning:

"Gobo—why a King Sword—now?"

Gobo blinked and fidgeted, twisting his cap in his huge, distorted hands.

"Because of the Dragon Fire," he muttered. Then, shrilly, "Gobo has seen it. Caw has seen, and Amil and Gerwent and Rianon."

"But here in the Outland hills, Lob *cannot* have seen. Gobo, what signal did you send to your people?"

Gobo began to back away.

"What signal, Gobo?" Celidon's voice was relentless.

"That—that—the Chosen One has come at last," Gobo muttered. Then his voice rose shrilly. "It is the truth—look, he wears the magic snake. I sent word only because he must be guarded now, guarded all the way. Master, do not take Gobo's cap. Do not take it!" and he hugged the dirty object close to his pigeon breast.

Celidon shrugged and shook his head.

"You deserve I should. Caw and Amil and Gerwent and Rianon saw the Dragon Fire, but *they* will keep silence. Gobo saw—and has told a secret thing to all the Little People of the Hills," he accused grimly.

Gobo drew himself up with a strange dignity.

"With the People of the Hills a secret is a secret. My master knows that. We *also* are the People of the Dragon

King," he said proudly. Then, his head on one side, wheedling like a child, "Gobo keeps his cap?"

"This time, yes. Another time, disobey me, and without permission send signals with the smudge-fire, and it will be no. Now go!"

As Gobo scrambled off, crablike, in a great hurry, Celidon laughed.

"To every man, his own magic!" he said resignedly. "Two things for you to learn from that conversation, Prince of Britain. To an Outlander his red cap carries all his luck. Take it from him, and the chances are he'll sicken and die, believing he has lost that luck. And secondly, always remember news runs faster under the fern than any emperor's post ever travelled. Your Hill People will know of every move you make and every word you utter, telling it from headland to headland with their small and secret smother-fires. Treat them well and they will serve you faithfully. Ill use them, betray them," he spread out his hands, "one of their poisoned elf-bolts brings a death that is not a good death to die. Now come, here is Caw with our noonings. When we have eaten we will ride over to one of their villages, and Lob the Smith shall alter that ring to fit your arm, Arthur. He is one of the very few I would trust to do it."

We rode up into the hills and came, after a time, across a great whaleback ridge, crowned with granite tors, to the edge of a steep valley. Celidon pointed down into it.

"Lob's village. Gobo, ride on and warn your people," he said.

Grinning, Gobo headed his pony downhill, and once he was out of earshot Celidon turned to us.

"They take fright like conies. Ride into one of their villages unannounced, you'll find it deserted," he said. "But keep your wits about you once we are among them—you too, Caw. They are notable thieves, and will whip the knife from your belt or the very shoes from your feet, and you none the wiser, if you are off guard. They do it for a pastime, like mischievous children. We want no trouble of that sort today."

Caw grunted agreement.

"I am knowing them, sir. From the pit they come and small devils they are. I will be watching them, never fear!"

As we rode downhill, letting the ponies pick their own way, I looked everywhere for the village. A stream brawled in sharp little waterfalls among the granite stones that littered the heather; and a sparrowhawk went sailing downwind, its shadow beneath it. The moorland rose on every side to the milky blue sky, empty of all life. Even Gobo had disappeared.

"I don't see any village. Where is it?" I asked. I dared ask questions again, and that was a happiness in itself.

"In the hollow. You will soon see," Celidon told me.

We came up over a small, sudden rise, and there, in the shadow below us, lay a round green basin, made uneven with grassy hummocks, and in the middle of it a ring of little men, black-haired, grimy and half-naked, but all wearing red caps, gathered about Gobo and his pony, chattering like a roost of starlings.

As we rode down towards them, they scattered in every direction, all except one, and seemed literally to vanish into the hillside. The one who waited our coming was taller than the others, which still gave him only the height of a fourteen-year-old lad. He was powerfully built, barrel-chested, with arms that hung almost to his knees. Grey elf-locks fluttered round a face so tanned and lined it might have been carved from a twisted root, and over his rags he wore the torn and scorched remnants of a smith's leather apron.

He limped forward to stand by Celidon's mule and, doffing his cap, ducked a greeting, then peered up at him sideways. One of his eyes was blind, covered by the whitish skin of a cataract.

"Greetings, Merlin the Master, and the greetings of all my people to him who rides at your right hand," he said in a gutteral growl. "What service does the Chosen One seek from Lob and Lob's folk?"

"Smith's service, Lob old friend." Celidon got down from the saddle, signing to us to do the same. "The serpent ring of Britain holds strong magic, Lob, and I would trust it only to a smith who understands magic as well as metalcraft. It fitted, last, the right arm of a king and a warrior. Now, it must fit a boy's arm. Can you spring it safely for me, so that he can wear it without danger of loss, yet so that it will stretch again as he comes to manhood? You understand such things. Give him the ring, Prince Arthur."

Arthur slipped the coiled ring off and held it out. Lob made the sign of homage, then stood for a moment, as if in thought, before he took it carefully into his big, callused hands.

"Strong magic and old magic," he said slowly. "Great kings and great warriors, back and back into the beginning of time—but none greater than he who shall wear it next." He glanced quickly up at Celidon, then turned the ring about, examining it, feeling it with a touch that was delicate and searching. Presently he said, nodding, "What needs to be done, Lob can do. But stand close while the fire touches it, Merlin, lest the fire spirits steal the magic."

He handed the ring to Celidon again, then turned and screeched a string of commands in an eldritch yell that made the ponies start and fidget.

Red caps popped up out of the grassy hillocks, as the little men we had seen before came scrambling out of their burrows. Lob roared orders in an unknown tongue and a flurry of activity began. Under cover of it I whispered to Celidon:

"Do they live *in* those hillocks?"

He nodded.

"Like conies in a warren. They dig themselves pits and roof them over with turf. No!" as I began to move curiously towards the nearest entrance, "don't go inside to look. You'd be lousy as a hedgehog in five minutes, boy!"

Lob's forge, however, he allowed us to enter, as Lob beckoned us within. It was a natural cave, running back into the steepest slope of the hillside, shored up here and there with rough granite blocks and thick old tree trunks. The stream we had seen before ran through it and at first that was all I could be sure of, for the place was dusky as late twilight and it stank (as did the smith himself at close quarters). But as the little men rushed in and out, carrying billets of wood and leather buckets of charcoal, the fire that had blinked only a few red embers at first began to crackle and roar, and flamelight reached out to show first a square anvil stone and the tools that lay on it, then strange shapes and glinting piles of stones and scraps of metal lying all about and white gleams of foam, swirling on the surface of the stream.

At first we were content to watch Lob as he began to work at the anvil. But he was a slow and careful craftsman, and a boy's curiosity is insatiable in such a place. Presently we wandered off to look at other things. I was squatting on my heels, examining a lump of stone that seemed to have sparks deep inside it as I turned it towards the firelight, when Arthur touched my shoulder.

"Come," he said softly. "Come and look."

I got up and followed him between two of the granite pillars into the very back of the cave.

"Look," he said again, and then, in a breathless whisper, "the Sword!"

It lay on a faded red cloth that was spread on a ledge cut out of the very roots of the great hill, and as the flamelight fought the shadows, it looked itself rugged and rough-hewn.

"Is it—real?" I whispered.

"Yes," Arthur answered with absolute conviction. "Real—but not ready. It is the sword he is making for the king. It must be."

"Your sword," I said.

"My sword," Arthur answered. Going forward, slowly, a step at a time, he put out his hand and laid it for the first time on the great cross-hilt of Excalibur.

The coiled snake ring fitted close on the young brown

arm, the red jewelled eyes in the scaled head catching life from the fire. Celidon the Merlin, who had sprung it into place, kept his hands cupped about it for a moment, and his voice held the harp note as he said:

"Remember always, Dragon of Britain, the serpent of wisdom lies coiled about the roots of the Tree of Life. Its magic is the oldest that we know, for it is the symbol of eternity that has no beginning and no end." Then he turned to Lob and his voice changed, as it so often did, to a brisk and businesslike note. "This work is well done, old friend, as only Lob could do it. Now the King Sword will take its final forging safely. Put aside fear. I am here. I will help you."

Lob looked up at him with his sideways glance that reminded me of a tame raven we had once had at home.

"If the Merlin says so," he growled, deep in his throat. "But with the sky-iron there is always risk. Lob waited the hour of the gods. Is it now, master?"

"It is now. Listen, Old One, the stream sings for it. The fire spirits call for it. Fetch the King Sword here, to the anvil, and finish its forging, while the power of the Dragon and the power of the Merlin are together in this place to give you strength. Better, if there were, as you have feared, fault in the star-metal, it should shatter now, than in the hand of the king who must wield it in the name of Light."

"True, master. True," Lob murmured. His face crinkled into an expression of excitement. Turning, he shouted:

"More fire, here! Much fire!" Then he began to sort among his tools, laying them out methodically, and giving orders right and left to his assistants as he did so in the gutteral language he had used earlier. Presently, when all was prepared as he wanted it, he motioned them back, and they melted, twittering together in whispers, into a circle, half hidden in the shadows. Lob took up a great stone hammer and looked across at Celidon:

"Let you bring the sword to me now Merlin, King Maker, and set your magic on it before Lob touches it again."

Celidon smiled.

"Let the one who shall wield it bring it. Prince Arthur, fetch me the sword Excalibur," he said.

Arthur looked up at him and their eyes met and held for a long moment. Then Arthur turned, and disappeared into the shadowed recess. When I saw him again in the red glow by the forge, he was holding the great black iron sword across his outstretched palms. In the flamelight his face looked grave and stern—and much older. Some trick of the light in that shadowed place showed me, for a brief moment, the face of the king I should follow down thirty unguessed years, until, at the last, the same sword passed from his hands to mine.

Much has been sung by harpers of Arthur's sword, Excalibur. Next to the Grail itself, it will live for ever in song as one of the Chief Hallows of Britain. Bards tell how its hilt flashed with jewels and the blade glimmered with runes, wrought in gold. I, Bedivere, who saw its final tempering, know these tales are folly. No soldier who knows his trade would choose such a weapon for use in a day-long battle. For parade, perhaps. Not for use. No, Excalibur was of an altogether different quality—one of those rarest swords only our Outland smiths know the secret of making—a sword forged from metal that does not grow on earth, but falls out of the infinite distances of the sky, when a star dies. The iron that, if it takes the third forging and does not shatter at cooling, turns darkly blue as the sky of midnight, and has a strength and a temper to it that no other metal will blunt or bend in the striking—a blade that will hone sharp as a razor and hold its edge, no matter what it bites. True, Lob, who knew its own magic, pricked strange, running patterns of spells that were old when men raised the standing stones, on hilt and blade. But that he did later, adding also another secret of his own, which only Arthur knew; and maybe the Merlin guessed. What I saw done in the cave was the hammering on the anvil, where the long blade glowed, red as a rose, red as the Grail, and then, at the last, the great clouds of hissing steam rising from the running water, as kneeling by the moorland stream, Lob called aloud to the old gods, as he drew the cooled metal out from its quenching, and staggered to his feet, his face white-runnelled where sweat ran in lines through the ingrained dirt, as he cried:

"It has taken the forging! Lob's work is done. Behold, Merlin, my master, the iron is blue!"

# Chapter Four

We had ridden some miles back across the hills, in the clear green light of sunset's afterglow, when a commotion among the slaves and a resounding oath from Caw made Celidon check his mule and look back, smiling:

"What's amiss?" he asked.

"The good bronze shoulder clasp that I have been putting into my pouch for safety—those small sons of the darkness have had it off me!" Caw complained. "It must have been at the very last, as I waited for the Prince to come to his horse, after you had mounted, master!"

Caw's sons stood grinning and Celidon laughed.

"I warned you to be careful," he said.

"And so I was, until that last moment. The wee thieving rascals that they are! And after we had given them meal and meat from our store, as well and besides the good payment yourself made to the smith. There is no gratitude to be had from an Outlander and never will be!" Caw grumbled.

"I'll give you another clasp—one of my best ones, Caw—when we get home," Arthur promised him, laughing, but kindly.

"Lucky if that's all we've lost." Celidon sounded philosophical. "Come—no use to go back now. We'd get no profit from the journey." And he urged his mule forward again.

Riding each side of him, through the spring twilight, the quietness of the great hills enclosed us. Only after a long silence, staring ahead, and speaking to no one in particular, out of a glowing happiness that shone from him like the last gold that was touching the high tors, Arthur said softly:

"They would be welcome to everything—everything I ever had—if one day I ride with *that* sword at my side! How long will it be, Celidon?"

Celidon shrugged:

"Who knows? The years will pass quickly, and will be short for all you must learn in them. You will remember what Lob taught you in the last moments, alone, while we waited?"

Arthur gave him a brief flashing smile.

"I shall remember the Secret of the Sword," he said, and added, under his breath, *"my* sword."

Three more days we rode through wilderness country, with the white clouds puffing up through the blue overhead, seeing no sign of life but deer and wild ponies and an occasional wisp of smoke on a distant tor that made Celidon raise his eyebrows and smile to himself.

I forgot I had ever been homesick and lonely. Though Arthur talked very little, he felt close again, as he had always been, and I knew the Dragon magic had not separated us. I chattered a good deal, I remember, telling him of Lancelot and Bors and the Boys' House on the Island.

Sometimes I thought he was not listening. Once, rousing himself from some deep preoccupation, he said:

"I'm sorry, Bedivere. Go on telling me. I was thinking."

"What about?" I asked.

He moved his head impatiently.

"Everything. There's so much." Then he smiled at me. "That my father was a king—and that I have a mother. It's still hard to believe. I was thinking of those things—and of the sword."

I stared at him—seeing, as one sometimes does, suddenly and very clearly, a face long familiar take on a new aspect. In that moment I knew, quite certainly, a thing he never afterwards told me or needed to tell, for he accepted that I must know it. I understood why I had recognized as a face I already knew better than I ever knew my own, or even Ygern's, the face of The Lady of the Lake.

On the third day the country grew steeper, more rugged. Everywhere great granite tors thrust up through the brown heather roots and thin, blanched grass. Ahead, a high blue ridge cut the sky, crowned with stones like fortress ramparts. We were no longer the only travellers. In the distance we saw, several times, other riders, singly or in little groups, and in the afternoon, a string of armed men dark against the western horizon. The slanting sun glinted on spears, and on a great, floating banner.

Caw, trotting at Arthur's stirrup, pointed and cried out a name. Celidon turned his head.

"Who?" he asked sharply.

"The Prince Geraint. There goes the Dragon of Cornwall, master."

"So!" Celidon shaded his eyes. "If you see right at such a distance, you see a good omen, Caw."

Caw nodded, his face crinkled in a smile that was grim.

"I am thinking this will be indeed a great Gathering —a Gathering to be remembered, if *he* comes to it!" he rumbled, and repeated again under his breath, "the Dragon of Cornwall—to *this* Gathering!"

Dusk had fallen before we came up between two great tors, high as watch towers, to a narrow pass, not to have been guessed at half a mile away, and looked down on the Place of Gathering. A wide valley, shaped like a shallow dish, lay beneath us, a river winding through it that reflected the last light like a gleaming pewter snake. On every side of the valley, enclosing it, rose the high hills, some steep and rockstrewn, some dolphin-backed and heather-covered. A secret place. A hidden place. But not lonely.

Celidon gave one of his sudden laughs, startling as a fox's bark on a winter night.

"So! We are not the first! The Branch has not gone out unheeded. Caw, you were right. We have come to a great Gathering."

The valley and the lower slopes of the protecting hills were alive with folk; winking with little cooking fires; busy with coming and going of men and horses. We could hear laughter and raised voices and the stamping of picketed ponies. There was a feeling of life, excitement, gaiety, in the very air.

"So many!" Arthur said, his voice awed and unbelieving. "So many *people!*"

Celidon laughed again, not as a fox barks, but softly and triumphantly.

"Your people, my Prince. They must have been gathering here since before the new moon—gathering from the four corners of Britain."

Again Caw's voice rumbled on that deep note of emotion.

"The new moon of Spring Sowing—and soon that moon will be at the full! They are knowing what it means for them this year, master."

"They know," Celidon nodded. "They have travelled long roads, old friend, but none longer than you and I have travelled from a snowy night and the beat of breakers on the cliffs of Tintagel. Take the High Prince's bridle and lead his horse down the track. It is an honor you have earned. We follow."

Few men, I suppose, even in their old age, forget their first Clan Gathering. Over the years I have taken my part in many—from the time I first competed in the boys' long race, to the days when I served as marshal and judge. Of those last I remember only the odd incident here and there—but always, when I hear the words spoken, clearly as if it had happened yesterday I see the secret valley in our western wilderness, where the Clans met for Arthur's King Choosing, and it is as though a hand squeezes my heart again with a boy's wild, almost suffocating excitement.

We had seen so little in our lives before, Arthur and I, of crowds and color and pageantry. It seemed to us that half the world's people must have come together there, and Caw made it plain that they had come to do honor to their High Prince, leader already, by right of inheritance, of the powerful Clan of Dumnonia, and appointed Pendragon of the future.

"Hold your heads up, both of you, and do not be staring everywhere about, grinning and asking questions as though we were nobodies," he warned us the first morning, with the careful anxiety for appearances a trusted family slave will show. "Remember, by the eagle feather in your cap, Prince Arthur, Dumnonia will know you for who you are. A proud and modest bearing they will be expecting, and if, by custom, none seem to salute you until the time of the Choosing for who you are, they will be taking note fair enough—they and all the others, also."

His advice was wise, but it was hard for us—Arthur as well as me—to follow. There was so much to see, so much that was new and strange. The soft, yet brilliant colors of the Clansmen's tunics—an infinite variety of combinations of greens, browns and sombre blues, laced through with the checkering lines of heather-purple and deep rose, or gorse-yellow. Colors by long experience chosen and woven by the women to merge into our island landscape and give a man protection when he needed to move unseen. Patterns of color that distinguished one Clan from another in tribal war. Men wear their best for a Gathering. Jewels flashed on shoulder and sword belt. The High Kings and Princes went about with great torques of red-gold about their throats, and many arm rings on the left arm, though on the right each wore only the snake ring of his Dragon initiation. Even those were of many differing designs. Among the crowds, mingling with them, were harpers and jugglers and peddlers, and on the outskirts one could always find a horse dealer, showing the paces of his fast chariot ponies, with here and there even a warhorse, larger than any we had seen until then, and always loudly vaunted as bred in direct line from the cavalry stallions of the legions.

Why describe it? Afterwards one saw it all repeated many times. Old men remember still—those who are too young to remember will never see the like again. The past is the past. There are no more Clan Gatherings since Camlan.

It was true that (by custom, as Caw had said) when we went among the people, Caw and his sons with us, close-faced but watchful, we might have been wearing the cloak of invisibility the harpers say the Merlin could assume at will. No one stared openly, but, like a rustle of wind in the ripe corn, I felt the whisper that followed us, and it made the hairs on my neck prickle.

For three full days, the distant Clans were still coming in. Down on the level ground in the valley bottom an arena had been marked out with peeled stakes. There were races and wrestling, spear throwing and archery, and best of all the chariot racing. We were given places on the outskirts of a stand where the judges of the games rewarded the victors, vying with each other, as Caw told us, in the liberality of their gifts. It was there we saw Geraint of Cornwall, a handsome, brown-bearded man then in his late thirties, who glanced our way with one quick, piercing look, after someone had whispered in his ear.

For those three days, we saw nothing of Celidon, but were left entirely in Caw's charge. Up in a cleft of the hills, at the eastern end of the valley, there was a walled village of round stone huts. It was sacred ground. A colony of the Wise Ones and the Merlin had withdrawn there for reasons, that, Caw told us firmly, were no business of ours.

"Himself will be there until the Warrior Making. They are preparing the boys for that. Since you are too young for it by more than two winters, it is not concerning us," he said, and shut his mouth close as a bear trap.

I knew a little about what it meant and told Arthur what I knew.

"Lancelot and Bors will be there and some of the other boys from the Island school. They have magic done on them first, and then there is a very hard test. You have to be fourteen years old."

Arthur frowned.

"What test? How hard?" he asked.

I had to admit I did not know.

When, on the third evening, Celidon returned to the

camp Caw had set up for us in a quiet place high on the hillside, screened by flowering gorse bushes, Arthur challenged him.

"Why must I wait two years to be made a warrior? Surely a Dragon should be a warrior? My Clan will expect it."

The lines on Celidon's face were deeply grooved. For the first time since I had known him, he hesitated. He put his hands on Arthur's shoulders, his strange, hooded eyes searching his face.

"There are reasons. You will understand them when your time comes. You are still too young."

"But I am very strong. As strong as most of the fisherboys of fourteen at home," Arthur said.

Celidon shook his head and walked away a few steps, standing with his back to us, looking out across the shadowed valley.

*"Please!"* Arthur said, softly but urgently. I believe it was the only time in his life I ever heard him plead for anything for himself.

Celidon shook his head.

"The risk is great. And yet . . ." Suddenly he swung round. "Arthur, there are some here who would agree with you a Dragon should show his mettle to the Clans. Some even spoke for it in Council—but they are not of your own Clan, and they are not altogether your friends. Certain things would have to be done later, but the Testing you could try—and that would prove you to them. If you failed . . ."

"I shall not fail," Arthur said, with absolute conviction. "Whatever the test, I *know* I shall not fail. It is something that is laid on me. Let me try."

Celidon spread out his hands in a gesture of defeat.

"Unless a man has courage to throw the dice, how will he win the wager?" he said softly. "If, in fact, you succeed, Arthur, at least those who say of the new Dragon that he is still only a child may have to think again. It is a risk indeed—but you and I may as well get used to taking risks together. Very well—I will grant your re-

quest, and I shall see to it all men know it *was* yours."
Again he shook his head and warned, "I tell you now,
you'll not find it easy!"

Arthur's eyes were blazing with excitement. As always, when he felt anything deeply, he said nothing at all.
He did not need to. Joy and gratitude were written on his
face.

Celidon became strictly practical.

"You will need a runner's short linen tunic. Caw
must see to that for you. Are your feet hard?"

Arthur's answer was to kick off his sandal and,
standing like a crane on one leg, display the leathery sole
of his foot.

"At home we always go barefoot. It saves our sandals," I interrupted. I'd been waiting eagerly for a chance
to speak. "Celidon, please, me too! Let me try, with
Arthur."

Celidon scowled at me, but I saw his eyes were
laughing. Before he could argue, I went on breathlessly,
"You said—you *did* say—that as I am Arthur's milk-
brother the Clan might accept me one day. Wouldn't this
help to prove I was worth accepting?"

(I'd forgotten, just then, the pride I should have had
in my Colonial blood. What I had seen of the Gathering
and the glamour of it had wiped out all memory of Uncle
Ectorius' parting instruction.)

Celidon shrugged.

"Unwise the man who lets house-reared wolfcubs
taste raw meat!" he said ruefully.

Arthur looked up quickly from refastening his sandal, and said with authority:

"Where I go, Bedivere goes, Celidon."

Celidon bowed, gravely mocking.

"As my High Prince orders," he said. Arthur flushed
scarlet. Celidon could always cut one down to size at the
age we were then—*and* for a long time after.

Warrior Making is a test of courage, strength and endurance. It serves a Clan to measure the quality of its boys
coming to manhood, both physically and as regards their
characters. I still think it a wise custom. I have served

among the judges for it many times and used similar tests as a commander to size up new recruits. One learns, by observation, that way to recognize the lad who has stamina enough to be trusted in battle and the one whose nerve may fail him. One can pick out the boy who, strong but too headlong, will need disciplining, and the type so eager for approval he'll cheat to win. They all take the Testing with deadly seriousness at fourteen. It is bound up for them with their religion, being part, always, of a solemn Gathering. To succeed, to be acclaimed at the end by the shouting of the whole assembled Clan, is something most men will agree crowns a day that stands out in memory all one's life. At the time, as the Merlin warned us, the thing is not easy.

Now, as I look back across the years, I see small, bright pictures—flashes only, that printed themselves on my mind, stamped there by stress, or terror, or pride. I accept again, earnestly, the order given as we gather in the early mist (shivering a little, because the dew-drenched heather is cold to bare feet) that all day we must go fasting. Even to drink from a spring is forbidden. I hear the short, sharp blast of the horn that scatters us, running, and think again it sounds like an old sheep coughing. I look up at a rock face I am told to scale, and reckon how far apart the holds are, for toes and fingers. Chosen for taller contestants than I am, they are going to mean a long, long stretch. I stand at the mouth of a dark cavern, where water drips from the overhang and gurgles, unseen, somewhere in the darkness ahead. A boy who has gone in before me suddenly rushes back into the light, his eyes staring, foam at the corner of his lips as he babbles horribly in uncontrollable panic. The judge at the entrance says to me impatiently:

"Your turn next. Get on with it! Wait until your eyes get used to the gloom. You'll see a spark of daylight ahead." Then, because he is kindly and perhaps I look small to him: "Don't pay attention to that bastard—some of them haven't the guts for this. Prove you have!"

I know Arthur is ahead of me and where he goes, I will go!

Outside at last, blinking, my heart hammering, my

knees raw and bleeding from scrambling about over sharp
rocks in the dark, I cannot see him anywhere. It is open
grassland, tussocky, with patches of gorse. There is shouting and wild yells. We have to catch unbroken ponies and
ride. I see a boy bucked off into a prickle clump and it
makes me laugh. Suddenly I feel better. I see Arthur
again. He has caught and mounted a pure white colt, with
wickedly rolling eyes. It rears and fights, but this is a
sport we've practiced often enough. He goes past me like
the wind, his knees gripping, his hands tangled in the
shaggy mane, his hair streaming out, bright and glinting
in the sun; and I yell encouragement to him louder than
all the rest.

It is late afternoon and oh, my belly flaps against my
backbone, I am so hungry! The thirst is even worse.
Everywhere in this boggy land little trickles of water run
to tempt me—but an order is an order. To fail because of
*that* would be too shaming. This must be the end of the
test—this long, gruelling race over rough country. How
much further? I flounder in a soft patch, and fall among
rushes and quaking yellow grasses. My legs are aching,
and I am slow, slow. A boy passes me and shouts back
over his shoulder:

"Bedivere, come *on!*"

It is Arthur. Where he goes I *will* go.

He shoots ahead. He can't win this race, though.
There were others far out in front. I am disappointed. He
should win. He is the High Prince—the Dragon.

The last barrier lies across our path. We are coming
to the river, where it divides into two streams, with
waterfalls. There is a great stone in the middle of it.
White water swirls on two sides, crossed by a chain of
black rocks, smooth, slippery, like seals' heads poking up
out of foam. There is a deep, dark pool, where the
streams join again, and the great rock hangs forward over
it, pierced through by a round hole. Warriors are waiting
on the near bank. The far bank is dark with watching
folk.

What is happening? A warrior stretches out his arm
as if to catch Arthur and hold him back, but Arthur
thrusts the arm aside, ducks under it. He is across the

stepping stones, going up the side of the great rock like a squirrel up a tree. For a moment he stands on its crest, his arms stretched up as if he is praying. Then I understand. He goes, head down, diving through the hole, and the dark water of the pool closes over him smoothly.

A roaring is in my ears and the ground is rocking under me. My breathing hurts my chest. The people are shouting on the far bank as Arthur comes up from that dive, laughing, shaking the water out of his eyes. I can hear words—rhythmic—almost chanted.

"Hail to the Twice Born! A warrior is born! A warrior for the Dumnonii!"

Where he goes—but I can't. Strong hands are on my shoulders. Though I wriggle frantically, they hold me in a vice. Over my head, a man's voice says, laughing:

"Keep still, will you! If we let another one your age through it'll cost us all a flogging!"

I am thrust down ignominiously into the heather.

"Sit!" a great, grinning Dumnonian Clansman orders me, as he would order a young, too-eager sheep collie. Then, kindly, soothingly, "You've had enough for one day, young 'un. It's by the Merlin's order I'm stopping you." Speaking across me, to another warrior: "I've got this one safe, so I have. The Merlin will have our hides off us. His orders was clear enough."

Hazily I see the other man's face. He is staring ahead of him, as if he has seen a god go by, and the light of that passing still all about him.

"Twelve years old—and he went into the Sacred Pool through the birthstone as gay as an otter at play. You can tell what egg that chick hatched from! He's our Chosen One, right enough. There's hope for Britain yet!"

His voice booms in my ears. The sky tilts above me and the ground comes up to meet it.

From a long way off I hear my captor's voice, suddenly anxious:

"Put your head between your knees, boy. You ran that last mile too hard!"

For the first time in my life, I go out in a dead faint.

In the years I worked closely with Celidon the Merlin he often surprised me. His ways were not the ways of ordinary men. It was half a lifetime before it ceased to puzzle me that he trusted me at twelve years old as if I were a grown man. Now I understand it. Having the Sight, time meant nothing to him. He saw the long pattern of past lives that had brought me to the Place of Gathering, and he knew, from the beginning, to what strange, unguessed end the path before me would lead.

On the morning after the Warrior Making I sat alone on a boulder in a little hollow below our camping place, picking bramble thorns out of my feet, and occasionally licking away a tear as it trickled down the side of my nose.

I was stiff, bruised and grazed all over. I was not Twice Born. I was very, very lonely.

I had come to myself, the night before, back in our sleeping shelter, wrapped snugly in blankets, and Caw had tended me with rough gentleness, feeding me broth and bread, plastering my various hurts. To my first question—"Where's Arthur?"—he answered briefly:

"No more talk now. Sup your broth and then sleep. It's been a rough day for one your age. Enough is enough."

Morning had not made him more communicative. I got nothing from him but a few grunts of rising irritation, and an order to keep my questions for the Merlin.

"And do not you be straying from this place, for when Himself comes, he will have need of you. Now leave me in peace to do my work," he told me.

I knew it was useless to argue. I thought he was despising me, ashamed because I had fainted like a girl in front of all the watching people; because I had not finished the course, and been hailed warrior and Twice Born as Arthur had been.

Licking up my tears, I brooded on the injustice of the failure that had left me outcast, separated from Arthur, who, being always just, would have understood.

A shadow fell across my hiding place. I looked up, then down again quickly.

It was Celidon—and Celidon, that morning, was my enemy.

Silence, when it lengthens, becomes unbearable to any child. At last I mumbled:

"I *could* have finished the course. Why did you order them to stop me?"

"Because, had you slipped, being faint and overweary, you'd have cracked your skull. Then in years to come, Arthur would have lacked a friend at need—and so should I," Celidon said gently.

I looked up and saw the kindness in his eyes.

He went on, his tone crisp and bracing.

"Come now. Yesterday you proved you are not a child any longer, but a strong lad, who will soon be a warrior. Get up and follow me. I've something to show you."

He turned, and began to climb the hill above us by a little goat path through the bracken. I got to my feet quickly and scrambled after him. Curiosity, at that age, is strong enough to overcome most other emotions, even wounded pride.

On the bare hillside, a clump of old, wind-twisted thorns, heavy with white blossom, bent their gnarled branches to the ground. Celidon drew one aside and, as I obeyed his gesture and ducked under it, the sweet, heavy scent was solid, like diving through a breaking wave. Within was a green and secret place, sun-dappled, loud with the sleepy murmur of bees.

I turned to look inquiringly up at Celidon, all agog to know what treasure I was to be shown.

He put his hands on my shoulders, and the green light made him look tall and strange, and magical.

"Bedivere, I am going to put a trust in you, because you have earned it. It is a great trust. Men's lives and their freedom could depend on it. Will you swear to keep faith with me, and never reveal what I shall let you see to anyone who is not, as we say, 'of the blood'—one of Arthur's people, and mine? Will you promise me not to forget, when you are at home again, and tattle of it carelessly—perhaps to Cai, or some Colonial friend of yours?"

I nodded vigorously, excitement and expectation bubbling up in me until I felt choked by it. What rare treasure was hidden in this secret place—gold, jewels? My imagination raced. I said eagerly:

"I have no friends except Arthur and Ygern, and I promise I will never tell."

He took my hand, and led me a few steps, over soft, cool moss, then parted the thorn branches on the far side.

"Look down. Tell me what you see."

I peered out anxiously. The thorns were rooted on an overhanging ledge. Below, the hill fell steeply—a clutter of granite that dropped sheer to the valley's western end. All I could see was level grassland, sheep-grazed, about a great circle of standing stones; one of those circles folk say giants must have raised, far back in the beginning of time.

I was puzzled, disappointed. What was I missing, failing to recognize? I looked up, questioning and confused.

"Well, what do you see?" he repeated.

"Only—only a lot of old standing stones," I muttered.

Celidon said gravely:

"Those stones, Bedivere, are a temple of my people. A very sacred, holy place. Tonight, we of the Old Faith shall meet there to celebrate a mystery. Because you are not altogether of the blood, but only Arthur's brother by adoption, I cannot let you take part in it. Because, however, of certain things, written in your stars, that will come to pass years hence, it is your right to be a witness of Arthur's dedication as the future Pendragon of our country. The Master Blaize, and The Lady, have sanctioned the privilege. It is their wish and mine. A little before sunset you will come to this place, quite alone, and secretly. Keep yourself well hidden, and watch. What you see, if you do not altogether understand yet, be sure you can remember. That is important. Now, listen to me

carefully. I will explain a little of what it means to us who
will be taking part. To us, and to Arthur."

The mind of a twelve-year-old is as receptive as a wax
tablet, new smoothed, and the alertness of the senses at
that age graves deep as a new stylus. I doubt if I understood the meaning of what I saw that night until more than
half my life had passed. But the picture remained, and remains still, a scroll of jewelled color, not one detail of
which I ever forget.

Late bees were still working the pink hearts of the
hawthorn flowers when I crept cautiously into the hiding
place on the hillside. The sun was low in the west and the
shadows of the standing stones stretched long and solemn
across the turf, as I peered down from my chosen vantage
point. Nothing stirred there. From the upper end of the
valley quiet sounds drifted to me. The thud of picket
posts being hammered more securely, subdued voices
calling to one another, the odd clatter of a cookpot. No
laughter. No singing. Since noon there had been a growing hush over the camp of the Gathering. A hush of expectation.

Gradually, as I waited, the silence deepened, until all
I could hear was the chuckle of little waterfalls in the
river, and once, a late lark singing. Light lay golden as
raw honey over a great emptiness. Slowly, imperceptibly,
the sun slipped down the sky, until its rim neared the
ridge of the distant hills. I watched it, dazzled, then
looked back, into the circle. Something was moving there.
A single figure. A boy in a white tunic, who carried a
great curling horn, like a ram's horn, only many times
larger. He took his stand behind a block of stone at the
centre of the circle, and rested the horn on it. He, too,
was watching the sun. I saw him lean forward a little and
set his lips to the mouthpiece.

The sound that filled the valley and sent echoes
rolling all around the listening hills was so tremendous, to
me so unexpected, that I grabbed at the hawthorn branch
beside me and did not feel thorns driving deep into my
palm until it died away. There is no sound in the world,

nothing I have heard in all my life since, so deep, so vibrant, so heart-shaking, as the blare of the sacred Aurucs horn, proclaiming the Hour of Appointed Death.

The last echo faded. A soft rustling, rushing sound filled the valley; hundreds of bare feet running quietly, swishing through the heather and grass. There was another circle forming itself—a sea of subdued color that lapped and eddied, yet left a wide green strand still about the standing stones, and a broad avenue leading to them. The warrior Clansmen were gathering in silence, moving softly, as men move who know they walk in the shadow of their gods.

From far up the valley, there came a new sound. At first it was only a pulse—blood beating in the ears. It grew, slow, insistent, to the throb of drums—small drums, beaten rhythmically with the open hand.

Down the long, sloping track, into the sunset, wound the procession of the sacrifice. First came young boys— the newly Twice Born, their short white tunics rose color in the low light. Then the Clan Princes, in full warrior dress, jewelled circlets, torques and arm rings glittering. Following them, strange and new to me, the robed panoply of a complete Druid College—Ovates in tunics striped blue, white and green, Bards in long mist-blue cloaks, Judges robed in green, and Priests in white, crowned with the sacred oak chaplets. There were women as well as men. The Old Faith makes no distinction of sex.

My eye was caught and held by the beauty of one young girl. She walked like a queen, alone, preceded by a child swinging a censer. Her long hair hung unbound, and the wind swept it smoothly back from her grave, intent face. In both hands she carried, lifted before her, a vessel covered with a cloth of rose color—or was the cloth white and transparent, and did the rose gleam through it? I could not tell, and had no time to wonder, for my eyes were caught by and immediately focused on the two who followed her.

Wand straight, his head up, his hair catching the deepening sunset's glow, so that it shone, red-gold above the yellow-gold of his short, belted tunic, Arthur walked to his King Choosing, led by the High Priestess of the Island—The Lady of the Lake.

I had no attention after that for those who followed. Only later the noble, dignified profile of the aged Arch-Druid of Britain, Blaize the Wise, struck me with the same strange hint of long familiarity I had felt when I first saw The Lady in the shrine of Ynis Witrin; and I had time to marvel at the magnificence of Celidon the Merlin's night-blue cloak, all sewn with stars. My eyes were fixed on Arthur, until momentarily he was hidden from my sight and, boylike, I could gape down, fascinated, at the drummers, who, still beating out their relentless slow-march rhythm, closed the procession; weird figures, dressed in wild-beast skins, their heads masked in the seeming of fox and boar and wolf and bear.

One does not speak lightly of the Greater Mysteries. The sacrifice of the king who goes consenting to death, that his life may pass into his people, and rises again, born in the vigor of renewed fertility, as the corn springs again out of the dark earth to be the life of men, is one of the oldest and most sacred of all initiations.

Celidon, being kind as well as wise, had warned me that what I should see enacted within the standing stones was only a play—a pageant—something the meaning of which I should understand when I was older. But the soul is old already in the body, and it is in the soul one knows the pull of the tides that run strongly between time and eternity, when the Power is invoked, within the standing stones, and builds up, deeper and deeper, like water rising in a well, as the interweaving wall of the slow-paced dance circles the sacred precinct, enclosing, concentrating, what must be guarded from all interruption because it is not of this world.

I, Bedivere, at twelve years old, saw the Wise Ones dance the Wheel of Protection in that lost valley of the Outlands in the magical hour of the long afterglow, and my eyes blurred with the swirling of it, so that it seemed to me I looked down on a great living flower, and the heart of the flower was a crimson spark, where a vessel in the shape of a chalice stood on the central altar stone, glowing as though carved from a single ruby.

I saw also, when at last the wheel came to rest, what was done within the circle, and it made me very much afraid, because the one to whom it must be done was not only the King Sacrifice. He was also Arthur, my brother, and where he must go now, I knew I could not follow.

All light had faded from the land and a red flare of torches ringed the standing stones when at last the play had ended, and the chanting of the Priests was taken up in the soft, lamenting dirge of the whole Gathering that mourns the king who, like the corn at each year's Spring Sowing, must go to his place in the dark womb of earth's renewing.

I saw him lifted on the black-draped bier, his face white and small above the covering pall, eyes closed in the long sleep that comes from herbs that, by tradition, are mingled in the cup from which the king must drink. I saw the Merlin seem to strike the death blow with his golden dagger, and heard his voice ring out, the cry of a night bird, relentless and triumphant, as he held the weapon high, and his cloak swung back from his raised arms in dark, threatening wings:

*"Behold, my people, the sacrifice goes consenting!"*

I saw the bier go forth between the torches, and the whole long procession wind away, down beside the river, away towards that unknown cave beneath a rounded mound of which Celidon had told me.

Lying on my face in the dew-soaked moss, a great shuddering shook me. I shuddered from the shock and the strangeness of what I had seen. But the cold that lay on me that night was not only the fear of a child, bewildered and very much alone. It was a warning—a wind that blew to me down the years from a battlefield between the mere and the sea.

Two days must have passed—the two days of traditional mourning that are the custom. For three nights the Chosen One must sleep within the cave and learn in dreams the wisdom that only the gods can communicate. On the mound above, the great watch fire burns and the High Princes stand their guard, each with forehead bowed against spear shaft.

Of those days I remember nothing. Perhaps Caw saw to it I was lulled with poppy juice. (It would have spared him trouble as well as me!)

It was still dark on the third morning when he shook me awake.

"Up with you now. If we are to find a place from which we will be seeing what comes next, we must be stirring," he told me.

"What comes next, Caw?" I asked, sleepy and bewildered.

He growled at me:

"No questions, now. It is Himself's order I should take you to the place of the Raising. Folk'll not notice you in the press, if you behave yourself and keep silent. It is a very great thing we will be seeing, so mind your manners, and not a word out of you."

When I dressed, he took me firmly by the hand and we went out together into the faint green light that comes in those parts just before the dawn.

The whole valley was awake and stirring. Here and there lanterns bobbed. Folk called to one another in low tones. Groups moved, whispering as they went, or single shadowy figures ran quietly past us.

"Follow and mind your footing," Caw muttered. It was an order. I obeyed as we had always obeyed him on the hunting trail. He led me at the loping run we had learned there for what seemed a long way. When at last he halted and, gripping my arm, bent to whisper in my ear, "Mind what I have said. Not one word, now," I realized we were standing close under the grass mound where the watch fire had burned. It reared above us against the growing light, dark, empty, deserted, but behind and about us people were gathering. Soon we were at the innermost edge of a vast crowd, that swayed and pressed on us.

I stared at the mound. There was a darker patch on its shadowy darkness—an opening—a door. But it was not a door—only a great round stone slab.

The light strengthened. The crowd swayed and tensed around us. Above the mound the dawn star, Hesperus, swam in a sky the color of young willow leaves.

Then I heard, faint and far away, but growing nearer, boys' voices singing—that lovely Celtic singing, where the voices twine and intertwine, intricate and sure as the running design upon one of their round, bronze shields.

Down a wide path the crowd had left clear, they came—walking two and two, flower crowned and garlanded, the Twice Born, in their white tunics, singing as they came. Their ranks divided, left and right, to line the way. Between them, preceded by a child swinging a censer, moved The Lady, alone and unattended. Her robe and veil shimmered like moving water; her hands were crossed on her breast, holding corn stalks of molded gold. She seemed to float rather than walk, a noble swan upon a windless lake.

Above the mound, Hesperus was paling, as a little stray curl of cloud, like a feather, flushed to rose color, and the sky turned gold.

High, shrill, unearthly, a trumpet sounded from the eastern hills, and others answered it, north, south and west.

Standing before the stone that closed the cave, The Lady lifted her right hand, and touched its rough-hewn surface. Deep within the cavern beyond there came a long, roaring reverberation, as of thunder that echoes in far hills. The slab rolled slowly sideways, and beyond it lay darkness. She went in, and following her went six of the Twice Born, carrying a flower-wreathed litter draped in white.

Caw's hand closed over mine, hard and horny, and I looked up at him quickly. His leathery face was working strangely; his eyes staring into the darkness were those of a man who awaits sentence, not knowing if it will be for death or reprieve. I realized he had forgotten who I was, and only grasped me so hard because, at that moment, he waited a verdict and must hold fast to his own courage. (I know now that not all come back from the ordeal of the cave alive and sane—and Arthur was still a child to him, the child of his heart.)

Then, deep within the cavern, a great gong boomed solemnly, three strokes, each one shivering the silence before the next began, and once more, all round the hills, the silver trumpets sang.

In the open archway of the cavern they stood together, a small figure of shining gold, and behind him, tall and protective, her hands on his shoulders, the shimmering outline of that other, the Priestess and the Mother.

Her voice rang, deep, commanding, every word audible to the furthest limits of the waiting crowd.

"Behold, my people, the sacrifice is accepted. The corn comes back to the land. Behold the Chosen One, who returns to you from the darkness. Behold your once, and future, king!"

When they are happy, the Celts always go a little mad. As the crowd poured up towards the standing stones, pushing and jostling, singing and shouting, surrounding the procession that wound its way there, carrying Arthur shoulder-high on the garlanded litter, Caw plucked me firmly out of the press.

"You have seen what you have seen. What follows first, within the holy place, is forbidden to those not of the blood—it is only, indeed, a thanksgiving that will be offered by the Wise Ones, and the swearing of allegiance by the Princes of the Clans. That is not for the likes of us, anyway. What will come next is the feasting—and that one your age is best out of, also, to my thinking. Come your ways, now, and we will watch all from our own place. Presently we will have a share of good things to eat. That I promise. But Himself may have need of us, and our place is back where he will look to find us."

"But—I want to be with Arthur," I pleaded.

Caw shook his head.

"The High Prince has his place today, and we have ours. Be thankful you have seen at this Gathering what no other of the Roman blood has ever seen. Enough is enough!" he said again, with absolute finality.

Caw had had his orders. Later I understood the caution that, in the wild rejoicing of that day, kept our small camp sober and alert. At the time I fretted, as any boy would have done, longing to be down among the crowds, part of the festival, thinking that, if I could not be with Arthur, at least I might find Lancelot and Bors again. Caw's sons and Gobo took the deprivation philosophically and I would not shame myself by grumbling before them. Our share of the feast was brought to us in the evening and it was very good. When we had eaten it, Caw sent me to bed.

"Sleep while you can. It is in my mind our time for sleeping will not be long tonight," he warned.

He was right. When he roused me, the stars were in their midnight stations and the embers of the feast fires still glowed all about the valley. But there was no longer the noise of laughter and singing, and the valley might have been a battlefield under the moon, so many lay sprawled and sleeping in the heather.

The ponies stood, saddled and waiting, our gear ready loaded. Caw handed me my cloak.

"Draw it up round your face. Mount and come. Himself and the High Prince are waiting," he said briefly.

"Where are we going, Caw?" I asked.

"Home, and fast," he answered.

"But why?"

He clicked his tongue impatiently:

"It is an order. Forby, Himself is needed. There is sickness there," he said, and after that would answer no more questions.

Men say, and the harpers sing it still, that after his King Choosing the Merlin spirited Arthur away by magic and hid him under a cloud of invisibility, deep in some enchanted forest.

There are those among the Clan Princes (Geraint, even, may have been one) who had their reasons to resent that magic. Some must have hoped for a chance to take charge of Uther's heir and mold him to their own ends, at that time. The Merlin used magic sparingly and did not need it to slip away from a Gathering where honey beer had flowed, day-long, as freely as the river flowed. He had his reasons. One, though perhaps the least, was that, back at the Dunn, Ygern lay at the point of death. Perhaps the inner sense that always warned Celidon of such things was a kind of magic—it is a convenient word men use to explain the things they find hard to understand.

# Chapter Five

Back at the Dunn everything was the same, yet everything was different.

On our first evening at home no one paid any attention to Arthur and me after the first half hour. The whole place was in panic over Ygern. She had fretted after our going, grown peaky and languid and then fallen into a high fever. She had raved so strangely that old Olwen had been convinced she had been "overlooked" by the evil eye, and could do nothing but patter charms over her. Father Gregorius had declared she was certainly possessed by devils, and sprinkled her with holy water to no avail. Our good neighbor, the Tetrarch Julius, more practical than either, had ridden into Totnesia and fetched a Greek physician he knew there, but the man could make no suggestion as to cause or cure of the sickness and, having taken his fee, departed, shaking his head ominously. For nearly a week now, they told us, Ygern had lain in a deep coma. The women in the slave quarters were wailing for her already as we rode in at the cattle gate.

My uncle met us, his face grey and old, his mouth set in a hard line of Stoic control. His expression lightened a little as his eyes went from Arthur to me, then met Celidon's.

"So you have brought me these two safely back? I feared I had lost all three," he said, and tried to smile.

I realized with surprise that he must really love us. I had taken it for granted, always, before, that we were a burden he carried for honor's sake, out of respect to the memory of the dead.

Celidon went at once to Ygern, and, turning Olwen and the other women out of her sleeping cell, closed the door and remained there alone with her for an hour. Then he called Arthur in and shut the door again.

I wandered about, miserable as a lost dog who returns to a familiar houseplace after it had been left empty and deserted.

Finding me moping, Cai growled at me:

"I said no good would come of all this! The whole place in uproar and no work done! At least, now you are here, you can make yourself useful. Find something to do. Don't just stand there like a molting fowl under a gutter spout!"

I went reluctantly to the stable to rub down my pony. But Rianon had done it for me already. A pony's flank is comforting to lean against when, tired out with hard travelling, hungry and desolate, one cannot hold back tears.

Arthur found me there. He was brisk and bracing.

"What are you crying for? There's no need. Didn't you guess the Merlin would know how to cure any sickness? Ygern's better, awake, and asking for you."

I blinked at him. The relief was too sudden and too great. His coolness, and something that seemed to me cocksure in his attitude, turned my misery into a blinding burst of temper. Here, in our home surroundings, he ceased to be Arthur, the Chosen One. He was the Arthur I had always known—my equal, and my brother who had roused me before (though rarely) to rebel against his lordliness. Without thought, and without warning, I hit him. We fought, all among the straw and the pony's legs, until Cai, coming in, pulled us apart and gave us both a beating.

After the strain of the past month it did us both good. We went to supper and bed sobered and settled, knowing that home remained safe and unchanged, a place where one knew what to expect.

For six years after the Great Gathering and the King Choosing, we three grew up together under the guardian-

ship of my Uncle Ectorius. They were not easy years, for
us or for him. Children, like dogs and horses, are quick to
sense an atmosphere. His tight-lipped silence soon warned
us never to speak in his presence of our journey with
Celidon, never to refer to anything that had happened
during our twelfth moon of May. As a result we lived a
double life—on its surface commonplace and ordinary,
but secretly rich with memories and shared experience—
experiences in which Ygern, from the first, seemed to
have an equal part. How much we actually told her in
words, how much she knew by the strange telepathy that
all their lives existed between her and Arthur, is impossible now to remember. The secrets of the Dragon Making,
of the sword and the King Sacrifice and the cave, belonged to the three of us, binding us in a jealous and
defensive kinship, closer and more lasting than any ties of
blood, a kinship that made us mature quickly in some
ways, and in others kept us younger than our years.

As we reached adolescence, we became restless, in-
secure between our two worlds: increasingly in conflict
with the rigid opinions of Uncle Ectorius, impatient of the
monotonous discipline of our lives. We must have been
unbearable then, as most adolescents are for a time, and,
like most adolescents immersed in their own problems, we
gave little consideration to the troubles of our elders.

It is to my uncle's credit that, Colonial aristocrat of
the old school as he was, he kept his oath to Uther the
King meticulously, leaving most of Arthur's education in
Celidon's hands. For long periods, though at irregular
intervals, Arthur would go away alone with the Merlin,
sometimes to the Island, sometimes elsewhere, to receive
the training of a Pendragon among his own people. When
he returned, without a word said on either side, his
Roman education would be resumed by my uncle, who
worked him harder for the interruption—to counterbal-
ance, no doubt, if he could, the nationalist and subversive
influences he must have suspected, and to instruct him in
a philosophy that should arm him against the backward
superstitions (as he saw them) of the Old Faith. Twenty
years later, Arthur said to me of those lessons:

"I owe him a debt for many lives to come, good man

that he was! Without the grounding he gave me in Roman law, how could I have given judgment in an island Rome had ruled for four hundred years? And how, without studying Alexander's wars, should I have guessed in time the value of speed, surprise and the right use of cavalry?"

Cai, burdened by the cares of our poverty, and lacking all imagination, made no secret of the irritation we, but more especially Arthur, often caused him. He had a way of mocking at Celidon's influence with caustic sarcasm, implying that Arthur would outgrow it "once he is in the army" (by which he meant Ambrosius' army). It was a long time before I realized—and then with surprise —that it was genuine love and anxiety for us, and anxiety for our future, that made him so critical and ill-tempered. We baited him, sometimes even we hated him, in those days—he, who hid the troubled affection of an elder brother so carefully we could not suspect its existence— he who was to prove it through so many years ahead, one of the most faithful and noblest of the Companions of Arthur!

In all families certain things are understood without needing to be put into words. I knew better than to hope I might follow Arthur again with Celidon, on the journeys they made together. Neither of us clamored for the impossible. Secretly, I hoped we might go, when we were old enough, to Ambrosius' legions together. That was to be my future and I accepted it without question. We of Maximus' line are born to a military career, and I looked forward to the time of my going, but more and more clearly, as the months passed, I guessed, and accepted, that I should probably go alone.

One friend the gods sent us in those six years: the Tetrarch Julius. To him we owed more than any of us, at the time, realized. Burly and white-haired, with the rolling gait of a lifelong sailor, and a sailor's far-seeing blue eyes, he had the tact to keep the friendship of Ectorius and Cai, yet win trust and affection from the three of us.

He still held some nominal post under Roman government then, and once or twice a month rode over from his farm ("Villa," as he called it), a mile or so inland from ours, to Totnesia on business. There he would harry the town council, drive a shrewd bargain or two in the market, drink raw apple beer with any captain of a local coasting vessel who happened to be in harbor, and return at evening by the river path to dine with my uncle and give him all the local gossip. His presence swept through the Dunn like a fresh salt wind and his great laugh would echo to the rafters, so that even my uncle could not help but smile and be cheered out of his melancholy for an hour or two.

Always aggressively optimistic, Julius had his own recipe for curing Britain's troubles.

"The only way to beat off pirates—Saxon, Irish, any of the spawn—is at sea. Found a navy again, like we had in Caurasius' day. Sink the enemy before they ever set foot on British soil. Some day the silly bastards who call themselves our rulers still will believe that. They'll have to! By Poseidon, if I'd been appointed Count of the Saxon Shore with enough galleys under my command forty years ago, we'd still be *holding* the Saxon Shore, and Ambrosius and his legions could be cultivating their farms like country gentlemen!"

We knew it wasn't true. More than forty years ago the land that fringes the Saxon Shore had been given by Vortigern to the Federate settlers, and my uncle, being a historian, reminded him of the fact. Then the two of them would be fairly launched into argument that went back over all the battles fought since the invasion, and both were happy.

For all his bluffness and his talk laced with seafaring oaths, Julius was a patrician at heart. Watching us grow up, still running wild as unbroken colts outside lesson-time, he grumbled to Uncle Ectorius that he was rearing a pack of young barbarians.

"Send them into society, and they'd have no more idea how to behave than a Saxon rower. It's high time somebody rubbed the corners off them, and since, with your nose always in your book rolls, you'll not do it, I must!" he roared cheerfully. "I'll have them over at the Villa once a week, to eat supper in a civilized fashion,

and in civilized clothes, not looking like unkempt fisherfolk, at that. Rising fifteen the lot of them, Ectorius, and
you can barely tell the girl from the boys. In the old days,
my lass, you'd have been weaving the last blankets for
your dower chest, if you weren't already married; looking
modest and sweet in pretty dresses, instead of a tunic that
shows your scratched legs above the knee, and with the
black mane of yours less well combed than a hill pony's!"

Ygern made a face at him, then said, with mock
demureness:

"We'll come, sir, whenever you invite us. The sort of
supper you give us will be worth combing one's hair
for!"

But it was the talk, not the food, at Julius' table that
tempted all three of us, at that time. We needed, desperately, to talk with someone like Julius, who let us speak
our minds on any subject, and whose discretion we could
trust. The most outrageous opinions, we knew from experience, only drew shrewd, twinkling-eyed tolerance, instead of the shocked response they would have raised at
home, and we could trust him to keep any of our raw
confidences as safely as if he had been a priest of Aes-
culapius.

I remember clearly an evening near the end of our
time together at the Dunn. It must have been June, for
the roses Julius cherished on the terrace outside his house
were in full bloom. (He was always a great gardener.)
Though his "Villa" was timber-built, and thatched like
our own, he kept the whole place in better trim, being a
bachelor, with fewer calls on his purse and more money
to start with than my uncle had after the Troubles.

That year he had planted a vineyard and, standing
with one sandalled foot up on the terrace wall, he lectured
us on its advantages. He kept hitching irritably at the
unfamiliar folds of his toga, while he talked. Being a
gentleman, he kept to the old-fashioned courtesy of wearing it when we were his invited guests. (Mostly he went
about in a scuffed leather tunic and kilt, and high horseman's boots, as most Colonial farmers did.)

"If we want wine, we must grow it, now," he insisted. "That's what I tell all my friends. Britain's an

island, thank the gods, and can stand on her own feet, if only she'd realize she's got 'em. I tell your uncle, Rome can't be expected to send an expeditionary force across the Channel, ever again, to get us out of trouble. Hasn't got the men. Hasn't got the money and, what's more important, hasn't got the will. With Rome itself full of Goths and the government perching in Constantine's city of Byzantium three thousand miles away, why should anyone bother about *us?* We're expendable as far as they're concerned and unless Ambrosius and the rest realize that and act accordingly, we'll bloody soon find we've been expended!" he boomed.

"Celidon says Britain stood alone, a free and independent state, for a thousand years before the Romans came, and could again. Do you agree, sir?" Arthur asked.

In the evening light his shadow stretched long across the scythed grass of the terrace. He had come almost to his full height; big-boned, lean and hard from exercise, but still with a lanky, boyish grace about him. Already he had to pumice his chin on the evenings we dined at the Villa.

Julius turned and looked at him.

"Celidon says that, does he? Well, he may be a ranting mountebank nationalist, as all Druids are, but by the gods, boy, he's got something there. Provided he and his wild Clans are prepared to work with us Colonials and not start bloody murder between the two factions, I'm with him. It's the only answer. Stand shoulder to shoulder, all of us, and rely on our own resources, and to Hades with Byzantium expecting tribute when we get nothing in return—and to Hades with their piddling interference in our affairs. Your uncle don't agree with me, I know, but he's got his head in the clouds as half the old fogies of our age have. Ambrosius and all of 'em."

I said, feeling loyalty demanded it:

"Surely you allow the General Ambrosius is a great soldier, sir?"

Julius scowled at me, his bushy white eyebrows working up and down.

"No offense, boy, but he's been a good soldier forty years now, and he's learned too little from defeat. 'Form

Tortoise,' 'Bring up the catapults,' 'The infantry will advance with full battle equipment' (which means hung round with a mule's load of pots and pans and picks and shovels and Zeus knows what else), a thousand paces to the mile, and twenty miles a day the furthest they can stagger, no matter if the enemy have landed at Rutupiae and they're in Aquae Sulis when they get the news. That's no way to deal with pirates from the sea, on an island with miles of undefended coastline. Or is it?"

Arthur laughed.

"That's what I say. On the mainland, in the old days, those tactics may have worked. We need light horsemen now—small bands, working independently, under leaders who can use their own initiative. Isn't that the answer?"

Julius grunted.

"Failing a fortress wall of stout war galleys, it well might be. Worth trying, anyway. Here's Ygern, with our garlands. Supper must be ready. I've got a barrel of fresh oysters for you—British oysters, the best in the world. The emperors in their great days used to have 'em sent, packed in brine, for their own table—and paid a tidy price for them, I'll be bound. I tell you, Britain's got resources enough, if she'll use 'em. Now remember, all three of you, no gentleman talks politics at supper until the slaves have left the room. Your uncle trusts you to me to teach you manners, not to listen to your seditious nationalist talk, picked up from native harpers!"

He winked at us, wiped the sweat from his forehead with the hem of his toga and led the way into the house.

All three of us got a little drunk that evening. Julius could afford to import wine while his vineyard matured, and, enjoying it himself, insisted it was part of our education to learn how to appreciate it. In me, even well watered, as we drank it, it produced a rosy euphoria that made me aware for the first time that I was in love with Ygern. She was wearing a long, Roman-style dress of pale green wool she had woven herself, and had knotted her hair up, low on her neck, under her supper-wreath of small pink rosebuds. She looked remote and ethereal, like a water nymph or the hamadryad of a birch tree, I thought, and remembered with distaste the warm, earthy curves of the little goosegirl who had recently initiated me into life's lesser mysteries in the hayloft. I lost myself in a pleasantly melancholy dream of lifelong, unrequited love, knowing she would choose, as she had always chosen, to put Arthur before me, when we, any of us, had time to think seriously of a thing so unimportant as marriage.

Arthur could carry his wine better than I could. It made him lucidly talkative, if a little reckless. The servants had left us before Julius poured the first libation with old-fashioned ceremonial, so Arthur felt free to speak of serious matters, instead of confining himself to the small talk Julius was teaching us was suitable while one reclined at table. Sitting up on his supper couch, his hands clasped about his knee, Arthur said earnestly:

"We trust you, sir. I'm going to tell you something I've decided. I'm not going to train with Ambrosius, though my uncle thinks I should. Bedivere must learn what is to be learned in the army for both of us. I mean to raise my own independent force in a year or two's time and prove what can be done with it. But first I shall spend at least a year travelling in disguise with Celidon the length and breadth of the island, getting to know the country and the Clans. That is necessary."

He spoke with decision and Julius raised his eyebrows.

"In disguise?" he queried.

"Yes. I shall go with Celidon as his apprentice—a young harper, learning the trade. I can play well enough —though nowhere near as well as Bedivere here," he smiled across at me. "If I darken my hair and wear the Bard's dress, no one need recognize me. We can go anywhere, everywhere—into taverns and farmhouses, market squares and High Princes' Dunns, and hear folk talk freely. I need to know how men's minds work, what they think and feel, what troubles them and what makes them glad, from prince to beggar. What it is they want from life. Those are the things a Pendragon needs to know."

Julius grunted again, a deep, rumbling sound.

"You'll find most men want peace and a full belly. Both hard ambitions to realize these days. A good commander in the field might give them both. Why not please your uncle by getting yourself some war training with Ambrosius first?" he queried.

Arthur shook his head.

"Ambrosius stands for continued allegiance to Rome. I'll not be identified with the Colonials, sir, until my own people have learned to trust me, and Ambrosius himself and the conservative Colonial element he represents are ready to accept me and my Clans on an equal footing."

"Celidon's ideas, or yours, boy?" Julius asked, his eyes twinkling.

Arthur flushed a little and admitted:

"Partly Celidon's. Mostly my own." He spoke steadily and added, on a rising note of excitement: "The ideas on strategy are mine. He is not a man of war. No Druid bears arms. Alexander believed in using fast cavalry and depending always on surprising the enemy, and *he* conquered the world!"

Julius chuckled.

"No harm in aiming high! Conquer the Saxons, the Picts and the Irish for us, and we can talk about making you Emperor of the World, if you're still alive at the end of that, boy!" He paused and shook his head. "Ectorius won't like your plans. I suppose you expect me to persuade him to them? I thought as much! Well, I'll think about it. I've heard plenty that made less sense."

He leaned forward and refilled our wine cups.

"That's the last round tonight. You've had enough already by the sound of you, but we'll drink a final toast. Here's to a Free Britain and"—he raised his cup and looked directly across at Arthur—"may the gods send her the commander she needs to win that freedom!"

The storm that brooded more heavily over the Dunn each year broke finally when Arthur made his plans known to my uncle soon after the three of us turned seventeen. For the first time—the only time—they quarrelled openly, and hard words were spoken on both sides. It was something that had to be—inevitable as the destruction of the egg when the young bird thrusts its way out into the daylight. But it was painful to both, and involved us all, at the time. Ygern and I took Arthur's part, while Cai stormed of disloyalty and ingratitude, and denounced the whole Celtic race with Celidon at its head.

"To throw up the chance of an honorable career under a general like Ambrosius, and instead go traipsing the country as a ragged mountebank, ending up, most likely, with a dagger in your back from one of your treacherous, feuding Clansmen—you must be mad!" he told Arthur.

But, white-faced and very quiet, Arthur went his own way, as he would always do. Ygern helped him to dye his bright hair black (which, curiously, suited his looks) and I lent him my harp, which was a better one than his own. In the grey dawn of a cold morning in early March, we said goodbye to him, and watched him ride away down the river path to join Celidon in the forest. As we went back up through the beech woods, I was ready to comfort Ygern's tears. But she was calmer than I was. Only his wolfhound bitch mourned for him all day, whining and restless, scratching at the door of his empty sleeping cell in a fashion that tore my heart.

Two weeks later I joined Ambrosius' army, still in winter quarters outside Caerleon. We were in action before I'd had time to learn the words of command, for Irish pirates sail in any weather, and had crept up Severn Water, hoping to surprise us. Luckily my men had veteran decurions and acquitted themselves well enough to earn a grim word of commendation from my kinsman. I suppose every man, if he is honest, feels his bowels turn to water at the start of his first battle. I was no different from others and luckier than some, for it was only a short, sharp skirmish. I saw dead men and raw wounds for the first time and, liking neither sight, found to my satisfaction I could stomach both. Round the evening cooking fire with the other young cadets, I felt the heady excitement of victory and comradeship and knew, with absolute certainty, I had found the life to which I belonged.

Ambrosius, at that time, must have been in his sixties, a hard-bitten, thin-lipped soldier, his face deeply lined, his grizzled hair, close cut in Roman style, thinning where the helmet's fret had worn it. His grey eyes, deep sunken, with brown patches under them like healing bruises, were keenly alert, but cold. One could never read his thoughts in them. Throughout my service I could not tell if I'd earned a reprimand or a commendation. He ranked, I suppose, as Count of Britain then, since he was supreme commander of the island, but I never heard him use the title. He was a hard man, who demanded unquestioning obedience and imposed a ruthless discipline. It surprised me, at first, to find how much his troops loved and respected him, in spite of the heavy punishments dealt out for the slightest fault. I've seen him have a man flogged for a rusted shoulder guard, and hanged for stealing a blanket off a market stall. Later, I understood. They loved him for his very strictness, which brought back to them the pride of the Eagles, and they respected his justice, which, being simple and unwavering, they understood. His senior officers were out of the same mold—Colonials of the old school; the ones near my age, cadets of the best families in Britain—those families that had stood firm throughout the Troubles. He seldom promoted from the ranks.

I fitted into military life easily, having expected hardship and being well prepared for it. By the end of my first year I'd got promotion and a couple of small battle scars. I counted myself a veteran, and thought I had seen war. Later, I understood better. That season was only a mild rehearsal of the real thing, for we had nothing but coastal raiding and no major, planned invasions to deal with.

We were in camp near Winchester early in the following year, just out of winter quarters and exercising on the Great Plain in readiness for the new season's offensive. The weather was vile, with heavy rain and mud everywhere, and I was glad to be going off duty one evening, when Ambrosius sent for me. I obeyed the summons uneasily, wondering what he wanted me for at that hour, apprehensively counting over several possibilities, for discipline is apt to slip a little when rain hasn't slackened for a week.

I gave the word of the day to the sentry outside his tent and ducked in under the flap. He looked up from the tablets scattered on a folding table before him, acknowledged my salute and went on with his writing. His face was inscrutable in the yellow light of the lanthorn strapped to the tent pole.

Rain drummed on the leather walls and wind flapped the entrance curtain. Outside, a trumpet blew and there came the squelching tramp of men going to collect their evening rations. I had plenty of time to rehearse to myself excuses for any faults I could remember. Then I abandoned the effort. Ambrosius never listened to an excuse.

When, at last, he looked up at me, the pale ghost of a smile twitched his lips.

"I see from my records you've been with us a year, kinsman. You are due for a spell of leave," he said. "Get off tomorrow and report back in a month and a half's time. Make the most of it, and say goodbye to your folk at home and any friends you have there. When you return I am sending you overseas on special duty. You'll probably be away three years."

I gaped at him, looking, I imagine, as goggle-eyed as a prawn, for again that swiftly passing glint of amusement tilted his lips. Perhaps to hide it, he picked up a small sheepskin roll from the table, and smoothed it out, but only glanced at it. His eyes were cold again when he lifted them to mine.

"Don't flatter yourself, Verus. This is not promotion. It's necessity. If I had an older, more experienced officer I could spare, I'd send him. But with the Saxons massing again for invasion in force, I shall need every senior centurion this summer. Young as you are, you have some of the qualifications needed. You are reasonably level-headed, your health is good, and being my kinsman and so of the line of Maximus you could be said, at a pinch, to hold senatorial rank. Do you know where Byzantium is?"

He shot the question at me, and frowned when I stammered.

"No? I didn't expect you would! It's a city three months' journey across the mainland. You'll have to find your own way there. I've a request from the notaries' office of the emperor to send a representative from our army to join the new Imperial guard. Mithras alone knows why they've remembered Britain. I'd call it an insult that they ask anything of us, after the treatment we've had. But it could mean the tide is turning at last. If you can stay alive until you get there (which will take some doing) and acquit yourself honorably when you arrive, it could be useful, to me *and* to Britain."

He paused, seeming to expect an answer. I said:

"I'll do my best, sir."

He gave me another of his searching, appraising stares: but a certain warmth had crept into his voice, as he said:

"This guard of the emperor's seems to be an experiment. From what I can understand it is being recruited from all that's left of the empire. You will be well paid and well equipped, and if you use your time wisely, the experience could be invaluable to you. The important thing for you to remember is that, to the court at Byzantium and to the emperor himself, you will represent a province they seem to have forgotten for too long. Remind them it is worth remembering, by good discipline, discretion and loyalty. I need not add, by courage. You've proved you have enough of that, or I should not be sending you."

I felt myself flushing with pleasure. From Ambrosius the comment was worth more than the coveted bronze Laurel of Honor from any other commander. I said again, my heart behind the words:

"I'll do my best, sir."

Surprisingly, he laughed—a low, pleasant laugh.

"It seems I needn't caution you to keep a quiet

tongue in your head. That's one point in favor of my
choice, considering your age, anyway! Now, get off to
your supper, boy. When you report back after leave, we'll
give you the best itinerary we can muster and money for
your journey. The seaways should be open by then. Remember me to Ectorius when you get home."

Greatly daring, encouraged by his manner, I said:

"My uncle will be proud to hear of this, sir, I know.
I am sure he'd want me to thank you for it."

"For sending you at your age three thousand odd
miles across country crawling with every sort of Barbarian savage, on what could prove (knowing something of
the Court of Byzantium) a wild-goose chase at the end? I
wonder? Well, you could be right! We are, all of us, of
the line of Maximus after all," he said. "Goodnight,
kinsman."

I went out into the driving rain, dazzled and bewildered by what seemed to me my miraculous good fortune.
Ambrosius Aurelianus, for all his harshness, knew very
well how to handle men. That night I would have died for
him gladly.

Ygern looked at me sideways through her wind-ruffled
hair.

"What will Arthur say to all this, Bedivere? He may
need you before three years," she said, in that cool, small
voice of hers, that, pitched to a certain note, always had
the power to bring one hard down against reality.

The two of us were sitting on a fallen log together,
eating barley cakes and goat's cheese companionably in
the thin March sunlight, down on the Telling Floor. I'd
been home a week. Long enough to see for myself that
things were harder than ever for them, back at the Dunn.
Long enough for some of the glamour of my first year's
soldiering to rub off, leaving me free to feel ashamed that
I had virtually forgotten, all that time, any concerns
except my own.

I said, defensively:

"He'll not need me yet. He wanted me to serve my
time in the army. *Where* I serve it won't matter—except

that I'll get more experience in this way—and good money, which the gods know we need, by the look of things."

She sighed, gazing away towards the woods where the beech buds were shedding their little brown scales like rain in the stiff spring breeze.

"It's been a hard year here, without you both," she said quietly. I glanced at her, noticing for the first time the shabbiness of the old tunic of undyed wool, gone yellow with age, that she was wearing. I must have grown and broadened considerably since I'd left home, for she seemed smaller than I'd remembered (she always had the bones of a little bird). Though she was thin almost to ugliness, she had a weather-tanned, whiplash look of endurance about her. Her hand, when I laid mine over it, and she turned hers palm to palm, was hardened by work, so that it gave me the quick grasp of a boy's, before she drew it away, impatient of sympathy.

"Uncle is failing, Bedivere. He has had too much trouble in his life. Cai does his best—but most of our slaves are growing old. Without Caw and his sons we'd never have got through this winter; and when Arthur comes back, he may need them. I think he will. I don't know what Cai can do without them." She brushed the hair back from her forehead impatiently and pushed the rush basket of food towards me. "Here—eat—we shouldn't waste time. I must go back to the house and you must get on here. We should be making the best of your help while we've got it."

I'd been felling and trimming young ash for fence rails all morning, wearing old clothes grown small for me, happy enough to be swinging an ax down there by the river, with only the birds for company, and dreaming of a future I found hard to imagine. I said:

"Julius will help you. If I can, I'll send back most of my pay. You'll win through, Ygern."

She shook her head, her eyes darkly troubled.

"I can't see the future. Usually I can, but now it's as though a curtain had dropped in front of me, or a thick mist."

She took a withered, last year's russet apple out of the basket and bit into it, rather desperately.

"I can't *see!*" she repeated.

I put my arm round her shoulders.

"You will. You're tired, my poor girl, and no wonder. Soon Arthur's wander-year will be over. When he comes back, he'll put new heart into you."

"When he comes back, it can't be for long. He'll have too much on his mind from now on to spare thought for our troubles," she said. There was no bitterness in the words, only a bleak certainty. She took the last bite out of the apple and threw the core into the undergrowth. "No, Bedivere, from now on we must think for him, not he for us. That's why three years seems too long for you to be away and risking, maybe, unnecessary dangers. I tell you, he may *need* you."

Still flushed with the pride of my promotion, and with more than half my mind caught up in what had become to me a way of life that suited me, her words nettled me.

"He'll understand better than you can that I've got no choice. A soldier obeys orders," I said.

She gave me a steady look, patient and oddly pitying.

"The orders of his rightful commander," she said gently. Suddenly her face changed, became alert and listening. "Hush, Bedivere, there's someone moving stealthily up behind us—I heard a footstep."

Startled, I jumped to my feet and turned. We'd chosen a place close under one of the grass-grown mounds of the villa ruins, to be out of the wind. Now a tall figure, wrapped and hooded in a ragged beggar's cloak, stood there above us.

"Spare a crust, good people, for a poor tramping man, who has not eaten since yesterday's dawning!" the apparition mumbled. The voice was harsh, with a northern accent that made the words almost unintelligible.

Angry, because I'd been startled, and on my guard, for there were plenty of thieves and vagabonds sheltering in the woods in those days, and I thought there was a look of strength about this man (I did not like the way he kept his face hidden—he might even be a leper), I said:

"Come down and show yourself, fellow. How dare you steal up on honest folk in that fashion?"

"Dare? Oh, I dare anything!" Arthur's voice answered me. The tattered cloak dropped, and he stood there above us, laughing down at our amazement. Just for a moment I saw him stand, the sun shining on his own red-gold hair, glinting on the Pendragon's ring, glowing on the soft colors of the familiar Dumnonian tartan. The silver-grey trunks of two tall ash saplings framed him against the pale spring sky, and the first primroses showed in the moss about his feet. It is a picture that has stayed in my mind for more than half a hundred years, bright and detailed and perfect, like one of the little paintings in a monk's book of prayers. Then he came down to us in a lithe, hunter's leap, and his arms were about both our shoulders, and all three of us were laughing and exclaiming, beginning to speak and falling over the words, stopping, and starting again to ask the questions not one of us stopped to answer.

Suddenly he broke away from us and pounced on Ygern's basket.

"Food! I spoke the truth when I said I'd had nothing to eat since yesterday. What have you got there, girl?"

"Oh Arthur! Come up to the house and let me get you a meal," Ygern said, her voice unsteady, for she'd been crying a little, as women do when they are suddenly, overwhelmingly happy. But he shook his head, sitting down on the log and already munching a barley bannock.

"No. I heard your voices as I came up the river road and blessed the chance of a word with you before I faced all the others. The Branch has gone out for another Spring Gathering. The Clans won't wait longer for a Pendragon. At Spring Sowing this year they'll decide finally whether to accept me or not." He paused, hunted in the basket for another bannock and laid a lump of cheese on it. "I think they will, for all there are some High Princes who think they have the better right," he said, confidently, then took a large bite of the rough food and munched it with a look of satisfaction.

Ygern sat down beside him.

"So that's the next thing? Of course! I wonder why I couldn't see it," she said, low-voiced.

I sat down on his other side.

"They'll accept you," I said.

He glanced at me, smiling.

"You sound certain. But there are those who'll contest the choice. They think I'm young for the task, for one thing. They'd prefer a tried war leader—Lot of Dalriada, for example. They plan to question my legitimacy. It will be—interesting."

Ygern said quietly, not looking at him, but away into the distance.

"You are the Chosen One. You know that, Arthur."

He put his hand on her knee, looking at her with an expression of such open tenderness I wished myself not with them.

"I know that, my girl," he said.

There was a moment of silence. I heard the voice of the river, which one forgets, being near it. Somewhere on the far side, a cock pheasant gave its sharp, clattery danger call.

Turning again to search the basket absentmindedly for what remnants it contained, Arthur said, with a lightness that sounded only a little forced:

"We shall see! I've come home now to bid Uncle Ectorius and Cai to the Gathering. The Merlin needs them to bear witness to my father's will. Did you know Ectorius holds that for me? It was signed on the battlefield at Verulamium and the Merlin left it in Roman safekeeping here with me. It's a mercy he did. Ectorius will feel honor demands he should bear witness to it and see justice done in the Roman tradition. If he and Cai will only stand by us now, openly, it will give weight to my King Making with the Colonials. I want that. From now on Britain must be one united nation, or else go down into the darkness for a thousand years ahead."

I looked at him, wonderingly. The year had changed him. There was a force, a decision about him he had lacked while he was feeling his way to his full strength. Now he was a man. The interests and the ambitions of a junior centurion suddenly seemed to be unimportant.

Whether I became a member of the emperor's guard in far Byzantium, or stayed in Britain to fight other wars, was out of my hands. It would be his decision, not mine. From now on, where I went, with him, or for him, would be his to say. Ambrosius might be my general. Arthur was, and would be, my king.

# II
# MARCH

# Chapter Six

Griffin tells me I have had the lung fever, brought on by cold and exposure, and aggravated by old wounds.

"Come spring you will mend, my lord," he assures me. For a Christian abbot he lies convincingly! He forgets I had a physician for my battle comrade. I know the wasting sickness. It took my singing voice a year ago. But the song goes on. Taliesen is a greater Bard than I have ever been, and he is young, with years before him still. I gave him my harp and the Merlin's jewel before I turned south from Yr Widdfa for the last time. Snow was already on the mountain at the dawn of our parting: the crest flushed to the color of rose petals—to the color of the Grail.

The fever that rises each evening in my blood makes me restless, until the sweating that follows leaves me weak and drowsy. Memory comes very clear at such times and for a little while I am young again, living the scenes it brings. Sleep too often casts the long shadow of Camlan and that I will not remember until I must.

Tonight that shadow lies still half a lifetime away. I am twenty-one years old, and the fever that burns now in my blood is the heat of a spring afternoon in the ruined magnificence of a city that once ruled the world.

Arthur's letter recalling me to Britain had taken half a year to reach me. Slowly the realization of that fact came to me, as I stood looking down at the empty wrappings on the bare barrack-room table. The leather packet was frayed and stained. Sea water had drawn wrinkles across it, and one corner was dark with dried blood. (Whose blood? I wondered.)

I turned sharply, the gilded fish scales of my cataphract armor clashing.

"Who brought this?" I asked.

Palomides, my auxiliary centurion, swung his legs over the edge of the bunk, where, since he was off duty, he had been resting through the midday heat of Rome, and looked at me curiously.

"The little yellow man with slanting eyes and hair braided like a woman's who serves old Bardeliez. Bardeliez is in Rome, Verus. I was just about to tell you. We are invited to dine with him. He is sending us an escort." He paused. "Is the letter important?"

"Yes," I said. "Yes. It is important."

I laid the strip of parchment beside its wrappings, and began automatically to pull at the side lacings of my parade armor. My fingers shook a little, partly from the fatigue of holding a spirited horse to a steady walk through four hours of ceremonial parade, but mostly from excitement.

"Let me do that." Palomides was at my side with one of his swift, silent movements. His slender, olive-skinned hands dealt expertly with the sweat-tightened thongs, and as I ducked out of the hooded neck opening he lifted the stifling garment clear, and dropped it with a clank on my armor chest.

"Phew! No wonder they call those things 'the soldiers' ovens.' Give me an archer's linen kilt in this climate!" he said lightly. His dark eyes were watching me, though, anxious and unsmiling.

"Thanks. No need for you to act as my orderly. Where is the lazy bastard?" I queried, busy peeling off my leg guards. "I'm dry as a corn husk and my throat full of dust. Shout for him to bring us some wine, Palomides, there's a good fellow."

"I'll find him. He'll be dicing or wenching somewhere. like all Goths, I'll be bound." Palomides disappeared through the door of our sleeping cell, and I heard his voice grow fainter down the stairs outside, calling for the man.

I stood up in my linen undershirt and breeches, wriggling my feet luxuriously on the coolness of the flagged floor. Then I sat down on one of the stools by the table and, pulling the clammy shirt away from my chest, picked up my letter again.

As I read it for the second time, I felt my breath come short and hard as it comes when one waits for the trumpet that will sound the charge. So long since I had heard from home—and now the news was good.

Ambrosius had appointed Arthur War Duke of Britain. It seemed unbelievable. He wrote simply, *"They* have appointed me"—but who, apart from Ambrosius, had the authority now? I'd reason enough to guess it was not the old self-promoted chamberlain-now-emperor in Byzantium. War Duke of Britain—and as such he wanted me home. Again there was no mention of Ambrosius—I supposed my general must have seconded me to him. Other letters evidently had gone astray. Perhaps several, since this one seemed to have been sent to me in Byzantium. Had they had no word from me in Britain, then? In three long years?

War Duke—second only to the Count of Britain, the supreme commander Ambrosius himself. That was promotion indeed! So the tactics had worked? I smiled at the closing paragraph. Arthur wrote as he spoke. In the close heat of the May afternoon I could hear his voice saying the words scrawled all across the parchment in his bold, clear script.

"The honor has reconciled our uncle and Cai at last to my tactics. I care little for it, except that it gives me authority to raise all the supplies I need. I have only to say to any reluctant owner of a villa farm, or well-heeled town council, 'Give me so much hay, so many fat porkers, so many bushels of barley—and the wagons and the horses for their transport. Here, my friend, is the order for them, signed *Arturus Dux Bellorum,* and we have what we need. So things are better for Arthur's men, and more and more of the Clan levies come in to join my standard. I need you home, Verus. This is the moment. Come as soon as you can, and come by way of Armorica. News of our victories is spreading there, and they promise us recruits. Tell them it is trained cavalry commanders I could do with. Get me also, if you can, information as to the price of mainland stallions. We have too few left of the old legionary stock. We must breed size and staying power into our native Icenian mares. Heavy cavalry will do more than anything else to end this forty-year-old war. Even the Berserkers go down before it. Just where I shall be, between Lyonesse and the Wall, when you win back to the Telling Floor, I can't say. But Ygern will know. She always does.

"Come fast, Bedivere, I need you."

He had signed the letter "Arturus. Dux Bellorum," and under the signature, bold and scrawling, half across the page, he had set the serpent sign of the Pendragon.

I looked up, startled, from my reading. I had not heard a sound, but Palomides stood at my elbow, holding two samian cups of water-thinned barrack wine. Half Greek, half Arab, he moved as quietly as a hunting panther, and there was something of the panther in his build, small-boned, lithe and tense.

"By the gods, Verus, you need to put that orderly of yours on charge. I ran him to earth at last, kissing a cook-slave in the kitchen courtyard, instead of guarding our stairhead. Kissing's a polite word for what was going on, too, let me tell you. If some of the holy begging monks who throng this town come on such a scene, they'll cry rape, I warn you (though the little slut was willing enough); then you'll have a hanging on your hands, and one hairy Goth the less. I ordered him back to his duty with an extra flea in his ear and brought the wine myself. He'd have drunk the half of it on the way else."

I smiled, accepting the familiar barrack jesting of auxiliary against regular legion, and taking the wine cup from him stood for a moment, holding it, while I met his eyes, that were dark and anxious.

"My thanks to you," I said. Then, answering the question he would not ask:

"This is where our ways part, Palomides. I am recalled to Britain."

"So." He set his own cup down untasted on the table. "I thought it might be that. The letter is from the General Ambrosius?"

"No," I said. "From my brother—my foster brother, that is. They have made him War Duke. He needs me."

"You are glad, Verus?"

"Glad?" I said. "Glad? Wouldn't any man be glad to go back and fight with his own people, for his own homeland, instead of selling his sword to the highest bidder, as I've had to do?"

Palomides said, very quietly:

"Of course. If he had a homeland to fight for, Verus."

"I'm sorry. I'd forgotten," I said. Palomides, like so many others on the mainland, had no home left to him now. My words had been thoughtless.

He gave me a quick, crooked smile.

"Think nothing of it! Come—let us both drink a toast to your good luck." He raised his cup.

I lifted mine. "I give you a better toast—to Arthur, my brother, Arthur the Pendragon, Arthur, War Duke of Britain!" I said and, draining the cup, dashed it down to shatter on the flagstones.

Palomides lifted one eyebrow, acknowledging the drama of the gesture, then, having drunk my toast, set his own cup aside and sat down.

"When do you start, Verus?" he asked.

"As soon as Theodoric will release me. Gods, I'll need to hurry! Arthur will have expected me when first the seaways opened. I'll have lost the best part of a campaigning summer already!" I said, my mind busy on practical details. "How in thunder did this letter take so long on the way—and how did Bardeliez come by it? Well, he can tell me at supper. I can't get an audience with Theodoric before morning, so we'll accept the old devil's invitation and see what news he has to give of the quickest route from here to Armorica. I'd like his advice on horses, too. My brother writes he needs mainland stallions for breeding fresh cavalry mounts."

Palomides nodded.

"Bardeliez will certainly help you there. If we are to dine with him, you should dress yourself. You can't ride through Rome in your underpants with an escort of Scythians, centurion," he reminded me, smiling.

"Neither I can!" I laughed, taking my cloak from its peg on the door, and throwing it over my shoulders. "I'll go down to the baths and be with you in half an hour."

"We wear civilian dress tonight?" he queried.

I nodded.

"Never again, if I can help it, will you see me in cataphract armor!" I told him. "Plain battledress is good enough for us in Britain, but tonight I'll do honor to Bardaliez and wear the toga for once. He'll appreciate the compliment."

"You are fortunate to have the right," Palomides said gravely, and again I could have kicked myself for a clumsy fool. Palomides was my good comrade. Why need I for the second time have reminded him of misfortune?

The baths attached to the old barracks of the IX Augusta, where we had been quartered for the past month, while King Theodoric of the Goths, whom we served, made a state visit to his capital, were, like most things in Rome that year, in poor repair. But the murky water in the cracked plunge pool was at least cool, and I floated in it for a time, letting my thoughts settle.

Theodoric would release me—it had been part of my contract with him when I offered him my sword two years back, that I should be free to return to Britain if and when I was recalled. I'd learned a great deal under his command, and I should be sorry to leave him short of an officer, when I knew he needed me. I'd knocked a modicum of discipline into the century of barbarian giants he'd given me to command. At least they were less lice-infested and quicker to obey an order than they had been. I should be sorry to part from Palomides too. He and I had been good comrades.

Bardeliez the merchant was a good friend of mine. As, clean, shaved and dressed, I knelt to fasten my sandal straps, I reflected it was a lucky chance that had brought him to Rome at the very moment when his advice was what I needed most. Since, very early in my time on the mainland, I'd done him a small service (which he was inclined to exaggerate), he had always been ready to give me his help.

Palomides was dressed before me (a trifle overdressed by my island standards, but in three years I'd grown reconciled to fashions that I'd despised as effeminate at first). His acid green cloak, heavily embroidered with silver, opened on a pleated tunic of white silk that emphasized the dark olive of his skin. There were jewels in the gold collar about his neck, and he wore several arm rings. We made a striking contrast. My only ornament was the purple stripe on the white woollen toga Ygern had woven for me. We of the Aurelian line have the right to it, being descended from Maximus the Emperor.

A thunderous knocking on the door announced my orderly, who followed it immediately, without waiting for leave. He came in, grinning broadly, a giant of a man, whose long, lint-fair hair, and ample beard and whiskers, hid most of his face.

"Escort is come," he announced, in his execrable Latin, and added approvingly, "Very fine! Much good horses!"

As we followed him out, he asked sociably:

"You go rich man's place? Good food, much wine, after, plenty pretty little flute girls?"

"Something like that," I agreed.

He patted my shoulder.

"Good! You deserve. You bloody nice fellow. Good officer. All of us say—we kill any man says different!"

He emphasized the promise by smacking his hand on his sword hilt.

"Thanks, Otho," I said. "Behave yourselves while we are away. We shan't be too drunk to have you all flogged in the morning if there is any disturbance in our absence."

He laughed uproariously at this and again smacked my shoulder in comradely fashion.

As we went out into the courtyard, where six wild-looking Scythian bandits, mounted on splendid, half-broken stallions, were caracolling around to the admiration of my cohort, I wondered what Ambrosius would have made of that interchange between a centurion and his orderly. Goths are superb warriors, but incurably democratic. Each one is a law unto himself. Prove to them your right to ride first and they'll follow you into any battle, at odds of six to one. Try to impose the regular and respectful discipline of the legion and they'll either laugh in your face or dash your brains out, according to their mood. I'd learned that early in my service with Theodoric.

We found Bardeliez and his caravan camping in the moldering magnificence of a half-ruined villa on the Pincean Hill. Two-thirds of the great houses of Rome had been abandoned, and lay open to squatters. A city that has been sacked three times is slow to recover.

We went in under a portico smirched from the burning, through an entrance that gaped, doorless, to find Bardeliez's "little yellow man" waiting for us. He was a slave from the land of silk, that lies three years' journey into the sunrise, and Palomides and I knew him well.

"The Master expects you. Be pleased to follow his poor servant," he greeted us.

We followed him through a maze of apartments and courts, all bustling with activity. Horses, mules and camels were being fed and watered, where delicate frescoes peeled from crumbling walls. Cooking fires burned on inlaid pavements. Everywhere men were carrying water, chopping wood, spreading blankets, chattering while they worked in a dozen different tongues. Saddlebags, panniers, bundles were piled wherever a roof remained to give shelter. Scythian guards lounged in off-duty relaxation, gambling, quarrelling, eating, or singing sad love songs. It was a scene Palomides and I remembered. Once, for months, we had been a part of it each evening.

The slave led us out onto an open terrace that faced

the sunset. All Rome lay spread beneath it. Advancing towards us, silhouetted against the light, came a dark, squat figure with the rolling gait of a spring-sleepy bear.

"Ah, my friends, my sons! So you have accepted the humble invitation of poor old Bardeliez? He is honored—he is enchanted! Good fortune attend you both!"

I found myself enfolded in a hug that also would have done credit to a bear, and a prickly black beard, redolent of jasmine oil, was pressed ceremoniously to each cheek in turn.

Gasping for breath, I was released and held at arm's length.

"So—so! You have not got yourself killed yet, my Verus? You are not, for once, in disgrace, in prison, in trouble? My, my, but how well you look—bigger than ever—and dressed like a senator—a sight to gladden the eyes! And Palomides the Beautiful, my son Palomides! Now the cup of happiness overflows for the poor old merchant!"

As Bardeliez released his grip on my shoulders to embrace Palomides, I reflected that he looked neither old, nor poor, but, as always, in whatever circumstances and whatever country, unmistakably a merchant and primarily a merchant who traded in horses.

All Scythians, they say, are half-Centaur. Bardeliez came from the wide steppes of the hinterland where some of the finest horsestock in the world is raised by folk who live all their lives in painted wagons, following their breeding herds. He looked tall on horseback, but on foot he stood a head shorter than I, for his legs had been shaped from childhood to a horse's back, and it was their wide bow that gave him his bearlike roll. His hair and beard were the grizzled black of a bear's fur, and he had small, twinkling eyes like a bear's, beady and expressionless, in which you could never read the next move of his mind, any more than you can in a bear's. His mouth contradicted them, a full-lipped, generous gash in the thicket of his beard, under the jut of his great hooked nose. Scythian dress, with its baggy breeches, square, sleeveless coat and voluminous linen shirt, all stiff with

brilliant embroidery, added to the width of him. He had
two curved daggers stuck through his scarlet waist scarf,
and he stank, as I remembered him, of eastern perfumes
and rank horse sweat. I found myself grinning in sheer
pleasure at the familiarity and warmth of recognition that
swept over me.

"Bardeliez, you old devil, what in the name of all the
gods are you doing in Rome, and how did you come on
that letter from Britain?" I asked.

He laid his arms across both our shoulders, steering
us towards an arbor, where wine waited on a cracked
porphyry table, and stone benches stood in a semicircle
among ankle-high weeds.

"What should I be doing in Rome, son of my old
age? Are not Theodoric the King and all his rich court
making festival here? It is written in the holy book of my
mother's people: 'Where the corpse is, there are the
vultures gathered.' Times are hard—very hard. One must
surely seek profit where it is to be found?"

I nodded.

"But the letter?" I persisted.

He sat down heavily, motioning us to sit one on each
side of him, pouring wine from an earthen jar into three
beautifully chased silver goblets. He pushed ours towards
us.

"The letter? Ah, yes," he said reflectively, and his
eyes twinkled. "Drink and I will tell you. It is a miracle
you received that letter. Have I not always said the stars
favor you?"

He drained his wine at one draught, wiped his lips
with the back of his hand and leaned towards me.

"It was of importance, was it?" he asked.

"Of the greatest importance," I said, with feeling.

He seemed pleased.

"So something warned me, when I found Timberlain
the Phoenician running about the quaysides of Byzantium
three moons back, bleating for you like a lamb bleating
after a lost ewe. I warned the fool he'd do himself no
good, shouting *your* name to the gulls, for Zeno's secret
police have long memories, and I asked him what ailed
him. Plenty did. He'd lost ship and cargo to the cursed

Vandal pirates, it seemed, and only got off with his life by diving overboard in the darkness. All Phoenicians swim like seals. A fishing boat picked him up a day and a night later and dumped him, penniless, on the dockside, with nothing in his pocket but that letter he'd been well paid to carry. He said if he could find the man it was addressed to, it might be worth at least one good meal to him. (In charity I saw to it he was not disappointed of that, anyway.) Also, being glad for your sake to have it, I recommended him to a friend of mine who needed a shipmaster. Byzantium is no city for an honest fool like Timberlain—no city for any honest man, come to that, as you learned, did you not, Verus?" and he rumbled with deep belly laughter.

I laughed too.

"Tell me something, Bardeliez—what did it cost you to get me out of prison there?" I asked curiously.

"It is something I prefer to forget, since anxiety blinded my eyes that night, and I paid the guards what they asked—which is bad business and brings the blush to my cheek when I remember it. A hurried bargain is always a bad bargain. Your execution was ordered for daybreak, though." He leaned back, his thumbs in his belt, shaking his head, "It was robbery, what they demanded—yet the price was cheap, my son, for the life of a brave man, who had risked his at odds of four to one, for mine, not so very long before."

"You exaggerate, Bardeliez. Those mountain brigands were cowardly thieves who ran like jackals at my first shout," I reminded him.

"Bah!—then how did it happen you had killed one, wounded two, and were covered in your own blood before my worthless guards rallied from their panic and came in to finish the affair? No, no, to the mad boy who came whooping over the hillside that morning two years back, Bardeliez owes his life. So there is no debt between us. The account is closed. Come—no more talk until supper is served." He broke off, clapped his hands loudly and, when a slave boy appeared, ordered: "Bring the food and quickly. We eat here."

When it came, a round iron cauldron, straight off the

fire, steaming with the savory smell of strange herbs and
hot spices, flanked by a battered but priceless antique
silver dish, on which were arranged a flat loaf and little
earthenware dishes of dates and sweetmeats, Palomides
and I smiled at one another. He said, exultantly:

"Desert food! Gods, how often, condemned to army
rations, we've dreamed of it!"

Bardeliez beamed.

"Sons of my adoption, so you too remembered the
good days when we travelled together? Dip in and eat
while it is hot. Lyn Ty would have sent to the cook shops
in order to honor you as guests. But I said—serve them
the food that is flavored with memory; for those shared
memories are good!"

We dipped into the cauldron together, and mutton,
stewed to rags in its own fatty gravy, burned the tongue
with spices as it used to do; the little balls of flour and
pot herbs swam with it, temptingly, and the bread had the
faint, smoky taste to the crust I remembered so well.

To Bardeliez, eating had always been a serious business. In the companionable silence, my mind went back
to that first day when, a month's journey out of Britain, in
wild country, I'd come suddenly over the crest of a hill, to
see a caravan in disorder, attacked by brigands, and one
man on the ground, surrounded by four ruffians, one with
a knife already at his throat.

I'd been in a vile temper that morning, for my
journey was going badly, and the fact that most of my
troubles were due to my own cocksure inexperience was
rubbing me like a saddle gall. Barely a third of my way to
Byzantium by then, I'd been fleeced at every inn so
ruthlessly that most of the money Ambrosius had given
me seemed to have vanished. My servant, a good lad, had
fallen sick of a fever, so that I'd left him with kindly
Christian monks in Armorica who, if he recovered, would
see him home again by some means. Fording a flooded
river, I'd somehow lost the military itinerary I'd been
issued as well, and, incidentally, lost my way as a result. I
was in just the right mood to take out, on the first enemy
that I met with, the seething frustration I was feeling.

Remembering it all, I chuckled softly.

"Gods, Bardeliez, when I think of that first day I met you, it seems a lifetime ago. What a green young fool I must have seemed!"

Bardeliez grunted.

"Younger by two years only than you are now, by my reckoning—but green? You were that! Riding alone, for all the world as though Rome's peace still guarded every road, and heading for Byzantium of all places. I told you from the beginning you'd get no profit there."

"You told me," I agreed. "But I was under orders. As a soldier I had to obey."

Bardeliez spat generously into the tall nettles.

"And what did I say? That the man who gave such an order could know nothing of Byzantium, to send a brave, honest lad there. That pisspot of a city, seething with politics and intrigue, lousy with superstitious priests, where I myself would not be venturing, except that the fever of its people for the Hippodrome always offers a little profit to a horse trader."

"You told me right. I know that now," I agreed.

Bardeliez licked his fingers clean of grease and, taking a handful of dates, chewed them meditatively, spitting out the stones.

" 'Member of the emperor's guard—good pay, fine military training, an honor to your country to be chosen for it?' Bah! *I* knew. There was no such guard and never would be! Zeno was always cautious. *He* would never trust his skin to a guard other than his secret police. I knew. But would you listen? No. Nothing would satisfy you until I'd got you to that cesspit, and you'd raised mayhem in the Imperial palace itself, half murdered a man (a holy man at that) and earned yourself a death sentence."

Remembering, I scowled.

"They drove me to it, Bardeliez. A month and more they kept me, day after day, kicking my heels in outer courts and frowsy warrens of clerks' offices, putting me off with bland excuses. Insults to myself I could stomach, but when a shaven-headed, fat priest with the voice of a eunuch spoke slightingly of Britain and of my general, Ambrosius Aurelianus, I admit I took him by the folds of his fat neck and shook him until his face turned blue. I'm still glad I did it!"

Bardeliez rolled on his seat, shaken by his own laughter.

"A Christian clerk, in the emperor's sacred palace! Ho, ho, ho! You tempted your stars that day, boy, you certainly tempted your stars!" he said. He wiped his eyes, passed me a bowl of sweetmeat made from crushed almonds and honey, and when I shook my head helped himself generously. "Well, we got you out of that scrape, even if your dignity suffered, driving camels in the caravan until we were well clear of the emperor's province! Have you found better profit and good soldier training in the service of Theodoric, my Verus?"

"I have indeed," I said. "You were right when you advised me to take it. He is a great general and a good man. What I've learned will help us in Britain, Bardeliez, for his problems are much like ours. He has built an independent state, free from the interference of an empire fallen so low it's not worth fighting for."

Bardeliez turned to Palomides.

"And you, my Palomides? You have been happy also?"

Palomides shrugged.

"Happy enough," he said quietly.

The sun had set while we were eating, and the sudden darkness of those southern lands shrouded the terrace. Below us, lights twinkled all over the sprawl of the half-ruined city.

A slave brought a lamp and set it on the table, clearing away the food, but leaving the wine cups and a fresh jar of wine.

Bardeliez went on staring thoughtfully at Palomides, picking his teeth with a silver toothpick.

"You are content, then, to be still only a commander of archers? You have not thought to volunteer for any other service?"

"Content enough," Palomides said briefly. His face in the lamplight had a wary, reserved expression I'd learned to know. For some reason, his guard was up, as I'd seen before, when he did not choose to be questioned.

Bardeliez sighed gustily and said, with sudden gutteral impatience:

"Waste! Me, I hate waste!"

Palomides laughed softly.

"Perhaps better to have left me to the vultures, after all, Bardeliez?"

Remembering that dark, handsome face of his, as I'd first seen it, cracked and sun-blistered, the face of a wounded man left after battle to die by a desert trail, I shuddered.

"Don't remind us of that, Bardeliez. Lucky we found him when we did. You never told me, though, where you two had met before."

"No?" Bardeliez's little eyes turned to mine, expressionless as pebbles. "It is not of importance. Tell me instead—this letter from Britain—what news did it bring?"

"This island, which your brother will rule one day—or so you say—tell me more of it," Bardeliez commanded me abruptly.

I'd talked for an hour or more, I dare say, arguing with him my reasons for leaving Theodoric's service, explaining to him the full meaning of the letter I'd received, and in the end giving it to him to read for himself.

"What more do you want to know?" I asked. "I've told you just about everything, Bardeliez."

"No—you have told me only of forty years' war and more war yet to come. What are wars to me? The whole world, now, is full of wars. I have heard, somewhere, that in the great days, Rome prized your distant island for the rich tribute it paid—tin, and precious metals, corn, slaves, noble hunting dogs. Is that true, Verus?"

I shrugged.

"It may be. A country raided by sea pirates hasn't much chance to think of such things. We're all poor in Britain now and I don't remember it otherwise."

He nodded.

"So? But what has been could be again. The re-sources, they are still there," he muttered. Tapping the letter which still lay before him under the lamp, he said: "I am old and a merchant. I have learned to judge men. The man who wrote this is a man who has it in him to succeed at whatever he sets his hand to, if his gods are with him. Verus, where will you buy these horses he asked for—from whom?"

I hesitated. Then I said frankly:

"I don't know. I need your advice on that—and on the quickest route I can safely take to get home fast. Advise me on both those things and I'll be grateful."

Bardeliez was silent a long time. When he spoke at last, it was half to himself.

"Every merchant I know would call me mad for this—*they've* wiped Britain off their books these many years. But some instinct tells me they could be wrong. Listen to me, Verus." He rose and, placing his hands on the table, stared across at me. "I've a mind, once my business in Rome is done, to travel north and see for myself what this new king who rules in Lutetia now—the Frankish king—has to offer by way of custom. A merchant caravan travels more slowly than you'd ride alone, but, big and well guarded as mine is now, at least you could count on arriving. Come with me, at least as far as Genabum where the old, good road branches west into Armorica. On the way, we'll talk of horses. If your brother would give me his bond to grant certain priorities to me when he has won his battles, we'd not talk of stallions by twos and threes, but a stud with mares that would not take him twenty years to raise the cavalry mounts he needs."

I rose to face him.

"Bardeliez, do you mean that?" I said.

"We Scythians are gamblers, all of us. I mean it," he rumbled. A wide smile broke across his face as I stared, hardly able to believe my good luck. "It is agreed then? You ride with us, again, when my business is done here?"

"I will indeed," I stammered. He had solved more than half the problems in my mind. Out of the shadows, where, for the moment, I had forgotten him, Palomides spoke quietly.

"I go also, Bardeliez. Verus, your brother asked for volunteers, did he not? Accept me as the first. Why look so surprised? You yourself have told me often that Caesar's assessment of the British climate was exaggerated!"

# Chapter Seven

"Palomides, are you sure it wasn't the wine speaking last night? You've good prospects here, and the best we can offer you in Britain will be hardship and danger in a climate that, if I'm honest, *can* resemble Caesar's description of it as 'unfit for human habitation' pretty closely six months out of every year! If you want to call the deal off, I swear I'll think none the worse of you."

We were waiting in an anteroom of one of the old palaces on the Julian Hill, where King Theodoric had made headquarters for his six months' residence in the city. (Ravenna was the capital he'd chosen to rule from —we'd joined his army just before he laid siege to it, two years before.)

Palomides said soberly:

"The deal is made, Verus. I've nothing to lose by it—neither home, nor country, nor cause. I have been thinking for a long time there must be something more worth giving one's life to than the career of a paid archer in a Barbarian army. The occupation bores me. I doubt if I'd have endured it even as long as I have, except for our friendship together."

The depth of feeling in his dark eyes embarrassed me.

"In Britain I doubt if you'll be bored—I doubt if you'll be paid, either," I warned him brusquely.

He smiled.

"I am not re-enlisting in hope of better pay. In

Britain I've an idea I may find something I have been looking for a long while."

"What's that?" I asked, made curious by his unusual gravity.

"A reason for living. Perhaps, even, the meaning of life," he said.

Before I could ask him what in thunder gave him that idea, an orderly came to tell us the king was ready to give us audience.

It was still early morning, but the palace was astir with comings and goings of both military and civilian personnel; the rooms we passed through were thronged with Goth chieftains, army officers like ourselves, of a dozen different races, and a host of minor officials, clerks and suppliants of all classes, many of them quite humble folk. Theodoric the Ostrogoth was a tireless worker, who kept the reins of government over his newly conquered country entirely in his own hands and—as far as I had been able to judge—was guiding it both wisely and justly.

That morning, he was sitting at a great green marble desk, in a high, light room, dictating to his secretaries, and I guessed he had had them at work since dawn. He must have been in his middle fifties—a big, soldierly man, with fair hair and beard already fading, so that it looked as if it had been dusted over with flour, and keen blue eyes that missed nothing.

He glanced up at our entrance, acknowledged our salutes and, with a gesture, dismissed his clerks.

"Well, what is it, lads? Trouble?" he asked briskly.

"No, sire—not trouble. A request," I said, and explained briefly what I had come about. Then I laid Arthur's letter before him.

Unlike most Goths, he read Latin as easily as he spoke it, having been educated at Byzantium in his youth, when he was a hostage there. After a few moments, he laid the parchment on the desk, leaned back and folded his arms.

"And you don't call this trouble, eh? Trouble for me, when I'm short-handed already. But, fair enough, you warned me, Verus, you'd ask for release if you were recalled to Britain." His keen eyes turned to Palomides. "Why must you go too? What business is it of yours to go gallivanting off to the ends of the known earth? You're a Greek of Asia Minor, aren't you? Are you two lovers?"

I felt myself flushing. Even after three years there were things I'd not grown used to on the mainland. Palomides, however, answered, with quiet assurance:

"No, sire. Tried battle comrades. I've an idea I'd like to see more active service than promises here, now you've conquered this country, that is all." He smiled suddenly, one of his strangely appealing smiles. "To be honest, I'd say with all respect, I don't much fancy police work in a land now virtually stable and at peace."

Theodoric's expression warmed.

"By the Hammer, I can understand that! I've fought all my life to get peace for my people and I mean to keep it, but I'll admit to a warrior the days of it can seem long." He took up Arthur's letter and read it again. "I know very little of Britain," he said thoughtfully. "Tell me something of this country of yours, Verus, and your brother who writes of it."

As I hesitated where to begin, he said sharply:

"Come. Give me a report. The first thing I taught you when you came to me, I remember, was how to give a report clearly and in few words."

The command steadied me. Automatically I came to attention and gave him, as briefly as I could, an account of the situation at home as I knew it. Put into that terse, unvarnished form, the facts of the case sounded pretty bleak—a small, sea-girt island, with miles of vulnerable coastline. A country where, for Barbarian pirates, there was still plenty of loot worth lifting; and, more desirable to many of them even than loot, hundreds of miles of fertile underdeveloped or neglected farmland. A country where two entirely different races still existed, not by any means reconciled to each other; and where law and order had broken down for more than a generation. A country that a foolish, usurping princeling had bedevilled for us all, forty years back, by land concessions to Saxon mercenaries all down its eastern seaboard. A land threatened by raiders of half a dozen races literally on every side at once. A country that had been written off as expendable by the civilized world.

Theodoric sat, stroking his beard, listening, with his eyes still on Arthur's letter, until I had finished. Then he looked up and said, with a glint of amusement:

"Stand at ease, centurion! Now, tell me, this foster brother of yours, how old is he?"

"Twenty-one years, last winter solstice, sire."

"And you—the same age?"

"Three days' difference, sire."

"Hmph." He nodded. "And you really believe, between you, you can fight a campaign that will make your island a free and independent country?"

"Success lies with the gods. We shall try," I said.

His eyes met mine and there was understanding as well as laughter in them.

"You are both very young, but who am I to find fault with that? I was eighteen when my elder brothers were killed and I led my tribe, thirty thousand of them, men, women and children, from their homelands beside the Great River, over the Alps in winter, the year the Mongol hordes swept down from the north on us, murdering and burning, a great host of human locusts no man could number. Now, the gods be praised, my people have a homeland again, and one where I, also, must teach two races to live and work together." He paused and glanced again at Arthur's letter. "High King of his own people and War Duke of the Romans as well. The best of both worlds if only he can hold to those titles; provided he's man enough. Is he, Verus?"

"He's a born leader, sire. Men will follow him anywhere. He's brave as a lion, but wise as well. A man very like yourself—only younger, of course," I said impulsively.

Theodoric smiled a little grimly.

"Is that so? Well, if he lives time will mend youth, that's one certainty at least. I can see you've set your heart on following him, so I suppose I must release you. You, too, Palomides, since you've caught the infection of restlessness and want adventure. I'll have a discharge prepared for you both, and give orders for someone to take over your duties as soon as possible."

He paused again, slipped an arm ring of red amber off his arm and sat for several minutes, turning it in his hands, looking down at it, then held it out to me.

"Here, boy, take this. If things should go badly in Britain, there'll always be a place for you in Theodoric's army, and for that warrior brother of yours and any more like you. Remember that. Bring or send this ring to me at need. I shall remember it, even if in the press of affairs, I may have forgotten you. Take it and good luck go with it—by the Hammer, from what you've told me, you are going to need all the luck the gods can send you!"

Harvest was over, and the first leaves were turning, when Palomides and I parted from Bardeliez and his slow-moving caravan at Genabum and, spurring our horses, thankful to be able to make our own speed at last, turned westward towards the Armorican border. The journey had not been uneventful, but I remember it only for the frustrations and delays that fretted me more each day as I watched summer waning and remembered that by late September the seaways would be closing.

At parting, Bardeliez embraced us with tears in his eyes. He had already loaded us with so many gifts our saddlebags bulged, and given his word to me that he would see to the choosing and shipment of the horses. I'd signed for him in Arthur's name a parchment promising him trade concessions in payment. It was something altogether outside my province, and I hoped I'd done right. But I trusted Bardeliez. If ever a man had proved friendship to me, he had.

At the very last moment he delayed our parting still further while he sent a slave scurrying to fetch two new hooded black goatskin cloaks for us. The Scythians have a secret of weaving them so that the cloth sheds rain.

Glancing up at a lowering sky, he exploded:

"Whatever other dangers await you, my sons, you need not die from the weather in that wild country to which you go. Take these, and the blessings of old Bardeliez go with you both!"

We were to bless him, indeed, for that gift. We were heading, though we did not guess it, into one of the earliest and stormiest autumns I remember.

Instinct and inclination alike urged me, for the next month, to cut short my remaining business on the mainland and push on to the coast, but Arthur's orders had been explicit and I did my best to carry them out. Armorica, at that time, was as packed with refugees from Britain as a pomegranate is with pips. Ever since the Troubles they had been crowding in. Each fresh wave of raiding brought more of them. Most were poor folk, whose farms or workshops had been burned, and who, facing starvation, came in search of work or fled blindly from the horrors that had overwhelmed them. We can never repay the Armoricans for what they did for those. The ones I'd orders to contact were a different breed, members of the great Colonial families, who had got out at the very beginning, with time to bring over their wealth and possessions and establish themselves again very comfortably in a pattern of life which we, of sterner stock, who had elected to stay and lose all except honor, held in contempt. My upbringing had prejudiced me against them for a start. I was one of the worst ambassadors Arthur could have chosen.

True, I was received with guarded civility in their comfortable villas, once I'd explained my connections. They respected the blood of an emperor, even an unlucky one. Palomides and I could have dined well every night for a year on that introduction. But I soon discovered they'd no belief in Britain's future, certainly not a future that depended mainly on a revival of Celtic nationalism. Their loyalty, now, was to their own small, exclusive, inward-turned society, where they could surround themselves with an aura of past grandeur, and indulge in sentimental nostalgia that cost them nothing.

They said, in effect:

"*Here* is all that is left of the civilization of Britain. Our fathers (or grandfathers as the case might be) brought it here in the time of the Troubles. Look at this silver, these bronzes, that statue—all originals, all priceless now! We preserve the best traditions—the literature, the music, the arts that the Barbarians have destroyed in our unhappy homeland. You will observe, young man, that *we* speak only the Latin of Courtesy still."

(They did, too, braying it through their aristocratic noses like Iberian mules, so that I was often at a loss to follow their affected conversation. I knew well enough they intended to humiliate me by it—drawing attention to my use of the vulgar tongue that gets you anywhere, still, from the Wall to Byzantium!)

They showed us with pride their comfortable, well-appointed, well-warmed villas; their flower gardens with fountains and potted rose trees in carved stone jars; sighing, all the time, with false humility, that nothing here, in the land of their exile, could compare with what their families once owned in Britain. But when I spoke of Britain's present need, and the hope, at last, of making it a free land to which they might return, they bunched against me, as sheep bunch against a strange collie, come snapping to round them up for the butcher's cleaver. In three long wasted weeks, I failed to gain a single recruit to Arthur's Dragon standard.

It was a white-haired, long-retired senator, who could remember Vortigern's rising, who finally decided me to stop battering my head against a wall.

"Send my grandsons to fight under a native Chieftain? I'd sooner see them dead! The average Saxon (and we've a largish colony of them settled on the west coast here, so I know what I'm talking about) is more trustworthy than any Celt. Civilize a Saxon and he'll make a good, honest farmer. You can't civilize a Celt. Rome tried for three hundred years—and look at the result. The Red Fox, Vortigern, stabbed us in the back! Tricky, treacherous, lazy devils, the lot of them, and always will be. I'm surprised a young man of the Aurelian family should have the effrontery to talk subversive treason in my house. 'Son of Uther,' indeed! The only son that blustering brigand ever fathered was a bastard got on a woman no better than she should be, the very night he had connived at her husband's murder. If you follow him, you

deserve to be crucified, Verus Aurelianus—and probably
will be! Now, get out, before I send for my house slaves
to throw you out!"

When I'd finished telling Palomides, in good barrack
Latin, what I'd have done to that one but for his venerable grey hairs, he said reasonably:

"Don't you think we have marched far enough down
a road to nowhere, Verus? My guess is that anything you
did recruit from among these families would not do your
brother much good."

"By the gods you're right there," I said. "I've had
enough of them. I'll make one last throw of the dice. King
Bann is supposed to be at Gesocrovate. I've found out
that much from three weeks' idle chatter. It's on the
coast. I'll make one last effort to get Arthur's treaty with
him sewn up, and then, win or lose, I'm taking ship for
Britain. If no ships are sailing so late in the season, I'll
damn well swim. I've had my bellyful of the mainland
and that's an all-time understatement!"

We rode north into the teeth of wild weather. A full gale
was blowing in from the coast, with vicious rainstorms
that made us thankful for our Scythian cloaks. Even with
them, we were soaked to the skin, as well as mud-
splashed to the eyes, on the evening we finally reached
Gesocrovate, a small port, tucked down between rocky
headlands, on a coast that reminded me of my own
Dumnonian seaboard. Once inside the gates, I began to
feel more cheerful than I had for a month, in spite of the
weather. The town was humming like a hive of bees
before thunder. Everywhere Armorican Clansmen in warrior dress were coming and going. I recognized half a
dozen or more who must be Clan Princes, to judge by the
cock's feathers in their leather war-caps, each directing
his own men. In the Street of the Smiths the forges were
at work, glowing in the wet dusk. You could not hear
yourself speak for the hammering.

"This looks like a gathering for war. With luck we'll
find King Bann somewhere in this place," I said to Palomides, as we turned our tired horses into a quiet street.

"Lucky if we find ourselves a bed and supper,"

Palomides warned. "Best look for lodgings on a night like this before you start to look for him, Verus."

He was right. The wind had veered and was rising with the coming dark. The showers were turning to hail. Along the harbor front we could see the caps of great waves rearing up, one behind the other, to break in spray the whole length of a stone mole.

"First things first!" I agreed.

There were plenty of inns in the town. The cross-Channel traffic had paid Armorican innkeepers well for years. We went from one to another, but all were crammed to the attics. At last we were directed to a small, clean place, tucked in under the ramparts, where the landlord, harassed but courteous, offered us beds in a converted outhouse.

"It's the best you'll find for the night, sirs. Tomorrow, when the army moves out, we can take you into the house. It's my two oldest boys' sleeping quarters by rights; but they've been called up for service and will be off to the war in the morning, may the good Christ protect them!" He crossed himself piously.

"What war is this?" I asked.

"The war against the bloody Burgundian settlers. They've come out in rebellion again. Hadn't you heard?"

"No," I said. "We've come from a distance. Is the king—King Bann—in the town still?"

The innkeeper scratched his head.

"I couldn't tell for sure. He was this morning. I saw him with my own eyes, addressing the advance guard in the square. Will you be wanting supper, sir?"

"Yes. But not yet. I've a message for the king I must deliver first. Where can I find him?"

"At the palace, sir—what used to be the prefect's residence. It's only a stone's throw from here, on foot through the alleyways. I can send our youngest to show you the way. Pardon, sir, but would a cut of venison suit your lordships? I know 'tis a fast day, but there's no fish, the boats not having been able to get out on account of the weather, so the bishop has given a general dispensation, you understand."

I stared at him, then said hastily:

"Very well. If it's all you have, venison let it be, and plenty of it!"

Armorica, it seemed, was as Christian as Byzantium. I had better take note of that, in dealing with its king.

I left Palomides to see to our horses and baggage, while a barefoot imp with inquisitive eyes led me, splashing through puddles, by stinking back lanes, and delivered me importantly to a sentry on guard at the gatehouse of what must have been once a handsome official residence. I was passed inside more easily than I expected, when I explained I carried an urgent message.

The inner court was alight with torches, flaring in the wet wind; and full of armed men, most of them, by their dress and weapons, officers in the tribal levies. I caught the attention of a young Chief, wearing bronze half-armor, whose single eagle feather distinguished him as of royal rank, and asked him where I should find the king.

He looked me over and shook his head.

"Not here. He left an hour ago. What's your business?"

"Urgent business. I've a personal message for him from Arthur the Pendragon of Britain," I said. Then, knowing that with a Celtic Chieftain it never pays to minimize one's own importance: "I am Verus Aurelianus, nephew of the General Ambrosius Aurelianus, and foster brother of the Pendragon. Where is the king?"

The boy—he was not more than sixteen—came smartly to attention and saluted.

"At the monastery, sir. I doubt if you'll get speech with him tonight though. He's keeping vigil—to pray for a blessing on the army. I dare say you could see the High Prince later. He's just gone in to preside at the War Council. They may be some hours talking, but if you would care to wait?" He paused deferentially, eyeing me with obvious interest.

The wind whipped my cloak about me. I was cold, wet and hungry. I met the boy's curious stare and smiled at him.

"See here," I said confidentially, "I've been in the saddle since dawn. I need to get myself dried and fed.

Will you do something for me? When your High Prince comes from Council, tell him who I am, and that I have something to say to him that can't wait until he has fought a war. If he will see me tonight, send a messenger to fetch me. I lodge at the Inn of Peter the Fisherman under the rampart. It's not five minutes from here. I'll not go to bed until midnight, and if he'll give me audience I can be with him in no time. I think he may, if you remember it is a message from Britain's Pendragon I have for him."

(I'd decided a High Prince in War Council would be more likely to listen to Arthur's requests than an ageing king who shut himself up among praying monks on the eve of a war.)

The young Chief's eyes sparkled.

"I'll tell him, sir. Without fail. And I'll come for you myself. I'm pretty sure he'll want to see you. We've heard great things of Britain's new Pendragon. Do you come from Britain? In this weather?"

"Never mind where I come from," I said. I'd made an impression, and meant to sustain it. "The important thing is that he should hear what I have to say. Can I rely on you?"

"Absolutely, without fail, my lord!" He saluted again.

I returned the salute.

"I trust the matter to you, then," I said.

As I splashed my way back to the inn, I felt my spirits rising. I liked what I saw of these Armorican fighting men. They were the type Arthur could use as allies. The admiration in that boy's eyes when he'd spoken of whatever rumors had reached as far as this meant Arthur's war must be going well, and his enthusiastic deference had warmed my blood after the Colonists' insolence.

Over supper in the crowded inn kitchen, I told Palomides what had happened.

"You'd better turn in and sleep. If I don't get a summons to the Prince tonight, it may mean we'll have to go chasing after a marching army to catch up with him tomorrow. I'm loath to miss the chance of settling his alliance now I've seen what it could mean," I warned him.

"I'll watch with you. Storms make me restless. We'll take some wine over to our quarters and wait on the event in comfort. I told the landlord to light a fire for us, and I'll warn him you are expecting a messenger," he said.

The fire, banked with good ash logs, was burning well, in the little timber-built outhouse, and the place was snug and cheerful, though bare as our barrack cells had been.

We stretched ourselves out on the two pallet beds, a jug of wine and two cups on the stool between us. Outside, beyond the rampart, we could hear the roaring of the sea. Wind rattled the door and heavy window shutter and hail hissed along the roof.

"What a night! If this storm doesn't clear we could be held up for a week, even if I do see the High Prince tonight," I grumbled. "You'll be sick as a dog, crossing to Britain, Palomides."

"Shall I?" Palomides raised himself on one elbow, drank some wine and looked across at me reflectively. His face in the dancing flamelight was hard to read. "What makes you so certain I'm no sailor, Verus?"

"Well, are you? Have you tried sea travel before?" I challenged him, surprised.

"Many times. I was born on the coast. I could handle a boat before I could ride, and do both by the time I was seven years old."

I turned on my side, propping my head on my hand.

"That's news to me. Remember, though I've talked often enough of my past, you've told me next to nothing of yours. Where *were* you born, Palomides?"

"On an island, like you—though a smaller one. Meliapolis, off the coast of Asia Minor. I doubt you'll ever have heard of it. My father's house faced the sea and behind it the olive groves and vineyards ran up into the foothills of the mountains. The sun shines warm there, year round. It is a good place. I had a happy childhood until I was ten years old."

He lay back, his hands behind his head, staring at the ceiling.

"And after?" I asked. As I've said, in the legion one does not ask a man questions, but I'd always been curious about Palomides. That night he seemed inclined, for once, to talk.

"After, not so good," he said quietly. "My father was an old man before I was born—a Greek of the Asian settlements—a rich merchant, come of a line of merchants. I was the only child of a late marriage, and my mother died at my birth. He doted on me and grieved for her. I dare say he neglected his business. When an empire falls apart, as Rome has done, money loses its value as fast as water runs through a sieve. I doubt he realized that. At any rate, when he also died, struck down between one day's dawn and dusk, his creditors moved in. I was sold with the rest of his assets."

He spoke so quietly I did not at first take in the meaning of what he had said.

"Sold—as a slave, you mean? At ten years old? Gods, Palomides! Can that really happen?" I asked, deeply shocked. "Can creditors do that?"

"Perhaps not in your country. In mine, yes," he said. "Sold as a slave to a brothel keeper. I'll not harrow you with details. I learned a lot I'd rather forget in the next four years. I was lucky, though, that I wasn't castrated. It's the usual practice. About the time I was due for that, one of my master's clients—a rich and cultured young aristocrat—fell in love with my looks, and paid a good price for me. He treated me well enough, by his own standards. At least he took the trouble to see that the education in philosophy and the arts my father had begun was carried on, while I remained his favorite toy. I shall always owe him gratitude for that. I was seventeen when his family arranged his marriage and, according to custom, my term of service in his household ended. To avoid future embarrassments, he sold me to a caravan on its way to distant parts. That was how I first met Bardeliez. He got me at cut price, to settle the bargain conveniently fast."

There was silence in the small, warm room. The

sound of the sea came back into it, and the rattle of hail.
I lay quiet, trying to picture something outside all my
experience.

Palomides sat up, poured more wine and pushed my
cup across to me. Clasping his arms about his knees, he
said gravely:

"I'd no special wish to talk of all this, but it seemed
best you should know. Perhaps I should have told you in
Rome, before you accepted me for your brother's army.
There's something else, though, that I need to tell you
now. I think I may be able to serve your king better than
as a captain of archers. I am a fully trained physician,
Verus. I worked my next seven years in the hospital of
Alexandria, under Archimandros, and *he* was one of the
finest masters of medicine even Alexandria ever knew."

I also sat up, so startled I gaped at him.

"You—a physician?" I said. "Why in the name of
Light did you never tell me before?" I paused, as a
memory struck me. "What a fool not to have guessed,
though! That time at the siege of Ravenna when you
stitched that sword slash on my arm?"

He shrugged and gave me an amused, sidelong
glance.

"I had to. It was an ugly wound, and the army
surgeon was a butcher, and drunk as an owl that night,
besides. It was your sword arm, Verus. I couldn't risk the
wound infecting so that you lost it, could I?"

I shuddered at the thought.

"I've always been grateful it healed clean and left no
stiffness," I said. "By the gods, Palomides, there'll be
work for a good army doctor with Arthur's forces. We've
very few doctors in Britain as far as I know. What beats
me is why you've concealed your skill. You'd have got
twice the pay of an archer from Theodoric, if you'd only
chosen to volunteer for the field hospital."

"I preferred not to. Comradeship means more to me
than money. I've had few friends in my life and in you I
knew I had found one. I preferred to serve as your
auxiliary," he said coolly. "No man should neglect a gift
the gods have given him. I shall be glad to use my skill
again."

I drank the wine he had poured for me, and lay down. Something puzzled me.

"You were not a physician when you rode into that ambush in the desert," I said. "How the devil did you get yourself from doctoring in Alexandria to soldiering out there?"

He frowned.

"Through mischance, as most men get themselves into an auxiliary legion. The Christians raised a riot in Alexandria, as they frequently do. Our hospital was wrecked and Archimandros put to death on a charge of heresy. I got away with my life by the help of a legionary prefect whose wife I'd attended in a bad confinement. He thought he owed me the son he'd wanted badly, and smuggled me out of the city with a draft going overseas, in the place of a man who'd deserted. It wouldn't have been politic to advertise my profession for some time after what had happened. A heresy charge is lethal enough to follow one a long way, in that part of the world. I always meant to return to doctoring, when I could. Britain may give me my chance." He got up and mended the fire, which had sunk to glowing coals. Over his shoulder he said "One other thing, Verus. Archimandros freed me before he died. That's one complication the less. At least I come to your brother a freed man, not a slave." Before I could answer, he straightened up, listening. "Someone is coming. This will be your messenger, Verus."

"Curse it—I'd forgotten him!" I said, and swung myself off the bed. I'd been absorbed in Palomides' story and did not relish the need to go out into the storm again.

I turned towards the door, hearing the landlord's voice, and then another—a deep, commanding tone that certainly did not belong to my young Celtic Chieftain.

"Very good, fellow. I thank you, and here's something for your pains. You may leave us, now."

There came a sharp rap on the door and Palomides crossed the floor in a couple of strides and opened it. As it swung back, the room came alive with torchlight. A young boy wearing the arm rings of a Chief's son stepped in and, holding the torch high, to show the entrance, announced:

"His Excellency the High Prince Lancelot of Armorica."

A tall man bent his head to pass the lintel, then stood, framed against the darkness outside, the torchlight on his face. He wore a long black cloak, and as he entered, threw back the hood with the impatient grace of a trained actor. Turning to the page, he said:

"Outside, boy, and guard the door. Let no one—no one, you understand—disturb us."

As the boy obeyed, he turned to me and held out both hands.

"So! They told me Verus Aurelianus had come to us with a message from the new War Duke of Britain. Greetings to you, Bedivere, my brother. We meet again. May it be in a propitious hour!" He laughed.

He let go my hands and with a quick gesture loosed his cloak and threw it aside. I stared at him, speechless with surprise. He was a magnificent figure of a man, tall, broad-shouldered, slim-hipped. Trews of a dark tartan and a close-fitting tunic of green wool emphasized the lithe grace of his movements, and the firelight caught the red-gold glint of the High Prince's circlet that bound his dark hair. His sun-bronzed face was handsome, with bone-deep beauty that comes from generations of fine breeding, and in it eyes I remembered, eyes of luminous, sparkling Celtic blue, gleamed with amusement.

"Come—you have not forgotten Ynis Witrin, the Dragon Making, the King Choosing? You have not forgotten Lancelot, still called by some 'of the Lake'?" he asked.

"Indeed I have not—and never shall," I assured him. "But I did not know—I never guessed—"

"That the High Prince of Armorica today was Lancelot of the Boys' House ten years ago? How should you? To be honest, I didn't recognize you under your Roman titles. But when that youngster you'd entrusted with your message stuttered out, 'He's the foster brother of the Pendragon himself, my lord,' I guessed." He crossed to the fire and held out his hands to the blaze, giving a sharp, inquiring glance at Palomides as he passed him. "What a night!" he said, with a shiver. "How did you get here in such weather? Did the Merlin spirit you over the water on a dragon's back, as men say he must have spirited the Lord Arthur and you away from the Gathering? Seriously, how did you make the journey?"

"On a horse's back, not a dragon's," I said, laughing. "I haven't been in Britain for three years. I'm on my way back there now, but I've a letter from Arthur, some of which concerns Armorica."

He glanced at me curiously.

"So? We hear great things of him and his men, Verus, specially this last year. I'll be glad to have word direct. But first, let me send that boy of mine for some wine, and more logs for your fire. I've been frozen to the bone in that tomb my uncle calls a palace, where the hypocaust hasn't worked since the last prefect left, twenty years back. How old men *talk!* I thought I'd never get his venerable Council to settle the battle order until the troops were too deaf from age to hear it!"

I caught Palomides' eye.

"The wine is our business. Palomides, will you see to it? And tell the landlord to bring more wood. This is a poor place to entertain you in, Lancelot. You should have sent for me to wait on you as I told your officer I would."

"Heaven forbid. I wanted our talk to be private," he said. Then, as the door closed behind Palomides, "That man—your servant—is he to be trusted?"

"Not my servant. A two-years-tried battle comrade. Yes, you can trust him as you would me. He's on his way to volunteer for service in Britain's army."

"I'll take your word for him. I have to be careful these days. Armorica has turned remarkably Christian lately and my Uncle Bann is under the thumb of our busy monks. He'd like folk to forget I was ever 'of the Lake,' since his sons died in battle and I became his only heir. The words 'pagan' and 'heretic' have an ill sound to his ears. So, since I'd like to rule Armorica after him, I mind my manners. That does not mean I have forgotten Ynis Witrin. A man need not deny the light his eyes have seen, because his work lies in a country where most men are blind. You agree, Bedivere?"

"I'm a soldier," I said. "I've had little time these last years to trouble about religious differences. I don't, frankly, understand them. It seems to me we've trouble enough, from Byzantium to the Wall, without making more for ourselves. What gods a man worships is surely his own affair?"

He laughed and laid his arm across my shoulders.

"You haven't changed!" he said. "Come, tell me what you've been doing all these years? But first, what does Arthur want from Armorica? The alliance, of course. That's pretty nearly settled, anyway. What else?"

"Volunteers for the army, he was asking for. But you were at peace when he asked it. He'll not expect them, now you've a war on your hands," I said regretfully.

"Not a war. A mere punitive expedition. I wouldn't start a war at the beginning of winter. No. The Burgundian settlers get ideas above their station, now and again— catch them, like fleas, from their Barbarian cousins. They've been giving trouble for years and I'm tired of it. I intend to give them a lesson that'll teach them some manners, and send them back to cultivating their vineyards. That's what we gave them land for in the first place. We delayed until now, to let them get this year's grape harvest in. That's the reason we are marching out when every other army is going into winter quarters. We shall make a quick job of it, for our own sakes. Tell me, how many men does Arthur want?"

I blinked. He was going too fast for me.

"As many as you can spare, I imagine. Remember, I've been out of Britain three years. You must know better than I do how the war goes there, now."

"Better than it did, but he's bound to be hard-pressed next summer. If all goes well, we should be able to put an expeditionary force across the Channel in the spring. Say five hundred men for a start—transports will be the problem. I'll lead them myself. I'll be glad to get out of Armorica and see Britain again. One can breathe in that country of yours, Bedivere. Ah, here comes the wine, and not before time. Talking's dry work and I've been at it half the night already!"

Palomides had returned with the landlord, the latter obviously flattered and flustered at the opportunity of serving such a distinguished guest, bringing his best pewter drinking cups and a fresh amphora, cob-webbed from the cellar. A goggle-eyed small son followed him, staggering under the weight of a great basket of logs.

Lancelot laughed and joked with the man, refusing his offer to clear the parlor of other guests and set it at our disposal.

"I'm a soldier, not a senator, and we're snug as mice in a larder, here. It's the quality of the vintage, not where one drinks it, that matters. Have you brought us something good?" he asked.

"The very best. From your own vineyards, my lord," the landlord assured him.

"Then it should be as warming to our hearts as a virgin's first kiss of passion. Pour for us, good fellow, then see we are not disturbed. Tell that young cockerel of mine outside he can dismiss and go home to bed. We march at dawn and he's too young to miss his sleep. He must be as cold by now, poor child, as a jar of Falernian that's stood all day in snow in preparation for a feast!"

When the landlord had bustled away, and the room was quiet again, I presented Palomides formally and we settled down to good talk for an hour or more.

There was something about Lancelot that created an atmosphere of ease and, at the same time, elation. The wine (some of the best I've ever tasted) may have had something to do with that, but I think it was the enormous vitality of the man, his enthusiastic, headlong acceptance of the challenge Britain offered, that made my heart sing.

He had keen, irreverent wit, and we laughed more than I remembered laughing since I'd been a carefree junior officer with Ambrosius. But it did not hide the fact that he'd a penetrating mind and a wide grasp of affairs outside his own country.

He questioned me shrewdly about politics in Byzantium and Rome and quite obviously knew more about

both than I did. Then he said, cocking an eyebrow at me
in a fashion I was to know very well in later years:

"You were at the King Making three years back—
before you left for the mainland? I was sorry to miss that.
We've heard some strange tales of it. Strange as the
rumor of flying dragons. By all accounts the Merlin
needed all his magic, and some quick thinking besides, to
get Uther's son accepted that day? To tell the truth, over
here, folk were surprised he succeeded. It was expected
the northern Clans and those from the far west would
vote for an older, more experienced war leader. Prince
Geraint was heavily backed as favorite, though a good
many put their money on Lot of Dalriada."

"Geraint is loyal to Arthur. Lot we may still have to
deal with," I told him cautiously.

He nodded.

"And some others, besides, at a guess. Well, it will
be interesting. He'll win in the end, whatever the odds. I
held my peace, here, knowing I could place my bet on a
certainty. Whatever men say of Arthur's right to rule, we
of the Island know it was written in his stars," he said
soberly. "Tell him, Bedivere, he can always count on me.
About the treaty my uncle must speak. Send us an embassy of venerable councillors sometime to wag their grey
beards at him, and I promise you it will be ratified. He
prefers to deal with old men like himself. But I'll be in
Britain next year, before the apple trees blossom on the
Island. Arthur can trust my word on that. Now I must go.
The night's turning towards morning and I've still work to
do."

He sprang to his feet, caught up his cloak and swung
it round him, then, with a few brief, courteous words to
Palomides and a hand lifted in farewell to me, was gone,
with a great swirl of shadows on the firelit walls.

I followed him to the door, but he was already
halfway across the yard shouting to the landlord for
torches to light him home. Outside, the wind had
dropped. It was raining steadily, with a plop and gurgle of
overflowing gutters all about the huddled buildings of the
inn. Overhead, stars were beginning to show, riding the
hurrying cloud-wrack. Without the wind, the sea sounded

louder than ever—a growl of caged beasts, prowling the length of the mole.

"Blue-haired Poseidon, if you ever existed, rein in those white stallions of yours. Send me a shipmaster who won't fear a wet back before this week's out!" I muttered aloud. I must have been more than a little drunk. I know I was very happy.

# Chapter Eight

In the years of peace that followed Badon Field, young folk who had not known war, and some of their elders, grown Christian-pious, used to reproach me for my cold, unyielding hatred of all Saxons. In those years, I would never sit at meat with a Saxon hostage, nor would I drink wine with Federate chiefs when they came to the conference table. I said, and did not care who heard me, that the only Saxon I ever cared to look on was a dead Saxon.

It was a weakness and also a foolishness in me. I understand that now. Weakness, because, though it shook me to the core at the time, what I found on the first morning Palomides and I landed in Britain was no worse than many others have come home to in war, and less terrible by far than some men experienced. Foolish since, Roman, Celt, Saxon, Pict, we are born into the shape and place we earned in other lives, and must learn lessons we ourselves have set. We can only act out the role that we ourselves wrote. Villain or hero, it is the way we play the part that is our responsibility. But hate dies hard in the heart, however, one may kill it in the mind. Most days, now, I can bear Paulinus about me with, at worst, a sick man's irritability. This morning, having lain awake all night, remembering things best forgotten, I sent him away abruptly, saying that, having slept ill, I was too weary to dictate. His immediate anxious concern makes me ashamed now. He was not to know that between us today drifted the smoke of a burning houseplace, and the pale, drawn face of a young girl, brutally misused.

A tubby little Armorican coaster, running in wine for the black market, braved the crossing from Armorica ahead of the regular galleys, and Palomides and I went with the wine casks. The wind had veered, but the sea was still running high. It was a quick crossing, if a rough one. I think the shipmaster was surprised we were neither of us sick and he was certainly grateful when, in mid-Channel, both of us were ready to give the rowers a hand. One fellow, missing stroke in the choppy cross-currents, got his arm smashed. As soon as we were in under the lee of the cliffs, Palomides set it for him. Watching the neat job he made, I thought:

"Though I am bringing only one recruit, Arthur will certainly find this one useful."

It was a bright, sparkling morning—white caps on the waves, and the coastline looking deceptively near, as it does when the weather is still unsettled and rain not far away. We saw smoke drifting up at the mouth of the Totnesia river as soon as we'd rounded the last headland. I guessed, when I saw it, we'd not hold the shipmaster to his bargain. I'd paid him well to take us in and let me pilot him up river to the landing place below the Dunn.

"I'm a poor man, soldiers, and I have a wife and children. Whatever the trouble on shore yonder, I don't want to mix my ship in it. If you've sense, you'll stay on board, and come with us to Isca. Where huts and boats are burning, I smell a pirate raid. Saxon or Irish, these gentry get on the track of a wine carrier faster than hounds after a hare. What do you want to do—come with me, or be put ashore? Make up your minds. There's no time to waste," he told me gruffly.

The ship carried several coracles for ferrying stores in shallow water. The man was honest, if cautious. I bargained with him quickly and he did not overcharge me, remembering we'd paid him the full fare already and a bit over.

Rowers dropped the little bobbing craft into the water and slung our baggage after it; Palomides and I followed. He landed less clumsily than I did, weighing less. Both of us got soaked and we had to bail before we could start paddling. Once we'd got the thing under control, I saw he was as used to handling a coracle as I, and more handy at it. We said little, being used to shared emergency. Only once he laughed grimly and shouted to me:

"The Hyperborean Islands at the end of the known world!" (It was a name the mainlanders called Britain sometimes and we had made a joke of it between us on the journey.) He added, paddling strongly, "You promised me I'd not be bored!"

I think he said that to hearten me. He always knew when I was anxious. The river is wide at first, then twists and turns about among wooded hills. The tide was with us. It cannot have taken as long as anxiety made it seem to, though we rounded each curve cautiously, keeping close into the bank. No careless spark from a cooking fire had burned the fishers' huts and boats to smoldering embers. We saw a dead man floating near the river's mouth and, on a little sandy beach, a child lay sprawled, face down, the small skull crushed in and bloody.

I think I only spoke once. I said, stupidly:

"It's twenty years since they burned the Villa. We never reckoned they'd come this far south again."

We smelt the thick smoke before we saw it, for the last bend is sharp. It had the greasy, sweetish reek anyone who has entered a sacked city can recognize. We had both been at Ravenna when Theodoric stormed it.

I ran the coracle into an inlet under drooping willows and led the way round the headland by a track that gave us cover. We carried our swords drawn, and went with hunters' care. Where the trees thinned out at the track's end, we saw the two galleys drawn, high above the waterline on the home beach. I had never seen a Saxon galley until that day, but I did not need to ask myself what they were. The black snake-headed prows told me. I looked up at the great cloud of yellow smoke that, billowing lazily, hid the Dunn above. I thought:

"We have come too late!"

Why dwell on old sorrow? The nightmare of the
search we made, Palomides and I, in the next hour,
proved to us the raiders must have left their boats unguarded, and gone on inland. It is something that haunted
my dreams for years—the silence and the emptiness, the
brooding menace of danger everywhere in that familiar
place, under the bright morning sky; a soldier's knowledge of what must be burning, beside wood and thatch,
within the Dunn; and the fact the raiders had left no
trace, save fire, of their passing. We found neither man
nor beast, alive or dead, anywhere about the place. It
gave the hour a horror of strangeness, because it was
something unlooked for. Something neither of us could
understand.

It was as we came down through the beech wood to
the Telling Floor for the second time that I said dully:

"There is nothing more we can do here. We must go
on up river to Totnesia. There we may still be of some
use."

Palomides laid his hand on my arm, motioning me
to silence, and pointed. Down on the Telling Floor, something moved. After a moment I saw what it was. The
rhythmic flick of a pony's tail, brushing away flies. In the
shadow on the far side of the pavement, two of them,
saddled and with small packs strapped behind the sad-
dles, were haltered to an ash sapling. They had not been
there when we had searched the place before.

Then I saw that a lad in ragged Celtic dress, a
bloody bandage about his head, was strapping on the last
package.

I went softly to the edge of the wood and whistled a
bird call I remembered. He turned in a flash, his hand on
the knife in his belt. I spoke in the Celtic then, and
stepped out where he could see me plainly, telling him my
name.

His face was very white, what one could see of it for
dirt, and he came towards me hesitatingly, a step at a
time, his eyes wide and startled. As I went to meet him I
said again:

"I am Verus, Verus Aurelianus who once lived here.
You need not fear me."

Suddenly, in a rush, he was across the pavement, and down on his knees, gripping my hand, kissing it and slobbering over it, like a dog that, finding its master, must whine and lick to show the joy of the meeting.

"Sir—oh sir—is it really you? We thought you were dead long ago. I feared you were a ghost coming out of the wood there!"

I pulled him onto his feet and shook him to quiet his noise.

"Silence, now, or you'll have the Saxons down on us! You're Tor, the swineherd's son, aren't you? Stop blubbering, you fool, and tell me what has been happening here. Which way have the raiders gone?"

He laughed wildly, hysterically at that, the tears pouring down his filthy face.

"Gone, sir? Gone to hell, all of them, if what Father Gregory tells us is true. To everlasting fire that burns hotter than the one they're burning in up there." He pointed at the Dunn. "Can't you smell the stink of them burning?"

I shook him again, and none too gently, a sudden hope springing in my mind.

"Talk sense, boy. Who killed them? Arthur's men?"

He shook his head, gulping and stammering.

"No—*she* did. She and I—alone—between us. She's wonderful wise—she knew what to put in their drink to make them sleep, and then I cut their throats for her. Easy as killing a pig it was!" He paused to make an expressive gesture across his own throat, his face alight with a glee that was purely savage. Then he went sober and troubled. "There was only us two left, see? They'd killed the others by then. The Lord Arthur, he's far away at the war, now, sir. Him and every man who can bear arms. Didn't you know?"

I did not pause to ask who "she" might be. Some instinct told me. I said urgently:

"Where is she now? Was she hurt?"

He blinked at me and his eyes dropped. Staring at the ground, he mumbled unhappily:

"They got her, sir. The big one—the chief. I'd have stopped it if I could, but—" he looked up, and his glance went past me. He said, sounding relieved: "She's coming now, sir," and he called out shrilly: "See, lady, see who is here! It is the Lord Bedivere come back to save us!"

If I had met Ygern that day in a crowded street, I think I should not have known her. She was dressed like Tor, in faded trews and tunic, her hair cut raggedly short of her shoulders, and by her face she might have been thirty years old. Only her eyes, deep sunk in her head, with shadows like purple bruises under them, met mine with a hint of her old affectionate mockery.

"Bedivere?" she said, on a little, questioning lift. "You're late! But you always came late. Cai used to beat you for it, remember?" Her voice was low and hoarse, and ended on a sobbing gasp. When I put my arms round her, she said sharply: "Careful! I think I've got some ribs broken."

I held her very gently and she put her head down on my shoulder, and we stood together quietly for a time. She did not weep, as most women would have done. Only I felt the grief and the right that were in her by a shivering that went through her now and again, as it will through a hill pony, newly saved from the menace of wolves. A sour smell clung about her—the smell of blood and sickness and something that was harsher—the faint reek that comes from a wild beast's den. It was hard not to press her close, close to me, to show the pain of my pity and my wonder and relief in finding her at least alive. But I remembered what she had said, and presently I called Palomides to us, and when I had explained them to each other, I asked him to examine her hurts and went away with Tor to get from him, if I could, some coherent account of what had taken place before we came.

Tor's story was simple enough, once shorn of the drama and repetition any Celt must employ in telling you a tale.

My Uncle Ectorius had died half a year back, peacefully in his bed.

Tor said, with peasant philosophy:

"He was very old. His time came."

(I was thankful Ectorius, at least, had been spared what that day brought us.)

Arthur was somewhere up country, with a great army. Cai had gone with him and Julius the Tetrarch and every man and boy strong enough to fight.

"They call it total war, sir. The Saxons took some island last summer end, seemingly, and have been coming in from it to burn and harry for miles up and down the shore."

He did not know the island's name. I guessed it was Vectis.

Since only the very old, the women, and the very young could be left, Arthur had ordered our Dunn evacuated, and all goods and gear sent over to the Tetrarch's place. Luckily, that had been done. Only a few able men had stayed at the Dunn to follow the army when the evacuation was complete.

"They were to ride with the mistress to join our army. She knows where to find it," Tor told me. He fidgeted, looking at me through his matted hair with eyes pleading as a mongrel's who begs to join the hunting dogs. "Sir, I only stayed to drive old sow across once she was ready, being she littered late and awkward on us. But I can go with you now, can't I? You'll take me, seeing I've proved I can kill Saxons clean, at need?"

"You can go with us, boy," I promised. From what I'd heard by then, he deserved that.

The raid had come at dawn, on a night of storm and without warning.

"We never heard aught until they were breaking the doors in. The roaring of the wind in the trees on one of those nights—you know how loud it is."

I knew well enough. Snug in bed, as a boy, I'd liked the sound of it.

Tor held up his two hands, fingers spread, four times, to tell me how many of the savages there had been. He had reckoned rightly, at a guess. The smaller war galleys mostly carried a crew of twenty each. Our folk had not stood a chance.

"I seen the big one—the leader—had hold of the mistress, and old Olwen (who was to have gone with us).

She was screeching and clawing at him. It was first light
by then, only still dimsy like. A giant, the man was. He
was laughing, and he pulled a little old ax out of his belt,
and crashed it down on Olwen's head, and I saw her fall.
Then something hit me, and I didn't know aught more for
quite a while."

When he came to himself, Ygern was bathing his
head, telling him he must get up and help her.

"There's only us two left, Tor. But I have a plan.
You and I may win a victory for the Lord Arthur still, if
only we keep our heads," she told him.

He said her clothes were all torn and bloody but she
seemed quite calm. "Like a warrior's, her face looked.
Like the Lord Arthur's," he told me admiringly.

(Ygern had always been part of our war games—
had always striven to excel us, making up by quick wit
and daring for the boy's strength she lacked. What followed I could well believe.)

The pirates, having ransacked the whole place, and
slaughtered the new-farrowed sow and her sucking pigs,
had lit a great cookfire in the courtyard and prepared
themselves a feast. By luck, they had not found a store
we had underground, on the north side of the barn, where
honey beer was kept.

"There was a batch we'd not bothered ourselves to
cart over to the Tetrarch's, seeing the bees had got in the
sycamore blossom, unbeknownst, and Sir Cai, he said the
stuff tasted like cat shit," Tor told me cheerfully. "It had
been there a good while and maybe mellowed—or maybe
Saxons, they'll drink anything. The mistress, she put magic in it—herbs and that. Old Olwen, being a witch, she
knew such things and I reckon the mistress had learned
from her. Then, by signs, she invited the chief man to
bring the food into hall and eat there—for it was evening
by then, and beginning to rain hard. She told me I must
bring over the beer jars and serve the stuff round, seeing
to it every man had a fair share. Wonderful steady she
was—and making believe she wasn't averse to the chief
pawing her and showing all she had was his property. He
stunned one man who tried laying hands on her when he
wasn't looking!"

I could picture the scene. I remembered it with care, often, sitting my horse at the head of the cavalry, waiting for the trumpet to sound the charge, when odds were heavy against us. It helped me, always, to kill fast and cleanly, giving no quarter.

What came after sickened me to hear. Some work is not for women to see, let alone take part in.

The honey beer worked the magic Olwen had taught. Slowly, one by one, the raiders, guzzling it, drowsed, then slept—the heavy, unwaking sleep of the deeply drugged.

Ygern told Tor to bring the knives kept for pig sticking.

" 'And see to it they are well sharpened. There are more beasts here than you and your father need to prepare for the winter salting. You must show me how the work is done.' That's what she said to me, sir—her face blue-white as milk twice skimmed. But, bless you, 'tis a bit of a skill, anyway—and not fit for the likes of her, that was gently reared. 'I'll do it for you. You stand by, mistress, and watch none stir to waking.' I said.

"After, when all was finished, she went outside and vomited cruel. Blood takes some that way, the first time they see the place aswim with it. It did me, when my dad taught me to help him with autumn slaughtering and me only a nipper. Doesn't worry me now, though. I was glad and proud, yesterday, to see all of it, after what that lot had done to us. So would you have been, wouldn't you, sir—they being Saxons and our enemies?"

I agreed. He would have been disappointed if I had not. I gave him the praise he'd deserved, and thought:

"This is what war does to a man from the very first. The lad's barely turned fifteen. He learns the lesson early."

But my soul shuddered that Ygern had been forced to watch the thing. I wondered what mark it—and other things she had suffered—would leave on her for life.

Before we left the Dunn, Palomides and I inspected the war boats. Both bore marks of storm damage. I guessed in the first place their crews ran in for shelter.

Probably all they'd aimed at was to clear the district by terror, while they patched and refitted, and maybe snatched up a little loot to pay for their trouble. I did not think it was planned raiding. Sheer bad luck had brought them to our river. It was one of those things.

One thing puzzled me. I said to Tor, who was scrambling about as boys will, finding odd, discarded trophies, and hoarding them in a battered Saxon helmet, with one of its horns missing:

"Tor, if the Saxons died as you say, who fired the Dunn?"

He looked guilty.

"It was an accident, that," he admitted. "That Saxon cookfire—we should have seen it was doused, but—well, we were that worn out and wearied—a spark must have blown up into the thatch, I reckon. When we woke this morning the whole place was alight. Sir Cai will blame us, sir—and him always so special and particular over fire danger. But the mistress, she only said, 'Let it burn, Tor. It is a good funeral pyre. None would have troubled to bury them, and dead bodies breed plague.' Then she cried a bit and said: 'Their armor and weapons, I should have thought of that! The army is so short of equipment. Arthur would have remembered. I'm sorry I forgot.'"

Palomodies confirmed what Ygern herself insisted, that she was fit to ride.

Privately, he said to me:

"She's not felt the shock of it yet. That may come later. When it does, I shall know what to do. It may be we shall need, then, to rest up for a day or so. Meanwhile, she'd be better away from here. Lucky for her the chieftain kept her for himself. In war I've seen much worse cases, Verus, and your foster sister has, I should say, a tough, resilient constitution. Best let her have her way, and ride with us to find your Lord Arthur and his army. Her mind is set on it, and she'll have less time to remember. Brooding is the worst thing for women in her situation."

We sent Tor to catch and bring in three more of the hill ponies, which, he said, had been turned out to run free on the cliffs above the Dunn. Palomides volunteered to go back and paddle up the coracle with our gear. Ygern and I sat together by the river's edge, waiting for him. We did not talk much. I put my arm about her shoulders and she leaned against me, resting. Presently she failed to answer some question I'd asked and looking down I saw she had fallen asleep. I sat very still, watching where late afternoon light glittered on the ripple of the outrunning tide. A kingfisher went by, with a flash of enamelled blue, bright as the Merlin's jewel. Across the water, a cock pheasant called. Behind us among the alder bushes a robin mourned softly for summer's passing. My heart grieved dumbly, seeing and hearing the familiar things of childhood, knowing that with the destruction behind us something had gone out of our lives that we should never quite find again.

# Chapter Nine

We reached Totnesia just as the sun was setting. Reaction had set in for me, by then, and I was in no patient mood.

A rundown little fishing port, its prosperity gone with the tin trade. I looked with a soldier's contempt at its neglected shore defenses, the crumbling earthworks and milling crowds that packed its narrow, hilly streets. Half the countryside, it seemed, must have got word of Saxon raiding and refugees were still coming in. Lost children screamed, sheep bleated, carts piled with household gear collided and blocked the way. Distracted middle-aged members of the voluntary municipal guard ran about, armed with anything they could lay hands on by way of weapon—I saw one waving a fishing trident.

Everywhere contradictory orders were shouted, while a shrill perpetual wail, like a Greek chorus, was going up from the women.

"Save us! The Saxons are coming! The Saxons are upon us!"

When, eventually, I'd run some members of the municipal council to earth, skulking behind closed shutters in a dusty office, arguing distractedly how to organize defense against "the Saxon hordes" advancing on them, they got the full brunt of all I'd experienced since morning.

"Defense?" I said. "You couldn't defend a henyard from one fox with what you've got here! Be thankful

you've no need. Your 'hordes' were two boatloads only—
and they've been accounted for. If they'd got through,
you and all those poor devils outside would be meat for
the ravens. Be thankful your work's been done for you.
You can tell your people the danger's over, the Saxons
are dead and they can all go home. I'd advise you to do it
quickly before somebody gets crushed to death in the press
out there or a herd of bullocks runs amok through the
crowd."

A fat little man, with a bald head and a face white
as wet lard, bridled and spluttered at me, demanding on
what authority I'd broken into a council meeting.

"The authority of the *Dux Bellorum,* Arthur the
Pendragon," I told him. "I am the centurion Verus Aurelianus, on my way to join his army now. A fine report I'll
have to give him of his own Dumnonian citizens!"

A tall, cadaverous individual in the background
muttered something. I swung round on him.

"What was that you said?" I challenged.

He waved pale hands like cod's flippers at me.

"Speak with more respect, centurion, to our chief
tribune. But for the army having taken all our young men
to fight up country we'd be better prepared this terrible
day," he bleated. I guessed he was a lawyer from his
clipped speech.

"But for the army, you'd have been wearing a slave
ring since you were a child," I told him. "If you'd kept
your walls in repair, here, and a chain boom across the
river, instead of spending every waking hour of your lives
scheming to make the last dishonest coin you could grab
out of the tax returns, you wouldn't be in this pickle."

I turned on my heel, went out on the portico and
shouted for silence in a voice that got it for me. When I'd
addressed the crowd and told them the raiders were dead
and the danger passed, you might have heard the cheering
in Isca.

The council changed their tune after that. I never
saw men so abjectly relieved. All the same, when I got to
the business I'd come about (I wanted those two war
galleys overhauled and kept ready, in case the Tetrarch
Julius had a use for them later), they had the effrontery

to ask me to sign for the repairs. (Civil servants are the same the world over. I was to learn that later. I'd only met the breed in Byzantium up to then.)

"Send your bill to the emperor's navy office on the mainland. You may get it paid, though I doubt you will," I said. "But I can tell you, if those galleys aren't ready for sea when the War Duke needs them, it'll be the worse for all concerned. I'll sign my name to *that*—and before witnesses if you want me to!"

I should have been wiser to put my pride in my pocket and accept the council's offer of beds for the night. But it was grudgingly given and I was at an age to consider my own dignity more important than the welfare of those in my care. We pushed on out of the town and slept in a hay barn beside the old Isca road. Ygern made no complaint —urged me, indeed, to hurry on—but in the morning her voice was gruff, and she complained of a throat too sore for talking. When, relenting and anxious, I suggested that at Isca we should find a comfortable lodging and rest until she was stronger, she rounded on me fiercely.

"Am I a soft Roman girl? I don't need rest," she croaked. "All I need is to get to the army fast, before Arthur hears rumors of Saxons in the west. If he does hear, he'll send men he can't spare to defend his rear— and that could cost him the battle that must be facing him, by now; that I *know* is facing him. I can manage well enough, if you don't make me talk," and she broke off, coughing, a small, dry cough that made her hold her side.

The journey took us a week or more. Floods were out round Isca and the many rivers that thread the flat, rich farmlands that lie north of Durnovaria were running deep even at the fords. We must have lost our way a dozen times. We came on signs of war two days' ride beyond Isca. First, more bands of refugees, heading westward; then burned villages and trampled crops. Finally, a land of rolling hills, and poor, thin soil, where the few folk we met were sullen and hostile, suspicious of strangers, unwilling to part with the little food or fodder left to them, and so confused by rumors that the directions they

gave us for finding the army were worse than useless. It
rained off and on all the way, too.

On the seventh morning, I was almost in despair.
We'd slept the night in a deserted farm, and Ygern had
been delirious, muttering and tossing, crying out now and
again in remembered terror. Palomides was beginning to
look grave.

"She's not fit to travel, Verus. How much further do
you guess we must go?"

He, himself, looked pinched and sallow, I noticed,
and was shivering in the early morning chill. We were
both hungry, having gone short of food most of the way,
and I guessed he was finding Britain's climate fitted the
descriptions he'd heard of it.

"Not much further. By the look of things we must be
getting close to the front. Provided we come up with our
own army before we trip over the Saxon host, our troubles could be nearly over," I said, feeling I'd better, as
leader, sound more cheerful than I felt. "I sent Tor off to
scout ahead before dawn. He's an intelligent lad, and one
peasant boy has a better chance of avoiding ambushes
than a mounted party. I'm hoping he can get some news
for us."

"Let's hope he does," Palomides said glumly.
"We've a very sick girl on our hands, Bedivere. You'd
better face it—she won't stay the course much longer.
Only her will has kept her in the saddle this far."

He turned and walked back into the farm. I went to
get in the ponies. They wouldn't last us much further
either, by the look of them. They were game little beasts,
but we'd pushed them hard. I was examining one I'd
suspected of going lame the evening before, when a shout
brought me round to the front of the building in a hurry.
Tor was racing up the track, waving his arms and calling:

"We've found them, master! We've found the army!
The old man says there's been a great battle and the Lord
Arthur's driven the sea devils back to their boats, and the
Tetrarch's fighting them at sea!" He'd reached me by
then, panting, for the track ran steeply uphill.

"Steady, boy! What old man? Where did you hear this news?"

I told myself this might well be only another wild rumor.

"A shepherd, master. I met him driving sheep for our army. Men—the Lord Arthur's men—rode into his village last night to buy corn and meat. They told his people. Three days ago, the battle was. Oh, sir—it's victory!"

"Where's the army from here? Did he tell you that?" Tor pointed.

"See that hill yonder? There's a good, hard trackway runs on into the woods on the far side. If we follow that it'll take us straight to them—an hour's riding, he said, or maybe two. Not more."

"Good. Help me now with the horses," I said.

He grinned at me, hugging his arms across his chest.

"If only we'd been there in time for the battle! D'you think there'll be food at the camp, sir?"

I laughed at his anxious eyes.

"Depend on it, they'll find us something to eat. No more rooting for musty eggs among the hay for us!"

(He'd found a deserted sitting the night before, well on its way to hatching—and we'd been hungry enough to be glad of them at that.)


"Go steady. If I know Arthur he'll have outposts stationed. We don't want to be knocked on the head by our own side at this stage of the journey," I warned.

I was riding close to Ygern, with my arm round her, supporting her in the saddle. We'd passed the shepherd and his flock some way back, and were going downhill, through a thin oak wood. All my instinct had been to hurry, but Ygern was in no shape for it. We'd had to lift her onto her pony, and now she was leaning against me and seemed hardly conscious.

Ten minutes after I'd spoken, we were pulled up short by a stockade of felled saplings across the track, and two young sentries rose up behind it, spears levelled.

"Halt! Who comes?" one challenged.

"Bedivere, the Pendragon's foster brother. Clear a way for us, boy," I ordered him.

He looked us over, then muttered something to his companion. They were tough youngsters, shock-headed, the beginnings of their boys' beards scrubby, their clothing ragged. Both carried serviceable hunting spears, well sharpened. One had a bronze dagger with no sheath to it stuck in his belt, the other an old-time flint ax, sharpened to a wicked blue edge. They were serious, unsmiling, and evidently heavily conscious of responsibility.

The elder said slowly, with country suspicion:

"Our orders were to let none pass without centurion's permission. You'll have to wait a while, until he comes, whoever you are."

"That we'll not do. I've told you who I am. Get those poles shifted now and quickly. My companion here is sick, and we've ridden far."

The lad shook his head, stolidly.

"Orders is orders. No more refugees in camp," he said, his eyes going from Ygern to Tor's bandaged head. "Leastways, not without permission."

His companion muttered something to him and they whispered together. The elder conceded grudgingly:

"If so be you *are* what you say, we could pass you through, sir, maybe. But the others, they must wait, that's for sure."

Ygern straightened up, drawing away from my arm.

"Go on, Bedivere. You go on," she said. Her voice was not much above a whisper, but she smiled at me. Her eyes very bright, two spots of color high on her cheekbones. "Find Arthur—tell him . . ." Coughing choked her words.

I looked across at Palomides, on her further side.

"Take care of her. I'll not be long," I said. "Open up for me, my lads."

They began to fumble at the barricade. I thought they were purposely taking their time. I reined back my pony a yard or two and shouted at them: "Stand clear!" Then I put the little beast at the jump and cleared it as if I'd been in the hunting field. Galloping down the track ahead I half expected a spear between my shoulders, but my patience had gone. Instead, I heard a shout from the younger lad.

"Straight ahead if it's the Lord Arthur you want, sir."

I raised a hand in acknowledgment and urged the pony on. Almost at once I was into the outskirts of a large, well-ordered army camp. Under the scrub oak and hazel, leather tents were pitched, baggage wagons drawn up, cooking fires alight. Armed men were everywhere, hurrying purposefully about, some seeing to a line of picketed ponies, some waiting their turn to sharpen weapons at a grindstone. Then, just ahead of me, the ground rose sharply to the left of the track into a small, rounded hillock and I saw red centurions' cloaks. I pulled up short, and heard a voice I recognized; Caius, bawling as he used to bawl for us from the head of the beech woods when we were children.

"You there—decurion—turn those folk away from the lower barricade. Tell them danger's over. Direct them to the monastery if their homes are destroyed. The monks have food. *We* can't spare them any. We've too many mouths to feed here as it is!"

I dropped out of the saddle, leaving the reins loose on my pony's neck and ran towards him.

"Cai!" I shouted. "You old grumbler, you, here's one more hungry mouth you must find rations for! Don't you know me? It is I, Verus!"

I would never have believed I should be so happy to see again the thin, familiar figure, and anxious, angry face, the well-remembered limping stride, as he came hurrying down to meet me.

"Verus—*you?* We'd given you up for dead!" he said, and I laughed aloud at the indignant accusation of his tone. He'd always mistrusted any surprise.

"No such luck. It's me, and very much alive—only late, it seems, as I always was."

He grasped both my hands and stared at me; then his queer, ugly face broke into a smile that warmed me through and through.

"My dear boy, what a surprise! What a wonderful

surprise. Arturus *will* be pleased! You got his message, then, recalling you?"

"I got it—eventually. Where is he, Cai?"

"Up there. Look!" He pointed, repeating, with emphasis, "He *will* be pleased."

I followed the direction of his gesture, and saw a giant of a man, in a ragged, stained red cloak, with a great iron sword at his side and his hair blowing in the wind, standing on the summit of the knoll above us, half-turned away, giving orders to a couple of young warriors.

"Arturus!" I cried to him. "Arthur! Bear! It is I, Bedivere. I have come!"

He turned, looked hard at me for a moment, then sprang down the slope, shouting, and folded me in his arms in an embrace that almost cracked my spine. He pushed me off and holding me at arm's length, shook me to and fro for a little.

"Late—always late, you! But I knew you would come. Oh, yes, they all pulled long faces, but I knew Bedivere, my brother, couldn't die while I need him. Where have you been all these years? What happened to you—laggard?"

"Your letter took long on the way. Then I had your business in Armorica to see to," I said. "Last of all, the cursed storm weather in the Channel—and then—other things . . ."

He burst out laughing and, dropping his hands from my shoulders, put an arm round my neck, and turned to Caius.

"What did I tell you? Always ready with an excuse, wasn't he? And always looked as if he knew nobody was going to believe it. Well—what news from Armorica? You haven't raised any recruits there? I doubted if you would."

"That can wait—first there's something I've got to tell you, Bear—and you, Cai," I said, searching for words to break the bad news I must give them. But before I could begin, we were interrupted. An elderly centurion, whom I thought I recognized, had come up and was hovering anxiously beside us.

"A moment—what is it, Ulfius?" Arthur turned to him.

"Sentries at the west barricade report recruits coming in—about a hundred men—armed with scythes and pitchforks, but carrying their own rations. Nobody knows where they're from—twenty days' journey from the west, they say."

"What Clan?" Arthur asked sharply.

"Don't know, sir—farm lads in leather and rags, mostly. Difficult to tell where from—but keen, the sentry said. Mad disappointed the battle's over seemingly," and the centurion smiled grimly.

"We can promise them plenty more!" Arthur said reassuringly. "Just a moment—from the west? Maybe Arventurians—so don't put them too close to the Ordovices lines or we'll be sorting out blood feuds all night. Wait a moment—" he moved a little aside and consulted with Ulfius in a lowered voice. I looked round for Caius, but he, too, had been drawn into conversation by a couple of lads, one of whom had an iron slave ring round his neck.

"You know your orders. All stores into the transport wagons, under guard. Make sure you get the grain well covered over. Corn's precious, every grain of it. We'll have to make it last. If it gets damp, it'll start to sprout and be wasted. Count the bags, and make sure the decurion has the tally—and you—why have you got that thing round your neck? Hasn't anybody told you once you're Arthur's man, you're a free man?"

The slave put his hand up to the iron collar.

"Hasn't been time, sir. Need a smith to cut it off and they're too busy. It doesn't bother me—worn it all my life, see? I'll get it attended to when the work's done."

"Good lad. That's the spirit!" Caius encouraged him.

While they talked, I had been watching Arthur. In the first moment of meeting, I had only been aware that I had found him again at last—the one man in the world I most wanted to be with. Now, seeing him as he talked, commander to subordinate officer, I realized the change three years had made in him. He had always been tall—topping me by half a head, and I not a small man—but

now he had filled out to his full strength, and in the rough
Celtic clothes and battered bronze corselet he was wearing he looked a giant. He had grown his hair long, and a
full beard in the Celtic fashion. Nothing remained of the
Roman about him but the old, faded centurion's cloak
that hung carelessly from his shoulders—no symbol of
command, since all his officers wore the same—but a
practical garment, slung on against wind and rain. Only
the gold circlet, half lost in his mane of red-gold hair, set
him above the men he commanded—that, and the easy
air of authority, the disciplined bearing that marked him
a Colonial aristocrat by training, and, by his very nature,
a king.

Caius went off with his storekeepers, muttering to
me that he really *must* attend to this himself, he'd see me
later. Then Ulfius saluted and hurried away, and Arthur
turned to me.

I told him what I had to tell, briefly and without
many words, as bad news is best told to a man who can
take it.

"I landed ten days ago, Bear—at the home Dunn. I
was too late there, as well. They'd been raided. A bad
business."

"Raided?" He went very still and his hand dropped
to his sword hilt. "What's the damage?"

"Extensive. All killed, except Ygern and Tor, the
swineherd's boy—and the place burned to the ground."

"Ygern's safe? Did she take to the woods as I told
her?"

"No," I said. "There wasn't time—and you might
have guessed she wouldn't, anyway. She and the boy
tricked the raiders and killed the lot—forty men—by a
clever ruse, before I got there. But I warn you, she's in
poor shape now. The leader kept her for himself—that's
the one bit of luck. She'd have been dead, else."

He stared at me, his eyes gone blank and hard, the
color draining from under the weather tan of his face.

I said—I couldn't help it:

"Why did you leave her, Bear? Why did you take
that risk?"

He said slowly, through clenched teeth:

"There hadn't been a raid on that coast for twenty years. There was so much to be done—and no time to do it. Aela would have been at Aquae Sulis by now if I hadn't raised an army and got here before him. Where is she now?"

I jerked my head towards the track by which I had come into the camp.

"Up at that barricade with Tor, and the one recruit I've raised. Your sentries only let me through when I put my horse at it. They obey your orders to the letter, Bear. You've trained them well."

"Damned young fools!" Arthur swore. "Keen as wolfdogs, but stupid as owls, all of them! You—Kerno," he shouted to a passing soldier, "run as fast as you can to the gate up yonder and tell the sentries it's the Pendragon's order the folk waiting are to be passed through on the instant!"

As the man went off, sprinting as though for a prize at the games, he said:

"How badly is she hurt? Tell me the truth."

"Two broken ribs and bruises—but we've ridden hard, and lived rough all the way, and the weather hasn't helped. The man with me is a trained doctor. He says she's got the fever beginning. She'll mend, once we're here and she's with you. It's been her one thought, to get here fast. Don't worry too much, Bear."

His eyes were on the track, and I thought he hardly heard what I was saying.

"There they are," he said, and went striding out to meet the travel-stained, bedraggled little party.

Bitterly I thought: "That was all I could bring him—that, and bad news, in his first hour of victory!"

But Ygern's face was alight, and she slid off her pony before he could get to her, leaning back against its flank, trying to laugh up at him.

"Tor here and I have killed twice twenty Saxons. How many have you killed, Bear?" she croaked, her voice rasping as she tried to force it to sound gay.

He put his arm round her.

"You little fool—obstinate little idiot!" he greeted her, his own voice unsteady. "I left you your orders, didn't I? Take to the woods at any threat of danger, I said. Oh, my girl, what have they done to you?"

"Only what you might expect. I'm all right now," she said. Then, fighting against a fit of coughing, "Don't fuss, please don't. We won—they're dead—Tor was wonderful. We're both of us Arthur's men now—your soldiers. You don't fuss over your warriors for a little wound, Bear."

"Stop talking. It hurts my chest to listen." He drew her close to his side, and his eyes went to Tor, kneeling at his feet now, pressing his face against the frayed edge of the red cloak; the dirty bandage making his hair stick up in tufts, while he babbled incoherently:

"The Dunn, my lord—oh, my lord, the Dunn!"

"Get on your feet, boy. I'll hear all that later. No need for tears—you're a warrior, proved, by what I can gather. Arthur's men don't cry for a burned-out houseplace." He put his hand for a moment on the boy's tousled head, very gently. "Now catch me those ponies, before they run amok through the camp. I'll talk to you presently."

As Tor jumped to obey the order, Arthur looked at Palomides, who had dismounted, but was standing a little apart.

"Are you the doctor?" he asked abruptly.

"I am, my lord—come to take service with your army, if you can use a surgeon—or willing to fight as a warrior for you, if that would be of more use." Palomides came forward, and I think would have knelt to the king, if Arthur had not stopped him with a quick gesture.

"*Can* we use a surgeon?" he said grimly. "Go down to our dressing station and you'll see soon enough. But first—what about this girl here?"

"She has fever, my lord. If there is some place she can be put to bed at once, with absolute rest and quiet and perhaps a woman to attend her? That would be best. I'll do what needs to be done—prepare better medicines than I could on the journey." He added, earnestly, "I was trained for seven years by Archimandros of Alexandria. I do know my trade, my lord."

Ygern began to argue she was quite well now, that she only wanted to hear news of the battle, but she began to shiver uncontrollably.

"It's only the cold," she whispered through chattering teeth. "It's so cold, Bear—so cold."

Arthur swept her up into his arms, and pulled his cloak round her.

"She shall have my tent. I can sleep anywhere. Come with us, doctor. You, Bedivere—find Cai and tell him to get extra blankets—and find me some good, motherly woman from among the camp followers." He bent his head suddenly and kissed Ygern on her poor, blistered mouth. "Be quiet, girl, will you? A warrior takes orders. You're safe, do you hear me? Safe with Arthur's men, and by the Light, from now on we'll keep you so!"

The belt of Orion swung low in the sky, and a waning hunter's moon hung just above it, before Arthur and I found an opportunity to be alone together. There is little opportunity in a war camp for private conversation—especially when the man you need speech with has given up his own tent, and refuses to trouble himself about other accommodation, saying impatiently he will find somewhere to sleep when the time comes for sleeping.

We had eaten round the fire with his section commanders at dusk. By then, Palomides had gone off to the hospital, telling me he'd already had some food, and that he was needed there.

"I think I can make myself useful. The white monks from the monastery are doing their best, but they're more experienced in comforting the dying with promises of heaven than getting out javelin heads, or amputating limbs before they gangrene. With your permission, I shall take Tor to help me. I gather he is not disturbed by the sight of blood!" he said, with a cheerful grimace.

I'd left him to his trade, and gone back to the cheerful talk of fellow soldiers, over a meal that was hot and ample, if roughly served, my spirits rising. I liked the company; a mixture of old, seasoned officers and eager young Chieftains, flushed with the excitement of their recent victory. The talk was all of the trap they'd laid for the Saxons, and for the first time I heard something of Aela, more than his name.

"He's been lying up on Vectis all summer—raiding inland, while more and more pirates joined him there," the old centurion Ulfius explained. I was sitting beside him, eating from a shared bowl of stewed meat with my fingers, for crockery, it seemed, was in short supply. "Done a lot of damage, curse him, before we could get here. You must have seen some of it for yourself, coming from the west?"

I nodded, but before I could answer, a raw-boned, freckled young Chieftain on my other side broke in, gleefully.

"Aye, but was it not worth a few farms burning, to give him the illusion of security? He'd not have chanced a landing of his whole host, else. That was what the Lord Arthur waited for—to make the great killing we have had!"

Half a dozen eager youngsters leaned forward, all talking together, describing the ambush in a deep gulley, well screened with gorse, and boasting of its paralyzing element of surprise.

"Three to one, they were."

"More like five to one, I'd say."

"Huddled like startled sheep—Saxons think slowly, thanks be. They could have massacred us if they'd realized how few we were."

"So they may think slowly, Gawain, but they can fight. More like wolves than sheep!" another grizzled veteran, with his arm in a sling, reminded the enthusiasts grimly.

"Och, they're bonny fighters!" the boy on my left agreed, his Highland accent getting more noticeable as his excitement rose.

From the far side of the fire, Arthur said, with quiet sarcasm:

"Bonny enough to get their chieftain safe back to his galley, I'd remind you."

Ulfius grunted.

"Young cockerels crow the loudest. Aela will be

back next spring, thanks to that stand of his house carls on the shore. You bungled that part of the battle, my lads."

"The Tetrarch may get him yet—our fleet was waiting for stragglers, don't forget. Another surprise for the sea-pigs!" An open-faced young centurion, in remnants of Roman armor, spoke up in a cultured accent.

"Our fleet, says Iltud!" growled Ulfius. "A dozen fishing boats and a captured galley with as many patches on its sides as a beggar's tunic!" I guessed he had the regular soldier's contempt for sea fighting.

"Aye, so it maybe is a small fleet yet—but with Tetrarch Julius in command of it—and himself the finest admiral since old Caurasius," Gawain countered buoyantly.

As Ulfius turned to answer some remark from another officer on his right, the dark lad leaned over to me and said, speaking courteously:

"Don't listen to that old pessimist, my lord Bedivere. Let me get you more food—I'll be bound you've been on short rations, if you've travelled from down country?"

"Half a moldy bannock and some eggs near to hatching—and that was last night's supper!" I laughed. "I'd be glad of another helping if it's to spare."

"Oh, we always have enough to eat in the army. With Cai as quartermaster we never go short for long!" Arthur had heard the last remark and was smiling across at me. "Sometimes we wonder what he can have found for the pot, but it always seems full enough, doesn't it, boys?"

There was a shout of agreement.

Somebody announced cheerfully:

"When all else fails, we reckon we get seethed Saxon, but there's always enough to go round. He's a marvel, Sir Cai is!"

"Nonsense!" Cai, sitting beside Arthur, was obviously pleased for once, but he hastened to add, "It's just a matter of forethought. Remember, victuals are half the word 'victory.' Good leadership, stout weapons and regular rations—those are the things that make Rome's legions invincible."

"Och aye. The *Roman* legions!" Gawain murmured under his breath. "But where are they now, I'm asking? If we'd bided for them, Aela would be at the Western Ocean, so he would!"

The meal was ending, and drink horns were being filled for the second time with thin, native barley beer. Someone called out:

"Isn't there a harper in all this host? Can't someone improvise us a victor's lay?"

Arthur rose to his feet.

"Make your own songs while the fire lasts, but don't forget you'll be up at cock-crow. One victory hasn't won us all Britain, and there's plenty of work ahead. Council of Companions at first light and then inspection of all troops. Understood?"

"Understood, my lord!"

He looked across at me, as the whole circle rose to their feet with respect to him as commander.

"Come with me, Bedivere. I must make the round of the outposts. After that I can hear your news."

His officers stood, while we moved off together into the darkness. From a little distance we heard a faint buzz of conversation break out again. Then a fine tenor voice began to sing a soldiers' song, and other voices took up the chorus in the Celtic harmony singing I remembered so well.

I said, a catch in my voice:

"It's good to be home, Bear. You'll never know just how good it is!"

We talked long and earnestly, that night, in the only private place we could find—a hollow among a pile of rocks on a little mound, so overgrown with scrub and bramble no tents could be pitched on it.

"Out of the wind, and out of earshot if we speak quietly," Arthur said, settling himself on a flat boulder. "Now, tell me your news, Bedivere."

I found a seat opposite to him, where I could just make out his profile in the moonlight. Briefly, but as clearly as I could, I told him the story of my three years on the mainland, what the state of affairs there was, and the conclusions I had drawn.

"We'll get no help from Rome. They've written Britain off as dispensable in Byzantium, and west of Byzantium now it's a case of every man for himself, as far as I can judge," I said soberly. "If we want a free country, we'll have to make *and* rule it, Bear. That's the report I've brought back for Ambrosius. He won't like it, but it's got to be faced."

"Ambrosius?" he said sharply. "Didn't you know? Didn't anyone tell you?"

"Tell me what?" I asked, startled.

"Ambrosius is dead. By the Light, I'd have thought you'd have heard *that* news, at least in Armorica! He was killed in the spring."

"God!" I said. "That's bad. How did it happen?"

"Caught in the marshes—those damned Anderita marshes, between the sea and the forest—he and the greater part of the Colonial army." Arthur's voice was harsh and sad. "He was a sick man, Bedivere—dying on his feet from the crab's disease, deep in his belly. I knew it and he knew I knew, but he'd never admit to it—not even at the last, when he'd got me my appointment as War Duke. That in itself told me the end wasn't far off in his opinion—he would not have been so insistent in the face of endless arguments from the civil administration (such of it as remains) to get the thing ratified unless he'd guessed his time was running out. We had our differences, but I think he'd learned to trust me, by then—he'd no one else to trust, if it comes to that."

"I'm sorry. He was a good man," I said.

"Britain'll be lucky if she ever sees one as doggedly faithful in the face of odds again," Arthur said. "Forty years, with more defeats than victories, and the damned nonsense of control from overseas weighing down his sword arm all the time; at the end, pain gnawing his guts like the Spartan's fox, but still he kept on. Last time I saw him he looked like death riding—nothing but a skeleton, with yellow skin stretched on the face of a skull. But he wouldn't give in—wouldn't let me take over the com-

plete command for him as I wanted to do. *I'd* never have
let an army be lured out into that swamp, latticed with
dikes and rotten with bog. Nor would he, when he was in
his right senses. It wasn't a defeat, it was a massacre. We
lost close on five thousand men, and the only good equipment left on the island. Worst of all, we lost the whole
division of cavalry—the last of the trained warhorses—
pretty nearly the last of the stock, even, bred from the old
legionary mounts. It hasn't been a good year for Britain
—I'm telling you that, Bedivere."

We sat in silence, hearing in the distance all around
us the faint sounds of a camp settling for the night. At
last I said:

"What else has happened? Remember—I've heard
nothing. More defeats?"

He made a quick, impatient movement.

"We didn't need more. No I gathered the remnants
of his army and we marched fast, collecting levies as we
went. But it's slow work, moving with infantry. Too slow.
I've always said so. Oh, we put in a good, hard summer,
and taught the Saxon Federals along the south coast it
doesn't pay to open the back door and crook a finger to
all their kin from the Rhineland. *They'll* have a hungry
winter, all right; and give no more trouble till they've
licked their wounds for a year to two, if we're lucky.
Then word came of Aela in Vectis. I'd hoped to leave
him there until after winter, but he was getting altogether
too sure of himself. Celidon warned me"—he paused, then
suddenly he crashed his right hand into his left with a
gesture of impatient frustration. "Do you think I'd have
recruited every fighting man of my own Clan—swept my
homeland bare as a monk's pate—if the need hadn't been
desperate? Why, we took the very slaves out of the fields,
boys from the sheep guard, greybeards who can remember Aetius' wars. I had to. Do you think I'd have left
Ygern to follow after us, if I'd had even a day to spare?"

In the moonlight his face looked drawn as he turned
to me. His voice sank almost to a whisper.

"I shall never forgive myself for that. Never," he said.

"You've nothing to forgive. Britain comes first.

Ygern understands that and so do I. We always have," I said.

He laid his hand over mine.

"Yes. You two understand. I've missed you, Bedivere. You don't know how much."

"Well, I'm home now," I said briskly, "and you've defeated this Aela. It's not like you to be gloomy, Bear. I like what I've seen of your army—especially your officers."

He nodded; then, clasping his hands round his knee, leaned back against a jut of rock.

"My army!" he said reflectively. "I like them myself. A rough enough crowd, with precious little legionary polish—but they're tough and they're keen, and if half of them are armed with boar spears and flint axes, at least they know how to use them. Tomorrow we'll sort out the battle spoils, and remedy some of our worst lack of weapons. Soon enough now winter should close the seaways and give us a breathing space."

I could tell he'd come out of the depression that recounting the rout of Ambrosius' army had momentarily thrown him into, and was back to his normal optimism.

"Celidon believes we can do it, Bedivere. Because we're an island, and a holy island at that, we can throw our invaders into the sea and win through to peace at the end. He never falters in his belief, and in some odd way I think he knows," he said slowly.

"It is going to be a case of fighting for our lives, I'd say," I murmured.

"Not only for our lives. For life itself. For order and justice and all the ordinary, decent simple things—the little things our people have been deprived of for too long, Bedivere," he said earnestly. Then, the old enthusiasm I recognized giving his voice a deeper note, "The things Rome secured to the world for so long—but never will again. The assured harvest, the safe sheepfold, roads a merchant may travel with security from thriving town to thriving town. Homes of richer folk where some grace of living may grow up again, giving scope to our craftsmen —where folk will read books, have good talk of ideas—

where lovers can grow old together, seeing their children
and children's children thrive and learn the gentler arts of
living. A land where justice and truth and understanding
replace violence and intrigue and petty, tribal jealousy.
That's my dream for the future of Britain. That's what we
are fighting for."

I pushed my hand up through my hair and whistled
softly.

"A tall order, with Britain—and the empire—in the
state they're in," I warned him. (He'd always gone too
fast for me. But I'd loved him for it, even when I'd
laughed at him.)

"I know it," he said quickly. "But we've got to do it.
I mean to do it, what is more. It's what I was born to do,
Bedivere. I believe we are the only people, as the Merlin
teaches me we have been before, who can guard the true
wisdom for the world, while the chaos of great changes
shakes all nations round about us. On a wild moorland, in
the storms of winter, one little rushlight kept burning in a
shepherd's cot shines out like a star. Poor and small this
island may be. But in it we must somehow keep a light
burning—a rushlight that will rekindle the lamps of the
world when the great storm of these times has passed
away."

We sat silent again. The night wind passed down the
hill, rustling the trees. Overhead the stars wheeled slowly, so that looking up at them, one seemed to feel the
earth wheel with them.

"We can try, Bear. We can try," I said softly.

Suddenly he got up, pulling his cloak about him,
laughing quietly, and stood, looking down at me, his hand
on the hilt of Excalibur.

"The Picts in the north, the Irish in the west, the
Saxons and all their kin—Jutes, Angles, Franks to east
and south of us—and here in Britain, what have we got?
The rags and remnants of Rome's rule, more hindrance
than help to any man, now. A hundred Clans, with a
tangle of old blood feuds and new, separate ambitions—
and Arthur's army, that must be disbanded soon to go
home and till next year's corn, all except a nucleus small

enough to winter in one half-ruined hill fort. Do you think I'm mad, Bedivere—nursing a madman's dream?"

I stood up and faced him, smiling, too.

"I seem to remember a triad the Merlin once taught us. 'Three things hold the Secret of Life—the corn in the earth, the child in the womb and the dream at the heart of the harp's song.' You were always a harper, Arthur the Pendragon."

He said, quietly and gruffly, his arm across my shoulders:

"Never so true a harper as you, Bedivere, first of my Companions." Then his voice changed. "Now—have I had all the news from the mainland?"

"Not all," I said. I'd kept the best to last. As we walked together, out from the rocks, and back towards the sleeping camp, I told him how he could expect Bardeliez's horses, and, from Armorica, in the spring, an expeditionary force led by Lancelot of the Lake. It was one of the happy—perhaps one of the happiest—tellings of my life.

# Chapter Ten

Today I slept late and woke to pale winter sunshine slanting across my cot, and to a good smell of woodsmoke and new-baked bread. A subdued bustle of activity outside told me I'd been spared the singing in chapel, for once. Presently Brother Paulinus came hurrying with a cup of milk for me, still warm from the goat, and the news that I was to be spared, also, dictating to him.

"So many poor folk are at the gate today, begging for food. All hands are needed to care for their wants," he told me apologetically. "It's the hard weather, coming after so poor a harvest."

It troubles me that I must be a burden on this little community. They are good men, and they work hard for the poor, between their praying.

The scent of woodsmoke and new-baked bread—it took me back a long way, to early mornings at the Great Fort, that first year Arthur's army made winter quarters in it. That was a hard winter, too, though luckily for us it came later than this one. What with one thing and another, it must have been well after Samain before we'd time to think about preparations for housing ourselves through bad weather. We had to clear Vectis and the shoreline of Saxon stragglers and chase out the Federates who'd been secretly spreading themselves into stolen farmlands all down the coast, secure in the promise of Aela's coming. After that, there was work still to do, strengthening the harbor defenses at Port Adurni, so that old Tetrarch Julius could get busy on his dream of tinkering up some sort of fleet there, ready for next year's campaign.

When all had been seen to, Arthur sent the main part of the war host home to get on with its own affairs.

"I know my Clans by now, Bedivere. As long as there is fighting and plenty of it, they'll stick together. Keep them idle from one new moon to the next and they'll melt away like a snowball in a warm hand, slipping off in the night to go and see how their homes and families are faring—those who don't begin to remember old quarrels or pick new ones—and blood gets spilt to no purpose. Besides, this country is too poor to support a host all winter. Better to let the men go and spread word of victory to hearten their own folk. We'll get double the number back when the Branch goes out next spring."

We were left, eventually, with a nucleus of officers and young unmarried volunteers—about three hundred fighting men, I suppose, and the usual tail of camp followers: boys, servants, slaves, and a few officers' wives and soldiers' women—to house through the winter months.

"Celidon's found me the place we need—an abandoned hill fort the legions once held as a signal station. I saw it for myself a while back. It's in the Durnovaria country. Folk call it Fort Camelot," he told me. "I want you to ride ahead with a small detachment and get the camp marked out for us. Lumbered with baggage wagons and Cai's precious catapults as we are, the main force is bound to move slowly, and we can't count on open weather for much longer. Do what you can to get things ready up there, will you?"

Old men forget the happenings of yesterday, but the first day I saw that place remains as clear in my mind, down to the last detail, as if one night's sleep only divided me from it. A gentle day of duck-egg skies, and big, rolling white clouds, it was deceptively mild, still, for the time of year. I'd asked for Palomides to go with me, knowing he'd more experience than I had in the laying out of a camp. We laughed and jested with our men as we rode, and I was interested to find how much Celtic Palomides had picked up in a short time. Once or twice he made mistakes that served to amuse them, but he was quite unabashed and always ready to explain his meaning by vivid pantomime. When I congratulated him on his fluency, he shrugged.

"Languages come easy to me. All my life I've had to work among mixed communities, and a dumb doctor is little use," he said.

The fort was easy to find. We saw it from miles away—a flat-topped mound, rising sheer out of the plain, with a range of lesser, rounded hills alongside. Any fighting man could tell at a glance that nature had designed it for defense, and when we came to examine it, later, we discovered that generations must have been at work there, long before Rome's day, improving the original shape, paring away sloping sides to make them steeper, and digging out three encircling platforms, each wide enough for four mounted men to ride abreast, where slingers, archers or spearmen could be stationed conveniently. It must have been neglected for years, however. Brushwood and bramble and quite large trees were growing up the sides, and we rode half round it before we found a track that led us to the top. Even when we'd located that, we had to dismount several times, and hack a path through breast-high tangles of blackberry and sapling willow, before we came on the half-rotted remains of fifty-year-old Roman defense works and two tall gate towers built of rough-hewn timber. One of these had collapsed sideways into a wreckage of fallen beams. The other still stood, stark and skeletal, against the sky.

"What a place!" I said, letting my sure-footed little mount pick its way delicately out onto the open grass beyond the towers. "Look at it, Palomides! You could house an army up here and hold it against attack for as long as you chose."

"Provided there's water," he said cautiously. (Most of his campaigning had been in desert country up to then.)

"There'll be a spring or well somewhere, depend on it. Celidon will have made sure of that, even if he's no soldier. Ah! There are the remains of the legion barracks.

They look in better shape than the gate. Turn the ponies loose to graze, men, and let's see what Rome left us in the way of shelter from the winter weather."

"Plenty of hard work for the carpenters, but better than nothing—a sight better than some of the places I've wintered in with the old general," a hard-bitten decurion from Ambrosius' army pronounced half an hour later, when we'd made a quick survey of the remains of the barrack buildings. He'd been testing the state of the wooden walls with his dagger. "Try for yourself, sir—good, solid oakheart. Must have used seasoned stuff at the start. Reckon the gate towers were an afterthought—green wood that warped and got on the skew, and the height of them caught the wind more."

"A draughty old rookery of a place, if you ask me," muttered the inevitable pessimist one finds in every army —a lantern-jawed veteran with a broken nose who was peering up through broken thatch that showed the sky. "We'd be dryer in tents than in here, sir. I'd have it down for firewood, myself. Never can tell what's happened, in a place like this. What do you reckon became of the last garrison? Murdered, the lot of 'em, most likely. Feels unchancy to me!"

"None of that talk, Moldaik," I said. "These outpost stations were evacuated by the army in regular fashion, when the legions went overseas. Be thankful they've left us what they have—a fine big hall, a range of sleeping quarters and plenty of storage huts. Even stabling for the horses, though that's rickety in parts."

"Och, it's no so bad," a cheerful youngster from the north reassured me. "Fine and snug enough for the Pendragon himself to sleep in, given some laced willow rods and a peck or so of mud spread on them. Besides a bundle or two of new reeds on the roof, maybe."

"Plenty of those, down in the marshes below," another youngster reminded us.

"What need? Turves cut on the spot will serve well enough," a native Durotrigian put in, in his soft, southland drawl. "That's what us uses, these parts."

"Find yourselves somewhere dry for sleeping, and

get in wood for your cooking fire; then cut me a pile of
stakes to mark out camp for the army," I ordered.
"Come, Palomides—you and I had better look the rest of
the place over. I want to find that water supply."

As we walked away together, across the short,
springy turf, Palomides glanced at me and shook his
head.

"Are you really as happy as you look, Verus?" he
asked, curiously.

I blinked at him, surprised.

"Why not?" I said. "It's a fine day. The men are
cheerful—and this is a grand defensible place. What more
do you want?"

He laughed.

"An eagle's eyrie, exposed to every wind that blows,
and a few ruinous huts to shelter an army from the
famous British climate! *How* long does your winter last
here, once it begins?"

"Oh, *that!*" I said. "Four moons, I suppose—five
perhaps, for I've known it to snow in April. But we'll do
well enough. I like this place. I like the whole feel of it. It
feels *lucky* to me."

"May it prove so!" Palomides said piously. "Look—
there's your well—down in that hollow. Better mark out
for the horse-lines well below it to avoid drainage, but not
too far away for the lads to carry the water."

He turned quickly to the business we had in hand,
and I was glad to have his advice. The work we had come
to do went well, but darkness falls too soon at that time
of year. When we had eaten our evening rations, there
was still an hour or two to fill before any of us would be
ready to sleep. Palomides and I sat with the men around
the fire they'd kindled in the old stone-ringed firepot in
the centre of the half-roofless hall. After they'd sung a
few songs, they began questioning us—at first tentatively,
but, once they saw we were ready to satisfy their curiosity, with eager interest, about the mainland.

What was it like in those far-off foreign places? Was
it true we'd actually been as far as Rome itself—been
soldiering with some king who ruled there now? How had
we managed to stay alive and win back home? Reckoned

Sir Palomides must be right glad to find himself safe in a
civilized country like Britain, even though Britain wasn't
rightly his home. *How* many days journey on the mainland was his own country?

When Palomides told them he'd been born in a land
three months' hard riding from the Coast of Armorica,
they stared at him with awe.

Then one, a sensitive-looking boy, with a long, fresh
scar, still red and angry, from ear to chin, grinned at him
admiringly.

"Lucky for some of us you chose to come here, sir.
That's what I say."

"You're right, Kerouac. You should all of you be
glad I brought him home with me," I said.

"Talking of homes, sir, may I ask a question?" the
decurion said portentously.

"Go ahead," I told him.

"Well, they're saying in the camp, like, that the Lord
Arthur's home was raided and burned back along. Down
somewhere in the Dumnonian country, if I understand
right?"

"Yes?" I said.

"Well, sir, if you'll pardon me for asking, was that
his real home? What puzzles me is this, if you understand. I was with the contingent of the guard the General
Ambrosius sent to the Lord Arthur's King Making. I believe you was there with him that day, sir. I seem to
remember seeing you?"

"I was," I said.

"Well, then." He scratched his nose and hesitated. "I
do seem to remember *that* day they said he was born a
long way further off—down in Lyonesse—in some great
fortress of the Pendragon Uther, his father?"

"So he was. The Fortress of Tintagel. But you'll
have heard tell how badly things went in those times. He
was carried off as a baby by Celidon the Merlin and
hidden away for safety in *my* old home on the Dumnonian coast. My mother suckled him with me. We grew
up together."

"Ah! That accounts for it, then." He seemed satisfied.

The boy Kerouac interrupted.

"Tell us about the King Making, decurion. Must have been a grand, fine sight, I reckon. All those High Kings there, every one of 'em hoping as *he'd* be the chap chosen for Pendragon—a lugging and tugging at the King's Sword stuck in that great stone and then the Lord Arthur, no older nor what I am now, walking up to it and by magic, out it comes, easy as kiss-your-hand. My, but I'd have liked to see their faces!"

The decurion laughed, deep in his throat.

"You got it wrong, boy. The others hadn't tried their hands, the *first* time the Lord Arthur drew Excalibur. That all came later, if I remember right. No. I'll tell you now how it really come about. I was there and seen it with my own eyes. Being in the guard of honor from the army, we was privileged to be inside the Basilica at Winchester. Mark of respect, we was there for—to show the Colonial army was going all the way along with the Clans about this here King Making lark. Can't say I liked—*or* approved—that by custom we had to pile arms outside, though. But there—it was the custom. No arms to be carried into the church, that was our orders.

"Well, it's a big building, the Basilica is, but that day it was packed out with everybody as was anybody in Britain, pretty near. I never seen so many notables all together, before or since. In front of the high altar they'd got a great black stone, with what I thought was a cross of iron sticking up out of it, and I wondered why, for the altar itself had a fine gold one, and a mort of candles burning—it being Christian Eastertide. The lord abbot, he said mass for a start (though I'll be bound some of those present hadn't much notion of what *that* was all about). Up in the front with him were the High Kings of the Clans, and the Lord Celidon (the Merlin, as we call him now) and some of the Colonial gentry in their togas —our Sir Kay among them, and him with the purple stripe on his, showing as he was descended from an emperor, same as the General Ambrosius, they being close kin.

"Everything goes along very quiet and orderly and proper, until, the mass being over, the Merlin makes a speech, explaining to the folk as they'd come together to proclaim the Lord Arthur Pendragon, him being the rightful heir of King Uther, and King Uther having had it put in writing as, so soon as he should be old enough, he was to succeed him, see?"

"'But,' says the Merlin, 'since some of you seem to want to question his rights' (or words to that effect), 'we will presently hold a test, me and the abbot, that we've fixed and agreed upon between us, as'll prove to you it's God's holy will who is the rightful next Pendragon. In this here stone,' he says (or words to that effect), 'is set a Kingly Sword. Now, only the true and rightful and appointed Pendragon will have strength to pull it out, and so I'm telling you. But before we come to that, I'm calling on Sir Kay' (Sir Caius, he called him, giving him his Roman name, see?) 'to read out King Uther's written will to you' (what the king had written down, and him knowing he was to die, just before the Battle of Verulamium, it was)."

The decurion paused dramatically. I looked round the intent faces and glanced at Palomides. Well, I thought, it's easier than trying to tell him about that day myself, and by the look of him, he's finding the story interesting—but I must guard my tongue later, for I'll be bound he'll have some questions.

"Well . . ." the decurion dwelt on the word, drawing it out, savoring the intent expressions of his audience. "No sooner had Sir Kay got out the will and unrolled the parchment, than there comes a great clatter and racket outside the Basilica—folks screeching and swearing and shouting, and a tramp of feet. The great doors burst open, and up the main aisle comes none other than King Lot of Dalriada (though I wasn't to know it was him then, never having set eyes on him, nor any of the men behind him, before that day). A tall, dark fellow he is, with the look of one used to being cock of his own dunghill. All swinked up and sweaty, him and his men were, just come from hard riding you could see—and every one of them armed.

"'Steady!' I says to my lads. "Stand steady. We're not too far from the doors we can't grab swords if we need 'em. But let this ride. They've got in. If need be, we can see to it none of 'em get out alive, but it's not for us to start trouble. This here place is sacred—and don't you forget it. Leave this to the abbot and the Merlin until I gives you your orders.' (They were a well-trained cohort— I knew I could trust 'em to move quick when I said the word.)

"Up to the altar goes his Royal Highness of Dalriada, with all the others that were gathered there shouting out shame on him for the disturbance, and his hands on his sword hilt all the way.

" 'So, Celidon the Wizard,' he says, and loud enough to be heard over all the din, 'you've had it in mind to make a Pendragon for Britain again? We in the northland heard of it late, but not too late for the Gathering. I and my men are here in time to see fair play.'

"Well, the Lord Merlin, he faced him out squarely, so he did.

" 'Lay down your arms,' he tells him. 'No man bears arms at the Gathering and well you knows that' ('tis the custom, same as I told you before).

"King Lot, he sneers like, and 'Cold iron's said to be good against magic. I'll keep my sword until I get a better one, Celidon the Magician,' he says. 'I've come to claim my rights,' he says. 'My rights as husband of the Queen Margause, as was eldest-born daughter of King Uther's queen.'

"Well, then the cat was all among the pigeons, as they say, and you couldn't hear yourself think for those great lords bawling at each other.

" 'Come on, lads—out and grab arms,' I says.

"We got outside somehow and I formed 'em up, proper and steady, and sword in hand, I leads them back in again, ready for action. But we'd missed some of the goings on, as you may guess. When I'd managed to push through the press of folk as were trying to hustle out the few ladies present, things had quieted down a bit. By all accounts the abbot had called for order—and *he's* got a voice you could hear above a battle. They tell me he'd ordered Sir Kay to read out King Uther's will, but *that* didn't satisfy my Lord of Dalriada.

" 'So!' he was shouting, as I got myself through that door, 'so you think the Free Clans of Britain'll take that stripling boy there for war leader, do you?' and he turns on a great scornful guffaw of laughter—snatches the parchment from Sir Kay and chucks it down, contemptuous. 'Why,' he says (and I beg pardon, my Lord Bedivere, for repeating his very words, "why, he's naught but a bastard, got before wedlock, even if (and there's doubt of *that*) he really is King Uther's son!'

"You know our Sir Kay—he's still one you couldn't insult and get away with it, I reckon. He snatches up that parchment, strikes Lot across the face with it and—'Take that, for the insolent troublemaking liar you are!' he says (or words to that effect, for I don't pretend I heard him that clear).

"Lot whips out his sword, of course, and there's a *wheep* of steel all down the line of his raggle-taggle ruffians as they do the same.

"I shouts to my chaps to come on, but before we can get moving, there's another sound of a sword being drawn and a great flash. 'Twas like as if lightning had struck down out of the roof, though most probably 'twas just the candles, reflecting on the blade of Excalibur. For our Lord Arthur had got ahold of what I'd thought was the cross above the black stone, and pulled the great sword out, easy as you'd pull your dagger out of a barrel of butter.

" 'Here you are, Kay. Take this!" he says, and his voice come across to me, clear and cool, and almost as though he were laughing."

There was a gasp from the decurion's audience. He'd got them living the scene, as a harper can, provided he tells his tale well enough. Like a harper he paused before he dropped his voice.

"Funny thing it was. Come to think of it after, I *have* wondered if some kind of enchantment was on that sword of our Pendragon's. All the noise in that great place dropped away, so you could have heard a mouse squeak. Sir Kay stood with Excalibur in his hand, just staring down at it, and Lot, he backs away, letting his blade sink. I seen the abbot whisper to the Merlin, and then he up and gets between them (Sir Kay and the King of Dalriada), facing out to all of us.

"'Clear the Basilica!' he thunders. 'This is God's holy house, and I'll have no more brawling here,' and he adds a good, strong bit of Christian cursing on all and every one of us, both inside and outside the Basilica, promising I don't know what of hellfire and burning for all eternity to any man who breaks Peace of Gathering from then on. 'The Council will meet, and a proclamation shall be made to all of you, what it decides,' he says. 'Until then, I declare a solemn fast, and prayers to be said and sung. A King Making is not a tavern brawl—and the great God I worship be my witness, there'll be famine, plague and pestilence throughout this land such as no man ever saw unless my words are obeyed.'

"That's how it was, Sir Bedivere, sir, and you can bear me out on it, can't you?" The decurion turned to me.

"That's how it was, lads," I said, and smiled at their solemn faces. "I couldn't have told it half as well myself. You've made a grand tale of it, man. You should have been a harper!"

The soldiers were not content, however, to let it go at that. There was a buzz of comment, and inevitably it was Moldaik, the grumbler, who raised an objection.

"'Tisn't how *I've* heard the story told. Folk always say as *all* the kings there were, they tried their hands at getting Excalibur out of the stone and failed. That's how it was proved our Lord Arthur was the rightful Pendragon," he insisted.

"Me, I've heard it that way—my father was there and he told us, back home." Kerouac sounded disappointed.

"Us didn't hear nothing about it taking place in a Christian church, neither," the Durotrigian shook his head, puzzled. "Us understood 'twas a proper Gathering, like, out at they old ancient stones, up on the Great Plain, with hundreds of folk there to see. How d'you account for that, decurion?"

The decurion snorted.

"'Course it was, but that was afterwards. Two, three

days after, it must have been. Oh, rumors was flying round, I can tell you, thick as gnats on a May evening, and all of 'em to do with the 'magic sword,' as they called Excalibur. Being a follower of Mithras myself, as I hold a soldier should be, I'm not a superstitious man. But what I seen, I seen, and I speak according. There *was* magic in what happened. The Lord Arthur's Excalibur's no ordinary weapon, and you can take that from me.

"I and my chaps, and a good few of the Prince Geraint's men from Lyonesse, we was put to keep the crowds back out of the Sacred Precinct, as they call the space inside the circle of the hanging stones. We was allowed ash staves to do it with, but nothing else, and a fine old job it was, as you can imagine. But, of course, we did get a front seat for the Games, as you might say. Could even see their faces, all of them—and I'll say they was worth watching." He chuckled reminiscently. "It's a queer old place—impressive, I'd call it—looks like the ruins of some temple of ancient times. They say it's the way it was built by giants, back along in the beginnings of the world—a circle of tall grey stones, joined to form arches, like. Anyways, they'd got the black altar out there, what we'd seen already in the Basilica, and the sword was sticking in it, up to the hilt, again, and a guard set round it of veterans (Centurion Ulfius, he was one of them). I've heard it had been kept guarded night and day ever since the do in the Basilica—and rightly so, considering all things.

"The Lord Merlin and the abbot, they took charge of the ceremony, both in their full robes, and very impressive they looked. The Merlin, he explained as it was to be the test for all and any as had the idea they'd some right to be Pendragon, for this here sword was to be the mark of the man appointed—only the rightful one could draw it, he said. Then the abbot, he prayed for God to give the Sign that way, and for the people to accept it, once it was given. ('Belt and baldrick,' I thinks to myself. 'The old magic ways, *and* the new Christian faith. Clever. Now nobody can't complain.')

"Up they comes, one after another—every Clan Chief in turn, and a good few Colonial gentry, for the

Merlin wasn't taking chances. He'd rounded 'em all for
the Test, willing or not, for the look of the thing. Some of
'em, you could tell, would as soon have ducked out, for it
isn't every man, Chief or not, would fancy the Lord
Arthur's calling—and some of 'em was shaking-afraid of
the magic in that sword. You could see the sweat on their
faces, for all the wind was blowing keen under a bright
sky that day. To tell honest truth, I was sweating myself.
You could feel there was something—well, odd; out of
the ordinary —about that place. Odder still, how none of
those men—great warriors many of them, used to the grip
of a sword's hilt for years—couldn't budge the thing. For
they tried—oh, yes, they tried. Prince Geraint, he was
smiling when his turn came. I noticed—at a guess, he'd
an idea he'd have the strength *and* the knack, too, maybe,
him being a famous wrestler, and maybe he'd an idea the
luck might be on his side for some do tell he'd a mind to
rule Britain. He took it well, though, when he'd no
success at all. Smiled, and shrugged, and says quietly:
'Let the gods choose a better man, Merlin.'

"King Lot, now, he pretty near lifted altar and all off
the ground. I never see a man put out greater effort, and
his face gone pale as a corpse with the sheer rage he was
in and his eyes like a wolf's eyes—glaring, with a red glint
in them.

"When 'twas evident he'd not a hope, he flung away,
swearing great oaths, muttering no man could win against
the tricks of wizard and monk, combined.

"Last of all, comes our Lord Arthur—very young,
he looked, that day—just a tall slender lad, but with the
promise of the shoulders and chest he's got on him now,
if you'd eyes to see it, and something in the way he
walked and held his head up that'd make you look twice
at him in any company. He tosses back all that bright
hair, looks up once at the sky, as if to say, 'Give me the
Sign, if it's mine by rights,' and then he curls his hand
round the hilt of Excalibur, and out the great sword
comes for all the world as though he just drew it from a
well-fitting scabbard. There's the same flash I'd seen in
the Basilica, and hard on it, for all there wasn't a cloud in
the sky, a great roll of thunder.

"After that, I can't tell you much, for I'd my hands full and more than full, keeping the crowd from breaking our barrier—and glad and thankful to have the Lyonesse men to help us. I've said their High Prince was a wrestler, and by the White Bull, so were the men he'd put on guard duty. They pitched in and did a proper job. We were all of us ready for the free wine that was flowing later in honor of the King Making—we'd earned it!"

The decurion drew his sleeve across his mouth, reminiscently, then added:

"I did hear it said the Gathering went on, with games and feasting, for a week or more, and there was talk how King Uther's queen was brought to the Council to bear witness to her son's legitimacy, poor lady. But that was all politics and no concern of the likes of us. Next day I and my lads were due to start back to the army—the general, he'd given orders not to outstay the leave he'd given us, him being short-handed then, as always. Discipline's discipline, and we rode off next cockcrow—half of us hardly able to tell which was head and which tail of the horses. I'll say when Britain makes a Pendragon, Britain makes a feast worth remembering, to celebrate! I'm right, aren't I, sir?"

I shook myself out of a cloud of memories to return his grin.

"You are indeed," I said, "and thanks for reminding me of it. It was a great day for all of us, and a great day for Britain. And now, since we've talked the stars down the sky," I glanced up through a ragged hole in the thatch above my head, "it's time for sleeping. I only wish I could issue you all a ration of the wine the decurion talks of, lads. That'll have to wait until we've won the Pendragon his final victory and the seas are clear of pirates, and galleys packed with amphorae come sailing into all our ports as freely as they did in the good old days—that's the best I can offer you!"

Sleep was long in coming to me that night. The decurion's story had brought back memories of Arthur's King Making, and one memory in particular that I shared only with Arthur, Celidon and Ygern. It was a memory I had buried deep, because at the time the happening had disturbed me, and, being young, and my mind set on my own affairs just then (I'd Ambrosius' orders to leave the Gathering as soon as the Pendragon was proclaimed, and report for my overseas service), I had resented interruption to my peace of mind. At that age, one can shelve problems, and forget them, if life is thronged, as mine was then, with new experiences.

Lying wrapped in my cloak, listening to a little wind that whispered about the ruins of the Roman barracks, I remembered vividly the eve of the King Making, and wondered how what had happened then had affected the two I loved best since, and how, in the future, it might affect me.

We had travelled to the Gathering in a dangerously exalted mood, we three. It seemed to me, looking back, even Arthur had been still very young and vulnerable. I could hardly believe three years had changed and tempered him to the war leader he was now. War matures men fast.

The King Choosing, six years before, had been deeply memorable. But this, the King Making, was the first very great occasion we had all three shared together, and the fact that my uncle and Kay went with us, ready to back Arthur's claim on behalf of the Colonists, gave it added importance.

Arthur and Ygern were in love that spring, both too young and inexperienced to hide it. The bloom of it lay on them like dew on a flower, and they were touched to beauty by it, as the young are by first love. I had accepted the fact with philosophy. There had been, earlier, a period when I'd rebelled against it, but my time with Ambrosius' army had given me at least a superficial sophistication. I asked myself, why break my heart hankering after the unattainable? Arthur meant more to me than my own happiness. All our lives I'd been ready to give up to him anything I'd even guessed he wanted. I told myself there were other girls in the world besides Ygern. Time enough to find mine, later.

On the eve of the ceremony she almost shook my resolution. She'd been wistful, as women will be, because she'd not, to her mind, clothes grand enough for such a

festival. Then Celidon (whose favorite she'd always
been) produced from somewhere a dress such as only the
richest Colonial ladies had ever been able to afford—and
they only in the great days before the Troubles. It must
have been old-fashioned, for it smelled sweetly of herbs in
which it had been long packed away. It was the first time
any of us had seen the shining cloth men call "silk,"
which is woven in a land three years' journey away, at the
world's end where the sun rises, and the colors in it were
unbelievably soft and shimmering, all running together, in
a design of strange flowers and branches and little birds.
It clothed her from neck to ankles in straight folds that
suited her slimness. With her hair loose, bound only by a
little gold fillet, her eyes wide and awed, she looked a
princess out of a harper's tale.

"Will Arthur like it?" she asked me.

"Go and ask him," I said gruffly, for she'd stirred
my blood in a way that angered me. "He was walking in
the orchard just now. I dare say you'll find him there
still."

(We were lodged in a little house on the town's edge
that my uncle had hired at more expense than he could
afford.)

She went without another word. I thought: "This'll
clinch the matter. Well, she'll make him a good queen.
They understand each other," and I waited for them to
come in together and tell me they were betrothed, expecting as lovers will that everyone would be surprised.

They did not come; but later Kay came, fussing over
some details of the next day's arrangements, saying he'd
mislaid his sword and Arthur must have put it somewhere.

"Where's the boy got to? Go and fetch him, Verus,"
he ordered.

I went, reluctantly, but thinking better I should disturb them than he should.

The orchard was small and enclosed—a very private
place. Old apple trees blossomed there, scattering their
petals on the long grass. Sunset glinted through the
gnarled trunks, and a blackbird was singing.

I went softly, but the gods know, I did not mean to

steal up on those two. Eavesdropping has never been a habit of mine. I came on them suddenly and what I saw held me at once spellbound and embarrassed, unwilling to go forward, afraid to betray my presence if I went back.

They were locked together in a close embrace—the first breathless kiss of passion new-discovered. When they broke away from it, they stood, holding each other by both hands, gazing with bright, bewildered faces.

Arthur said slowly, almost arrogantly:

"Now I know. Now I understand. I shall marry you, Ygern. You will be my queen."

She answered, on a low, breathless note:

"Yes," and then again, "Yes!"

The sunlight, slanting level between the tree trunks, was suddenly darkened. A shadow fell across their linked hands. The Merlin's voice said, speaking slowly, heavily, as a man speaks who is in pain:

"The thing is forbidden. In this life you two can never marry."

I saw the linked hands loose and fall apart, then looked higher, and Celidon's face made me afraid. He was deathly pale, sweat beading his forehead. In battle I have seen men look so, who feel the spear they had not known was aimed their way sink deep between the shoulder blades.

He spoke again, and in his voice there was the desolation of the wind when it comes across the lonely Outlands in winter.

"I should have foreseen this—I, who am the Merlin! Why have I still thought of you as children? The union you desire was forbidden before you were born. Uther the Pendragon was father to you both."

Late that night Ygern came to me—no longer a princess robed in fairy color, but a little white ghost, in an old woollen tunic, who crept into my arms and cried there, incoherent and inconsolable as I had known her a few times when we were children and some disaster had temporarily shattered her small world.

Frankly, I had not been able to make head or tail of what she tried to tell me. The story she sobbed out

against my shoulder sounded too wild and too improbable
—strange as some old legend of forgotten rites, and fated
lovers.

It seemed her mother and Arthur's had been twin
sisters, born at one birth—hers was Uther's queen, once
wife of Gorlois of Lyonesse, that Ygern who all men
reckoned had borne Uther's heir so soon after Gorlois'
death that some still dared to call Arthur "bastard" to his
face. Arthur, in very truth, was born of a different marriage rite, a rite shrouded in the ceremonial magic of the
Old Faith, the Chosen One, fathered by Uther the Pendragon, but born to that twin sister of Queen Ygern, the
dedicated Priestess of the Island—The Lady of the Lake.

That much I understood. How the thing had come
about and why, and what its meaning might be, I could
not get clear then, and it was to be many years before I
did. When a girl's defenses come down and all she can do
is cry inconsolably, because her life seems to her to lie in
ruins and yet stretches ahead of her, an endless length of
empty years, one cannot press too hard for detailed explanation.

I was sorry for Ygern, that night—but more than
half my mind was on Arthur. The morrow was the vital
day of his King Making. I cursed the gods, and Merlin
their messenger, who had brought knowledge of this thing
on him at such a moment. How would he react to it, I
wondered? Would his nerve be shaken, his determination
undermined?

I did him wrong. He came to the next day's ordeal
as the decurion had seen him and described him. With
him, all his life, the Matter of Britain came first. He had
the royal power in him, which can put aside personal gain
or loss in moments of crisis, as unthinkingly as a man,
trained to arms, will get up from the meal just spread for
him (and he hungry for it) at the first call to arms.

It did not mean he loved Ygern less than she loved
him. She was the one great love of his life, as well I know.
The link between those two must have been forged before
the beginning of time. But for a woman love is enough to
fill all life. Few are strong and wise enough, as Ygern,
our comrade, proved herself, to learn its deepest lessons

and, walking empty-handed down the lonely years, give all its strength to the one she loves, asking and expecting no reward.

I was up and about early next morning, and left the others sleeping. There was still much planning to be done and I needed time to look the fort over for myself, undisturbed by well-meant comment and suggestion.

It was a soft, grey day, with a wet wind blowing in from the west. A hare went leaping across the long, drenched grass, and a big dog fox turned to stare at me with appraising amber eyes, before he slid soundlessly to cover. The wild things must have had the place to themselves twenty years and more since the last legionary marched out under the ruined north gate.

I had made about half the circuit of the upper rampart, my mind busy on calculation of the amount of timber we'd need to replace the rotting palisade, and where would be the nearest place to fell it, when, glancing out across the surrounding plain, the view I saw brought me to a sudden halt. It was strangely familiar. A wide, flat land, laced with dikes and slow, winding rivers, with far away in the distance a silver shining sheet of lake water with a green island rising from it.

I narrowed my eyes, though the light was kind and the prospect clear, promising rain to come. There was no mistaking that largest island's shape—long and narrow, like a galley, with the blunt hill rising up where the mast would have been. Ynis Witrin, the Holy Island—the place of Dragon Making.

I knew then why, out of all the hill forts there are in Britain, Celidon had chosen the Fort of Camelot to be the centre of Arthur's rule.

# Chapter Eleven

One advantage of legionary discipline was the uniformity of equipment and maneuver that existed throughout the empire. Men knew what to expect when they moved into standing shelter, because all barracks were laid out on the same plan, and varied only in size.

When Arthur and the main body of the army caught up with us at the Great Fort, we had less confusion getting them allocated to their quarters than I'd expected, thanks to the leavening of Ambrosius' veterans. Granted, there was more democratic comment and cheerful argument than the old general would have permitted. Celts are incurably talkative, and Arthur treated every man who served under him as a brother in those days.

Understanding the independence of his native levies, he never stickled for form so long as the spirit of discipline was preserved.

By evening on the day of arrival the last heavy supply wagon had been hauled up the track, the horses were picketed, the Shrine of the Standards was erected, and the cooking fires were alight. The whole place was still a bustle of activity, but I had time to find Ygern and make sure she'd been shown the centurion's cell I'd reserved for her and her serving wench, at the end of the women's quarters. (I'd seen to it myself, the roof was sound, and the door could be closed and barred at need. It wasn't much by way of preparation, but it was all I'd had time to do.)

I found her there, competent and practical, unstrapping the saddlepack a soldier had dumped on one of the wooden bunks built into the wall.

"This isn't much of a place—but the best I could get for you," I told her. "Things will improve when we've had time to organize ourselves. At least this gives you some privacy."

She smiled at me over her shoulder.

"Better than I'd expected. I like this fort, Bedivere. It has a good feel to it—a lucky feel," she said cheerfully.

She still wore Celtic boys' clothes—most of our women did, on the march. She looked tough and resilient, though she was thinner than I liked and her face had a fine-drawn pallor under its outdoor tan.

"Not too tired, girl?" I asked.

She shook her head, and made a quick grimace at me.

"Don't fuss, Bedivere. I've told you before, there's no need."

I had been inclined to fuss over her since I'd come back from chasing pockets of enemy resistance and been met by Kay with news that troubled me.

Always quick to foresee gloomy possibilities in any situation, he'd been the first to guess a reason when Ygern, mended from her fever, was still plagued between bouts of her usual energy by turns of faintness and vomiting, and days of unaccountable weariness.

"Mark my words, Verus, the worst's happened. That girl's with child. I know the signs. Best see if the man what's-his-name—the fellow you brought over with you from Armorica—can do something about it for us. He's a doctor, isn't he? He ought to be able to prevent us being landed with a Saxon bastard. He must prevent it!"

Shaken, I'd consulted Palomides. He was sympathetic, but grave.

"There are things I could do, yes. But the risk would be one I'd not advise. She's not fully recovered from the shock of all that happened to her, and the conditions of life as she must live it would not help. No, Verus—if you want my advice, better let nature take its course. Archimandros advised it in such cases, and we had a good few through our hands in Alexandria. An unwanted infant can always be exposed at birth—unless that is against the custom of your country?"

I'd not enough experience to know for certain. I'd an idea slaves and the peasants put out unwanted girl children on the hillsides in times of poor harvest, I told him.

I'd found Ygern brusque and short-tempered, as she'd been in our childhood whenever she's hurt herself keeping up with us in some game too rough for her.

"Don't make such a coil about the thing, Bedivere. Thousands of women in thousands of wars must have faced the same problem. If Olwen was still here, she'd have helped me, but I trust your Palomides. I'll do what he says. You are all going to need me this winter. I can't afford to go sick again and be a burden. I'll manage."

Watching her sorting out her few possessions in the wretched little hutment that smelt of mildew and long disuse, I admired her courage. Outside and all around us there was the noise of the host, settling itself for the night. Shouts, laughter, running feet, the thud of mallets driving in tent pegs (half of us must be under tents, still). Dusk was falling early, and the cell was already full of shadows.

"I'll get you a lantern," I said.

"No. They're in short supply and the men need them." She was quite definite. "I've a rushlight somewhere. That'll serve. We must make a good supply of those as soon as Kay will spare me enough fat. There's going to be a lot of work for women this winter, I can see. I've been planning what must be done. Arthur's army is short of many things we can make—blankets, pots and pitchers, baskets and saddlebags. Some of the wives have skill enough, but the soldiers' girls will need teaching. Never mind—they're willing. They only need to be given a lead."

She spoke like some young centurion considering his first command. I smiled to myself. She and Arthur were very alike. No wonder that, as I'd noticed from the first, all the host treated her with the respect due to one close kin to their commander. The dangerous inference that some might draw from the position he gave her and the trust he put in her, I did not altogether realize.

We were interrupted by a crash, as the door of the hut burst open and two palliasses stuffed with straw were thrown in at it, followed by a tall, strapping, red-haired young woman, whose weather-tanned face cracked into a cheerfully impudent grin at sight of me.

"Sorry to intrude, sir, but we need this bedding in while it's still dry. Going to rain cats and dogs any minute now. Always rains first night in winter quarters—noticed that? Be worse when it snows and that can't be far off now." She heaved the palliasses onto the bunks and addressed herself to Ygern direct. "Come and give us a hand in the hall when you've time, dearie, will you? It's like the morning after a town's been sacked over there— the silly buggers keep on bringing in stuff and piling it up regardless, and Sir Kay'll burst a blood vessel soon, if somebody don't calm him down. If you ask me, we'd do better without some of the centurions' madams giving orders what stores they need, 'stead of belting up and lending a hand with the work. We all need a bit of your coolness to get things organized. In your own time, of course—don't want to interrupt anything!"

With a wink at me, the wench hurried out, kicking the door to with a bang that shook the rickety walls.

"In the name of the gods, Ygern, couldn't they have found you a better servant than that trollop?" I asked, frowning. It was obvious to me what section of the camp Alfia came from.

Ygern laughed.

"I chose her. The woman Kay recommended had a face like a half-cooked bannock, and was so pious-proper she depressed me as much as I shocked her. Alfia's been with the army all her life. She can teach me things I need to know. She's had three children by three different fathers, and marched twenty miles the day before the last one was born. She's got the sort of courage that stiffens mine and she makes me laugh. Alfia and I understand each other!"

That first winter at the Great Fort we were short of most things except faith in ourselves and our cause, the vigor of our youth, and good fellowship. Arthur worked us hard, officers and men alike, rain, shine or snow, and by spring we'd got the fortifications temporarily repaired, the gate towers rebuilt, and the trackway from the north gate widened and made passable for cavalry in formation. A day's hunting, when we could spare time for it, had been our only relaxation. We never lacked meat, for the woods were full of wild pig in those days. They'd bred there for years, descendants of the ones that must have escaped when the great villa-farms were burned in the Troubles. Just below the fort we found the ruins of one of these, a wealthy place in its day. We took anything we could plunder from the materials that were left, but there was not much except a load of broken conduit pipes that made good foundation for the track. Later, where gardens had run down to the river, Palomides discovered herbs growing still that he was pleased to have, since they were rare ones in Britain, he said.

Spring came early. Sooner than I'd dared hope, Bardeliez made good his promise. He shipped us the horses over in the first spell of good weather, reckoning the Saxon fleets would still be icebound in their northern waters, and the seaways reasonably safe for a valuable cargo. Arthur went down himself to Adurni to see them unloaded, taking Kay with him. The two of them were away longer than I'd expected and came back in so serious a mood I was afraid at first something must have gone wrong with the shipment.

Arthur laid my anxiety to rest swiftly, his eyes kindling with pleasure as he spoke.

"Magnificent stock and they'd stood the voyage well. Safe down in the Dumnonian valley pastures we'll breed the cavalry mounts I've dreamed of, Bedivere, thanks to your Bardeliez. He's a man after my own heart. He's taught me a great deal I needed to know and never fully understood until these last few days. He sent greetings to you and Palomides, and I've gifts from him for you both somewhere, besides."

"Bardeliez? *He* came over with the horses?" I said,

surprised. "I'd not thought of that possibility. He's always feared sea travel as Gregorious feared the devil!"

Arthur laughed.

"By his looks when he landed, he'd not enjoyed the journey. Nothing I could do would persuade him to come on inland this year, though he's promised to spend time here in the future, if our news is good enough to make the risk worth taking."

We were sitting together round a charcoal brazier in the hut where Kay kept his records and accounts, and where he slept to guard the army's small treasure chest. Now he grunted, reluctantly.

"The man seemed honest. If he does the half of what he promises, some of our troubles could be over. But I don't, myself, see Britain giving him the profit that will make it worth his while—or any rate, not for many years to come."

Arthur glanced across at him sharply.

"War's our trade, Kay, and the only one, so far, we know. Give this merchant credit for knowing his at least as well. Things he said made sense to me—and I liked his straight speaking." Smiling suddenly at me, Arthur added, "He called me a fool to my face, Bedivere, then praised me for not taking offense. Why should I, when he spoke of things he knew and I'd never troubled to give my mind to?"

"Such as?" I queried, smiling too. I knew Bardeliez.

"The fact no king can win victory by the sword alone. An army must be fed, clothed and armed, and for that one needs money. After victory comes peace, and for maintaining that, it seems, we'll not have enemy loot to fill our treasure chests. By his reckoning, Rome's empire began to crumble from the day the legions had stripped the conquered nations of their gold, from the Scythian borders to the deserts of furthest Africa. He said" (and Arthur's eyes were thoughtful, fixed now on the red flicker of the glowing brazier), " 'There comes an end to plunder, and to tribute, squeezed from subject peoples. Tax men too hard, and they sink under the burden. Either they rebel, and die, or, having eaten next year's seed corn because they starve, famine comes and after famine, plague, so, that way, too, they die. Believe me, Arthur Pendragon, Rome the all-conquering has fallen, fallen, as I believe, never to rise again, not because her armies were weak and the Barbarians' strong. Not because divisions occurred, splitting the empire apart, as an old coat rips at the seams, but because for years not one man among her rulers was a merchant who understood the skills of barter and exchange. Despise these skills at your peril, War Duke of Britain. Let me, Bardeliez, teach them to you; employ them on your behalf: and where Rome falls, Britain may rise up, and in some far future to hold all, and more than all, that Rome has lost.' "

"Fine words!" Kay growled. "Merchants are glib talkers! When you get down to the bones of the thing, what does it all amount to? A promise to get the export trade we had here before the Troubles started up again. That'll take him all his time, even given command of the undertaking you rashly signed over to him, Arturus. It'll be years before *we* see profit from it."

Arthur shook his head, and I could tell his mind was worrying at some problem, as I'd seen him in the past mastering an idea that was new, but seemed to him good.

"I trust that man," he said slowly. Repeating as a boy repeats a difficult lesson, he murmured, " 'The wealth of your mines, corn, Icenian chariot teams, great hunting dogs and fine metalwork of your Celtic craftsmen, and a river of gold flowing steadily back in payment for those fine things, a river out of which a king may dip at need to meet the calls of government.' Yes. It's all a new idea to me. A magic Celidon has not taught me. A magic I need, and intend to learn!"

As I remember, we'd little time to speculate and discuss the nebulous possibilities of Bardeliez' golden river, for Celidon came in soon after with news the Picts were for certain mustering north of the Wall and had made strong alliance with Lot of Dalriada.

We sent out the Branch, and were lucky, for levies came in fast, encouraged by the last season's victory, and heartened by the rumor we'd got the Armoricans promised as our allies. That was the year we went north with such a good show of strength that Leodogrance of Rheged, who had been sitting on the fence ever since Arthur's King Making, uncertain which horse he'd back, came down finally on our side. By the time we reached the Wall, we'd three of his fifteen sons leading a rabble of half-naked Clansmen on our flank. They proved savage warriors and kept faith with us, not deserting to the enemy as we half expected. (In fact, they stood a chariot charge better than our southern Clans, being more accustomed to that outdated style of warfare.) But we had trouble and to spare with them in other ways, for they were notable thieves, and when Arthur hanged half a dozen of them for torturing a farmer who they suspected had hidden money, their High Princes seemed bewildered and were inclined to take offense, evidently thinking he made much of little.

That was the first year Palomides and I saw the Great Wall—Hadrian's Wall, as men call it still. Palomides was impressed by the skill of the old-time engineers who built it. To me, then and always, it seemed a melancholy, unchancy place. East to west it runs, right across Britain from sea to sea, a guard tower every mile along its length. Once it took a full legion to man it, and was the most unpopular posting in all the empire, for the country up there is bleak and desolate indeed. Looking north through a mist of cold rain, across barren hills, Palomides said, laughing:

"This is the Britain men on the mainland picture, Verus. *This* is their Hyperborean Island at the world's end!"

I shivered and did not answer. It seemed a place of ghosts to me, for the wind howls there through the weed-grown ruins. Doors creak and bang on broken hinges in the fire-scathed towers, and the rotted leathers of great abandoned catapults wave and flap with sudden gestures of despair against an empty sky. A place of ghosts to me, even that first evening, with Palomides jesting at my side. How much more haunted the last time I crossed it, two years back, a ragged ghost myself, with only my harp and my memories to bear me company.

Brother Paulinus has the facts of that first victorious campaign we fought in the north. Ashamed of my ill temper, I took care to give them to him fully and precisely, for our victory at the forest's edge, which folk call Silver Wood, has always been accounted one of Arthur's twelve great battles. I commanded our light cavalry, but it was Lancelot and his five hundred trained Armoricans on their big battle stallions who turned the day for us. I think that was the beginning of the lifelong friendship between Arthur and Lancelot. Those two were commanders who, in war, thought with one mind, that day and ever after. Their one regret (and mine) when the battle ended, was that Lot of Dalriada was not among the slain. By a ruse, changing cloaks with one of his men, he fled the field, and the head of a commander who wore the High King's yellow Clan tartan when Lancelot's men brought it back in triumph from a wild pursuit was red-haired, so we guessed we had been tricked at the finish.

There was no time to pursue fugitives, even if Arthur had cared to risk his troops in unknown country, thick with forest and rotten with bogs. Runners had come from Celidon with news of Federates in revolt on the east coast, and a Jute landing there, on the march to cut off our rear. We went south by forced marches, and beat them where a river-mouth, wider than any lake, comes in from the sea. It was a tough encounter, for our men were weary, and we'd lost more than we could spare at Silver Wood. Our casualties were heavy, that year, and the march back hampered by the slow pace of the ox wagons, carrying the wounded.

It was high summer by then, and we'd left Kay at the fort with only a skeleton garrison. Arthur sent me on ahead of the host with two centuries of cavalry. We were not expecting trouble down south, but in good sailing weather we could never rule out the chance of it.

There is nothing quite like coming home to one's own people with news of victory. That was the first time it happened to me. I can still hear the trumpets sounding above me, from the new-built gate tower, while the whole population of the fort pressed about our horses, shouting, cheering, laughing, sobbing. I can still see their

faces, all turned up to me, awed and joyful, etched by the
glow of sunset, the homeliest touched to strange beauty.
Even those to whom we brought bad news took it proudly, counting no cost too great since at last the army of
Britain was turning the tide of a forty years' war. I felt an
elation that throbbed in my own heart and in all the
crowd about me, beating as one pulse—a great wing-beat
that reached up into the fiery sky. Even Kay felt it. When
I had dismounted, he stood grasping my hands until the
fingers tingled, saying exultantly over and over again:

"He's done it! The boy's done it, Verus. There was a
time I never thought he could!"

With Kay, elation seldom interrupted for long the nagging
worry of small everyday anxiety. Once I'd given him an
account of the campaign, his face began to work in the
fashion I knew so well.

"Things have been quiet enough down here, bar one
troublesome disaster," he told me.

"What was that?" I asked, expecting to hear nothing
worse than news of weevil in a consignment of corn, or
maybe a few barrels of salt meat gone maggoty.

"Ygern," he said grimly. "Little fool! She went out
riding—in *her* condition—without my permission, alone
with that wild wench Alfia. She was thrown, and bore her
brat untimely, in some native hovel, and none to blame
except the pair of them!"

The glory of the day turned cold and grey about me.
I gripped his arm.

"Where is she now? How bad is she? Tell me!" I
said.

He shook off my hand testily.

"She's well enough. Ashamed to face you, I dare
say. She's come through the ordeal as scatheless as if
she'd been a field hand or one of the soldiers' girls who
follow the army. But it was three days before we found
her and then it was too late."

"Too late for what?" I asked. In my anxiety I could
have shaken him.

He scowled, his whole face twitching.

"To put down the bastard half-breed bantling she's

brought into the world, of course. You know her, Verus. The scenes she used to make when you were children if even a litter of unwanted kittens needed to be drowned! I blame Alfia. She should have seen the thing was done quietly and at once. She knew my orders. I'd have had the silly trollop stripped and whipped, if I'd had my way. Women—no sense, any of them! Now she's feeding the thing herself, and all the other silly females in the fort are cooing over it. Where are you going, Verus?"

Over my shoulder I said, laughing with relief:

"To find her, of course. Don't you remember we two always comforted each other when you'd been scolding us, Kay?"

# Chapter Twelve

It is the spring starving time. Although Griffin makes light of it, I fear I am a heavy burden on his little community. The brothers' white habits hang loosely on them now, for what they have they share with all who come and there cannot be much left in their store at this season. When Griffin sits at my bedside he sits like a tired man, I notice, and the lines on his face groove deep. I wonder, sometimes, what fresh troubles have broken out, that he knows and keeps from me. What use to ask? The days when I could give help to any man are over. I listen to his cheerful talk of small affairs and somehow we still find matter for laughter—though I have to be careful, for if laughter sets me coughing, I see his eyes are troubled. Alone, I lie and drowse and dream, hardly knowing night from day, living again the years when none of us was lonely.

"What shall I do with the child?" Ygern repeated my question, her head on one side, mocking me above the swaddled bundle in her arms.

I'd found her, waiting for me, so she'd said, in the barrack cell she'd made homey as women will, with woven hangings on the bunks, and at the tiny window, a flowering plant of some sort on the sill.

"We saw you ride in, Bedivere—Medraut and I. I stood at the edge of the throng and heard the news, my dear. The shouting frightened him, and he started to yell, so I came away and waited. I knew you'd guess where to find me," she'd said.

"Him—Medraut?" I'd queried. "Why 'Medraut'?"

She'd laughed at that, parting the woollen shawl to show a tiny dark head.

"Have you forgotten your Celtic? Ratling—small rat. One day, maybe, he'll earn himself a better name. It's what Kay called him, in temper, the first day—'that Saxon rat.' He said it in Latin, but 'Medraut' sounds better. Come and look at him."

The thing looked much like other babies to me. Tiny, smudgy-featured, but healthily pink, with a thatch of black hair, thin and soft as kitten fur. When its eyes opened, they had the same unfocused blueness as a very young kitten's, with the hint of a cast in one, and it mewed a little before the lids drooped and closed again.

"Well?" she challenged me, "What *shall* I do with him? Should he have been strangled at birth as Kay insists? Will Arthur blame me, too, because the thing wasn't done that way?"

I sat down abruptly on the spare bunk. Suddenly I realized that I was very tired.

"The gods know, my girl. All I know is it's too late to talk of that now."

She nodded, suddenly grave, no longer defensive.

"I'm sorry, Bedivere. I've managed badly, for myself and everyone. It was selfish of me to ride out that day, as I did. But, oh, I was suddenly so weary of this place, and of the long waiting for news, and the endless, idle chatter of women! I felt I must get away, just for a day. How could I guess a hare would cross my path and make the pony shy?"

"A hare?" I said. "That was a sign of bad luck anyway."

She shrugged.

"It certainly seemed so, at the time. But I don't know. The poor folk who took me in were kind and Alfia knew what to do. It wasn't as bad as most women make out, having him. He's healthy and not much trouble. He's only half a Saxon, after all, and they make good warriors.

Even Kay admits that. Time enough to decide his future when he's weaned!"

Bardeliez used to quote a proverb of the Silk People: "A journey of a thousand miles begins with a single step."

So, lightly, almost carelessly, unknowing the end, the first step towards Camlan had been taken.

I seldom saw Arthur so put out by any happening as he was when Celidon brought us news, early in the autumn, that Lot of Dalriada had died mysteriously, it was said of a wound, thought slight at first, he'd received in the battle.

"That man! All his life he cheated, and he has cheated me at the last. Celidon, I swore to you, when I was a child, I'd avenge my father's death on him—and he must die in his bed and rob me of my oath.

He was in one of his sudden passions, his hand on the hilt of Excalibur, his eyes blazing.

We'd been out on the exercise ground, watching some new hill ponies being broken in to replace the ones we'd lost in the northern campaign, and Celidon, whom we'd not seen since he harped us into battle at Silver Wood, had come quietly on us there, with his news.

He stood, swaying heel to toe in a way he had, smiling a little.

" 'Three things are matters for rejoicing: the love of a woman; the faith of a friend; the death of an enemy,' " he quoted softly. "Don't tempt your luck, Arthur. You'll find your path run the straighter without Lot of Dalriada in the way."

"Shall I? *Shall* I?" Arthur stormed at him. "You know what it will mean, for one thing. Gawain came to me as hostage, but he defied his father to stay and become one of my best young commanders. Now, I suppose, I must let him go back and lead that unruly Clan. He is—or thinks he is—my nephew, but he's Lot's heir, Celidon."

Celidon shrugged, his smile deepening.

"Calm yourself. Margause, who reckons herself your

sister, having disposed of the husband to whom, so she swears to me, she was far from devoted, will not deprive you of your commander. The Clan of Dalriada still worship Earth Mother, and it was their custom, until Lot took the High King's crown by force in your father's day, to be ruled by women. She has had herself proclaimed queen in her own right, and as such, she is on her way, now, to sue for peace, and cement a strong alliance with the Pendragon brother she has always admired and longs to meet."

*"What!"* Arthur stared at him. His fury would have been comical, if it had not been also terrifying. "Margause of Dalriada coming here? That I will *not* suffer, Celidon. I'll have no embassy from that treacherous Clan spying out our defenses. Have you gone mad?"

"Guessing that might be your answer, I persuaded her the journey was too long and perilous, especially so late in the season. I appointed the meeting at Caerleon. The voyage there by sea from Dalriada will be less fatiguing for a woman, and from here it should not take you more than a week's easy riding."

Suddenly Celidon dropped his light manner and spoke with authority:

"Take this chance while it offers, Arthur. Dalriada will give us a strongpoint in the north and, with Rheged, that Clan could hold the Picts back for a time, at need. That need could come, if the Saxons pressed us hard."

"Yes. Yes, that's true," Arthur said reluctantly. His eyes met Celidon's and for a moment it was as if two swords touched, blade to blade, each swordsman keeping equally his guard.

"So I must meet this—sister—of mine, Celidon?" Arthur said between his teeth.

Celidon nodded.

"The thing is written. A man cannot avoid his stars," he said.

A week later, we set out for Caerleon. I doubt if there was an unpatched tunic or a pair of sandals fit for marching in left between the whole garrison at the fort when our embassy and the guard we took with us had been fitted out. It was the first time I ever knew Arthur careful of appearances. To satisfy his new insistence, most of us had to borrow from friends. Kay even opened up the treasure chest and loaned Saxon plunder to those who lacked sufficient ornaments to make a showing. I myself wore some pirate's sword belt, sewn with gold plates and great lumps of red amber that matched well with Theodoric's arm ring.

Brusquely, Arthur ordered Ygern to choose a half a dozen women she could trust to behave themselves from among the officers' wives and see to it they were furnished with necessary clothing for an occasion.

"I'll need you and them to help me. I can't entertain a queen and her attendants with only the warriors of my staff present, even if she is close to kin to me. It would not be seemly," he told her curtly.

When she protested she could not go on account of the baby, there being just then no wet nurse she could leave him with, Arthur gave her one of the hard blue looks he used to turn on us when we were children together and had balked some challenge to adventure.

"Bring him with you, if you must. He'll take no hurt. That serving girl of yours can see to him most of the time, surely? I need you," he repeated.

She answered his look with a long, thoughtful glance, then agreed. She had always accepted his challenges. I thought, for some reason, she doubted the wisdom of this one. That, and the fact he was on edge, still, over the whole affair, made me vaguely uneasy.

Caerleon had been Ambrosius' chosen headquarters and still kept his memory green. It had a clean, prosperous look, old-fashioned Colonial, with municipal buildings dating back two hundred years or more and small trim villas, set among gardens and orchards. A pleasant, secure, civilized little town, that hadn't changed much since the days of Maximus. I could understand why Ambrosius loved it.

The citizens gave us a loyal reception, hanging out flags and garlands and lodging us all in more comfort than we'd known for a long while.

Three days after we got there, the embassy from

Dalriada sailed up the river, and Arthur received them in the great hall of the legate's palace.

No pains had been spared to make that reception impressive. We were inclined to jest, among ourselves, on the journey, we of the Companions, over Arthur's sudden demand for outward show, but one glance at him, as he entered the hall that morning, showed us an Arthur we had not seen before: a man in no mood for jesting. He looked magnificent, wearing a hauberk of bronze, inlaid with gold, over Celtic warrior dress, and, for the first time, the great white cloak that is the insignia of a War Duke. (It had been woven by the women of Caerleon, as a gift for Ambrosius, and left unfinished on the loom when they had news of his death. I heard they'd worked day and night to finish it since first they'd had news of Arthur's coming.) He'd had his hair and beard close-trimmed, but the Pendragon's circle, and his royal arm ring, were all the jewels he would wear. He took his place on the dais at the hall's end, attended by two pages, one carrying his helmet, the other his shield, and beside him stood old battle-scarred Ulfius, with the Dragon standard; Ulfius, who had seen Uther fall to Lot's sword, and (to judge from his grim expression) did not forget that fact. We of the Council were ranged behind them, and there was a guard, shoulder to shoulder, all down the hall.

Only Celidon was missing from our company—he, in his role of Merlin the Messenger, the peacemaker, had the task of meeting and escorting Dalriada's queen.

I remember the tense few moments while we waited —early sunlight falling through tall Roman archways, the sound of a cavalcade reining in outside the doors. Then Kay snapped a word of command, and the guards came to the salute, spears sloped. Deep and gay, and utterly startling, came the sound of a woman's voice beyond the doorway, and a soft, husky laugh.

"*Ought* I to be afraid of my brother, Lord Merlin?"

Arthur started, laying his hand on the hilt of Excalibur to still the grate of the scabbard point on the marble floor, and I heard him draw in his breath, sharply.

I don't know what we had been expecting—a daunting, masculine matron, in the hideous mustard tartan of Orkney, I suppose, or else a suppliant robed in sombre black. The woman who came in through the great doors, her hand just touching the Merlin's arm, her head up, her eyes alert and curious, shone, tawny and golden as a wheatfield at harvest. Tall, deep-breasted, hair the color of Arthur's swinging in two heavy braids down the front of a pale yellow tunic that caught the light, jewels glittering about her waist, on her arms and in the royal circlet that proclaimed her rank, she swept up the hall, a cloak of deepest wine-purple swinging out behind her, to kneel at Arthur's feet. With a gesture at once dignified, yet apparently impulsive, she lifted the queen's circlet from her head with both hands and held it up to him.

"Pendragon of Britain—Arthur my brother—accept the homage of Dalriada!" she said, and her voice rang through the hall like a deep harp chord.

If Arthur was nonplussed, he did not show it. With dignity that rivalled hers, slowly and deliberately he took the crown, held it up a moment for all to see, then set it back, firmly and gently, on that shining hair.

"I accept the homage. Rise, Queen of Dalriada. Be welcome, Margause, my sister!" he said, and raised her and kissed her ceremonially on both cheeks.

As they stood together, both smiling, I saw a likeness between them. It was unmistakable. Only the eyes of Margause were different—velvet-brown, dark and unfathomable as a mountain tarn—and, for all the softness of her wide, clever mouth, I thought, as cold.

"More like a priestess of Dionysius than of grim old Earth Mother, that one. It's a good thing she *is* the Lord Arthur's sister, otherwise we'd be blowing for trouble if you ask me," Palomides remarked flippantly, a few days later, as we were strolling back together across river fields towards the town, after a review of our troops by the king and the Dalriada embassy. "I'd never have guessed he had such a soldier's eye for a good-looking baggage, Verus!"

I laughed.

"The Bear's no monk and never has been! It hasn't

softened the terms he's meted out to her council. Admit
that. They looked like men biting into a sour lemon when
they put their marks to the parchment this morning."

"But they put them," Palomides said, approvingly.
"Did you notice the queen, herself, was the only member
of that contingent who could write? I admired the flourish
with which she did it. She's a good loser—if she counts
this treaty a loss. Perhaps, unlike her council, she
doesn't?"

"Perhaps not," I said. "By her own account, alliance
with us has always been her dearest dream. She's even
happy to leave two more of her sons as hostages, did you
notice? Where else could they learn so well the arts of
war and the manners of a court?' was all she said, when
the clause was read to her."

"But she's kept back the youngest one—Gareth—
playing on the king's kindliness with that dewy-eyed plea
about the boy's youth and her loneliness. Dalriada is sure
of an heir. If I'd been the Lord Arthur, I'd have made
sure of the whole brood," Palomides said meditatively. "I
don't trust that woman, Verus."

I shrugged.

"Who does? Not Celidon. Not Arthur. But at least
she's gay and amusing and good company. That goes for
something in these hard times. I haven't laughed so much
for years as I have the last few days—and neither have
you—neither, for that matter, has Arthur. We'd grown
intense and earnest at the fort this past year, I'm thinking.
We needed a holiday!"

Palomides shook his head.

"Shall I ever understand you islanders? You meet
the envoys of your most implacable enemies, enemies of
twenty years' standing. I expect stern looks, harsh words,
hands on the sword hilt, and what happens? Gaity, feasting, and we go hunting and hawking together to 'show
them good sport.' The king makes a present of his own
rare white gier-falcon to the wife of the man who killed
his father, and she confides that man's sons to him for
their future education. Well—we can only hope it all turns
out for the best!"

"It will—as long as Arthur's men go on winning

battles," I said cynically. "If they don't—parchment burns in fire! That's about the size of it, and for all he's enjoying his new-found sister's company more than he expected, you can depend on it, Arthur's got the facts clear enough—he *and* Celidon."

"I'm glad you're so confident. I'll tell you one person who is not—and she's a shrewd little judge of character— that's Ygern. She, at any rate, hasn't been fooled by Queen Margause, Verus. She hates—and fears her. Did you know that?"

"Jealousy. She's always wanted that white gierfalcon!" I said lightly.

My task, as Arthur's Chief Companion, during that meeting at Caerleon, was to play sheepdog to the council of Dalriada.

"Keep watch on those dour greybeards, Bedivere. They were my father's enemies, and I've a feeling none of them has much love for my father's son," Arthur told me, after the first day. "I'll not have them poking and prying about, maybe feeing our men with drink money to learn just how matters stand with us back at the fort. Let them return to Dalriada believing we are as well founded and carefree as the show we have put on here would lead folk to believe."

The work was wearisome, but I think I did it successfully. Glum and sour at first, very watchful of their dignity, the northlanders thawed towards me when I'd taken some pains to let them know I was Colonial born and descended from an emperor of whom even they had heard. Their kind set store by a man's ancestry. They set store, also, I discovered, by good living, not being accustomed to it at home. The citizens of Caerleon must have strained their resources to feast us as royally as they did each evening. By the week's end I had begun to count days until the Dalriada galleys were due to sail. It did not please me that, the weather having fallen flat calm, it looked as if their departure might be delayed.

I was on my way, after a last day's hunting with them, to change my clothes before the evening's entertainment, and looking forward to the luxury of a bath (which the villa in which I'd been lodged provided), when Alfia waylaid me.

"Sir Bedivere, sir, could you come to the mistress? She's wanting a private word with you."

"Where is she?" I asked. Then, noticing the woman's face, "Is there anything wrong, Alfia?"

Her usual cheery impudence was lacking. She looked flushed and glum.

"Wrong? I'll say there is! Proper taking she's been in since morning. The gods know what's biting her, for she won't tell *me*, but if she goes on as she is, her milk'll turn on her, and then we'll have trouble and to spare. That precious little lamb of ours is puking as it is, his stomach all upset with his feeds being irregular—not that that can be helped, with all the carry-on there is here, and her for ever at the beck and call of all and sundry. See what you can do with her, sir. She listens to you. She's waiting over yonder in the orchard—down that path and there's a gate in the wall at the bottom."

Ygern and I lodged next door to one another. I crossed the small garden that lay behind my own pleasant quarters, and went through a postern, in a wall of mellow brick, direct into the orchard of the adjoining villa. The place was small and neat and Roman-orderly, the trunks of the apple trees freshly whitened, red apples thick among the turning leaves, the grass close-scythed. In the exact centre was a well, with a low marble surround, and a fancy ironwork bucket-wheel.

Ygern had been sitting there, but she got up quickly, and came towards me.

"At last! I thought you'd never come!" she greeted me. "Bedivere, you have got to help me. That woman Margause—she frightens me."

Her face looked pinched and white, her eyes large and shadowed.

"You, frightened?" I said. "That's not like you, my girl. What's the trouble?"

"Don't make a jest of it. It's serious." (I could tell from her tone she was seething with impatience.) "I hate that woman—she's a sly, designing bitch, and she's got the Bear wound round her little finger. I'd never have guessed he could be fooled so easily. Men!"

I took her wrist and led her back to sit by the well.

"Tell me then. What's happened? But keep your voice down, girl. No need to tell all Caerleon."

She laughed angrily at that, then bit her lip. I realized her laugh was not far from a sob.

"Bedivere, Margause thinks I'm Arthur's light o'love, and the Ratling's his. Do what I can, I can't convince her otherwise. She just smiles at me sideways, strokes my hair, and calls me a 'sweet, discreet little soul.' I *hate* her!"

I stared, dumbfounded for a moment, then, as the full meaning of her words struck home, I burst out laughing.

Her face flamed.

"It's no laughing matter—not to me," she said tensely.

"I'm sorry," I apologized, sobered. "I only laughed because, whatever you may be, at the moment 'sweet little soul' hardly describes you. It *was* an insult, my dear, but I doubt if Margause the Queen meant it as such. You and I have lived too far out of the world for too long. This is something both Arthur and I should have foreseen. If we had, we could have saved you from it. Don't take it too much to heart."

She shook her head impatiently, staring at me.

"What would I care for that sort of insult? Don't be Roman-stupid. No. It was what she said next that made me afraid. She asked me why in the world Arthur did not marry me and make me his queen? She watched me while she said it as a cat watches a bird. I said I doubted if we should do well married. Having grown up together we knew each other's faults too well.

" 'Like brother and sister, aren't you?' she said softly, then.

"Bedivere, that woman suspects the truth. She was old enough, before Uther married her off, to have overheard some careless word—even a look, a gesture, can betray a great deal to a girl who hates as she must have

hated Uther. Remember, she may well have blamed him
for her father's murder (many did), and it can't have
endeared him to her that he bundled her off to marry a
man twice her age at what must have seemed to her the
world's end. No wonder if she incited Lot to turn against
him—I might have done the same at the same age, given
the same incentive. She and I are close kin, remember,
though I'd rather we were not!

"When I did not answer her, she walked away from
me and stood looking out of the window. I think she may
have been as angry as I was, but she hides it better.
Suddenly she came back, put her arm round me and
whispered:

" 'Keep your secret, if you must, obstinate child. But
I'm your friend and Arthur's. Trust me, and I'll take that
little indiscretion of yours back with me to Dalriada. I
promise you he would be gently reared—given the education of a High Prince. Someday, one never knows, Arthur
might be glad to acknowledge your—Saxon bastard. Until
then, you and I could keep the matter close. What do you
say to that?' "

"What did you say?" I asked.

Ygern made a grimace, half apologetic, half defiant.

"Nothing. I took a woman's way out of a tight
corner. I burst into tears and fled. But the gods know
where we go from here. What will she do, Bedivere?"

"Nothing. What can she do? She may, as you imagine, have some vague suspicions of a mystery surrounding
Arthur's birth. She can have no proof, or she'd have used
it before now, while Lot was alive. She can hardly kidnap
your Ratling out of hand for whatever purpose she wants
him. If that's what you fear, I'll set a guard round your
lodging tonight. Tomorrow, the gods being good to us,
she'll sail home. There's a wind stirring the apple trees
already, and the weather's on the change. Back at the fort
we can forget Margause, my dear. There'll be better
things to think about."

I sent her indoors comforted in the end, convinced
she'd let her imagination run away with her reason. Indeed, at the time I thought she had. The only thing in the
whole story that seemed to me of importance was an

abrupt realization that others, beside Margause, might well be interpreting what they saw by their own standards. I wondered, startled, if perhaps half the fort gave small Medraut credit for better blood than a Saxon pirate's?

# III
# ALLEGRO

# Chapter Thirteen

Brother Paulinus' record grows too slowly. I see his eyes fixed on me sometimes with the anxiety of a hound who, having waited patiently through an evening's feast, begins to fear after all the bones will not be thrown to him. I weary quickly, and when I am weary, my mind becomes confused. I remember the scenes of the past, but not their sequence. His insistent questions as to the exact place, the exact year, sting like horseflies at midsummer, and irritate as much. I welcome the clanging of the little bell that calls him to his prayers and rids me of him. Old men grow selfish!

Once he is gone, I lie at peace again, and the winters and the summers of those early years run together in my mind, bright as April raindrops, sliding, many-colored, down a flowering branch. Those glittering, glinting years, when we were all young, and danger threatened every hour, giving life a quality Paulinus can never know, the taut, singing tension of a stretched harpstring. Years when the blue flash on a jay's wing passing, the song of a storm cock in winter twilight, the scent of fresh-mown hay on some upland meadow, struck home, sharp as a spear-thrust, breathing always the whisper: *"This may be the last time. Beyond death who can tell how much we shall remember?"*

No chronicler—Paulinus least of all, for I, certainly, can never give him the facts—will set down a complete record of the fighting of those early years, for we fought

more than half our time in small, scattered, independent
bands, each reckless young commander trusted to use his
wits. It was hill fighting in the west against Irish pirates;
forest fighting in the south, where bandits and broken
men lived by plunder and thieving; coastal patrols fought
often up to the knees in breaking surf, or floundering and
cursing among bog and reeds along the banks of some
marshy inlet, where we turned back single prowling Saxon
raiders. There were skirmishes that seemed like battles,
and battles we counted at the time as mere skirmishes.
We were so few, still, for all that needed doing. Speed and
surprise were always Arthur's watchwords. To implement
them, he sometimes had to spread his forces dangerously
thin. Not all who rode out from the Great Fort to answer
urgent distress calls, brought by the Merlin's messengers,
those tireless, barefoot runners, came back again, to hear
the trumpets sound "All's well" at evening, and smell the
homely welcome of the cooking fires. But the tactics paid
steadily more interest every year, as the rumor spread
that wherever need was desperate, there, miraculously,
Arthur's men would appear. After a while, the common
people themselves grew bold enough to grab what weapons they could find, and hold out until help came to
them.

I remember the first time Arthur and I had proof of
that, ourselves. It was late on an afternoon of early
spring, though which spring of which year I could not
swear to. For once we were together, leading a little band,
somewhere away on the Durotriges coast, foraging for
supplies. I remember the clatter and clanking of our
equipment, as we rode at ease down a stony combe
between catkinned hazel bushes, and I know I was glad to
smell the sea again and hear gulls crying.

With a jolt, I realized it was not only the gulls that
screamed. Women were screaming to each other, as well,
in the Celtic, and we'd ridden, before we knew it, full tilt
into a bunch of refugees. They were all round us—young
women, with small children and babies. Some I saw
carried one baby, with a toddler riding on their backs,
and half a dozen little boys and girls clinging to their
skirts.

I've never forgotten their faces—thin, hungry-looking, tearstained—but all lit up at the sight of us, unbelieving, illumined, as if they saw a vision. They pressed in against the horses, kissing our feet, plucking at our cloaks, catching at our hands, urging us on, begging us to hurry, all pointing down towards the shore. I looked that way, over their heads, and saw, though only for a second, small and clear, like a picture painted in a monk's prayer book, the silver of the calm sea in the late afternoon light, the flash of oars, and the black snake's head of a war galley turning in to beach. On the wet brown sand, between the galley and a little cluster of huts, the men of the village, and the young boys, and even a few grey-haired women, had ranged themselves: not more than a score at most, their homespun rags fluttering from half-naked bodies, and in their hands such pitiful weapons in the face of Saxon seaxes—pitchforks, scythes, a blacksmith's hammer, and the curved bronze knives that fishermen use to gut ther catch.

I thought incredulously, "Gods! They mean to fight!"

I only got that one, short glimpse. Then there was a flash, between me and them, as Arthur drew Excalibur and gave us the battle-cry:

"*Britain and Freedom!*"

We killed quickly, and as cleanly as we could that day, and we left no wounded. (Desperate folk, with long scores to pay, cannot be trusted not to prolong that payment, and Arthur never countenanced torture.)

When all was finished, and the freckled ripples of the outgoing tide ran red under the glaring black prow of the stranded galley, Arthur, on foot, embraced those ragged, ill-smelling peasants as though they had been his dearest companions, and the tears were running down into his beard, unheeded, while he praised their courage, and swore to them they had given him, the War Duke of Britain and their king, new strength of heart, and more happiness than the arrival of an army of trained warriors, coming in to join his standard.

"I and my men will fight for you, and the like of you, all our lives. But today you have shown me Britain is ready, at last, to fight for herself, to fight *with* me. This is the proof I have been waiting for, my friends, since the first day of my Choosing," he told them.

I doubt if they understood him. Even his speech must have been strange to their ears, set against their slow, slurring accent. But they understood that he loved them, cared for them, was proud of their will to resist the enemy, who, but for our chance coming, must have overwhelmed and slaughtered them where they stood.

We left them the galley, and all the spoils and weapons of the dead—wealth, for them, beyond their wildest dreams, it must have been. We took nothing back from that victory but the assurance of their heartfelt loyalty and the love in their eyes as they pressed about Arthur's horse at parting. We needed nothing more. They had given us the promise of new times.

We did not always have reason to think so highly of our own people. I remember a day when Arthur came back from a foray, with a face so pale and set I thought he must be wounded, until I realized anger at others' pain, not the drag of his own, was what ailed him.

"Get me Palomides, and quickly. Every man of my band carries a child who needs his tending," he said to me.

He'd come, by chance, on slavers, driving a gang of boys and girls they'd aimed to sell cheap to the Irish pirates down in Lyonesse.

"Chained by the neck, barefoot and starving—and the brutes with them our own people. Children, Bedivere, some not eight years old! By the gods, I was never so tempted to flay men alive!" he exploded furiously. "We'll stop that filthy trade. I'll not have Britain soiled by it!"

Later that day Palomides came to him and asked leave to lead whatever mopping-up operation was contemplated.

"I'd like to make it the first proof that the lads I've been training have learned to shoot straight," he said grimly. "Those children have broken ribs where they've been kicked, and backs where the flies have got into the lash strokes, my lord. One boy's been forced to walk on a poisoned foot until it has gangrened. They are all scabrous, filthy and starving."

Arthur looked from his face to mine and said between his teeth:

"And the men I hanged seemed surprised when they saw the rope! They said, as if it excused all, that they only bought from parents willing to sell since most, if not all, those children were chance-gotten by Saxon raiders, and shamed the villages where they were born. 'Such children bring bad luck. Best out of sight and out of mind, folk think,' one fellow told me. When he begged for mercy, I gave him as much as he had given."

I thought of Medraut and wished Ygern need not hear of this, but knew she must.

Surprisingly, of all the Companions, Lancelot seemed the one most deeply moved to pity. He spent hours with Palomides in the hospital block, the next few days, tender as a woman. Later, passing the open doors, one heard laughter and shrill little voices calling to him by name. Once I met him coming out, and he smiled at me, half apologetic.

"Children soon forget. I teach them to play again," he explained.

I had not known before that he loved children so much. I said something of the sort to Palomides. He looked thoughtful.

"That man has healing in his hands. I wonder if he knows it?" he said.

When, later, Palomides went westward into Lyonesse, I went with him. Geraint, whose territory it was, had welcomed the offer of our help along his northern seaboard.

"To tell the truth, it's work that's needed doing a long while. For years the Irish have been setting up robber-holds among the cliffs and crags, where slave-trains such as you came upon are guarded until they can be shipped to the markets of Tara. My Clansmen drag their feet whenever the question arises of cleaning out the pirates. There's money to be made by slaving, and I suspect more than half the petty Chiefs are bribed to turn a blind eye to it, and the poorer folk are too much afraid of those bandits to lift a finger against them. Do what you can, and you'll deserve nothing but gratitude from me!"

Wild work we had of it for a month or two. (That was when Palomides taught me to shoot with the powerful Persian bow. I'd never thought of it as a weapon suited to a man of any standing before. But I learned from him its uses in mountain warfare, and in those days Arthur was the first to mock anyone among us who put his dignity above practical necessity.) We took and burned a dozen or more stinking eyries, using fire arrows to set ablaze places that had been considered impregnable for years. Our lads called it "burning out wasps' nests." On occasion we discovered wasps sting, for the Irish are savage fighters. What we found in those places turned the stomachs of some of our raw youngsters, and persuaded every one of us that night marches through bog and forest and the scaling of dizzy crags in the dawn was labor well spent. When we caught native slave traders we hanged them where roads met, and gave orders they should be left hanging as a warning. Arthur's men intended to police the highways of Britain at least as well as the legions had policed them for four hundred years. Slave traffic is old as time, and no reasonable man expects it done away with. But it can be carried on decently, as Bardeliez proved, without barbaric torture of the unfortunate.

The poorer folk who had lived under the shadow of those pirate dens left us in no doubt of their feelings, by the end of our campaign.

"No shepherd alone with his flock; no farmer returning late from market; no girl washing clothes in a lonely Outland stream, has been safe for years, my lord," an old headman of one of the villages told me earnestly. "Now we have proof the Pendragon remembers us, there is a new heart in the people here. Tell him Lyonesse is grateful."

It seems to me now that I returned to the fort from that expedition to find a ship had sailed that never reached the port in Armorica for which it had been chartered. But I must be wrong, for the bracken had turned and the last leaves were falling as Palomides and I came up from the west country that year, well pleased with ourselves and our small, seasoned troops. The ship we always called "the children's ship" sailed on a May Day. I remember Kay telling me that, for it is a day Roman superstition has always held to be unlucky.

I know he met with the news when I'd been away some time and come back happy, and that what he had to tell took all the brightness from my day.

He fidgeted about his small, cramped quarters, where I'd gone to report to him, for, as often happened, Arthur was absent at the time and he was in command.

When he took a jug of home-made blackberry wine out of some secret nook and poured us both a drink, I know I was surprised at his unusual hospitality and wondered what was coming next, for he was seldom lavish with his stores.

"Sit down, Bedivere. Something unpleasant—very unpleasant—has happened here, while you have been away. You'd better know the facts from me," he said. I thought he looked older, and more careworn than usual.

"Bad news? A defeat?" I asked.

"Oh, no, no, no! Nothing like that," he said irritably.

Then he told me, in his own roundabout, jerky fashion, losing the thread of the story here and there, while he apportioned blame, partly to Lancelot (who, as a foreigner, he'd not learned to trust in those days) but, surprisingly, even more to himself.

It happened that Lancelot had come back from wintering in his own country with an offer to give a home out there to the children rescued from the slavers, and to any other unwanted half-breed bastards parents cared to sell to him. He'd made generous arrangements for them to be adopted into some Christian community of his uncle's founding, where he promised they'd be well cared for.

"Raised as monks and nuns, I suppose. A good idea it seemed to me, since it'd ensure at least they'd not breed more bad stock," Kay said grumpily.

A galley had been chartered to take them. But it had

not reached Armorica. There had been a storm. Wreckage had washed up on the Armorican shore.

"I blame myself. The shipmaster was a Phoenician. One of those insolent, blustering fellows who thinks himself a sea-god and will take advice from nobody. Our folk warned him the weather would worsen, but he seemed to be in a great hurry to be gone, and swore he knew the coast and where he could run for shelter at need. I should have *ordered* him to stay in port until the storm had blown itself out. I blame myself. Yes, I blame myself for the whole disaster!" Kay said, and I could see the thing weighed heavy on him—more heavily than seemed reasonable.

"Well," I said, "accidents do happen, Kay. It was a sad tragedy, I agree. But it can't be helped. No use brooding on it."

He looked at me and I was shocked to see there were tears in his eyes.

"Ygern's child was on that ship, Bedivere. She sent him, and the nurse-girl Alfia to care for him on the journey. I went down to the port to see them safely bestowed for her—I'd not have gone, else. I'd been very much impressed by her courage and common sense in parting with the brat. She knew how I felt about the whole business from the start, though. I only hope she doesn't think I let them sail because I'd always felt that child would be better dead!"

"Where is she now?" I asked.

"Celidon took her away after we got the news. I believe to some holy island or shrine or something. 'A place of healing,' he said. Poor girl! She took it very well, I will say. Father would have been proud of her. But I was sorry about the whole thing. I always shall be.

The winter before the Battle of the Blackwater came in early. The cold began soon after Samain, and it was March before the snow thawed. It was one of those rare great winters (much as this has been) which come every twenty years or so in Britain and stand out in the memory, a talking point every autumn, until the next one comes. A little before the shortest day, a blizzard blocked even the legion roads four feet deep in snow, and froze the marshland hard enough to bear a loaded bullock train. The fort was well provisioned and we'd wood enough to keep us warm twice over; once in the cutting and hauling, and again when great fires blazed in hall and cooking pits.

On a glittering morning, when the sun turned the long icicles to rainbows, but gave no heat at all, so that an ungloved hand laid carelessly on the sword hilt stuck to the iron with the pain of a burn, a hunter came to the north gate, carrying two wild geese. He was the first visitor we'd had in weeks and the gate guards called me, as centurion of the day, to look him over.

I liked the look of his geese better than I liked the look of him. He was a rough type, bundled up in black sheepskins, with a hat of the same stuff pulled low over scowling brows, and a beard that covered what little of the rest of his face might have been visible. He spoke civilly enough, in an accent I could not place, asking as a favor that he might present his Midwinter gift of the birds to the High King as a good-luck token, for he had, he said, a desire to see so great a warrior as the Pendragon for himself. I guessed him an outlaw and had the guard search him for weapons. Though Arthur never refused any man audience, there were those who might fee a bandit well to take his life, in those days, and something about the fellow made me uneasy. Then I took him myself across to the Great Hall.

Arthur was standing by the fire that burned night and day in the centre of it, with Gawain and some of the youngest commanders round him, showing the boys how to read an itinerary map. Gaheris and Aglavain, Gawain's hostage brothers, were pressed close in on each side of him, their alert faces for once solemn with concentration, as they peered at the scrap of parchment they held between them, and Gaheris, with twelve-year-old cock-sureness, was proclaiming:

"Aye, there's some point in book learning if a wee scrap of sheep-skin like yon can show a man the way to lead his armies from Vectis to the Wall. I see fine now what you mean, my lord."

In the background Gawain murmured, with elder-brotherly mockery: "He sees it fine, since he's looking at it the wrong way up! Move over, now, and let the others have a turn."

Aware suddenly of interruption, the group broke apart and turned to stare at the stranger I brought with me.

Arthur gave the man one of his keen, assessing glances, then smiled.

"What's this, Bedivere?" he asked.

"A hunter, with tribute for your Midwinter feast. Speak up, fellow, and doff your cap before the Pendragon."

The man shambled forward, made a sketchy obeisance, and a gesture of the hand as if to a forelock, but failed to remove the sheepskin from his head.

"Greetings, lord king. I bring you good eating in hard weather. I bring also a message—but it was to be for your hearing alone," he mumbled.

"Do you, now?" Arthur's hand shot out quick as the dart of an adder's tongue, knocking off the black, enveloping headgear, then he took the man by his beard, and wrenched that, also, away, and held it at arm's length, while we all gasped in amazement. He threw back his head and laughed—a great, echoing shout of laughter that rolled up to the smoke-darkened rafters.

"Next time, Celidon the Merlin, remember to cover your hands, I'd know them anywhere! Wasn't it you, yourself, who taught me on our first journey together that hands can betray any disguise faster than faces? Now—what is all this? A Midwinter jest, or what?"

My "outlaw," with a swift gesture, pulled off shaggy false eyebrows, and, giving the geese to a goggling Gaheris to hold, shrugged out of his padded sheepskin tunic.

"Fair enough, Arthur. You made a good pupil and you remember your lessons well. I should never have saluted you, but Bedivere was so insistent I must show respect!"

I joined in the laughter.

"You fooled me, Merlin the Magician," I admitted.

"I'm sorry—I'd never have had you searched if I'd had
even a clue who you were.

His strange eyes met mine, with a rare glint of
warmth in them.

"Arthur is guarded as he should be." Then—"Mind
those geese, boy! They've been singed well enough. No
need to start them roasting until the hour of the feast is
nearer!" Celidon grinned at Gaheris, who, his eyes almost
out of his head with amazement, was backing dangerously
near the fire. "Now, tell me—are you set for good sport
here to mark the solstice? I've travelled a long, hard road
to be in time to share it." He held his hands—those long,
thin harper's hands—to the warmth of the fire and shivered.

"A festival that needed only our own harper to make
it the best we've had in years. We've missed you, Celidon.
Where have you been since summer's ending?" Arthur
asked.

Celidon shrugged.

"Where indeed?" His eyes swept our faces, and
came to rest on the half-scared, half-admiring stares of
the two youngest. "Up to the gates of the Northern Star,
and down into the pit of Anawn, maybe. My travels are
for the king's private ear. Bedivere's hunter said he had a
message, remember?"

"Come with me. We'll go to my quarters." Arthur
laid an arm about his shoulders, and they moved off
together. I heard him say, in a lower tone, "We've been
starved for news, here—but I never dreamed you'd get
through to us in this weather."

As they disappeared through the far door, Aglavain
drew a deep breath.

"Has yon old wizard *really* been to the Northern
Star?" he whispered, awed.

Gaheris shook his head.

"I'm doubting myself he meant it—though that kind
can do the like if they've a mind, folk say. Would you
think these two great birds are just magic, Lord Bedivere,
or would they be for real? You never can tell with a
wizard, now, can you?"

I laughed.

"Take them to Kay. They'll not fly off the spit and vanish up the chimney, I promise you that."

He swallowed and licked his lips.

"If they dinna, they'll make fine eating for someone," he said, hopefully.

When the solstice was over and, though the days began to lengthen, the weather, if anything, got worse, I searched about for ways to keep up the spirits of the garrison. The notion of a mock attack on the fort, half of the men a side, occurred to me. I'd detected a weak spot in the ramparts, I thought, so laid a plan, and went in search of Arthur to ask if I might lead the attacking force.

I found him on the signal tower of the north gate, sitting on a pile of slingers' stones, drawing patterns in the snow with a hazel rod. He listened to my suggestion without looking up, then shook his head and said curtly:

"Waste of time. We've no leisure to play at war. Real war's coming again in the spring—total war. We've got to prepare for that now."

"What makes you think it will?" I asked.

He glanced up at me.

"I don't think, I know. It's my business to know. You don't imagine geese were all Celidon had been hunting since summer end, do you? He brought news, and it's reliable. There will be a full-scale invasion in the spring—Saxons, Jutes, Frisians, the lot. They've made an alliance, under a new man—Cerdic. They'll come in somewhere where the Federates are strong and well established—and the Federates will rise with them. Sit down, and I'll show you."

I blinked, taking in the size and shape of the threat.

"It sounds serious," I said slowly.

"Of course it's serious. Sit down before I have to knock you down—I want to show you how it'll go. I've been working out the probabilities. Look at this map . . ."

I sat down quickly beside him, wishing he could have chosen a warmer spot for a conference. It was one of those bitter, still afternoons, of iron frost, when the cloud cover is like a pewter cauldron inverted over the earth, and the snow holds more light than the sky above it. But when he was occupied, Arthur never noticed weather. I saw the sketch he had been drawing made the outline of a map.

"See here—that's roughly the shape of Britain. Here's Lyonesse and Dumnonia, coming up from the Land's End, with the Durotriges country widening out above. Not more trouble than we're used to expecting, there. Now, follow the southern coastline along this way. You come to Vectis and the estuary. That's a danger point. They landed there before, they may try again, but I doubt it. They'll know of our fleet, for what it's worth, waiting at Adurni. Up here, round Onna and Clausentium, at the head of the estuary, if our scouts are right, there are bands of Jutes, roving around in the forest. They got cut off up there, last year, by all accounts. They'll have to stay where they are until they choose to come out. I don't believe in hunting wild boar in a thicket. If the attack does come up Vectis water, we'll watch out for them, though. They'll be on the flank of the old Novemagus road, and we'll need to hold that, and keep it clear all the way, for transport.

"Now, where I expect trouble is further up here." His stick prodded the snow. "It's those cursed Federate farmers, along the Cantii coastline, towards Anderita, where there are shallow landing beaches, who've been getting into cahoots with Cerdic for a year past. (They're kissing kin, after all, so that's no surprise to me.) Do you see what it'll mean?"

He'd taught us all some of his skill with maps, and I'd ridden over most of that coastal country a dozen times in the years since I'd got back from the mainland, either fighting or patrolling. I saw only too clearly what he meant.

"That's bad, Bear," I said slowly. "We can't defend a line as long as that. We haven't got the men."

"Of course we can't, and we shan't try," Arthur said impatiently. "What we need to do is this . . ."

The stick moved again, in quick strokes, and sharp, prodding dots.

"By my guess, they'll attack from the south and east at the same time, calling up their Federate allies from the

Londinium river valleys to protect their flank. It's what I should do, and Cerdic by all accounts is a good war leader. If I were in his shoes I'd try for surprise and march fast inland for Calleva. Look. It commands five roads—good roads. Once get those, you can smash northwest, up this way, to Corinum and Glevum, south to Venta, southwest to Isca. If once we let them get to Calleva, they'll be all over us at once; and there won't be a harvest in the Heartland this year *or* next. We've got to hold Calleva at all costs, and in depth. It shouldn't be too difficult. The one weak spot is *here*," he pointed, "but we've got the river line along the Blackwater, from where it crosses the Calleva-Londinium road, down to Trisontana ford. That's going to be where the crunch is bound to come, and that's where we'll start digging ourselves in, as soon as the buds turn grey on the willows. The War Branch must go out early, this year."

I studied the map closely.

"One thing I don't like. Suppose they turn our flank and get up behind us?"

He chuckled.

"You'll make a general, yet! Thanks to Ambrosius, who met the same trouble ten years or so ago, we've got the Dike—fifty miles of it—to keep our backsides warm. Kay can take charge of that for us, patrolling night and day with fast pony patrols. He can have a few of his precious catapults with him. You and I know they're antiquated lumber to cart around in these times, but he's got a passionate faith in them still and they'd look forbidding mounted on a Dike wall—to Saxons, anyway, who've never seen better!"

He paused, frowning down at the crisp little ridges of the map, where its edges were already freezing over.

"I think we can do it. We've got to do it. We've got to keep those murdering devils out of the Heartland, Bedivere. It's always the bait that brings them."

I nodded.

"You can't be surprised. Every Saxon's a farmer. After their bleak homeland our corn country must seem like the Islands of the Blest. If the Frisians are coming, *they've* been living on dunghills in the sea, by all ac-

counts, for years, eating their fish raw because they'd no
fuel to cook it with. I don't blame any of the bastards for
thinking Britain's worth a try! One other thing, Bear—
with all this on our plates, what about the north? Can we
trust the Rheged to hold the Picts for a season, and the
Dalriada not to see this as the moment to forget their
treaty?"

Arthur shrugged and gave me one of his quick,
sidelong glances.

"I'm not a proud man, Bedivere—not when I'm in
as tight a corner as this one. The first galley that can get
out of Vectis water is going to carry word to Lancelot
that I need him again (or any good commander like Bors,
if he can't come himself), with enough Armoricans to put
some extra starch in old Leodogrance's tunic until summer's end. We ought not to need them longer. If I know
him, he'll be happy to do our Pict-hunting for us this
season."

He got up, brushing the snow from his tunic. A look
of concern crossed his face, and he felt the back of his
leather breeches.

"Christian devils! That snow was *wet*," he remarked
in an affronted tone  "Brr, it's cold up here! Why in the
name of the gods must you gossip for a sentry-watch in a
place like this when there's fire and food in the hall?
Come on down, before we both freeze."

So it began, the struggle that was to prove the first major
turning point in the fortunes of Free Britain.

Four pitched battles we fought against Cerdic and
his combined war host, along the Blackwater river, and
we didn't win them easily. All summer through, the enemy attacked again and again, as a bull attacks, charging
and charging, until he falls from sheer exhaustion. I
wonder if men today, or in times still far off, will guess
the weariness of hearing those cursed Saxon conches
moaning dawn after weary dawn through half a year,
while the outcome of invasion hung in the balance? I
wonder how many old men still wake, sweating, when
they dream they face a charge of Berserkers? Palomides
swore a chariot charge was more unnerving, but I did not

agree. There's something eerie about those naked, demented suicide squads that still makes my stomach heave when I remember it. I never discovered if the Oden priests drug them before battle, or if it is genuine religious fervor that drives them on, glassy-eyed, howling like wolves, froth on their lips, stepping on the piles of their own dead as if they didn't see them. They are like mad beasts, those men, and like mad beasts they are the most dangerous of all fighters.

I got my first serious wound from one of them, oiled, as they all are, from top to toe, who slipped through my hands when I thought I'd finished him and, with his last dying snarl, jabbed up at me, and laid my right thigh open to the bone on the inner side. Luckily it was nearing the end of the campaign, and Palomides got me mended enough to be in for the final, decisive confrontation, though I was glad to get out of the saddle when it was over, and leave the youngsters to finish the job of chasing the last fugitives right back to the coastal settlements. They enjoyed that, and by the Light, they'd earned their fun! We thought, that night, the whole war was over. Lucky for us we hadn't the Merlin's Sight and could not guess that twelve more long battle-years still lay ahead, for we'd paid the price of victory high. There would be more empty places set at the board on Samain night than most of us cared to think about. But the Blackwater campaign turned the tide for us. Word of it rang through Britain, and the new men who flocked to the Dragon standard because of that word filled the gaps that were left ten times over. We did not forget the faces we should never see again. Caw the Hunter's was one of them.

# Chapter Fourteen

It was Arthur's custom from the first to call those of the senior command he had named as his Companions to Council and discuss with them whatever plans he had in mind. Often the meeting would be short—a matter of briefing each of us for the day's duty. But after Blackwater, they grew longer.

"Having won an interval of peace, let's use it to advantage. There's a lot needs doing in Britain besides making war," he told us briskly.

I remember a morning when, to my consternation, he looked round the rough, scrubbed table, at the upper end of the fort's Great Hall, where we met, and said, quite casually:

"Well, my friends, the last link's broken. Like it or leave it, Britain is independent. Yesterday I sent word to Byzantium, in answer to a demand, the tone of which I did not like, that since Rome sends us no help, we pay no more tribute."

"Tribute?" Kay, at his right hand, spluttered. "Tribute? They dared demand that—after all these years?"

Arthur laughed.

"After all these years!" he repeated, "*and* for all the years it has been owing, what's more. Oh, the account was long and detailed, I can tell you! Some clerk in the notary's office must have burned oil and to spare reckoning it. He sent, as well, a list of the offices of government, requiring to know (for his files, he explained) the names

of those who held them at present, since he doubted his
record was something out of date. Forty years and more,
it must have been! But that is something we can put to
use."

He proceeded, briefly and clearly, to outline the
structure by which Britain had been governed before the
time of the Troubles.

"Good, solid Roman foundations, on which we can
begin to rebuild. Sound as a legionary road, to my way of
thinking." His eyes swept round the circle of doubtful,
attentive faces. "Granted, like the roads, we'll need to
patch them in places. This is how I propose we do it."

I realized, as he went on speaking, that what he said
could not be the outcome of one night's thinking. It was a
plan he must have been perfecting in his head for months,
probably years.

(When I questioned him curiously about that, later,
he drew his eyebrows together and growled: "Well, what
of it? Do you imagine when I sit by the fire on winter
evenings all I do is warm the soles of my feet?")

He met some opposition to his plans at first. Geraint
and Gawain both questioned the need to govern by Roman methods, while Kay and the Colonial commanders
grew angry defending tradition. He got his way, though.
Not one of us could fault the logic of his reasoning. What
was more important and, as I look back, surprises me
more, he'd managed, at the finish, to convince every man
present there was no cause to grumble or take offense for
the honor of his Clan or his Colonial status. The new
Britain, as Arthur made us see it that day, had place and
need for the best each one of us could give.

We went out into the noon sunshine laughing and
joking together over the new appointments he'd made,
giving each of us some part in civil government as well as
our army commands.

"If I'm to be Prefect of Menaevia, I'd best find what
Menaevia amounts to!" I remember saying to Palomides.

When I discovered it was the largest of the old Five
Provinces—an area that stretched pretty nearly from the
Land's End to the Dike—I sobered considerably. Com-

bined with my cavalry command I guessed, even then, I was likely to find my hands rather more than full.

It is strange that, try as I may, I cannot remember exactly when it was in time that Arthur first spoke of his intention to revive the Roman title of "Knight." I remember the occasion very well. We had been hunting deep in the forest and it was autumn. Early autumn, it must have been, for Lancelot had not gone back to Armorica, and he always left before the seaways closed for winter.

The four of us, Arthur, Lancelot, Palomides and I, sat together about a fire of birch logs, in a glade where the first leaves had fallen from great beech trees, and there was a smell of woodsmoke, and the first hint of frost in the air. (It *must* have been the autumn after Blackwater.)

We'd got Lancelot to sing for us some of the Armorican fisher songs. They have a haunting strangeness. Later, when I'd learned more of the harper's art, I came to realize they must be very old, before men tuned strings to the voice, for the notes fall somewhere between anything one can match to a harp's range.

When the last song ended, none of us spoke for a while. Then Arthur stirred and, clasping his hands about his knees, said softly:

"That music lifts the heart. When I listen to it I get to dreaming of a world where men walk simply, without deceit or subterfuge. A kindlier world than ours, where the strong defend the weak, and to have some manners is not thought to be beneath a warrior's dignity. Truth, justice, mercy—one cannot impose those things—they must grow out of a man's own striving with himself."

"*Pietas,*" I quoted, remembering Ectorius' lessons. "We Romans had a name for it."

I saw Palomides' eyes, bright in the firelight, watching, intent and questioning.

Out of the shadows Lancelot murmured again that one word which means so much and translates so ill:

"*Pietas!*"

There was a note of laughter in his voice. I thought

he mocked, not at us, but at the distance Rome had fallen
below that stern ideal.

Arthur said abruptly.

"We need to rouse that spirit again, to set a standard; and create a pattern that even the dullest can
comprehend and strive to achieve. I have decided we will
revive the order of knights, but change and shape it to
meet the needs of the new age. Listen—this is how we
can do it."

I felt the old eager excitement welling up in him as
he leaned forward in the firelight.

"It was the only honor Rome gave without regard to
a man's birth, or wealth or the standing of his family.
That we will keep to. It was good. King's son or beggar's
son, what a man *is* shall determine, alone, his right to be
called a knight, with us. Of her knights Rome expected
standards of conventional good behavior. I shall expect
more than that—but not too much, for it must be clear to
such a man as Tor, the swineherd's son, as well as to you,
Bedivere, or to Lancelot here, what this thing means.
Since a vow clinches the good intent a man may have
when he is moved (as we were, just now, by Lancelot's
singing) and holds him to it after the bright moment's
passing, they shall give their word to a few straight,
simple rules. A promise is a promise. Once given, they
must keep it, live by it, or forfeit the rank they've
earned."

"How will they earn this rank, my lord?" Palomides
spoke for the first time, and there was a vibration in his
voice akin to Arthur's own excitement. (He always kindled to talk of ideas.)

Arthur paused, then said, as if thinking the thing
through, weighing it:

"By courage, since in all of life, to my mind, courage
is the principal thing. By service, given without grudging
and without hope of reward, to this island, and to me as
its Pendragon. By the quality of their lives and the respect
they've earned by it.

"The vows could be something of this sort—I'd have
them swear loyalty to their own gods and respect to other
men's. They must seek truth and speak it always, even to

their own hurt. They must be worthy of trust and trust each other, and I would have them use their strength to protect the old and the weak, the widows, the fatherless. And I'd have them what's more, each one, behave himself with some heed to manners, as if he were and knew it a man of worth, the equal of any High Prince in the land and so above idle wenching, rough speech, drunkenness and guzzling, because of it."

He paused and Lancelot whistled softly.

"You call those vows simple?" he asked. "I've an idea Rome asked less of her knights and still, sometimes, got short measure! Men who held to such vows, Arthur, might, in truth, bring the land a little nearer to the Light we learned on the Island to seek before all else. Found your order. I'm with you. The world has need of it!"

At Caerleon, where we kept Spring Sowing (which the Christians call Pentecost) the next year, the order was founded, on a day of sun and blowing wind, when the hawthorn was in bloom, and buttercups lacquered our sandals gold-over in the water meadows. Celidon devised the way the thing should be done, for he was wise in the meaning of ceremonial and knew the power and magic it can generate. I can feel that power still, run through me, tingling, as I felt it that day, when I knelt in the flowering meadow before Arthur the Pendragon and, laying the blade of Excalibur on my bowed head, then, lightly on each shoulder, he bade me rise up, the first of his new knights, as I had been the first of his Companions.

I have heard the Merlin warn, and I myself have proved the warning true, that after any advance in initiation a man may expect an attack from the Powers of Darkness. It came to me soon enough after my return from Caerleon. All of us had been lifted a little out of ourselves, had passed through one of those inner gates of experience which the Merlin's kind name "initiation," when Arthur made us his knights. I was happy and, being happy, the more vulnerable. I was not ready for the darkness that fell on me when Ygern told me one evening, as we walked together on the lower rampart:

"Bedivere, the time's come when I must go away from here, and for good. I have made up my mind. I can help the Bear and all of you best if I take my training as a Priestess of the Old Faith. My place is on the Island."

I stared at her, not believing I'd heard her right.

"A Priestess? You?" I said. "Don't be a fool, my girl. Your place is with Arthur. Why, neither he, nor Kay, nor any of us here could do without you. What's put this crazy notion into your head—is it Celidon's doing?"

"Partly," she said calmly. "Yes, Celidon made me look into my own mind and see the truth that had been waiting there a long while—a truth I did not want to recognize."

I took her hand, as we walked slowly along the grassy terrace in the late golden light.

"Girl darling, you've had a hard time of it these last years. Too hard for most women. No need to talk of it, you and I, for you never cared for sympathy when you were hurt, and knowing that, I've said little, on purpose. When that thing happened last May Day, Celidon was kind to you. You always loved and trusted him. I understand that. But don't let him persuade you to something so wildly out of reason—so against all I've ever known of you, as to try and turn yourself—you, of all people—into a Holy Island Priestess!" and I laughed.

She looked at me, her face small and set and grave.

"You don't understand. It isn't any question of 'holiness.' It's a question of learning certain skills, certain wisdom, that will be of use to Arthur and to Britain in the future. I've got the Sight, Bedivere, and I must learn how to use it. There are not so many who have that gift, these days. It's a long training—twenty years. I'm old to begin, but I've always longed to learn. It is my moira—and one cannot avoid that, once one has recognized it."

A small, cold fear began to grow in my heart; and it made me angry.

"Who, do you imagine, can take your place here, if you choose to desert us now?" I asked. "Who will see to the women folk for us, entertain Arthur's guests, give him comfort and support and advice when things go ill, and he's weary and depressed?"

She drew her hand out of mine, and looking straight ahead, quickened her step a little.

"His queen," she said. Her voice was tight and hard. "He *must* marry, Bedivere. He knows it and I know it. The Pendragon owes Britain an heir. Maybe he'll not bring himself to it for a while yet, though he should. But he'll come to it more easily if I have gone away. With me here, the thing is impossible. You know what folk think. Margause first opened my eyes to that, and as it is, I've let the whole matter drift too long. Don't make this harder for me, my dear."

But I did. I could not help myself. I was like a man clutching at straws when a torrent is sweeping him towards the weir. I argued and reproached and stormed at her. Then I grew calm and very reasonable and persuasive.

"Ygern, listen to me. You know I love you, have always loved you. I've no illusion that what you feel for Arthur you'll ever feel for me. But we understand each other. Marry me—now, soon, at once, and that'll stop all idle talk. As my wife, you could stay here in all honor, queen or no queen. Whoever she may be, she'll need another woman to counsel her, coming strange to her task. Marry me, and we three, Arthur and you and I, can be as we've always been. Don't leave us, Ygern. Don't go away."

She laughed a little, looking up at me again with eyes that were kind and sorrowful, dark with woman's wisdom, that is as old as time, the mother-look that pities all men, recognizing the child in the man.

"I must go. You know it. It is the only way. But there will still always be the three of us. That you need not doubt, and that nothing will ever change," she said.

For a time the enemy left us quiet enough for me to ride out with only a small escort and begin to get the measure of my duties as Prefect of Menaevia. I asked for Iltud as my deputy—the young Colonial centurion from Am-

brosius' army who had been my second-in-command on
several expeditions. He was steady and efficient, a man
I'd come to trust. If he found me poor company he did
not show it. He had the courtesy in him patrician breeding gives, that neither intrudes nor expects intrusion. We
got on well enough together without ever becoming more
than superficially acquainted with each other's deeper
feelings. At that time I should have found Palomides'
too-sensitive comradeship an irritation, even if he could
have been spared from his physician's duties. All I needed
was hard work in a field so new to me that it would absorb
all my attention. I was not disappointed. Menaevia is a big
province, and its civil administration was in chaos, just
then. By the time we'd ridden over the half of it, making
some rough assessment of what would need doing there,
I'd enough problems on my mind to set any personal
frustrations in their right proportion.

That same year of threatened and uneasy truce,
Arthur set the garrison of the Great Fort to a furious
activity of rebuilding. It was an opportunity the first war
had given us, and the task was overdue.

"I'm sick of giving judgment in a hall cluttered all
about with cookpots and the clacking of the women's
looms. We'll make ourselves something more in keeping
with a Pendragon's dignity, and while we are about it,
pull down the worst of the men's quarters and lay out the
whole place to better advantage. We may not have another season when it can be done in good summer weather," he told us.

He went at the task as he always tackled a fresh
project, with ruthless energy, setting his whole mind to
the practical details as they arose, ready with a solution
each time a problem appeared to be insurmountable,
driving himself as hard as he drove the men. Stripped to
the waist, he would lend his giant strength wherever a
timber-tug bogged down, or a big beam needed lifting,
encouraging the work with jests and oaths; his great
infectious laugh making light of toil so that, for very
shame, even those who were weary or inclined to shirk
hard labor by nature strove to emulate his endurance.

I wondered, coming back to find the whole fort loud

with the ring of ax and hammer, a hive of orderly disorder, if he, too, had felt the need to escape from loneliness.
When all the normal patterns of life are in upheaval one
misses a familiar presence less. It was a thing we did not
speak of together. Only Kay lamented aloud the loss
Ygern's going was to all of us.

"I miss her at every turn! I simply cannot understand this affair. It's beyond me altogether. Arthur should
never have sanctioned it. That man Celidon! I just hope
they all know what they are doing, that's all," he grumbled to me unhappily.

The work went on all winter and into the next
spring. It was a mild, wet winter, luckily. Before we were
through, we'd had enough of discomfort, overcrowding
and the general chaos that follows reorganization on such
a scale. By March tempers were growing short, even
Arthur's. I'd an idea he'd more on his mind by then than
impatience to get the building project completed before
open weather promised the start of the new season's
campaign. Though he still jested with the men, I could
feel some inner conflict smoldering in him like a fire
banked with wet peats.

A morning came when he called us suddenly to
Council. Celidon had come in the night before, stayed an
hour or two with him and gone again. That was not
unusual, but I'd heard their voices raised in argument,
which was rare, and glimpsed Celidon's face by torchlight
as he rode out under the north gate. He had looked
strangely bleak. I was uneasy, and the other Companions,
as we squelched through the churned mud towards the
hall, were glum and silent. The weather had broken again,
with thunder in the night, leaving a grey, warm drizzle
behind it. Most of us had been about since cock-light, and
were damp, sweating and surly. The hall itself was still in
disorder, for a number of folk crowded in to sleep there
during the building time. Tables and benches were
stacked against the walls, and bedding still lay in heaps
where men had crawled out of it at the dawn trumpet
call. The place stank of stale blankets, the night before's
cooking and our wet goat's-hair cloaks. It was always
gloomy in there on a dark morning, for the windows were

small and high, and the steady drip of rain, plopping through the smokehole on the dead ashes of the fire, added to the depression.

Arthur, coming in hurriedly, paused and stared round, his lip curling in disgust.

"Is this the hall of a High King or the ill-kept sty of a Saxon holding?" he thundered. "What have those damned boys been doing? It's their duty, surely, to see to things here?"

Knowing very well (for I'd just come from there) that every boy on the place was down in the water meadows, goggling at a string of unbroken horses that had just arrived from the Outland horse-runs, I said:

"I'll go and call them."

"Stay where you are. We've work to do. This isn't the time to have the nursery under our feet with all their ears flapping to catch every word we say. Pull out a table and some benches and let's get to business," Arthur ordered.

I saw some of the younger Companions glance at one another. They thought themselves above page's work and were ill advised enough to show it. Arthur saw the raised eyebrows and roared at them to hurry. I kicked the bedding aside while the lads jumped to it to bring out the benches, Aglavain and Gaheris making a notable clatter at the job to prove they, at least, were present. Then, grinning, they sat down on each side of Arthur's Council chair, that Gawain had moved over to the table's head. (As High Princes they were admitted to Council as messengers.)

Old Ulfius, who'd been irritable since he'd got himself a head wound in some minor skirmish a month before, took offense.

"Is it usual for the youngest to take precedence?" he growled. "Get down to the far end, you two. Make place for your betters!"

Arthur, who had taken his seat, and was glancing at some notes he had made on a wax tablet, looked up and smiled—a tight-lipped smile I knew promised trouble.

"In my father Uther Pendragon's Great Hall at Tintagel he held Council at a round table, Ulfius, where all companions sat down as equals. Perhaps you remember it?" he said. "Quite soon we shall be in a position to resume that good custom. King Leodogrance writes me that he proposes to send us that very same round table (which he had of Uther for safekeeping in the time of the Troubles) as part of his daughter's dowry." His voice changed from smooth sarcasm to imperative command. "Sit down where you can find room to sit, all of you. Let's have no more talk of precedence among brothers and comrades."

We sat down, and fast. In the ensuing silence the regular *plop* of the smokehole leak sounded very loud. I think we were all too startled by the implication in his words to speak.

He looked round our solemn faces, and laughed grimly.

"Well, which of you is going to ask me the question that's in all your minds? *Why should Leodogrance be considering a dowry for his daughter?* I'll tell you. Because I have grown tired, this year and more, of hearing the whispers all about the camp, from Council to kitchen boy—*The Pendragon should be getting him an heir. When will he marry?* My answer is—now."

We still gaped at him, dumbfounded. I, for one, felt as if I had been winded by a body blow.

Geraint, who ranked as the most senior officer present, recovered himself first. With the grave courtesy of speech he always used in Council, he said slowly:

"Are we to understand, my lord, that the honor of the royal alliance has been offered to the Rheged Clan?"

"Yes. That's the size of it," Arthur said. "For a long time, now, that old rascal Leodogrance has been angling for it. Some of you, at any rate, must have guessed as much, if you've kept an ear to the ground. I had his final offer half a moon back. Well, I've been considering it— and it's a good offer. In the face of the Merlin's advice, I'm taking it."

We glanced at each other, up and down the table.

"Celidon advised against it?" I asked. "What were his reasons?"

Arthur gave me a stern, hard look.

"Less important than mine for acceptance. He let me persuade him, at the finish. He sees some risks in the match, but not for Britain, and it's for Britain I'm thinking now," he said. He leaned forward, his eyes keen and commanding, with the flash of steely grey in them one saw, usually, only just before a battle.

"Leodogrance, now, and probably for years to come, holds the most important sector for us in this war. While we fight to free the south of the island, he *must* keep the Picts occupied in the north. Oh, I know—" his fierce glance had caught the expression on Gawain's face and a restless movement from Gaheris and Aglavain—"I know well enough the Dalriada share the task with him. I'm not casting any slurs there, you lads, so no need to scowl! But the fact remains, we can't fight on two fronts—not yet. We haven't the strength. Until we have, we need to be sure of the Rheged."

"That's common sense. Your father would never have gone under, but for the north betraying him," Ulfius muttered.

"I don't forget it," Arthur said. He leaned back, drumming the fingers of his right hand on the table. "Leodogrance, as you know, has been well furnished with tall sons, but has, living, only one daughter. His ambition runs to seeing her the Pendragon's consort before he dies. Very well. She's young, strong and healthy. She should bear sons, for that line runs to boys. Do you ask anything more from Arthur's queen?"

The mood he was in froze comment. It was a long moment before Geraint asked tentatively:

"You spoke of a dowry, just now?"

"Ha! That!" Arthur smiled, mockingly. "You are thinking, no doubt, we'll be better magicians than the Merlin, if we squeeze gold out of the Rheged? Well, my friends, you're right. Leodogrance writes that his people are poor—very poor, in money. He will not insult us by offering the paltry sum they could raise in coin. But, he says, they are rich in courage, in fine young fighting men and in horses. He offers, with the Princess Guinevere, to send us a hundred fully trained and equipped heavy cavalry, with their horses and remounts, led by three of his sons. What's more, he'll keep up the strength for us, each year, with fresh recruits as they are needed. Considering our losses at Blackwater, that clinched the bargain for me. An entire heavy cavalry cohort is something we can't afford to sneeze at. Do you agree?"

A gasp of amazement greeted his words. Faces that had been tense and anxious broke into wide, half-incredulous smiles. Even Gawain whistled softly, murmuring:

"A hundred armed cavalry—now that's talking!"

Geraint said:

"A royal dowry indeed!" He, in his turn, glanced round the table. "I think it is for all of us to approve this match—and to wish the Pendragon all happiness with his bride."

As the murmurs of assent threatened to rise into full-throated cheering, Arthur put up a hand sharply. His smile twisted his lips, but did not reach his eyes, as he said:

"A king's marriage, except in rare cases, must be dictated by policy, and happiness has little to do with it, Geraint. If this serves Britain, that's all I ask. But I thank you, just the same, for your good wishes. I take it the matter's settled? Let's get to other business."

When Council ended, and Arthur, shrugging on his wet cloak, went shouldering out abruptly from it, I left the others to discuss and exclaim together, and followed him into the rain.

Keeping step with him as he strode to his own quarters, I said quietly:

"Bear, I'll not question this decision of yours. You know your own business best. But tell me one thing. Why does Celidon oppose alliance with Leodogrance's daughter? Does he distrust the Rheged? I'd have expected he'd be the first to see good reason for strengthening the northern frontier."

Arthur checked for a moment and looked me straight in the eyes.

"He tells me the stars predict I'll get little happiness from the marriage. Since I expect none from marriage to any woman save Ygern, that is altogether irrelevant. I'll

get a hundred armed and mounted men, and, with luck,
the heir Britain needs. It is a good enough bargain. Now,
fetch me Lavain, will you? He must ride north tomorrow
with letters to clinch the matter. And, Bedivere, pick a
couple of your own decurions, and a trustworthy veteran
escort for me, will you? Men who know how to behave
themselves. I want this thing done with some order and
dignity. Oh, yes, and tell Kay I'll need the keys of the
treasure chest. I must look out a suitable bride gift for the
girl, I suppose. That's customary, isn't it?"

I agreed, with due seriousness, that I believed it
was.

I'd as soon have jested with a three-days hungry lion
as risk a smile just then, for I sensed Arthur's mood.
Whatever had brought him to the decision he had made,
the road to it had been hard and dark. He had never, in
all the years before, flouted a warning given by Celidon
the Merlin.

# . Chapter Fifteen

Men who have not known war think of it, if they think of it at all, in terms of battles lost and won. The hardest part, as I remember, is the waiting time between. It is like watching lightning play night-long over the Outland hills, wondering if and when the storm will move down, to crash about one's homestead in the valley.

That spring, for the second time, thunder rumbled in the distance, rumor contradicting rumor of Saxon fleets at sea. We waited, and did not send out the Branch, hoping (as we always did) to get the harvest sowed, and maybe even reaped, before we called men away from the fields.

On a blue and gold morning, when the larks were loud overhead, I heard the sentries challenge and the groan of the north gate being rolled back. All unannounced, Lancelot rode into the fort, a couple of dozen armed followers behind him, each leading a loaded pack pony. Once inside, he pulled up short and sat, gentling his horse, and looking about him with a pleased, half-mocking surprise.

I hurried to greet him.

"Man, what brings you here?" I asked.

He leaned down to grasp my hand.

"Boredom!" he announced cheerfully. "Armorica is full of old men who never laugh, a land where, for the moment, nothing is happening. I said to myself—'In Britain, even if they've no great war on their hands, they'll not be sitting idle.' So I came. Besides, I heard certain whispers of changes in the wind over here, that roused my ever-inquisitive curiosity. At a guess, they were true." He looked meaningfully at the new buildings, bright and clean in the sunlight. "A High King's hall for a High King's bride—is that the meaning of all this that I see, Bedivere?"

"Now how in the name of Light did wind of *that* blow as far as Armorica?" I questioned. (Lavain was not yet back from his mission, though we expected him daily.)

Lancelot shrugged and slid off his horse, throwing the reins to Griffin—a freckled, frog-faced eleven-year-old, then, newly appointed to serve me as page and assiduous in carrying out his duties.

Lancelot paused to smile at him and made a quick, measuring gesture.

"A full foot taller since I saw you last, eh? Do you feed these youngsters royal jelly from the hives, Bedivere, to make them grow so fast?"

Then, as Griffin, grinning happily, led the horse away, he turned to me, his face grave. "It's true, is it, what we've heard? Arthur's to marry? Who is it to be, Bedivere?"

I told him, quickly, how matters stood, and added:

"Best not make a jest of it with Arthur. He takes it hard. A matter of policy, not choice."

Lancelot nodded.

"So? Well, he could have done worse than settle for Leodogrance's girl. I'd a suspicion that one-eyed old rascal was playing for the match as long ago as the summer of Silver Wood. Let us be practical—love is one thing, marriage, after all, another, for most of us. He may be lucky. I heard it said, that year, the princess was beautiful and high-spirited . . ."

"Did you?" I said, nettled. "I'd not heard it, and neither, as far as I know, has Arthur. She brings a hundred armed cavalry as her dowry, the sworn alliance of a powerful Clan, and the hope of heirs for Britain. Those were the reasons for Arthur's choice."

Lancelot cocked an eyebrow at me.

"Good reasons," he agreed. His expression was solemn, but his eyes were snapping. "All the same, a woman who is easy to look at and amusing to talk to—with him, those things may count. Ah—here comes Kay. Kay, most honored Master of the Victuals, where's the storehouse now? I and my men, hearing rumors of festival ahead, bring with us a small tribute."

Kay welcomed him warmly, all in a fluster.

"What? What's all this? All those bales and bundles? What are they, Lancelot?"

"Be tender with them. They're mostly breakables. Wine from my own vineyards and crocks our Armorican potters make, these days, near as good as the samian stuff that (to judge from my last visit) is in somewhat short supply with you. I thought you might find a use for both."

Cutting short Kay's thanks, he laid his arm about my shoulders.

"Come! Lead me to Arthur. Ah, but it's good to be back with you all. I swear this place is more home to me than Armorica. Britain has always been the country of my heart!"

It seems to me now that Lancelot's presence that summer blew through the fort like a warm gale. He was everywhere at once, admiring, advising, suggesting.

"Thanks be to the gods, you've built separate kitchen quarters at last! Now a man will be able to warm himself in hall without forever tripping up on a dripping pan or getting black looks from the cooks. An upper storey to the new hall to sleep the womenfolk? That is a precaution I regret! Count your maidens up to bed and guard the stair so none slip down again before morning, eh? What's this about the barrack privies? They don't drain as they should? Now, the answer to that I can tell you, for we've had the same trouble. The secret lies in the packing of the outfall pits."

For a week, he was busy as a dog at a Gathering fair. He even set every youngster in the place to lime-washing the new hall.

"This you must do, believe me. It gives light and discourages fleas. But it's not men's work. Children can do it." he assured us. "Me, I am expert and I will take charge of this for you."

He had all the small boys in the fort clambering up ladders, as daubed with whitewash as Picts with woad.

"Ho, we laugh! The Lord Lancelot makes us laugh!" Griffin shouted down to me from a perch among the rafters.

Lancelot made us all laugh, but outside in the sunlight that day, where he and I had gone for a quiet word, he said to me, suddenly serious:

"Children and dogs, Bedivere—surely there are more of both about this place than I remember?"

I shook my head.

"Too many of both. Ask Kay! But what can we do? The men bring them in from every patrol. We can't leave them to starve, the only things alive in some raided farm or burning village. I got my Griffin that way—pulled him out of a smoking cellar where he'd hidden, while outlaws killed and brutally mutilated his whole family. I covered his eyes with my cloak as I carried him through the yard, but he still starts and whimpers in his sleep."

"I see." He nodded. "War's a bad business. There are times when I understand why men turn to the Christian religion and become monks or hermits. If I had not been Lancelot of the Lake I might even be tempted to it myself."

I thought it unlikely. War was in his blood. Within a week, he'd grown restless, I could see, and when rumor reached us that the Forest Jutes at the head of Vectis water seemed to be on the move again, he jumped at the chance of action.

"Let me take a patrol down there. I'll rout them out for you," he offered.

Arthur laughed, and let him go. Not putting much faith in the seriousness of the rumor, for we'd heard it before and it had proved groundless, he said:

"Take young Gaheris with you. He's been plaguing me to let him see action and it'll be good field training for him. I doubt you'll find much in the forest but some good hunting."

They went off with Lancelot's men and a score of our own new recruits.

A day or so later Lavain, sleek and gay as a cock pheasant, rode in with his party. I could tell by the look of him his embassy had been a success. Arthur called Council and announced briefly the Rheged alliance was sealed.

After, he said to me:

"I'll get away north as soon as maybe. That Rheged cohort will need a full winter's training in our sort of discipline. It's my guess we shan't have another idle summer next year. We shall need those men."

Late that evening I went down to the horse-lines to see to a pony of mine that had a swollen hock. I heard young voices in the hay barn, raised in an eager babble of questions, and then Lavain's Colonial drawl:

"Oh, they welcomed us as though we were Companions of the Council! Nothing's too good for Arthur's men as far as the Rheged are concerned."

I paused, amused to hear Aglavain's shrill, girlish treble demanding insistently:

"But will you tell us what we want to know? This king's daughter, now, is she beautiful?"

"Beautiful? Old One-Eye's daughter?" Lavain mocked.

There was a general groan. Someone said, resignedly:

"Oh well, plain women make the most faithful wives, they say. Maybe in this fort just as well she should be homely."

Aglavain, Highland-persistent, piped up again:

"*Is* she homely? Not plain ugly?"

Lavain laughed. By the sound of him, I thought he might have celebrated his return with more than one horn of heather beer, for he sounded recklessly elated.

"The Princess Guinevere, my children, is plain as moonlight on the snows of Yr Widdfa. Plain as the evening star, rising in a sunset sky. Plain as a perfect wild rose, with the morning dew on it." He whistled a long wolf whistle. "I'll tell you a secret. When that one rides in under the gate tower there'll not be a man in this fort who wouldn't give a year's share of plunder from the richest campaign we ever fight to be in the Pendragon's shoes—or rather, in his bed! We've always said the king was lucky —and by the gods, he is, to be getting an armful like her at his age. Why, he must be close on thirty, and she not more than eighteen! Hair of spun gold, a face like apple blossom and a figure . . ." he whistled again, and proceeded to elaborate in soldier's terms.

I tramped, heavy-footed, round the barn end into their midst.

"What's this? A meeting of gossiping girls round the wellhead?" I asked. "Have none of you anything better to do than discuss the king's private business? Get back to your duties, and one of you find me a horse-boy. I need help with a pony gone lame."

That broke up the meeting in a hurry. Sheepishly, muttering apology, they melted away.

I stood for a time in the twilight, smelling the sweetness of mounded hay in the warm summer night.

*"A man of his age,"* they'd said.

Arthur and I would share our thirtieth birthday next solstice.

For the first time in my life the realization struck me: one day he and I must both grow old.

Some weeks must have passed, because I know I was beginning to suspect Arthur, for once, was dragging his feet over a task that needed doing. Each time I brought up the question of his starting north, he had an excuse for further delay.

One evening I went to look for him about some other matter (I forget what it was; a question the decurion in charge wanted clarified about the signal beacons, I think).

I found him up on the rampart, in one of the catapult bays, leaning on the palisade rail, looking out towards the Island. It was rare to see him idle. Something in the brooding stillness of his figure, alone there, outlined against the last light, made me pause, reluctant to disturb his thoughts. A pebble rolled under my foot and he turned his head.

"Ah, it's you, Bedivere. As well you've come. That new moon yonder reminds me it's more than time I turned the fort over to you. Before it wanes I must get this marriage of mine over." He pointed to the little slip of silver that was climbing a duck-egg sky.

I went and stood beside him.

"Since the thing must be done, best get it over with, Bear," I said. To cheer him, I added, "From all I hear, your bride is beautiful, gay, and still young enough to be molded to your ways. A man might hope for less."

He laughed a little, deep in his throat.

"The poor child!" he said unexpectedly. "If she's fulfilled the promise she had when I saw her, her looks won't disgrace her new station."

"You've seen her?" I asked, surprised. He'd never spoken of it before.

"Oh yes," he said calmly. "When I was playing the harper, that year I went wandering with Celidon. A pretty, fairy creature, she was then—not above eight years old. The Merlin awed her, but she came to me, one evening, in her father's hall, and leaned against my knee, asking me to play for her some northland song I'd never heard of. When I did not know it, she sang it for me in a voice true and clear as a little wren's. She'd a great cloud of silver-fair hair, I remember, that clung to my fingers, when, bending to me, she'd let it tangle in the harp strings." He paused and said again, on a sigh, "The poor child!"

"Why pity her now?" I asked. "Surely every woman in Britain will be envying her, chosen to be the Pendragon's queen?"

He shrugged.

"Maybe. But I've little to offer any woman, Bedivere, apart from that empty title. You know how it is. Besides, her life cannot have been easy. Her mother was of the Mountain People, that strange, wild race that live in the hidden valleys about Yr Widdfa. Some say she was a witch, and cast a spell on old Leodogrance that lasted

only a given time, as such spells do. The truth of it is she
was of a faith older than even the Merlin's—a Priestess of
the Moon. When Leodogrance's folk blamed her for
blight on their corn and murrain on the cattle, he hurried
to put her away and marry his present bustling, half-
Colonial, wholly respectable Christian consort. Guinevere's mother died by her own hand, and I doubt the
stepmother was kind. Now Guinevere must marry a soldier, years older than she is, who'll have little time or
thought to spare for her in the years ahead. We must try
to be kind to her, Bedivere."

A little impatiently, I said:

"She'll do well enough. Given luck, there'll be children in a year or two."

He was not listening. I saw him stiffen, his head
up.

"What's that? Do you hear it? A single horseman on
the track below and travelling fast. It's ill light for such
speed, and on an uphill path. This must be an urgent
message."

I leaned far out over the palisade.

"A wounded man—he's reeling as he rides," I said.
My eyes were always keen. I could just make out the
figure before a turn in the track hid it. "Gods, Bear—I
believe that's Gaheris!" I exclaimed sharply.

We ran together, and reached the Great Gate just as
the guards were opening up. The pony, sweat-dark and
foam-flecked, stood, feet apart, head drooping. I was just
in time to catch Gaheris in my arms as he fell from its
back.

"Pain—I didn't know pain could be like this!" he
muttered thickly, then moaned as I laid him on the
ground. I thought he was dying.

Arthur bent over him.

"What's happened, boy? Try to tell us. Remember
you are a soldier," he said. His voice was gentle, but it
held urgent command.

Gaheris responded to it.

"Saxons. They're back. Jutes with them. Six hundred
about—on the Calleva road, heading north. Oh, the
pain!"

He had his hand pressed to his side and suddenly
drew his knees up in a spasm of agony.

The decurion of the guard, peering over Arthur's
shoulder, said in a hushed tone:

"I've sent a man for the surgeon, my lord," then
turned back as Palomides came hurrying, and added in an
aside, "He's bad, sir. I think he's a goner."

Arthur, kneeling beside Gaheris, took the boy's hand
and held it.

"Listen, lad. Palomides is here. In a moment he'll
give you something to ease that pain. But first, try to tell
me—is Lancelot dead?"

"No—he sent me. He said they—making for Aquae
Sulis. He'll follow—but to come quickly."

His head rolled back against my arm. I said:

"He's dead."

Palomides pushed me aside as I laid the boy back,
and took my place at his side.

"Bring torches," he said urgently. "I think he's still
breathing."

His examination was quick and deft.

"An arrowhead, buried in his guts. He must have
broken off the shaft himself. No wonder the pain was
bad! This can be dealt with if we are quick about it—
with luck it's not gone deep enough to touch a vital spot.
We may save him," he said, looking up at Arthur.

Arthur nodded, his face grim.

"See to him, then. Bedivere, as soon as you can be
spared here, I'll need you," he said, and turned away,
back into the fort.

I waited to help them get Gaheris on a stretcher. As
we eased him down, the trumpets on the watch towers
above answered each other across the fort, sounding
shrilly: *"General alert! Stand to arms."*

It was not an invasion. Rather, a wild, dashing raid
planned to catch us unprepared (as for once it did) by
two of Cerdic's younger sons, and a following of warriors
their own age, eager to snatch some plunder after a long,
lean summer. They'd slipped up Vectis water at the dark
of the moon, and joined with the Forest Jutes. Most of

our fleet were out on patrol, and the rest comfortably
asleep, trusting it was near enough the season to lay up
their boats for winter.

By the time we'd scrambled across country at break-
neck speed with three-quarters of the fort's garrison and
every man we could muster on the way, our tempers
balanced the fact we were outnumbered. (It stings any
soldier's pride to be caught napping by the enemy. Besides, we'd seen the damage already done, on our way.)

We got ahead of them and cut the road just south of
Calleva, having picked up Lancelot and his men on the
way.

The only thing that stands out clearly in my mind
now is Arthur's face, as he stood beside a heap of Saxon
dead, at the end of the battle, methodically cleaning off
the blade of Excalibur with a bunch of grass. He'd got an
ugly, deep scratch across his forehead, and had been
smearing the blood out of his eye with a dirty hand. He
looked rueful and surprised, much as I'd seen him when
we'd been found by Kay raiding the home orchard years
before.

"Well, that was a near shave, and no mistake!" he
admitted. "But for you, Lancelot, and young Gaheris,
Aquae Sulis could have gone up in flames. They fairly
caught us with our breeches down, man, and nobody to
blame but the War Duke of Britain!"

I began to laugh and suddenly all three of us were
laughing.

Lancelot said:

"We have a saying in Armorica, 'He who never
makes a mistake never makes anything.' "

I finished knotting a strip torn from my undertunic
round a gash on my wrist.

"Hot work while it lasted, but the end of it until
next spring if I'm not mistaken. You can still get to your
wedding, Bear."

He scowled at me, but his eyes were sparkling.

"Time to talk of wedding when we've cleared up the
last of this mistake. Call off the pursuit for tonight,
Bedivere. I'm going to rest our men, then we'll make a
sweep south of the whole country down to the coast. This

time we'll shift the last of those Jutes, if it means gutting the whole forest."

What with one thing and another the first leaves were turning before we got back to the fort. It looked as if there would be no royal marriage that year.

Surprisingly, Lancelot pressed for it.

"You cannot afford to offend the Rheged's pride, Arthur. They'll take delay as insult. Besides, you need those cavalry replacements more than ever now. If I'm to train them for you this winter . . ."

Arthur interrupted him.

"You? You mean to winter with us this year, then?"

Lancelot shrugged.

"I had hoped. Armorica does not need me—and I have told you, in Armorica I am bored," he said, smiling.

Arthur was pleased and showed it, but he still hesitated.

"There's much to do here, now. With winter coming on I must go down to Adurni and cheer old Julius. He blames himself he let the enemy past his guard—and there are other things, besides, I must see to," he said, frowning.

Why I said it, I don't know. I never have known. The thought came to me suddenly, and I, who as a rule think slowly, spoke on impulse.

"If you can't be spared, send Lancelot to escort your bride here, Arthur. It's a good old Colonial custom, when all's said, for the bride to be brought to the bridegroom's house for her marriage by his best friend and a handsome escort. Lancelot's the man to persuade Leodogrance there's no insult in that—rather, honorable Roman manners."

Arthur looked at Lancelot, his face brightening.

"Would you do that for me?" he asked hopefully.

Lancelot spread his hands and lifted his eyebrows.

"But willingly—if you trust me with such an errand, having knowledge of my reputation with women!" he said, and laughed. Then he turned serious and immediately practical. "Spare me some Saxon loot to make suitable compliment to Leodogrance and I'll see to it he takes the change of plan in good part. With that one, money will always talk—and we shall save him the expense of a marriage feast, besides. With good horses and a small escort, we can make a fast journey, both ways. I'll go, Arthur. How soon can I start?"

So, lightly, almost carelessly, the matter was settled. At the time I did not doubt the wisdom of it.

That evening I went to visit Gaheris and cheer him with the tale of our victory.

I found him, propped up in bed comfortably enough, clamorously demanding food, though he looked pale and drawn still.

"There's naught wrong with me now but sheer starvation, so I'm telling you. How can a man get his strength on broth and milk slops?" he grumbled, scowling at Palomides, who stood by smiling.

"How can a man with a gash in his stomach digest aught else? Maybe you shall have some broiled fowl tomorrow—a small portion, anyway," Palomides promised.

As we went out together, he laughed.

"That one is making a quick recovery. If I can prevent him bribing one of the orderlies to smuggle him in full army rations, he'll not remember that wound by spring, unless he looks at the scar. You breed a tough race here, Verus."

As we crossed the newly paved square outside the hospital block, he glanced at me curiously.

"Is it true, what I hear, the king is to send Lancelot to bring his new queen south to him?"

"True enough," I said.

"I should have thought, if he could not go himself, he'd have sent you." Something in his tone warned me he did not approve the matter, but I thought he'd read in it a slight to me. He was always jealous for my honor. I said lightly:

"Lancelot's the better man for the job. He's a good talker and has the charm to handle a delicate mission. I haven't."

"Oh yes. Lancelot has charm. All the same, in Arthur's place I'd rather have sent you." Palomides sounded thoughtful.

"If" is a small word. The pebble that, turning under a runner's foot, loses him victory when the race seems almost run.

If the messenger Lancelot sent ahead to warn us at the fort of his return had not been thrown from his horse in the forest and broken his neck, we'd have had the place in at least some kind of order. Any woman has the right to expect preparation made to welcome her on the day she is brought as a bride to her husband's house-place. Celidon was right when he warned that the marriage would be star-crossed from the first.

I can see the fort now as it looked that mellow, golden evening of late October.

Arthur, Palomides and I had just got back from Port Adurni. Julius the Tetrarch was dead, and sorrow for our old, trusted friend had cast a shadow over us. We'd stayed down at the port longer than we'd intended, for after the funeral rites there'd been a deal of reorganization to see to (Julius always kept everything in his own hands, and his sea captains appeared stunned by his loss).

The three of us had made haste on the road back, and were travel-stained and weary.

We found chaos at the fort. A patrol under Gawain had clashed with outlaws in the forest, and just ridden in bringing a few wounded with them and a bunch of prisoners. There were messengers waiting—one from Geraint. who'd been kicking his heels for three days, waiting to deliver news of trouble down in Lyonesse. To crown all, a party of youngsters, hilarious after a good day's hunting, had driven in a herd of wild pigs and let them get adrift all round the camp. They'd brought fresh-killed deer as well and, the weather being unseasonably warm, the women were hard at work, skinning and jointing the carcases, ready for salting down against winter. The whole place smelt of entrails, swine, and the sweat of men and horses.

Palomides went at once to see to the wounded, and Arthur to deal with his messengers, and take Gawain's report. I used my full battle voice to bawl out the lads who were enjoying themselves in a holiday mood that

threatened to extend their pig hunt round the place in-
definitely. A squealing old sow swerved across my path
and sent me sprawling. I got up, swearing and muddy, to
find Griffin, breathless from running, his eyes popping out
with importance, stammering at my elbow.

"Don't stand here. Head off that blasted pig!" I
roared at him. Then, his words penetrating my fury
*"What* did you say, boy?"

"Report from the sentry on the gate tower, sir. A
party of horsemen coming up from the plain. They've got
women with them. He says, sir—it's the Lord Lancelot
and the new queen, he reckons."

"Dear gods!" I said. Then—"The king's in his quarters. Get him out here—and all the other commanders.
Send the news on by any pages you meet, but don't hang
about looking for them. Get the king—and hurry!"

I grabbed a passing small boy and shook him into
attention.

"Pass the word round, quick as you can, that Lord
Lancelot and the new queen are at the gate. Turn everyone out to greet them."

"I will, sir!" He shot away, yelling the news.

I myself lifted up my voice again to full battle
pitch.

*"Turn out the Guard! Turn out the Guard! The
King's Guard to the Great Gate!"*

My decurions were well trained. We had two lines of
warriors flanking the entrance by the time the gates rolled
back, though their appearance would have made Ambrosius weep. Half of them had been on the hunt and
were still splashed with mud and deer's blood; the others,
on rest, were buckling belts and straightening sword slings
as they hurried into line. I drew my own sword and gave
the centurion's salute, which signals the "Present spears."
It was the best I could do, and I was tinglingly aware of
what I must look like, bare-headed, dishevelled and plas-
tered with mud, doing it. I only prayed all the gods
Arthur had my message and was close behind me.

They rode out from under the shadow of the gate
tower, into the sunlight, a tall girl on a magnificent
chestnut, and Lancelot beside her, smiling encourage-

ment, his hand on her rein, his shining black charger tossing its head, as he checked its pace to a stately walk.

I looked up at them both and my heart turned over, as the salmon turn in a deep pool. The harper in me recognized perfect beauty and for a moment forgot everything else. Lancelot was always the handsomest man I ever knew and in the honey-gold of the late October sunlight he seemed to glow as if lit from within by even more than his ordinary shining vitality. And Guinevere? There was a quality of magic about her that dismissed Lavain's description as adolescent vulgarity. She was dressed in green that day, the fairy color of the fern, that belongs to the People of the Hills. She rode bare-headed, as a virgin should, her hair—that moon-gold, glinting hair—rippling down to her waist, little, soft curling tendrils blowing all about a face grave, intent and wary as a new-roped yearling's. Her beauty was no passing charm of youth—it went bone-deep. I saw that. She would still be beautiful, even in extreme old age, I thought, with that clear line from ear to chin—the wide, clever mouth, the eyebrows, darker than the hair above them, etched like the curve of a swallow's wing, above eyes of deepest violet. And her coloring—there, at least, Lavain had found the apt word—apple blossom on a morning of May. Eighteen? Yes—the small, high breasts, the slender waist—the look in the eyes that alone betrayed how strange, how daunting this moment must be. She was still very young. But there was a dignity about her that could have belonged outside time—something withdrawn and secret, old as the hills of the Outland are old, even when clothed in their spring grass. The magic of a Moon Maiden, that set her apart, with Lancelot, two figures outside time, caught in a rainbow's circle—figures in a harper's dream.

Then they were past me, and the horsemen of the escort were pressing in behind, and I left the guard to the decurions and hurried to take my place at Arthur's side. He had come quickly enough, Kay, Gawain and the Companions crowding behind him. All were in rough clothes, bare-headed. Because the moment had caught

him unawares, he looked grim and alert, towering above
the others, his hand on Excalibur's hilt. Lancelot reined
in the horses before him. I saw Guinevere's glance go
from one to the other, her eyes wide and questioning, and
I saw, too, the quick, reassuring gesture, as Lancelot laid
his hand for a moment on her arm.

"My Lord Arthur, Pendragon of Britain, my mission
is accomplished. I bring to you your betrothed bride, the
Princess Guinevere, her royal brothers and the fighting
cavalry cohort of the Rheged," he said. His voice was
clear, ringing, ceremonious; his eyes mocking and
amused.

Arthur smiled at him grimly.

"My thanks are none the less heartfelt because, as
you can see, you've caught us unprepared," he said.
Then, stepping forward, he lifted Guinevere down from
the saddle himself, and kissed her on both cheeks. "Welcome to Camelot, my dear. You've come to marry a
soldier, so you must forgive the rough welcome of a
soldiers' camp. You and I are old friends, though I dare
say you hardly remember our first meeting? Later, over
supper, we'll get better acquainted. Now, you must be
tired from your journey. Kay, here, will show you and
your women to your quarters and you can rest for a time.
Bedivere, see to the new cohort. You know where they
are to pitch camp and set out their horselines. Palomides,
can your deputy surgeon see to those wounded men of
Gawain's? I need you to take charge of a detachment of
archers for Lyonesse. You'll have to start at dawn, so
come over to my quarters now, and I'll give you your
orders. Lancelot, my friend, I'll see you later. There's
trouble in the west again and the messenger's been kicking his heels for three days while we were down on the
coast. You understand?"

"Oh, perfectly!" Lancelot said pleasantly. As Arthur
turned away, he caught my eye and gave me one of his
quick Armorican shrugs. "In this country work comes
first. One cannot begin too soon to understand that!" he
murmured softly. Then, shaking his head, "For a woman
—and a young woman—perhaps a hard lesson? Bedivere,

my brother, I foresee things are not going to be too easy here, for any of us, for some time!"

It took me until well after dark to get the new cavalry contingent settled for the night. As a precaution, until our garrison and the Rheged recruits had time to get acquainted, I was camping them outside the fort, on the slopes of the nearest signal hill, beyond the south gate. On one excuse or another, I noticed, most of the senior Companions dropped in while we were at work, to take a look at both men and horses. Curiosity had been mounting as to their probable usefulness from the very first. For myself, I liked what I saw of them better than I'd expected. The three sons of Leodogrance are, it is true, brash young men, still in their teens, unsure of themselves in strange surroundings and anxious their rank should be appreciated. I'd met plenty like them among the High Princes of the Clans. Tact and firm handling should turn them into useful officers presently. Their Clansmen impressed me—young, lithe lads, with quiet voices and alert eyes, who went to work intelligently, and knew how to handle horses. As Leodogrance had promised, they were well armed and equipped. The old man must rate both his daughter and the alliance high to have given her such a dowry.

Our last visitor was Lancelot, come to see all was well for the night. As we strolled back to the fort, he asked:

"What do you think of them, Bedivere?"

"I like them," I said.

He nodded.

"So do I. By the Light, it was a pleasure to ride with recruits who could handle their horses. A change from some we've had in the past, that needed to be taught how to stay in the saddle without falling off at the first trot! That's how we made such good time—too good time, I rather thought, when we first rode under the gate tower, to judge by all your startled faces?"

I laughed, embarrassed by the memory.

"Gods, man, you could hardly have chosen a worse

moment! The place must have looked a shambles—wild
pigs and deers' entrails everywhere—hardly the welcome
we'd have planned for the royal bride. We could have
done with a warning messenger."

"I sent one. What's become of him I must try tomorrow to discover. I set a fast pace, I admit—too fast for
the princess's women, I fear. The older ones complained
like hens when the fox is in the chickenhouse. Not too
fast for her, though. That girl rides like an Amazon. I
never saw a woman handle a horse of spirit so well. It's
been a pleasant embassy for me, and I'll tell you something. Arthur is lucky, say what the Merlin will. That
girl's got the making of a Pendragon's queen. She has the
pride and the courage for it, and she's witty as well as
beautiful."

"The embassy went well, then?" I questioned.

"From the start. Granted, there were moments of
difficulty. Since I was determined to get back here before
the weather broke, Lavain and I overrode our messenger
the other end, also. Rumor was in Rheged before us, and
they'd got it in their heads (understandably) that Arthur
himself would be the leader. The princess greeted me
most charmingly, as her intended husband—and fainted,
poor child (with relief, I don't doubt—though it could
have been from embarrassment) when I had to explain
the mistake. But we got over that and both of us laughed
heartily afterwards. I'd forgotten Arthur dyed his hair my
color when he played the wandering harper. She tells me
she'd pictured the Pendragon swart as an Armorican ever
since.

"The second bad moment I had was over his famous
bride gift of Uther's round table, which Leodogrance had
had loaded on a wagon that needed twelve yoke of oxen
to drag it. I ask you—am I the man to lead a hundred
horsemen at a solemn walk three hundred miles and more
across Britain to accommodate the pace of twelve yoke of
oxen? Oh no, my friend! That bullock wagon, it will
arrive when it arrives, believe me! We started out with it.
Yes. The Princess and I agreed we should not give offense. We agreed, also, that it was unlikely a table of
wood, however traditional, would tempt the hardiest out-

laws. It comes, with skeleton guard. I've promised double pay for their journey. Let us hope it arrives before the first snows fall!"

"Let's hope so, indeed," I said, a trifle shocked. I knew that, as one of the few heirlooms from his father's time, Arthur set store by that gift, and I said so. But Lancelot was impatient.

"A piece of furniture—poof! What is that, when I bring him safely his hundred cavalry, and such a bride?" he said airily. He laughed. "Believe me, time will pass quickly for Arthur for the next few months. He'll have less time for business. How fortunate to marry at the season when nights are growing longer and days shorter! We must see to it, Bedivere, that the king's wedding festival makes up, in grandeur and gaiety for, shall we say, the somewhat terse and preoccupied quality of his first greeting to his bride?"

As things turned out, I had no part in Arthur's wedding feast, for I left at dawn with Palomides for Lyonesse. As Prefect of Menaevia, the trouble there was in my province, and it seemed it was serious. The slavers had been stirring up rebellion, headed by those who profited from their traffic inland. Geraint's call had been for a force strong enough to show who ruled Britain now.

I was not sorry for the excuse to leave the fort. I'd little heart for feasting and merrymaking over a marriage that, for all its obvious advantages, rang hollow to my heart. War was my trade, in those days, and nothing warned me I was riding westward towards a great and lasting loneliness. Palomides and I were very close on that last ride together. He was the comrade a man needs at such a time. I parted from him and his archers somewhere in the heart of the wild Outland country beyond the Tavy river, and rode on south with my men to join Geraint at his Fort of Deva. A month later, with the rebellion settled, and winter closing in so that I was impatient to be turning back towards Camelot, Palomides' chief decurion reported to us there, bringing in what was left of the archers he had commanded. They'd been badly cut up—caught by a landing of Irish pirates in dawn mist on a lonely, remote shore. Commanding the rearguard himself, to get his men away, Palomides had been surrounded and taken prisoner.

"They killed his horse under him, sir, dragged him off and got him out through the surf and onto one of their galleys—then up anchor and away. We dared not shoot for fear he should be hit. He was wounded already, I think—stunned by the fall, most like. It was a sorry business. There wasn't one of us wouldn't have died to save him if we could. He was one of the best."

The decurion who made the report had tears in his eyes, as he spoke. He himself was wounded, his right arm in a sling and a gash on his forehead that had narrowly missed blinding him. He added, bitterly, "Almost better he'd been killed, I'd say. If he lives, it's slavery—and in that outlandish country."

It was no time for tears. I said, to hearten the fellow and his downcast following:

"If he's alive, the chances are he'll find some way to escape and get back to us. You did well to bring off the best part of his command, decurion. Let's hope one day he'll thank you for your loyalty."

But I did not believe it.

Slowly, on the long march back to the fort, through driving, sleety rain, the full impact of the loss closed in on me, cold, inescapable, dark as the winter ahead. In all probability I should never see Palomides again. My horse's hoofbeats, squelching through the mud, pounded out the sentence. He, who had come to the end of the known world with me for love of freedom, had found, for the second time in his life, the iron of slavery, instead. Each day I thought, at waking, "To what suffering does this dawn wake him?" Sometimes, like the decurion, I wished, for his own sake, he could have met a soldier's death.

That journey was the end of my youth.

# IV
# INTERMEZZO

# Chapter Sixteen

At last, though slowly and reluctantly, this winter is loosening its hold on the land. Griffin looks happier because I have been a little stronger lately, and coughed less. Today, with my bowl of pottage, he carried in the first snowdrops to cheer me.

"A poor woman brought these—all the offering she could afford," he told me, touching them gently with his big, chilblained hands, as he set them in a cup beside my bed. "They bring the promise of better weather. Come warm days, you'll mend, my lord."

"I'll do my best, for Paulinus' sake. I dare say, now, I'll last until his story's told," I said.

We both laughed. (How often we have shared laughter, Griffin and I! When he was my page, when he was my armor-bearer, when he rode with me, a fellow knight. Memory, for both of us, goes back a long way.)

I lie now, in the cold spring twilight, watching the flowers gleam green and white, withdrawn and secret, their hearts hidden. Green and white—the chosen colors of Guinevere, the queen. She, too, hid her secret heart, withdrawn, untouchable, remote. I did not understand her. For years I distrusted and, distrusting, came to hate her. I am glad that, at the last, we parted friends.

In the years that followed Arthur's marriage, except in times of total war, I was away from the fort more often than I was quartered there. Menaevia is an important

province. Men said I administered it justly. Much of it, in
those days, was Colonial country. My birth and the standing the Aurelianii had had, back to the time of Aulus
Plautius, helped me there. With small-town councils and
fossilized civil servants who still dreamt of Byzantium I
had a reputation for harsh discipline. I'd little patience
with their petty complaints, and I taught them taxes were
for the king's treasure chest, and not gathered to stick to
*their* fingers. The common folk and honest traders learned
to trust my justice. On the whole, all of us came slowly to
an understanding over the years.

Lyonesse was a different proposition. There, Rome's
rule had never been more than nominal, except for the
mining tribute. It's a wild land. I must have been prefect
close on five years, I suppose, before I'd time to give my
mind to it fully.

Geraint warned me, the first time I planned a progress there.

"Forget you were Roman-born among my people,
Bedivere. They are a rough, independent lot of savages
and they bear a grudge still against Rome. If you don't
want your throat cut, remind them you are their Pendragon's Chief Companion, his milk-brother. They may accept you as that. Take my advice. Use Uther's Fort of
Tintagel as your headquarters. It's impregnable—or nearly so. You'll find cold comfort there, for it's a bleak, wild
spot, but at least you can hold it with a score of trained
men, if you *do* stir up a hornet's nest." ·

I thanked him for his advice. Geraint was a man I
trusted.

I came to that grim fortress on its sea-washed crag
in a black mood and wild weather, I remember. I'd ridden
there straight from Camelot after the Midwinter festival.
The season had stayed deceptively mild, and though my
men grumbled we'd likely meet snow on the way, I'd have
risked worse to be quit of the fort that year.

Guinevere's coming had brought changes; changes I
found irked my patience and roused doubts I did not wish
to face. Though, at the time, I could not lay my finger on
a just cause for complaint, there'd been a hollow ring to
the noisy mirth of the solstice, to my mind. Arthur

seemed content enough—preoccupied as he always was
with work, treating his young queen more like a spoiled
and favorite daughter than a wife, maybe, but amused by
her flashing, sometimes mordant wit, tolerant of her restless, avid demand for amusement.

Lancelot, wintering in Britain again, had been master of the revels, and every day had devised fresh entertainment. It was not difficult, for there were many young
folk in the place. The whole fort seemed full of the
queen's girls, shrill-voiced and giggling, for every Clan
Chief was competing to have a daughter in attendance at
the Pendragon's court in those days—a son, too, if one
judged by the eagle-feather caps, and the varied tartans
that brought color to the hall in the fire-lit evenings. The
girls were herded up the ladder to the women's bed-place
every night by stern and careful matrons, before serious
drinking started. (One could hear them up there, even
through the harp music and the loud laughter, rustling
and squeaking like mice among the rafters.) But a good
deal of lovering went on by day. One came on couples in
every shadowed corner, and the young men made a cult
of the queen, besides, sighing and posturing for her notice, praising her beauty with extravagant compliments
she seemed not ill pleased to receive, even when she
laughed and mocked at them.

I'd been inclined to agree with Kay when he grumbled under his breath to me, at the supper table, after one
such lively exchange:

"Beautiful she may be, but that young woman will
look better to me when her girdle needs lengthening. The
years pass and still no sign of an heir! Celidon could have
been right about this marriage, Bedivere. He could have
been right!"

I was glad to be done with the festival and ride
westward into driving mist, with only a score or so of
seasoned veterans, Griffin and my own thoughts.

Tintagel did little, at first, to raise my spirits. Where wood
is hard to come by, and stone lies ready to hand, men
must use it, even if their skill is small. Some Chieftain,
long before Uther's time, had piled himself a round tower

out of the crag's end, above a little cove. He had a good
eye for defense. The rock stands sheer up out of the sea
on three sides, joined to land only by a narrow causeway
two armed men could hold against a hundred enemies.
Later, others enlarged the place, with haphazard additions, until it could have housed a sizable force—provided they were hardy and cared little for comfort.
There's a good well, high up, where the spring never fails,
and a few acres of flat turf for grazing. But the wind
scours the rock face and whistles through the unmortised
stone nine months out of every year, and salt mists
shroud it for days on end, even in summer.

I took one look at the king's bedchamber—a curious
look (for I remembered it was the place where Ygern had
been born)—and turned away, shuddering.

I took up my quarters in a small round room, where
two unglazed windows, with heavy shutters, looked clear
out to sea. Once it had been cleaned and sparely furnished, it suited me well enough. There was a hearth with
a stone chimney to carry off the smoke. With a good fire
burning in it, one could have found worse billets on a
winter night. Just beyond the door there was a little
closet. Griffin slept there, on a straw pallet—to be within
call, he said, but I think he was still young enough to feel
the eeriness of the place at night, and prefer to know
there were two of us to face whatever ghosts might haunt
it.

Poor Griffin! He must have found his master dull
company those first days—unreasonably short in the temper, sunk in a depression nothing seemed to lift. He did
his cheerful best, bringing me, boylike, gossip of our new
surroundings even the first morning. Did I know that
under the rock there was a great cave, running clear
through from the cove to the open sea on the far side?
Folk said a dragon had lived there once—before King
Uther's time, that must have been. And did I know (his
head on one side, watching how I would take the news)
that we had *hermits* on the rock.

"Hermits?" I said, my mind elsewhere.

"Yes. Old men—and very holy. They say—the people say—Prince Geraint gave them leave, when the place

was left deserted. You want to see their little huts, right out on the cliff's edge, like bees' houses, all built of stones, roofs and all."

"What in the name of Light are they doing there, anyway?" I asked.

Griffin shrugged, wide-eyed.

"Praying, I suppose," he said. "But they work in their garden sometimes, I'm told. When folk are sick they tend them—and they go fishing."

The Clans down in Lyonesse are of different blood from the main run of our Celts. You can tell it in their speech, which has a harsh, spluttering accent, and is sprinkled with words that to me, at first, were foreign. I found them wary of strangers, and gave them time to learn confidence, as I would let a savage dog sniff my hand before I stroked it. It seemed wisest to let them come to me, rather than forcing myself too busily on them. They had their grievances and when I'd settled some of those justly, others heard of it, and thought the risk of consulting a stranger worth taking. All the same, when I had ridden out a few times and made myself and my purpose known to the local headmen, I found myself sitting at home, with more time on my hands than I'd had in years. Later, when the weather made travelling less hard on the horses, I must go out, prospecting mines for Bardeliez. It was a thing I'd promised him some long time. Each year when he came on his annual visit to us, he'd grumbled that the work had not been begun.

Perhaps the fact I had taken a fever back in the autumn, from drinking bad water in a little town where the magistrates were too careless (they said they were too poor) to repair their broken aqueduct, accounted for my depression. I had a return of it soon after we got to Tintagel, I remember, with gripings in the belly and a throbbing pain in the head that felt for a day or so as though my skull was full of hot coals. An old servant woman and Griffin between them nursed me and dosed me with a vile draught they'd begged off the hermits. It tasted of mildewed hay, and even the smell of it made me retch; but when I had got it down, I felt better, and certainly I recovered quicker than I had the first time.

The sickness left me with a weariness in all my limbs, glad to huddle over the fire in my tower room, brooding in a great loneliness.

One afternoon, when the light was beginning to fail, and the logs in the grate had fallen to grey ash because I'd been too idle to lay on fresh ones, Griffin came with a basket of wood and glanced at me anxiously, as he knelt to rekindle a cheerful blaze. Then he fussed about the place, lighting my lamp, drawing the curtains of peeling, painted leather over the shutters, longing, I could tell, for me to give him encouragement to speak.

"Well, what is it?" I grunted at last. His busy care broke in on gloomy thoughts and I wished him away. "Haven't you anything to do? Take my arms and burnish them. This sea air breeds rust."

He looked reproachful.

"I will, sir, but—"

"But what?"

"There's an old man below, a harper. They say he was part of the household here once—in King Uther's time. He's come back."

I hesitated. Harpers are protected by custom and, because they are wanderers, gather news. But I was in no mood to be disturbed. I said:

"Tell them to give him food and a place to sleep. I'll see him in the morning."

Griffin still lingered.

"He did ask admission to you tonight, sir. He says he has a message."

My mind went to the Merlin. I sat up attentive suddenly, remembering Celidon's gift for disguises.

"What's he like?" I asked.

Griffin blinked.

"Tall—and very old—with a bald head." He grinned at me. "He's not the Merlin, sir. *I* thought of that!"

"Damn your impudence, boy. Who spoke of the Merlin?" I said, disappointed. "Did he say from whom he brings this message?"

"From the gods." Griffin's face was solemn—his eyes wide.

I slumped back in the chair.

"Which gods, I wonder?" I said bitterly. "I've heard stories like that before." Then, partly because the boy looked at me as a hound will that pleads dumbly for a bone until its pleading breaks one's patience, partly because I remembered all that lay ahead before bedtime was another evening listening to the wind and the roaring of the sea, I relented.

"Bring him up here if you must. At least his tall tales will serve to pass the time. But tell him to leave his harp below. I'm in no mood for music. He can keep that for the guard at supper."

Griffin was gone like a flash and presently returned, leading in a frail old fellow, in beggar's rags, who saluted me humbly enough, and yet with a certain dignity.

"The blessing of the Bard upon you, Lord Bedivere, and upon all in this house," he said gravely.

He spoke without accent, except for the Celtic lisp, in good Latin, his voice much deeper than the Merlin's. His eyes, grey as the winter sea under their bushy white brows, searched my face, and looked about my little room vaguely, as though he were short-sighted, even partially blind. He was, as Griffin had said, a tall man, and though his head was bare of all but a fringe of hair behind, and that thin as a powdering of snow on a brown rock, his white beard swept down to the knotted thong that bound his colorless robe about his gaunt frame. His face, darkly tanned and grooved with wrinkles, might have been carved out of a weathered oak root by some country craftsman, who had made the nose too big and hooked, the chin too jutting, so that together they reminded me of the bird from Africa a Phoenician sailor had offered to sell me once, as a rarity, in the port of Ostia.

I greeted him with the courtesy harpers expect in Celtic lands, and told Griffin to set a chair for him by the fireside. When he had sat down, stiff-jointed and slow, I asked his name.

"Diarmed of the Isles, my lord. I was once harper to Uther Pendragon—on whose spirit may the Light shine."

"Why have you come back to Tintagel, Diarmed of the Isles?" I asked.

I thought he would beg, then, for employment—or at least permission, as I had given other old servants, to make himself a home about the place. His story of a message I took to be a trick to get himself admission—though it was still possible he brought word from one of Celidon's people.

He looked at me again with that vague, wandering glance.

"I was sent," he said. "I do not know why. I was far away, in the mountains of Yr Widdfa, when the whisper came to me. I have travelled a long way to reach you, my lord, and the road was a hard one. They said I should find you in the hall of Uther, but they did not tell me your name. That I have learned only since I reached the journey's end."

" 'They'? Who are 'They'?" I asked.

"My voices," he said.

He seemed simple to me—perhaps, like old Gregorius at home, his wits wandered. Looking at his face, it struck me that if they did, it was sorrow more than age that had scattered them. The lines on it had a suffering look.

A gust of wind howled about the tower, making the curtains stir from hidden draught, and the lamp flickered, sending tall shadows clawing up the wall.

To humor him, I asked:

"What did these voices say of me, harper?"

He clasped his hands on his knee and turned his head a little, as though listening.

"That it was the time when paths divide, and a guide is needed. They sent me here to be your guide, my lord."

The lamp steadied, and its light caught the goldwork on my harp, which Griffin had hung up on the wall when he unpacked my gear. I had brought it with me on an impulse, thinking I might need to keep my men's spirits up in the long dark evenings. Diarmed gazed at it.

"You are a warrior now—your men say a great warrior and a leader of warriors. But my Voices tell me that a time will come, though it is still far off, when the

sword can no longer protect the flame—the flame that
must be kept alight in the darkness, or the people perish.
When that flame burns low, the breath of song alone can
fan it back to life. I am sent to teach you a mystery, my
lord—the sacred mystery that only a thrice-crowned
Bard, such as I, can impart. Take your harp from the
wall and sing to me. Then I shall understand what it is we
have to do together."

I hesitated. It was my habit, by then, to give orders,
not take them. Then, seeing he meant no insolence, but
was wrapped deep in some far-off dream, I shrugged and
got to my feet. As I took the harp, I said:

"It is a long time since I played on this. Both it and
my voice are out of practice."

He made a small, dismissing gesture.

I sat down again, the harp on my knee, and while I
tuned it thought what I should sing to this mad old
beggarman. It was in my mind that, having always been
acknowledged to have some skill, even by the Merlin, it
would be pleasant to surprise him.

I struck the loud, resounding chords that any harper
uses to still the chatter in a Chieftain's hall, and went
straight into the Battle Hymn of Hu Gadarn, that had
often brought me applause from our warriors at the fort.
After the first few verses, he put up his hand authori-
tatively.

"No! Any man can sing that. It tells nothing. Sing to
me from your own heart, Lord Bedivere."

I stopped the strings abruptly, with the flat of my
hand, so that a humming filled the room for a moment.
My face and even my ears burned, as they had not done
since I was a boy, taking a sharp reprimand from my
uncle at lesson-time. I was in two minds to order the old
man out of my sight for his impudence and have him
turned from the fortress at next day's dawnlight. Then, as
silence flowed back into the small, warm room, I heard
again, beyond the walls, the desolate crying of the wind,
the relentless hungering of the great waves, breaking,
defeated, on the rocks of the cove. All the dumb sadness,
the loneliness that had weighed on me in the past weeks
seemed to well up in my soul, seeking the expression no

words could ever give it. I remembered Palomides, my comrade, to whom those words might just possibly, once, have been spoken. I remembered Ygern, who had never needed words to tell her what was in my mind. And from somewhere, out of the long past, out of the forgotten time before the King Showing, when I had begun to guess at love, and life and loss, there came back to me a little, sad song I had made—a lament for the Corn King's dying— for the golden youth, who must go down alone into the dark earth-cave, and give up his life to make the next year's harvest.

I sang it softly—and not well, because now and again my voice was near to breaking. But my fingers felt for the near-forgotten notes and found them surely, and my heart went into it, so that I knew, at the end, I had been eased as if by long weeping.

While I played, the old man sat staring into the fire, hardly seeming to listen—listening, rather, to some voice within himself. His head sunk low, until his beard jutted out from the chin, resting on his chest, and I thought he slept.

When the last echo of the final chord had died away, he stirred and sat up, but did not look away from the fire. Speaking briskly, a master taking charge of the lesson he must teach, he said:

"You have much to learn. I understand now why I was sent here. What time we have, we must use together wisely. But I can teach you all you need to know."

I laughed, nettled by the calm authority of his tone.

"I have not been altogether untaught, Diarmed the Harper," I said. "When we were boys together, Arthur the Pendragon and I, Celidon the Merlin was our teacher."

He seemed quite unimpressed. Without taking his eyes from the fire, he said:

"For the son of Uther it was enough. But for his chosen Bard—not enough. Give me the harp."

Again, I hesitated, feeling the unaccustomed jerk of an order that took obedience for granted. But the man was old, and obviously more than a little mad. He meant no harm. I rose and handed him the harp, going back to my place again without comment.

He took the instrument in his thin, earth-colored hands, on the backs of which dark veins crawled, corded blue. Shaking his head over it, as I have seen a woman shake her head over some piece of weaving, where the pattern has been botched by a beginner, he tuned it again delicately, leaning his ear to each string as he thrummed it, taking his time. Then he settled it on his knee and began to play.

Note for note, chord for chord, he gave back to me my own song. His voice was deeper than mine, and for all his years, he had it under far greater control. There was a quality in it, and in his harping, I had never heard before. It was as though he had peeled away some rough outer covering, and shown, beneath it, a running pattern of pure and shining gold. He added nothing to the thing I had made. Rather, he stripped it clean, for me to see all I had meant by it, and gave me back my own truth again, clear-cut and transparent—a stone burnished to show a perfect, flawless crystal.

When he had finished, he turned and for the first time looked me directly in the face. Then he smiled.

"You see?" he said.

I got to my feet, went over and knelt beside him in the fireglow. "You are right, my father. I have much to learn," I said humbly. "Teach me!"

To every man the gods apportion his mystery, and make it known in his own appointed hour. Mine did not lie in the cave of Mithras, the Druid circle, the rites of any religion. It came to me that winter night in the tower room of Tintagel, and my whole soul rose out of darkness to meet it, recognizing a calling I, a soldier, had never dreamed would come to me.

By day, and to all outward seeming, Diarmed the Harper remained what I had first judged him, a gentle old madman. He melted into the pattern of life in the fort, so that he seemed to go unnoticed—sleeping in some nook or cubbyhole he found for himself, getting his food from the kitchen, wandering, a great part of the time, over the cliffs or along the shore in all weathers; tolerantly and even respectfully accepted by my people, for whom, at times, he would tell stories and sing as any other harper might. But each evening—and sometimes by day, when I had leisure for it—he came to me and we shut the door of the tower room and worked together, craftsman and apprentice. I think both of us knew our time was short.

To my surprise, I found he rated my harp, that I had thought a good one, very low. I found myself working with tools that at first came awkwardly to my hand, making me a better. Though I offered him money to do the work for me, I got no help, only a dark, quick glance.

"The harp of a Bard is a part of himself. What hands other than his own should shape it? A man buys himself a whore. He must court the woman he would make his wife with love and long patience," he reproved me.

So I labored away patiently under his direction, spoiling good wood, and wounding my thumb with gouge and chisel, until I could get the skills of the thing. While I worked he talked, in short, crisp sentences, very different from the vague and wandering speech that came from him at other times. I learned, amazed, how much there is for a Bard to know, outside and beyond his music, and I began to realize the power that lies in the harper's hands; power greater than a king's, reaching beyond a man's own death-day, into the tomorrow of the world. Like all mysteries, one cannot speak of it, except to a fellow craftsman, for it has to do with hidden things, that must not be profaned. Like all mysteries, its core is the truth in man, and in his relationship to the world he knows, and the universe beyond it. At its deepest level it is concerned with the harmony, the measure, the rhythm out of which all things were created, and by which they must be governed, consciously or unconsciusly. It is the life thread that holds us suspended safely above ultimate chaos, and the navel cord that joins life to eternity.

I do not pretend I understood all this in the few months of my apprenticeship in the tower room at Tintagel. Nor that Diarmed alone taught it to me. As he said himself, he pointed out to me a path. It is all any man can do for another.

What I did learn from him—and that is something that one needs to be taught—was the strict, meticulous discipline, harder than weapon training, that gives to a Bard the secret of control over his instrument and his voice, so that the truth can sing through him, and touch the spirit of those who listen. For the harper and the harp must be one instrument in the hands of the gods, if he is to become, at the last, the Bard thrice-crowned. Only when both are tuned rightly can they sound forth the Note of Power. I know this power. I have felt it. The breath of the god, going through me and out to the people. It comes seldom, and then like a white fire—the fire of heaven, from whose spark the flame is rekindled. The flame that does not die.

# Chapter Seventeen

Things having gone more smoothly for the Prefect of Menaevia in Lyonesse that winter than I'd been led to expect, I'd almost forgotten Geraint's warnings. On a bright spring morning, when the spray of the great waves glittered, clawing up the rocks below Tintagel Fort, I remembered them.

I'd returned from a dawn ride over the cliffs to a village where, so it was reported, a murder had been committed. I'd not been able to make much sense out of the evidence, and ordered my men to bring in witnesses, and I'd try the matter later. Telling Griffin to fetch me breakfast, I ran up the stairs to my tower room, unlocked the door (of which, since it housed the pay chest, I always kept the key) and paused abruptly on the threshold.

"Who are you? What are you doing here?" I asked, my sword already half out of its scabbard.

A figure, standing by the window, turned without haste.

"Seeking sanctuary. Also, I bring a message. You can put up your sword. I am unarmed."

It was a light, husky voice, more like a woman's than a man's. I stared at the slim youth in the white hermit's robe. With his back to the light, and the cowl drawn over his head, I could not see his face, but both figure and voice were too young to belong to any of our hermits on the rock. They were old and humble men, and would never, from my experience, have dared enter the precincts of the fort uninvited. Besides, who could have admitted one to the room of which I, alone, had the key? I smelt treachery, and closing the door, set my back against it, wary and alert.

"Tell me how you got in here before I hear more,"I said grimly.

The shoulders under the woolen robe moved in a quick shrug. The voice sounded amused.

"There are ways into Tintagel only gulls and conies know—and children. I was a child here. Since today I was being hunted for my life, I took the way I remembered. I've grown since last I came up the rock funnel from the cave, though. It was a tight squeeze at the turn, this morning."

The lad turned back the loose sleeve of his robe and examined a long graze on his sunburned arm with casual interest.

I strode across the room, took him by the shoulder and swung him round to the light, jerking back the cowl so that I could see his face.

"I am Bedivere, Prefect of Menaevia. Don't try playing the fool with me, or it'll be the worse for you," I warned.

I felt him go taut under my hand, but he looked up, cool and unflinching. His hair was dark, without the hermit's shaven forehead, his eyes dark, too, in a small pointed face that was so like Ygern's that, for a moment, it stopped my breath, and my hand dropped to my side. He stepped back, and stood facing me, smiling a little.

"I'm sorry I startled you, Lord Bedivere. With a mob at one's heels one can't be too mindful of the civilities! I've a message from the Merlin for you. My orders were to see you had it at all costs, and privately. I am Mawgan of Cornwall. You may have heard that name?"

"Yes," I said slowly. "Yes, I have heard it. But—"

"But this meeting's taken you aback, and no wonder! May I sit down? That climb's left me giddy. If you'd a glass of wine to offer, I could do with it."

I saw, then, that for all her apparent self-possession,

this messenger of the Merlin's was trembling, and had gone suddenly pale.

Bewildered and utterly taken aback by the whole affair, I muttered an apology, and, as she sat down in my chair by the hearth, hurried to open a small cupboard where I kept a flask of wine and drinking horns.

Mawgan of Cornwall—Gorlois' daughter—sister to Margause of Dalriada, half sister to Ygern! That explained the likeness. Indeed, I had heard tales of her in plenty. One of the Merlin's most fearless underground workers; a woman with a mixed reputation, who some said was a witch and a whore, others a heroine fit to lead warriors in the field.

As she took the wine-horn from me and, having pledged me, drank from it, I looked at her more closely.

Older than Ygern by quite some years—a face more mature and harder, now I'd time to study it. The mouth, wide and clever but reckless, the eyes watchful, but with laughter lines at the corners. A face, now the color was coming back under the deep, outdoor tan, that could have passed for that of a youth, until one looked closely.

"Well?" I said, smiling down at her as, having finished the wine, she set the horn aside.

"Well indeed! I needed that. My thanks for it," she said. Dipping her fingers in the wine's dregs, she spread a little on her grazed arm, wincing and screwing up her face with a rueful expression: "Wine's good for wounds—cleans them and staunches the blood. But you're a soldier so you know that," she said. "Now—my message. Celidon sends you a warning, my lord. He says Menaevia must shift for itself for a while, whatever work's still to do down here in the west. This season the king will have need of his Chief Companion, both in Council and in the field. The sooner you return, you and your men, the better for Britain."

"Thanks for that warning. I'll heed it," I said. "Is it the Picts or the Saxons this time?"

She shrugged.

"He did not say. Both, most likely, from what I've heard elsewhere. The chief reason you're needed is that there's trouble in Armorica and Lancelot's been re-called."

I nodded, reckoning the odds.

"They'll need me for the cavalry, then. Very well. I can start before this week's end."

I saw her studying me. She seemed to approve what she saw.

"Good!" she said briefly.

We were interrupted by a scratching on the door. I went to it hurriedly, opening it a crack, to find Griffin, whom I'd forgotten, with bread, meat and ale for my breakfast. I took the platter from him and said briefly:

"I've a messenger with me. Go down and keep the stair. Let no one interrupt us."

He goggled at me, but obeyed without a word. He was wondering, I guessed, how a messenger had come and he not known of it.

"That was my page, with breakfast. Will you share it?" I asked.

Mawgan laughed.

"If you've enough to spare. I've not eaten since noon of yesterday."

She ate fast, but tidily, like a hungry soldier, sharing my food without embarrassment, as men do in camp.

Abruptly, she said:

"Can I stay here till dark? Yesterday I made a fool of myself—which is something I seldom do, and something one can't afford to do when one's on the Merlin's business. Half the countryside's looking for me, intent on a witch-burning. I'll need darkness to slip away from the fools."

"Tell me," I said.

She shrugged.

"Oh, it was nothing important. I'd thought to get through to you disguised as an old woman, selling wound ointment and lotions against the spring itch. One can usually get the men off duty in any fort talking with those wares at winter's end. I'd have found some way to get word through to you easy enough once the ice was bro-ken. I've done it before. But passing through a village a mile or so away, I saw a man beating a little slave-boy almost to death. It was no business of mine—but I never learn! I interfered, and when I got what I might have expected, foul words and a promise to loose the guard dogs on me, I must needs up and curse the great brute. How could I guess he was near an apoplexy already, what with the rage in him and the drink he'd taken? The end was, he fell down, foaming at the mouth, went black in the face and died. The village blamed my curse (which was a good, comprehensive one, I admit, and included his farm, his family and all his stock!). Now they're hunting me for a witch. I took refuge in their Christian praying place, thinking they'd not expect a witch to head for that burrow, found this handy garment hanging on a nail and slipped out the back way. But they were beating the gorse on the cliffs at night, *and* using dogs. I'd an idea I'd be safer in the fort here than outside it. That was when I remembered the way I used to come and go here in Uther's time. I was lucky you lodge in this room, not, as I'd expected, below in the old royal quarters, and keep your windows wide. When I saw the harp and the book rolls, I guessed if I waited long enough I might be lucky and get private speech with the Lord Prefect of Menaevia."

I pushed my hand up through my hair and laughed.

"For a woman, you've certainly got courage and resource, Mawgan of Cornwall. It's what I've heard tell of you. Your story explains the complaint of murder that took me abroad at dawn today. Stay close until I've dealt with the storm you've raised, and by evening I and my men can escort you wherever you need to go next on the Merlin's business."

She said at once, with decision:

"No. I must go alone. My work's 'under the fern,' as we say. My next contacts would not relish an armed escort. You can help me best by keeping my presence secret. Can you trust that page of yours not to talk?"

I nodded.

"If I give him an order, he obeys me," I said.

"Then go about your business. Lock the door on me, since that's your custom. I'll sleep here until evening. May I lie down on your bed?"

She went across to it, without waiting an answer, sat down on the side, and laughed up at me.

"Soft for a soldier's—and the covering lined with wolfskin. The Prefect of Menaevia understands comfort!" She stretched out without another word, drew the covering up to her chin and closed her eyes, sighing contentedly. Then she opened them wide and murmured, "Ygern, my sister, told me you were kind. Now go to your day's work. I'll do well enough until you return."

When I'd gone out and locked the door, I stood for a few moments, gathering my wits. There was a stirring in my blood I'd not felt in a long while. Like the flick of a lizard's tail over a rock, the wonder went through my mind, how long was it since I'd had a woman? I put it from me and went down to deal with the witnesses, who should be waiting below, by now, to tell me their confused and contradictory stories of the "murder" I was beginning to understand.

"Well, you certainly rattled a stick in the beehive last night! But the matter's settled now—and to everyone's satisfaction. You must be a white witch, Mawgan, for the man who died was a petty tyrant, feared by his family, and hated by his neighbors. It was fear for their own skins, not grief for him, sent them out witch-hunting," I told my guest that evening.

We were sitting together over a good hot supper Griffin had conjured for us from the kitchen (I did not ask what excuse he had given as to why it was for two and not, as usual, for me alone). I could tell he was bursting with pride that he shared a secret with me, and I guessed the construction he'd put on it. For all her hermit's robe, the sex of my messenger was obvious enough, for she was taking no trouble to hide it. His face as he served us was so importantly discreet I could have boxed his ears, if I'd not been hard put to it not to laugh. A boy does not grow up in the army without learning commanders are men.

When I'd dismissed him to his post on the stair below, I leaned back at my ease, finding it very pleasant in the little room, that, lit by the sunset and warmed by the burning logs on the hearth, had a cheerful homeliness that night. Mawgan had greeted my return as casually as Ygern might have done. I'd a feeling we'd known each other all our lives.

I told her the outcome of her last night's adventure.

"Your curse must have been impressive. No one had much regret, I think, for the man who died of it, but his family certainly feared its effects on themselves and their stock. They were insistent only the witch's burning could lift it, until I had one of the holiest of our old hermits here, a man they know, who serves their church, brought out to reason with them. He girded up his robe forthwith and went off with bell, book and holy water to lift your dark spell. He's a wise old fellow and owes me something for leaving his community undisturbed. His promises and a small money present from me cleared up the case to everyone's content." We laughed together. She questioned then if I'd thought to ask after the little slave.

"For a child you'd told me beaten near to death, he looked remarkably spry to me. My men had brought him along as one of the witnesses. Since I saw some sidelong looks at him and there was a muttering about magic having been put on him by you, I bought him and gave him to the hermits. They can do with help in carrying wood and water and he'll be safe enough in their care."

Mawgan looked at me curiously.

"Yes, you are kind. Wise, too."

"What did you do to that boy, Mawgan?" I asked. "I saw his back. The weals on it were ugly enough proof he'd suffered, but they looked half-healed already and he was too talkative for a child in pain."

She shrugged.

"I've good hands. I know how to use them, for Celidon trained me. Some folk have healing in their hands, you know."

I nodded.

"I've had experience of that. Lancelot has the gift." I bared my arm and showed her a scar. "That was sliced deep by a Saxon seaxe, and I spouted blood from it like a stuck pig. Lancelot charmed it for me, and the bleeding stopped. I was grateful, for one can bleed to death fast enough when a vein's cut."

She laid her finger on the scar, tracing it, her expression interested and impersonal, but I'd an idea she knew her touch disturbed me.

"Yes. Lancelot has the gift," she agreed.

"You know him?" I asked.

She met my eyes and laughed.

"Oh, yes, I know Lancelot!" she said. At some time, I thought from the way she said it, she had probably known him more than well.

Suddenly, she was grave again. Pushing aside the empty platters on the table, she rested her elbows on it, and putting her chin in her hands, gave me a long, measuring look.

"Bedivere, tell me. What's the truth of rumors I hear that the queen mistook Lancelot for the king, when first they met—and, some say, might yet take that mistake further?"

I blinked, as at a sudden thrust in swordplay.

"Idle gossip," I said, too quickly. No man likes a vague anxiety he'd taken trouble to repress in his own mind brought suddenly into the open.

"So?" She lifted her eyebrows. "Is the queen a barren woman, do you think then? Or is it the king's fault there's no heir yet?"

I frowned, and seeing me ready to take offense, she said bracingly:

"Come! You must know that's a question half Britain is asking."

"What's half Britain's answer to it?" I asked.

She laughed.

"Arthur's a proven sire to common knowledge. Does not Lein, who carries his standard now, favor him beyond disputing—and I've heard of others. Most men blame the queen."

"I see," I said. "Well, there's time yet. You speak more like a soldier than a woman of these things, Mawgan."

"Why not, since the work I do for the Merlin is

hardly a woman's task? We live in rough times, Bedivere. A comrade is a comrade, of whatever sex. You and I have been comrades a good few lives back. No need for pretense between us, because, this time, we've only met since morning."

The sun had set, and the room was growing shadowy. She got up suddenly, and walked over to the window, looked out over the tossing expanse of water below and shivered.

"Call that boy of yours to light us candles. This place grows ghostly when dusk comes. I always hated it!" she said, with sudden violence.

When Griffin had cleared away supper and closed the shutters, I told him to bring extra candles as well as lighting those in iron sconces each side of the hearth. He returned with two tall ones of pure wax, in bronze holders, which he must have borrowed from the hermit's chapel. I remembered I'd seen them there. I supposed the old fellows must be grateful to lend them—or perhaps it was just Christian charity.

Mawgan sat down again beside the table and, drawing one of the candles nearer, gazed fixedly into its still, crocus flame. Her neck and throat rose out of the folds of the cowl, very white and delicate against the yellowish undyed wool. Her hair, where it caught the light, had the polished gleam of a jackdaw's wing. I watched her brooding, withdrawn expression and asked her:

"Were you so unhappy then as a child here, Mawgan?"

She looked up sharply.

"What do you imagine? I was eight years old when my father, Gorlois, was murdered. I'd been his pet, the spoiled latecomer, youngest of a marriage that can never have been happy. He'd given up hope of a boy, by then. But my mother still longed for a son, and to her I was just one more disappointment. His death shattered my world, and he was not a week buried before Uther was here in his place—a tawny, impatient leopard of a man, loud-voiced and masterful—and my mother," she paused, and her smile was bitter with memory, "my mother a woman I'd not known before, a stranger, all lit from within by some strange fire of emotion I was far too young to understand."

"They were in love, then, those two?" I asked.

She shrugged.

"Don't all the harpers sing it so? Yes, they were in love, right enough. Ruthless, too, as all great lovers are. My elder sisters Uther bundled out of the way as fast as he could make their marriage alliances. I was too young for marriage. He tripped over me, as a man is tripped by an unwanted hound-pup, until I learned from being kicked to keep from underfoot. I need not bear him a grudge. At least I learned early to expect little and rely on myself. I learned, too, to be wary and sly, to fade into the shadows and listen at keyholes, and draw my own conclusions from what I overheard. All useful lessons for the life I live now," and she smiled across the candle flame at me.

I asked, wondering how much she knew:

"What was the ending of it?"

She clasped her hands before her on the table, and sat, looking down at them, then gave me one of her sudden searching glances.

"Bedivere, how much do you know?"

I met her glance steadily, holding her eyes until they dropped again.

"I see," she said softly. "Well, that's another bond between us, anyway."

Men say of her still that she was a witch. I think she must have cast some enchantment on me that night. I, who had never spoken to any living soul save Ygern the secret thing I knew, felt impelled to speak of it to her, a stranger, chance met, and one of whom I'd heard strange tales.

"Mawgan," I said, "tell me the truth, if you know it. What happened here at the winter solstice the year Arthur the King was born?"

Again our eyes locked, as blades lock and hold when the swordplay is well matched.

"How much *do* you know?" she questioned.

"That Arthur is the son of Uther Pendragon, but his mother was not Uther's queen. The child she bore him was Ygern, whom you called this morning your sister, and who was brought up with me. She was my foster sister, Mawgan. We two have been very close, all our lives. She told me something of this—but the whole of it, I admit, I have never understood."

I felt her guard drop. She leaned back in her chair, relaxed. Her voice when she spoke again had regained its light, half-mocking ring.

"Right enough, as far as it goes. You were Colonial-born, weren't you? I can tell it in your speech. The fact that Uther was Island-trained and of the Old Faith I suppose you know by now. But do you understand our customs, our beliefs, well enough to know that once every so often (and always when the country is in danger) the king can be called upon by our Wise Ones to re-enact the old rite of the Traveller at the Ford? It goes back beyond time, that custom, older than Rome or Greece before Rome. I suppose men always dreamed of a god-begotten hero, who might be sent to rescue them from troubles of their own making."

I nodded.

"That I know something about. One of the advantages I had was a teacher who beat into my memory tales of Hercules and Theseus with a good stout rod," I said.

"Then, if I tell you that, at the very height of his infatuation for my mother, on the eve of leading an expedition into Lyonesse to carry her off from her husband, Gorlois, Uther was called by our Masters of the Wisdom to Ynis Witrin to perform a duty held to be sacred, and went, you'll not be surprised."

"I suppose not," I said.

"That was the way of it, Bedivere. When all else fails, our Masters of the Wisdom invoke the Great Light, and, having regard to the aspect of the stars, a night is appointed when their High Priestess, the ruling Lady of the Lake, must go alone to the little shrine on the Island's shore, and give herself to the first traveller who comes that way. Once, it was believed, that traveller was always

a god, disguised. But later they grew more cautious, or
their faith grew less, and they made certain their Chosen
One would at least be sure of royal blood."

She laughed, and her eyes were wickedly, mali-
ciously amused.

"I've often wondered, did they keep at least one
lamp burning in that Island shrine, or was the thing, by
custom, wrapped always in discreet darkness? If Uther
saw the bride of the god, that night, he must have thought
the god loved his deputy, for they do say Arthur's mother
and mine, being twins born at a single birth, were like as
peas in a pod, so that even Blaize the Wise, who'd
fathered them, could never tell them apart!"

I laughed too and, rising, fetched wine and poured it
for us.

She nodded an acknowledgment, and we drank to
each other.

"So it truly was Ygern who came to birth here, in
that grim chamber below, where the rats scuttle now, and
cobwebs wave from the roof beams?" I asked.

"Yes. Deep winter it was, and a long, hard labor my
mother had with her. I was banished, up to this very
room, and very much afraid, for the women whispered
she was like to die, and even though she never loved me,
I looked on her as some protection against Uther. He'd
been away for a time, he and most of his men. I knew
there was war and I hoped he might be killed in it.
Children are better haters than most people imagine—at
least I know I was. There came a night of loud noises, the
tramp of armed men, the fiery, red reflection of torches. I
fled down the stairs and, finding the doors of the great
bedchamber open, that had been barred against me for
three days, crept in and hid myself in some hankings
where I could feel safer than up here with only a nurse-
girl for company. My mother lay in the wide bed, a
swaddled bundle in her arms. Beside her stood Uther,
bare-headed, in full war harness, a bloody rag round his
head, his great shield still on his arm.

"He bent to my mother and his voice was husky, as
it always was—he was far on in the wasting sickness,

already—but that night it sounded triumphant and yet oddly gentle.

" 'Well, sweetheart, we've both had a hard fight of it. Another girl, is it?'

"Her answer was so low, I could not hear it, but Uther laughed, his harsh laugh that always ended in a cough.

"He straightened up and beckoned into the shadows.

" 'Olwen, take it away,' he said.

"Our old nurse came forward and lifted the babe from my mother's arms. I saw a puckered red face and hair dark as my own as Olwen bore the bundle away, clucking and muttering. Then Uther swung his great shield aside, and in the crook of his arm, where the shield had hidden it, I saw another swaddled babe. Uther bent over my mother, laying it beside her.

" 'No tears, now. Remember you hold Uther's son and Britain's Chosen One. He's a fair, strong child. We've had a rough voyage from the Island and fought off two pirate ships by the way, but we had a good wet nurse and the child's none the worse. Things are getting desperate for us now. When I've called in the Council to bear witness to the Pendragon's heir, he must go, as we planned, to safer keeping for a while. Celidonius is below, and he knows what must be done. Heart up, my girl, and put a brave face on the thing. We must play this out to the end, or all our labor's lost.'

"I craned forward and got a glimpse of a sleeping face within folds of white wool—a tiny face, fair and rosy, with hair like the bright halos monks paint in their singing books. I must have made some sound. Uther was always quick as a stooping kestrel, and that night, I can guess now, his nerves must have been stretched to danger. I can still feel his hands round my throat, as he dragged me out and shook me."

Mawgan paused, running one finger round meditatively inside the hermit's cowl.

"That was the end of Tintagel for me. Uther sent me back on the galley that had brought him, with orders I was to be raised an Island Priestess, well out of harm's way. I don't altogether blame him. Children talk. His was a secret too dangerous then—as it is still, Bedivere, for any man to take risks with." She paused and I refilled the drink horns.

"It's a secret that'll be safe with me. I'm glad to know the whole of it," I said. "Only one thing's not clear to me still. *Are* you an Island Priestess, Mawgan?"

She shook her head.

"Not me, though I had the training for it, and I'll always be grateful for the skills it gives. There were certain obligations to the life that never fitted me— virginity, for one! The Merlin doesn't hold that against me. I serve him well enough in other ways."

She looked at me over the rim of her drink horn, her eyes snapping, then tossed back her wine and, getting up, stretched, supple as a cat that suddenly wearies of the hearth and thinks towards a night's hunting.

"Enough of the past. If I'm to be on my way before first light, it's time for bed. But here's another warning for you—mine this time, not the Merlin's. Be watchful, if your path ever crosses that of my sister Margause—be *doubly* watchful—of the secret we've talked of tonight. She'd give half Dalriada to know the rights of the thing, suspecting a little, and that little hard to prove. One other word to you, remember the name Allisander. If ever one comes to Arthur's court who is called by that name, watch him well and be wary of treachery."

"Allisander?" I repeated curiously. "Very well. I've a good memory. I'll heed that warning."

"Then let's say goodnight," she said, and began to unfasten her hermit's habit at the neck, as casually as Palomides might have started to take off his tunic before me when we shared a sleeping cell.

I moved toward the door. She looked up quickly.

"Where are you going?" she asked.

"There's a pallet outside that my page sleeps on. It'll serve me well enough for once," I said.

She laughed, then said, irritably, fumbling with the thick woollen folds beneath her chin.

"Here, help me to get out of this. I can't find out how it unfastens."

I met her eyes.

"Don't be a fool, Bedivere. The bed here is very soft and wide enough for two," she said.

I helped her then, as she'd asked me. The time until dawn was short. She taught me more in it than I'd learned in all the years since I'd first tumbled the Tetrarch's goosegirl in his haybarn. Men say rightly Mawgan was a witch, for we parted, after, casually as soldiers do who, having shared food and a cooking fire, go their different ways next day, without regret, neither expecting nor seeking any future meeting. It was an incident, only, in both our lives. Few women are wise enough to know, as a man knows, that some experiences are for once only, and can lose meaning if clung to after the hour is past.

# V
# ALLEGRO
# MOLTO

# Chapter Eighteen

Paulinus tries my patience. I dare say I try his even more! It is the plodding pace of his Saxon mind, forever preoccupied with the non-essential detail, and seemingly unable to grasp the wider issues at stake. It is like talking to a blind man of color when I speak of battles fought up and down the length of Britain. I doubt if he ever travelled twenty miles beyond this Island's shore in all his life. What can it mean to him when I talk of Chester of the Legions, the Bassus river, the estuary of the Glein, or the wild mountain lands of Dyfid? Despairing of getting the shape of our campaigns into his thick head, I tried myself today drawing an itinerary map for him, of the sort any commander in Arthur's armies could read. He stared at it suspiciously, as if it were some heathen rune, then brightened and asked me for the tenth time to give him the exact year of every battle that we fought.

"*That* is the important thing for a chronicle, my lord," he repeated mulishly.

Well, I've told him, as best I can. With an effort, I can place most of them in their order, but for a year or two either way I'd not take a knight's oath now.

Tribruith was the last but one of the great battles before Badon, and there was a good long gap between those two. I'd confused it in my mind at first with the campaign Mawgan came to warn me was pending, that spring at Tintagel, then I remembered, in time, it could not have been that year, or we'd not have had Lancelot with us. That year would have been Chester of the Legions.

Tribruith, I know, was fourteen years after my landing in Britain, for I've a peg to hang that date from. One I'll not forget.

The whole of the north boiled up that spring. News came in from Leodogrance, from Dalriada, from Celidon's underground workers, and all of it was bad. The Picts were massing for a major attack again, only waiting for the weather to favor their allies. They'd made a pact two ways on for help. A sizable Saxon fleet was anchored in the mouth of Rhine River, and they'd got the whole of northern Wales in ferment, besides, fomenting rebellion among the Ordovices.

Gawain looked grave when that report got through.

"The Ordovicii? They're Vortigern's Clan—men with a grievance. A grievance they've been nursing for two generations, forby. They've not forgotten the burning of the Red Fox's lair, with him and his queen inside it, *or* the laying waste of their lands that followed. They were brought so low, in those days, I've heard tell, they invited the Irish to come over the sea and settle along their coastline—though I'm thinking myself those reivers needed no invitation, seeing there were too few of the Ordovicii fighting men left to oppose their settlements. In any case, they've been blood brothers to the Irish ever since. We'll be fortunate if there's not an Irish fleet fitting out for attack as well as a Saxon. I'm no Merlin, but I'm predicting this summer will be a hot one for Arthur's men, Bedivere!"

Arthur himself appeared unshaken by the odds stacking against us. He was more cheerful than I'd seen him in a long while. I suspected that the call once more to total war had come at a time when he was weary of life in the Great Fort. Guinevere had been plaguing him for a year and more to build new quarters for the court, with a grand great justice hall, down on the meadows by the river. She'd discovered the foundations of the old villa there, with the vestiges of its pleasure garden and orchards all run wild, and nothing would serve but we must raise up a Roman-style palace fit for a king—built in stone in the grand Colonial style. It had seemed to me a woman's idle fancy—unnecessary and extravagant. The threat of large-scale invasion put it out of the question, for the place would be all but indefensible.

"Poor lass—she's little enough to occupy her time. She's young and impatient, and longs for more grandeur than I'd ever planned to have round me. Someday, if the gods are good to us, I'll let her indulge her fancies. But this year we've other matters to attend to," he told me. "Now I propose to divide our host into three for the march north. You'll take the eastern wing, Lancelot the western and I'll command the centre. Lancelot's Armorican cavalry will be the smallest contingent, joining with Dalriada, for Dalriada will need stiffening, if the Irish do mean to invade. The Rheged must hold the Ordovicii off us. We'll settle their account later—and in full."

Once again we were poring over maps—and once again I'd reason to marvel at his grasp of strategy. He'd made war his trade, and in it he was by then a master craftsman.

All summer long, tirelessly, patiently, he worked our host as a good shepherd works his dogs. Holding us in check, avoiding casualties, with the old familiar tactics our men knew by heart, he harried and harassed the enemy up and down the border country north of the old Wall, alternately luring and driving Saxons and Picts alike, with a wide, slow, relentless pincer movement, until at last he had them where he'd planned from the start, backed against impenetrable forest to the north, cut off by bog and marshlands to east and west with Tribruith River south. Then, and only then, he threw the whole weight of the main force directly on them and we went into the attack with the Merlin harping us into battle. It was Celidon's home country. He'd long scores to settle with the Picts, for they'd burned his home and murdered his kin when he was a young child.

There was something about Celidon's harping ahead of an army on the move—a magic no one of us

lesser Bards ever quite achieved, for he played on the
strings of a man's soul with his wild music. I felt it sing
through me that day, a white, freezing fire that burned up
fear and all reasonable caution. I understood at Tribruith
something of the Berserkers' madness—for I felt my very
soul stripped naked to the rushing wind of battle, and my
horse a winged creature under me. Men say I led the light
cavalry well that day and I'm still glad to believe it. I've
scars to remind me I was not impregnable, as I felt myself
to be. But when at evening I dismounted, I'd no thought
that the blood covering me was, at least in part, my own,
for I'd felt no wounds at the time. Griffin and I discovered
the gashes on my body with equally concerned interest as
he helped me to disarm.

One notable piece of good fortune helped us to that
victory. I only knew of it after the battle was won. An
unexpected ally had come in from the west to join forces
with Leodogrance to hold the Ordovicii off our backs.
The Irish war fleet changed sides at the last moment.
Three days after our victory, runners came in from the
Rheged bursting with praises of a wild Irish Chieftain and
his men, who'd landed, not as enemies, but friends, and
saved the day for the Rheged at a moment when they
were hard-pressed.

When Arthur heard the news, he took one of his
lightning decisions that always pleased the troops.

"By the Light, we'll not go tamely home again with
no celebration to mark the luck we've had this year! We'll
march westward to Luguvalium, where the good roads
meet, and send word to the Rheged and to Dalriada to
meet us there for a seven-day Games."

So we went westward by easy stages, resting men
and horses, and camped all about Luguvalium on the
bare, rolling hills, while we waited for the men of Dalriada and Rheged to join us. It was summer's end and
glorious weather. They came in, eager and triumphant,
decked out in their bright Clan colors, with the great
Dragon standards floating in the warm, harvest air.

The Dalriada were the first to arrive, Margause the
Queen riding out ahead, with a whole bevy of girls about

her, escorted by her sons and Lancelot. She fell on Arthur's neck, embracing him and calling him the savior of Britain, swearing that, though she came uninvited, he must welcome her, for she had not been able to resist her longing to see again the dearest and most glorious brother any woman could have. We'd not expected her coming, and it caused us some headaches, but the presence of women, most of them young and gay as kingfishers in their many-colored dresses and glinting trinkets, added to the holiday atmosphere. Margause herself, whatever her faults, was always good company, and though Arthur had her measure, he enjoyed her wit.

Lancelot was the only one who seemed to be out of tune with the mood of the moment. He looked gaunt and weary, and there was a brittle quality to his humor, that had sharp edges to it. I gathered he'd not found his part in the year's campaign made easier by Margause.

"God defend me from a land ruled by a woman!" he said darkly, when I questioned him. "I feel as though leeches had sucked my blood, for I've fought on two fronts all summer. Don't ask me about it. It's a campaign I shall be glad to forget!"

I guessed his meaning when I saw him with Margause. It was obvious his famous charm had worked too well, and landed him with the embarrassment of an infatuation he'd not mind to reciprocate. I wondered, with ironic amusement, if he'd been offered the post of king consort outright, or eluded that final confrontation by tireless tact all summer. That he was in full retreat from an untenable situation was evident when Arthur sent for me on the day following his arrival.

"Lancelot's anxious to lead a scouting party into the Welsh mountains and take aid to High King Pelles of the Gwynfid, who's said to be cut off in some remote hill fort, holding out against the Ordovician rebels. They're a small, loyal Clan, the old man was a friend of my father's. If he's truly in danger we must help him. But it seems hard Lancelot should miss the Games—could we find some lesser commander for the job?"

"Let him go," I said. "He has his reasons, and with

his experience, he'll make light work of it. We can't afford to lose the loyalty of any mountain Clan through neglect in an hour of need. Take his generous offer."

Arthur gave me a long look, and I saw his lips twitch.

"So? I trust your judgment. As you say, a generous offer and one in strict accord with his knight's oath!" he said.

We both laughed. Arthur, truly, had the measure of Margause.

I laughed again to myself that evening (though the gods know, it was to prove no laughing matter) when Lancelot came to my tent with a request that told me he'd had to give some hostage to fortune, avoiding the main issue he'd no mind to face.

"I'm loath to ask it of you, Bedivere, but will you do me a favor? Will you take one of my pages into your service while I'm off on this business of old King Pelles? The boy's an orphan, not overstrong, too young for mountain warfare. I took him to please the Queen of Dalriada—he's a child she'd reared out of charity, and since he's quick and clever, she wants to have him educated for a time in one of our Armorican monastery schools. Let Griffin have a care of him back to the fort, and I'll pick him up again as we pass through on our way home. It'll not be long. He's a harmless quiet little lad. He'll give no trouble."

"Very well. If I must," I said. "I've too many pages already, since I made Griffin my armor-bearer, but one more shouldn't be beyond patience. What's his name?"

Lancelot hesitated, then said, with studied carelessness, "They call him Allisander. A thousand thanks, Bedivere! I'll send him over to you before we leave."

He swung out of the tent, with a quick glance of farewell, looking more relieved than, I felt, the favor warranted.

"Allisander?" I thought. "Allisander? I've heard that name somewhere."

It was some years and a long, hard campaign since Tintagel. Memory brought me no enlightenment. I shrugged. I'd probably heard the name somewhere and remembered

it only because it was an unusal one. It amused me that
Margause should have managed to shuffle off an unwanted responsibility, if nothing more, on the man who preferred leading a perilous venture in tricky mountain country to being longer in her demanding company.

I noticed the boy for the first time a few days later, on the
morning we'd turned out the whole host to give the
Rheged the sort of welcome Leodogrance would expect
from us. Vaguely, I'd been aware of a dark, smooth head
among the three towheads I was used to round my tent.
But I was Marshal of the Games, with plenty on my
mind, and Griffin knew his job (and me) well enough to
keep the small fry from under my feet, on such occa-
sions.

   We'd formed up on level ground below the camp in
a hollow square: the infantry in their cohorts, with the
centurions out in front, on two sides, Arthur, with the
Companions, Margause and her ladies, mounted, at the
centre. The cavalry were flanking them, all except Gawain
and his escort who'd already ridden out to meet and bring
in the two kings, Leodogrance and the Irish Chieftain,
Niel Long Sword, who counted himself a High King in his
own land. Arthur had learned the value of ceremonial
display by then, and he intended this occasion to be
remembered. There was a flash and glitter to the whole
array that morning—a sense of excitement and expectation—yet the discipline was good. My place as marshal
was out in front of the cohort commanders, at the end of
the left wing of the infantry, where all could see me
clearly, and take their timing from my signals. I was on
foot, with my armor-bearer and pages in attendance, and
I could feel the ranks behind me steady as if waiting to
repel a charge. I could see the Rheged host coming out
through the gates of Luguvalium (the road from the
south runs through the city, straight as a spear shaft)
with the sun glinting on their shield bosses, and our own
escort and the leaders riding ahead. I gave Arthur the
signal, and he and his staff, with the queen and her
women behind them, began to come slowly down the
field; a dignified and brilliant company, half-armor glit-

tering, jewels flashing—the horses, reined to a walk, tossing their heads, jingling their trappings, Aglavain, with
the great Pendragon standard, riding close behind the
king.

It was at that moment a small, stammering voice
piped up hoarsely, close at hand.

"Is that one him? Is—is that Arthur the King?"

Griffin's affronted growl, "Quiet, you!", made me
turn my head just long enough to glimpse Lancelot's
page, craning forward, and Griffin's hand pulling him
roughly back.

I was half angry, half amused. Arthur was a legend
and a hero to every small boy in Britain by then. The
child's interest was understandable, but the brief glimpse
I got of him startled and, in some odd way, repelled me.
He was thin and weedy, and looked tense as a cowed
whippet, his small face, with a lock of black hair falling
across it, pale as skimmed milk. It was the expression on
it that disturbed me, convulsed by some conflict of emotion far beyond his years, that twisted his features and
made them ageless as a monkey's.

I'd no time to notice more, for the king was level
with me and the moment had come when I must draw my
sword for the salute that would bring all the centurions'
swords flashing up together. As I did so, I heard a scuffle
and a smothered oath from Griffin. When I was free to
look over my shoulder again, annoyed by the renewed
disturbance, I saw two of my own pages backing out
through the ranks, carrying our new lad between them in
a dead faint. Griffin was where he should be, staunchly at
attention, his face scarlet, his eyes apologetic as a span-
iel's that's forgotten its house manners. I scowled at him
and within minutes forgot the incident. I'd other things to
think about. The kings were meeting, and it was time for
me to signal to the host to raise the threefold ringing
shout of victory, before I mounted the charger my groom
was leading out for me, and joined the other Companions
in the procession.

Niel Long Sword was the only man I ever saw who stood
half a head taller than Arthur. Beside him Leodogrance

looked like an Outland dwarf. His was a warrior's face, beak-nosed, square-chinned and reckless, with hair the red of a new-cut carrot curling back from it and bushy red brows sprouting out above eyes green and glancing as spring bracken. His clothes were careless and shabby as any Arthur had worn in our first campaigns, faded by weather, the leather of belt and breastguard scuffed with use. Only the circlet half hidden in his hair, the great gold torque about his neck and his magnificent arm rings proclaimed his rank.

I thought, "Here is a man after Arthur's own heart. They might be brothers!" and I wondered just what had worked on him to change from enemy to ally, in our hour of need.

The host had been dismissed. The cohorts were being marched away and, having dismounted, we were walking up the field towards the place where wine and cold meats had been laid out in readiness for a light, informal meal. Leodogrance was talking volubly, describing with great gestures the landing of the Irish and the battle that had followed. Suddenly, without ceremony, Niel interrupted him—pausing in his tracks, bringing us all to a halt.

"Sure, now, I was forgetting—I've a gift for the Pendragon. So I have! Brian Hen, where is he? Where is that man?"

An old warrior with white hair pushed forward out of the throng.

"He is here, Niel Long Sword. He is here!"

Then I saw, and for a long moment the whole bright field dipped and swung around me, like a galley meeting a heavy swell. For my mind could not believe what my eyes told me.

"Palomides!" I breathed.

He was thinner than I remembered. So gauntly thin his clothes hung on him. His face was older, more heavily lined. Most striking change of all, the difference that for the first moment almost made me doubt if only a likeness to the dead was mocking me, his hair was iron-grey, with one pure white lock running through it from front to back on the right side.

I thought:

"He has suffered! What have those Barbarians done to him?"

Then, as Arthur caught him by both hands, preventing him from kneeling, and folded him in a close embrace, "But he is not a sick man. He is well. I never remember him so happy, so utterly alive!"

The next minute, releasing him, Arthur was shouting for me.

"Bedivere—Bedivere, where are you? Look who is here! Look at the gift the Irish have brought us!"

There were tears in my eyes, making bright prisms all about him as I grasped his hand, feeling again its slender bones and hard, firm clasp.

"Is it you? Is it really you, Palomides?" was all I could say.

Then they were all about him, the Companions, pressing in, forgetful of ceremony, careless of the presence of three kings, greeting him with shouts of joyous recognition that, as his name was repeated from one to another, sent rumor of his return running back through the guards, to be caught and tossed from mouth to mouth among the common soldiers.

I knew they had loved him and mourned him. How much, the wild cheering that broke out on every side told clearly to every stranger present.

Niel stood by, smiling broadly, while old Leodogrance grinned and gesticulated for all the world like a showman at a fair.

"A good gift, a welcome gift? A gift you would have chosen above gold and riches, is it not, my Lord Arthur? Aye—and there's more to it than that. Here stands the man who brought Niel Long Sword over to our side in the nick of time. The man who saved the day for us of the Rheged."

Arthur looked from Palomides to Niel.

"A kingly gift, indeed!" he said, his voice gruff and deep with emotion. "No man has ever brought me a better. Come, let us drink to it, and you shall tell me between you the whole of the story; for I've a notion, Niel of Tara, we in Britain owe you a debt we'll find it hard to repay."

Niel laughed, a great, infectious, rollicking laugh.

"Sure, and the debt's on my side, entirely. Fine sport we've found so far in Britain, I and my men, and this is the finest Gathering we've had the luck to see in all our lives, so it is! From now on, count the men of Tara your allies, Pendragon, until the sky falls and the earth sinks under the sea!"

"Gods, Palomides, let me look at you. I still can't believe you're alive. All this long day I've been waiting in fear I'd wake and find it only a dream. You don't know how I've missed you!" I said.

At long last the evening feast was over, and I'd got him to myself, sharing my tent again, my comrade, returned to me from the dead. The feasting had gone on until long after dark, and both of us had drunk enough to break down the restraint that ties the tongue from speaking out from the heart.

A little dizzy, between wine and so much gladness, I sat down abruptly on my low, soldier's cot, and stared up at him. The shaded lantern on the tent pole frosted the grey of his hair with little points of light and darkened the hollows under his cheekbones.

He smiled down at me, beginning to unlace the soft leather tunic, embroidered with many-colored Celtic designs, that he wore.

"And I you—and I you, Bedivere," he said softly.

He had a trick—I'd noticed it all day—of running one finger round inside the standing collar of his tunic. Now, as it parted at the throat, I could see the skin of his neck was rough and peeling, with a line, pale as a leper's scales, running between the dark tan of weatherburn.

He saw my look and laughed.

"I only got the slave ring off a week back. There was no time, and no smith I'd trust, to do it before. I can't get used to being without it yet," he said, and pulled the garment up over his head. Then I saw the scar on his right arm. It ran from wrist to elbow and beyond, and as he moved, laying the tunic aside, it seemed to crawl and wriggle in the lantern light like a snake, blue-black and ragged, with odd lumps standing out on it, livid as a dead man's flesh. I'd seen plenty of battle scars in my time, but that one made me shudder.

"In the name of Light, how did you get *that?*" I asked.

He looked surprised, glancing down at the hideous thing indifferently.

"That? Oh, you can't stand the wolf guard six winters and never get clawed. I was careless—but lucky. There's venom in the brutes' claws, and it festered. I might have lost the arm—but thanks to good nursing I can still do a surgeon's work."

"Lucky for all of us," I said grimly. "Get to bed, man, and I'll do the same. Then we can talk in comfort. I need to hear more of the years we've lost than the modest account you gave Arthur and the Companions at supper."

When we were both snug in our blankets I got the story from him. He made light of much of it, and some things I only learned later, but he'd had a rough enough time. Sold as a slave in the markets of Tara, he'd been bought by an Outland farmer and carried off to a remote steading on the coast.

"He wanted a slave trained in the use of weapons, to lead the wolf guard in winter and help with sheep year round. It was a hard, rough life until one got used to it, but I've known worse. He was a good, honest master. The first year was bad and the second, worse. It takes time to come to terms with complete loneliness—the loneliness of the mind, cut off from all communication with one's own kind. I learned to speak the language fast enough, for it's near the same as yours in Britain, once the ear gets accustomed to its accent—but I'd not a soul to talk to, but Ug the shepherd and his boys."

"No chance of escape?" I asked.

"What chance? The sea between that land and Britain is not one I'd choose to navigate in a coracle and we'd no other type of craft I ever saw. Besides, with an iron ring riveted round your neck, that needs smith's craft to get off, to attempt to escape is to court the runaway's punishment. That's blinding with red-hot irons. I'd sense enough, even in my blackest hours, not to take that risk," he said. He laughed softly.

"Archimandros, my wise teacher, once said to me: 'No man who has not known despair knows himself, and no man who does not know himself, can find the truth.' I came with you to the end of the known world, Bedivere, seeking for truth. I hoped to find a master among your Wise Ones who could lead me to it. I did not guess I should learn its deepest meaning from an old, unlettered shepherd and a crazy Christian hermit."

I propped myself up on my elbows and looked across at him, puzzled.

"What truth?" I asked.

"The rhythm of the universe, and the secret of the love which sustains it," he said softly.

I lay down again. This was all beyond me.

"Whatever that may mean, I'm glad if it eased your captivity," I said. "Go on—tell me more. When did you get that scar, and how?"

He laughed.

"That was the second winter. I'd a death wish on me by then, for I could see no hope of ever regaining freedom. I drowsed one night and let my watch fire sink. A big dog wolf came over the wall of the fold behind me as I bent to mend it. I caught up my spear, but held it too short, having no time to shift my grip. It was my own fault. Ug the shepherd fetched Brother Gregory to doctor me when the wound festered, and so I gained a friend who healed more than my clawed arm."

Palomides paused, clasping his hands behind his head, smiling to himself.

"A little wizened old man who looked like a grass-hopper faded brown at summer ending—as active and as talkative as one, too. All his life, he told me, he'd been gadding about the world, searching for truth. He'd walked to Rome and further in his young days, studied there, and been accounted a notable scholar. I've an idea his adventures lost little in the telling, but discounting the half of them, his stories served to take my mind off my own

troubles, and set it working again. We argued philoso-
phies together for a night and a day, while he patiently
heated and reheated the trough of herbal waters in which
he steeped my arm until the poison was all drawn out. By
the time I could flex the fingers of my right hand again
(and that was two full moons or more), I'd learned a
hearty respect for his knowledge of medicine at least.
He'd learned it in a different school from mine and so we
each had something to teach the other. His skill was
mostly empirical, drawn from experience—invaluable to
me, since he worked with herbs one can find to hand in
these islands. Later he taught me to recognize the ones
that were strange to me. We got on famously, though
we'd argue the sun down the sky on most subjects other
than physic. He'd a laugh like the cackle of a hen an-
nouncing a new-laid egg, and would mock even at his
own religion at times, which seemed to me shocking in a
priest, until I understood his reasons.

    " 'Hate the Christian church, do you, boy? So do
I—so do I!' he said to me one day, when I'd thought he
was hoping to convert me, and so had told him outright
what had been done to Archimandros.

    " 'The Church—what is it? A man-made, botched-
up affair, grafted before the cutting was ripe by the
Emperor Constantine (God rest his soul) onto the deep-
rooted superstitions of the old Roman priesthood. No
wonder the briar grows up and chokes the rose now.
Why, the Bishop of Rome's taken over the very robes of
the Pontifex Maximus—and without waiting to shake the
fleas of politics out of them, either. Constantine handed
over the title in all good faith. Pontifex Maximus had
been one of the emperor's titles time out of mind. Well,
it's a temptation to any man who holds it now to dream
himself spiritual emperor and act accordingly—and what's
the result? Scheming for power that'll back the claim and
grabbing for money to finance it. Oh yes, I saw these
things happening. Rome's church has no use for any
Christian who isn't prepared to go along with it blindly all
the way. Arians, we all are, or Pelagians, or Manicheans,
or any other label they choose to stick on a man who
thinks for himself and uses the intelligence God gave him.

No wonder they burned your Archimandros. They'd have burned me, if I'd chosen to speak out all my mind. But I wasn't a priest in those days—just a pilgrim, looking for truth. I didn't find it at the bishop's grand house, so I slipped quietly off and worked as a day laborer in the docks down at Ostia till I'd money enough saved to buy me the book the bishop should have been studying, and tramped back home to my own country where I could study it in peace. Have you read, since you can read I suppose, Johannes' History of the Christ?'

"I told him I had not. So he lent me the manuscript. When I'd read it through for the third time, I'd no more wish to die."

"Why not?" I asked. "Don't tell me *you* have turned Christian, Palomides?"

He shook his head.

"A man can perceive the truth of a mystery without necessarily declaring himself a neophyte. But the truth that was in Johannes' writings healed my bitterness and nourished a new faith in me that behind all the seemingly senseless pain of living there is stretched a web, a pattern —a design of ultimate perfection which only great souls glimpse and interpret. One pattern, sketched by an intelligence far beyond man's. Plato knew it. Archimandros knew it—and this Jew, Johannes, the friend and chronicler of the Christ, he recognized it very clearly. Since I'd no ink or parchment, I learned his words by heart (I've a good memory). One of my first tasks will be to make a fair copy of his history before I forget one word of it."

Palomides paused, shifted over on to his side and said, meditatively:

"Yes, I learned much from Johannes' writings—and much, too, from my work with the sheep."

"Your work with the *sheep*?" I repeated.

He laughed.

"Aye. There's rhythm to a shepherd's life that brings a man close to understanding the very heartbeat of the universe. When old Ug watched for the right stars to rise over the standing stones so that we might know when we should put the ram to the ewes, and, though he could count in numbers no higher than the fingers of his two

hands, foretold from the circling of the heavens to within
two days when we might expect our first lamb, there was
a wisdom older than time behind his skills. The trust of
the dumb beasts in him—in me, too, after a time—the
faithful service the dogs gave the flock, trained to interpret our every order—Bedivere, there is a pattern, a
design, behind all living, that if we could only trust
ourselves to it as that old shepherd knew how to do, would
heal the sickness of our world."

I shook my head.

"You may be right—you probably are—but I'm a
soldier, not a philosopher. I'm glad, at least, that you
found comfort in having such a man as your hermit for
friend in that wilderness. But tell me, how did you escape? How did you come into Niel Long Sword's company?"

Palomides sighed and yawned suddenly, as if his
weariness had suddenly hit him.

"By sheer good luck. My master was a thriving
farmer, and had no mind to leave his farm and go to war.
Since, in that country, a man may provide a deputy in his
place when his Clan sends out the Branch, he ordered me
to serve in his stead. I'd no notion what this war was to
be about, but, when I learned we were to sail against
Britain, I told the Chieftain I'd been assigned to I'd serve
as a doctor if they needed one, but I'd not draw sword
against Arthur the King, having sworn an oath of loyalty
as one of his Companions. They were in two minds to
hang me for insolence, at first, but the Irish have respect
for an oath. They hauled me up before Niel for judgment,
and when he'd heard what I had to say, he sent everyone
away and we talked together half a night."

"And you persuaded him to fight for Arthur, not
against him?"

"I did my best. To be fair, he was half persuaded
already. Do you remember Iltud?"

"I do, indeed," I said, frowning.

"It seems he'd been in Tara some time back (I never
got the rights of it, as to exactly why, or how he'd fetched
up there) but he'd made an impression. Niel's not a man
you could turn from his own gods easily and if it was

conversions Iltud was trying for, he'd failed. But he'd talked of Arthur in a way that had caught Niel's imagination—and he talked, too, of one of Arthur's Companions missing in Ireland, a pirate's captive, sold into slavery. You must have seen for yourself the type of man Niel is—a warrior, first and last. Raiding and fighting are his chosen sports, and which side he's on is relatively unimportant, provided there's plenty of adventure and some loot to be had. I didn't find him hard to persuade."

"Well, thank the gods you achieved it!" I said. "Since I'm Marshal of the Games tomorrow, I suppose we'd better get some sleep. Thank the gods, too, that I've got you back, Palomides!"

Through sudden, overwhelming drowsiness, I heard him murmur quietly:

"And I you—and I you, Bedivere."

Griffin was late the next morning. I was dressed before he put in an appearance. I greeted him gruffly, my head still ringing from the last night's wine.

"Where in the name of all the Christian devils have you been and where are the boys? I need messengers. We've a hard day's work ahead of us."

He was red in the face and breathed as though he'd been running.

"Sorry, sir—we've had a bit of bother. Our lot have been bullying the little new lad. I've had to give all three of them a beating," he panted.

"Mithras! Need you choose the first day of the Games? Boys always bully each other, don't they? *You* were bullied. Let him learn to stand up for himself, as you had to," I grumbled.

"Yes, my lord. But this was serious. Young Allisander had got hold of a halter from the horse-lines and was trying to hang himself when I found him. Luckily he'd tied the wrong knot and only fell out of the tree. But if he'd managed it—well, we'd have had to answer for him when the Lord Lancelot got back, wouldn't we?"

"Tried to *hang* himself?" I said, startled. "What in the name of Light had the others done to put that into his head?"

Griffin grinned reluctantly.

"Well, sir, they *have* been giving him a rough passage. He's too softly reared, if you ask me, for our sort of life, and yet got a very good opinion of himself. An annoying little bastard, though you'll not have had time to notice. That fainting business yesterday put the lid on it with our boys. They—well—they caught him in the privy this morning and took his breeches down, to see if he was really a boy at all or one of Lord Lancelot's girls in disguise, they said. He took it very hard. Carried on about being shamed for life, and having no home— wanting to die because the only person who ever loved him died a while back. D'you think that'd maybe be his mother, sir? If so . . ."

"If so he'll have to get over it. It's hard, Griffin, but we can't afford to pander to a spoilt brat. There's too much to be done. Where is he now?" I said, anxious but impatient.

"I told him to wash his face and get himself some breakfast and report for duty as quick as he could. I'll keep an eye on him from now on, sir. The others'll let him alone after this or I'll know the reason why!"

"Good!" I said. "See to it they do. Now get me the pennants. We must start measuring out the field for the foot races."

In the back of my mind a memory nagged at me. Why did the name "Allisander" bring with it a feeling of uneasiness? Where had I heard it before? Curse Lancelot! I'd enough on my hands without being lumbered with his shrugged-off responsibility and I'd more important matters to put my mind to than a squabble among small boys!

It was not until we were back in the Great Fort, and some weeks after that even, I gave any serious consideration to the boy Allisander. Griffin, I suspect, had gone to some lengths in the interval to keep him from troubling me. I'd noticed him now and then doing some minor page's task, apparently industrious and docile enough. He was smooth spoken and well mannered, but he looked up at me sideways under that limp black forelock in such a startled fashion if I spoke to him suddenly that I wondered if he'd been ill-treated, rather than pampered in the past. He'd got a pale, peaky little face, and an odd, slight cast in one eye that gave him a furtive expression. If I thought of him at all, it was to commend Margause's decision to send him to the monks in Armorica. He'd neither the physical stamina nor the spirit to make a warrior as my other three tough little rascals had, by my reckoning. They'd taken to fighting among themselves for the privilege of burnishing my arms, and indeed, over most of their other tasks, and generally one or other of them seemed to have a black eye or swollen nose, at that time. When I asked Griffin why they were so quarrelsome, he looked resigned.

"It's that boy Allisander. He's a born troublemaker, that one. I'll be glad when we're rid of him. When's Lord Lancelot coming back, sir? If he delays much longer the seaways'll shut down for winter," he complained.

"They will, indeed. You're not the only one asking that question. I wish we could get news of him," I said.

When it came, it was bad news. The mopping-up operation in Arphon had proved more costly than expected. The Armoricans had done their job successfully, and reported back in time to catch the last sailing weather, but they'd had casualties, and Lancelot was one. He'd been severely wounded—a deep spear thrust in the side. He'd not be fit to travel before spring.

"Bors says it was a close shave, but he's out of danger now," Arthur told me, "and they've got the country up there quiet enough. King Pelles' people are caring for Lancelot well. But he'll have a dull winter, cut off in that lost and forgotten mountain province. I wish they'd brought him back here—but Bors says he wouldn't hear of hampering them by being carried down by litter. They've force-marched all the way, as it is, and we must get them started for Adurni tomorrow. The men want to get back to their families before the weather closes in."

Bors, when I found him later in the day, was harassed and anxious.

"Lancelot's been desperately ill, Bedivere. Those deep body wounds are always the worst. He lost so much blood when they were getting out the spearhead, he looks like a ghost. But he's very cheerful. Swears he'd rather stay behind until he's recovered. Seems to like it up there—though I can't think why. It's a weird set-up. Primitive beyond words—all inaccessible mountain peaks and waterfalls, and the old king more like some odd breed of Priest than a High King. But the atmosphere's peaceful in a way. Lancelot says it reminds him of when we were boys on the Island."

"Talking of boys," I said, "what I came to find you for is this—I've Lancelot's page on my hands. Will you take him back with you, or must I keep him?"

Bors looked more than ever harassed.

"Oh, keep him, will you? Can you? We're going to be packed in the galleys as close as oysters in a barrel by the look of things, and the crossing's bound to be rough. I'd sooner not have an extra youngster to fall overboard. He'd be better off with you for the winter, if that's not asking too much. Can he muck in with your boys until Lancelot gets back?"

"I suppose so," I said.

I'd always liked Bors, with his downright manner, and plain, open face. It seemed a small favor to grant a good comrade who, I could see, had enough on his hands getting his men away against time.

"Very well. I'll keep him," I said.

# Chapter Nineteen

That winter I stayed on in the fort. Lacking Lancelot, Arthur had need of me there, so I left Menaevia to Dinas, who by then was my deputy. I'd lost Iltud some time before, under circumstances that still made me angry to remember. The young fool, having got himself wounded in some skirmish, was taken in for nursing by a Christian hermit, who so worked on him, that, recovered, he'd begged Arthur's leave to resign his commission and enter the Christians' church as a priest. Arthur, tolerant of men's beliefs, let him go. Before he went I told him in no uncertain terms that to me such a choice came perilously near desertion and I reckoned Ambrosius would have counted it the same. I missed him, for I'd chosen Dinas, a middle-aged Colonial veteran, on the rebound, and he lacked both Iltud's breeding and his quick insight. Still, I found him conscientious and doggedly persistent—both useful qualities for the task we shared.

Arthur and indeed all of us were in good spirits after Tribruith. I was happy, that winter, having Palomides for my good comrade again. Only Guinevere the Queen seemed out of tune with the general mood. There was a cruel edge to her wit, and a restless impatience that broke on slight provocation into waspish irritability. Some days she'd abandon every pretense of gaiety and sit for hours, sunk in melancholy brooding.

"She grieves for Lancelot," Arthur said, indulgent as

usual. "Well, we all do—but women take anxiety harder. I tell her he's strong and will recover well enough, given rest and care."

Palomides, when I spoke of it with impatience one night in our quarters, laughed at me sideways.

"Maybe, knowing Lancelot, her anxiety is less for his sickness than for how he is employing a long convalescence?" he suggested. "Bors, who is sometimes naif, did lay stress on the charming nature of King Pelles' daughter who nurses him, remember!" Then, more gravely, he added, "I'll tell you one thing. Whatever the cause of the queen's anxiety, it is eating her heart out as a grub eats the core of an apple. It's to be hoped this marsh fever we have in the garrison does not strike her down, for she's no strength to resist it. Have you noticed how thin she's grown?"

We'd had an epidemic that year, as one often does in winter quarters—an ague, that started with shivering fits and high fever, and brought with it pains in the chest and a racking cough that lasted for months. We'd had reason to be thankful Palomides was back to deal with it.

As the year turnëd, and the days lengthened, there were more cases. I took the infection, but lightly, and threw it off after a week or so, but it left me irritable. It was then that I began to find the boy Allisander pricking my temper like a thorn stuck in a soft sandal strap.

I'd hardly noticed him until then, for as long as their duties were carried out I left my pages to Griffin's training, and he always saved me annoyance where he could. That is part of the duty of a good armor-bearer. But two of my older boys went sick, and suddenly I found myself brought more into contact with Lancelot's lad.

There was nothing I could complain of in his behavior. True, he was clumsy, fumbling when he helped with arming me, spilling wine when he poured it at table, but the gods know, one gets used to bearing with those things in a page's first year of service. It was rather his manner, at once nervous and defiant when he was at fault, and the ready lie he could always find to pass blame slickly onto another when I chided him, that made me impatient. If I spoke roughly, he'd cringe, as a dog will that's been badly handled as a pup, then throw back his head with a gesture of mute defiance, and an odd little smile, as though some secret sense of his own importance armed him against rebuke.

One day Kerouac—who was master-at-arms that year—complained to me he could do nothing with the boy.

"He'll not take correction, that's my main trouble with him, sir. His spear throwing's poor, and his sword-play's a disaster. Had you noticed he's left-handed?"

"No," I said. "Only that he's more awkward than most. That could account for it."

"I've had them left-handed before, but for the most part they'll take pains to overcome the disability, if only to catch up with the other boys of their age. But this one, you might say he glories in it. Turn your back, and his practice sword's in his left hand again, and he's got an insolent smile on his face, as though *he* were in the right of it and all the rest of us wrong. Near on half a year I'll have had him in the class, time Sir Lancelot's back, and what's to show for it? What *he'll* say I can imagine, sir."

"Cheer up, Kerouac. Allisander's marked out to be a monk, not a warrior," I comforted him.

"*Is* he so, sir? Well, I'm glad to know that. To listen to him you'd never guess it, I must say. Carries on alarming, sometimes, about how his father was the greatest of warriors, and he's all set to be even greater. Very mysterious about just *who* this famous warrior was, I might say—and the whole story probably a pack of lies, for he's a sly little bastard, *and* a troublemaker, besides. Got an ugly temper, too, when it's roused. Would you speak to him, sir? I was thinking he'd take more notice of you than he does of me."

"Have you tried beating him?" I asked.

"A score of times. Doesn't seem to make a blind bit of difference, except he'll give a look like a snake that's rearing to strike, and then go off and whisper to the other boys, and set them against me, I've a feeling. That's another thing. He's a bad influence, sir, specially with the younger ones—he and that Aglavain between them, they've got together a gang, you might say. Don't get up to mischief, exactly; not like Gaheris and your Griffin and those used to, honest mischief a man can settle with a quick clout round the ears and no hard feeling on either side—more inciting each other to dumb insolence, if you know what I mean."

I did know. Dumb insolence, and a hostile, wary suspicion of all authority. Instead of noisy, thoughtless, but eager small brothers, ambitious to excel each other in winning our approval, the gang Kerouac spoke of behaved like hostages in an enemy camp, watchful and secret, whispering among themselves. I'd noticed, with mounting exasperation, how often when we of the Companions were discussing something important, there seemed always a small page quite legitimately underfoot, bringing logs, tending a lamp, waiting with a message, escorting wolf-hounds in or out for exercise. Later I'd see the same small boy reporting to Allisander and then Allisander murmuring in a corner with Aglavain.

That evening I had Allisander up for reprimand, and talked to him for his own good about the reasons for learning to wield sword and spear right-handed as we all did.

"In a cavalry charge, riding in close formation, a left-handed swordsman could be a menace to his comrades," I told him severely.

He looked at me, his small, white face attentive, his strange eyes, shadowed by the limp-falling back forelock, oddly unfocused.

"A greater danger to the enemy, sir. A man doesn't think to guard against a thrust from the left," he said, and sniggered nervously.

Taken aback I said, "Maybe not, but it's bad discipline. You'll do as you're told—as Kerouac tells you, and not question it, understand?"

He sighed and said in a martyred tone:

"Kerouac picks on me—on all of us who come from Dalriada. His Clan and Dalriada have been at feud time out of mind, Aglavain says. Did you know that, sir?"

"Kerouac is one of the fairest men I know. That's nonsense," I retorted briskly.

He gave me a quick, upward glance and changed his ground.

"If I am to be a monk, it doesn't matter? I'll not need warrior training for that life, will I?" he questioned innocently.

"It'll do you no harm to learn. Bishops have led armies to victory before now. Germain of Auxerre did," I said.

He nodded.

"That's true. May I ask a question, sir?"

"Yes," I said.

"Can *you* fight left-handed?"

"Damn you, yes, if I need to," I said, my patience exhausted. "From now on you'll do an hour extra practice with Kerouac each day and obey him as you would me, or I'll know the reason why. Now get out and send Griffin to me."

I suppose my tone was harsh. He shivered, and his bottom lip trembled. He looked suddenly very young and miserably brow-beaten. Relenting, I said:

"Heart up, lad. The thing's not so impossible. You say you come of warrior stock. Remember that when a task is difficult, and see to it that you don't shame your own boast."

His head went up, and he flushed a deep, dusky red. His eyes met mine in a cold unchild-like stare. In a choking voice he said:

"My father—if you knew who my father was, you'd not dare—" then suddenly turned, and ran out, sobbing loudly, the noisy, uncontrolled sobs of a much younger child.

Next day he was missing when he should have come on duty. Griffin reported resignedly:

"Young Allisander's down with the fever now, sir. No end to it, is there?"

I was surprised at the feeling of relief that swept over me. One should not be so vulnerable to the atmosphere one small page can create, I thought—and thought no more about him for a while.

Some days later I missed Palomides at suppertime, and going back to the quarters we shared found him still not returned. I went to bed and must have been asleep some hours when his hand on my shoulder roused me. I sat up, blinking in the light of the lantern he carried.

"Bedivere, I need you. That boy of yours—Lancelot's lad—he's in high fever. I've had to move him out from the others, for he's delirious. Will you come?"

I muttered an oath or two, then, looking at his face, sat up, fully awake.

"Bad is he? How bad?"

"Bad enough. This fever runs high for a little, specially with the young, but he'll recover. It's the things he's saying I think you should hear."

Palomides was never one to make much of little. I knew that.

"I'm with you," I said.

Outside the stars were paling towards dawn. It was later than I'd guessed, and cold. Suddenly, out of nowhere, a memory came back to me. I heard Mawgan's voice saying urgently: *"Remember the name Allisander."*

"Gods!" I said aloud. *"That's* where I'd heard it before!"

I'd stopped in my tracks and Palomides turned.

"What did you say?" he asked.

"No matter. A warning I'd forgotten too long. Lead on," I said.

There were some little huts we'd built near the hospital to house cases of suspected plague or leprosy. A light was burning in one of them, and as we entered one of Palomides' assistants got up from beside the bunk and made some signs to him, then went silently out.

Palomides said in a low voice:

"Rainault—I chose him to help me. He's dumb since that head wound he got at the Blackwater Ford. Anything he hears he can't repeat."

Then he went forward, hung his lantern on a peg on the wall and bent over the bunk.

A querulous whimpering came from it.

"Alfia—Alfia—I want Alfia."

I moved round to where, myself in shadow, I could see the small figure tossing restlessly under rumpled blankets.

"Alfia is not here, Allisander. But you are quite safe. Lie quiet and try to sleep," Palomides said gently.

The boy stared up at him with bright, unseeing eyes. His face was flushed, his lips swollen and cracked. Suddenly he shrieked and struggled up to a sitting position, clutching at Palomides' arm.

"She's dead. Alfia's dead! They killed her. *She* had Alfia killed. I hate her, I hate her, I hate her."

"Quiet, quiet." Palomides pressed him gently down into the bed. "That's all over now. You're not in Dalriada. Here no one will hurt you."

Allisander tried to push aside the restraining hands.

"Let me go! I must get to Sir Lancelot. He'll save me. He's my father's friend. The king's friend." He was fighting to get off the bunk, his thin bare legs thrust out over the side, his face distorted with terror. Suddenly he collapsed, whimpering again, trying to shield his head with an upflung arm.

"Don't! Don't! Not the hot irons. I swear—I swear—I swear by the Cross I won't tell, ever. I'm not mad. I'm not. I'm not."

"Hush!" Palomides soothed him. "Come, you're thirsty, Allisander. Lie down, now, and you shall have a cool drink."

"Yes. Yes. Thirsty," the child muttered, licking his lips with a furred tongue. "So thirsty."

He went limp, and Palomides tucked him back into the blankets, then, reaching for a cup from the shelf at the head of the bunk, raised the thin little body against his own shoulder and let the boy drain its contents. Allisander drank greedily, choking a little. Then his face changed, looking up in a puzzled fashion at the man who held him.

"I'm not Allisander. I'm Medraut," he said. "Medraut." A crafty little smile twisted his face. "*She* thought I didn't know. But Alfia says I must never forget I'm Medraut, the great king's bastard." He clutched at Palomides again. "Don't say I told. Don't! *She'll* put out my eyes and sell me for a slave. She said she would if I told. Oh, she used to love me—when I was little. Then—then—" his voice weakened and grew indistinct. He muttered something, then cried again "Alfia!" and his head rolled against Palomides' shoulder, his eyelids flickered and closed, and a long shiver went through his whole body.

Palomides laid him back on the high-propped pillows and straightened up.

"Dead?" I questioned. I'd seen wounded men go out like that.

Palomides shook his head, looking down at the boy closely.

"No. The draught I gave him brings sudden sleep. I'd not risk his raving longer. He's not the strength for it. Better, perhaps, for him, if it was death, poor child."

In the broken light our eyes met and held.

"Gods!" I swore softly. "What treachery lies behind this, Palomides? Margause the Queen? Lancelot? Mawgan warned me. How did I forget? 'Remember Allisander,' she said."

At his name the boy stirred and murmured again. Palomides said softly, but with authority:

"We must not disturb him now. He's a very sick child, Bedivere. I'll call Rainault to watch by him until morning."

Outside the night had clouded. A fine mist was driving in across the hilltop, rising from the marshes. I waited the few minutes until Palomides rejoined me, trying to grapple with the shock of the thing. That small, pointed face, peering out through dark hair. The strange cast in the boy's eye. Mawgan's warning—and yet, the whole idea seemed fantastic—impossible.

"The boy's lying," I said harshly, when Palomides was beside me again. "He must be. He's picked up some rumor—heard some garbled camp gossip and thought to make himself important, play-acting the thing until he believed it himself. He can't be Ygern's child. That ship foundered."

"Perhaps," Palomides said calmly. "In delirium he might remember a fantasy. But to me the symptoms point to his having suffered some great shock, some terror, that he has kept secret, as children will, and that the fever has released. I wanted you to hear for yourself, at any rate."

"Yes. I see that," I said. "By the Light, Palomides, if the thing *is* true . . ." I paused, anger welling up in me so that my hand instinctively felt for the sword that was not at my side. "Lancelot shall answer to me for whatever part *he* had in it. I'll not be made a fool of by any man!"

"It was because of Lancelot I needed your witness," Palomides said, a certain bitterness in his voice. "I am still Palomides the Foreigner. You, he will have to believe."

"You never trusted Lancelot, did you?" I asked curiously.

"Not wholly. No. But I could well be mistaken. It is not his fault that both his looks and his charm, from the first, reminded me too vividly of the master who sold me to Bardeliez," he said.

I glanced at him, startled, but in the bobbing light of his lantern I could not read his face.

"So? I never knew that. Lancelot and I have been good battle comrades, always. I'd not like to think he's conspired with Margause to make a cat's paw of me. That *she* might have had the child stolen away seems possible—Ygern said she'd a mind to take and rear him up."

"I know," Palomides said quickly. "I remembered that, when he began to talk. It could have been done, Bedivere."

"But the ship foundered—lost with all hands," I insisted stupidly.

"So we have always believed. But do you remember how Kay said the shipmaster was so anxious to sail, even in the face of coming storm? That's rare in a Phoenician. He argued he could put into port down the coast if the weather worsened. Maybe he'd been well paid to do that anyway. Maybe he'd orders to be at some lonely haven by a given time and put one child, with his attendant, ashore? Afterwards," I felt the shrug in his voice, for in the swirling mist I could not see it, "well—who knows?

Perhaps the ship *did* founder. More likely, having thrown overboard a few recognizable bits of 'wreckage' where the currents would carry them across to Armorica, he sailed for some distant port and made good profit selling his cargo into slavery. Questions would have been asked, otherwise. A Phoenician I would *never* trust, that's certain."

We'd reached our quarters. I lit the lamp, and stood staring down into the flame.

"One thing—we must keep this problem to ourselves until Lancelot returns. I'll not have Arthur troubled with it—much less Ygern—until we know if it's more than a mare's nest." I turned and looked to him for agreement, and saw, suddenly, how grooved and drawn with weariness his face looked. "Gods, man, you're dead on your feet! Get to bed and get some rest. You've been losing sleep for nights, tending all these sick folk. We can talk in the morning," I said.

He smiled at me.

"A physician is accustomed to long hours. But, as you say, there's little we can do, except wait on Lancelot's return. I'll keep the boy in isolation until then. It will cause no comment, for Lancelot's due any day now, and the child's sickness will mend slowly, in any case. He's little behind him by way of constitution, and even now could solve the problem for us by slipping out with some complication I've not foreseen. Don't let it trouble you too much. You've more important things to give your mind to, when all's said."

"Maybe," I said. But I could think of few, just then, that weighed against a threat of treachery in Dalriada and Lancelot involved in it. Lancelot, whom Arthur trusted and loved above all the rest of the Companions.

As luck would have it, I'd no time to brood over that night's happenings. I was called up again before I'd been in bed an hour to lead a cavalry patrol scouring after cattle raiders. In the mist, they'd had the impudence to drive off one of our best herds, pastured below the fort on the water meadows. We always had trouble at spring starving time, in those days. The forests still housed too many colonies of outlaws—roving bands of runaway slaves, who'd made off back in the time of the Troubles, and bred for two generations, living in the wild. When game was scarce, they'd grow bold enough to come out of hiding and plunder for food. They were a savage lot, a menace to the small lonely farms, where they'd murder the menfolk and carry off the women as well as the stock. It took me and my men a week or more to track down this tribe, though we caught up with the cattle and got those sent back fast enough. Hunting the dense forest for an outlaw camp was mostly labor lost. Nine times out of ten all one found was a cluster of deserted huts, their hearth fires cold. We'd burn the place out on principle, but the owners faded like shadows into the undergrowth. Men, women and children, they'd travel miles in a night, leaving no trace in the trackless wilderness. We hanged the men we'd caught with the cattle, on an oak where four paths met, to discourage any of their kind passing that way, and got back to the fort on a bright, blowing morning to find the whole place in a stir of excitement.

"The Lord Lancelot's back, sir—rode in last evening," the decurion of the gate informed me, grinning with pleasure.

"How is he?" I asked, knowing that query would be expected of me.

"Looked the same as ever, to me, sir. But they say the journey's tired him—proper touch and go that wound he had must have been, by what his chaps tell us. Lucky to have got him back, by all accounts."

"Lucky indeed," I agreed, and rode on in. Lucky for me, I thought, to have missed his actual arrival. I'd have found it difficult just then to greet him with enthusiasm.

It was not until evening I had an opportunity to see him alone. All the womenfolk in the fort had been fussing over him, day long, but he'd excused himself from supper and gone to rest in his own quarters. I reckoned I'd get myself some food later and take the chance of speaking with him uninterrupted.

I found him lying on his bed, wrapped in a furred robe of soft red cloth. Very much the interesting convalescent, I thought mockingly, until I saw his face. The change in it startled me, seeing him off his guard as I entered (for I'd not let his page announce me). He'd aged five years and, having lost the deep tan of an outdoor life, was austerely pale. With his clear-cut features emphasized by loss of flesh, he'd a new dignity—a strange serenity; he was lying against heaped pillows, his eyes closed and dark smudges of weariness beneath them.

I hesitated in the doorway, my old and real affection for him warring with the impulse of exasperation I'd been feeling all day.

He opened his eyes, and his whole face came alive.

"Bedivere! How good of you to come! I've been wanting so much to see you—and alone," he greeted me.

"So I should think!" I said, relenting. "How are you? By the look of you in no fit state to explain yourself for the pretty prank you seem to have played on me. Shall I come back in the morning?"

He heaved himself up in the bed, wincing a little as he did so.

"By no means. I'm well enough—damnably stiff from the saddle, that's all, and riding's started my side throbbing again. But it'll pass." He motioned to the table beside his bed. "Help yourself to a cup of wine."

I shook my head.

"I'll not drink with you until you've heard what I've come to say. Lancelot, tell me straightly—what did you know of the boy Allisander when you so lightly put him under my protection that day at Luguvalium?"

"What do you know of him?" he countered quickly. "I suppose, from your expression, the little wretch has talked?"

"Not intentionally. He's down with marsh fever, and last week he was delirious," I said.

Lancelot grimaced.

"That would happen! So now the whole fort knows who he is?"

"No. Only Palomides and I. He's quarantined, with a dumb orderly to care for him. So it's true that he's Medraut?"

Lancelot nodded, biting his lip.

"Sit down, for God's sake, and I'll explain it to you. I'm sorry, Bedivere. When I left him with you I'd expected to have him off your hands and safe in Armorica out of harm's way in a matter of weeks. Believe me, that was what I intended."

I sat down on a gaily painted chest, facing the end of the bed. (Lancelot's quarters were always better furnished and more elegant than any of the rest of the Companions'. He'd a love of fine things and a natural good taste I'd always admired.)

"Why, for my sake, didn't you confide in me from the first?" I asked.

He shrugged.

"What time was there? It was a long story, and I'd barely time to remember the boy existed, with a whole new campaign—mountain fighting at that—to organize. Besides—it was safer for him—and possibly for you— that he should merge into the background, with no special notice taken of him just then. Margause the Queen might have changed her mind. As it was, I reckoned she'd not risk showing her hand by demanding him back from *you*, of all people—and I knew I could trust you to hold him safely for my sake, if she ever did."

"Well and good. But there's time for his story now," I said.

He nodded.

"I owe you that. It's not a pretty story, Bedivere, and I don't blame you for taking the thing amiss. I'd be angry enough in your place. The boy's Medraut, worse luck. There's not a doubt of it. You remember Alfia. Ygern's red-haired serving wench? Margause does not know it, but I'd had the essential facts from her before she was murdered. She'd meant to tell me more, but Margause saw to it she'd no time, poor soul. I'll not forgive myself for her death. I should have foreseen the danger and prevented it. But somehow one doesn't expect such utter ruthlessness from a woman."

"Margause is ruthless enough. You can see it in her eyes," I said. "But how did the thing happen?"

Lancelot sighed, moving restlessly. I could see his wound still pained him.

"Oh, I'd been at the queen's Dunn for a while before
the battle, getting the Dalriada recruits drilled, seeing to
the remounts for my own men, you know how it is? I
suppose the boy was about the place, but I'd never
noticed him—how much does one notice a child of that
age separately from the background of pages always
around? Then, one day—one night, rather—I'd been
down at the horse-lines late and when I got back to my
tent he was there, waiting for me instead of my own page.
He stammered out some story that my boy'd gone sick,
then suddenly took it back and confessed he'd bribed the
lad to let him take his place, because he'd a favor to ask.
Very earnestly, with tears in his eyes, he begged me to
take him into my service.

" 'The queen will let me go if *you* ask for me. She'll
do anything you ask. Everyone says so, sir,' he stammered out." Again Lancelot made a comical grimace.
"My friend, you will guess just how that news endeared
him to me! I suppose it's no secret that the Queen of
Dalriada—well, shall we say shows her preference for a
man a little overwhelmingly? I'd suffered excruciating
embarrassment all summer, and had hoped I'd passed the
matter off with Armorican tact. To know even the pages
had it for common gossip!" He shrugged and laughed, his
face wickedly alight with all its old sparkle. "So! I said
briefly and firmly I would *not* grant Sir Impudence's
request—and what next? The wretched boy is grovelling
at my feet, begging, imploring, sobbing his heart out. Me,
I cannot stand to see a child in real distress, and there
was no mistaking—I lifted him up and comforted him a
little and, to stop his blubbering, gave him some wine.
That, I agree was foolish. It was good wine and strong,
and he was too young to have the head for it. It loosed
his tongue with a vengeance. He poured out to me his
secret heart, and I—I was thunderstruck and appalled.
Not so appalled, you understand, that Margause the
Queen should have tricked us all ten years ago, but that
for ten years, through all his growing time, this boy must
have lived two-faced always. One life on the surface,
one—and evidently so tumultuous, that second life—in
his secret heart. For, on the surface, Margause treated

him, in fact, as Allisander, one of the orphans she raises out of charity, and such he believed she thought him. And then, his secret life, nourished by the tales of the good nurse, Alfia, that he is someone better than all others, the Pendragon's bastard, one day, perhaps, the Pendragon's heir Such a conflict—such a secret—in the mind of a child—it is impossible—it is impossible!"

The genuine concern, the kindly indignation in Lancelot's voice, touched me. He'd shown that surprising side of himself once or twice before—that tenderness towards the weak and unfortunate and real love for children. After all, it was he who had first thought of shipping the unwanted half-breed children to Armorica for safe upbringing, and I'd seen him, grave and intent, using his gift of healing on the wounded.

"So what did you do?" I asked.

He shook his head.

"A foolish thing, for which I blame myself. I soothed the child as best I could, promising him I'd do my best to grant his wish and take him with me, so that he could see the great king and the Companions But I warned him straightly that the king was not his father, and he must never think, much less speak of, such an idea again.

" 'Your mother was a great lady, and close kin to the king,' I said. 'It's true you share some measure of royal blood. But your father was a Saxon pirate, who took her by force and died for it. No blame or shame to you, lad. Saxon blood is warrior blood. You'll never be the Pendragon's heir, but, if you choose, you can rise to be one of his loyal Companions.' He seemed to take it in, after a time, though it's hard to tell, with children. He stared at me with those queer eyes of his, blinking like a small owl. Suddenly he said, 'I'm going to be sick!' and I only got him ouside the tent just in time.

"It was the wine, of course. After, he was shivering, and his legs gone from under him, so I wrapped him in my cloak and carried him across to the back quarters of the Dunn, where I sent a servant for his attendant. There was little light in the passageway where I waited and when the woman came I could hardly see her, except she was brawny and grey-haired. She knew me, though. She clutched at my arm, calling me by name, asking what was wrong with the lad, scolding him, and me too, for that matter, making a great to-do, but more, I thought, for the benefit of other servants passing to and fro than anything else.

"Medraut climbed down out of my arms, went to her and whispered.

"She said, staring at me: 'He's told you, sir? For God's sake, take him away from here then. For God's sake, sir!' Someone passed us and she began scolding again, then leaned close and whispered: 'Let me speak to you, sir. I must. I'll slip out later. Can you be down at the horse-lines when all's quiet?' "

Lancelot paused, frowning.

"I should have waited until I'd seen her, but," he shrugged, "one does things on impulse. The opportunity offered at supper. The queen was flattering me with her attentions, and said in two-edged jesting: 'Ask what favor you choose, Lancelot. Nothing can repay the help you've given Dalriada this season. Ask the half of my kingdom if you will—it's yours.' Her eyes said 'And so is its queen, for the asking.' I said quickly, thoughtlessly: 'Madam, I've no need of a kingdom, but I *have* need of a page. Give me Allisander, your orphan, and I'll cry you quits.'

"Her eyes narrowed like a cat's. 'Why Allisander?' she asked.

" 'My own page was sick and tonight the boy served me in his stead. He's quiet and deft and I could see would serve me well,' I said. 'We'll talk of it in the morning,' she said, and called loudly for the harper to strike up the evening lay."

He paused again.

"I met Alfia. I suppose we were followed. The night was overcast, it would have been easy. She was nervous and hurried in her talk, but she told me enough to convince me. The shipmaster put her and the child ashore at some little harbor down the coast, where an armed band waited. They travelled fast, by back ways and lonely tracks, to what must have seemed to her the world's end. Margause paid her well, and promised her a good husband and a farm to keep a still tongue.

" 'She persuaded me, sir, it was for the boy's good. Said you'd planned to have him put away, like Sir Kay wanted done. I believed her at first, but I've grown to know her better. Take him away, sir. I've a feeling whatever she wanted him for, she's changed her mind. Take him back to his own folk, for I've a feeling there's danger for him here and I do love him so. You take him and I'll slip off when the chance offers and join up with the army, like I used to be, so I can stay near him, in case he needs me. Will you do that?' "

"Bedivere, I promised I'd do my best. What else could I do? But next day we went on full alert, with news of a Pict war party sighted in the hills. You know how it is. First things must come first in war. I was away from the Dunn maybe a week or longer. When I returned it was Margause who reminded me of the request I'd made. All gentle, womanly concern, she seemed, commending her orphan to my care. 'Such a chance for any boy to train under the greatest of Arthur's Companions. Take him and welcome.' I looked her in the eye and asked his parentage. She gave me, pat, a story to move a heart of stone. All of it lies, of course. Then she said 'He's delicate and clever. Maybe he'll not make a warrior. If you think it wiser, have him trained as a clerk in one of your great Armorican schools and I vow I'll have him back in my service later, for I love the little fellow as though he were my own blood kin.' I thanked my stars the matter had gone so smoothly, but when the boy came to me (and it was the eve of our march to join you at Luguvalium) he looked like a little ghost.

" 'What's wrong? Are you regretting your request to come with me? Would you rather stay here?' I asked. I'd not much time to spare just then, as you can imagine.

"He looked at me blankly, as though he was half-stunned, then said: 'They found Alfia's body in the lake yesterday. She's been missing for days and days. They say she must have slipped drawing water and drowned by accident. But Daraik, who helped pull her out, says there

was a knife stuck into her back. Take me with you. I'm
frightened here.'" Lancelot sighed, leaned back and
spread out his hands. "So you see? Will you drink with
me now? I could do with some wine."

I hastened to pour for both of us from the jug set
ready beside the bed.

"I'll drink with you and willingly. I'm sorry if I ever
doubted you, Lancelot," I said.

When I'd drained the cup and set it down, I asked:

"What now? What are we to do with the boy?"

"What I'd planned from the first. He shall go back
with me to Armorica and I'll see to it he's put in the care
of an abbot I can trust. As a vowed monk he'll be under
obedience, and not trouble anyone here again. The life
should suit him, once he grows used to it. I've not
forgotten the Merlin's prophecy. Medraut must never
come back to Britain."

"When do you leave for Armorica?" I asked.

"As soon as may be," he said, with an emphasis that
startled me. "I doubt if I'll be back this summer. Bors
must lead our contingent. I've been away too long."

I was surprised and I suppose my face showed it.

He said, with an odd gravity:

"Bedivere, there are times when some unforeseen
accident can change the course of a man's life. I think
that may have happened to me. They say old King Pelles
is mad, but if so, it is a madness sent from God. That
place—it has an atmosphere, a holiness past all describing. I have been close to death and close to God, in the
mountains of Powys. I have found a new and precious
meaning to my life, and listened to wise advice. I must go
home to Armorica, and give more thought to my duty
there. You will not see me in Britain again for some
years."

"Some years? But Lancelot, we need you here!" I
said, knowing how Arthur counted on him.

He looked at me very gravely.

"If ever the *king* needs me, I shall come back," he
said. "Be easy in your mind. I shall not fail him," and he
sighed.

The emphasis on the one word told me much.

("Given time for thought, he's seen the danger of the situation that was developing. This means he intends to break with Guinevere. More honor to him!" I thought.) Aloud I said:

"We shall miss you. But every man must make his own decisions. I think yours may be right."

He held out his hand and, as I clasped it, I saw, with embarrassment, his eyes fill with tears.

"You were always a staunch comrade, Bedivere—be kind to her!" he muttered.

I said awkwardly:

"I'll do my best."

He pressed my hand until the bones almost cracked, then let it go and, leaning back, closed his eyes. Seeing the great tears slipping down his face, from beneath the dark lashes, I turned away and went silently out.

It was the only time he ever came near speaking openly to me of his love for Guinevere the Queen.

For three full years Lancelot kept to his resolve. Each season the Armoricans came over under Bors' command. He was a man of few words, a reliable commander, but lacking Lancelot's dash and initiative. I thought him more reticent than usual, when folk pressed him to say when Lancelot would come to Britain again, and if anyone asked him directly why his cousin lingered so long in Armorica, he answered shortly, with a gruffness that was unlike his usual placid good humor.

The reason became plain enough, the third year, when a scandal burst upon the fort that, for a time, rocked it to the foundations.

I came back from one of my journeys round Menaevia to find the thing still a nine day's wonder. Lancelot, it seemed, was married. Had been secretly married the year of Tribruith, to the daughter of King Pelles, the Princess Elaine. There were already two children of the marriage, a boy and a girl. So, folk said (wagging their heads and counting dates), he must certainly have returned to Carbonek at least once, without any hint reaching us he'd been in Britain.

That was not all. He must have deceived the poor girl

grievously as to the real state of his affairs, for while I'd
been away she'd come on a visit to Camelot, in all
innocence, believing the king, and indeed everyone else,
must know Lancelot had a wife, thinking she'd be welcome, hoping to get news of him.

The story, with exclamations, comments and exag-
gerations, was poured on me from every side.

"A most unfortunate affair!" Kay called it. "*Most*
unfortunate. Quite impossible, under the circumstances,
to keep it quiet. I'm afraid it will have created a very bad
impression. These foreigners!"

Gawain took the thing more lightly.

"You canna altogether blame the man. This Elaine
was a sweet, gentle lass, and nursed him back to health
when he was verra sick, by all accounts. I dare say, what
with her rank and the holy old father, he couldna have
had her any way except by marriage. The folly of the
thing was trying to hush it up, once done. To my mind, he
dared'na face the queen's anger at finding she wasna his
only heart's darling. You should have seen that one's
face, Bedivere, when he came hurrying from Armorica
for the funeral rites last month. A marble statue couldna
have looked colder on him, with a curl to her lip, besides,
that put him lower, by her reckoning, than any worm that
crawls."

"Funeral rites?" I queried, more bewildered than
ever. "Whose funeral rites?"

Gawain looked surprised.

"The Princess Elaine's. Has no one told you? She
died, poor lassie. Of a broken heart, they're saying,
though Palomides gives it some longer name. Better ask
him, Bedivere. There was some mystery about her death,
but the king insisted she must be buried with the solemn
pomp becoming a High King's daughter and the wife of a
High Prince."

I ran Palomides to earth just coming out of the
hospital and we went across to our quarters where we
could be private together.

"Tell me the simple truth about all this uproar in my
absence, for the gods' sake! I'd best know it before I see
Arthur," I said.

He nodded.

"The worst's over, now. A nine days' wonder. Folk will forget it, once the next scandal catches their interest, I don't doubt. The king handled the situation magnificently, Bedivere. He's a great man. Great in every way."

"Tell me something I don't know," I said rudely. "What actually happened?"

Briefly, the facts were much as Gawain had reported them. A secret marriage during the winter Lancelot was recovering from his wound, one or more visits paid in disguise, to Pelles' Fort of Carbonek—then silence and neglect. A young girl, with no experience of the world, in love and trusting, coming to Camelot to look for her missing husband, believing he might be wounded again, since she got no word from him.

"She was very young, Bedivere. Not yet nineteen, and I should say far from strong at any time. She'd borne the second child, a girl, not long before she made the journey here, and not had the best of care. She looked pale as a lily, and as slender, that day she rode in here, asking audience of the king. Her reason for coming must have shocked him, but *he* gave her no sign of that, but received her with great kindness and respect."

"And Guinevere?" I asked.

Palomides shook his head.

"That, I ask myself," he said grimly. "On the surface, all sweetness and concern—but with women it's hard to say. Somehow that girl must have learned the truth, I believe. After childbirth, any physician can tell you, there is sometimes a period when a woman falls into deep melancholy, even when conditions about her are most favorable. To a girl, gently reared, in a remote hill fastness, where, by all accounts, the atmosphere is one of rarefied and mystical religious devotion, the shock of finding herself deserted and neglected by the man she obviously adored may have been enough, without necessarily a hint she'd never stood, or was likely to stand, first in his affections.

"Enough for what?" I asked. I could tell he was keeping something back.

He hesitated, then shrugged.

"Best you should know it, Bedivere. Since the king could give her no promise of Lancelot's return, the Princess Elaine, after some days, asked his leave to return home. That night she wrote two letters, one to the king, one to Lancelot. At dawn next day, a couple of your guards found her body floating in the river."

"Gods!" I said, horrified.

"Luckily they were your men, Bedivere—Lysas the decurion and another veteran. They came for me and made no clamor of the finding. They'll not talk. No one knows of it, otherwise, except the king—and Lancelot. I bore witness to the Council that a sudden stopping of the heartbeat caused death—since that happens in drowning anyway, the diagnosis does not contradict my physician's oath. There are times when such discretion is necessary. But that you should know the facts without his telling may save Arthur distress."

"Yes," I said. "It's a bad business, Palomides." After a few moments' thought I asked him:

"Where is Lancelot?"

"Gone back to Armorica—for the present," he said.

"What of the children?"

"In Carbonek with their grandfather. I imagine he'll leave them there, though with him there's no telling." Palomides smiled a rather bitter smile. "It's my prophecy this will all blow over in a year or two, and you'll find Lancelot back with us. Possibly the best thing that poor girl could have done for him was what she did, Bedivere."

Palomides' prophecy was fulfilled. With his unerring sense of theatre, Lancelot came to our rescue, a year or two later, sailing the whole Armorican fleet round the coast and into the mouth of the Glein river with a force that turned what had looked like defeat into a smashing victory. We'd got ourselves cut off in the old hill fort of Agned, partly by an invading army of Angles and Frisians, but mainly by a rising of the Iceni. (Horse traders for generations, one can never trust that Clan. They'll back what looks like being the best bet for any day's race!) When the battle was over, rescued and rescuer were far too glad of the meeting to remember old scores. We marched back together to Camelot as one host, and from then on things were, at any rate on the surface, exactly as they had always been. There was no question in my mind Arthur was glad of it.

After Agned there must have been one of those lulls in the war that lasted several seasons. Harvests were good, and Bardeliez had prospered, for that was, as far as I can remember, when building began on the villa-palace, down in the water meadows. I'd my province to occupy my time, and I never approved that project, in any case, thinking it both extravagant and unpractical. Once built, the place would be impossible to defend (as indeed it proved.) It did not reconcile me to it that, each time I returned to the fort, it seemed to me Lancelot and the queen together were the moving spirits behind the work there, and in that shared interest had apparently agreed to sink all memory of differences and grievance.

Arthur, busy with more serious problems, looked on the whole thing with tolerant amusement.

"They're good playmates, those two, Bedivere. They always have been. The gods know, I am dull company for any woman these days. Women need occupation, amusement. Since she lacks dearer things to fill her days, I'm glad my poor lass can find happiness planning me this grand judgment hall she's set her heart on. It's little comfort beside the joys she'd the right to expect when she first came to me," and he sighed.

Again I was reminded of an indulgent father, speaking of a headstrong, wilful daughter. The bitterness of his disappointment that he remained childless I knew, though he never referred to it except by some such brief allusion. One does not lay a rough hand on the unhealed wound of a comrade.

I knew by then he'd resigned himself to the inevitable. Palomides told me so, one winter day, when we were riding home together after we'd been hawking out on the marshes.

"Guinevere will never bear a child, Bedivere. I doubt Leodogrance knew it, but her mother vowed her to the Moon Goddess at birth as an offering, hoping to win back Leodogrance's love through the Goddess's favor. Secretly, as a gesture of defiance and revenge—you know how wilful she is—after Leodogrance put her mother away and took a Christian wife, Guinevere persisted in the rites of that strange, ancient cult. The girls vowed as Moon Maidens go through a certain initiation at puberty that assures, if not their imposed perpetual virginity, at least the outward seeming of it, since there will never be the embarrassment of a babe to prove vows broken. It's very old magic, barbarous and dangerous. Some die. Those who survive are barren for life and there's no remedy."

I remembered the bleak look on his face, in the grey light of the late afternoon, as he said it. Snow was threatening. The hawk on his wrist ruffled its feathers in the cold. We'd had poor sport that day.

"By the Light, if that's true, and Leodogrance knew of it . . ." I said fiercely.

Palomides interrupted me.

"No, I think you may count him guiltless. I'm not even certain Guinevere herself understood the intention of 'The Dark Draught,' as they call it, when she accepted it, unquestioningly, at thirteen years old. Maybe the step-mother suspected something, for soon after she sent the child away to Christian nuns at York, for her education, and worked on Leodogrance to banish the moon cult from his country. But she did it too late."

Thinking back, I said:

"This is what the Merlin knew—or guessed. This is why he warned Arthur against the marriage."

"Very likely that man knows most things," Palomides agreed.

"How did you come to knowledge of it?" I asked.

"The queen, privately, came to me for a remedy against her childless state. I examined her. Certain things made me doubtful and when I questioned her, she confessed to the whole affair. From her distress, I deduced she'd secretly feared the truth but hoped I'd tell her the fear groundless. Those draughts used in the mysteries are deadly, Bedivere. The drugs of which they are composed are a secret handed down in the priestly caste of more than one cult. We learned of them in Alexandria. Archimandros called their magic black, for it destroys the very source of life."

# Chapter Twenty

Twelve great battles Arthur fought to make Britain a free and independent land. That is how the harpers tell it. Now, at last, Paulinus, to his satisfaction, has recorded the twelfth on his parchment sheets, bound together in their heavy cover of brown bull's-hide.

Today he was disappointed, for I had to admit to him I, myself, was not at Badon. (It is the landmark, Badon, still, in men's minds, when they speak of Arthur's wars.) Paulinus felt himself cheated that he could not have from me an eyewitness account. I did my best, searching memory for every detail of the strategy I'd heard so often recounted by those who were there, telling him how Cerdic and his sons, with the last and greatest invasion force we were ever called upon to encounter, got themselves as far as Badon Hill, below the downs, in country where the white horse sprawls all across the sheep-bitten turf (a strange beast, cut in the gleaming chalk by the Old Men, time out of mind).

He listened and scratched away attentively, his quill squeaking with his haste of writing in the fashion that sets my teeth on edge. When I thought we'd done (for I'd told him all I knew), he looked at me reproachfully with his pale-lashed Saxon eyes, and prattled some rigmarole about a Christian charm he'd heard gave us our victory.

"Surely, my lord (for all men tell it so), at Badon Hill the king rode into the battle wearing the picture of

Blessed Mary the Virgin on the shoulder of his hauberk?"

I was weary to exhaustion with all the talking I'd done, and muttered that I knew nothing of that.

He seemed crestfallen beyond common sense.

"But my lord, it is of the greatest importance we should record that fact. There are evil-minded folk who seek to put it about that Arthur was never a truly *Christian* king. If I could write in my book that he wore openly Our Blessed Lady's badge in the hour of his greatest victory, and that her intercession gave him, miraculously, power to break the heathen host, then men for ever would know such rumors false," he murmured.

He sounded so downhearted about it and he is after all a good, faithful fool. I took pains and searched my mind again. Then I remembered.

"You can write it that way," I said. "It may well be true. The queen did give him such a picture, I believe. Made in enamel work, it was. He could have worn it to please her that day. Leave out talk of miraculous help in breaking the Saxon onset, though. There are a few cavalry veterans left alive who would prefer to think *they* were responsible for that!"

I laughed and set myself coughing. I never yet met a Saxon, monk or otherwise, who had a sense of humor. Solemn as an owl, he wiped the blood from my chin and assured me he would set down exactly what I had said. He wanted, above all things, to stick to the *facts*.

Closing the heavy book, and preparing to carry it away with him, he added with smug satisfaction:

"Now that leaves only Camlan to record."

"Yes," I said. "Only Camlan."

I think something in my face warned him. He scuttled off in a hurry, and sent his abbot to tend me. He lives in daily fear still that I shall die before his record is quite complete, poor Paulinus!

It was pleasant and restful, for a little, to talk with Griffin of how surprised we all were to find which of our battles, now, are counted the most famous. Badon, in fact, gave us peace of a sort for more than twenty years. But the spring it was fought, I doubt any of us would have wagered it would prove of such importance to our cause. Wars are like that, when one is fighting them.

Communications had been bad, that year. We got word early that the Saxons were gathering a fleet, but just where they meant to land seemed to be anybody's guess. By Spring Sowing reports were pretty equally divided—some said it would be Vectis water, but a reliable source predicted the Thames river and the Kentish beaches. Arthur gathered two war hosts and went northeast with one, taking Lancelot and half the cavalry. I stayed in charge of the second, camping them around the fort, with Gawain and the rest of the cavalry sweeping the country southward on regular patrol. Rough weather at sea delayed the attack, and everyone's nerves were at full stretch, waiting on into spring, with the Clansmen getting restive, as they always did, when the time of sowing or harvest drew near and tempted them to chance taking dog's leave to their homes, in the hope they could scramble back in time for any battle with their corn in the ground and their haybarns well stocked behind them. Arthur's task was the easier that year, for his host was at least on the move! My temper was frayed to breaking point, holding my lot in check—but somehow, between regular maneuvers and some providential brigand-hunting, we managed. By late April the news was definite that a considerable force had landed on the Kentish beaches and it looked as if Arthur would meet the brunt of the attack. Half my Clan Chiefs wanted to go scoring off to share the fun, but there was no guarantee a second fleet would not be coming into Vectis water any day, so I held my hounds on a close leash, and wished Palomides had not gone with Arthur's host. It was lonely work being the most unpopular commander in Britain. It would have helped to have someone I could grumble to when I'd heard other people's grumbles from dawn to moonset!

What with one thing and another I'd paid very little attention to the queen and her girls, except to forbid, absolutely, that any woman should leave the fort without my knowledge, and to ensure that whenever any of them rode abroad, it should be with a proper escort. Guinevere had her own guard by then (all Rheged men) and my orders to them had been explicit from the first. She was to go nowhere without my permission. If I gave it, she would be accompanied by the centurion of the day, a full cohort, and a scouting party of auxiliary archers.

She had not liked my order, I could see that. Since I had given it, she had not eaten with us in hall, but kept to her own quarters and been served there, separately.

Guinevere and I were not friends the year of Badon. Women, like dogs and children, sense disapproval. One does not need to show it. For me, I could not have disapproved of her more, for it seemed to me that, deliberately and recklessly at that time, she played with fire.

Challenge any woman in love with threat of a rival, and the hunting instinct shows itself. Since the affair of Lancelot's marriage, I'd watched her using every weapon in her woman's armory to draw him into complete bondage—and Guinevere was well armed. At the beginning it had been, on his part, I do believe, a courtly game, played by an older man, flattered by the headlong devotion of a lovely girl. That was over. Now in the full maturity of womanhood, she knew how to rouse in him the response she'd craved from the first. One had only to look at the man to see the strain that was being put on him, torn between desire and his loyalty to Arthur. Both of them were moths, flying ever nearer to the candle's flame. But Arthur, not they, would be the one who would be scathed by the fire. That was the fear in my heart, and had been a long while.

By chance (and it was a lucky chance) I'd business that took me abroad soon after daybreak on May Morning that year. A native smith, whose work I respected, had his forge in a clearing in the forest. He was a dour, independent old devil, but a master craftsman. I'd commissioned him to make me a new set of half-armor for the opening of the campaign, and he was taking his time over the job. When I'd sent Griffin to collect it he'd come back, flushed and indignant with the information that I must call for it in person.

"He says you can please yourself, sir, but if you want it to fit you, you'd better ride down and let him do his work properly. He's not a magician, to guess the placing of the buckles, he says, and he's too busy to lose a day's labor traipsing up to the fort—I told him you'd make it worth his while, but he says it's not the money— it's the fact everyone wants their work done before our host moves out. Shall I take some of the guard down and bring him up by force?" Griffin looked hopeful.

"Certainly not," I said. "His skill is needed, and I'm comparatively idle. I'll ride down early tomorrow morning. You can come with me."

I was glad of the excuse to get away from the fort, if only for an hour or so.

It was a perfect May Morning, and as we left the river road and plunged into one of the green forest tracks, I felt a twinge of compunction that Gawain and I had agreed it would be folly, that year, to allow the youngsters to keep the usual May Day festival. Discipline forbade it, for we'd known what it would mean, girls and pages straying off, gathering green branches, hunting for blossoms and accidentally-on-purpose losing themselves in couples all over the woods. With our own host in camp, I knew there were all manner of landless folk prowling the forest—beggars hoping for camp scraps, thieves and vagabonds hanging on the outskirts of the army, hucksters and peddlers, harpers and gypsies. When the queen had sent to me, asking what plays we were making for the Maying, I'd sent back a curt answer that, for this year, there could be no plays, and had added, unkindly, that, though she might not have noticed it, this was a time of war.

As the dew-drenched forest grass, starred with small, bright flowers, brushed my horse's fetlocks, and a cuckoo called among the golden-green of the branches overhead, I thought that perhaps I had been too harsh.

We must have gone about a mile, when, ahead of us, beyond a stand of thickly growing holly scrub, I heard a woman scream. A moment later there was a thud of hooves, and a riderless horse bolted along the tracks towards us, shied and swerved off between the tree trunks, the reins hanging loose on its neck.

It was one of our own good horses, not a native pony, I'd time to see that. Saddle and bridle were crimson leather, with shining ornaments. Either it had been stolen, or else . . .

Griffin cried out shrilly:

"That was one of the queen's horses, sir! Did you see?"

I shouted to him to follow me and rode forward at a gallop.

Beyond the hollies, the track widened to a clearing, where bluebells were trampled and there were signs of a recent struggle. On the far side of it, the track ran on into the shadow of thick evergreen—spruce and fir and more holly. Coming out of the sunlight, I'd only just time to rein back my horse on his haunches, or I'd have ridden clean over a small boy in the green tunic the queen's pages wore, who was running, staggering and sobbing, towards us.

He can't have been more than eleven years old—a thin elf of a child, with a dead white face, clutching his right arm, which hung awkwardly at his side. But he'd got the makings of a warrior. He let the arm hang and pulled at my cloak, left-handed.

"Sir, sir, don't stop! Ride on! It's the queen! They've got her, sir. I couldn't stop them. I went for them but they twisted the dagger away from me. Oh, sir, please hurry!"

"How many men, boy?" I asked, not wasting words.

"Three." He was swaying again.

"Armed?"

"The leader was. He pulled her up across his saddle. He had a sword—the other two only hurling spears I think—and on foot. Oh! My arm!"

"See to him, Griffin. Take him up in front of you and ride back for the guard. Mind his arm—I think it's broken—but ride like the wind, boy!" I ordered.

"Sir, let me come with you!" Griffin clamored. *"Please,* my lord. It'll be three to one . . ."

"Damn your impudence! I can manage that many! Do as you're told!" I roared at him, and kicked my horse forward again. There was no time to lose. I knew the track ran straight through almost impenetrable forest for a couple of miles. I must catch up with the quarry before they reached open woodland and I lost the trail.

Round a bend in the track, a quarter of a mile on, a man jumped from cover and grabbed for my rein, missed it and fell. I rode over him and heard him scream. Ahead of me another was running steadily—a tough, shag-headed fellow. I drew my sword; glancing over his shoulder, he must have seen it and, diving into cover, vanished from sight, shouting something as he went. A short hunting spear whistled past me and buried itself, quivering, in a tree trunk.

I urged my horse on, but the mounted man must have had a longer start than I'd reckoned. Round each curve the ride showed, empty and mocking in glimmering green shadow. Then ahead, I saw open sunlight again, and a gleam of white. I'd come to the end of the fir trees, and into a place where charcoal burners had been felling trees at the edge of the great oak forest.

The going had been soft. I suppose it had muffled the beat of my horse's hooves. The man thought he was alone with his prey, and had no reason to suspect pursuit. He was still well ahead of me. On a patch of open ground, in front of a half-ruined hut, I saw him pull up. A woman's white dress fluttered; then she was down on the ground and he was on top of her.

I shouted I don't know what—oaths, curses, threats—and saw him get first to his knees, then to his feet. He was ready for me as I threw myself off my horse and went for him, and I saw, as I ran in with my sword already drawn, that he was no ordinary brigand, but a man I remembered: Meliagrance, once a junior officer at the fort, whom Arthur had outlawed for robbing and half murdering a comrade. He was a big, red-faced bull of a man, with black hair curling close like a ram's fleece and thick wet lips. But he'd been well trained in our army. I'd my work cut out to hold his first furious rush and it was minutes before, by a feint and twist he wasn't expecting, I sent his sword spinning out of his hand and harmlessly away across the grass. I've never had much stomach to kill a man unarmed and suddenly I saw the fear in his eyes. I slammed my own sword home in its sheath and before he could draw his dagger, went for him again, bare-handed. All the frustration of the past weeks, all my rage with an idle woman's folly, had blazed up in me. I fought exultantly, furiously, glad at last to have something tangible to hit out at. Geraint's men had taught me to wrestle. I got him face down, with my knee in his back and my arm under his head. Then I jerked upwards and heard the neck bones crack. He went limp under me. If you know the trick of it, that hold always ensures a quick finish.

I got to my feet, panting, my wrist streaming blood where he'd bitten it. (One should avoid that, but I was a little out of practice and too intent on the finish to be careful, that day.) Then I saw his handiwork and for a long moment my rage, that had been an exultation, turned cold and deadly, so that I wished I'd taken time to make his end harder.

Guinevere had always been beautiful. Now, cowering on the trampled ground, clutching her torn dress across her breasts, she was ugly. He'd ripped her white tunic from neck to waist and below. It was muddy and draggled and stained with blood. Her hair hung loose and matted, and there was mud on that as well, and her lips were swollen and bruised, gone oddly square as she gasped and sobbed for breath, her eyes half closed in a face that was pinched and blue-white.

The sight of any other woman brought so low would have roused pity in me. But the whole episode had got me badly shaken. Arthur had left her in my charge, and I had somehow, I did not stop to think just how, allowed this thing to happen. She might very well have been killed. It might have proved a plot to kidnap her and hold her hostage, involving us in the gods knew what problems of intrigue, or what vast demands by way of ransom. All these things had been thundering through my mind on that two-mile ride, beating time with the galloping hooves of my horse. Predictably, my anxiety exploded into rage. I was very, very angry!

"In the name of Light, madam, how did this thing happen? What were you doing, outside the fort, without

my permission, without a guard?" I said. "Come, pull
yourself together. At a guess, I came in time. You may
thank the gods I did. How much are you hurt?"

She drew a great shuddering breath and looked up at
me, recognition dawning slowly as her eyes widened.

"Bedivere! It would be you!" she said in a harsh
whisper. "That man—that brute . . ." and she shuddered
again, her voice failing her.

"Is dead," I said briefly. "I've sent for the guard.
You've nothing to fear."

She pushed back her hair and her face changed,
became suddenly alive to more than her own condition.

"Bedivere—the boy . . ."

"What boy?" I asked.

"Nicki—my little page. He's only a child, but he
tried to defend me. Oh Bedivere, did they kill him?"

"His arm is broken—but it'll mend," I said grimly.
"No thanks to you he's alive though. How dared you—
how *dared* you wander abroad with no other attendant at
a time like this?"

She blinked, and again tried to pull her torn dress
about her. A little color began to come into her face. She
said, with a strange simplicity that held an echo, for all
her draggled looks, of her usual haughtiness:

"It was May Morning."

I drew a deep breath. "Women!" I thought. Well,
the guard would be coming, and besides that, there was
the fellow whom I'd let slip, who had run off into the
woods. He might be part of an outlaw band, and even
before the guard could get to us I might have a hornets'
nest about us. I glanced round. There was the charcoal
burner's hut.

I unslung my cloak.

"Come," I said. "Get up and put this round you.
You don't want the guard to see you in this state. We'll
shelter in the hut over there until they come. Can you
walk?"

I helped her to her feet and wrapped my centurion's
cloak round her.

She'd got command of herself quicker than most

women would have done. I had to admit that. Once on
her feet, though she was trembling all over, she drew
away from me a little.

"I can manage," she said proudly. "You don't need
to help me."

But when she tried to walk, the faint color left her
face and I saw her bite at her bruised lower lip. She was
limping badly.

"My ankle—it must have twisted when I—when he
threw me down off the horse. Oh, I'm sorry, Bedivere!"
she said, miserably, and I saw she was blinking back
tears. I put my arm round her, and suddenly my anger
evaporated.

"Come," I said again, more kindly. "You've had a
nasty toss and a bad shock, my lady. I'm going to carry
you."

She shrank at my touch, then quite suddenly went
limp in my arms, as I lifted her, and dropped her head on
my shoulder with a little sigh, like a hurt child.

She was lighter than I'd expected. Though she was
tall, she was very slight—I felt how thin she'd grown and
the smallness of her bones. She must be badly bruised, I
thought, dragged across a galloping horse and then flung
down, as I'd seen her, like some bundle of merchandise.
Besides, the brute had been all over her—I could smell
the stink of him, rank as a fox, in her hair. As I carried
her easily across the clearing and into the hut, I'd begun
to wonder if, perhaps, I'd been a little rough with her,
myself.

The place was bare and dry and there was a pile of
hay in one corner. I laid her down on that. As I did so, a
trickle of blood fell from my bitten wrist, and she saw
it.

"You're hurt," she said. "You too—let me look."

Before I could stop her, she caught my hand in both
hers and examined it, then looked up, as I knelt beside
her, her eyes gone suddenly very dark and startled.

"But this isn't an ordinary wound. It's . . ."

I drew my hand back quickly.

"It's nothing. We wrestled and I was clumsy. The
man bit me, if you must know. I'm sorry I let the blood

drip on you. You'd had enough today without that!" and I laughed awkwardly.

She shook her head.

"It's no laughing matter. It's deep. It could fester. The brute—that *animal*," she said fiercely. "Oh, I'm glad you killed him! That was well done. He—he used to follow me about at the fort. Did you recognize him, Bedivere?"

"I did," I said grimly. "Meliagrance."

"Once, years ago, he even dared to speak to me. He must have been drunk—the thing he said was—unrepeatable. Today, any woman would have served for him. He did not recognize me until I was up on the saddle in front of him. But all the way he kept gloating that he'd got me in his power at last. He said he would teach me I was only a woman like any other woman and that in the forest there are no queens." —

"He'll not boast again. You were lucky," I said, and got to my feet. "Now I'm going to make sure we have not been followed."

I went outside and looked around. The forest slept in the level sunlight. Nothing was stirring, except my horse, cropping the lush spring grass. There was a little stream, trickling among watercresses. I went and washed my wrist in it, then tore some strips from my shirt. I used one to staunch the bleeding and soaked the others in water.

When I went back into the hut, I saw she had got herself in some order, winding my cloak around her over one shoulder and under the other cleverly enough, so that, held in place by a brooch off her own dress, it made her completely decent, and she was sitting forward on the hay, examining her foot, wincing a little as she prodded at it.

"Not broken—only sprained," she said, and gave me a wry little smile. I liked her courage.

"I've wet linen here. Let me bind it for you," I said, and knelt down again. Her foot was long and slender, and very white, but the ankle was already puffing up and turning purple-black.

One learns some skills in soldiering, and I made a

firm job of the bandaging, while she watched me, pushing
back her tangled hair, and trying to comb it into place
with her fingers, with a certain impatient distaste. When
I'd finished she said, curiously:

"You're kind, Bedivere. Arthur always told me you
were kind. The cold water is taking the pain away. If you
could put me up on your horse, I think I could ride
now."

I shook my head.

"With permission, madam, we'll wait here until the
guard finds us. Meliagrance must have been living an
outlaw's life. He may have a band of ruffians somewhere
not far off. I'm not taking chances."

She accepted that.

"Lie down and rest. I'll keep watch in the doorway,"
I said, and went over to where I could get a view across
the clearing, without being seen from without.

She sighed and I heard the hay rustle, as she settled
herself back into it. There was a long silence, and deep in
the forest I heard the cuckoo calling again, and the
cooing of ring doves.

She said, suddenly, in a small voice:

"Bedivere!"

I turned and glanced at her, then went back to my
watching.

"Yes, my lady?"

"Do you understand why I *had* to come out to the
woods on May Day?"

There were several answers I might have made to
that. If I had said, "Because you are no better than a
spoilt child, who must always have its own way, at
whatever cost," it would not have been far off the mark.
But one has to be angry to speak that kind of truth. I said
simply:

"No, I do not understand."

"My mother was of the Hill People, a Priestess of
the Moon, and so, once, was I, Bedivere. It would be
unlucky for them—perhaps for Arthur and—others—
who are in danger if . . ." she paused, then went on more
quickly. "There is a fountain in the forest that the Little
People here hold sacred. There are certain rites an initiat-

ed Priestess can perform that bring good luck to the corn
sowing, if they are done truly on May Morning. I have
always seen to that for Arthur's people. They are *my*
people, Bedivere. If I had known you could be kind, I
would have told you—tried to explain. But you always
seem so stern—so distant, I didn't dare. Arthur understands."

I looked round at her again in real surprise. This
was a thing that would never have crossed my mind.

She went on, gravely:

"It is a very old faith. The oldest in the world,
perhaps. A woman's religion, but still it has power. It is
to do with the earth, and the mystery of all life—the
growing crops, the fertility of the cattle and"—she caught
her breath on something like a sob— "and of the women.
Truly, it is important still."

I was puzzled.

"You believe that? But—you are a Christian, surely? Didn't you give Arthur a holy Christian relic to wear
on his armor—a shoulder brooch, surely, for his cloak,
with a Christian picture done on it in enamels? He
showed it to me the night before he left."

She smiled at me—and it was a strange, mysterious
smile, that lit her face to beauty again and wiped out the
memory of the tattered woman, cowering on the ground,
I'd seen so short a time before.

"That's true. A picture of Mary the Virgin Mother.
What difference? The difference only of a name men use."
The wise, seeing look passed and she laughed, a bitter
laugh. "Oh, I'm Christian enough. My stepmother saw to
that. She had me christened after my own mother died
and sent me away to York to be educated by the nuns
there. I needed it. I was wild as a mountain hare in those
days. They taught me a great deal, but one cannot un-
learn the lessons of childhood—the truths that go deep
into one's very roots. I loved my own mother passionately. For her sake, secretly, when I was fourteen, I went
back to the hills and was fully initiated as a Moon
Maiden. Arthur knows." She sighed. "He has good reason
to know. It is why I have failed him, Bedivere. A girl who
has been set apart by the Great Initiation, to serve Earth

Mother, takes risks. The Dark Draught, which gives one magic to fertilize the crops, the cattle, the people can sometimes exact a bitter penalty. One has the magic, but—one cannot bear a child. I was thirteen, lonely, headstrong—and they did not warn me. I nearly died. Better, perhaps, for Arthur, if I had. Palomides understands. He made me understand. But I knew too late. Now, having nothing else to give, I try to give Britain my magic. I *had* to go down to the forest on this day, Bedivere. You are a Bard—perhaps that will help you a little to forgive me."

"Women," I thought again. "How they complicate life. Their own *and* other people's!"

I said, as gently as I could:

"I am a soldier, madam, who knows little and understands less of any religion, except loyalty to my country and my commander. If you had trusted me with your reasons yesterday, I have enough respect for the beliefs of others to have helped you to your wish, I hope. It is a pity you could not, and that, I suppose, was my fault. I'm sorry for it. We might have saved you from an ugly experience. Will you try to trust me in the future?"

She said, solemnly:

"Yes. Now that I know you better, I think I shall always trust you."

A sound caught my attention. I turned to the door again.

Through the trees I saw the glitter of spear points, and as the horsemen came out into the clearing at a fast trot, I said, over my shoulder:

"The guard is here, and somebody has had the wit to send a closed litter. Now we'll soon have you home and safe."

I went across to her and put out my hand to help her up. It was the bandaged one. She startled me by taking it and holding it for a moment up against her cheek with an impulsive little gesture that was oddly maternal. I've seen mothers do the same thing to "make the hurt better" for a small child.

Palomides said, later, I'd been lucky that that bite

healed so cleanly. Even the scar of it ceased to show within the year.

Three days later, the news of Badon came through. Celidon the Merlin brought it to me. He slipped into the fort, between moonset and cocklight, passed in without question by the guards on the gate, as he always did, and stood beside my bed, a ragged black figure that made me start out of sleep and grasp the sword that always lay close beside me in those days.

His high, cackling laugh mocked that instinctive gesture, and I sat up, throwing back the covers, and caught at his cloak.

"What news?" I croaked, still only half awake, and not sure if he was dream, or ghost, or reality.

"Good news, Bedivere. Victory. But we've paid for it."

I reached for my tunic, shivering in the dawn chill, and pulled it on all anyhow over my nakedness, afraid to ask him the price we'd paid. Then, nerving myself to the question:

"Arthur—is he safe?"

"Safe enough, boy. Hacked about in places, as they all are. You can't fight a three-day battle without giving blood. But we've lost a third of the men—centurions and warriors. Palomides has his hands full. Lamorak's gone, and Geraint, and Ulfius. It was a bloody business."

"Lancelot?" I asked.

He shrugged, and in the faint glow of the shaded lamp I kept burning all night when we were on alert, his shadow wavered up the white wall of my sleeping cell.

"That one bears a charmed life," he said, and there was a hint of bitterness in his tone.

He sat down on my armor chest and something in the abruptness of the movement made me look at him more closely.

"You're hurt," I said. "Your hand?"

I'd seen, as his cloak fell back, that he carried his left wrist in a scarf and the hand was swathed in bandages.

He glanced down at it and laughed.

"Yes—you'll have to give them the Lay of Victory this time. I was careless. It'll be some time before I'll be able to make harp music for the host again. But it'll mend."

I began to pull on my clothes. It was the first time I'd ever known him take a wound in battle, and it shook me.

"How bad is it? Gods, Celidon!—we always thought our Merlin bore a charmed life if anyone did!" I said.

"I tell you, I was careless. Lamorak was carrying the Dragon standard. As he fell, I caught it from him. I forgot in the heat of the moment a Bard must take no active part in any battle, being unarmed. It's bad to tempt the gods. Saxon seaxes are sharp when one forgets for a moment to keep the ring-pass-knot about one," and he laughed again.

Then, as if dismissing an irrelevance, he said briskly:

"The worst I've told you. The best is this—Cerdic's dead and so are his sons. The Saxon war host's broken. There'll be no more trouble this year. You can take the fort off alert." An urgent scratching at the cell door interrupted us. Griffin's head came round it, tousled, his face anxious:

"I heard voices, my lord, and—my lord Merlin!" He stopped, halfway into the room, his whole attitude changing into one eager question mark.

"Come in, lad. It's victory," I said quietly. "Cerdic's dead and the Saxon host is broken." Then, as his whole face lit up and I saw his mouth opening to let out a yell of joy (he was still young enough for that): "Be quiet, you fool. Time enough to rouse the whole fort when we've warned the queen. Go over now, and tell the centurion of her guard to wake one of her women, one of the reliable matrons, and break it to her quietly that all's well. The king and the Lord Lancelot are safe and there's nothing more for her to fear. Then roust out the trumpeters and tell them to stand by. I'll come over to the gate tower and announce the news to the whole fort from there when I'm ready. And, Griffin, send two of our boys to me at once.

The Merlin needs attendance—food, wine, a bath."

"Yes, my lord—I'll see to it all, my lord." Griffin made a hasty reverence to Celidon and was off like an arrow.

I called after him.

"Go first of all to the queen, mind."

I turned, and in the growing dawn light, saw the Merlin's eyes were measuring me with their old, sardonic amusement.

"The king—and Lancelot?" he said softly.

I felt my color rising, and frowned.

"She—she has been under great strain from the long anxiety. Despondent. Full of woman's fears and omens," I stammered. "It was only right to give her the news before a general announcement. The shock—"

"Oh, yes, yes, I understand!" he said, lightly. He stretched, winced a little and settled his bandaged hand more comfortably in its sling. "I'll come with you to the gate tower, Bedivere. They'll want to hear all I can tell them of the fight. Then I'll be glad to let this body of mine rest for a time. I'm not as young as I was when we rode to Arthur's King Choosing. Age tells even on a Merlin when he's careless and forgets his magic!"

I looked at him anxiously. It was true. His face was grey with weariness, and the lines on it were grooved deep as scars.

"By the Light, they might have sent another messenger—and you wounded!" I said.

He smiled at me.

"I come and I go," he said. "It was my own choice and I had my reasons. Besides, with this hand I could be no use to them and they need every whole man they've got at the moment. Badon will be remembered as long as Bards sing, Bedivere—but they've bought it at a heavy price. I may be able to help some of those here who will be paying that price as long as their hearts hold memory."

After the first few days of wild rejoicing and stunned realization of personal losses, a strange lull fell on the fort. I waited until I was sure my half of the command

would not be needed again that summer, then sent the
greater part of the men on leave to get in their hay
harvests while the weather lasted. The regular garrison
went back to normal duties and once again we were
waiting—this time for the return of the host. I found
myself with some leisure on my hands, and began, in odd
moments, composing the Song of Victory that would be
expected of me by Arthur's host, since the Merlin would
be in no shape to give it them when the time of feasting
came.

There was a place I had found for myself years
before about half a mile distant from the foot of the
ramparts—a quiet and secret place, in the heart of a little
wood by a stream-side. Some hermit, long since dead, I
imagine, had built himself a Christian chapel there of clay
and wattle. Half buried now, in eglantine and a luxuriant
overgrowth of wild white roses, I had come on it out
hunting, and kept its existence to myself. Only Griffin
knew of it and knew when I went there, so that I could be
found if need arose. He had an odd, boyish reverence for
the little shrine and had taken some pains to sweep it
clean, and even repaired the roughly carved crucifix
above the doorless opening. I suppose, even then, he had
a stirring of the urge to that religion in him, though I gave
no thought to the matter—and should certainly never
have guessed he would one day turn to it enough to wear
his present abbot's robe and cross.

On a golden afternoon when the scent of the hundreds of small, white flowers was sweet in the warm air,
and trout were rising in the shadows of the stream, I lost
myself in a new song—a song that had nothing to do with
the battle lay I had gone there to work upon. It was a
small, haunting tune, that had been teasing in my mind
for a long while. Words fitted themselves to it—the song
a girl sings, wandering at dusk on the shore, holding a
seashell to her ear, asking it which of two lovers she shall
choose, and hearing only the roar of distant waves, echoing in it—the waves that have carried both of them out of
her life for ever. There were three verses to it—no more.
When it was complete, I bowed my head on the carved
pillar of the harp and felt the tears prickle against my

closed lids. For the girl I saw on the dim sea edge was Ygern as I had known her long ago—Ygern, with her wild dark hair, her great sad eyes and her small, pointed face set in a white, determined acceptance of inevitable pain.

"It is good when the harper lives in his song. Play that for me again," a voice said above my head. I started, and looked up into the face of the Merlin.

"It was nothing—a trifle that came into my head. I should have been shaping the Victory Lay by rights," I said gruffly.

"Time enough for that." He moved away to where a fallen tree trunk lay across the little glade and sat down on it.

"Diarmed taught you well," he said. He was prodding with the long staff he carried at a patch of moss on the ground. Suddenly he looked up at me, with one of his old, flashing glances. "Ygern has also passed into the degree of Bard this year. She's happy in it," he said.

"I am glad," I said, looking down at my harp.

"You'll see her again, and in this life, Bedivere. She does not forget you, any more than you forget her. The years will pass," he said.

He went on looking at me. I could feel his eyes, though I kept my head bent. Suddenly he said, his voice sounding old and irritable:

"Well, well, every one of us must face his moira. Three things no man can rule: the flight of the wind; the rise of the tide; and the fate written in his stars. Make no mistake, Bedivere, the years ahead of us are not going to be any easier than the years behind."

I looked up then. If he would talk of other things than Ygern, I could meet his eyes.

"Who ever imagined they would be?" I said. "Does it matter, provided we win through to final victory?"

"You'll do that. Up to a point, this Badon Hill could even prove to be it. There may be peace of a kind for a good while ahead now."

He went back to prodding at the moss bump.

"Fewer invasions. Less fighting. Plenty of other troubles. At the end, darkness—and then one small spark that

burns steadily on—a spark on which will depend the
lighting of a flame down the long centuries." He paused,
then, with one of his sudden movements, was on his feet
again. "Go on with your harping, boy. We shall need it!"
he said, turned on his heel and was gone, disappearing
into the shadows of the little wood as though he had
never been there.

I sat for another half hour, striking odd, disconnected chords only, wondering what he had been foretelling.
Had he spoken of what the true Sight told him?

I comforted myself in the end with the thought he
was human after all, and not used to war wounds and the
battle fatigue that any soldier knows leaves a depression
on the spirits. Besides, he was getting very old.

At last I got up and went back to the fort to check
that all was prepared as it should be for the return of a
victorious host. Something told me I should make little
headway with my Song of Victory. Those words—*at the
end, darkness*—had laid a quietening touch upon the
strings of my harp.

# Chapter Twenty-One

Much changed after Badon. If Paulinus needed to know just how and when those changes took place I could not give him his facts. Only the small, unconnected pictures flit across my mind, now, as the swallows used to flit about the Great Judgment Hall of Camelot on summer evenings—that must have been long after Badon, though, for swallows will not nest in a new building for seven years or more.

The first time Arthur brought back prisoners from a pitched battle was after Badon. That was the first change.

Riding awkwardly, slumped like meal-sacks and obviously saddlesore, six hairy, sullen young giants rode in under the north gate, surrounded by a strong guard.

"What are *those*?" I asked Gaheris, who was in charge of the detachment.

He grinned down at me.

"Hostages. Hostages from the Federates. Earnest of good behavior until we've time to go in state and sign a treaty. They're all Chief's sons, and if there's any trouble, we hang them. Simple as that!"

"Simpler to hang them now, and be done with it!" I muttered. "What's to be done with them here, anyway?"

Gaheris's grin widened.

"They're *hostages*, man. To be treated with all courtesy. Eat and sleep with us, and have plenty of opportunity to have a look at the strength their folk have been

defying. I'd advise you to keep upwind of them. Stink like
polecats and every one of them as lousy as a cuckoo;
forby not a word do they speak of any language but their
own barbarous tongue. But they're here by the Pendragon's orders, so who are we to complain?"

"Who indeed?" I said. "Carry on, Gaheris. Tell your
men to look to those ponies, though. Every one of them's
saddle-galled at a guess."

He saluted still laughing, and trotted smartly forward at the head of his century.

The prisoners looked at me with hatred as they
passed. I don't doubt my expression was equally grim.
The very thought of sitting at meat with a Saxon turned
my stomach. I could not understand why Arthur should
forgo the custom that had served us so well all through
the war of never taking prisoners.

I told him as much at the first opportunity. He gave
me a hard, blue look, and said briefly:

"Times change. From now on we don't only fight for
Britain, we *rule* Britain—and that includes the Given
Lands, which, in honor, I cannot take back from men
whose grandfathers earned them, and who have farmed
them for three generations. Rome gave justice to men of
all races in this island. So must I."

"You aren't planning to use them as Federate auxiliaries—as Rome did—by any chance?" I said. I was
angry, and so was he.

He paused, looking away from me into the distance.

"No," he said quietly. "No, I shall never do that. I
might, some day, learn to trust a Saxon. But for a reason
you know well enough, I'd not trust myself—ever—to
fight beside one."

Badon brought loot enough and the promise of sufficient
future stability to justify finishing the building and fur-
nishing of the queen's palace in a style that satisfied even
her taste. I came, reluctantly, to admit there were some
things to be said in its favor. Men say Caurasius' Imperial
villa on the coast was grander and larger in its day, but
materials and craftsmanship must have been cheaper and

easier come by then. At least a judgment hall on the level
land saved old poor folk the long steep climb up to the
fort when they wanted justice, and visitors of importance
could be housed in a style that impressed them. Palomides was lyrical in his admiration for the place.

"A building with the solidity of Rome, and the
Celtic genius for color and craftsman's work. A palace fit
for your Pendragon, Bedivere. Something folk will remember us by, long after we are dead, and say 'Out of the
ruin of war, Arthur the King raised up a new Britain and
this noble building marked the beginning of it!'" he
said.

Indeed, all down the years, it was never entirely
completed. New additions were always being made to it
to meet new needs. Even the year of Camlan, I remember, men were at work enlarging and improving the
queen's pleasure gardens along the river.

Once, when I asked Celidon his opinion, he rocked,
heel and toe, the way he had and, staring out across the
terrace at the pillared portico of the main living quarters,
and the bronze doors of the judgment hall, said, with his
quizzical smile:

"It will serve a purpose. The dream, not the fabric,
will endure."

After Camlan it was the one place, so they tell me,
the Saxon war host took trouble to raze utterly to the
ground. They had, I suppose, a superstitious horror of it,
for the rumor of the king who might return from his
enchanted rest always haunted them. Last time I passed
that way the brambles grew waist-high and nothing remained. Even the tessellated pavements they must have
dug up and scattered in their haste to wipe out all trace of
even a foundation.

War did not stop short for us who lived through it,
at Badon Hill. I'd plenty of trouble with the Irish, down
in Lyonesse, after, and so had Gawain (Arthur had
revived the Province of Valentia by then and made him
its prefect) with the Picts.

They are a strange race. Not like any other enemy
I've ever been up against. More like the wolfpacks of

winter, which, well hunted, will vanish into the forest for
months, sometimes years. But they always return.

Gawain's appointment made him responsible for the
whole strategy of northern defense, and left Margause the
Queen with a good deal less power to interfere than she'd
been used to having.

"Go north with him for a season, Bedivere," Arthur
said. "I've a notion he may need support. My sister has a
strange hold on all those boys of hers, even Gawain, still.
I've never known him give ground in battle, but he'll
fidget and look apprehensive whenever there's a question
of outstanding his mother on any point of policy. I need
him out of leading strings if, as seems likely, he's ever to
make a Pendragon."

"Have you appointed him your heir, then?" I asked,
startled.

"Not I, but the Clans would, if I were to fall in
battle. Who else is there? And I've no belief I bear a
charmed life, for all the army's faith I do. I'd die the
easier, if it came to it, thinking Britain would be ruled
by him, and not by Margause through him!" and he
laughed.

So one summer I went north and spent a season in
and about Dunedin Fort, and on the whole enjoying the
exercise. To be honest, I remember very little about it.
I've an impression I found Margause as floridly charming
as ever on the surface, and suspected her of being no less
devious than usual beneath it. I suppose I must have
convinced her she'd no option but to accept Arthur's
orders gracefully, for I do recollect her assuring me she'd
no wish to be a second Boadicea, and only longed for the
day when she could resign all responsibilities and live a
life of quiet contemplation.

"Like that dear, sweet girl, Ygern. So *brave* of her to
give up the world. I'm sure she was right to do it, you
know. Arthur could never have succeeded without the
Rheged alliance. But such a *pity* the queen is childless.
Such a tragedy, Bedivere."

Her eyes, brown and hard, watched me with birdlike
calculation and held no hint of sympathy to match the
velvet crooning of her voice.

One incident stands out in my mind, harshly clear. The campaign was virtually over and summer waning. I was back at the Royal Dunn, preparing to go south with my own men, and leave Gawain to follow later. He'd taken out his cavalry to make a final sweep and my fellows had mounted night guard for him, as we sometimes did. The Royal Dunn of Dalriada is a good place for defense, built on a steep man-made mound that rises from a tongue of land running out into the deep water of a sea inlet.

I was surprised, accordingly, to hear some disturbance going on down at the palisade entrance, while I was finishing my dressing, early on the last morning. It sounded as though the decurion on duty was turning out the full guard. Before I'd finished buckling on my sword, there was a thundering on the door of my sleeping cell, and one of the guards, a young recruit, with a sunburned face and a harassed expression, stood to attention as I opened it.

"Well?" I questioned.

"Decurion Lysas says could you come, my lord? We've a party of Saxons below. At least he reckons that's what they must be. Come in bold as brass they have, carrying green branches—about thirty of them, I'd say."

"*Saxons?*" I repeated the word unbelievingly. "Lysas must be wrong. There aren't any Saxons in these parts. Are they armed?"

"Fully armed, sir. By the look of their footgear they could have marched a fair distance, though."

"What do they want with us? You say they are carrying truce branches?"

"Yes, sir. They *seem* peaceable enough. Wanting something, but Lysas can't make out exactly what, seeing none of us speak their lingo."

"I'll come," I said.

They stood outside the palisade, faced by a wary Lysas, and his watchful, curious guards. (Lysas was a veteran and took no chances. His men, I noticed, had their spears ready and their bucklers up.) There were a score or more Saxons, big, hulking fellows, whiskered to the eyes and armed to the teeth. I'd faced hundreds like them in the past across a shield rim. Their drab, loose clothing hung on them, and I noticed their felt foot wrappings were worn through, filthy toes poking out at one end, scaly heels the other.

Their leader, at sight of me stepped forward, raised a grimy clenched hand to his horned headpiece respectfully enough, and began to speak, earnestly and doggedly. His speech, deep and gutteral, conveyed only a word or two here and there I could understand, though I'd mastered some Saxon over the years. He was evidently pleading for a favor, but all I could get was the word *"Bretwald"* which I knew was their equivalent for chief or leader, and something about "war" and "hunger."

"I suppose they must be a ship-wrecked crew, come in to give themselves up—they're asking for the king's mercy, at a guess," I said.

My decurion, who'd been watching me hopefully while the Saxon talked, looked reproachful.

"Thought you spoke Saxon, sir?"

"So I do—after a fashion—but I think this must be some kind of dialect," I said. "Wait, I'll see if *they* understand *me*."

I got my tongue round a question or two, phrased awkwardly enough.

"You come from the sea? Your ship's lost?"

"No ship. Farmers. We dig." The leader made the action of a man using a spade, then went off into another incomprehensible explanation.

"He says they're farmers," I translated, totally at a loss.

"Look like it, don't they?" Lysas was unimpressed. "Farmers! With those bloody great seaxes *and* swords and spears? If I was you, sir, I'd forget about their bits of greenery and round 'em up quick and tidy, before any more like them show up from nowhere. Whole set-up smells fishy to me."

"We can't arrest men under the truce branch. Send up to the fort and see if you can raise me an interpreter," I said, and added, impatiently, "We'll only buy trouble otherwise. Get moving, Lysas."

The decurion snapped out an order and a guard set off uphill in a hurry. We waited, but not for long.

He came down the slope from the Dunn at a loping run—a tall, slender young man, dressed in a tartan I did not recognize, with a Prince's eagle feather in his small round cap, and the usual glitter of arm rings, torque and shoulder brooches. He halted beside me, saluting casually.

"Can I be of service, my lord Bedivere? I understand most Saxon dialects and can speak them after a fashion. What's the trouble?"

I explained, briefly, and he turned at once to the Saxons' spokesman, firing a brief question, repeated more than once in different words, until the man's face cleared, and he answered in a long, gutteral response. My interpreter listened intently, his head on one side, fidgeting from foot to foot, and gesturing all the time with his left hand, as if to show he understood. Then he turned to me.

"Simple enough, my lord. These men are a deputation from one of the East Coast settlements—not Saxons, Jutes. They say their harvest has failed for the third time running, and their homefolk are in very low water. Can't hope to live through another winter without help. These men have been chosen by lot to offer themselves as auxiliaries to fight the Picts for pay. They say the money they'd earn would serve to buy food for the settlement, and seed corn for their spring planting."

"Well, that's a new one!" I said, taken aback.

Behind me Lysas gave a short bark of laughter.

"Reckon we've just about heard everything now!" he muttered.

The young Clan Prince raised a supercilious eyebrow in his direction.

"A normal request, surely? We'll be shorthanded as usual, up here, when the host goes south. This sample look useful to my mind. I think we should let the queen's council decide."

"Decide? Decide what?" I asked.

He looked at me with raised eyebrows, and answered, perfectly courteously, but with a hint of patience, as though explaining something that should have been obvious.

"Decide if Dalriada can accept these men as paid auxiliaries. Why not? It's been done before."

"In Vortigern's day—yes. And look at the result! No, we use no Saxon auxiliaries in Arthur's host," I said, in a tone I reckoned final.

"Not in the king's host, perhaps, my lord. None of us could presume to suggest it. But"—he shrugged and smiled—"different Clans, different customs. Dalriada rather leans to hired auxiliaries. I'm one myself, as a matter of fact. You don't recognize me, do you, my lord?"

I stared at him, while the Saxons shuffled their feet in the dust, and Lysas coughed discreetly behind his hand.

The thing was that I half remembered—but could not place the man—nor where I'd seen him before. A small, arrogant head, the chin hidden by a well-trimmed beard. A sallow skin and blue-black hair cut to his shoulders. Something strange and faintly repellent about the cold, grey-blue eyes.

"Maybe I should know you—but at the moment I can't recall," I said stiffly. His brash manner annoyed me. How could I be expected to remember every princeling of the hundred small Clans who'd fought with us over the years? The less important, the more touchy and arrogant they all were!

He laughed, half apologetically. "Why should you remember? I was your page for a short time only—and that's years ago. Thank God, I've changed past recognition from the miserable little brat you knew—Allisander, they called me then. I've another name now—and reason to believe you knew it at the time, sir? I'm Medraut—Medraut out of Armorica."

"Why did he come back here? Where else should he go, poor boy, when he found they wouldn't keep him as a monk? Lancelot, the dear, impulsive man, carried him off in a *most* high-handed fashion in the first place. I never thought a monastery was the right place for Medraut.

Remember his heredity—warrior blood on both sides, whoever his father was, *and* there's still a tiny doubt about that in my mind, you know. Oh yes, there is, Bedivere. Women have intuitions about these things! But I'm discretion personified—I'd never breathe the suspicion to anyone but you—certainly never to the boy himself. I said to him: 'Medraut, you're a Saxon bastard. You must accept the fact and forget any nonsense your old nurse told you.' I can be very direct when I choose."

Margause and I sat alone together in a small upper room that looked out over the still water of the lake through a window cut deep in the rough-hewn wall. She was still a beautiful woman, though she'd put on a good deal of weight with the years, and small crow's-foot wrinkles were beginning to show around her eyes.

I'd not minced words with her, for I was very angry. It had not taken me long that morning to discover from some of her council that in a quiet way they'd been building up a private force of paid auxiliaries in Dalriada for a year or more.

"Only a *small* force, my lord—only one full century at the most. How could we afford more? We are a poor Clan. But since the Pendragon calls out our warriors under the queen's sons to fight his wars, we need some guards we can depend on here. Prince Medraut of Armorica commands them—a fine young officer, with experience of Saxon auxiliaries overseas," one old greybeard with shifty eyes assured me and, seeing my expression, added hurriedly, "Only a temporary expedient, ye'll understand."

"One that is directly against the High King's policy. I'll speak with the queen herself on it," I'd said.

Now Margause smiled at me, and leaning forward tapped my knee playfully with a plump, ringed hand:

"Bedivere, don't scowl at me. I adore my brother, but it's time he, and all of you at Camelot, learned to move with the times. The young folk, now, are all for cooperation, and letting bygones be bygones. King Bann is *encouraging* Saxon farmers to settle and farm wastelands down his western coast; and he's recruited an entire

auxiliary legion from among them to guard his frontier
from the Franks. Medraut served for three years with
them before he came to me. That's where he learned their
language. He's a *brilliantly* clever boy—reads, writes, and
absolutely magical at figures! I was touched and proud he
chose to come back and offer himself to my service. But
there—Dalriada was the only home he'd ever had. So
many of my war orphans tell me that. They are a great
comfort to me, since Arthur has deprived me of all my
own boys. Not that I grudge them to him—not even my
naughty runaway Gareth!"

I'd no intention of being deflected from my main
purpose by talk of her favorite youngest's latest prank of
running off to join Arthur's host. That could wait.

"Tell me," I said sternly, "how did it come about
Medraut was dismissed from the monastery? Lancelot
planned he should stay there for life."

"Oh, Lancelot!" She shrugged and laughed with
malicious tolerance. "Lancelot I adore—but admit he is
apt to believe God made him his deputy here on earth?
One cannot dictate to a high-spirited boy that he must
leave the world, when he has already seen the glamour
and the glory of war and victory, and a High King's
court. Medraut wearied of the dull routine—and to be
frank with you (and I am always honest)—I'm inclined
to guess he took steps to enliven it in ways the pious
abbot found—shall we say—disturbing?"

"You mean he was thrown out of the monastery for
bad behavior?" I said. (I could guess the abbot's reasons.)

Margause spread her hands and raised her eyebrows.

"He says they told him he had not the vocation,"
she said primly, and added, glancing at me sideways, "I
doubt Lancelot knows of it. He is so *seldom* in his own
country now."

"So Medraut stays here in Dalriada?"

She gave me a long inscrutable look.

"Why, yes, Bedivere. He is invaluable to me," she
said innocently, and added emphatically, "With my sons
now all at Arthur's court, quite invaluable."

*"Checkmate,"* I thought.

We might be able to nip the use of Saxon auxiliaries in the bud. Gawain would have to attend to that. But I could see no way, at the moment, to forestall whatever scheme she was weaving round Medraut. I guessed she must have kept watch on him through the years and offered some bribe to get him back. As a child he had feared her—but men forget childhood fears, and, at a guess, he was ambitious, for I'd sensed the vanity in him even when he was my page. "Lancelot must advise with me on this—he and Palomides," I thought. "For myself, I cannot see the ending to it."

Abruptly I got to my feet and, pleading an early start in the morning, took my leave of Margause the Queen.

It is easy—too easy—to be wise after the event. Not knowing what to do about the problem of Medraut's return I did nothing, putting off any decision with the excuse to myself that I would be doubly watchful of Margause's every move in the future. A great deal was going on in Britain that seemed, at the time, more important, or at any rate to have more urgent a claim on my attention. With Arthur's rule growing stronger and more far-reaching every year, surely no grave threat was likely to arise from an ageing woman's scheming in far-off Dalriada, where, each year, Gawain's influence was growing. If he, as seemed then most probable, was to be Arthur's acknowledged successor, Medraut's spurious role as an illegitimate pretender for the future was irrelevant. He must be reduced, even by Margause's tortuous imaginings, to the status of a mere pawn in the complicated game of power politics. Why rake up an old scandal by revealing to anyone at Camelot that he still existed?

I said as much to Palomides, who, after a longer silence than I liked, finally agreed with me.

"Let sleeping dogs lie, Bedivere. But it might be wise to warn the Merlin of his existence. In view of his prophecy that the boy's stars were crossed with Arthur's, I'd do that—though I dare say you'll find he knows it already."

A little reluctantly I agreed, and got small satisfaction from Celidon's reception of the news.

He gave one of his inscrutable looks, shrugged, and said:

"Medraut? Yes, he's in Dalriada, I know that. What must be, must. No ocean is deep enough to drown a man's appointed destiny. This life or another, we must face the enemy we left behind us. For Arthur that time is still a long way off, and the outcome will be in his hands, not yours," and he turned away as if the matter ended there.

I caught at the sleeve of his gown.

"Tell me, Celidon—what *is* this danger you forsee? By the Light, there must be something a man can do to guard against it!" and instinctively I laid my hand on my sword hilt.

He half turned and glanced at me with one of his strange, white-hot gleams of anger that shot through my consciousness like a flash.

"Leave well alone, soldier! No earthly sword can turn the edge of Fate," he said, and for a moment I saw, in his veiled hawk's eyes, a terrible desolation. My hand dropped from his sleeve, and he went away, leaving me to stand, bewildered as a man stands when under him the solid ground has rocked in an earthquake.


Margause moved her pawn very quietly out across the board, when, in the press of other business, I'd let the memory slip my mind for a time. I'd been in my own province half a year and more, travelling from place to place, out of touch with the fort. Those of us who could got back to Camelot for the Pentecost Spring Gathering each year. It was our custom. In war we had drawn together to be ready for the summer campaigning, but afterwards we continued to come in from the four winds to make our reports, and to enjoy the fellowship of the greatest Gathering of the year.

That particular spring I was delayed (I cannot remember how), for the Games were over when I got back and so, I discovered, was the marriage of Gareth, Margause's youngest son, to a pretty, pert little piece on whose account he'd recently earned knighthood by rescuing her from a bandit kidnapping attempt.

"Why, Bedivere, you've missed great doings here!" Palomides greeted me, his smile welcoming, his eyes mocking. "Never was there such a feasting and merry-making. The Queen of Dalriada came junketing to bless and forgive her truant child, and purr and exclaim over her brother the king's great new palace! A shame she left this morning for her return journey. I'm sure you'll be disappointed at that!"

"Devastated!" I said. "The gods must have a grudge against me! How was she?"

"Overwhelmingly charming to everyone. Enraptured over the queen's palace by her own account, and managing to underline just how much of its elegant good taste we owe to Lancelot. Guinevere reminded me of a beautiful white cat I once saw sitting safe in a window embrasure with a bowl of cream, while a pedigree wolfhound bitch barked at her from the rushes below."

I laughed.

"Bitch is the right word for that one! Well, what trouble's she sown this time?"

He grimaced.

"You'll not like the news, Bedivere. But I may as well warn you at once, for you're bound to learn it soon. We've Medraut at court again—come ostensibly to earn, his knighthood."

*"What?"* I said, flabbergasted.

"I'm sorry. There was nothing to be done about it. You know how Arthur is with Margause—she amuses him and, to avoid granting her political advantages on which he'll not budge an inch, flatter him as she may, he's always ready and glad to meet what seem to him harmless whims."

"And she persuaded him Medraut's having a place at court was a *whim?*" I questioned. "But how in the name of all the gods did she account for him? For his being alive still, and grown to manhood secretly, mainly in Dalriada?"

"Nobody knows. The explanation—if there was one—passed between those two in private, though I believe they called Lancelot into the discussion at one point. I only know what Medraut told me this morning—that

the queen, his gracious benefactress, has given him ex-
tended leave of absence to serve her royal brother and
pursue the greatest ambition of his life—to become a
Knight of Arthur."

"We'll see about that," I said grimly. "If I've any
influence at all . . ." I left the sentence unfinished.

I had none, I discovered. Arthur, to my surprise, expected me to be as relieved as he himself appeared to be
that Medraut had survived infancy.

"I've always felt uneasy when I've remembered that
shipwreck—almost as though some corner of my conscience cried 'murderer' at me out of the dark. Oh, I
know well enough Margause tricked us—but what of it?
Women do these things. She'd asked quite openly for the
child and been refused—she wanted her own way—
women always do—*and* mostly seem to get it in the end!"
He laughed, and I could see he was thinking of Guinevere
and the new palace.

"So you mean to have Medraut here? The Merlin
warned against it, remember?"

He shrugged.

"A man must judge his own risks. The lad seems
harmless enough and anxious beyond most to make himself useful. I can do with a man who can write and figure
for me, on occasion, and Gawain can give him junior
rank in the cavalry under Gaheris. They'll judge him as a
warrior for me. Bedivere, he's Ygern's son—it must
weigh for something, that?"

His tone was oddly pleading.

("Yes," I thought, "he's Ygern's son—and *you* are
childless.") Aloud I said:

"Be careful, Bear. He's half a Saxon pirate, and I'm
telling you now, I who had him for my page, he'll never
be a man you can trust."

Arthur scowled at me.

"How can you tell that? Let him prove himself,
fairly, without prejudice. Every man deserves that much
justice."

"You'd make a knight of him some day?"

"If he deserved it—yes—and a Companion of the

Council as well if he proved himself worthy. Now, quit playing the Merlin, will you, and let me follow my own mind, at least in a matter as unimportant as Medraut. I sometimes think the king has less freedom of choice, once he's come to power, than any hind in the land, who at least can decide without asking which beast goes to market and which he'll keep to swell his growing flock! Come, tell me about the state of things out in Menaevia this year. How much corn can I count on for the army? Last year's harvest was good?"

I saw any further argument was useless. The pawn was out on the board. Only a pawn, after all. But a pawn, moved with skill, by the player one cannot see, may serve to finish a game checkmate.

It's strange how places can affect a man's mind and spirit—and that for no sensible reason. I always felt oppressed by the queen's palace, and though I was given quarters there—spacious and comfortable quarters—I seldom used them. To me, the fort, high up on its hilltop, with the winds blowing round it, was home. There the memories of the good years belonged. Kay agreed with me. He was beginning to feel his age a good deal by then, and was as set in his ideas as he was stiff in the joints.

"A lot of unnecessary extravagance! The judgment hall—yes, we needed that, and I will say, they've made a good job of it. It's spacious and dignified, and I admit it looks very fine when it's properly set out for feasting. There's room to serve the tables without jostling, and the lighting from the long windows and the great door is good. And, of course, one has to have proper cooking and storage space to serve a great company with food and drink. But that should have been the beginning and end of it. All this proliferation of guest chambers and bath-houses and courtyards and grand apartments—where's it going to end? It'll all have to be paid for. When I think of the expense!"

Palomides still approved all the changes, though he, too, chose to keep to his own austere way of life, up in the fort, to be close to the hospital.

"Rome is dying, Bedivere. On the mainland more

and more is being destroyed each year. Here, on this island, a new civilization is being born. Lancelot, for all his faults, has the eye of an artist. And he's maintained what Rome's learned through the centuries of civilized comfort. Thank the gods for hypocausts that work, and baths where a man can get himself comfortably clean!"

"And tessellated pavements instead of rushes where the dog's bones molder and the fleas breed—I know," I admitted, laughing. (I'd heard his views on that before.)

He nodded, gravely and unsmiling.

"A king holds his power from the gods, Bedivere. Something of the dignity and the mystery of a god should surround him in the eyes of subjects who cannot know at first hand the greatness of the man himself. I tell you, when the bronze doors of the judgment hall swing back, so wide and high a mounted man can ride through them, and between the rows of stone pillars (that golden native stone, the color of run honey) one sees, far up at the end, the round table of the Council on its dais, with Arthur's carved Dragon seat facing down the long aisle of the inlaid floor, all patterned as it is with the mysterious running designs of your Celtic craftsmen, something of the magic of Delphi catches the heart. A man who enters there knows that he is entering a Presence, and the awe of it reminds him that he, too, though he may be ignorant and poor, is still a man, with a man's right to walk, now and again, with his gods."

# Chapter Twenty-Two

Geraint's death at Badon left a questioned succession in Lyonesse. For some years unrest worked below the surface there. With the help of the Merlin's spies, I kept a wary eye on it. Suddenly, it erupted in Clan warfare, on a scale that could not be tolerated, and I found myself heading westward with a force of cavalry strong enough to restore law and order before the Irish should get wind of shore defenses neglected and rivalries to their advantage.

The problem—and while it lasted it gave me a spell of brisk campaigning—was the spurious claim of one of Geraint's nephews to the Dragonship of Lyonesse. Geraint had warned me of the man.

"Watch my cousin Milas, Bedivere, when I die. He's made trouble for me, time and again, and once I'm gone he'll make more. He's a treacherous, ambitious blackguard, strong as a bull and wily as a fox. He's got a certain swagger to him that attracts the common folk, and he's always had a following. I could handle him—but I doubt Carados is man enough."

He proved right. Carados, the rightful heir, for whom Geraint had stood regent, and then served loyally as advisor, was a gentle, studious man, who would have made a better monk than High King. When he died suddenly, under suspicious circumstances, that year, he left a wife and one young son, Constantine, kin to Arthur on his mother's side. The boy was obviously a case for

royal guardianship, and it would be my place to act as
protector to him and his mother until he came of age. But
Milas saw a golden opportunity to appoint himself regent,
and once in his care I'd a notion Constantine was likely to
follow his father before he had a chance to grow to
manhood. Leonore of Lyonesse, the boy's mother,
thought the same, and being a woman of spirit and
resource shut herself and the child, with a band of loyal
Clansmen, into the ancient hill fort of Dor and put up a
very creditable resistance until I and my men could hurry
westward to her rescue.

It took a season's hard fighting to sort the matter out
and the best part of another to persuade Lyonesse that
Arthur, not Milas, would rule there for the future. We ran
Milas to earth at last and I had the satisfaction of seeing
him personally to his hanging, as an example to any other
would-be rebels against the Pendragon's justice.

I was sick of the business by then. Civil war is an
ugly aspect of my trade, and settling the troubles it leaves
behind a long and wearisome task. But the campaign was
lightened for me by the short, yet wholly satisfactory
relationship it brought me with Carados' widow. There
have been fewer women in my life, I suppose, than in
most men's. I'd loved Ygern too deeply and too young
ever to find me another woman I could wholly give my
heart to. There had been others since Mawgan—brief
interludes of war, the sort every soldier knows—and I'd
asked myself sometimes why I could not be content, like
other men, to accept the comfort of second-best. Always
when it came to a decision, I found I shrank from making
it.

I could have married Leonore. She had a quality in
her that was kin to Ygern and to Mawgan—a gay, re-
sourceful, independent woman, whose mind marched with
mine; and she was beautiful in her own way. She had the
tawny coloring of Uther's line, and a slim, lithe tallness.
Her Clansmen called her "The Lioness," playing on her
title as Queen of the Westlands. She'd come to maturity
married to a man with the instincts of a monk, and in the
heat of shared danger passion flared up in us both, fierce

and short-lived, like fire in midsummer heather. We took
what the gods gave us and the memory of it is still sweet.
When I would have prolonged the affair and made it
permanent, she was quite definite.

"No, Bedivere. We've had our enchanted hour. We'll
not spoil the memory. Go back to your own life—you are
Arthur's Companion before you are any woman's lover,
my dear. Take Carados' boy to Arthur's court and train
him for the work he must do there. Rule Lyonesse for
me, with the rest of your province, until he is ready to
take his place as High King. He and the Clan will be safe
in your hands."

"And you?" I asked. "Leonore, what will you do?"

"What I can to help you both by civilizing at least
one corner of this wilderness country. Carados had it in
mind that one day we'd found a community of Christian
monks and nuns somewhere in the wastelands, that could
teach folk how to live in peace together with order and
some dignity. A community where the widows and the
orphans of war could come for help in time of need, old
folk could be cared for, and the sick healed," she said
gravely.

"You—*you* would be a nun?" I said, and laughed.
"My dear, let Carados sleep in peace. You don't owe him
such reparation. Think of me—not of the dead!"

But I could not move her.

"I do think of you. We have given each other a year
neither of us will ever forget. Leave it at that. Give me
my freedom as I give you yours. Don't try to hold back
summer when the leaves are falling, Bedivere."

In my heart I knew she was right. The wrench of
parting was sharp while it lasted, but the slow withering
and long winter of a relationship that belonged, for both
of us, to that one period of shared stress and danger
would have been harder, and would have dimmed the
bright memory of shared enchantment.

I rode soberly back to Camelot, taking with me a
small, red-haired, sturdy boy, with a freckled face and his
mother's grey-green eyes, who, after the first day of the
journey, forgot homesickness enough to be as much and

as little trouble to Griffin, in whose care I had put him, as the average healthy seven-year-old. I remember looking at him one evening, when we'd drawn rein to breathe the horses on a hilltop, and being suddenly reminded of Arthur, when we'd ridden with the Merlin to the Island. I suppose it was the sunset light, glinting on that mop of red hair, and the square set of his shoulders. It came to me that here was a child of Uther's blood, close enough kin to be in some sort in line of succession, and I wondered what Arthur would make of him. It came to me, also, with a sharp stab of regret, that here was Leonore's son and other sons of hers and mine might have sat their ponies, solid, straight-backed and eager-eyed at some future time, had she been less obstinate.

"Women!" I thought bitterly.

Suddenly he turned and looked at me eagerly.

"Sir—when we get to Camelot, Griffin says there is a river. Will you take me fishing?"

"Yes, when there's time, we'll go fishing," I said.

It was Arthur's custom, once in every few years, to hold Justice Court at Caerleon. In the press of my own affairs I'd forgotten that time had come round again. I found Camelot all in a flurry of preparation and though they gave me welcome, all of them, I had a feeling of disappointment and flatness. I was battle-weary, for one thing, and not pleased to find I must take the road again, to Caerleon, so soon.

Lancelot was in Armorica, they told me, and Palomides gone north with Gawain. Most of the Companions had taken up their new quarters in the palace, and one ate there now, by custom, if one was of the Council, I was told. The palace seemed to be all aflutter with Guinevere's girls, and giggling pages, helping them prepare for the impending royal progress. Arthur himself was absent —gone, they told me, as he went more and more often these days, to the Island. He was not expected back before morning. I handed a subdued and awed small boy over to Griffin's care for the night and went back to the fort, where I was content to get my supper from the decurions' mess and would have gone to bed, feeling myself ill used, but that the men I'd brought home had, it seemed, been talking big about some of our exploits. In the end I was persuaded by some of my old friends among the decurions to sit drinking with them, and they eventually fetched my harp and I sang them the Lyonesse story as I'd put it into rough verse. So I went to bed in the end more than a little drunk and slept without dreaming of Leonore for the first time since we two parted.

The next morning I found Arthur already at work. He was eating breakfast while he dictated a letter. I saw that, instead of the white monk who had always served him before as secretary, Medraut sat on the low scribe's stool, writing carefully on a tablet. He rose, with respect, when I entered, and Arthur waved the bannock spread with honey he was holding at me in cheerful greeting.

"Bedivere—it's good to see you! Wait a moment while I attend to this—there's a messenger waiting. Help yourself to food. I shan't be long." Then, impatiently but pleasantly, to Medraut, "Sit down and get on with it, boy—we've no time to waste today on ceremonies!"

I took a chicken leg from the plate beside him, and walked across to the open doorway on the far side of the room, biting into it as I went. It was still strange to find him here, instead of in his old quarters up at the fort. It was a pleasant room—small, but light and convenient for business, with one entrance direct off the Great Hall and the other leading, by shallow steps, out to the new gardens. He could come and go, and receive messengers without the whole court being aware of his movements, or of who visited him. He had stamped his personality on it, I thought. No fancy frescoes or elaborate mosaics, here. Walls plain washed in a cool green, and skins of wolf and deer on the stone-slabbed floor. Furnishings of the simplest, though solid and pleasant—a heavy desk of painted wood, with the red Dragon ramping along the front of it. Some carved chairs, cross-legged and comfortable, with no woman's fuss of cushions to them, and along the walls copper-bound chests. Pegs on the wall behind him held his armor and his white cloak with its deep gold border catching the early sunlight, and Excalibur, hanging by the broad, embroidered belt and shoulder sling. The only signs of luxury were the bronze brazier where a small fire of apple wood, recently lit, crackled still, with the charcoal above it beginning to glow, and two tall Roman lamps of fine design set one on each side of the hearth. A room for use, not show. A commander's quarters. Idly, I watched a peacock on the scythed grass of the terrace below spreading his tail for the admiration of his dull-colored wives, and reflected, with a certain wry nostalgia, how far we had come from our first winter at the fort. I heard Arthur's voice dictating. The letter seemed to be ending, and I did not trouble to catch its drift—until he said in a different tone:

"That's all. Get one of the monks to put it on parchment and bring it for my seal when it's done, Medraut. I shall need you again later, but while you've time, rout out the tallies of what's due from us in pay to those Armorican lads. They'll be wanting to get down to the coast in a hurry, I dare say."

Medraut rose with lithe obedience, pausing only to say, in a confidential undertone:

"You've not forgotten the queen goes hawking this morning, my lord?"

"What? Oh yes—I remember now. I said I'd go with her, didn't I? Well, of course I can't now. See a message goes to warn her not to wait for me. I don't want to spoil her morning's sport."

Medraut bowed and then, turning, gave me a respectful inclination before going silently from the room.

"A good boy, that. You were wrong about him, Bedivere. He's been making himself so useful I don't know how I ever did without him!" Arthur said, getting up and stretching largely. He came across and laid his arm across my shoulders. "Now let's look at you, man—gods, but it's good to have you back! Come and tell me all your news."

I threw the picked drumstick out to the peacocks, and turned to face him, feeling all the old warmth of homecoming and comradeship begin to flow back from his great, radiating personality. We smiled at each other. He said:

"Well? All quiet in Lyonesse, or you wouldn't be here, I suppose?"

"All quiet—for the time being, at any rate," I told him. "I've brought the boy."

"Good. What's he like?"

"Much like other boys. Needs discipline."

"Don't they all? We'll see how he shapes. Considering the uncertain future, he'd better take his Dragon training on the Island in a year or two."

"I'd thought of that. But with four of Margause's sons before him—and *their* sons after them . . ." I left the sentence unfinished.

He said, quite cheerfully:

"You've heard Gawain's latest is another boy? That makes four of *them*—and Gareth's hard behind him—a second baby expected at summer's end. That blood runs to warriors! Tell me, though—what of the Queen of Lyonesse, my little half cousin Leonore? Did you bring her back with you?"

He was smiling at me in a way that told me he'd heard rumors. I said gruffly:

"She had her own plans. She's for founding a Christian convent to 'civilize' Lyonesse. She'll make a good abbess."

"I see," he nodded. "I'm sorry. I'd hoped—but never mind—you know your own business best. Tell me more of the fighting. Milas gave you a run for your money, I gather, but did you—?" he broke off as the door from the Great Hall opened, and one of the king's pages announced:

"The queen, my lord."

Guinevere came into the room with a quick, impetuous grace, her eyes alight and eager, her color high.

"Is it true there's a messenger from Armorica? When is he coming? How soon?" she asked breathlessly, before the door had closed behind her.

She was dressed for riding, in the bracken-green she favored, a little green cap with the royal eagle feather in it set on her shining hair, that she'd caught up under it in a silken net. She had a white falcon Lancelot had given her, hodded and jessied in scarlet, on her gauntleted left wrist, and the necklet of gold set with great emeralds which had been his prize in the Games we held for Margause's amusement, two years before, clasped about her white throat. She looked as slender and brilliant as a young birch tree in May sunlight.

Arthur shook his head.

"I've a disappointment for you, sweetheart. This year we shall have to make do without Lancelot, or Bors and their men. They've trouble on their hands in Armorica."

The color drained from her face and she went very still.

"Bad trouble?" she asked.

"Bad enough. Clovis of the Franks has invaded them, with a strong force—claims Armorica was part of Gaul in Caesar's time and should be again. I doubt it's mainly bluff on his part and will end in a show of strength and then some more treaty-making. If it isn't, the Armoricans will be in for tough fighting. Clovis is no mean enemy."

She said quietly, decisively:

"You'll send reinforcements, of course? You'll go yourself?"

She was perfectly steady, but her face had gone pinched. She had looked like an eager girl when she came into the room. Now one saw that in fact she was a woman past thirty, her beauty burned to a transparent flame by the tension under which, for so long, she had been living.

The shadow had touched Arthur, too. His face was suddenly masked and expressionless.

"They've not asked for help. Lancelot knows my rule. We send no troops out of Britain. We can't afford to. He'll not expect it."

She stared at him, her eyes wide and angry.

"But that's betrayal," she said slowly. "After all he has done for you—for us—I can't believe it!"

Arthur said, gently, but with an edge of impatience to his voice:

"Don't get the thing out of proportion, my dear. The Armoricans can defend themselves. They've a fine war host and experienced commanders. It's not a plea for help Lancelot's sent me—only word he can't be spared, nor any of his men, this summer. He'll do well enough. You'll see."

She bent her head, looking at the ground, fighting some secret, inner battle. Up to then she had given me no greeting and I had thought she was unaware of my presence. Suddenly she threw back her head and her eyes came directly to mine, tears trembling on the long lashes, but a quick, little smile contradicting them, forced yet pathetically winning.

"Bedivere, he listens to you. Tell him he *must* send help. Tell him you'll lead an expeditionary force—now—today, before it's too late."

"Madam," I said, "you know it is for the king to decide in a matter like this."

Suddenly she lost control. Stamping her foot she flashed out:

"Cowards, both of you! To leave a man friendless when he needs you—to leave him to die. There are men who *will* go—my brothers. The men of Rheged will go. We do not forget the debts we owe to an ally who has always, *always* been there when we needed him. *We* don't betray our friends . . ."

She turned as if to leave us, quickly, as she had come.

Arthur did not raise his voice, but the command in it was peremptory.

"Stay where you are. Listen to me, my girl. I'll not be called 'coward' and 'traitor,' nor hear such insults hurled at my best friend by any hysterical woman—queen or wife to me though she may be. Take a hold on yourself and listen. War is men's affair, and Lancelot would tell you the same. He and I understand each other—yes, and better than you can ever hope to understand either of us. He was my trusted battle comrade, and Bedivere's too,

half a score of years before you ever set eyes on us. Do
you think we'd leave him friendless if he needed help? If
he asked for it?"

She stood, turned away from us, her head bowed
again, her shoulders drooping.

Arthur's face softened. He said, suddenly gentle:

"Come, sweetheart, be reasonable. Give that
damned bird to Bedivere. You'll have it baiting any
moment. Here"—he caught up his falconer's gauntlet
from where it lay on one of the chests and tossed it to
me—"take that hawk out, Bedivere, and give it to one of
the boys to put back on perch, until the queen's ready to
ride. Now sit down, my dear, and let's talk sense. I can't
have you upsetting yourself this way."

She obeyed him, holding out her wrist to me blindly.
I'd some difficulty getting the great falcon from her, and
then transferring it, outside the door, to Baudwin. It had
caught the infection of her nerves, as Arthur had seen it
was doing, and was beginning to ruffle and beat its wings.
By the time it was quiet and I'd seen the boy could
manage it, I found the argument within no nearer solution.

The queen sat, rigid and unyielding, in one of the
carved chairs by the hearth. Arthur was prowling up and
down the room, saying, as I entered:

"Three generations we lost that way. I've told you
before, I'll not send men overseas unless I must. It's
against my policy. Britain comes first. If Lancelot were
ever in extremity, that would be different."

"Would it? How would you know? How will any of
us know unless we are *there,* with him, and sharing his
danger. Oh, Holy Virgin, Mother of God, if only I were a
man!" She suddenly sprang up, wringing her hands.
"How many days' ride from the coast to Caerleon for a
messenger—and then the time lost gathering the men
you'll grudgingly send? If he needs help, if he sends for
help, it'll all be too late!"

Arthur went to her and put his arm around her.

"Steady now, lass." He spoke as I'd heard him speak
gentling a nervous horse. "Steady! You've had a shock

and you've taken it hard. I should have broken the news differently. Go to your bed and rest for a time. Bedivere shall find one of Palomides' assistants and he'll give you something to calm your vapors. At this rate you'll not be fit to travel tomorrow except in a litter."

She drew herself away from him with a sharp movement of such physical repulsion that it shocked me.

"Don't touch me! Leave me alone! If you are heartless enough to ride off to Caerleon tomorrow as though nothing had happened, you can go alone. I shall stay here—here, where the messengers will come first. Here, where I can see to it. I, the queen, will see that men are ready, if it's only my own Rheged guard—ready night and day, to march at a moment's notice."

She burst into a storm of sobbing, buried her face in her hands for a moment, then stiffened, and with her head held high went quickly out by the door that led into the gardens.

Arthur looked at me and shrugged, then sat down at the table, drew a parchment towards him, and seemed to be studying it. I saw, with concern, that his hand shook. The silence lengthened.

"Bear," I said at last, "is it often like that between you two now?"

He looked up at me, his eyes troubled.

"Too often. It's her woman's nerves—she frets her heart out, poor lass, because she's barren, and cannot give me the son I need. Talks wild talk when the Council plague me to appoint an heir, begging me to put her away and take another wife. The thing preys on her mind, and because of it small matters become great ones, and scenes like the one you've just witnessed happen too often between us. This war in Armorica's come at a bad moment. Lancelot's better than I am at lifting her spirits. We'd both counted on his coming."

I bit my lip, then, taking a risk and knowing I did, I said:

"You've never considered doing as she suggests? Divorcing her with all honor, for Britain's sake, and raising up sons while there is still time?"

His face flushed darkly and he slammed his fist down among the papers before him so that they scattered and some fell to the ground.

"Not you, too?" he exploded. "By the Light, I thought *you* knew me better! Am I a man to break my given oath to a woman who has been a faithful wife to me, because the gods deny us the fruits of marriage? She blames herself—some nonsense Palomides told her, to do with moon magic when she was little more than a loyal, bewildered child. If there's blame, it's mine. I defied the Merlin's warning to get us a hundred armed and mounted men when Britain needed them, and I must pay the price. Who among my wise Council set *you* on to persuade me to this, Bedivere?"

I said evenly:

"There's none among the Companions who'd be rash enough, Arthur, to interfere between us two. You must know that. Why? Have the Council advised you to divorce? I've been away some time, remember?"

He looked down at his hand, lying on the table, as if surprised to see it there. After a moment of hesitation, he said wearily:

"Some of them—yes. Kay's forever nagging at me —and others, too." He looked up again, and smiled crookedly. "Let's not quarrel, we two. I know you mean well, but this is not a matter on which I'll take advice, even from you. Two wrongs never made a right. I wronged that girl when I married her. I'll not wrong her a second time. Besides"—he scowled and burst out with a renewed irritation—"I've no mind to be treated like a stud bull, who having failed a service is put to a different cow to prove his mettle!"

I laughed at that. It was the only thing I could do.

"You've sired good stock in your time, Bear. No need to read a slur where none's intended. I doubt any Companion of the Council, or any man in the host, for that matter, lays the blame of failure at your door."

He nodded, amused, but grimly so.

"Maybe you're right there. The subject's a sore one, and I suppose I've grown touchy and fanciful, brooding on it too much alone. Forget it. We've other things to think of—where were we, when this interruption began? Ah, yes, you were just about to give me your report on Lyonesse. Get on with that before Medraut comes back to plague me with a whole sheaf of routine matters I must settle before we leave for Caerleon. By the gods, man, if Guinevere would only believe it, I wish I *was* free to lead a host into Armorica! This everlasting labor of governing a kingdom in peacetime's harder, far, than a slave's labor in the salt mines!"

Woman-like, Guinevere got her way. Next day she'd taken to her bed, with a nervous fever, and we rode to Caerleon without her. I'd an idea Arthur was not sorry to be free of the delays and complications women who are pampered create about them. We travelled faster without her, and, though the citizens of Caerleon were disappointed of some of the fine show they'd grown to expect, we got through the business there with a dispatch and efficiency that pleased Arthur. We'd settled the western councils and judgments a full week ahead of expectation, and with only the three-day Games still to come, he said to me suddenly:

"Bedivere, I'm uneasy for some reason. I've been thinking that maybe I did take the matter of the Armorican invasion too lightly. I must see these Games out—I can't be spared until they're over. But Kay's getting old, and if a quick decision had to be made, he'd likely hesitate and waste time sending to me for orders. Get back, will you, and see if any fresh news has come through? The Franks are a force to be reckoned with, by all accounts. Lancelot *could* need help, and though it's against my custom to send men overseas, the gods know, after all he's done for us in the past, I'd break my own rule to help Lancelot fast enough if he's in real need. I can trust your judgment better than Kay's, these days. Use it. Take command of as many men as are needed— and get across the water as fast as you can, if you think circumstances warrant it. Understood?"

I was surprised, but I agreed readily enough. After

Lyonesse I'd found the little walled town of Caerleon,
with its old-world Colonial atmosphere, oppressive. One
had to mind one's manners there, being always on show,
stared at from morning to night as though one were part
of a travelling circus.

With Griffin, now a new-made knight (I'd recommended him for that after the good service he'd given me
in the Lyonesse campaign), and a small escort, I enjoyed
the fast ride across country in sweet June weather. We
made record time, but I still found leisure to notice how
rich and well ordered the countryside was becoming.
Everywhere there were signs of vigorous life, crops growing where I remembered neglected fallow, thatchers at
work repairing long-ruined farms and barns, fat sheep
and cattle and geese, under the care of well-fed, sunburned children, who laughed and shouted at the sight of
our fluttering pennants and glittering equipment.

I'd a feeling of homecoming when we rode up to the
fort very early on the morning of the last day. The mists
that promised more glorious weather were rising off the
marshland and the sun, glinting through them, gave a
feeling of enchantment and mystery. The red, curled tiles
of the judgment hall, fringed with a flutter of white doors,
glowed above the treetops. We skirted the queen's palace
unchallenged, and rode straight up to the fort and in by
the main gateway. There was some sort of a stir going on
there—I thought we'd probably caught the guard napping
and decided I'd turn a blind eye.

Only when we were well inside and riding over to the
stables, something struck me as odd. I reined in my horse
and looked about me.

"Where in thunder is everybody? No sentries on the
walls—no ponies in the picket lines—what's been going
on here?" I said.

Griffin's eyes met mine.

"Looks like they've had a general alarm, doesn't it,
my lord?"

"Yes. But—" I began, then I saw a familiar figure
hurrying towards me. I threw my reins to Griffin, slipped
out of the saddle, and ran to meet Kay.

He was limping painfully. His face, grey and puckered, looked as if he hadn't slept for a week. Without any greeting, he panted:

"Where's Arthur? Where's the king? Is he with you?"

"Still at Caerleon and will be for half a week at least. Why?"

"Thank the gods for that! Come inside—I can't talk to you here." He gripped my arm and steered me towards the old barrack quarters that he still used. As we went, he was muttering to himself, "If only Gawain's in time! If only he can get her back in time!"

"Get who back? What are you talking about?" I asked. I was startled, but half impatient. I knew so well his capacity for translating some minor crisis into a cataclysm.

He pushed me through the door into his sleeping cell and banged it behind us. Then he turned to face me.

"She's gone, Bedivere. The queen's gone. To Lancelot."

*"What?"* I couldn't believe I'd heard him right.

He nodded, his mouth working.

"Gone, and taken her guard, and the full cohort of Rheged. Close on five hundred men, with their horses and arms. She, and those infernal brothers of hers. Deserted us. Gone. Just gone—to join Lancelot in Armorica."

I put my hand on his arm.

"Sit down, man. Tell me this thing from the beginning. When did it happen? Why?"

He dropped down on his sleeping cot, where the coverings lay all heaped anyhow, and put his face in his hands.

"My fault. All my fault. I'm getting old," he groaned. Then he looked up at me, his face dark and twisted with rage, so that the veins on his forehead stood out.

"They foxed me! The traitors! *An exercise—the queen's orders her troops should go on exercise.* That's what I gave permission for. Then, alone, by night, without even one of her women with her, only a groom and a couple of pages, she slipped away and joined them. That three times over cursed 'palace,' as they call it! Impossible to guard. You always said so, from the first. If only she'd been up here in the fort! By the gods, I hope this'll show Arthur—if it doesn't kill him. The two-faced bitch! The whore! She's been playing him false for years. I've always doubted her and this proves how right I was. In his place I'd see her burned at the stake for adultery. That's the Roman penalty, you know. That's the penalty!"

I put my hand on his shoulder, feeling it so thin and bent and shaking that a dart of pity went through me.

"Steady, Kay. Steady!" I said. It was in my mind he'd give himself an apoplexy this way. "Just tell me one thing. How long ago, all this?"

He drew a deep breath.

"Two nights—no three, now. But the fleet's in Vectis water—and she had the king's signet ring. She got it from Medraut, tricked the lad into giving it her, he says. How could he refuse the queen? *He's* not to blame."

"Maybe. Maybe not. But in any case, loading five hundred men and horses takes time, Kay. You say you've sent Gawain?"

He nodded, passing his hand across his forehead with a gesture of despair.

"Gawain and every man I could muster. He'd only got fifty of his own advance guard with him. The rest of the northern host should be back soon. I risked it, Bedivere, and I sent every soldier on the place except the gate guards. I said: 'Bring her back by force if there's no other way. You can kill every man of Rheged, High Princes and all if they resist.' That's what I told him. Gawain's a good, reliable fellow. He understood. If only he's in time!"

"Wait," I said. "A trumpet at the gate! They may be back, or some news of them. Stay here, I'll go."

The moment I set eyes on Gawain's face, I saw his news was bad. He'd ridden in alone, and by the look of him, he'd ridden hard. His first question when he slid stiffly from the saddle was the same as Kay's:

"You here? Is the king with you?"

His reaction, when I told him, was the very opposite of Kay's, however.

"Curse on it! That'll mean more delay. He'll have to follow and bring her back himself. No one else can—at least, not without orders."

"They got away from you, then?"

"Hull down on the horizon, with a fair, following wind. Forby, they'd taken every craft in the harbor, down to the wee fishing smacks. Nothing left but coracles."

He leaned back against his sweat-darkened horse. Some of the pages had run out and were hovering. He motioned them off angrily.

"This'll mean war with Armorica, I'm thinking, and we canna afford it. The randy besom! The king'll have to get her back for his honor's sake, if it's only for her burning. Aye, I've seen this coming, we all have—and for a long time. She putting shame on him and he refusing to see it. Is he clean daft, do you think, or just wilful blind, maybe?"

"Neither. He trusts Lancelot and he could be right. This may be no more than an ill-timed effort on Guinevere's part to take help to the Armorican army. Come over to Kay. He's half out of his mind."

Gawain nodded.

"I ken that fine. Like an old henwife, who's had the midwinter goose stolen by foxes, he's been! Well—the fox has gone to earth, sure enough. Best get the news told."

I rode out, accompanied only by Griffin, to meet Arthur. I was determined he should hear what had happened from me, and without witnesses. It was a thing for which, in common decency, a man must be given time to put his face as he would have it seen: not take the shock with the curious eyes of half the fort watching him.

When we saw the dust cloud and the gleam of the Dragon standard, Griffin fell back and drew his horse off the road without my having to tell him.

Arthur greeted me gaily enough, but his eyes went alert and wary. My expression warned him, I think.

"You've news for me, Bedivere? We'll ride ahead together. By your leave, friends—" and he lifted a hand to his following.

We spurred out of the press and galloped for a mile or more, back along the road I'd come. Over the rise of a hill, out of sight of the main body, he drew rein.

"Well, what is it?" he asked.

I told him, briefly, without ornament, then sat looking straight between my horse's ears, staring at a clump of gorse that shone golden in the afternoon sun.

A bee whirred past, and my horse tossed its head, making the bridle ornaments jingle. Crickets clicked in the dry grass. I thought his silence would never end.

At last he said:

"So!" And again, after a long pause, "So! Well, we'd better ride on, Bedivere. There'll be work waiting at the fort."

At last I dared to look at him. His face told me nothing. It might have been cast in bronze.

We were half an hour's ride from home. Neither of us spoke. His silence was like the stillness of a night when the snow has fallen, and the frost is just beginning.

The queen had left a letter. Medraut gave it to the king as soon as he was in his own apartment. It was the first I knew of its existence. In fairness, I had to admit that discretion could have prompted that concealment.

We were alone together, Arthur and I. Medraut would have lingered but I dismissed him curtly.

It was a short letter, but Arthur took a long time reading it, and I watched his face go grey and old as he read. Then he let the slim parchment roll itself again, moved heavily across to the brazier and dropped it into the glowing charcoal, watching it curl and blacken, then flake to yellow ash.

When he raised his head, his eyes had a blind look.

"Lancelot!" he said, very low. "This means I've lost Lancelot."

He turned without another word and walked out of the room.

Ten minutes later Baudwin came to me, white-faced.

"My lord, the king has dismissed us for the night. He asks that you will set a guard on the door of the great bedchamber and see that he is not disturbed," he said.

I gave that guard to Griffin. I'd rather have taken it myself, but I knew there would be questions that night, and I was the one who must answer them.

Arthur came to the Council next morning more finely dressed than was his custom, freshly barbered, and with an expression on his face as grimly impersonal as the closed vizor of a cataphract's helmet. He drummed us through an accumulation of business that had mounted while we were in Caerleon with cold and ruthless efficiency. It might, but for the tension all round the table, have been any ordinary working Council. As each item was settled and dismissed, I felt the Companions waiting, with indrawn breath, for him to speak directly of the one matter uppermost in all our minds. He referred to it only once, and then the reference was oblique.

"Since the cohort of Rheged is no longer with us, we must call up a fresh levy for training. It's time the Trinovantes served a term of duty. See to that, will you, Bedivere?"

"My lord," I said, acknowledging the order formally.

It was Aglavain, youngest and most inexperienced member of the Council, who, in the momentary silence that followed, lost his nerve. Always highly strung and undependable, he glanced around at the grave faces about him, and flushing to the roots of his hair, stammered suddenly:

"Will none of you ask what is to be done? Sire—this matter of the queen?"

Gawain growled in an undertone:

"Silence, you!"

"But—but we must know. How else can we—?"

Arthur looked at him for a long breath-stopping moment.

"Speak on. You have the right," he said with dangerous patience.

Aglavain's voice cracked on a shrill note (it had not fully broken).

"For your honor's sake, sire—for the honor of Britain," he pleaded.

Arthur said, very quietly:

"This Council is dismissed," and rose to his feet. Towering above us, he stood silent for what seemed an eternity, then, his eyes fixed on Aglavain's scared face, he spoke with absolute finality, as I had heard him speak only once or twice before and then when he was pronouncing a death sentence.

"The Pendragon's honor and the honor of Britain are in the Pendragon's keeping. Who questions his guardianship of either, I will challenge to single combat and the gods must decide the issue."

He turned and left the Great Hall, his two pages, pale and solemn, following him.

Aglavain put his head down on his crossed arms and burst into loud sobbing.

Gawain said again, this time with exasperated violence:

"*Silence,* you!"

We got up, one by one, and went out without a word. At the door, Gawain caught up with me, and muttered:

"I'm gey sorry that happened, Bedivere. The young cub! But for all I could murder him and gladly, ye must admit there was some excuse for his questioning! What *will* the king do?"

"I don't know," I said. "I don't know, Gawain. Before the gods, I wish I did!"

I have lived through bad days in plenty. The worst I remember, barring the aftermath of Camlan, were the days that followed Guinevere's going.

Rumor, conjecture and, in some cases, sheer blind panic, seethed through fort and palace. Every hour of the day, and often late at night, I was waylaid by questioners.

What was to be done? Would this mean war with Armorica? Would it mean blood feud with Rheged? The queen's matrons flocked about me, voluble with anxiety, and the queen's girls sobbed out their personal problems of parents who would, certainly, never allow them to stay at court once the scandal became known.

"What scandal?" I asked a damp and incoherent little group of them crisply.

They blinked at me, blushing, then looked sideways at each other, until the boldest whispered:

"The queen, and the Lord Lancelot?" and another, seeing my face darken, explained primly:

"*My* father will say that a woman who leaves her husband for another man is no fit guardian for—for a virtuous maiden."

They all nodded at that and one, a pretty little puss, wailed:

"Oh, and I *did* want to stay at court until I found me a husband!"

"See here!" I said firmly. "You served the queen, all of you. You knew her for a kind and gracious mistress. It does not become you to think ill of her at the first breath of rumor. Go back to your quarters, say your prayers and do your needlework, and for pity's sake leave idle gossip to scullions and serving wenches. We don't know—none of us knows yet—what moved the queen to do what she has done. You are sensible girls and so I'll say this to you. She is a great-hearted, generous lady, and it may be she had reason to believe that in Armorica the Lord Lancelot, our noble ally, was hard-pressed, and in mortal danger. She had authority over the warriors of her Clan and, though some may hold she was impetuous to lead them herself, that's a matter of opinion. Myself, I'd say it was bravely done, and no shadow of other interpretation should be placed on her action. Do you understand?"

Again they eyed each other sideways. The one who'd wished for a husband looked at me with great, reproachful blue eyes, and murmured earnestly:

"But they *loved* each other—we all knew."

I smiled at her wearily.

"Baby-face, what do any of you chits understand of loving? Some day you'll learn it's a greater matter than the romantic nonsense harpers sing. True love begins with loyalty. See to it, all of you, that you are loyal, discreet and maidenly, as the queen would have you be, and set an example to all by your behavior, as women should, in times of anxiety. We'll have no talk of scandal or"—and I frowned on them sternly—"I, myself, will see to it the rod's not spared on any flighty, ill-tongued little gossip who utters the word, and what's more, bag and baggage, she'll be packed home without delay."

That silenced the women's quarters. My friends among the decurions were just as curious, but more outspoken. I ordered the first man who used the word "whore" in my hearing fifty lashes and put two others in irons for twenty-four hours for jests I did not care to hear. I had a certain reputation with the army, and the rumor that it was not wise to try the Lord Bedivere's patience just then must have got around, for discipline, after that, was almost oppressively apparent everywhere.

The Companions were a different matter. I had no authority to silence either their questions or their comments. I bore both with what patience I could and wished myself anywhere but at Camelot. Once, indeed, I found myself turning Theodoric's arm ring in my hands, remembering thoughtfully his promise that there would always be a place for me in the army of the Goths. But somewhere, out of the long past, I heard my own voice—a boy's voice—say: *"Where Arthur goes, I go!"*

But Arthur had gone very far away, into a wasteland of icebound silence, where not I, nor any man, dared follow him. He moved through the days wrapped in impenetrable dignity, courteous, attentive to all his duties, aloof and utterly terrifying. It would have taken more courage than anyone among us could muster to question what his next move would be.

Then the Merlin came from Armorica. There was a day when Council was called again in Great Hall and the Merlin, instead of Arthur, took the Dragon chair.

He wore his ceremonial robes, and the Merlin jewel, and he spoke to us in the king's name.

The war against the Franks, he said, had ended in truce and treaty. King Bann, wishing above all things to maintain alliance with us in Britain, had ordered the Rheged cohort, under their High Princes, to return to their own Clan country, and there wait the Pendragon's pleasure and the will of their own Clan council.

He looked around the grave anxious faces that watched him, and I felt him focus our attention, as a man gathers his horse under him, for some dangerous leap across a flooded river.

"My lords, there is this thing more to be told of King Bann's message. He says that against his will, and to his deepest distress, the High Prince Lancelot has withdrawn to his Fortress of Joyous Guarde, deep in the Forest of Broceliande, taking with him Guinevere the Queen, who goes of her own free will, and under no duress. For which act, the High King of Armorica has disinherited him from the succession and declared him outlaw, and the Christian Church has pronounced against him and the queen the sentence of excommunication."

The Merlin paused a moment, his eyes watchful, his mouth stern. Then he said, and suddenly I thought his lip twitched, in some unaccountable amusement:

"King Bann wishes us, in Britain, to know that he will give free and safe passage to any army we choose to send across the sea to lay siege to this Fortress of Joyous Guarde, that no assistance will be given by Armorican arms to help in its defense and no reparation or vengeance exacted for the death of its outlawed garrison."

A rustle went round the table. We of the Council looked at each other.

Gawain said, abruptly:

"Yon's clear speaking, and no mistake! What are the Pendragon's orders, Lord Merlin? Which of us is to take command—or will he go himself?"

There was a pause that lengthened until the tension of it seemed to ring like a taut harp string. Then the Merlin rose to his feet, his cloak flowing back with a rustle like a hawk's wings as the bird settles on the falconer's gauntlet.

"I pronounce the Pendragon's judgment," he said.

"There will be peace between Britain and Armorica. There will be peace between us and the Clan Rheged. There will be no force sent from Britain against the Fortress of Joyous Guarde. From this day forward, the Pendragon rules alone and there is no queen in Britain."

Kay leaned forward.

"You mean—he'll divorce? The king will put away his wife?" he asked. His voice was hoarse, his eyes eager.

The Merlin shook his head.

"We of the Old Faith hold that a vow once made cannot be unmade. That is the Pendragon's belief and mine. It is written in our triads, *'Three things no man can alter: the stars in their courses, the flow of the tides; and the pattern that unrolls from the given word.'*"

# VI

# ANDANTE

# Chapter Twenty-Three

Two years went slowly by. Things changed, some for the better, some, to my mind, for the worse; but for Britain they were good years. The Saxons, except for pirate brigandage, held off, and Dalriada, under Gawain, kept the Picts at bay. Slowly, Arthur's men cleaned the Heartland of robbers and bandits, so that honest farmers prospered there. Trade flourished in the towns that were busy rebuilding the damages of war. The wealthier folk became, the more everything seemed to cost, but since most men were well off, one heard fewer complaints of that than might have been expected. One thing I noticed, in my work as prefect, and it made me uneasy. Many of the old Colonial families, and especially the patrician ones, seemed to be emigrating; selling up and going overseas to Armorica. They could always produce to me good and apparently purely personal reasons, but it made me wonder, just the same. I got the truth of it, in the end, from a distant kinsman of mine, whom Arthur had created chief magistrate at Aquae Sulis—Flavius Aurelianus. He was about thirty years old, and one of the younger generation born just too late to remember the Troubles, a hardbitten, cynical young man, with few illusions. I used to lodge with him in the magistrate's quarters whenever I was in that part of my province—and he made me feel welcome, which was more than could be said for all the Colonials I had to visit.

Over a good supper, one evening, he said to me, abruptly:

"Old Martius Flaminius has sold up and is pulling out like the rest. Did you know?"

"No," I said. "What reason is *he* giving?"

"He'll find you one. I can tell you the real cause, if you haven't guessed it."

"Well?" I said.

"The same as all the others. They've given up hope of another Emperor of the West from Britain, at last. If the king (and I mean no offense, Bedivere) will not cross the water to fetch back an erring wife, they've at last got it into their thick heads he's not likely to lead a war host overseas to try his luck for the Purple. That was what they were hoping for after Badon. Didn't you know?"

"I did not!" I said.

He nodded, reaching over to refill my wine cup.

"They're disappointed in the king, Bedivere. Too much the Pendragon, too little sign of Arturus Maximus about him. They don't appreciate his custom of promotion for merit, irrespective of birth and breeding, for one thing. Britain's going altogether too native Celtic these days for their taste. They pinned their hopes on the queen to lead a Roman revival, for they'd all heard about her palace villa. Now," he shrugged, "not enough class distinction, Roman blood at the top and everyone else a steep step lower down the ladder." He paused and laughed softly. "Mind you, the price of land, goods and gear, at the moment, is encouraging them to indulge their prejudices. Old Martius has made a pretty penny out of that villa of his. I'd a notion to bid for it myself, until I heard what he was asking. Phew!" he whistled, "it takes one of the new tin lords to produce that kind of cash!"

I thought the information over. It fitted pretty closely with a lot I'd noticed.

"What about you?" I asked him directly.

He looked at me and smiled.

"I stay. Most of the men of my age will stay. It's the old brigade from Ambrosius' time who can't stomach changes. Let 'em go. Armorica may suit them well enough to molder and die in. I and my friends are ready to try our luck with Arthur. We owe him too much already not to trust our future with him. Independent Britain suits me better than anything I'd have reason to expect on the mainland. I don't see another Emperor of the West taking Rome from the Goths in a hurry, do you?"

I shook my head.

"That's finished," I said. "You can thank the gods Arthur knows it."

He looked at me, his head on one side.

"Which gods, my friend?"

I could not follow that, and my face must have shown it. He smiled.

"That's another complaint, you realize? Rumors breed fast in an ingrowing community. The Colonials of the old school, when they can't find any other complaint of him, whisper darkly that Arthur consorts with wizards and Druids on some unholy island and has plans to bring back the Old Faith. For your private ear, some of King Bann's tame priests from Gaul could have started that story. Our king isn't above ordinary tactful dealing with foreign clergy, to judge from what I've heard some of them recount at the end of a good supper in my pious great-aunt Drusilla's house. Tell me—*is* he likely to declare himself a second Julian the Apostate one day?"

"Unlikely," I said. "Tell them to ask Abbot Iltud. *He's* one of the Companions."

"Ah, yes. The Abbot of Llan Vawr? Now there's a man after my own heart. A soldier and a gentleman; but with all the wrong ideas about the date men should keep Easter, my aunt tells me!" Suddenly he looked grave, and abandoning his mocking tone said, sternly, "I am a soldier, born of a line of soldiers. I worship Mithras, as my fathers did before me. By the Great White Bull, Bedivere, I swear to you that I, and men like me, will stand by the War Duke of Britain. He is a king and a warrior. We trust him. I hope he'll realize he can trust us. For the rest—I wish Bann of Armorica joy of the new colonists *he's* getting!"

When, during those years, the need to report on my province took me back to Camelot, I was reminded of that conversation with Flavius. It was apparent to me, increasingly apparent as time passed, that Arthur was turning more and more back to the influence of his early years; to the Merlin, and to the secret teachings of Ynis Witrin.

"I had too little time, when I was young, to learn all that a Pendragon should know. *I* never spent years in the Boys' House on the Island as a High King's heir should have done," he told me. "Now, perhaps only for a little while, I've the chance to put that right. Besides—my mother is ageing, and she's very dear to me, Bedivere. I want the support of her wisdom while I can have it."

It was the first time, since before his marriage, and one of the very few times, in fact, since we were children, that he'd spoken to me openly of The Lady. It was winter, and we were sitting by the hearth in his room off the Great Hall.

He looked across at me with a sad, half-defiant expression, and added abruptly:

"I'd Lancelot's training in the Wisdom to depend on in the old days. Don't forget that."

Before I could make any comment he'd switched the talk, deliberately, to my work in Menaevia.

I noticed how often, in the course of the conversation that followed, he referred me to Medraut.

"Ask Medraut for those figures; I'll tell Medraut to see that's attended to. Medraut has the keys of the treasure chest—he'll issue you what you need."

"You give that young man a lot of responsibility these days, Bear," I said at last.

"Why not? He's proved able to carry it. I can't attend to details, with all I have to do. He's got a memory that never fails, and a grasp of affairs that is invaluable to me. Besides, he's quiet and unobtrusive and knows how to keep his mouth shut."

"Not likely to be beguiled into indiscretion by affairs with women at any rate?" I said, lifting an eyebrow.

Arthur frowned.

"Oh *that!*" he said impatiently. "What of it? We've

had cases of the same sort before. Remember Balin and Balan—good knights if ever I had such. Besides, Aglavain's changed considerably for the better, as you should have noticed, since he attached himself so closely to Medraut."

"So we are to have the Theban Band?" I said sarcastically. "Well, if Medraut takes some of the drudgery off your shoulders, I suppose I should be grateful, but I'd watch young Aglavain if I were you, Bear. I can't say I agree with you he's improving. If anything, I'd say this passionate attachment is making him more insufferable than ever. We don't want those two setting a fashion."

But they'd set it already, in some directions, and what was worse, it seemed to me, Medraut and his boyfriend were gathering a faction, very much as Medraut had done in the days when he was a page. I could have offered no solid proof of my suspicions, and no reasonable explanation of the uneasiness they caused me. Just, once again, I sensed a division being emphasized all the time between two generations.

*"We, the young. You, the old."*

Medraut's following, if following he actually had, were scrupulously respectful to me—to all the veteran Companions. Perhaps too respectful. Their very courtesy, their marked consideration, emphasized their awareness that we needed and perhaps deserved their tolerance. They granted us, generously, the reputations we had achieved in the past. But their manner reminded us that the new world, their world, was one we could not be expected to understand. It was a very subtle atmosphere; and it irritated me inordinately. I was always glad to get away from them, back to Menaevia, where I could forget I was growing older every year.

At intervals I would tell myself that, for Arthur's sake, I should try to overcome what might be—what surely must be—an unworthy prejudice. After all, Medraut was the son of the one woman I had ever loved. He was serving Arthur with a patience and devotion that were admirable—in ways that none of the rest of us was qualified to do.

I would set myself then to try once again to establish

some understanding, some kind of working relationship at
least, with him. But always he repelled me. Fundamental-
ly his attitude to life, whenever I glimpsed it under the
suave, deferential exterior, seemed to contradict every
truth in which I believed. There was a savagery, a blind
admiration of material success, that seemed to me wholly
and dangerously Saxon. Money, position, power; these
were the standards he understood and respected. Success,
in any field, and at whatever cost, was what gained praise
from him. I remembered later, too clearly, one particular
instance, though at the time it seemed unimportant.

I was walking with him at evening by the river in the
palace gardens.

We had been discussing again, fairly amicably and
impersonally, the case for and against using Saxons and
Jutes as paid auxiliaries. It was a question that came up
periodically in those days, and opinions were sharply
divided. Most of the younger generation could see nothing
against it, while we, who had fought the Saxon wars, still
saw plenty.

Suddenly he laughed.

"There, it's a subject on which we'll never agree, my
lord! I'd shock you more, I dare say, if I were to speak
out all my mind on it. If I had my way I'd not stop at
Saxons. I've always had a mind to command an auxiliary
cohort of Pictish archers."

"Picts?" I laughed also, thinking it a jest. "My uncle,
Ambrosius the General, used to say the man who could
tame a Pict could tame a python. Your cohort would
desert at the first onset!"

He shrugged his quick, supple shrug.

"It would depend what troops you set behind them
in the battle, wouldn't it? I've thought, often, the effect on
enemy morale would be worth the risk. Think of Pict
arrow poison, my lord. It's the deadliest thing I know.
Even a scratch brings slow-creeping paralysis—blindness,
deafness, speechlessness; a very cold and lonely death!
The antidote for that poison's so rare you might say it's
unobtainable."

The tip of his tongue swept his lips, as a cat's will,
watching the quivering mouse between its paws.

I shuddered.

"Enough! It's a barbarous weapon. No civilized fighting force should tolerate it!" I said, and glanced at him with disgust.

His expression shocked me. It had the withdrawn, entranced look of a man remembering his enjoyment of a night of love.

It was a momentary impression. He felt my eyes on him, and was instantly grave and decorous.

"Of course you're right, my lord. It's a weapon we, of the Pendragon's host, could never contemplate," he agreed sedately. "And yet—in total war, I've heard the king himself say it does not pay to be squeamish. Victory is the aim; and in a just cause, surely the aim justifies the means?"

He could twist words, that one. After I had left him I found myself still puzzling over the rights of the argument, while I steamed myself clean in the new bathhouse of the palace. There was something about Medraut that always made me feel I needed to wash off contamination. I wondered how Arthur could tolerate the smell of the man, forever about his rooms. But I knew the thought unjust. One of the things about Medraut that grated on me was his fastidiousness. He would never welcome a hound's warm head laid on his knee, but push the creature aside and dust his clothes for a possible hair. He was the only one of the Companions who never, to my knowledge, owned a dog.

That idle talk with him must have taken place soon after the queen's going, and I forgot it for a long time. Forgot it until the fifth autumn of those shadowed years, during which no word came out of Armorica, and the names of Lancelot and Guinevere were seldom spoken at Camelot, and then only in low tones, with caution, as one speaks the names of the dead, fearing to open again a wound that will bleed inwardly.

That autumn, Dinas and I, with a handful of troops, found ourselves weather-bound in the fort at Tintagel. We'd been riding the western boundaries and a gale had blown up suddenly, as it does in those parts, with thunder, hail and torrents of rain, and we'd made for the

nearest shelter. Three days it blew, and with no one
expecting us, there was little food fit to eat and smoking
fires, and the men grumbled and Dinas and I grew weary
of one another's company. He was a trustworthy enough
deputy, but stolid and lacking conversation when there
was no work to be done.

On our third evening I'd looked out at dusk, over
the waste of tumbling water, visible from my old tower
room, and watched pale, livid wisps of cloud racing
across the lowering horizon.

"Three days usually sees this kind of weather out,
but by the look of it, it'll not clear before another twenty-
four hours," I muttered. "Winter's coming early this year,
Dinas."

He'd drawn out a dice box and was shaking it in a
hopeful way. Resigned to another dreary evening, I sat
down to play one of the soldiers' gambling games that
bored me excruciatingly but were his answer to passing
time.

We cast once or twice. The howl of wind and roar of
breaking surf must have drowned the sentry's challenge
and the clang of the opened gates below. The first I knew
of any disturbance was the running feet of my page on the
stairway, and his urgent scratching at the door.

"Enter!" I shouted. Then, at sight of his popping
eyes, and air of importance, "Well, what is it, boy?"

"My lord—a messenger—from Camelot. He's ridden through all this, his horse near foundered. It's Sir
Griffin. Will you please to come at once, sir?"

But heavier steps, steps that faltered for all their
haste, were hard behind him. Griffin, his long black cloak
shining with wet, mud-spattered to the thighs with
splashes of it on his face and dripping hair, pushed the
boy to one side and stood framed in the doorway.

"My lord—it's the king," he croaked. "The king—
he's dying."

Then he staggered, and I thought he was going to
fall.

I caught his arm and steered him to the chair by the
hearth. I had a glimpse of Dinas' horrified face and the
page, hovering, his mouth fallen open.

"Get wine. If there is none, hot broth," I ordered. My mind had gone clear and cold and very still. "Now, Griffin—one last effort, man. Tell me what's happened."

He looked up at me.

"He asked for you. It's taken me near on a week to get here. Every ford's flooded. Oh, my lord, my lord, I did my best." His eyes filled with tears, and he rubbed his hand across them like a child.

"Where's his wound? How did he get it?" I asked. No other explanation occurred to me.

Griffin drew a hard, sighing breath.

"No wound. A sudden sickness. He fell from his horse and lay like the dead. Sir Palomides said to tell you he fears it's"—he paused, and, as if repeating a lesson he'd got by rote—"*the bolt of Apollo.*" His eyes clouded again and suddenly he gripped my hand. "What is that, Sir Bedivere, sir? Is it some foreign witchcraft?"

"No," I said quietly. I'd been with Palomides long enough to recognize the diagnosis. "Not witchcraft, boy—but a sore ill enough," I said.

Griffin swallowed twice before his voice would come and then it was little more than a whisper.

"He was alone with his page when he fell. By the time we got to him he was past speech, but the boy swears he asked for you, sir. I waited for nothing when I heard. Just got my horse and came."

I gripped his cold, wet hand.

"You've done well, Griffin. By the gods, you've done well, in weather like this!" Then I stared at him. "How the devil did you know where to find me?"

"The Merlin's men—the Outlanders," he muttered. Then, urgently, "Oh sir, the king's asking for you."

"Yes," I said. "I shall start as soon as a horse can be saddled. No!" as he made a movement to rise," my orders to you are to stay here. You've had enough. See to him, Dinas, and bring the men back as fast as you can, once he's fit to ride again. Griffin, you'd be a hindrance and no help to me. You've done your part."

I remember very little of that ride. I killed one horse under me, I know, and another was swept away in a

torrent, where the ford was lost in yellow, churning water
that should have drowned me, but I am—I was—a strong
swimmer. I remember small, dark hands that grabbed me
at the further bank. I lost my cloak there. I did not notice
the loss at the time. All the way across country, from
Lyonesse to the Great Fort, Merlin's men were ready
when I needed them most. Fresh horses (they must have
stolen them, for they were good horses) were led out of
hidden hiding places, food was handed up to me to eat as
I rode, and strong sweet mead was held to my lips in
leather cups that stank of the Outlanders' huts. Once a
dark woman, slight as a wraith, with eyes like Ygern's,
gave me a long draught of warm milk, seethed with honey
and yeast, that put new strength into me. No man, they
say, has ever covered the distance as fast before or since,
not even in summer weather. It was the worst journey I
ever made, save only one.

There were torches burning all about the entrance to
the palace, torches that smoked in the mist and did not
flare. The wind had dropped. The whole world was still:
a heavy, dripping stillness, that seemed to wait, as men
waited all about the queen's gardens; dark figures of
warriors, silent and ghostly in the gloom. The bronze
doors opened before me, as I dropped out of the saddle,
and someone said:

"This way. He's in the great bedchamber."

I was so stiff I could hardly walk, and my eyes were
swollen from the wind and rain so that I could barely see.
I remember I blundered against the carved doorpost of
the king's chamber, and an unknown hand came out and
guided me through.

It was dark in there, after the blaze of torches
outside. One lamp burned on a table beside the great
painted bed and there was a sharp smell of herbs and a
heavy quiet.

Palomides came out of the shadows and took my
hand.

"Bedivere? Thank the gods you've come. We did not
dare expect you so soon," he said in a low voice.

I looked past him at the bed. Under the embroidered
cover I could just see the outline of a form.

"Am I in time?" I asked. My mouth was dry and I had to swallow twice before the words came out in a whisper I did not recognize as my own voice.

"You are in time," Palomides said. "But I warn you, he may not know you."

I went forward and fell on my knees by the bed.

At first all I could see, in the ring of the lamplight, was a hand, lying outside the covers—the strong, dear hand I knew so well, looking strangely white, except where the corded veins showed it the hand of a man no longer young. I took it up, holding it between mine, feeling the hard calluses on palm and fingers that the hilt of Excalibur had made. It lay there, heavy and cold, and when I pressed it I felt no answering pressure.

"Arthur!" I said, and then, as once before, "Arthur—it is I, Bedivere. I have come."

Fearfully, I looked up, searching the face, shadowed by the fall of the silken hangings. His head was tipped back a little on the pillows. It was hard to see. I thought the closed lids flickered. But it was only a trick of the light. There was a stubble of beard on the chin and the nose looked pinched and sharp, with bluish lines running down from it and around the lips, that were parted, as though already the jaw had dropped. I'd seen men too often look like that, in the dawn light, who had lain dead all night on a battlefield. Then I realized that the quilt, folded back so neat and straight over his great barrel chest, was stirring ever so slightly. He still breathed.

In the semi-darkness on the far side of the bed, a white figure moved quietly away—some assistant of Palomides, I supposed, withdrawing at a sign from him.

I said again:

"I am here, Bear—I am here!"

Slowly, reluctantly, as if with enormous effort, his eyes opened and he looked directly at me. But there was no recognition, and the lids drooped and closed again.

Palomides' voice behind me said:

"Best not to disturb him. Come away now, Bedivere."

I rose heavily and went with him. Outside the door, I turned, seeing him clearly for the first time.

He looked ghastly, but very calm. His eyes, hollow, with dark swollen pouches under them, met mine with gentle and concerned understanding.

"He will live, Bedivere. The worst is over now. He will live," he reassured me, repeating the words as though he knew I found it hard to take in any meaning.

"In the name of the gods, what is it—what caused it?" I muttered.

"Arrow poison. An elf-bolt struck him on the side of the neck, shot from cover of an alder thicket, as he was riding back here from the Island."

"An *elf-bolt?* A Pict arrow?" I queried.

He nodded.

"A deliberate attempt on his life. From what quarter we don't yet know. Unfortunately there was confusion and delay. He rode on, unaware of the wound, we think. Suddenly, almost at the gates, he fell from his horse without warning—a heavy fall. They guessed only that he had struck his head against a stone. When I could find no injury, I thought: 'This is the bolt of Apollo, that strikes out of a clear sky, and strikes often when a man, no longer young, having suffered some great shock or sorrow, lives on under secret stress of grief.'

"But the symptoms, to a physician, did not altogether tally with that. It was his page who gave me the clue, when I questioned him closely a second time. He said: 'As we passed the alder copse I heard a hornet buzz, and my lord put his hand up to his neck and swore. Then he laughed and said: "The little beast has stung me! Well, better the king than the king's horse! A hornet's sting would set the quietest mount dancing!" He rode fast after that, and drew ahead, for I was afraid of more hornets and looking about for them. Suddenly I saw him sway in the saddle and then he fell. I dismounted and ran to him. He said: "Fetch Bedivere!" then he coughed and whispered, "Fetch Lancelot!" and his mouth drew down one side and his eyes rolled upwards and I was very much afraid. I didn't know what should be done, so I rode fast and called out the guard.' "

Palomides gave a quick shrug.

"Having that account to guide me I found the

scratch on his neck; the arrow must have glanced. By the time men had gone back and searched and the bolt was found, I'd already given him the antidote. But it was fully late by then."

"Palomides, *is* there an antidote? Don't try to spare me. *Can* a man ever truly, fully recover from this?" I asked, searching his face.

"I think Arthur may. He is very strong, and the bolt did not lodge. But it'll be a long, weary sickness, and I'll be honest with you, there may be aftereffects. He'll never be quite the same man again."

"Gods!" I said softly, hopelessly, "and he has no heir!" Palomides put his hand on my shoulder.

"Come—come and rest. You've had a bad journey. We can only hope now. I promise you, I'll do my best."

"I know you will. Thank the gods you were here!"

"Thank them, rather, that my time in Ireland gave me the opportunity to learn the secret of the antidote. Few have it, but it's a good medicine," he said, his voice cheerfully firm.

I went with him blindly, and presently found myself sitting by the brazier in Arthur's own room, shivering as though I had an ague.

"Stay there. I'll send you wine and food. I must go back to him," Palomides said.

"Yes. Yes, don't leave him. Don't leave him for a moment," I begged helplessly and selfishly. By his looks, he'd not slept for nights, but I'd no thought, just then, for anyone in the world but Arthur.

I had never before, in all our shared lives, faced fully what the world would be like without him. I had seen him wounded, it's true, and that often. He had always made light of wounds, recovering in half the time any other man could hope to do. I did not recall his ever suffering a day's sickness since we were children. His strength and health had seemed as impregnable as the granite tors of the Outland, that will outlast time. A tempest of darkness rushed over me, as on a winter night it rushes through the forest gap where a great oak has fallen.

*"He may never fully recover from this,"* Palomides had said. If he did not, who was there to take his place?

Who but Arthur could hold the Britain we had fought so hard to win?

I buried my face in my hands, and groaned aloud. Against the darkness of my closed lids the picture stood out relentlessly of his face as I had just seen it—the face of a man very near to death.

"No one can ever take his place," I said aloud.

"No one but you, Bedivere. You, his brother, must hold Britain for him now. You are the only man who can," a voice said quietly.

It was a voice I had not heard for so many years, except in dreams, and had thought I might never hear again. Crouched there by the brazier I did not dare to move, lest the sound of it should prove a fantasy.

"Speak to me again. Speak to me," I prayed in my mind.

"Bedivere," Ygern said. Slowly, I raised my head, and saw her at my side.

She had changed. How much she had changed, I did not realize until much later. All I saw then was the light that seemed to shine around her, in her white, straight robe, and the strength and serenity of her face.

I turned, as a hurt child turns, and clung to her.

"Ygern! Girl darling—oh Ygern, help me!" I begged.

I felt her hand stroking my hair.

"We must help each other, and him. He will live, and he will need us both," she said tenderly.

"He can't see. He can't hear. He doesn't know me," I whispered, and felt my tears soaking into the soft wool of her tunic, that smelt of sweet herbs like a June meadow.

"Hush, my dear." Her hands, strong, compelling, gripped my shoulders—a comrade's hands, drawing me back to sanity. "He knows you. I promise you he does. He came back to you from the cave. He will come back out of this darkness. You're exhausted now. I've brought food and wine. You must eat and rest. They need you, here. While his sickness lasts, it is you who must take command."

I looked up at her.

"Don't leave us again. Don't go back to the Island. Stay with me, Ygern," I implored her.

"I shall stay here as long as I am needed," she said, and bending down, kissed me on the forehead. Then, smiling, drew out a kerchief, and wiped my face with it simply and quickly, as if I had been a child and she my mother.

I laughed shakily at that, suddenly aware of the sane reality of her presence in the warm, comfortable room.

"Girl, I'm filthy—I'm not fit for you to touch. I haven't been out of the saddle for days," I said brokenly.

"Hush!" she said again, and held a cup to my lips. "Drink this. You must eat, and then get out of those wet clothes before you take a fever. Palomides has enough on his hands, without you for a patient."

She was calm, staunch, the comrade I remembered. A great peace flowed over me. As she turned away, to fetch me food, I noticed with no sense of shock the light from the lamp behind us shone silver on her hair.

# Chapter Twenty-Four

It was a strange time, that winter of Arthur's sickness. We lived at first from hour to hour, then from day to day, while Palomides and Ygern fought for his life, and the Merlin came and went, a presence in the background, a strength, a quietness, to which, instinctively, all of us turned for reassurance.

Without Ygern, I doubt if that grim battle would have been won, for all Palomides' skill and all the Merlin's wisdom. It seemed to me, standing helplessly by, aware only of my own uselessness, for I had no experience of sickness then, as if a slender cable stretched between those two. A line of light, tenuous but strong, which slowly, slowly drew Arthur back, out of the far places where his soul roved, back into the body that lay so stiffly inert on the bed in the darkened room—back to pain and struggle and a world that could not go on without him. The strength that had always been in her, the fighting will that had carried her through the hardships of her own life, the courage that had made her leave him years before, to temper her spirit in the Wisdom of the Island training, she lent to him.

Long afterwards, she said to me:

"The hardest thing I ever had to do was to make him go on living, Bedivere. Only the Merlin's direct order at the critical moment could have given me courage to bring him back into a body, crippled and helpless, when he was free and beyond all pain. But the time had not come when he could be spared. So many needed him and his work here was not finished. It was the test of our obedience, his and mine."

"Your obedience to the Merlin?" I asked puzzled.

She flashed round on me then with something of her old impatience.

"To all the Merlin stood for: to the Light; to the Pattern; to our moira," she said.

By then I could understand, at least a little, what she meant.

At the time, I only saw that, in some strange way, the link there had always been between those two held firm in the shadow of death—and when no other living soul could reach him, who neither saw nor heard, and from whom the power of speech and movement had been taken away by the vile venom of the arrow's poison. Ygern could still communicate with him and translate that communication to those of us who tended him.

For myself, I turned resolutely to the only thing I could do for him. I accepted the unanimous vote of the Council of Companions and ruled Britain as his deputy, while his sickness lasted. It was not easy—but the loyalty of the whole brotherhood of the Companions made it possible, and we worked together, each man lending his best, in experience and skill, to keep the hard-won fruits of Arthur's victories intact.

In those months I came to depend, in a way I would not have believed possible, on Medraut. Methodical, orderly, indefatigable, he labored eighteen hours a day at the detail of government for me. His memory was prodigious and without him, coming new and unprepared to my task, I should have been utterly at sea. I never wholly trusted him. Some instinct in me recoiled from the cold, calculating mind that preferred figures and statistics to the human problems they represented. I was uncomfortably aware, more than once, of a lifted eyebrow, a contemptuous side glance, when I gave judgment in Arthur's place and tempered it with mercy to some poor wretch as Arthur himself would have done. Once or twice I suspected, in Clan disputes, he was at his old trick of stirring up rather than avoiding trouble. But he was always ready

with an excuse so reasonable I decided I'd not let prejudice sway me, and so was content to let matters stand. He
had a way of making himself indispensable at any moment when he had roused my impatience. Without him,
that year, I doubt if I could have carried the load so
suddenly laid upon me. In justice I would still remember
that.

    In justice, too, I remember how, for the first time, I
came to understand, as I had not fully understood before
(my mind being on other things), the part the Little
People had played from the beginning in the intricate
organization of Arthur's government. It was the Merlin's
genius that had seen in them the possibility of a secret
network, spread throughout Britain, well suited by their
inveterate curiosity to gather news, and having their own
methods of conveying it over great distances. In the old
Imperial days their very existence had been almost forgotten. Withdrawn into the pathless forests, and moor and
mountain fastnesses, they knew every track and long
disused by-way, and could travel unnoticed, using often
the bewildering maze of waterways that penetrate,
through swamp and lake and silted stream, the unex-
plored Outlands, carrying messages faster than even the
emperor's post in the old days when it thundered down
the legionary roads with fresh horses waiting at every
guard post. Their trust had been given, long before Rome
ruled, to the Wise Ones, and they looked still, in our day,
to the Merlin and the Island as their traditional pro-
tectors—the only authority they had ever willingly acknowledged. Because the Merlin directed them to serve
Arthur, they served him well—just how well I had realized on that ghastly ride from Tintagel. They served me
with equal loyalty during the difficult months when I was
his deputy, and asked for no reward, through all their
years of service. While we ruled Britain we saw to it that
their hunting runs were respected, their skilled smiths well
paid. In times of famine, from the first they knew they
could come to us for help, and what we had we would
always share. They were grateful, but never subservient.
A strange, secret people. When the bad times came, they
did not complain, only withdrew and once more became

invisible to the invader. That lesson was in their blood.
They must have learned it over a thousand years before
they watched, unseen, the first Eagles of the first legions
carried into the Heartland of Britain.

Slowly, very slowly, inch by inch, it seemed, the darkness
rolled back from us. Painfully, with setbacks and re-
lapses, Arthur's enormous physical vitality asserted itself,
and he regained first his senses, and then the power of
movement. A time came, as the year turned to the spring
and the days began to lengthen, when he could leave his
bed for an hour or two each day and sit, wrapped in a
fur-lined robe, by the brazier in his own room. But he
had changed. There was a patience, a docility about him,
that was utterly out of character. I, indeed all of us, had
expected him to be a difficult convalescent. Recovering
from wounds in the past we had known him impossible to
restrain, impatient always to be up and doing. But now a
lethargy seemed to hang over him, a deep, brooding
melancholy. He would sit for hours at a time, gazing into
space, and sometimes tears ran down his face unheeded,
into his beard that was now streaked with grey.

If, at such times, I tried to rouse him with talk of the
day's happenings, bringing some problem forward in the
hope it might catch his interest, he would look at me in a
bewildered way, as though I spoke a foreign tongue, and
say, helplessly:

"See to it all for me, Bedivere. You can judge what
should be done better than I can."

Once or twice, when I pressed him, thinking it might
be as well to force him into attention, he shook his head
restlessly and muttered:

"If only we had Lancelot! Lancelot would know,"
and once he cried out hoarsely, like a man in sudden pain,
"Why did they leave me? Why? Why could they not have
told me, trusted me? Between us three it was so small a
matter, and there was so much besides!"

And then he bowed his head down into his hands
and when I tried to speak, though I could find little of
comfort and the words I said sounded foolish to my own

ears, he did not answer, so that after a time I left him and went to find Palomides.

"For the gods' sake, man, find something in your skills that will serve to lighten this darkness that is fallen on him," I said roughly. "What use to cure his body, if his mind is clouded by old sorrows best forgotten? Have you no drug, no draught, that will bring back the Arthur we knew, the leader, the soldier? Every day that he sits brooding, the task of holding the Clans together, of keeping up the spirits of the army, grows harder. I tell you, I can't be responsible much longer for the state of affairs in Britain without proof of his recovery. Don't you realize rumor of his condition will get across the sea soon, and bring down the Saxons on us again in force, or the disaffected Clans will get wind of it, and start a rebellion, or the Picts plan a mass attack and persuade Leodogrance he's little to lose, now, by giving them free passage south?"

Palomides' eyes, dark-shadowed with weariness, never left mine while I spoke, searching my face intently. His mouth was stern and unsmiling, as I'd seen it when, on campaign, things were going badly for the host.

"There is *one* remedy that *might* serve—but," he paused and shook his head, "a desperate one. If it failed . . ."

He paused, and I felt a cold shiver of anxiety.

"What remedy? What danger in using it?" I asked.

He did not answer that, but asked abruptly:

"Is Iltud in the fort at present?"

"Iltud? Yes, I think so," I said, startled. "Why?"

"Find him for me, Bedivere. He's the one man who might be able to get the cure I need. But I warn you, it may take time to find it and I cannot promise . . ." He stood, frowning, deep in thought. Then, raising his head like a man who has taken a decision: "Yes, send Iltud to me."

"What *is* this remedy," I persisted. "Where is it to be found? Why Iltud?"

Palomides said sternly:

"The only remedy left to us, and until we have tried

it, I, the king's physician, cannot tell what its effect will
be. Do you trust me, Bedivere?"

I looked into his eyes and saw how deeply they were
troubled. For what seemed a long moment I hesitated.
Then I said:

"Who else can we trust? Things can't go on as they
are. You've saved his life for us. Now you must save his
reason, Palomides."

"Then find me Iltud," he answered, "and when you
have found him, be patient. He may have to make a long
journey to fetch this cure I need."

It was the full moon of April and Ygern had left us to go
back to the Island to take part in the mysteries that
prepare for Spring Sowing. Her departure and the Merlin's (for he had gone, also) Arthur accepted with the
same patient indifference as he showed towards all outward events, saying only:

"A month to Pentecost, is it? You'll have to take my
place in hall for that this year, Bedivere."

"A month is a month and you're mending. It may be
you'll sit with us at the feast yourself, Bear. I think you
should try," I said.

But he only shook his head and said bleakly:

"I doubt I could face it. This sickness has done
something to me. I'll need time to find myself again. If
only Lancelot were here." And although the night was
mild, he shuddered, holding his hands, that were grown
white and bloodless, over the brazier's warmth.

I made some excuse and, leaving him, went out from
the close room where Excalibur hung on the wall above
his burnished armor, and a bowl of posset left neglected
on the table beside him gave off a sickly smell of honey
and herbs. I felt stifled and very near despair.

In the Great Hall the pages were still clearing the
tables from supper, and Gawain, passing through, paused
to ask me:

"How is he, today?"

"The same," I said.

He scowled anxiously.

"It canna go on like this, Bedivere. Spring's on us

now and the seaways open. Who's to say what this summer'll bring?"

"Who indeed?" I agreed, and left him before he could say more.

Outside, the air struck chill, and moonlight lay like frost on the scythed terraces of the queen's gardens. Owls were hunting down by the river.

"Lancelot!" I thought bitterly. "Always Lancelot! Ygern, whom he loves, the Merlin who has given a lifetime to his service, we the Companions; we count as nothing beside that one who betrayed him in the fashion no man who *is* a man forgives. This is madness! The poison has touched his brain. Will he ever be anything but an old man, warming hands grown soft at the embers of a dying fire? And he has no heir!"

A great restlessness was on me. I paced up and down the lower terrace, glancing now and then towards the lighted windows of the palace, seeing one after another darken, where folk were going to bed. At last only the lamp in the king's chamber remained burning, and the moonlight stared at the long white walls, and struck a gleam from the helmet of the decurion on guard outside the king's door. I had passed below the steps that led up to it when I heard the rattle of his armor, and his gruff voice giving a challenge. I turned back sharply. Who was seeking entrance at such an hour to Arthur's private apartments? Palomides, probably, returning from the hospital at the fort, I thought. I'd turned back in time to see, for a moment, a tall figure in a white monk's robe, the cowl drawn up, speaking with the sentry. Then the door yawned inwards, closed, and the sentry came to attention again.

I knew our guards were reliable—picked men, who understood their duty—but I went up the steps two at a time, and said to the decurion:

"Who was that you admitted to the king's presence?"

He came to attention and saluted.

"Abbot Iltud, my lord." His voice was startled. He added, laboriously explaining, "He's one of the Companions, sir. My orders were to admit . . ."

I cut him short.

"Fair enough. I didn't recognize him, that's all. Carry on with your watch."

I walked slowly along the upper terrace. The owl hooted again from the willows by the river. The peacock, roosting on the parapet wall, a dark bump of feathers, head under wing, stirred, and its shadow stirred on the white stone of the path below. A group of young cypresses cast long bars of blackness across the way just beyond it, and where the moonlight shone between those bars, another shadow stirred.

"Who's there?" I asked sharply.

No one answered. But the shadow was not cast by a cypress.

My hand on my sword, I moved forward.

"Answer me. Who are you? What do you want here at this hour?" I asked, every nerve in me tingling with some premonition I could not explain. "Come out and show yourself."

Still utterly silent, a tall figure, cloaked and hooded in black, moved slowly into the moonlight and stood facing me, then, with a quick impatient gesture that was oddly familiar, raised a hand and flung back the cloak's hood.

A voice I had never thought to hear again said hoarsely:

"He asked for me, Bedivere. I have come."

"Lancelot!"

There was no mistaking him. His height—that gesture—but his hair shone silver in the moonlight and his face, hollowed by the shadows, had a gaunt, ghastly pallor. For an endless moment I stared at him, thinking:

"He is dead. He has come back from the grave. This is a portent!"

Then he laughed, a short, harsh sound, more like a sob, deep in the throat, but unmistakably human.

"Strike if you must. I deserve no other welcome from any of you. But I had to come."

There was a small, rustling sound, like the wind

passing through poplar leaves, and suddenly she was there beside him, more ghostly even than he, a woman clothed from neck to ankle in a straight nun's robe of undyed wool—the penitent's robe—her hair unbound, falling about her thin, strained face.

"If you kill him, Bedivere, kill me too," Guinevere said. "That is the only mercy I ask of you—you, who were always kind."

"Gods!" I said softly. "Gods! So this is what Palomides meant!"

I looked from them to the sword in my hand and saw the moonlight glitter on the naked blade I had not known I'd drawn. My head felt empty, full of a strange lightness, as though the whole night's immensity was rushing through it. Very slowly, feeling the weight heavy in my hand, I sheathed my sword.

"Go to the king. He asked for you," I said. It was as though the wind of some great distance spoke through me. I, Bedivere, who loved Arthur as my own soul, would liefer have killed them both. But there are times when the gods speak through a man—and Arthur, in the hour when death struck him from the saddle, had called for Lancelot as well as for me.

What passed between those three that night none of us ever knew. I dismissed the decurion and took the guard on the king's door myself. If the man was surprised, he did not show it. I was, after all, his commanding officer and it was not for him to question an order. After a little, Iltud came out and seeing me, gave me a nod, as if it was natural to find me there. He looked radiantly serene, like a man who has been in the presence of some great mystery. He beckoned, and the two figures, the black and the white, came, close together, up the steps, and passed me into the king's chamber, and Iltud closed the door very softly behind them, lifted his hand in the Christians' blessing, and padded away into the night without a word.

I watched until the sun rose, and Palomides came to tell me that I need not keep the guard longer, for the night had passed and the king was sleeping.

"Eh, it's a gey queer affair, no danger, and what folk'll make of it is past predicting. I'll say this much—there's not another man in Britain, no, nor in the whole empire, maybe, who'd carry such a high-handed, unheard of judgment off, against the whole precedent of normal behavior and get away with it. Only Arthur could outrage every convention so completely, I'm thinking," Gawain said to me, doubtfully, a week later. Then his face cleared and he grinned at me, his expression changing to conspiratorial delight. "Eh, but it's proof of one thing, Bedivere. The sickness has left him at last, or he'd not be showing himself so gey headstrong and determined!"

We had just come from Council and were strolling across the queen's garden to the palace gateway, where pages held our horses. I glanced at his leathery, hollow-cheeked face with warm affection. The sun was shining, white clouds raced overhead and all the birds were singing.

"The king is the king!" I said. "The Chosen One, Gawain. It's not for any of us, man or woman, to question his judgment of his own affairs, and that I'll uphold in arms against any who may come."

"Oh, aye, and so will every Companion among us," Gawain agreed solemnly. Then he chuckled: "Abbot Iltud may preach, as he did just now in Council, that to forgive is the Christ's greatest commandment, and to follow it sets man above the beasts, on a level with the gods, but I'm thinking, to the common folk, proof of the pudding's in the eating. When, yesterday, the host saw Arthur in the saddle again, and riding among them, do you ken what they were saying?"

"What then?" I asked.

"That whatever evil magic has lain over the king this six months past was too strong even for the Merlin to lift alone. It needed Lancelot's luck, and the queen's witchcraft, to break it. Did ye note how they thronged to Lancelot's stirrup, shouting luck had come back with him? Aye, there's some straitlaced sticklers would have it there should have been punishment meted out for sin and a' that—I've heard a complaint or two that Roman custom demands burning for an unfaithful wife and an ill, slow death for him that seduced her—or maybe was seduced *by* her more like! But, man, if the king had laid a finger on Lancelot yesterday he'd have had a mutiny on his hands. Forby, this reconciliation and forgiveness will cement the Rheged alliance just when we're like to be needing it most. The king's himself again, Bedivere— magic of the Old Faith or miracle of the new, you can take choice which you believe, say I, so long as we've our Pendragon at the head of the war host again, and the enemies of Britain knowing of it."

He swung himself up into the saddle, and together we trotted our horses out along the river road. Overhead larks' song trembled in the blue air. The willows were gold-over with pollen, the water meadows glittered with buttercups. Life had come back to Camelot.

"My lord, is it true that there will be no official trial held on the matter of the queen and the Lord Lancelot?" Medraut asked me.

It was the eve of Pentecost and he and I together had been working to clear routine business before the festival, in the scribes' room at the palace, after the copyists had left. I looked up from the list of pleas before me and said briefly:

"That is the decision of the Council."

"It is the king's wish that everything should be as it used to be before the—thing—happened?"

"Yes," I said.

"I only ask, my lord, because, as you can guess, questions may come my way at the festival. I needed to know how I should answer them."

I looked at his closed, impassive face.

"Well, now you know," I said.

He fidgeted for a moment or two, stacking wax tablets with meticulous neatness.

"My lord, do you believe that the queen did, in fact, dwell apart from the Lord Lancelot, in a nunnery in Broceliande Forest, all those years they were in Armorica?" he asked softly.

"I believe what I have been told," I said, and felt my hand itch to strike him in the face.

He nodded.

"She is greatly changed, is she not, poor lady? One would say she had practiced great austerities among the good nuns, by her looks?" He glanced up at me with his blank eyes, then down again at the last tablet he was adding to the pile. When I did not answer, he went on, speaking carefully as a man will do who chooses his words. "They say the Bishop of Rome himself sent an emissary at King Bann's plea to persuade her to leave Lord Lancelot's Fortress of Joyous Guarde, and seek the protection of Holy Church."

"They say a great many thing, Medraut," I answered him, steadily. "Take my advice, and let them say. All that concerns us is the king's order—that here, at Camelot, things go on as if the past five years had never been."

"Of course, my lord. I understand," he said.

Again he glanced up at me, a cold little smile on his lips, a smile of complicity, as though he were tacitly suggesting we shared some subterfuge.

I picked up a list of the Clans from my desk.

"Take this to Sir Gaheris. He's Marshal of the Games. He should have had it before," I said curtly.

When he had gone, with his catlike, sinuous walk, and too-ready obedience, I sat for a few moments, feeling a grey depression stealing out of the shadows of the long, bare room, where the scribes' tall writing desks and the shelves of stored tablets and parchment rolls against the walls stood, half seen beyond the circle of lamplight cast by the one lamp beside me.

What was it about the man that made feel as though I had watched a slug trail its slime across the petals of a flower in bloom? His questions had been reasonable enough.

I remembered the day after Lancelot and Guinevere had returned. Arthur had slept late, watched over by Palomides anxiously until his waking. Then he had sent for me. I went to his room not knowing what to expect. I have never seen a man so changed. He was sitting up in bed, his eyes bright, his hair tousled, his expression as alert, as intent, as I remembered it when we were boys together and he was planning some adventure.

He held out his hand to me.

"Bedivere—they've come back!" he said.

Just that. No questions. No doubts. A deep, shining happiness that he needed to share, that he took for granted I *must* share.

I took his hand and held it up against my cheek, saying nothing, feeling resentment and jealousy and smallness dissolve from my heart in that great, living warmth of love.

He gripped my hand with a strength I had forgotten, half crushing it in his, then, laughing, let it go, and threw back the bed coverings.

"Here, help me up, will you? I'm still stiff in the joints, but by the Light, it's time I stopped skulking in this sickroom like some old gaffer with the rheumatics. Where are those idle pages of mine? Shout for them, will you? I need a bath, and proper clothes and a horse saddled. By all the gods, I've wasted too much of life already. Today I feel like a man new-born!"

"Yes," I thought, turning out the lamp in the scribes' room, and feeling my way to the door through the sudden darkness, "to those who love greatly enough, there is a simplicity, a directness that cuts through all the webs of convention and custom and the care for other men's opinions. But the web, sticky and clinging, is still woven all about that shining greatness by little minds like Medraut's."

I remembered again the simile that had risen in my mind, and instinctively, as I stepped out of the dark room into the night air, I ground my heel against the outer step, as I should have ground it on a slug.

# VII
# SOLEMN MELODY

# Chapter Twenty-Five

Griffin and his monks are preparing for the festival of
Pentecost. Somewhere outside my cell hawthorn must be
in bloom for the sweet, heavy scent of it comes in waves
through the door that they have left open to the mild
spring air.

So many memories it brings. Pentecost at Caerleon,
that long-ago year when Arthur first created the order of
knights, and I felt the fire of a new life run, tingling, down
the blade of Excalibur when he gave me the accolade.
Pentecost as it was kept with ever-growing ceremonial in
the Great Judgment Hall, where the Christian rite and the
rites of Spring Sowing were combined, after Badon, into
one solemn observance. The Pentecosts of the Grail . . .

Today, while Griffin sat at my bedside, cheering me
with his homely chat of small happenings, I interrupted
him abruptly.

"Tell me," I said, "for I've often wondered—now
you are a Christian abbot, what do you teach your people
was the truth of the Holy Grail?"

He was silent a long time. Then he said, reluctantly:

"I do not speak of it to them, my lord. How can I
teach what I, myself, have never fully understood?"

I saw my question had troubled him, but, perhaps
unkindly, I chose to press it further.

"Suppose one of them were to ask you concerning
it?"

He shook his head.

"They are poor, simple folk, and ignorant. I doubt if they'd remember, now, any talk of that strange happening." Then he brightened. "If one did ask, I should answer as Abbot Iltud (God rest his soul) always did. He spoke of the Grail as a holy vision, granted to those only who were worthy to behold it. A vision of the Cup from which our Lord drank at the Last Supper, and which later the great saint, Joseph of Arimathea, brought to Britain for safekeeping, in a time of persecution. I should explain that a relic so precious, lest it be profaned by heathen hands, had been caught up to heaven in the time of the Troubles, and was only sometimes shown by God's mercy to his elect, carried by angels, and surrounded by a great light."

"And that is all you would say?" I asked, still curious.

He got up and began to busy himself, raising me higher on my pillows, setting a cool drink within easier reach.

"That is all I should say, my lord," he answered steadily.

"Yet, Griffin, *you* know how much more there was to it. You were in the judgment hall that day of Pentecost. Have you forgotten?"

He stepped back, and crossed himself.

"How could I, how could any of us, ever forget?" he said harshly. Then, suddenly, in a voice that was not the voice of the abbot, but of Griffin, my armor-bearer and my comrade, he said brokenly, "No one who was not with us in those days will ever understand. Best not talk of it. It was the beginning of the end!"

Outside, the little sheepbell began to ring insistently. He took up the worn shepherd's crook he carries by virtue of his office, and went out, without another word, to lead his cross-bred flock once more in their tuneless chanting.

His words startled me. Pondering over them, I saw how, to one as simple and direct, they must seem the only answer, now. But it made me lonely. The hardest part of age is losing the companionship of minds and hearts that shared one's understanding of life's deeper mysteries.

Now the square beyond the open door has turned from daylight to deep night-blue. The seven stars of the Bear—Arthur's stars—swing low above the apple trees that crown the little hill I can just see from my bed. In my mind, it is as though the curtains were to be drawn aside, and against that solemn backdrop, I saw the drama beginning in which each one of us played our part, line by line, as the gods dictated it, not knowing the meaning of the play, nor how its plot would develop, until, the Chorus having spoken the epilogue, the theatre was empty.

For me, that play began on a morning after Lancelot and the queen returned to Camelot, when, having come in overnight from a long tour of my province, I'd slept late, and so missed the dawn Council meeting.

Things were very quiet and orderly at Arthur's court in those days. Whatever life Guinevere had led in Armorica during the years of her absence (and the truth of that time I never fully learned), they had laid a deeply Christian mark on her—and on Lancelot also, it seemed. Both behaved with dignity and gentleness, taking Iltud for their friend and advisor, so that he had become, again, a permanent part of our community. Arthur treated him as one of the Companions, giving him his old place in Council, as a matter of course. He was a good man, honest and tolerant, and it was natural enough that those three should love him. (They owed him their reconciliation, after all.) Arthur seemed happy and at peace, and preferred, I dare say, the almost monastic atmosphere of austerity and good works that surrounded him, to the restless gaiety and craving for display that had marked Guinevere's earlier years. It suited well with his own soldierly discipline. With his deeper beliefs even Iltud never dared to interfere. On the whole, I suppose those years were the most personally peaceful Arthur ever knew.

I was surprised, accordingly, and at first amused, that morning, when I went to report to him, to find him striding up and down his own room in one of his old royal rages. He was cursing a couple of his small pages roundly

when I entered. They, it seemed, had dawdled over their
duties while he was at Council, and were scuttling about
like puppies in a panic, hanging up the armor they'd been
burnishing and getting under his feet in the process.

"Out, both of you! Get out and leave me in peace!
Where's Constantine? He should see to it you attend to
your duties better than this. Be careful what you're at,
boy—if you've dented that shield I'll have the hide off
you!" This as, with a mighty crash, his great bronze
buckler fell to the floor.

"I'm sorry, my lord. The peg's come out of the wall.
It wasn't my fault, really it wasn't," a scared small voice
piped, aghast.

"No? If you'd stood on a stool to hang it instead of
swinging on the thong like a mad monkey the peg would
not have given way. Leave it now, and tell Constantine to
see to the repair. Where *is* he, anyway?"

"G-gone rabbiting, my lord. Don't you remember, he
asked permission and you said—last night, you said—"
the second small boy stuttered reproachfully.

Arthur laughed suddenly.

"Maybe I did! Well, tell him from me that until he's
trained you two better to take his place he'll have no
more time off to chase other game. That should ensure
me better service for the future. Now, go!"

He turned, saw me, and his face lit up.

"Bedivere! They told me you were back and the
gods know you've returned at a time when I need you.
Come in and sit down. Menaevia can wait" (he'd seen the
parchment lists in my hand), "Medraut'll see to that
report of yours later. There's another matter we need to
discuss. Come and sit down—and you, boy" (to the elder
of the two pages, who was sidling quietly out of the
door), "see to it we aren't disturbed."

He went over to the hearth and with a gesture of
impatience threw a couple of cushions out of his great
carved chair.

"Women!" he muttered. "Anyone would think I was
an ailing dotard—she means well, my Guinevere—but all
this nonsense of *cushions!*"

He slumped into the chair and passed his hand over

his forehead with a sudden gesture of weariness. Then, as obeying his order, I took the seat opposite him:

"Irritable as a spring bear, aren't I? Well, I've reason to be. No man enjoys being reminded he's growing old. The Council have been rubbing it into me for the past hour and more. The damnable part is they're right, of course, and I know it. A draught blows all across Britain from that empty chair custom sets on my right hand at the round table, Bedivere. The chair the Merlin named too many years ago 'the Perilous Seat.' I've got to make my decision who's to fill it."

"They've been plaguing you again about the succession, have they?" I growled.

"Rightly enough," he said at once. "No man lasts for ever. It's time Britain had assurance who the Pendragon's heir will be; time for a new Dragon Making."

"I see," I said. "Well, who is it to be, Bear. Gawain?"

He did not answer. I said, feeling my way:

"He's the nearest to you in blood, and has sons to follow him. Is he the one they want?"

Arthur shrugged.

"Some do. You can guess the ones who don't."

"Easily enough. Who then? Young Constantine? His claim could be shown to be valid, but is he old enough?"

"No. A nice enough lad. He's got the makings of a warrior, but he'd hardly fill the Perilous Seat this year. He'd likely as not liven the Council's debates by letting out a capful of mice on the round table, or set a hedgehog in the Merlin's seat from what I know of him. He's a scamp after my own heart, that one, and I've had worse armor-bearers, but I doubt he's the makings of a High Prince yet."

"Who, then?"

Arthur sat, leaning forward, his hands clasped between his knees, his eyes on the ground.

"It was in my mind for a time that I might do as the emperors did in like case and adopt me an heir," he said slowly. "There's one, after all, who has Uther's blood on the mother's side (though that's not a claim I'd care to put forward, seeing the circumstances). He knows the

work of government and is not a bad war leader, though
without experience. He's the son of the one woman I'd
have chosen to bear my children, Bedivere, if the fates
had been kinder. I could have adopted Medraut."

I drew in my breath sharply.

"You could," I said, and my voice was grim. "If you
did, Bear, count me out as one of the Companions."

He looked up at me.

"So?" he said. "Like that, is it? I thought others
might feel the same. In any case, the question doesn't
arise. The thing's settled, though the Council doesn't
know the full story yet, and won't until Pentecost. The
Clans are gathering for Spring Sowing now, as they gathered for me, and a Chosen One goes to his Dragon
Making this year, as I went to mine."

I stared at him.

"You mean?"

"That the choice is not mine or the Council's to
make. It lies, as it has always lain, with the Masters of the
Wisdom. Lancelot's son, Peredur, will be the next Pendragon, Bedivere. He is the Island's choice."

"*Lancelot's* son?" I repeated stupidly, stunned by
the utter unexpectedness of the news.

Arthur nodded, his face grave and alert, his eyes
very bright.

"Lancelot's son by Elaine of Gwynfid, the grandson
of King Pelles, descended on his mother's side through a
line of royal blood that goes back to Heilyn the Mighty
and counts kin somewhere, so the Bards tell, with the
saint, Arimathean Joseph, for good measure. He is
Island-trained and the Merlin bears witness that the stars
confirm his destiny. He is the Chosen One, the next who
will come to the heritage of Britain, as I came, by way of
the Fire and the Cave."

It was very quiet in the sunlit room. Far above us,
faint with distance, a trumpet sounded high noon from
the ramparts of the Great Fort.

A dozen questions rose in my mind, and sank into
silence, unspoken. What use to question an accomplished
fact?

At last I said:

"Are you happy with this choice, Bear? Is the Clan's Chosen One a man *you* would choose?"

Arthur leaned back, clasping both hands about his knee in the old, familiar gesture, and smiled a little.

"To be honest, I'm not sure. He's a strange lad, one I know at least I'll find it easy to love. I've watched him grow up on the Island these last six years, and he's stood out, always, from the rest. He's Lancelot's son, after all, so one might expect that. I think he'll make a warrior, for he excels in all the arts of war, is strong and swift and skillful, with a shrewd mind, too. But . . ."

"But what?" I asked, as the pause lengthened.

Arthur shook his head.

"There's something I don't understand about the boy. An odd remoteness—a touch of the Bard, perhaps, or maybe it's something bred from his early years in that lost and forgotten mountain country, under the influence of old Pelles and his odd ideas. He's a bit of a dreamer, I'd say, lives in a world of his own. But he's young yet, barely eighteen. Time and experience should serve to bring his head down out of the clouds. With any luck I'll be at hand to guide his way for a good few years, despite the Council's croaking," and he laughed.

"You kept his identity secret from them, did you?" I asked, puzzled as to his reason for that.

"From those who do not know it already, yes," he said decisively. "I'd not have the Island's choice questioned and mulled over, with endless chatter and discussion that might leave room for old jealousies and rivalries to raise their heads. You know how matters stand—not all those who follow the Christian Faith have Iltud's wise tolerance and not all the Colonial element will be ready to welcome a High Prince out of Gwynfid until they've learned to know the man for himself. I've not forgotten my own King Showing, Bedivere. I've a mind to have this feast of Pentecost kept with decent order and dignity, if I can, and with no brawls. By the gods, man, you know my method's always been the same—speed and surprise. I believe in it still, be it in time of war *or* peace!"

Easter fell late that year, and Pentecost was two weeks
into May. The hawthorn was white-over on all the hedges
and the elder flowers were in bloom. It was hot as
midsummer, after a three-week drought, and there was a
hint of thunder in the air. Buttercup petals lacquered our
sandals with fairy gold again, crossing the horse-field, and
in the woods below the fort the cuckoos were calling all
day, through a mist of small birds' song.

A feeling of excitement, a presentiment of something
out of the ordinary impending, pulsed through the whole
of Camelot, and preparations for the festival were on a
scale more elaborate than I ever remembered. More than
twice the usual number of Clans came in for the Gathering, and I'd my work cut out quartering them all about
the hillsides and water meadows, remembering which
could be trusted to prove good neighbors, and which were
wisest kept with distance between them. I missed Lancelot's help for that. He'd been absent for some time, I
could guess where, and Gawain, who did his best to help
me, was oddly absent-minded and on edge. Medraut, too,
I'd noticed, looked white and strained. I wondered with
grim amusement if both were waiting under equal stress
to learn who would sit down at the feast in that long-
empty chair at Arthur's right hand. I'd an idea one
dreaded and one hoped against all reasonable hope that
he might be the man.

On the vigil of the feast I got back late to my
quarters in the fort, and was glad to find Palomides there
before me. Thoughtful as ever, guessing I'd have missed
supper in hall, he'd a plate of bread and meat and some
wine ready for me, and I sat down to it hungrily, glad of a
comrade I could grumble to over the happenings of my
day. He let me talk myself out, than looked at me with
one of his quick, half-mocking smiles.

"Since I take it you've more work to do already than
you count one man can accomplish, you'll not be pleased
with a message I have for you," he told me. "Lancelot's
been here with a request that, if you grant it him, will
mean both of us must be up at cock-light tomorrow."

"Christian devils take the man! What for?" I asked.

"A strange matter. He was very earnest and oddly humble in asking it. He wants us, you and I, to stand as sponsors for his son, who is to receive knighthood tomorrow, before the feast."

*"Before* the feast?" I said. (It was Arthur's custom to give the accolade to the year's new knights when the feast in hall was near its ending. But I saw, with Peredur, there might be reasons for making an exception.)

Palomides spread his hands in the quick gesture I knew so well.

"Bedivere, I understand the situation now. Lancelot's explained it to me. The lad insists that it is from his own father, whom he calls 'the best knight in the world,' that he wishes to receive the accolade. Lancelot was most deeply moved—in tears, protesting he's unworthy to perform so high an office. But the king's persuaded him— ordered him, in fact—to accede to the request. Lancelot came looking for you and, not finding you here, poured out his soul to me (you know his way!). Nothing will serve, it seems, to outweigh his own unworthiness, but to have us two stand sponsors. (He added, I must say, some very pretty compliments at that point!) I promised to persuade you to it, for he was terribly wrought up and insistent, and I think it might be wise to go with him if we can. Wise for the boy Peredur's sake."

"Very well," I said, resignedly. "I'd enough to do already—but if you say so—gods, Palomides, I wish I knew what to make of all this! Lancelot's son to be High Prince and Arthur's heir—how will Britain react to that, do you imagine?"

Palomides' dark eyes were thoughtful, his tone graver than I'd heard it for a long while.

"That must depend on one person only: Lancelot's son," he said.

We rode out at dawn, just the three of us, attended by two of Lancelot's pages to hold our horses. This matter of giving the accolade had, by custom, been considered a ceremonial occasion from its first institution at Caerleon. All three of us wore full military dress, with half-armor, and rode together in silence, our minds on the solemn mystery of a young knight's initiation into the brotherhood.

I'd seen what Palomides meant about Lancelot when we joined him at the north gate. He looked magnificent, in the Armorican tartan that suited him so well, his breastplate of burnished bronze inlaid with gold, a jewelled sword belt of crimson leather clipping his waist and the red-gold High Prince's circlet shining against the iron-grey of his hair. He was grave and quiet, as he wrung my hand, and in a low tone thanked me for my coming, then explained we must ride into the forest to a meeting place already appointed. But I could feel the tension in the man, taut to breaking point. His face, white and set, was that of a man facing some great ordeal.

The forest, when we came to it, was full of birdsong, and the glint of sunrise on new young green. Under the tall grey columns of beech trunks, bluebells smoked away into the distance. A little breeze rustled overhead.

We rode some distance, then crossed a stream, and on its further bank Lancelot reined in his black stallion.

"We leave the horses here," he said briefly.

We dismounted, in silence, and the three of us went forward alone down a broad green ride that led out into a clearing where a granite monolith, carved roughly with a cross far older than the Christians' symbol, leaned sideways above thin woodland grass.

"This is the place appointed," Lancelot said, and we waited with him. Minutes passed. Some distance away a little bell, very silvery and sweet, rang, and ceased, and rang again, three times, as is the custom at the saying of the mass. Lancelot crossed himself and stood with bent head, as though he prayed.

Again, time passed. On the far side of the glade I saw something move among the trees. An old man, very bent and frail, in a long white hermit's robe, came slowly out of the blue early shadows, leading by the hand a tall youth, dressed from head to foot in the dull red that is the Celtic color of kingship. He moved slowly, accommodating his pace with courtesy to the aged hermit beside him, but he held his head high, and the level rays of the morning sun shone full upon his face.

Such a quiet face. That was my first thought. Lancelot's features. The same hawk nose and strong, cleft chin. The same deep eye sockets and delicately flaring brows. But the mouth different—a beautiful mouth, wide, tender and vulnerable. (His mother's mouth, and *she* died for love, I thought.) The hair was different, too; soft and very fine, the color of a winter oakleaf, falling straight to the shoulders, curling in a little at the tips. He was bare-headed, and unarmed, an empty scabbard hanging from the plain belt at his waist, and he wore no jewels, except the Dragon ring on his right arm, and round his neck on a slender chain an equal-armed cross of carved rock crystal that caught the light in a prism of rainbow colors. There was strength in the set of the shoulders, the narrow waist, the long, lithe hips, and he moved with the controlled grace of well-trained muscles.

"Lancelot's breeding—yes, he'll make a warrior!" I thought.

Then, as he came closer, I saw his eyes, wide and strangely intent; hazel eyes, clear as an Outland stream, curious and innocent and searching; the unguarded eyes of a child.

I thought: "He is the most beautiful young man I ever saw—but from what strange place has he come to us? Surely, out of a world that is not our world—he has the look on him of the Land of Heart's Desire, the People of Sidhe, who dwell in the Hollow Hills. Now I know what Arthur meant!" and a strange shiver went through me as it does each year when I hear the wild swans' cry overhead, flying northward on a night of early spring.

The impression was only momentary. It passed as the lad stepped forward alone, and knelt before Lancelot. Big-boned, a little awkward, with the uncertainty of all young things not yet come to their full growth, still at the stage where clumsiness and promise meet, he went down on his knees, and said, simply:

"My father, I, Peredur of Gwynfid, ask of you the accolade of knighthood."

His voice was deeper than I expected, mature and assured. Though the gesture had the humility of youth, the voice claimed the respect of manhood, and I felt suddenly reassured and content.

"He may be Lancelot's son, but Arthur might well have sired him. The Wise Ones have made us a good choice," I thought.

Back at the fort that day I'd little time to reflect on the morning's happenings. A score of practical matters needed my attention. Towards noon I noticed the breeze had dropped and the sun hazed over. It was very hot again, and beyond the marshes thunderheads were building up. Great towering mountains of cloud, edged with copper. A storm would spoil the ground for the Games, I remembered, and hoped it would pass over.

By custom, we went to dinner early on the day of Pentecost, for the feasting was preceded by a certain ceremony, which, begun very simply in the early days, had grown with the years into a rite of some magnificence. It had been devised to stress the essential unity that bound Arthur's followers together, no matter what their individual beliefs might be: the underlying truth that Spring Sowing, Pentecost, or the mystery of the great Bull Slaying lead all alike to one essential truth—the dependence of man upon a power greater than his own—the life that brings back summer to the world, ripens the corn and puts the bloom upon the grape, that mystery of the circling seasons' changeless order, the patient, tireless rhythm of earth's yearly renewed fertility, without which man must surely die. A mystery symbolized in all faiths by the Cup, which, held elevated in human hands, can only be filled from above.

So, each year, our Great Hall was hung with garlands, and the tables were spread for us, but before meat was served, a procession passed through the hall, and there followed the admission to knighthood of those who had earned that distinction; and the renewal by all present of the vows of fealty we had taken to the king and to the cause of Britain.

Most folk were already gathered in hall when I

crossed the queen's gardens to the palace. The air was close, and there was a stillness of waiting over the land. Only the willows down by the river fluttered their leaves, showing the silver of the undersides, and a blackbird startled the silence with its sudden harsh cry of warning.

I was the last of the Companions to take my place at the round table on the raised dais—my accustomed place at Arthur's right hand, with the vacant chair between us, which down the years the Merlin had placed there awaiting the Pendragon's heir.

The hall was filled that day, fuller than I ever remembered seeing it, not a place vacant save that one waiting chair, and the Merlin's throne, facing Arthur's. It was dim and shadowy, for the late afternoon outside lowered with coming storm. As I reached my station, the silver trumpets sounded and through the wide-flung doors of the Great Hall the procession entered and we rose to our feet in reverence. First came singing boys, swinging censers, then white monks and Priests of the Island and of Mithras, walking in pairs, alternately. Iltud, in his abbot's cope of crimson, his cross-bearer before him; the High Priest of Mithras, wearing the bull's-horn headdress and jewelled sun-rayed breastplate. After him, another incense boy, and then three of the Island's youngest Priestesses—slim, lovely girls, with unbound hair and straight white robes, bearing corn sheaves. And behind them again, taller, a little older, one whose robe shimmered with gold as she moved, carrying aloft the great crystal Cup of Life, tinged rose-red by the wine within it. The Cup each man might reverence in the belief of his own faith, symbol equally holy to those who saw in it the Druid wisdom, the victory of the Bull-Slayer, or the sacrament of that Christ-God who went to death, consenting, for the renewal of the life of the world.

All of us paid homage, as the procession passed, with the sign of his own belief—some crossing themselves, some raising clenched fist to forehead, and others with the secret signs of their degree in the Mithraic or other mysteries. It was simple enough and yet, each year, I found it moved me strangely.

Three times they circled the hall, then passed, singing, out through the great bronze doors that were closed, clanging, behind them. When the voices of the singing boys had died into distance, Arthur gave the Pentecost Challenge: *"Let any man in Britain who claims a favor of the Pendragon ask admittance now!"*

The waiting silence that always followed the Challenge seemed, that year, to throb like the humming of a stretched wire. Three knocks sounded and as Arthur signed to the waiting pages to open, a rustle of expectation passed round the hall like the rustle that passes through a forest before rain. Beyond and behind it I heard the first growl of thunder.

One of the palace doves, disturbed, perhaps, by the coming storm, flashed through the opening doors, and fluttered down the hall. Then I saw him again, Peredur, the Chosen One, walking between the old white hermit and the Merlin. He was dressed as he had been in the morning, except that now he wore a sword at his side, a King Sword, long and straight as Excalibur, and binding his soft, leaf-brown hair close to his lifted head, the thin gold circlet of a High Prince. He moved with dignity, but his face still had that look of calm wonder, as he came slowly up the hall. His eyes were raised, following the flight of the dove, and he seemed totally unaware of the many all about him who watched his coming.

Arthur had moved to the edge of the dais to meet the three. When they stood before him, the hermit spoke, in a clear, trembling voice—the voice of extreme old age:

"Arthur, Pendragon of Britain, I, Nazien of Yr Widdfa, present to you Peredur, son of Lancelot, High Prince of Armorica and of Elaine of Gwynfid. I bear witness for him that he is, in truth and verity, the legitimate grandson of King Pelles the Holy, come of the line of Heilyn the Mighty, descended on his mother's side from that sainted Joseph of Arimathea who first brought the faith of Christ to this island."

He drew back a step and the Merlin moved forward. His deep, harper's voice rang out:

"Behold, Arthur of Britain, the Chosen One, Peredur of Gwynfid, who comes to you from the Cave, acclaimed by the assembly of the Gathering. Recognize him by virtue of the Dragon ring he wears as the one appointed to fill the vacant seat at the right hand of the Pendragon."

Again that rustle went through the hall, as Peredur knelt and Arthur laid his hands upon his head.

"By the Dragon ring he is recognized. In the name of Light I receive him," he said solemnly. "I receive him. I accept him and here, before you all assembled, I declare him to be, from this day forward, the Pendragon's son by adoption. Rise, Peredur of Gwynfid, High Prince of the Island of Britain and my dear son."

Close on the words a flash of lightning lit the hall from end to end and thunder crashed above the roof.

Raising the boy, Arthur embraced him and turned him to face the assembly.

"Behold, all of you, the Chosen One, whose seat is the long-vacant chair at the Pendragon's right hand."

For a long moment they stood together, two tall, warrior figures, briefly illumined by the blue levin's flash, while rolling thunder half drowned the fanfare of silver trumpets and the great shout of acknowledgment that we raised; then Arthur returned to his place at the round table and the Merlin led Peredur to the vacant chair beside it.

Arthur called for lights and music, and for the feast to be served, in a voice that told us ceremonial was at an end, and the time had come for relaxation and rejoicing. But in the storm's glare I had seen the startled and amazed faces of the Companions all about me, and among them the face of Medraut, white and distorted, the face of a madman, who, wandering among mountain peaks, perceives, before he falls, a great chasm opening at his feet.

I stayed on longer at Camelot that year than was my custom. It was Arthur's command I should. He'd taken a risk and he knew it.

"I'll need you near me, Bedivere, until we see how matters shape. We may have trouble and as you know well enough, where there's trouble, I like my Chief Companion close at hand!" he told me, with one of his quick, half-smiling grimaces.

Surprisingly, we had very little. I'd expected it, too, for by any reckoning he had taken a high hand, deciding the succession as he had, and springing it on both the Council and the country.

We owed the lack of trouble to the love and respect all but a very few had for the king, but we owed it also to Peredur. There was a quality about him from the first that was oddly endearing. He had won the host to his side before the three days of the Games were over. They measured a potential war leader by his physical prowess and in that their new High Prince did not disappoint them. His handling of a team in the chariot racing proved he had not wasted his opportunities, reared as he had been among the famous horse-runs of Arphon. His javelin cast broke all our previous records by a full three feet, and he wrestled as if he had been born in Lyonesse. What made him lovable was the quiet surprise his success seemed to give him, and a certain shy pleasure with which he received congratulation and acclaim. He was courteous to all, of whatever rank, and showed well-mannered respect whenever he spoke with us older Companions, but there was an eager, naif curiosity about him, that reminded me again of my first impression that he had come to us out of some other world. He would ask unexpected questions, that left folk puzzled by their directness, and listen with grave attention to the answers, but sometimes, under the quietness of his manner, I suspected there was something of Lancelot's humorous shrewdness. He could be disconcerting, when pressed for an opinion, for he always gave it seriously and directly, without the slightest concession to convention.

I had wondered with some misgiving before he actually came among us how Guinevere would react to Arthur's choice of heir. I never pretended to myself I could understand the workings of a woman's mind, but it seemed to me the boy was bound to cause her at least some emotional stress. He was, after all, the son of a man she had loved too well, by a woman of whom she had been fiercely jealous. He had been chosen by the husband she'd betrayed to take the place of the son she'd failed to bear. If such thoughts occurred to her, she hid them with a control I could only admire. Her manner to Peredur, from the first day, was gentle and welcoming. Sometimes I thought it was tinged with bewilderment, but that was true of all of us.

Once, on a summer day, when we three were walking together on the palace terrace, I remember he left us abruptly in the middle of a serious conversation to race down the steps and rescue one of the small wolfhound pups, waddling purposefully towards disaster in an ornamental fountain; then lingered, the wriggling bundle held carefully in his big hands, watching as if entranced the sun make rainbows in the fountain's spray.

Guinevere shook her head, and said, with indulgent amusement:

"What a dreamer that boy is, Bedivere! Look at him. He is like a child to whose eyes everything—the wild flower in the hedge, a bird's shadow on the grass, a sunlit wave, are all new, all touched with wonder!"

There was a wistful sadness in her voice that for some reason irritated me. I said gruffly:

"Let's hope he soon grows out of such fancies. He can be practical enough when he chooses to set his mind to more serious matters."

She turned to me, her eyes startled and questioning. I noticed, not for the first time, how well the fashion she'd adopted of going always in unadorned white suited her still haunting beauty. As if thinking aloud, she murmured:

"He's got Lancelot's charm, but something of Arthur's blunt, downright directness, hasn't he? Sometimes he frightens me, the way he can go right to the heart of a matter, and make one almost shockingly aware of the truth behind appearances. There are some folk, I'll wager, will always find that disconcerting. He could make enemies." Then, as if shrugging off too serious a mood, she added lightly, "Thank God, Arthur seems to understand him. Peredur, I truly believe, is, at last, the son he always longed for, and if I loved the boy for nothing else, I must always love him for that."

Palomides, I discovered, shared the general feeling that we entertained in Peredur some kind of changeling. He said to me, after the first Council meeting at which Peredur had been present:

"He looks at life with the unclouded vision of a child or a god, that one, Bedivere, and I'm not sure which. It is as though he had wandered here from some distant star, and found all our customs exhilaratingly strange!"

"Give the lad a chance!" I said. "Gwynfid is a remote enough area, and the gods know, a century and more behind the times. His grandfather, by all accounts, lives in a world of his own, wrapped in strange Celtic dreams and mystical visions. (One does not earn the title 'holy' from our mountain people for nothing!) What other experience has the boy had? Six years in the Island school, yes—but that's hardly training for life as we know it. Give him time to find his bearings, and he'll settle down and get his head out of the clouds."

"Perhaps," Palomides said meditatively, then he smiled. "Can one break the winged horse of Apollo to draw an army transport wagon, Bedivere?"

I watched closely for signs of hostility to the new order of things, during the first months. It existed, if at all, among Medraut's following, and took the form of shrugged shoulders and covertly cynical mockery, which I hoped might pass. Medraut himself behaved with impeccable discretion during the first weeks, then fell sick of the yellow jaundice, was duly doctored for it by Palomides, and, when he was convalescent, asked for leave to go north to Dalriada for a while.

"The queen, my dear and noble patroness, has been failing in health, and they tell me may not live the year. I long to pay my respects to her once more and tell her again of my gratitude for all she has done for me before it is too late," he told Arthur, and added, with a show of humility, "That is, if I can be spared from my duties here, my lord?"

I wondered if Arthur found it as irritating as I did, how very ill we found we could spare him in the weeks that followed! I said something of the sort to Gawain, when we two had spent an hour sorting out a query over a decurion's accounts that Medraut would have settled in five minutes.

Gawain snorted.

"Aye! He has the pull on us all, that canny laddie, when it comes to this weary task of figuring. I'm riding north myself, soon, and I'll see to it he makes this visit in Dalriada a short one. You shall have him back before leaf-fall, never fear, for if you must have it, I've no mind to thole his presence in my domain. I couldna oppose his going, for I doubt my mother'll last the year, from what they tell me. She's had an affection for him, always, and it could be his feeling for her is one of the few genuine things about him. But you, here, need him, and Dalriada doesn't! When *she* goes, I'll have problems enough, keeping the Clan loyal and the Picts at bay." He scowled. "Not all Dalriada was pleased by the king's choice at Pentecost, Bedivere. I'll need to make it gey clear to them up there that no insult was offered to their touchy pride by it."

I looked at his dour expression, and asked, curiously:

"You, yourself—how did you feel about it?"

His face cleared and he grinned engagingly.

"About being passed over for the succession? Glad as a man reprieved from lifelong imprisonment. What else?"

"Do you reckon Peredur is the High Prince we needed?"

"Aye, he'll do well enough. A thick head's no great disadvantage to a warrior. That lad's clean daft, times, but if he rides at a Saxon war host as straight as he answers any questions he's asked, he'll make a Pendragon some day. He canna help being slow in uptake, now and then, seeing the lost and forgotten, backward place Gwynfid is, and him brought up by old King Pelles, that's mad as a hare in March. But he's a likable lad. Give him time, he'll grow to fill that chair of the Merlin's better than I could have done, I dare say."

There was no doubting the sincerity behind the words. I admired him for his generosity and was content no lurking jealousy would threaten the future peace of Britain from his direction, at any rate.

An outbreak of cattle raiding up on the Trinovantian border took me away from Camelot for a short spell. It was endemic as marsh fever, most summers. The young Clan warriors looked on it as sport that enlivened the boredom of peace, and we never wholly stamped it out. It led to blood feuds and murder and general mayhem, if allowed to go unpunished. I turned a tolerant eye on it sometimes in spring starving time if a Clan known to be poverty-stricken raided a rich neighbor. The Trinovantes were not poor and it was high summer, so I made an example of them, with fines and reparations, all very judicial and impressive. By then it was time to go on to Aquae Sulis and preside over the yearly hearing of criminal cases from all over the northern half of my province, and what with one thing and another it was late autumn before I got back to Camelot.

I found the whole court in mourning for the Queen of Dalriada, and Samain was kept with great solemnity that year. It falls about the same date as the Christian remembrance of the dead, and there was a deal of mass singing, and processing, and keeping of fast days to the queen's memory and the memory of all the fallen of our wars. I thought of Margause as I'd known her and guessed how depressing she'd have found it all.

Medraut was back, going about dressed in black from head to foot, which suited his dark good looks in a sinister way. He seemed subdued and genuinely grief-stricken.

"The Queen of Dalriada was a wonderful woman— more than a mother to me, my lord. I'll never forget her kindness, and I owe her so much for the wise advice she gave me," he told me piously, but there were genuine tears in his eyes when he said it.

"At a guess she advised him to abandon vain ambitions, and make the best of the situation as it is, to judge from the way he's working!" I said cynically to Arthur, who'd overheard the conversation.

He frowned.

"Why must you always be so hard on Medraut, Bedivere? I can tell you, I value that man above most of the Companions, these days. Why can't you forget your prejudices for once and trust him, as I do?"

"Don't trust him too far, Bear. Remember the Merlin's warning," I said, risking an angry response.

"Oh, *that!*" he said impatiently, and turned to other subjects.

I watched Medraut closely, trying to assess his reactions to Peredur, for I'd an ugly memory of his face at Pentecost. But I had to admit I could find no fault in his behavior. He went out of his way to smooth the new High Prince's path in a fashion that was tactful and unobtrusive, as far as I could tell, and they got on well together.

Peredur got on well with most folk, from the highest in the land to the scruffiest bare-foot beggar who waited for kitchen scraps at the north gate. He reminded me of Arthur in his disregard of rank, and yet he kept a quiet dignity which few would have been rash or insensitive enough to presume upon. He lacked Lancelot's sparkling good fellowship, but he had a quiet gaiety of his own, and where he was there generally seemed to be laughter.

His beauty, inevitably, had made him a nine days' wonder among Guinevere's girls. Since her return to court there were fewer of them, carefully chosen and strictly kept. But they fluttered about him like convent doves, at first. I never saw a lad of his age so modestly unaware of his own attraction. He treated them all as if they were his sisters, and as far as I could see never took notice of one more than another. All his short life, I doubt if he ever took any woman, gentle-born or slave, to his bed. His indifference troubled me a little and, thinking of the future, I asked Palomides:

"What's wrong with the boy? He seems not to have the natural instincts of a man where women are concerned, and yet, as far as I can see, he doesn't favor any of the pages. With his opportunities, he should have been in and out of love half a dozen times by now!"

Palomides' eyes were thoughtful.

"Your Wise Ones chose a man out of the common mold, Bedivere. Some fire burns in him that I don't altogether understand and I doubt if he does. Have you noticed how little things—the flight of a heron, a rainbow over the marshes, some small hedgerow flower—kindle him to ecstasy? It's as though he saw the world more vividly, lived more intensely, than the rest of us. It may be that inner fire burns up the lusts that most men feel—or it may be that a lonely childhood and the influences that surrounded it have driven him too deeply into a world of fantasy. If that's the case"—Palomides paused and shrugged—"well, let's hope he'll come out of it gradually, and not with some violent, rude awakening. He'll need a steel core, if that happens, to face the squalor and cruelty and brute stupidity of our world. Provided he's got it, he could be a great king some day—greater perhaps even than Arthur. If he lacks the strength to face reality when the test comes on him"—again Palomides shrugged and shook his head—"there's instability in his blood—mental instability; the old grandfather, remember, his mother's suicide—and I'd not trust Lancelot under certain strains!"

"You mean—madness?" I asked, startled.

"Not madness as you'd count it. I said 'instability.' That's something different. He could be thrown off balance, become obsessed with an idea, maybe, or even with some great, overpowering passion . . ."

Palomides checked himself suddenly, fell silent, and then said briskly, in the tone he used when dispelling the anxiety of a wounded man:

"Maybe I'm wrong about all this. We physicians get the habit of looking for symptoms. Like as not there's nothing in the world wrong with the lad but bewilderment and strangeness at the sudden turn things have taken for him. Leave well alone. Forget what I've just said. With Arthur to guide him through the next few years and what support the rest of us can give now and then when it's needed, Peredur should do well enough."

I said, doubtfully, for I'd been shaken by the things he'd hinted at:

"I hope you're right, for Arthur's coming to love him, I believe, as if he were indeed his own son."

Palomides gave me a long, strange look.

"Who could help loving such a one—who could help it?" he said quietly.

# Chapter Twenty-Six

Two years or it may have been three after Peredur's coming, I wintered in Tintagel again. Lyonesse always gave me more trouble than all the rest of Menaevia put together. That year a man I'd appointed to hold Tintagel for me and keep order down in that area murdered his young wife and her lover and fled the country. (It is a tale all know, and it has been made into a harp song now, for the lover was himself a harper.) At the time I found little romance in the happening and less in the blood feuds it left behind for me to settle. Lyonesse is bad country to hunt fugitives from justice in, specially during a wet year, which that one was. Communications with Camelot were poor the whole season and broke down completely, once the autumn floods were out.

When, on a cold November afternoon, with a promise of more wild weather to come, I heard the sentry's challenge and the clang of opening gates, I was ready to welcome any break in the gloomy monotony of the old fortress, now more than ever haunted by sad ghosts.

I left the fireside in my turret room and went out to the stairhead. My page came leaping up, two stairs at a time, his face eager.

"My lord—it's Sir Lancelot, come from Camelot!"

In the shadows behind him I could just make out a tall figure, cloaked in grey.

"Lancelot?" I cried. "Why, man, come up, come to

the fire. You must have had a rough journey in this
weather. What brings you—not bad news?"

"A rough enough journey, and a long one. The boy's
got it wrong. I'm not from Camelot, Bedivere. Does that
make me less welcome?" he asked. His face, staring up at
me, looked gaunt and pale, I thought, but it might be the
winter twilight.

"Welcome a thousand times, wherever you come
from," I told him heartily. "How many men are with
you? But no matter—my fellows will see to them. We're
well provisioned. Come, yourself, up into the warm,
where I can see you."

He passed the page and followed me into my room,
saying, gravely for him:

"I ride alone at the moment. There'll be no strain on
your resources. All I ask is a bed for the night and forage
for my horse."

"That we'll gladly furnish!" I laughed. "Draw to the
hearth. You look perished."

In the lighted room I saw that his cloak hung on
him, sodden through and muddied, and that it was such
as poor men wear, grey wool and not over-thick, at that.
He unclasped it and threw it aside, moving to the fire and
holding out his hands to the blaze. He was shivering, and
when he turned to smile at me, I thought he looked ill.
There were bright spots of color on his cheekbones and
his eyes were feverishly bright.

"Whatever errand you ride on, you've taken a chill
by the look of you. I'll send for some hot mulled wine
and food," I suggested. "Wait while I give my page the
order."

He stayed me with a quick gesture.

"No wine, Bedivere. Food I could do with. I've not
eaten since yesterday, and the flesh is weak. Some bread
and maybe a morsel of cheese, with a draught of spring
water, will serve my turn. We who ride on the Quest are
vowed neither to drink wine nor touch flesh meat until
our search is ended, remember," he said.

I stared at him.

"Don't be a fool, man! You can't travel Britain in

this weather on a hermit's diet. No wonder you look starved with cold! At least let me send for hot broth or pottage of some sort."

An uncontrollable shivering took him and he crouched over the fire.

"To be honest, that tempts me. Maybe they've something of the sort without meat in it, since today's a Friday?" He laughed apologetically. "My belly clamors for hot food, I'll admit. But I cannot break my vow."

"Damn your vow!" I thought. "What bee has he got under his helmet now?"

I hurried to give an order to my lad on the stair outside. He went off looking as bewildered as I felt.

When I returned to the room, Lancelot was lying back in the chair by the hearth, his eyes closed. He looked so exhausted I did not disturb him until, after a longer delay than I'd expected, the boy came in, carrying a tray with a bowl of steaming soup on it, a platter of new-baked bread, with cheese and some garnishings. He looked at me anxiously.

"It's bean-pottage, my lord, with kale and herbs in it. Our folk had nothing of the kind you asked for, but the cook begged this off the hermits. Will it serve?"

Lancelot roused up and smiled with something of his old, swift charm.

"Bless the good brothers for their charity! Here, boy, take this to them in thanks, and beg their prayers for me. I need the prayers of such as they to help me on my search—ask them to pray that some day—some day—unworthy as I am, I may find what I seek," he said earnestly.

Round-eyed, the page took the gold piece offered, glanced helplessly in my direction and, when I nodded dismissal, bowed and scuttled out in a hurry.

I watched Lancelot, as he wrapped his long, beautiful hands about the bowl and began to sup the thick brown liquid from it.

"Now, tell me, what's all the mystery? What is this search of yours? Remember I've been cut off down here since early spring. Who's lost—or what, and why are you, of all men, ranging the country alone, in that disguise?" I asked him, eventually. (For he was dressed like a peasant, in grey trews and tunic, with no ornament. Only his sword belt showed his rank.) He looked at me above the bowl, drank again, then said slowly:

"You've had no news from Camelot since early spring? Is that possible?" He seemed amazed.

When I nodded, impatiently, he drained the bowl and set it aside, beginning to eat the bread hungrily, but absent-mindedly.

"Then you don't know what happened last Pentecost?"

"Not at Pentecost, or since. What with the weather and chasing rebels through forest and fen, our communications have broken down here completely this year, I'm ashamed to say."

"I see. I didn't understand that," he said. "It explains the urge I felt to come here tonight. God uses even a man's weakness for his own wise purposes. When you've heard all, you, the first and greatest of Arthur's Companions, must surely ride upon the Quest with us."

"What 'quest,' and for what?" I asked. "Stop talking riddles, in the name of Light, will you? *What* happened last Pentecost?"

I was beginning to lose all patience.

"A great mystery was revealed to us, a great opportunity suddenly made plain to every one of us. We saw a vision, Bedivere," he said solemnly. "Oh, my friend, if only you had been there!"

"Well, I wasn't," I reminded him. "A vision of *what?*"

He looked at me with eyes clouded, as though I'd roused him from deep sleep, and the dream he had been dreaming was not yet distinguishable from the reality of waking.

"A heavenly vision of the true Grail—that Cup of all wisdom, all knowledge, all love, the earthly symbol of which we'd just before seen carried in procession through the hall."

He leaned towards me, the fever-flush on his cheeks deepening, his expression wild and exalted.

"Peredur saw the Cup—the Cup itself—rose-red and glowing, borne by great winged spirits of the air. We others, we saw only the shining cloud that veiled it—that must veil it from us until we are purged of mortal sin— purified and worthy."

"This *is* madness," I thought. "Well, Palomides warned me. Best let him talk!" I said soothingly:

"Tell me more. Explain this thing to me, Lancelot. Remember, I've been more than half a year down here, fighting a soldier's war in desolate, god-forgotten country, and thinking of nothing else. How should I, of all men, understand heavenly visions and what they may portend?"

He nodded, as if the explanation was reasonable enough.

"It began with the coming to court of my little daughter, my own white lamb," he said, and his lips trembled. "Oh, Bedivere, she's dead—my child I neglected all those long years. The child I never knew until it was too late!" He wrung his hands together with a gesture of such despairing sorrow that I thought, "This must be it. He's suffered some great bereavement that has unhinged his mind." I said, as gently as I could: "I'm sorry, Lancelot—deeply sorry. But you, who are of the Island training, know death is not the end."

He nodded, bracing himself with an obvious effort.

"Yes, yes, I know. She was too good for this world. Her bright spirit was only lent to us to show us the way. Have patience with me, my friend. Let me tell you the story as God gives me strength, for it is strange and of great moment, believe me, to you, as well as to us all."

Years have passed, so many years, since passionately, often incoherently, Lancelot poured out to me, with all his Armorican exaggeration of metaphor and gesticulation, the strange tale of the Pentecost of the Grail. I have heard it since many times, from the witness of more sober men: from Griffin and Gawain, from Palomides, from Arthur himself, even, with far different interpretation put upon it, from Medraut.

How it came about, what lay behind it, I learned

slowly to understand. Perhaps I do not fully understand
even now. It arose out of so many different causes: from
the long-pondered, visionary imaginings of an old, half-
mad hermit-king; from the Merlin's cherished dream that
all faiths must one day be united into a shared wisdom;
from Arthur's sickness, that still lingered on, robbing him
now and then (though we had not guessed it) of the
lightning-quick power of decision in unexpected emergency; but most of all, I believe, from a hidden weakness in
Peredur, which Palomides had half-foreseen, that could
not take breaking strain in a moment of crisis. Peredur,
on whose bright innocence was laid, through Medraut's
guile, too suddenly and too heavily, the weight of worldly
reality and shattering disillusion. Peredur of whom life
asked the question he could not answer and, failing to
answer it, retreated from his true heritage into a dream
world that laid Britain waste.

Griffin tells me that I must forgive all men their sins,
now that I am near to death. I do not find that so very
difficult. What I find hard is to forgive them their follies.
It still seems to me that it was headlong folly that made
Pentecost that year what Griffin called it today: "the
beginning of the end."

Briefly and not at all as Lancelot told it me at
Tintagel, colored by his own emotional involvement, what
had happened at Camelot was this:

The weather was untimely. The great gales of the
equinox came late, after a cold, reluctant spring, sweeping
the whole country, tearing the young green from the trees,
leaving a trail of wreckage and disaster everywhere. There
were floods out and fewer Clans than usual came in to the
gathering. The crowd in the Great Judgment Hall was less
than normal, though most of the Chief Companions were
present, and no new candidates for knighthood came
forward at the king's challenge. When all had just sat
down to meat, some kind of whirlwind hit the palace,
tearing off a portion of the roof, and wrecking the outer
colonnade. The bronze doors burst open of themselves
and wind filled the whole building, so that the torches
were extinguished and even the Roman lamps about the
high table flickered and went out. Then the freak tempest

died and a beam of moonlight, clear and silver-white, struck down through the hole in the damaged roof, and seemed to move along the whole length of the hall. Peredur leapt to his feet and cried out—

"See—see where it goes—the Holy Cup, carried by three bright angels—oh Rose of the World—the Grail!"

What vision the boy saw—whether it was some magic beyond our understanding, or some inner revelation, meant for him alone—who can say? All who were there that night must have been shaken already by the wildness of the storm. The conviction of one man can impress itself on the minds of others at such a time. When, later, I asked about among the Companions, all the satisfaction I could get was that every one of them had felt the wind's blast, and seen the white shaft of light that travelled down the hall. Each one affirmed that others had seen the Cup within the beam, but that it had appeared vague and shadowy—a rosy shape, veiled and covered as if by blowing mist. Each man I questioned told me (believing what he said, I could tell) that he himself had not been of sufficiently holy life to see the Cup as the Chosen One had seen it. All that is, except Medraut. He shrugged and his half-smile told his contempt.

"*I* saw nothing, my lord. But then I'd not expect to. I've trained myself for years not to be swayed by mass hysteria. If it was anything it was a case of hypnosis. Maybe the Merlin could explain it—if he would!"

Had that been all, maybe the awe and the excitement of the thing would have passed after a little while. But it was not all.

What, away in Tintagel, I had not heard, was that the old king, Pelles of Gwynfid, had fallen sick and died that year, at the time of the Christian Easter. It seemed he had died, as he had lived, in a cloud of strange dreams, and he had laid upon his young granddaughter, Lancelot's second child, a solemn oath to travel, after his death, to Arthur's court, and proclaim his dreams, as prophecies, to the king, to her brother and to all the court.

Away there in the mountains of Gwynfid, he had

been building up, for a long time, a secret and hidden
cult—a new religion, that, so he believed, could bring
inspiration to Britain, and through Britain, to the whole
troubled, broken empire. I never altogether understood it.
He'd studied for years, the good old man, both with our
own wise men of the Old Faith, and with others who
came to Britain from the deserts of the East—hermits out
of the wastelands beyond Alexandria, refugees, perhaps,
from the Christian persecutions of which Palomides had
told me. His contention was that no man who had not
received a training in these matters and reached enlightenment in his own soul was fit to govern others, and it
was lack of such that accounted for all the troubles of our
times. I believe now that there was a great deal in the
essence of that notion—it was the manner in which it was
translated that was unwise.

In any case, the girl obeyed his wish and came to
Arthur's court as he had commanded. She was young,
beautiful, dedicated—and very, very frail. She had been
reared as a priestess of his new faith, which demanded
austerities of so severe a kind that her health had failed
under the burden of them.

"She was the loveliest thing I ever saw," Palomides
told me, long afterwards. "Fragile as a wood anemone, a
creature out of this world. It was the shining spirit of
utter conviction, of complete dedication, that shone
through her like a flame shining through a little alabaster
lamp that I shall always remember. But it was a lamp
that had burned away its oil. I knew, the first time I set
eyes on her, that her days were numbered."

She begged Arthur on her knees to let her give
Pelles' last messages to the full assembly of the Companions. Her speech to them must have been very moving; it
swayed so many I would never have guessed would be
vulnerable. In it she urged them to renounce the world in
order to learn how they might most truly serve the world.

Lancelot, in the firelit room at Tintagel, repeated
that message to me, his voice trembling with emotion.

"Go out, all of you, alone, unattended, and put your
souls into the hands of God. He will guide you, in the
wastelands and the forests, and bring you to those who

dwell in secret, hidden places—in caves and mountain fastnesses—the Enlightened Ones—the Knowers. They will teach you the new secret—the secret of the Holy Cup, the Grail, which alone can heal the sorrows and dissensions, the strife and the hunger of the nations. In it is the secret of all wisdom, all plenty, all peace. Only when you, each one of you, holds it between his hands, can he be a rightful servant of the people—a shepherd—a ruler over the toiling, the ignorant and the starving."

I listened to him. I had been listening a long time and the room was growing cold. I bent and piled wood on the fire, then sat back, and looked at him.

"So that's the explanation?" I said slowly. "I'm not sure if I've got it clear, even now. You mean you've left the court to search for these reputed Masters of Wisdom, who'll instruct you in Pelles' new branch of wisdom? That's your search?"

He nodded.

"By your own account, you've been six months on the road. Have you found any of them?" I asked.

His eyelids flickered. A nervous tic that I'd noticed earlier jerked his mouth now and then at the corner.

"No, Bedivere—no—not yet. I rode first to Gwyn-fid, but the priests there told me what I knew too well already, that for such as I enlightenment can only come after a long struggle with the sins of the flesh. They advised me to subdue lust by the willing endurance of austerities, to fast and meditate and to keep myself from the interruption of human contacts. Perhaps I should not have come here tonight—perhaps I yielded to a temptation." He drew his hand across his brow with a movement of utter weariness, then shook his head, as though he were a swimmer trying to clear water from his eyes, and smiled at me sadly. "It was weakness, and I knew it—but oh, suddenly I hungered so to talk to someone who might understand!"

I smiled back at him.

"I doubt if I do that—but I'm glad you came. Loneliness is bad for all of us beyond a point. I was lonely, too!"

We sat in silence for a time. A rat squeaked and

scuttled in the wall and outside the sea sighed quietly.

He brushed his hand across his eyes again, and I saw this time it was to wipe away tears.

"I shall persevere in the search until I achieve the vision. That's all I can tell you, Bedivere. I gave her my word, when she was dying—my sweet child, my daughter. It was all she ever asked of me—all I ever gave her. No toys when she was little. No pretty trinkets or jewels or loving caresses. I neglected her all her short life—that saint whom God inspired. How can I ever atone for that? How can such as I ever hope to achieve the Vision that she saw so clearly? The least and lowliest of those who set out with me have greater right to it than I!"

"Lancelot," I said, startled. "How many others have become involved in this thing? You aren't the only one?"

He looked up at me, surprised.

"Why, no. More than forty of us left Camelot immediately after Pentecost—more, I dare say, have taken the oath since then."

"*Forty?*" I said. "What others that I know—not any other of the Chief Companions?"

"Oh yes," he told me gravely. "How can one refuse the command of God? For a year and a day, we took the oath—Gawain, and Gaheris, Palomides, Lavain—most of Arthur's first Companions. You'd have taken it yourself, it you'd been with us, Bedivere."

"But this *is* madness!" I said. "It's utterly fantastic! You mean to tell me Arthur permitted it—he gave you leave?"

"Peredur called on us to swear the oath, and we drew our swords and swore. Arthur could not forbid us after that and make us all forsworn," Lancelot said simply. "One does not ask even a king's leave, when a messenger from another world asks for one's allegiance to God."

I got up and went across to the window and with a quick gesture pushed back the shutter. I felt as if I were suffocating. The dead, still cold of a winter dawn poured into the close room. I saw we had talked all night. Far below, the sea lapped at the rocks and a long bar of grey light showed along the horizon. I said slowly:

"What if there were war? What of Britain's justice? Who, in the name of the gods, is doing all the work, while you, who should be serving Arthur, run hither and thither about the land saving your own souls?"

I don't think I have ever felt quite so angry in all my life—or so utterly bewildered. I turned on him.

"Have you all gone crazy? You—in charge of the cavalry on which again and again our victories depend. Gawain, who should be keeping the northland safe. Even Palomides, whom I thought I could trust as well as I trust myself—they, and all the others. A year and a day! How many years has it taken to build a free Britain? Twenty, thirty—more, if you count Ambrosius' work before ours—and you'd throw it all away because you saw a phantom cup in a beam of moonshine, and had a message by a green girl from an old man driven mad by too much studying!"

Lancelot said, very wearily, with the same gentleness I'd found so different all evening from his usual manner.

"You weren't there, Bedivere. You can't know the power—the overwhelming strength that swept us like a great tidal wave."

"Tell me one thing," I said. "Where does Peredur stand in all this?"

Lancelot shook his head.

"He was the first to take the oath. He'd no need, for he had seen the Vision—he was Initiate already. He has gone out, the first to carry news of the Cup to the common people."

I turned back to the window and leaned there, defeated. I felt utterly drained and exhausted by my own anger. I watched the dawn light grow, sullen and reluctant over the sea. So must a sentry feel, I thought, who watches the sky lighten over a doomed fort, after a cold night's guard. Then I shook myself awake. Despair is the coward's retreat.

"One thing's certain," I said. "With all of you gone, Arthur needs me at Camelot. I must put things in order here, and leave today."

I'd turned to face him again. In the first glimmer of

daylight his face looked ghastly and a reluctant pity swept my rage aside.

"I shall ride fast and with few followers. I'll leave a strong guard here. Get to bed, now, and rest. My people will see to you."

He got up stiffly and came across to me, taking my hand.

"Bedivere, you're wrong. Only the fulfillment of this command we have received will give us the inspiration Britain needs now. Come with me. Let us ride together, at least for a time, on this most urgent and most holy search," he pleaded earnestly.

I pressed his hand.

"I'm a plain soldier and as a soldier I must serve my country and my king," I said. "Follow your fate, my friend, since obviously it must *be* your fate. May you find what you seek, since it means so much to you. But I tell you one thing straight. If this Grail is something without which I cannot serve Britain, it must come to me, for I've no time to ride in search of it!"

I felt his hand still cold and shaking and, as I let it go, I turned to close the shutter behind me.

Far out on the horizon, below the long bar of shadow, a crimson spark rose out of the sea and grew and expanded. My mind told me it was only the reflection of the rising sun upon a small wisp of cloud. But for a long moment, to my eyes, strained by sleeplessness, it took another shape—the shape of a cup I had seen long ago in a secret valley of the Outland, carved from some strange and flashing substance; a crystal cup, glowing like the heart of a rose.

I drew the shutter close and turned, forcing my mind to practical affairs. But somewhere, far back, a memory checked me, and I paused. Tintagel tower does not face the dawn. Whatever I had seen out there, I could not explain by the sun's rising.

# Chapter Twenty-Seven

Directly I got back to Camelot, that first year of the Grail, I resigned my prefectship of Menaevia, turning the work over to Dinas and two young deputies, one a cultured Colonial, the other a Celt with a quick wit and personal charm. I reckon they could do well enough, between them. My place from then on must be at Arthur's side.

More than half the Companions were absent and, to add to the confusion, Kay had died during the winter. Very quietly, still in harness, he had died at his post, working late over his accounting. They'd found him, slumped across his desk, the quill still in his hand. I'd known for a long while he was failing, but I grieved for his lonely end—he, who had always hoped to die gloriously in battle. Lucan, his deputy, a middle-aged Colonial centurion, knew his work and did it with smooth efficiency, but he was a pompous person, and to the end I found him tiresome.

For the rest, temporary promotions had been inevitable, and to my mind too many of Medraut's young men given posts they were not adequate to fill. Finding discipline poor, I treated them as Ambrosius would have done, forgetting (as Medraut reminded me with careful tact) that times had changed. Some took offense and rode off home to their Clans in dudgeon. The better sort, once they'd got over the first shock, accepted hard training and shaped well enough, though I'd no illusion they loved me for it. As the year turned and the days started to lengthen I began to see some improvement, but I was glad, Pentecost falling early, we might expect the return of the Companions from their Quest before the seaways opened.

Well before Easter, as it proved, a trickle of those who'd taken the vow began to come back.

Gawain was the first. He rode in under the north gate, shamefaced, inclined to bluster, declaring he'd had enough of hunting phantoms and wearied to be at work again.

"I canna think what got into me to go off in the first place," he confided, as we two sat over a cup of wine in his quarters. "After a month I was asking myself if yon old warlock Celidon had put an enchantment on us all, or what? I found neither Grail, nor any Master that could explain to me what like thing I was seeking, nor where I should start looking for it. All I found in the forest was good hunting to no purpose, since we'd vowed to eat no meat. I soon wearied of that, and of my own company. I'd the luck to bide the night over with an old hermit-body who civilly invited me into his cave out of pouring rain. When I'd told him all my tale, he advised me I'd serve heaven better by going home to Dalriada and minding the business God assigned to me in the first place than running about wet woods like a hound that's lost both slot and pack. I was minded to heed him, since he seemed a holy man, and a sensible (forby I'd begun to be uneasy in my mind how things might be fairing up north). A gey good thing I went home, so I'm telling you! You'd have had the Picts down on you this summer, else. The whole country north of the Maund was in turmoil. They'd heard rumor I'd left Camelot and decided I was after deserting Arthur's cause, so it seemed to them a moment they might start hosting without fear of reprisal. Well, I've taught them different and all's quiet again. That's why I'm here. Tell me, who's commanding the cavalry? Is Lancelot not back yet?"

He reminded me of a man returned to work after a drinking bout, his temper still uncertain and touchy. I found the mood easy enough to tolerate because I was so glad to have him back.

The others came in ones and twos after that, all of them lean and bearded, and with varying tales to tell. Some few claimed they had found the guidance they had sought for, and a few of the more impressionable swore to strange, mystical experiences. Most had met only such hazards as any man might encounter who ranged alone for months through the wilder forests and Outlands of Britain. Early on the exact day appointed by their oath, Peredur and a few others returned together, having met on the last lap of their journey. They rode in, with him at their head, and about them something of the joyous air of a wedding party. Arthur welcomed them with affection and no hint of reproach, listening with grave attention to the reports of their experiences. But all that day he was restless, waiting for those who had not come. At supper the empty places at the high table were the more noticeable because one tried so hard not to look towards them. Midnight came and passed, and of the Chief Companions Lancelot, Palomides, and three others were still missing, as well as a score of the younger knights.

After that we began to send out search parties. It was like looking for a flint arrowhead on a shingle beach, trying to trace lone riders who'd started more than a year before. Some we found, and others gradually straggled back, mostly in poor shape from wounds or fevers. Some we heard had died and kindly folk had marked their graves for us. A few vanished completely, leaving no trace, and to this day their end remains unknown.

Hay harvest came and passed and corn harvest began. It was on the evening of blazing day, when farmers everywhere had been busy since dawn, that Arthur finally put into words the bleak, inevitable conclusion I'd been trying to avoid acknowledging to myself.

"Bedivere, we must face it. If Lancelot were alive, he'd have got word to us somehow by now, and so would Palomides."

We'd been up at the fort, and when we'd finished our task there, he'd suggested we should take a turn on the ramparts, where there was always a little breeze at evening, before we went down to the sweltering heat of the plain. He'd seemed preoccupied, and I'd been in no mood to break silence, for depression hung on me like a cloud, and I'd no wish to burden him with it, for he looked tired and drawn enough already.

He turned into his favorite lookout in the catapult emplacement, where the breast-high palisade faced towards Ynis Witrin, and leaned there, staring into the distance.

Suddenly he brought his clenched fist down on the rail with such violence that the wood splintered.

"Why in the name of Light did I let them go? It was wrong and I knew it. The wrong time, the wrong way—too soon, too headlong, too unprepared!"

I said bleakly, for I'd no comfort to offer:

"You had no option. They'd sworn their oath, Bear; all of them. An oath is an oath. Even the king cannot interfere, when a man has pledged word to his god."

He glanced at me sideways and nodded.

"That's true. In the past it was my pride, always, that I could think fast—faster than most other men, when need arose. But that night the thing came on me suddenly, like an untimely birth. Their swords were out and the words of the oath spoken before I'd seen danger threaten. I'm growing old, Bedivere. I must be growing old!"

He leaned again on the palisade, and I felt the heaviness of his brooding weigh on my heart, but could find no words of comfort.

Below, the plain spread wide in the golden evening, checkered with little fields where figures no bigger than a child's mommets moved purposefully, piling the last of the garnered sheaves on slow-moving sleds. In the tree-tops of the palace gardens, ring doves cooed drowsily, and a cloud of gnats danced in the clear air before us.

At last, more to break the silence and turn his mind from grieving than for any other reason, I said:

"Bear, tell me something—this visionary Cup—this Holy Grail which Peredur saw—do you believe it exists?"

He turned slowly and looked at me, a long, measuring look.

"Do you?" he countered.

"I'm not sure," I said. (I was remembering dawn over the sea of Lyonesse.)

He shook his head.

"Neither am I. It could be. You and I know there are things in this world outside and beyond ordinary experience. I'll not dispute Peredur's vision, for the boy has the Sight, and he is one who does not know how to lie. But since the beginning of time, it has been taught by the Wise Ones that certain truths may not be revealed indiscriminately to all and sundry, but must be come at slowly, patiently, as each man is ready to receive them, and not before. *That* is the meaning of Initiation. Truth snatched too soon, half understood, misunderstood, brings only confusion, dissension, madness. One cannot feed strong wine to a suckling babe. But Peredur is young, eager, inexperienced, and judges all men by himself. The light his eyes saw dazzled him, so that he could not judge the shadows in which most men walk. I don't blame him, Bedivere. I blame myself that I was not quick enough to guard him from the danger of his too-great innocence."

Dusk was running over the fields below, grape-blue, lapping up to the foot of the hill, though the sun still shone on the rampart. Arthur sighed, and set his hands on the cracked rail, looking down.

"The Cup," he said slowly. "We chose it, Celidon and I, as the symbol all faiths could share, and sharing, bind themselves into one brotherhood, each respecting the beliefs of others, yet drinking together from the one Cup, sacred to all, begin to understand that those who seek the Light are all equally the children of that Light. Unity, tolerance, understanding—those things grow slowly, as the corn down there grew, from the buried seed to the full ear, brought to final harvest only by slow, patient, sweating toil."

I laid my hand over his.

"Bear," I said (and it was the Bard in me gave me the words, suddenly, I think, for in one part of me I was still too much the soldier to understand all his thought), "remember one thing. There are years when the harvest fails, for all the farmers' honest toil. It must depend on sun and rain, and the hazard of untimely tempest. But to the husbandman there is always next year's Spring Sowing. If he is wise he ploughs the winter furrow, and commends the future to the will of whatever gods custom has taught him to trust."

Arthur's hand gripped mine.

"Yes," he said slowly, "yes, I must remember that. To the end of time, there will always be next year's Spring Sowing!"

It was the eve of Samain when Palomides came back—a cold, still evening, with mist lying in swathes over the marshes, and the last leaves fluttering down, though no wind loosened them from the black, dripping branches. He rode in quietly, on an old, foot-sore mule, muffled in a ragged cloak, so that the sentries took him for a beggar and would have directed him to the hostel for the homeless that the queen and Iltud had built just outside the palace gates.

When he put back his hood and they recognized him, we heard where we sat at meat in hall the cheering run back through the guardroom and spread all round the outer walls. I left my place at table and hurried out. They'd got torches by then, and were pressing close, greeting him, kissing his hands and the hem of his cloak, patting the old mule, wild with joy and relief at having their beloved physician back among them. In the smoky torchlight I saw him, sitting there, smiling down at them, very quiet and serene, mocking them a little in his Celtic that still had its foreign accent, because they were (so he said) withdrawing the good offer of a free bed and a bowl of broth they'd promised him at first.

"Palomides!" I cried. "Oh, Palomides, my brother, where have you been all these months? Are you safe—are you well?" I'd pushed my way through the crowd to his side. "Get off that deplorable animal and come into the warm!"

He looked down at me for a long moment, his eyes searching my face.

"Is all well here? Have the others returned?" he asked.

"Most—not all," I said.

"Lancelot?" he queried.

I shook my head.

He gave me a brief, understanding nod. In a low voice he said:

"I was afraid of that. I've been searching for him for months. Let's go inside, and I'll tell you."

He got stiffly out of the saddle and patted the mule.

"Take this one to a warm stable and feed him well," he said to the nearest soldier. "He's served me faithfully, poor beast."

"We'll do that, sir," the man promised.

Somewhere in the crowd a voice asked earnestly:

"Did you find the Holy Grail, sir? If anybody deserved to, you did. We all said that."

Palomides paused, his dark face lifted so that the torchlight played strange tricks with the lines and hollows on it.

"Yes, my friend, I found it," he said. "But it is a Great Mystery—one of which no man should speak."

A rustle and a sigh, like the sound of a small wave running back on the sands, went round among the soldiers, as each man drew in his breath, awed by those words.

I put my hand on Palomides' arm and we went forward through the opening ranks quickly. As we passed in through the doors, a man called after us:

"God bless you, sir!"

"Come to my quarters. You'll need a wash and some dry clothes before the whole court starts to eat you alive, they'll be so glad to have you back. I'll send my page to tell Arthur you're safe and coming to him as soon as you've got rid of your wet clothes," I said.

"I'll agree to that, gladly enough." He smiled. "I'm wet to the skin and chilled to the bone, and feel as if I've been both more or less continuously most of the year!"

Once my pages had brought hot water and towels and laid out a winter tunic and trews, and my best sleeveless overtunic, lined with squirrel fur, I sent them packing, and while he washed and towelled himself before the fire in the small room I used when I needed to sleep down at the palace, I questioned him further.

"What in the name of Light induced *you* of all people to go off on this search in the first place? I've never been able to understand it," I said.

He paused for a long moment, the towel limp in his hands, the firelight gleaming on his naked scarred body.

"I told you long ago that I came to Britain searching for truth. I suppose I thought some portion of it might lie hidden in this Grail," he said slowly. He finished drying himself and began to dress. Suddenly he looked across at me and smiled. "There were other reasons. As things turned out, I'm glad I went. Bedivere—when did *you* last see Lancelot? Was it the time he told me of, at Tintagel?"

"Yes," I said. "No one seems to have set eyes on him since. You have, since you know he was there?"

"I have, indeed." He shrugged his way into the fur-lined tunic and wrapped it round him gratefully. It hung loose, for I'd noticed already that every bone on his body showed like a man's at the end of a long siege. Gathering its wide skirts across his knees, he sat down and held his hands to the fire. "Bedivere," he said seriously, "I needed to talk with you before I saw Arthur and the queen. Lancelot has gone out of his mind."

I grimaced as one does, hearing bad news that's been expected.

"I'm not surprised," I said. "He was near enough to that, when I saw him. Where is he now?"

"I left him, near a month back in the care of good, holy men, on a little island off the coast of Wales. He knows no one, and has forgotten his own name and who he is. The abbot there knows the truth about him. If he comes back to himself, they'll see he is brought safely home to us, but until that happens, *if* it happens, he's best where he is. At least there, if the frantic fit takes him again, he can't go wandering."

I suppose he saw the question in my face, for without my asking it, he nodded.

"Yes—it was violent madness at first. When I came on him, around Midsummer, he was wandering mother-naked in the forest, a danger to himself and a terror to the few poor folk in the vicinity."

"Gods!" I said. "That must have been bad, Palomides. How did it happen that you found him?"

"I'd been following him for months," Palomides admitted quietly. "We met by accident—not so very long after you'd seen him. I'd been for a time in Gwynfid—not at the new king's court, but up in the mountains. It had been in my mind that the place where Peredur was reared, where he first learned the ideas from which his Vision sprang, might be the best place to discover more about this whole mystery of the Grail. In those mountains I did find wise priests, with whom I had a deal of useful, interesting conversation. Lancelot, not unnaturally, had had the same idea as mine. He'd even more reason than I for thinking of it. But it was a bad place for him to choose." Palomides paused.

"How so?" I asked.

"Too many associations. Don't forget it was in Gwynfid he was nursed after that battle, the year of Silver Wood. The place where he wedded Peredur's mother and then deserted her."

"Of course," I said. "I'd forgotten. The memories troubled him?"

"They were a part of the heavy sense of guilt he carries; all interwoven with his infatuation for the queen, and what came after." Again Palomides paused, and shook his head. "Obsessional madness, the Greeks held, is a sickness of the mind sent from the gods to punish hubris. The one night we spent together, Lancelot and I, alone, lodging in a mountain cave, I knew, from all the signs, that he was very near to that. He could not rest. I doubt if he'd slept for weeks. He was haunted, devoured, by the desire to see and touch this Hallows of which Peredur had spoken—this Cup we all went seeking. To him, it was no longer a symbol, but something actual, concrete. He raved for hours, describing it to me, walking up and down, constantly spreading out his hands before him, as though he were trying to grasp something out of the air.

" 'The Grail, Palomides, think of it—think what it

must look like! A cup, carved from a single ruby—a ruby from another world, fallen from some distant, purer planet than ours—falling through infinite space beyond the stars that we can see. A jewel, struck out of the helm of Lucifer, the rebel angel—Lucifer, that banished son of Light, who stormed the gates of heaven in desperate longing for his lost beatitude—Lucifer, so full of pride, but full, ah God, how full of utter loneliness—of cosmic homesickness!'

"I could tell he had identified himself with that great rebel angel (as only Lancelot could!) but the thing that troubled me was that in doing so he revealed the sense of separation in his own soul. And what troubled me yet more was his conviction, unshakeable by any reasoned argument, that only in finding an actual, magical cup, concrete to his earthly senses, could he find healing and peace.

" 'I have sinned more than any man on earth. How can I ever hope to find the Grail? Yet only it can liberate me, purify me, save me,' he kept repeating." Palomides sighed. "I did what I could, knowing it was little enough. I persuaded him to drink a draught of poppy syrup and lie down to sleep. I made it twice the strength that would have kept most men unconscious for a day and a night. But I should have reckoned how immune insanity can render a patient to normal drugs. I was very tired myself. I sleep lightly, as a rule, so I risked lying down for a few hours. When I woke, he'd vanished, slipped away so quietly I never heard him go, and left no trace of the way he'd taken."

"But you still followed?" I queried.

"What else could I do? The crisis of his sickness—and sickness of that sort is real and desperate as any battle wound—was, by my judgment, near at hand. Though I lost track of him for a time, I followed what rumors I could get and at last I came on this story of a madman in the forest; a man of more than mortal height and strength, who ran naked among the trees, howling sometimes like a wolf, muttering at others in an unknown tongue. A man who'd been seen striking his head against trees, climbing among the branches like an ape. A man of whom, understandably, the charcoal burners and wood-cutters were very much afraid."

I shuddered.

"You don't tell me you tackled him alone? Gods, man, you've more courage than I have! He might have killed you!"

Palomides shrugged.

"I've dealt with madmen before. It is always a risk—but one has certain skills—certain remedies," he said quietly. "What I need to decide now is how much of all this it's wise to tell Arthur? I'm thinking mainly of the queen. If she loves Lancelot still, will she feel she must go to him? That, it seems to me, would be a bad thing on all counts."

I considered for a few moments. Then I asked him directly:

"Will he recover?"

"That I cannot tell. He may. At present the sickness, as I told you, has passed into the passive state. Brought on, as it undoubtedly was, by years of strain, and not by any injury to the brain, with complete rest in a quiet and holy place, and men about him well skilled in healing of the body, I think he may, slowly and gradually, come back to normality. But any emotional shock, anything suddenly reminding him of all he has, for a time, so mercifully forgotten, would be the worst thing that could happen just now. Nature has her own methods of healing men's minds as well as their bodies. Complete forgetful-ness comes sometimes as the natural cure."

"Then do not tell even Arthur *all* the truth," I said. "Tell only that you found him very sick, and having stayed with him through the crisis of his illness, have left him in good hands, in a house of holy men to finish his cure. Tell him it may take time—that he may choose, even when his strength returns, to stay on and—what is the expression?—'save his soul.' Even, if your conscience will let you, tell them that that was his intention, and that he begged the king's permission for it. Guinevere will accept that, Palomides. I don't think she'd agree to any-

thing short of rushing to nurse him herself, if you told her
the whole truth. You know what women are! Though her
passion's spent, and I think all her love and tenderness
now have turned to Arthur, and all her devotion to her
religion, one can't ever be sure that the mother in a
woman won't be roused by a story as tragic as this." I
paused, and said urgently, "Palomides, don't tell her.
Arthur can't lose her to Lancelot a second time. He's not
young, any more. There's too much at stake."

Palomides nodded.

"I agree. I'd thought much the same thing, myself.
Thanks, Bedivere. Now I'm dry and warm again, and
have your advice to back my judgment, I think I should
go to the king. They will be waiting for news."

He rose, straightening his shoulders like a man preparing to lift a heaven burden.

I said softly:

"One question, Palomides—and not about Lancelot
this time. A while back I heard you say something to the
soldiers, outside."

"Yes?" he turned and looked at me, the serene smile
I'd noticed before lighting up his face.

"You told them you had found the Grail. Did you?"
I asked him.

The smile deepened.

"Yes. I found it. But not the Grail that Lancelot
seeks," he said.

It must have been spring again, since the seaways were
open. Going into Arthur's room on some errand I forget,
one morning, I found him reading a letter, and so deeply
engrossed he did not hear the question I asked.

Looking up after a few moments, he said:

"Eh? What was that? Never mind it for the moment,
whatever it was. Did you tell me once you'd served on the
mainland in a town called Ravenna?"

"Yes," I said, surprised.

"So! Well, I've a communication here from a fellow
who signs himself 'Hilarion, Bishop of Ravenna.' Read it,
will you?"

I took the parchment he handed me. It was a long

screed, the writing crabbed. When I'd got the gist of it, I exploded violently.

"May his own devils fly away with the man! Who gave him authority for this kind of insolence?"

Arthur smiled, his eyebrows raised.

"He's archbishop in Rome, he says. The lineal descendant of the Pontifex Maximus, since Constantine's day, Bedivere. A power to be reckoned with, so Medraut tells me. You see rumor has already reached that far of Britain's new heresies. Like Bishop Germain in Ambrosius' day, Hilarion proposes to save my people from what he calls a 'heresy more outrageous even than that of Pelagius.' I can only suppose he's heard some version of Peredur's Vision and the Quest."

I bit my lip, fuming.

"Have the meddlesome fool stopped at the port and put on a fast war galley back to the mainland," I advised.

Arthur shook his head.

"I thought of that. But Medraut advises against it. Since Armorica has welcomed the black-robed brothers, their teaching's spreading, even over here. With the Colonials they've influence. Medraut tells me (and he should know, having been in their schools) they are better educated than our white brothers, and Guinevere agrees with that. To insult this man Hilarion would be bad policy, I'm told. We'll have to put up with his visit, and treat him with honor. For his accusations—well, Iltud must deal with those. I acknowledge, as you know, the loving wisdom of the Christ's teaching—but the squabbles men enter into over it now they must settle among themselves. As the Merlin says: 'Truth is the light your eyes can see.'"

Hilarion of Ravenna came, accordingly—a smooth and well-fleshed man, with small, observant eyes and a hard mouth. We entertained him courteously, and took his visit lightly, leaving Iltud to dispute with him and calm his disapproval with soft speech and truly Christian forbearance. He spent much time with Medraut, who showed him great respect.

It did not seem a matter of importance then. Arthur,

being occupied with other matters, may have slighted his
self-importance. When he took leave of us, I did not like
his smile. Medraut, humbly holding the rein of his mule
that day, was the only one to whom he gave a bishop's
blessing, I noticed.

# Chapter Twenty-Eight

It is the eve of Midsummer. I have lived, already, half a year longer than I'd the right to expect when I fell across the threshold of this little sanctuary in the snows of winter. Even Griffin has had to acknowledge I'll not last much longer. I see it in his eyes, for the sickness has lain heavy on me these past weeks. I was never one to leave a task unfinished. Tomorrow, Paulinus shall have the facts of Camlan. Then he, as well as I, may rest in peace!

The facts I can tell him. Some things are graven so deeply that even an old man does not forget. The steps that led us, slowly, inexorably, to that last, lost battle in the west are what tread my heart tonight. Even now I ask myself, with bitterness, could we not have avoided the end? Could we not have foreseen, in time, the hand of fate and turned it aside? Should not *I* have seen it?

I remember a day—how long was it before Camlan?—two years?—three?—when Arthur sent for me very early, having his page rouse me from sleep. When I'd dressed and joined him on the terrace outside his room, the palace gardens were still grey with dawn. It must have been high summer, for there was a scent of roses and wild honeysuckle in the air.

He was pacing up and down and I saw from his face that something had disturbed him deeply. He came to a halt, facing me, and said without preface:

"You must be the first to know this, Bedivere. We've

got to find a new High Prince for Britain. Peredur has resigned the title."

I stared at him, not able to believe I'd heard him rightly.

"How can he resign it? He is the Chosen One," I said, stupefied.

"Chosen by our Wise Ones. Chosen by the Clans, yes," Arthur answered grimly. "Not, so he tells me, chosen by God. He has had a call from heaven, another of his visions. He is ordered to leave all earthly things, and go to Jerusalem, there to worship at the place where the Christ died and learn the final secret of the Holy Grail."

"The boy's crazy," I said. "Jerusalem is at the world's end, with half the Barbarians of the mainland warring between us and it. Besides, to forswear his solemn duty to you, to Britain—it would be betrayal of his knight's oath, if nothing else. You'll not let him go?"

Arthur took my arm, and began to pace up and down again, drawing me into step beside him.

"All night I've pondered this thing. I've made up my mind. For Britain's sake, I *shall* let him go," he said. When I would have spoken he pressed my arm imperatively, checking the protest he must have known was coming. "Bedivere, I love that boy. Maybe I've loved him too much and that love blinded me to what I'd no wish to see. His charm, his gentleness, his shining honesty all point to a greatness of soul that sets him above and beyond ordinary men. But they are not, and I realize now I've known it some time, the qualities that will ever make him the Pendragon Britain needs. He is a dreamer, living in a world outside the harsh realities a king must face. I let him lead the Companions out, away from all their duties once, because I was taken off my guard. If you and I and a few others had not been here to keep the ship afloat and man the helm until they returned, what would have happened? When we are gone, what might not happen, with a Pendragon whose eyes are lifted to the stars, to the Grail, who cannot, blinded by that light, see the rocky path of duty beneath his feet?"

"That's true," I admitted reluctantly. "What's to be done, then, Bear?"

"Spring Sowing's past and the Merlin's in Armorica. This is no time to call a Gathering." Arthur spoke with the impatient decision I recognized. "There's only one thing I can do. Take the opportunity the boy's given me. Accept his challenge. I've always sworn I'd not stand between any man and his god, and the Council knows it. Peredur must go to Jerusalem, since he sees that as his moira. I shall confirm Constantine High Prince, with you and Gawain joint regents in case of my death before he's of warrior age."

We walked in silence the full length of the terrace and back before I found the words I needed. There was so much at stake. I wondered if, for once, Arthur was making too swift a judgment. Playing for time, I said:

"Bear, before you put this to the Council, have you thought that Peredur's been plagued with the marsh fever he caught that year of the Quest lately? Maybe that accounts for this vision—maybe it's a mood that will pass. Ask Palomides what he thinks."

Arthur shook his head.

"I've consulted Palomides concerning Peredur's health before. He's not satisfied with it; hinted there was more wrong than an ague got from sleeping in bogs. It's another reason for letting him go. No man who hasn't the endurance of a plough ox can bear the weight of the Pendragonship on his shoulders, for years at a stretch. I should know! Young Constantine's sturdy enough. He'll grow into a man fit for the job."

I nodded, remembering Leonore's resilience.

"He comes of good stock, it's true. He should be tough, for he has your blood, Bear—but I doubt he has your brains, or ever will have."

Arthur laughed.

"Barring accidents, I'll be there to guide him until he's learned his trade. If I'm not, he'll have you and the Companions—Gaheris, Gareth, Medraut—as well as the veterans. Though not the son of my heart Peredur's grown to be, he's a grandson I'd not be ashamed to own as mine."

He sighed as he said it.

I thought:

"The old wound still aches!"

Frowning again, but with a look I recognized meant his mind was concentrating on a new task, he said:

"We must see to it that boy marries early. I've not spoken before of another matter that's troubled me with Peredur. He always balked the issue when I spoke of marriage. Put me off with some rigmarole about celibacy being a part of the discipline he wished to keep a while longer, so that he might give all his mind to his search for truth. It was one of the signs, to me, that his calling all along was rather to priest than king, but I hoped one day he'd grow to being both, so I said nothing and let him take his time. Sensing the greatness that was in him, I was content to wait, for the Priest Kings of the ancient world were something we could do with again, I thought.

"That's over. With Constantine I'll have no nonsense. An early marriage and an assured succession. *He* shows no indifference to girls, you may have noticed!"

"I have noticed it," I agreed. "He's a normal enough youngster. Since a choice had to be made, you've made the right one, Bear. I don't think you'll have much trouble in convincing folk of it, once they've got over this shock."

Without hesitation he said:

"It was the only decision I could make. Britain had to come first, Bedivere."

The sun had risen and was casting long shadows across the queen's gardens. The Council must have gathered, I guessed, and would be waiting. I said:

"It's a bad business. Let's hope good comes out of it in the end. Either way, you know I'm with you, whatever judgment you proclaim—now and always."

"I know that. I shall need you more than ever now, Bedivere—you and Medraut." He paused. The level light shone full on his face, showing the sadness and the strength grooved deeply in the lines about his mouth. "I shall miss Peredur. There was a brightness in the air about him—a shining quality beyond what I've known in any other man. He *has* greatness, never doubt that. But it is the greatness of another world, not ours. The greatness of a Merlin, perhaps, or a Christian saint. Constantine will make Britain the better Pendragon."

That evening, when I went to the quarters I still shared with Palomides, I found the place in confusion.

"What's to do? Are you going on a journey?" I asked, seeing a strapped saddlebag, and folded clothes on the bed, with book rolls laid beside them.

Palomides looked up from the table, where he had been packing doctor's stuff into a small leather chest.

"Yes. A long journey, Bedivere," he said. The lamp was behind him. I could not see his face.

Some instinct warned me. I asked abruptly:

"Where to?"

"Jerusalem," he said, as quietly as though he spoke of a two days' ride.

I sat down on my own bed.

"It just needed that!" I said bitterly. "Arthur loses his High Prince and you, his physician, the man he trusts and depends on since the arrow sickness more than he realizes, must desert him the same day. Don't be a fool, Palomides! You'll not find truth (if that's what you're still searching for) any more in Jerusalem than Britain. Don't let Peredur deceive you as to that. I doubt if you'll ever live to get so far, either of you. *You* know the state of the mainland—and better than I do."

Palomides tucked a square of cloth down over the pots and packages and shining instruments in the chest with care, then closed the lid and locked it.

When he turned I saw his face was haggard.

"I've the king's permission to go, Bedivere. It is because he, as you say, trusts me, he's given that permission. Bors also goes, and a small guard of picked Armorican volunteers. Peredur cannot ride out alone this time."

"In the name of the gods, why not?" I asked. "Need his madness infect sane, useful men, like you and Bors? The boy *is* mad—his behavior proves it."

Palomides looked at me, his eyes dark and sorrowful.

"He is not mad, Bedivere. He is dying," he said.

He sat down on a stool beside the table, like a man suddenly too weary for longer standing and repeated slowly, "Dying, though he does not guess it. I've known it a long while; ever since he returned from the Quest. His spirit has burned out the lamp that holds it. That's the true fact, though in medicine we give the symptoms another name."

I stared at him.

"The wasting disease?" I questioned. (Peredur had grown wraith-thin, I remembered, and tired easily, though I'd not noticed him cough.) "*A* wasting disease. Not the one that rots a man's lungs. This turns the blood to water, and settles in the very marrow of the bones. It is the same his sister died from, and the cause the same. Maybe the ascetic practices of the old King Pelles' court, when they were children, gave them both less stamina than is needed to take the impact of powerful mystical experience— maybe the thing runs in families. I do not know; nor did Archimandros, my master. All I know for certain is the disease is rare and there is no cure for it."

I was shocked, remembering the bright promise of Peredur's first Pentecost among us.

"That's a hard thing for a man his age," I said slowly. "Will he last this dangerous journey? Can he ever reach Jerusalem?"

Palomides shrugged.

"I doubt it. Deterioration sets in suddenly, as a rule, with devastating weakness and pain in all the joints. That I *can* help to save him, and that is why I must go. By ship most of the way, we might get there. If not . . ." he smiled a strange smile. "For a man like Peredur there may still be the city he dreams of at the end."

I said, bleakly:

"I wish you need not go. We shall miss you here, and it's a dangerous, crazy venture."

Palomides said gently:

"Since his god calls him, he believes he must go. Since I love him—have loved him since the first moment I set eyes on him that day in the forest—I must go with him, Bedivere. Do you understand?"

Our eyes met. After a long pause I said sadly:

"Yes. I had not guessed—but yes, Palomides, I do understand. May his god, and yours, go with you, and bring you safe back to us when your work is done."

I rode with them down to the coast. I remember the glitter of sunlight on water, the crying of the gulls, the smell of salt water and fish, and the cheerful bustle of the little port from which they sailed.

At the last Palomides slipped a ring off his hand and onto mine.

"Keep this for me, Bedivere, until we meet again. It came to me from Archimandros and is a ring of healing. It will be safer in Britain than with me on this journey."

We embraced, and he followed Peredur and Bors up the gangplank of the waiting galley.

It was a ring of heavy gold, the green stone engraved with the caduceus and twining snakes of Mercury. Griffin knows what I want done with it and with Theodoric's arm ring when I am gone. They are all I have to leave this little community, to whom I owe so much.

The stir that Peredur's going caused settled gradually to general acceptance. Peace brooded over Camelot, and over Britain for a time. The peace of an October day, when the last flowers glow in homestead gardens and the robins sing, so that folk, feeling warmth still in the windless air, forget that behind that hazed brightness winter waits.

Lancelot, healed of his madness, though strangely quiet and sometimes inattentive to the point of vagueness, had been back at court some time. Iltud, who had visited him regularly after Palomides left us, had been finally advised by the monks in whose care he remained so long that he was fit to return to ordinary life. His memory, they admitted, was still impaired, but to all seeming, he was a whole man otherwise, and had begun to fret for his old, active life.

Arthur and Guinevere, who had never doubted Palomides' story that physical sickness afflicted him, received him with joy. After a time, even I forgot the grim reality that lay behind his protracted absence. Surrounded by friends, and lovingly cared for, he soon slipped into his old place among us, even, on occasion, commanding the cavalry at exercise, though I made it my business always to see to it that an experienced officer I could trust acted as his second. When he grew tired, he sometimes had difficulty in remembering the words of command, I'd noticed. As time passed, he, the queen and Iltud were much occupied with good works, founding a house of nuns in the forest and building a chapel, high up in the fort, where it should have served as a landmark. It was, so they said, to hold a replica of the Grail, and the light within the shrine would burn day and night, reminding all men of the Holy Vision. (That building was never finished, I remember. Our winter came too soon.)

I made it my business, too, having time on my hands, to keep my promise oftener to take Constantine fishing. We got on well together, and fishing is a sport where one can learn a good deal of what is passing in a boy's mind.

One evening, when we sat together, waiting for the evening rise, he said restlessly:

"Why does the king insist I must take lessons in statecraft from Sir Medraut? I'd rather learn from you."

"Because Medraut understands figures and diplomacy, which I don't," I said briefly.

He thought that over, and I watched him, amused. Like me, he thought slowly. He might well have been my son, had Leonore and I met in time. At last, frowning, he said:

"I don't like Medraut. He's clever, but he's a left-handed swordsman. Dogs and horses don't trust him. Have you ever noticed? I'll tell you something. I don't trust him either!"

I was glad his judgment chimed with the unerring instinct of horse and hound.

Only once in those last years did Medraut let the mask of his subservient humility slip with me. He was drunk, though from his manner one would hardly have guessed it. I was a little drunk myself. It was the night of the solstice and we'd feasted late. By chance, the lot had fallen on the two of us to make night rounds at the fort—a thing one can't neglect at that season for fear of fire, when the cold and the festival combine to make the men careless.

Coming out of the warmth and noise of the Great Hall, into the raw winter night, I saw him stagger a little, and take a few steps waveringly. Then he straightened up and laughed, falling into step beside me, his black cloak muffled close up to his chin.

"I'm with you, my lord! The wine was strong to-night, and when one first meets the outer air is when one feels its potency. As a rule, I drink little, you may have noticed—but at festival time one cannot refuse to pledge one's friends."

I laughed too.

"You sound sober enough to me for the task before us, at any rate. Let's get it over, and then to bed. Sleep'll clear our heads before morning."

He glanced sideways at me, his face a white gleam in the starlight that was just bright enough to show us the steep upward track.

"My lord, since for once we two are alone, and no eavesdroppers, may I ask a question?"

"If you must," I said, on my guard.

"I've often wondered, should things fall out in such a fashion that you were called upon to share the regency for the young High Prince with Sir Gawain, what changes would you be prepared to make in the policy of this country?"

"None," I said, unhesitatingly. "The country's stable at last after years of unrest. My chief and only aim would be to keep it so."

"Yet, I think, some changes will be inevitable in the future. Time doesn't stand still—not all folk are satisfied with things as they are at present."

"Who, for instance?" I questioned. ("Now what trouble is he trying to brew," I wondered.)

I felt, rather than saw, his supple shrug.

"There's unrest nearer the surface than the king will admit. He should take more heed of what younger men believe. We're behind the times in many ways here. The new generation's weary of so much talk of war, and the need to be forever preparing for war. That's one thing certain."

"Are they? Tell them they'll see the reason next time the Saxons gather a war fleet," I said.

"*If* the Saxons do," he said, and I heard the sneer in his voice. "When I rule Britain—" he caught himself up, much as he'd retrieved those first, stumbling steps of his, "*if* I ruled Britain with you, my lord, who are, after all, a man of experience, and have seen the world beyond these shores (as I have, myself), I'd say: 'Let's try what policy will do, not force, to end this Saxon menace and the threat from the north as well.' " His voice was smooth as oil. "Saxons are, when all's said, men, and have some qualities, let's face it, that our people lack. For myself, I see no reason why we should not make lasting treaty with them—use them to subdue the Picts (who, I give you, are savages still) and pay them with grants of land, where the country is still wilderness. Britain's wide enough and fertile enough, God knows, to support twice, ten times her present population."

"Your Christian God also knows, if he is as all-seeing as Abbot Iltud would have us believe, that, once we'd let them in on us, it wouldn't be long before they ruled all Britain, and we found ourselves enslaved," I said impatiently. I'd drunk enough to make me quarrelsome and I felt my temper rising.

"That's a matter of opinion, my lord. Many of the young folk now might be prepared to risk it. It's in tune with the spirit of the time. Half the countries of the mainland have had to accept Barbarian infiltration. Peaceful co-existence has been proved possible in Italy, for example. You yourself must have seen that."

"Under a Barbarian king," I reminded him.

"My plan would bring prosperity. The Saxons have proved themselves better farmers than our folk. You need only visit the Federate Given Lands (as I've done) to see how they can transform forest into rich cornland. We could double the tax returns in five years. But you'd not be ready to make the gamble?"

"Never," I said.

"Nor, at a guess, would you willingly change the king's policy on the religious question?" he asked, an edge, I thought, to his tone.

"What policy?" I asked.

"This flouting of the acknowledged right of the Bishop of Rome to dictate Christian doctrine everywhere. The open encouragement he gives to our white fathers in their declared heresies and his tolerance towards such prescribed practices as take place on the Merlin's Island. Those things are unacceptable to many now, my lord. They foster unrest. The rumors of that farce of the Grail search did untold damage. Thank heaven, Peredur's disgrace and banishment came in time to repair some of the scandal. *I* saw to that."

"Peredur's *what?*" I stopped short, swinging round to face him.

I thought he shrank a little and he'd good reason, for only the fact we were by then near enough the gates of the fort for any disturbance to have brought the guard running saved me from knocking him headlong into the bushes.

"Forgive me, my lord. I've learned to use diplomacy. Both the so-called search for the Grail *and* the sudden change in the succession needed explaining, you'll admit, to some outside Camelot—hard-headed Colonials and Clan chiefs who don't believe in dreams and visions, nor understand heavenly leadings. If the king had, truly, sent his heir into exile as punishment for instigating the search, it proved him a man of common sense, whom they could still trust. It only needed a hint from me in the right quarters, I promise you that."

"Medraut," I said, "you were always a liar. If you weren't drunk, I'd challenge you for such a lie as that. May the gods grant Arthur lives until Constantine's of age to rule, for I can see tonight that you and I could never work together. Come, let's do the rounds and get to bed. I've answered the question you asked me. Let you remember what my answer is. While there is strength in my body, I'd consent to no strategy of appeasement and I'd see to it Britain was guided along the straight path that Arthur has laid down. Moreover, and you may as well be clear on the point, I'd see to it Constantine made no drastic changes either. You'll not rule Britain while I live, Medraut—and neither will any other Saxon bastard!"

We faced each other for a long moment, and I had my hand on my sword hilt, for I could feel the anger in him, as one feels the heat from a fire.

Suddenly he shrugged, gave a short, mirthless laugh.

"Forgive me, my lord. I let the wine talk. Far be it from me to quarrel with one to whom I've owed so much, ever since I was a whining little rat of a page. You, the king's first and greatest Companion, whom all men hold in honor, have never needed to stoop to shifts of diplomacy. I realize that. If I've taught myself the craft, I swear to you it is only because, being as you so rightly remind me, base-born and a half-breed at that, I'm perhaps nearer to the common folk, and so understand how their minds work, how they think and feel, and how one can use their failings to the best advantage. The king is the shepherd of the people, but a wise shepherd needs a dog (even if it is a mongrel) to snap at the heels of the flock; to drive the sheep where they should go, and round up the stragglers. All I've said tonight, forget. Remember only that, should ill chance bring young Constantine to the Pendragonship before he is of age to rule, you'd have, as the king has, a dog who'd do his best to serve you well."

I did not trust one word of that, but he spoke with such earnestness, such apparent sincerity, I found myself constrained to accept the assurance. What help would it be to quarrel openly with the man? Arthur had grown to depend on him, and he had his uses.

"Let it go at that, then, Medraut," I said. "You and I are both the worse for midwinter revelling tonight. Best forget all that's been said."

Before I knew what he was about, he caught my hand and put it to his lips.

"Thank you, my lord! Believe, if you can, that from the day I first came to your service as a lonely, bewildered child, I've honored and revered you above all men. You can trust me, if only you will."

He sounded moved to the point of tears.

Embarrassed, I thought, "I wonder?" Aloud I said:

"Now I know you're drunk, man!" and laughed. "Come, let's get on with the work we're here to do."

We were at the north gate by then. Before I answered the guard's salute I rubbed the back of my hand on my cloak. His lips had been cold and wet as the touch of a toad, new crawled out of slime.

On a spring evening two years after Peredur's going, about the hour of lamp-lighting, one of Arthur's pages brought me a message that the king was asking for me. The boy looked solemn.

"He's in his private chamber, my lord. He said to tell you Sir Bors is with him."

"Sir Bors? Alone?" I asked. I felt a sinking in my heart.

The boy nodded.

"Yes, sir. I—I think he's brought bad news, sir."

I knew, as soon as I entered the familiar room, how the boy had guessed. Arthur's face had a grey, pinched look, and his mouth was set. He was in his usual chair by the hearth and Bors sat opposite, but rose to his feet and greeted me with a silent handclasp.

Arthur said, his voice tight and controlled:

"Bad news, Bedivere—the worst. Bors has won back to us, as you see, but—" he stopped speaking, and I could tell it was because he could not trust himself to go on. His voice was steady again, but very low, as he said: "Peredur is dead—the boy's dead, Bedivere."

I looked from him to Bors.

"Palomides?" I questioned.

Bors nodded. "He also. I'm sorry, Bedivere. I did my best," he said heavily.

Arthur broke in abruptly:

"Sit down, Bors! You've had a rough, hard journey. Bedivere, there's wine on the side, yonder. Pour it, will you? It may help us all, while we hear what Bors has to tell."

As I obeyed him, memory stabbed me. Instead of the fine silver goblets, I saw a cup of red samian ware, and Palomides' hand holding it out to me in a barrack room. That is how the first bleak realization of "never again" strikes home, like the pain that wakes in a wound after the first numbness has passed.

Arthur said quietly:

"I suppose I needn't ask whether you reached Jerusalem?"

Bors shook his head and, having drunk from the goblet I'd served to him, set it carefully aside, and sat, his hands on his knees, burly, dependable as ever, obviously grieved by the sorrow he must bring us, but seeing no way to soften it, for words had never come easily to him.

"No. We did not cover even half the journey. But Peredur seemed content. Maybe he thought the place we came to *was* Jerusalem. I'm not sure. It was a beautiful place."

His face, deeply tanned under the thistledown whiteness of his thick, straight-cut hair, looked faintly puzzled. I noticed for the first time a deep scar across his forehead, that showed the angry red of a wound not long healed. Noticed, too, the scuffed shabbiness of his leather jerkin.

"What place was it?" Arthur asked.

"A small hill town in the mountains of southern Gaul. They call it Saras, I believe, and it must be a holy place, for the folk round about hold it in respect and have built a chapel on the spur of the mountain above. Great peaks rise all about with snow on them and there's a torrent leaps down the rocks and away through the gorge below. A spot where mists rise up and the clouds come down, so that it's hard to tell where earth ends and sky begins, and the sun on the spray of the waterfall makes rainbows." Bors paused and leaned forward, clasping his hands between his knees. "Yes, a holy sort of a place and shining. It's how a man thinks of Jerusalem."

"Southern Gaul?" I said. "You took the overland route? I'd thought you planned to travel by sea, through the Pillars of Hercules."

"That was our plan. It would have been easier. We got some way down the coast in a wine galley, going home to Bordeaux, but the wind set against us and the weather turned rough. It looked as if we might be delayed for weeks. I said, 'Best push on overland down to Marseilles. We can take it in easy stages.' Maybe I was wrong. The weather cleared inland and it gets hot in summer in that country. Peredur's fever came on him again, but he was restless; desperate to push on each day, until, suddenly, he collapsed. It was as though he'd suffered one of the Three Great Wounds and near bled to death. After, he complained of pains in all his limbs, and seemed weak as a three-day-old kitten. But he would travel on. Nothing else would serve. So we hired a litter, and went very slowly, resting one day in every three. Palomides tended the lad, but I could see he'd no more hope than I had we'd ever reach Jerusalem. I blame myself. The sea voyage would have been wiser—less tiring—but I'd little experience of sickness. To me Peredur seemed well enough and I thought Palomides overanxious. But he knew."

Bors looked from one to the other of us, anxiously, as though expecting blame.

Arthur said quietly:

"Palomides warned me the boy's sickness was mortal. That's why I let him go. We agreed that all any of us could give him was this chance to follow his heart's desire as far as his strength would take him. You say he thought, at the last, this place you reached was the city of which he dreamed?"

Bors sighed.

"Yes. I think in some sort it satisfied his dream," he said heavily. Then he brightened a little and repeated, "It was a beautiful place. We'd the habit of starting out very early each day, while it was still cool, and resting through the noon heat. On the road, that morning, early as it was, we met a throng of country folk. They told us they were on their way to worship at a shrine in the mountains, it being festival time.

" 'It is the Chapel of the Holy Spirit, served by the good monks. Many miracles of healing have taken place there, sirs. Surely you have heard tell of it? When we saw you carried a sick man with you, we thought for sure you must be on your way to ask for a cure.'

"Palomides said to me: 'The mountain air is pure, and if the place they tell us of is served by healer-monks, they'll likely let us rest there for a while. He can't go much further, Bors.'

"So we turned off the road and took the mountain track with the pilgrim folk all about us. As we climbed, we saw the little town stand out above us, all the houses white, and the chapel on the rocky spur above touched rose color by the rising sun, and the mist coming and going round about, so that it seemed to swim in space, like some heavenly vision. A bell was ringing, and all about us the poor folk were singing as they walked. Oh, it was a strangely wonderful place!

"Peredur sat up in the litter and stretched out his arms. 'Jerusalem—the holy city!' he cried out strongly. (We were amazed, for he'd not spoken above a whisper in a great while, and had seemed unaware of all about him.) 'Oh, my friends, let us hasten! Let us kneel and worship in that place from which the King of the World went, a sacrifice consenting, through the gates of death, for the healing of mankind.' "

Again, Bors fell silent, drawing a deep breath, brushing his hand across the angry scar on his forehead, as if his effort of speech had set it throbbing. Then he went on steadily, his voice gruff with emotion.

"When we'd reached a terrace before the chapel door, Peredur signed to us to help him from the litter. He could only stand and walk with great pain, by then. He leaned upon our shoulders, and so we went into the shrine, the press of people making way for us, and some of the good monks in their brown habits coming forward to help us and clear a way up close to the high altar, where the mass had just begun. We knelt down, the three of us, and presently a silver bell rang for the sacring. Peredur had been leaning against my shoulder. He whispered to me: 'Do you see the great Angels of the Presence, Bors? Oh, the colors! Their wings are flames!'

"Then he got up, off his knees, with no help from either of us, and went forward alone, moving steadily and strongly, like a whole man, except that he trembled a little, as though deep awe was upon him. He knelt before the altar step and received the bread and wine, with humility and devotion, as he always did. Suddenly he stretched out his arms with a great cry that rang through the hushed chapel:

" 'The Grail! See where it passes, the Holy Cup, red as any rose!'

"He looked upwards as he spoke, then swayed and would have fallen, but Palomides caught him, and the two of us, the monks helping us, carried him out into a little courtyard, where a spring rose out of the rocks and there was an arbor of vines.

"He was conscious, his eyes open and very clear. I brought water, and we bathed his face and knelt beside him, holding his hands. He looked into our faces and smiled and said: 'The Grail—it passes, but it will come again.' Then he murmured something about having reached the holy city, his head fell back against Palomides' shoulder and he was gone—just like that—quietly as a child falls asleep."

We sat silent a long time. Then Arthur said, very low:

"You buried him there?"

"On the mountain ledge, where the monks have their graveyard. It's a well-tended place. There's a stone cross to mark the spot, with his name and title carved deep, and (those monks being skilled craftsmen) the design of a cup within an open rose, where the arms of the cross meet. He'll not be forgotten. Already, before we left, simple folk were laying flowers and praying at the graveside, having heard his story, and accounting him a saint."

"And afterwards?" I asked.

"We started homeward, both of us sad and weary. Palomides seemed stricken. He'd worn himself out, tending the boy day and night. We came to an inn in a walled city, where, hearing the innkeeper's son was sick of a fever, Palomides must needs offer to see to him. He came out and said to me: 'It is the yellow plague. Take the guard and ride on. I shall be needed here.'

"I was for all of us flying the accursed place, but he'd have none of it. The end of the matter was that we sent the men with us away and I stayed. Soon the infection was raging, and many died, but many also survived who owe their lives to having Palomides among them. He worked himself to death, I think, for when, at last, the pestilence had burned itself out and there had been a day and a night with no new cases, I went to rouse him from sleep, and he did not stir. His face was calm, with a smile upon it, so I could tell it was not the plague that had killed him. Plague victims don't die that way." Bors drew out a linen kerchief, and mopped his eyes. "He'd worked himself to death," he repeated in a muffled voice.

I turned the ring on my finger, and green fire in the stone woke, behind the carved caduceus of the healer.

In my heart I said: "I will wear it until we meet again, my battle comrade." Aloud I said:

"Don't grieve for him, Bors. He followed the road he would have chosen. You did all you could and no man can do more."

Bors blew his nose loudly, stowed away the square of linen, and looked at me gratefully.

"That's all there is to tell. I saw to it he was buried decently, away from the cursed plague pits, and took the road for home. No man in his senses rides alone on the mainland these days, so I joined a merchant caravan. They were glad to have some help from an armed man, for the roads are infested with brigands. I did what I could a couple of times when we were attacked and got myself knocked about a little, which delayed my journey. I only wish I could have brought happier news. It was a sorry business—a sorry business, from start to finish."

"Sorrier still, had you not been with both at need. You did well, Bors—no one of the Companions could have done better," Arthur said, gently. "May the Light shine on them in the place of Light to which they have gone, for truly, I think the end came for both in the way each would have chosen. Though their graves are far away, Britain will remember them."

# Chapter Twenty-Nine

The mark of the potter's thumb on the soft clay remains, an indelible imprint on the fired wine jar. Margause of Dalriada had set her mark early on the unstable character and ambitious mind of a bewildered child. From her, over the years, Medraut learned the cynical distrust of men's higher motives, the devious methods of political intrigue, the long patience that never loses sight of a coveted material advantage. Too late for her planned personal satisfaction, her dead hand reached out from the grave, and through the tool she had fashioned, dragged down a greatness she had been intelligent enough to recognize, but always too jealous to accept.

Like a worm in wood, like a moth in a clothes chest, Medraut worked under cover of darkness in those last years at Camelot. Secretly, tirelessly, he used every means to undermine and destroy, and only later, too late, did the evidence of his cold, methodical industry become clear.

Arthur's trust gave him his opportunity. When he asked leave to go himself and deal with Clans whose taxes were in arrears, or whose levies had not reported for duty, Arthur praised his diligence. When he offered, humbly, yet eagerly, to act as mediator between the king and the Federates, he had the qualification we others lacked in his fluent command of their barbarous dialects. (I remember his making a jest of it, once, he who so seldom jested: "Who better could you send to deal with Saxons than a Saxon bastard?" he asked in Council, and, laugh-

ingly, Arthur gave him, gladly, the task no other among
us would have welcomed.)

When, pleading policy, and the need to reassure
Colonial opinion, he changed the white brothers in the
Scriptorium for black brothers from overseas, Arthur let
him have his way. When it was necessary to make contact
with Armorica, who better than Medraut? He had spent
his youth out there, and understood its politics.

So dissensions were sown, rumors spread, suspicion
and hatred fomented. Medraut, who all his life had
nursed a secret grievance, until it grew into lust for power
so obsessional that only the Pendragonship would satisfy
it, moved among us, those last years, protected by the
greatness of the man who refused to see in others integrity
less absolute than his own.

For me, those last years held happiness, a strange happiness, that took my mind away too often from the vigi-
lance that, as a soldier, I should have maintained towards
possible danger. On the surface, they were prosperous
and peaceful years. As I recall them now, they have the
dreamlike quality of an October day, when the last
warmth of summer lulls the mind to a belief that winter is
still far away.

Having more leisure on my hands than I could well
remember since childhood, I turned again to the music
Diarmed had taught me. Lacking the Merlin, it pleased
the Companions to hear, in hall, the great battle lays that
recalled our early victories. If, now and then, I became
aware of an undercurrent of inattention, a lifted eyebrow,
a whispered comment that produced shrugged shoulders
and a smile among the younger men who aped Medraut's
outlook, I paid little attention. The rousing applause I
could always depend on, when I sang for the Clans at the
great Gatherings, reassured me too easily that there was
little to fear from changing fashion in a small, if aggres-
sive minority. The memories of that time I cherish most,
the ones that come to my mind still as clearly as though
they had happened yesterday, are of rare evenings when
Arthur would call on me to sing to him and a few of
those closest to us in the warm intimacy of his private

apartments. One such occasion haunts my mind particularly—a winter night, not very long after Lancelot had been restored to us. Wild weather had made us glad to draw close about the brazier, where juniper chips, scattered on the blazing ash logs, sent up their flickering, aromatic blue flames. Arthur was in his accustomed chair, and Guinevere, as she often did in those last years, had settled herself on a cushion at his feet, sharing the brazier's warmth with a couple of favorite wolfhounds. Bors and Gawain went out after a while to do night rounds and Lancelot, in the chair opposite Arthur's, had fallen into a doze. We'd been talking of old times, singing together or in turns as the fancy took us, songs we all remembered. Now the four of us, though the hour was late, were reluctant to break the spell of shared nostalgia.

Very softly, Guinevere began to hum a little haunting tune, looking up to smile at Arthur, as she broke off to ask him:

"Do you remember?"

He nodded, answering her smile:

"Well enough, sweetheart. The first song you ever taught me. Can you still remember the words? I doubt if I ever learned those—all I can recall now is your little wren's voice piping them. Sing it again."

She glanced from him to me, brows lifted in question, and nodding I touched the harp's strings gently, giving her the opening chords.

Her voice was still sweet and true, though age had thinned it a little, and I knew the tune well—a shepherd's song of her people, with the strange, haunting cadences of the northern hills. The shepherd who sings it is old, and he tells of a long, hard life. A strange choice for a child to have made, all those years ago, when the wandering harper came to her father's hall, I thought, watching the worn beauty of her face, while my fingers found the familiar chords. On the last verse her voice rose a little—

> *I had three wives*
> *But all are gone before me.*
> *One by one, like the sheep at evening,*

*Through the gates of sunset,*
*To the fold of Erda.*
*Now I follow, follow,*
*But my feet are weary.*
*Now I follow, follow,*
*Through the sunset's gate.*

I let the last note die, and sat watching the firelit scene, while silence settled back, and the wind's sound flowed by above the smokehole, the flames fluttered, and one of the hounds groaned, stretching in an ecstasy of content.

Guinevere bent her head, perhaps to hide sudden tears. Arthur's big, gnarled hand went out to stroke the soft silvery hair that caught and clung above his fingers, as once, he'd told me, an eight-year-old's bright hair had clung.

He said dreamily:

"I, too, have had three wives. Did you know that, Bedivere? You should put it into a song one day. *The king had three wives. The name of each was Guinevere.*"

"How so?" I asked, humoring his mood.

"The first was a wild, wild girl, so young she felt to me like a daughter. A gay, glancing, laughing lass, wilful and wayward, dearer to me than I'd time then to guess.

"The second was a woman, beautiful and proud, who came to maturity in a loneliness I'd not the wit to guess at. A woman who suffered because, in the weight of a country's needs, I was too blind to know love needs cherishing."

As she raised her head sharply, about to interrupt with some quick protest, he shook his, gazing down at her intently.

"No denials, sweetheart. I've had long enough to cast the account. The reckoning stands against me. No man, whatever the pressures life puts on him, had the right to be so wilful-blind as I once was, making the two nearest and dearest to him suffer, and not having wit enough to know they suffered.

"Past such a man's deserving, Bedivere, I found my third Guinevere—a wife still beautiful, still young to my eyes, who by some miracle has learned to love me at last for what I am, with all my faults."

Guinevere had caught his hand and laid her cheek against it. I could not see her face. But Arthur, as he glanced from her to Lancelot, was calm and smiling, his expression quiet as a winter sea after a night of storm, when it breathes softly under a windless dawn. Turning to me, and shaking his head again, he muttered, on a different note, with a hint of gruff apology for so rare a show of emotion:

"Gods, man, how the young suffer, and how soon the years pass! Why do men dread age? It seems to me I never had time to be happy until now, when all of us are growing old!"

It must have been soon after that evening Arthur broached the matter to me, without preface, and very much to my surprise, which was to bear more closely than I then guessed on all my life ahead. It was his wish, he told me, and the Merlin's advice, that I should be appointed the Pendragon's Bard.

"Times change, Bedivere. As long as he lives, Celidon will remain the Merlin of Britain. But he is old and he knows his powers are failing. More and more, now, he's withdrawing from public life, hiding himself away in the remote and lonely retreats of the Wise Ones. Before it's too late, he'd have you learn some of the secrets of a Merlin, for he foresees a time when there will be no other but you to follow him. He counts you, thanks to the teaching Diarmed gave you, ready for the Bard's initiation. Will you take it?"

I said, doubtfully:

"I am Roman-born and have been a soldier all my life. Surely the training for a Crowned Bard takes twenty years? Celidon's had the thought too late, Bear!"

Arthur swept the objection aside.

"That one knows his own business. He always has. Go to him on the Island. They've orders to receive you."

For a day and a night I wrestled with doubts. Then I went.

I found that I, who all my life until then had shun-
ned commitment to any of the mysteries, was already
committed. These things, like birth and death, come to a
man without his willing them. In the short time that was
left to us, I was made free of the Sacred Island. Sometimes Celidon, more often Ygern, instructed me in those
hidden things which, beside his craft as harper, a
Crowned Bard must know. One does not speak of them,
save to a fellow craftsman, but I found no strangeness
there. Rather, they seemed to me memories, once precious, that had been buried deep, that I was glad to have
recalled. Frail as he was, then, the Merlin taught me what
I needed to know as clearly and as ruthlessly as a good
master-at-arms teaches weapon-play to an apt pupil. He
knew, and I think I knew, that for both of us the time of
my learning would prove all too short.

News of disaster hit us in the last summer, storm out of a
clear sky. Medraut saw to that. It was not by accident so
many of the underground, who should have brought us
earlier warning, died mysteriously. He knew too much of
the Merlin's secret network, and used his knowledge to
bring them to their deaths.

Medraut himself was in Armorica on an embassy
when at last word got through that once again an invasion
fleet was gathering. Angles, Saxons, Jutes and Frisians
were all converging on their old anchorage in Rhine
rivermouth. They'd made a signed treaty with the Picts,
besides—Aela's sons, who led the invasion fleet, had
insisted, this time, it should be signed in blood.

"Though it'll take more than blood dropped on
sheepskin to keep a Pict to his word!" Gawain growled,
grimly cheerful, when he heard of it.

The Branch went out the length and breadth of
Britain, for the first time in twenty years, and the Clan
levies began to come in. A new generation, young, without battle experience. They came less promptly, and there
were fewer than there should have been. I sensed reluctance to leave home territories unguarded even among
those who came. (They had, after all, so much more to
guard than we had ever had.)

In Council that reluctance flared openly, voiced by Medraut's faction and led by Aglavain. The burden of the argument seemed to be that the Branch had gone out too soon—by making preparation for war we were precipitating a war that might still be avoided, by careful negotiation, and possibly some few concessions.

"Why not wait until Sir Medraut returns? Let him suggest terms. The country does not want war, my lord," Aglavain stated with conviction.

"Do any of us?" Arthur asked. "Some of us have seen enough of what it brings, the gods know!"

"I've heard it hinted there *are* some," and Aglavian glanced from Lancelot to me with open insolence, "who have lived so long on the reputation of it that their fame grows threadbare, and they'd be glad of the chance to renew it."

"So?" Arthur questioned, with dangerous quietness. In the seat at his right hand young Constantine gripped the edge of the table and half rose to his feet, his freckles standing out on a face gone white with rage.

Arthur motioned to him, as one waves down a young, too-eager sheep collie.

"So—we disband the host and let the Saxon fleet land unchecked—is that the advice of the Council?" he asked.

A growl went round the table from the older Companions. Aglavain flushed, but Medraut had trained him to speak softly and keep his temper. In a tone that copied Medraut's own carefully reasoned logic, he said:

"We let them land, my lord, as allies, not enemies. Offer them the things they're prepared to fight us for, land grants and loot, in exchange for *their* help in destroying the northern menace. Let them annihilate the Picts for us, lay waste the whole savage northland once and for all, and pay them for doing it. Britain can afford the price now."

"No," Arthur said, evenly. "No, Aglavain. Their price would be too high. Our children's children would still be paying it, and their children after them, a hundred years from now. Freedom is too precious a thing to be bought with any price but blood and suffering. Bedivere,

which of the Clans are missing? How many men have we
in arms so far—and what's lacking in their equipment?"

Medraut's absence prolonged itself, and grew tiresome. A
messenger had been sent to him with news of the impending invasion, and then another with urgent orders for his
return. Meanwhile his staff of monkish scribes twittered
and flapped like hens disturbed at feeding time when I
went to them for the weapons and stores we'd always
kept ready, in the past, for emergency. I cursed Arthur's
trust, and my own preoccupation, that had left so much
in Medraut's hands. We were short of essential supplies in
a dozen directions. Blacksmiths' gear and trenching tools,
leather thongs for securing loads on the baggage wagons,
cooking pots and storm lanterns. Small things, but the
very lack of which can cause confusion and delay on the
march.

We'd sent out the Red Branch by then, following the
Silver, which meant immediate mobilization. That startled
the Clan Chiefs awake to the gravity of the situation.
Fresh levies poured in and the signal hills and the level
land below the fort were once again alive with noise and
activity, and watch fires blinked all about us in the nights.
I felt my heart grow lighter. The spirit was still there, I
told myself. It had only needed rousing. The conviction
did not make me tolerant of frustrations and obstructive-
ness on the part of Medraut's clerks.

Things came to a head one morning when the monk
in charge of army stores, a sleek, cautious man, put me
off with excuses that goods in short supply were unobtainable. He was delaying matters intentionally, I felt
certain of it.

"If you can't get what I need from your usual
sources, duplicate the orders elsewhere," I told him
curtly.

He smiled cunningly.

"Oh, my lord, I've not the authority for that. Think
of the expense! Only Sir Medraut could authorize it. I
fear we must wait for his return."

Behind me, Arthur's battle voice, which I had not
heard for years, roared with all his old authority:

"Do as you're bid, man! Don't you know that in time of war Lord Bedivere as my second-in-command takes precedence of all the other Companions—and that includes Sir Medraut. Whatever he ordered you just now, do, and do quickly!"

He turned briskly to me.

"Now, Bedivere, what is it you need? What's in short supply?"

I told him, and the clerk, his face gone sickly green, wrote down items and quantities on his tablet with a trembling hand, while Arthur and I discussed briefly the nearest and most likely sources where the things could be obtained.

At one point the monk raised a squeaking protest (torn, I guessed, between fear of Arthur and fear of Medraut):

"But—but—those are not our regular suppliers now. Sir Medraut has found others whose terms are more advantageous."

"By the gods, that may account for the complaints I've had of the shoddy stuff you've been issuing!" I growled.

Arthur ignored him.

"Bedivere, detail reliable patrols to go out and fetch what's needed." He grinned at me suddenly, and added, "Put veteran decurions in charge who haven't forgotten how to organize a forage for supplies, and tell them not to return empty-handed! Now come outside—I want a word with you."

This was the Arthur I remembered: the War Duke we'd lost too long in the Pendragon. Even his appearance had changed in the past few days. He'd discarded civil dress in favor of an old leather battle tunic, trews and studded army sandals. Bare-headed, his grey hair cropped close, his face clean-shaven, he looked ten years younger.

"A messenger got through an hour ago—a man we can trust," he said, as soon as we were out of earshot of the monk. "The fleet from the Rhine will sail with the first fair wind after the new moon."

"Their objective?" I asked.

Arthur shook his head.

"That we don't know for sure. Anywhere along the Federate beaches, I'd say, but it could be Vectis water again. The fellow risked his life to find out as much as he did."

"If it's the beaches, can we trust the Federates to stand by Medraut's precious treaties—or not?" I asked.

We had been walking together across the exercise ground. Arthur stopped abruptly, his face clouding, his mouth stern.

"They may. So much the better for them if they do. But there's another thing. The man brought with him a letter. It's from an agent you know, one the Merlin always trusted. Read it."

I took the parchment from him. The writing was small, precise, very clear.

*"Be warned, Arthur. In Armorica Medraut is raising an expeditionary force. Remember the cross-bred hound that scarred the hand that fed him. Mawgan."*

I drew a deep breath.

"Mawgan *is* to be trusted," I said.

He looked at me, frowning. "I know she is, but Bedivere, is this possible? Ygern's son—the man I've grown to depend on, all these years, as if he had been *my* son?"

I said nothing. He read my answer in my eyes.

Suddenly he shrugged and walked on.

"Well, I'll condemn no one without evidence. We shall see. He could be raising reinforcements for us, now Lancelot's outlawed and has no authority in Armorica."

"If so, why has he not sent a message, and so explained his delay in obeying your order to return?" I said, and added, because I felt I must, "You know I never trusted Medraut, Bear?"

He glanced at me, still frowning, then squared his shoulders and his head went up in the old, defiant gesture with which he'd always met the challenges of the past.

"Let it stand! We've more to consider than one man's possible defection. The moon's at the full now—

that gives us two weeks, three if we're lucky. Not much time, but time enough." Suddenly he laughed, and clapped his hand on my shoulder. "Heart up, man! Don't look so solemn. Badon was our last victory, but by the Light, I think I've always known, and you must have guessed, it wouldn't be our last battle!"

In Council a majority overruled the young dissidents, and Aglavain was silent, showing his feelings only by an occasional sneer. But there was an undercurrent, a whispering in corners, a sense of something moving in the dark. Gawain must have felt it, too. Unexpectedly, but with highland obstinacy, he refused to take command of the north.

"Let Gaheris and Gareth have their turn. With Leodogrance's brood to back them, they'll do well enough. Something tells me I'll be needed here before all's through," he said, and nothing would move him from that decision.

Quickly, surely, Arthur laid his plans. Rheged and Dalriada between them were to hold the north. Lancelot and Bors with light cavalry would take Kay's old post, patrolling the Great Dike that is the Heartland's second line of defense. The bulk of the levies were to be divided into two hosts, one under Arthur's command, with Gawain in charge of the heavy cavalry, destined to meet the main brunt of invasion, wherever it came, while I held the second half in reserve, in case the enemy attacked us on two fronts, or Arthur needed reinforcements. A great deal was going to depend on communications being fast and reliable. I saw to it that only officers and men I personally knew to be reliable were assigned to that duty, and personally inspected every one of the Icenian chariot ponies. (In peacetime we'd used them for the postal service—in war they would keep communication lines open.)

The fleet in Adurni was the last link we needed in the chain of defense.

Arthur said to me:

"I'm going down there myself to see to their briefing. A lot will depend on them, and I need to be sure they understand the part they must play. With led horses, so that we can change mounts every twenty miles, I've time enough for the journey. See to things here for me, Bedivere."

"You can trust me for that," I said.

"I know I can always trust *you*," he said briefly. That was the only reference he made to Medraut in that week.

He went off at cock-light, with his small cavalry guard, and for the three days that followed I'd work enough to keep me busy all the hours of daylight, and well on into the night.

The third evening I was delayed on my last round of the camp by some problem of a dispute over quarters between the Chiefs of two minor Clans. The spirit of the host was good, by then, for Arthur had been about among them himself all week, and they'd caught the infection of his grim gaiety. I'd learned long before that time and tact were well spent, placating the touchy dignity of minor Chieftains, and I'd stayed to drink brotherhood with the two I'd reconciled, and half a dozen more who were their friends. As I rode back alone in the dark along the river road I remember thinking the only ones I'd failed, so far, to make good relationship with were the new commanders of the Rheged levy—the three youngest of Leodogrance's brood, who, banking on their rank as the queen's brothers, were giving themselves airs that might well breed trouble. Tomorrow I must attend to them, I thought.

An owl hooted and swept low along the dark path under the trees, and my horse shied, bringing me to instant alert. Something had startled the bird from its night's hunting, I guessed. I drew rein, and heard the muffled hoofbeats of another horseman, riding fast from the direction of the palace. Horse and rider loomed up alongside me and came to slithering halt.

"Is that you, my lord? Thank God I've found you!" Griffin's voice panted breathlessly.

"What's wrong? News of a landing?" I asked.

"No. Trouble at the palace. Bad trouble. A quarrel. Two dead and five wounded; Sir Lancelot's one, and

badly by the look of him. Oh, sir—they surprised him in
the queen's bedchamber—in her bed, they say. It's Aglavain and his lot."

"Tell me as we ride," I said. He wheeled his horse
round and we went forward at a fast trot.

"I was with Sir Gawain in the doorway of the Great
Hall when it happened. Supper was over, not many people about. Suddenly Aglavain and some of his gang ran
past us shouting: 'Treachery—Treachery to the king! The
king is betrayed!'

"They burst open the door of the great bedchamber,
but it was banged shut again directly. They started to
hammer on it with their sword hilts, yelling: 'Shame!
Come out, lecher!' and other such filth.

"Sir Gawain swore and we drew our swords, but
before we could get across the hall (you know how the
hall is at that time, all cluttered up with tables and
benches, and the boys unrolling bedding and so on), the
door of the bedchamber swung back, and there stood Sir
Lancelot, all but mother-naked, my lord, with only a
cloak flung round him, unarmed except for one of the
heavy spinning stools swung up in both hands to defend
himself. Aglavain and the pack set on him, six armed
men to one, naked and unarmed. I couldn't believe my
eyes. I've never moved so fast in my life, but Sir Gawain
was in before me. Lucky we *were* armed. As it is I think
they may have killed him. It was filthy fighting while it
lasted."

"The queen—was she there—was she hurt?" I
asked.

"She was in the bedchamber, sir. I heard her cry
out. I think those two must have been alone together.
Dame Helena rushed up behind us, screeching, and one
or two others of the queen's women. Dame Helena went
in, as soon as we could clear a way, stepping over the
dead and wounded and cursing us all. She's a grand old
warrior, that one! But it's a bad business. If only we'd Sir
Palomides, still, to tend Sir Lancelot!"

"If only!" I muttered. ("If only I had you, my battle
comrade, the man who could always keep my head for
me—show me what must be done," I thought.)

There was a double guard on the palace gate and commotion everywhere. I pushed my way into the Great Hall through a gaping crowd of pages and squires, past two of Guinevere's girls who were having hysterics and being comforted. Lucan plucked at my sleeve, babbling, his Colonial dignity gone all to pieces.

"Sir, sir, what's to be done? This is a most terrible thing!"

"Hold your tongue!" I snapped at him. "Send everyone here about their business. Get this panic quelled somehow."

"But, sir—under Roman law it's a burning matter. The queen and the Lord Lancelot, alone together, and him naked—"

"Silence!" I thundered. "Remember I command here in the king's absence. If any man impugns the queen's honor or the Lord Lancelot's, I'll have him flayed alive. This is some plot—some mare's nest. Those who hatched it shall suffer for it, and not the innocent. You, Lucan, stop your braying and see order is restored. Where's Sir Gawain?"

"In his quarters. The doctor is seeing to his wounds, sir." My own armor-bearer, a reliable, quiet lad, had materialized suddenly at my elbow.

I shouldered Lucan aside and went quickly to find Gawain.

He was in a room off one of the small courtyards. A serious-faced young surgeon, one of Palomides' men, had just finished stitching a sword cut from his left wrist to elbow. He sat, slumped in a chair, his face sallow—pale under the summer's tan. The bead of blood on his lower lip showed where he'd bitten into it, as one does when pain is bad.

"Well, this is a pretty business!" I said.

"Aye, it is that," he agreed.

I waited while the surgeon finished his work. He was deft and quick at it, and discreet, for he made haste to gather up his gear and go quietly from the room. As the door closed, I said:

"Are you fit to tell me what happened?"

"Och, it's nothing. A deep scratch," he said impatiently. Then, frowning: "If you're wise, you'll hang that devil's brat of a brother of mine, before Arthur gets back to pardon him. I tell you in all honor, I'll hold no blood feud against you if you do. This time he's gone too far. I and my Clan disown him for it."

"Where is he?" I asked.

"Under guard at present, he and those of his cata-mite friends left alive. You'll have heard two were killed, maybe?"

"I've heard," I said. "Medraut is behind this, Gawain."

"Aye. I'd the same thought. It would serve that one's purpose to set dissension among us, just now. Raking up a scandal twenty years cold!" and he spat his contempt unceremoniously on the squared pavement beside his chair.

"What in the name of all the gods was Lancelot doing naked in the queen's chamber, the two of them alone together? Tell me that," I queried.

He grinned a little.

"You may ask! He wasna naked, mind—only stripped to the waist. She'd been putting unguent on his back for him. Yon new stallion he's training for battle threw him this afternoon. He was as stiff as an old hound by suppertime. The queen would have it she and the old beldame widow-woman Helena must rub the hurt for him with some of the stuff Iltud's nuns brew from herbs and such. I suppose she'd sent Dame Helena for more or different liniment. That's all there was to it, Bedivere. It's long past the time those two had need of a bedchamber alone together; and, to give them credit, they'd not have chosen the king's for their need even in the old days."

"Well I know that," I said. "But there are some who'll not choose to believe it. There couldn't have been a worse time for the old scandal to be revived."

"There couldna be a worse time for us to lose Lancelot." He grinned reminiscently. Gawain was always practical. "Man, ye should have seen him! Like a lion he fought. He'd smashed one fellow's skull in with no weapon but that wee creepy stool before I got to him. With naught but his cloak for buckler. I'm feared he'll not ride

again, though. There was blood all over him when they
carried him away. We should go to him, Bedivere."

Gawain made as if to rise, but I stopped him.

"Stay where you are. You'll need your shield arm
soon enough. Don't risk a chill on that wound making it
fester. I'll go to Lancelot," I said.

"Maybe you'd better. The room reels round me
when I stand," he admitted. "It's naught but the loss of
blood. I aye bleed like a stuck pig. You'll mind that from
the old days."

I found Lancelot's large, luxurious apartment looking indeed as if a pig had been slaughtered there. A trail
of blood on the tessellated floor showed where they'd
carried him in, and the elegant coverings on the bed were
dabbled and darkly stained. The most senior doctor from
the fort was bending over his long, sprawled body, and
the widow Helena, grimly efficient, stood holding a bowl
into which, presently, the doctor wrung out a reddened
cloth.

I went forward on tiptoe, and asked softly:

"How bad is he? Will he live?"

Before the man could answer, Lancelot muttered:

"Is that you, Bedivere?" then, impatiently, to the
surgeon, "Take that thing away—I can't see. *Is* that you,
Bedivere?"

"Yes. I'm here, beside you," I said, going up close
on the further side of the bed, where I could see his face.
It was not a pretty sight. He must have caught the blow
of someone's fist full in the mouth, for his lips were
puffing up and turning blue. The surgeon was swabbing
blood from his forehead, where a flap of skin had been
turned back, and the blood was rushing into his eyes, but
he appeared to be fully conscious and in the worst possible temper.

He snatched the cloth from the surgeon and himself
mopped his forehead, and then, holding it clamped there,
so that he could see, struggled into a sitting position,
blinking, and with his free hand grabbed for mine.

"Why are you here? God's death, haven't you anything better to do than come croaking 'Will he live?' over
me like some old corbie crow? I'm right enough if only

these fools will put a bandage round my head. You should be with the queen. She may be in danger still. This place is seething with treachery, Bedivere."

His voice was thick and a small trickle of blood ran from one corner of his mouth down his chin. I thought of internal bleeding and looked at the surgeon. Lancelot caught the look, swore with Armorican fluency and took the cloth from his head momentarily to spit into it.

"What do you imagine? A sword through my guts, is it? You'd spit blood if you'd had three teeth knocked out! Here you—" he let go of my hand and clutched at Dame Helena's arm, "you tell him there's no harm done that won't mend in a week. Go to the queen, Bedivere, and tell her so, for the good Christ's sake!"

The old dame frowned down at him sternly.

"Calm yourself, my lord, and do not blaspheme. Let the physician do his work. You help no one by setting yourself in a passion that's like to bring on a fever."

Firmly, as if he had been a rebellious small boy, she pressed him back upon his pillows. Then, facing me squarely, she said in a quiet voice:

"There's little harm done, compared with what might have been expected, my lord Bedivere. A few minor cuts about the body, that the doctor has already attended to. Will you tell the queen that? She is bound to be anxious. There was much blood upon him, and at first we feared he was badly hurt."

Lancelot spluttered impatiently:

"Of course there was blood on me and brains too! You can't crack a man's head open with a spinning stool at close quarters and not look like a butcher boy in a slaughter shed! All I need is a bath and a change of clothes!" and he shuddered fastidiously.

I laughed.

"If that's the case, I'll leave you in good hands and get to other business," I said.

"Go to the queen," he repeated, and as I turned to leave him he added, his tone suddenly grave and imperative, "and Bedivere, see the man who started this is well guarded. I've an idea there's an adder's brood loose in the fort. They could strike again."

The great bedchamber was closed and guarded. Two of Gawain's centurions stood outside the door with their swords drawn, their dour Highland faces gazing straight ahead, trying to appear unconscious that a little knot of women and pages were gathered at some distance, huddled together and all on their knees. There was a low murmur of prayer coming from the group, punctuated by the desolate sobbing of one very small page. A sensible-looking middle-aged matron got up from her knees, came to meet me and made me a dignified reverence.

"My Lord Bedivere, these centurions say they have orders to admit no one. Is that order yours? The queen has suffered a great shock. She is terribly disturbed. Surely you would not hold her like a prisoner, with no woman to attend on her?"

"Madam, there's no question of the queen being a prisoner," I said. "The guard is set for her protection, since there seems to have been trouble here I don't yet fully understand. I must speak with her now, but I promise you later she shall have full and proper attendance."

The woman's face crumpled, and she made an odd grimace, mastering tears with an effort. (She was a Roman Colonial, I remembered, and obviously held to the traditional control of the Roman matron.)

"Then—it's not true? We'd heard—they said—my lord, if the queen were to be accused—"

"She will be accused of nothing," I said sternly. "If she were, I myself would defend her innocence in arms. There has been treachery here tonight. When the king returns, he will see justice done on those responsible for it. Take my word on that."

"Thank God! Our prayers are answered, then," she said steadily. "Thank you, my lord. God bless you!"

The guards saluted and let me pass. I scratched on the door and when no one answered, tried it, and finding it unbarred I went in and closed it behind me, standing with my back against it, until my eyes could grow accustomed to the dim light within.

"It is I, Bedivere, madam. May I speak with you?" I said.

She did not answer. She was sitting facing me, a little

table inlaid with colored marble for the game of chess between us, on which one tall candle guttered in a gilded sconce. Her hair was unbound, falling all about her, and she was dressed as she so often was by choice, in white. She looked like a ghost, in the shadowy, richly appointed place, her hands clasped before her on the table, her eyes wide and watchful.

"Have you come to take me to my burning, Bedivere?" she asked.

Her voice was low and hoarse, and sent a shiver through me.

I said abruptly, to cover my disquiet.

"Why speak of such a thing? The fools should never have left you alone in here after such a terrifying experience. Why are there no lights? Wait while I call in your women."

"No, Bedivere! No! I want no one. Leave me alone. Tonight by thoughtless folly I've brought death on a man I once loved better than honor; better than life itself; and shame and grief on the finest, noblest husband any woman ever had. Leave me alone with the darkness of my own soul," she said dramatically.

It is a fault in me that I've never had patience with women's megrims. Self-pity, in man or woman either, has always raised the opposite of sympathy in my heart.

I moved quickly into the room, and taking flint and steel from my pouch, set about lighting the two great ornamental Roman lamps, and the sconce of candles by the wide, disordered bed. The room sprang into life about us, and I saw where a pitcher of wine and silver drinking cups stood in a recess by the window. I filled one of the cups, brought it to the table and set it down.

"Drink that, and take a hold on yourself, madam," I said sternly. "This is no time for wild talk. Call up your courage and remember you are a queen!" Then, as she looked up at me, startled, and I saw her face, still beautiful, but ravaged and gone old with a grief that, surely, was not play-acting, the eyelids swollen and red with weeping, my heart softened and I smiled down at her.

"Drink your wine and listen to me. All's not lost, for Lancelot's very far from dying. I've just come from him.

The blood you must have seen on him came mainly from
the scoundrelly young ruffian he was forced to kill. He
may have been stunned for a time, for he's caught a blow
on the face that'll mar his good looks for a while, and he's
got some minor cuts about the body. But he's very much
alive and in a towering rage—as all of us are, for that
matter. Have no fear. Those responsible for the fright and
the insult you've had tonight shall pay the price of it."

She closed her eyes and swayed against me so that I
put my arm about her shoulders.

"Bedivere," she murmured. "Oh, Bedivere! Is that
really true? He is alive and not badly hurt? Well enough
to be angry still? He was so terribly, so madly angry! I
think that was partly what terrified me—those men's
hatred, that I'd not guessed at ever, and his violence. He
fought like a madman."

"So would any of us have done," I said quickly (for
I'd remembered, uncomfortably, that Lancelot had once
been in truth mad).

She stared at me.

"Yes. I suppose you would. Perhaps no woman ever
wholly understands—" she murmured.

Suddenly she sat up straight, freeing herself from my
support, took the wine cup and drank from it. A little
color came back into her face.

"I must go away from here, Bedivere. I can't face
the court again—not a second time. The curious glances,
the whispering—the knowledge that there may be those
who, secretly hating me, plot to hurt the king and the
king's cause through me. I'll go to my nuns in the forest—I'll go tomorrow. Arthur will understand."

I thought, suddenly impatient again: "Women! Do
they never think of anything but their own feelings?"

It would mean arranging for an escort, detailing a
guard about the forest nunnery. I should have to go with
her myself and see to it she was safely established, if only
to prove no possible shadow of scandal clung to her and
that I, Arthur's second-in-command, honored her still as
Arthur's queen. All that must be done when the threat of
total war was upon us and I needed every moment to
oversee the preparations for it. But common sense told me

we'd do better with her away from Camelot, at least for a time.

I said, accepting necessity:

"If you, and such of your attendants as you choose to go with you, can be ready at first light, I'll ride with you myself. You've made a wise decision."

The queen's nunnery was deep in the forest, further off than I'd reckoned, the tracks that led to it narrow and winding, swampy in places, even in that high summer weather. We took near half a day to reach it, for no matter what is at stake, women must always carry baggage, and the hundred guards I'd detailed had their own equipment and supplies. One can't hurry led pack ponies, where there's only room for horsemen to ride single file.

When we reached the place and I'd seen to the disposal of the guard about the clearing where it stood, nothing would serve but that Griffin and I (I'd taken him with me that day) must eat with Guinevere and her nuns before we set out on the return journey.

Women, other than those like Ygern and Mawgan, who have proved my true battle comrades, have always amazed me by their volatile changes of mood. On the journey, Guinevere had been sunk in depression, nervous and apprehensive. But once we'd reached our destination, she became animated, apparently forgetting the reason for her coming, all eagerness to show me the place and explain the purpose for which she'd founded it. The nuns in their white woollen habits fluttered about us giving her a great welcome, honored and at the same time much put about by the importance of being chosen to give her refuge, I could see.

"We all love her so much, my lord. But I fear things here will be sadly different from Camelot," the prioress told me anxiously. "Of course we have our vegetable garden, the hens, the goats—but our life is austere and very quiet. At least, up to now it has been very quiet." She bent closer to me and asked anxiously: "All those soldiers in the forest—forgive me asking you, my lord, but are they—trustworthy?"

I guessed she was not doubting their loyalty as warriors, but their behavior as men.

I said, solemnly, in an equally discreet tone, "My lady abbess, I myself will vouch for it. You'll have no trouble from them. I chose veterans and sober, married men, at that. Their orders are to keep their distance and attend strictly to discipline. Security must be ensured, you'll understand, for war is imminent. The king will be in command of the host. He must be assured of the queen's safety."

She crossed herself.

"God protect him, and all of you, my lord. We'll do everything we can to care for his sweet, saintly lady. Having her with us will be a great privilege and a great happiness."

It all took time. Courtesy demanded that it should. But time, just then, to me, was precious as though the sands running through the hourglass were gold dust.

When the sun was already well down the sky, Griffin and I managed to get away. He'd been much impressed by the place and by the thriving orderliness of it.

"Poor lady, she'll find peace there, surely," he said piously.

"She may. She'll find enough interest to turn her mind from brooding, and that's more important at the moment," I answered impatiently. "Come now—the shortest way back, and no more time wasted!"

Forest tracks are bewildering at best. My mind on other things, I'd not marked any too well the way we'd come that morning and I questioned Griffin's memory of it. Overriding his advice where two paths forked, I lost us the way. Dusk had turned to full darkness when at last we got clear of the trees, out on the old paved road from which we could see the fort standing up from the flat marshland, a mile or more distant. An orange glow lit the sky above it.

"That's more than reflection of the watch fires. Something's burning up there, sir," Griffin called out sharply.

"More trouble!" I muttered, and swore as I urged my horse to a gallop.

When we reached the foot of the hill, though all seemed quiet about the palace, there was a tossing flare of torches on the ramparts of the fort, a clamor of shouting and the clash of arms as though the place was under attack.

"My God, sir—the Saxons!" Griffin shouted to me.

"It can't be!" I shouted back. "Don't be a fool, boy!"

We urged our laboring horses up the steep approach to the north gate, and I shouted again, more loudly, to the gate guard, to tell them who we were. As they opened up, I saw Lysas was the centurion of the day.

"Praise be it's you, sir!" he greeted me.

"Quick—what's wrong?" I asked him. "Is it an attack?"

"No, sir. Bloody mutiny. Those Rheged bastards! They got some rumor about last night's trouble. Heard you'd carried off the queen prisoner. Some blasted nonsense she's to be burned alive along of—well you can guess what for, sir. Stormed the south gate shouting they'd have Prince Constantine as hostage for her release."

"Have they got him?" I cut in.

"I can't rightly say, sir. Couldn't leave our post here, see. But all hell's let loose by the sound of things, and there's more behind it than meets the eye, if you ask me. Somebody's been issuing free liquor down at the camp and half the Clans are at each other's throats. We got news of that first and Sir Gawain and Sir Lancelot are down there with their chaps, restoring order. The Rheged attack came later. It's a proper messup all round, sir."

"Right! Stay where you are and hold this gate with your lives," I said, dismounting and drawing my sword. "Come with me, Griffin."

Lysas warned gruffly:

"Be careful how you go, sir. The Rheged are in an ugly mood. Take some of my men with you."

"They can't be spared. Attend to your duty and I'll attend to mine," I said shortly. We smiled grimly, understanding each other very well.

"Along the rampart—the trouble's up there by the

sound of it," I said to Griffin over my shoulder, and took
the steps three at a time.

Once on the rampart I could see it was the south
gate tower that was burning. Between me and the fire a
dense crowd surged around one of the catapults. The
fighting, if there'd been fighting, appeared to be over. A
man was standing up on the catapult shaft, haranguing the
crowd, a black figure, lit by tossing torches and the fiery
sky beyond. There were shouts and boos and a dull
muttering undercurrent of noise, but the voice of the
speaker could be heard above it—a shrill, hysterical,
screaming voice, more like a woman's than a man's.

Griffin, beside me, panted:

"That's Sir Aglavain. Christ! How did he get free?"

We were up to the fringe of the crowd, packed close
and intent, their backs all turned to us. Below the rampart on the under side there were more, their faces white
blurs, looking upwards.

"Wait!" I said to Griffin.

The screaming voice carried, now, so that I could
hear the words.

"Which will you follow? An outworn, impotent king,
fallen so low he'll let himself be cuckolded in his own
bedchamber by the lecher he's tolerated twenty years, or
a leader for the New Age—Medraut, the man who has
ruled Britain for the old Pendragon this long time past,
and ruled it wisely? Medraut, the king's son, robbed too
long of his heritage, Medraut, the man who has given you
stable government, prosperity and security, while Arthur
dreamed away his days on the Druid's Island, under the
enchantments of Merlin the Wizard.

"Listen to me, all of you. There's no need for this
war. Only the vanity of the veteran Companions leads us
into it. Proclaim Prince Medraut Pendragon and he'll
save you from war. With him the Saxon chiefs would
make treaty tomorrow, for they know and trust him. They
could be allies, not enemies—allies against the Pictish
menace, as the honest Federates were in Vortigern's
day—a strong shield-wall between your homes and the
painted savages of the north."

"And who'd pay for them doing it?" a voice shouted

out of the darkness. Heads turned; a mutter, that was half agreement, half protest, went round.

"Britain has the resources, if we had the right man to use them. How much do you think the queen and her lover have spent over the years on the great palace below there? How much will war cost you—and you—and you? Your farms burning, your fields trampled, your children starving, while your own lives are thrown away, squandered, sacrificed to the vanity of old men, who were great warriors once maybe (at least they would have you believe they were), but are now not able to sit a battle charger without being thrown and needing other men's wives to tend their bruises after!"

There was a guffaw of laughter. Someone shouted:

"If Prince Medraut's to lead us, why isn't he here? Where is he?"

"He is not far away. When he comes, he'll come with an army—a well-paid army—behind him. Take the fort and hold it until he reaches us and he'll reward every man among you—reward you richly, with gold and land and spoil from the houses of the rich who have grown fat on your honest labor this twenty years past. The Clans have declared against the oppression of the outworn few who've ruled Britain too long. Swear allegiance to Medraut now and he'll lead you to peace and prosperity!"

They cheered him, the fools. A ragged cheer, at first, but men are like sheep. The cheering grew to a thunder. As it died down, a voice I recognized as that of one of my own decurions bellowed angrily:

"What about the king? Haven't we sworn allegiance to him?"

Aglavain's voice rose to a hysterical scream:

"Arthur's day is over. Can a man rule Britain who can't rule his own household? Merlin the wizard, Guinevere the witch and Lancelot the lecher rule Arthur now. Will you let those three lead you, blindfold, to bloody death?"

Ahead of me on the edge of the crowd, I'd noticed one of the archers I knew well. In the torchlight his face had told me by its cynical expression Aglavain's oratory was not swaying him to the general hysteria. I tapped him on the shoulder and said in his ear, as he turned his head, startled, and I saw he'd recognized me:

"Lend me your bow and a good sharp arrow."

When, at Midsummer, a hound goes mad, the only thing to be done is to put it down, before its venomed bite spreads infection to man and beast.

It was a long shot, and the torchlight tricky. But Palomides had not been my teacher for nothing. I breathed a prayer to his watching shade, and drew the strong war bow full stretch.

The arrow took Aglavain in the throat, as I'd aimed it. The shaft must have stood out two-thirds of its length, for when I saw his body later, only the flight feathers showed between his clutching fingers, crooked rigid in death.

As he pitched down off the catapult shaft I put my shoulder to the crowd, burst my way through and sprang up to take his place. A white blaze of anger blinded me, playing round me like a levin flash. I'd no idea what I was shouting down at the pale sea of faces below me. Words came to me, that night, as sometimes my music came. It is the sign the gods mark upon a Chosen Bard. Griffin told me, afterwards, admiringly, he'd never heard anyone, save Arthur before battle, rouse soldiers' hearts with such a trumpet call to action. (But Griffin has kept, all his life, something of the exaggerated devotion he gave me when he was my frog-faced page!)

Whatever I said, it got them quiet and listening. Once that was achieved, I dropped my voice, and spoke the cold common sense I guessed they were sobered enough by then to understand. I reminded them of Arthur's twelve great battles.

"Most of you are too young to remember those times. But remember this—you've lived soft because we fought hard. You've had security and plenty, because men paid with their lives to buy those blessings for you. Will you let all your fathers earned be robbed from you by clever rascals, who care for nothing but their own ambition? You aren't fools. Use your heads. Reckon what the cost would be of buying off invasion—of hiring wolf to eat wolf for us. I tell you, it is you who'd find yourselves torn to pieces, a flock of silly sheep caught between two ravening packs. The Saxons and the Picts would eat Britain whole, and you'd get an iron slave collar, every one of you they left alive, for your share of the plunder. Your children and your children's children would wear the same, and curse your memory as they starved and shivered.

"Britain—a free Britain—is still ours tonight. Tonight, each one of you is free. United under the Dragon standard of Arthur we can keep things that way. Let treachery divide us now, and all will be lost.

"I Bedivere, who have never lied to you, tell you now that the price of freedom is heavy. I know, for I have paid it, in my time, with blood and pain and hunger and hardship, and with bitter sorrow for friends who fell in battle beside me, missing the good days we'd hoped to share. But I tell you never, never once have I grudged that price. A free country was worth it to me, and will be to every one of you who survives the inevitable conflict we must all face, and that cannot, now, be avoided.

"I am old, and so are the greatest of the Companions who are left. So is the king. But we are not too old, yet, to remember what past wars taught us. Arthur the Pendragon, Arthur the War Duke, the one man the Saxons ever learned to fear, alone can lead us to victory. Who will swear again the oath of allegiance to him? Who is for Arthur and Free Britain tonight?"

Any man who was convinced enough of his cause, as I was, could have swayed them. Half-drunk and mob-happy, they'd have been easy enough prey to anyone with the gift of words. At the finish I had them all on their knees, swearing by their various gods, with sobs and strange soldiers' oaths, to follow Arthur to the death and beyond, if need be.

By the time Gawain and Lancelot, with a flushed triumphant Constantine, fresh from his first taste of action, riding between them, got back, reporting all quiet in the camp below, we'd no difficulty in restoring discipline. But the hospital was busy all night, and burying parties were at work next day, both at the fort and down at the camp. For us, war had begun before it was declared. The first casualties were men mauled or killed by those who should have been battle comrades. That was not all. Worse, to my mind, was a fact that we only fully realized by noon the following day, when we found gaps left where before the camp had been close-packed. The Rheged Princes had deserted, taking their whole Clan levy with them. So had a few minor Clans, whom I'd been none too sure of from the first. The loss in numbers was not great. But it was something that had never happened to us before. I asked myself, if it was to Medraut they were going, just where did they have reason to believe they might rally to his standard?

# VIII
# REQUIEM

# Chapter Thirty

The wind changed with the new moon. It was still blowing strongly, east by north, at the end of the first quarter.

"A Saxon wind—they'll not be long now," Arthur predicted. "Well, we're ready for them."

He'd come back from Adurni grimly gay, content with what he'd found there. Our fleet was at sea, beating up and down the coast, ready to fight a running sea battle, if need be, with the Saxon galleys.

"They'll be outnumbered, five to one, if the reports of the enemy's strength prove correct. That's unimportant. Their task is to confuse and delay the attack, so that we have time to prepare a welcome wherever the landing is directed," he explained. "Hang on their flanks and snap at their heels. They've got to the task, keen as hounds on a hot scent."

I was glad that, at least, had cheered him. The report I was forced to give him of the happenings at the fort in his absence, he took with fatalistic calm.

"What must be must be! You handled things as I would have done myself. It's over and can't be helped now. First things must come first from now on, and the first thing for us is to see we smash the invasion fleet, and do it on the beaches, with no chance of the enemy getting a bridgehead and harrying inland."

"And Medraut?" I asked.

Arthur frowned for a moment, then said with decision:

"The gods willing, there'll be time to deal with him later. He's cautious by nature. I think he'll wait to attack us, if attack is in his mind, until he sees which way the cat jumps. A decisive victory might well decide him to change his tactics and sue for a pardon. Otherwise he's your pigeon, Bedivere. You'll have to hold him off somehow until we can get reinforcements to you. Understood?"

"Understood," I said.

"One other thing. Constantine stays with you. We must divide the risk as well as we can. If Medraut shows himself with an army, put the boy in command here, while you march to meet the rebels. It will salve his pride and keep him safe for Britain's future. No man's luck can last for ever, and if mine fails me this time—well—" he shrugged.

"Your luck will hold," I said. "Bear—will you ride to the nuns' house in the forest before you go?"

He shook his head.

"Impossible! There's no time. Guinevere will understand. Let her know that I make nothing of that damned poppycock affair of Aglavain's, will you? And Bedivere, tell her my love is with her, even though I've not time to say farewell."

"I'll tell her. But she'll grieve," I warned him.

He made a quick, impatient gesture.

"In war there is always grief. This is not going to be an easy war. It is one we have got to win," he said sternly.

There followed a few more days of feverish activity. Lancelot and Bors with the light cavalry went off first. Then word came through that the invasion fleet had been sighted and was heading for the Federal beaches. The main body of the host struck camp and marched away. I did my best, on the final morning, to persuade Gawain to change command with me. His arm was painful and inflamed, for he'd got a blow on it during the mêlée down in the camp on the night of the mutiny.

"You'll not take the weight of a shield on that in time for battle. It smells of pus through the bandages as it is. Don't be a fool, man!" I urged him. "Stay here and give it a chance to heal clean."

He scowled at me, his eyes smoldering.

"I'll no have it said *two* of my house were traitors. Leave me to win back some kind of respect for the Clan of Dalriada, will you?" he growled. Then his face softened. Suddenly he reached out and wrung my hand. "Thanks for the offer, just the same. It was kindly meant. I'll no forget it."

Half an hour later, his arm in a sling, he trotted through the north gate at the head of the cavalry, his standard-bearer behind him. I watched them wind down the long, steep track, four abreast, the men well armed, the horses groomed and shining, the centurions' red cloaks catching the early light. They were a strong, well-disciplined force. Most of them looked very young to me, that day. Perhaps that was why a strange sadness twisted my heart and the clang of the closing gates behind the rearguard sounded loud and hollow.

The waiting time began. It was the worst of many I remember.

I sent Griffin to carry Arthur's messages to the queen. He came back with a reassuring report.

"She wept a little, poor lady—that's only to be expected. But she is most piously resigned and busying herself about the convent's affairs. The nuns say she's an example to them all."

"Are the guards behaving themselves?" I asked, being practical.

He laughed.

"Indeed they are! The queen's set them to clearing the forest round about, cutting great stores of firewood and building barns and byres. The whole place hums like a hive at the honey-flow. If she hadn't been a queen, she'd have made a grand abbess, sir!"

That took one weight off my mind. I set myself to practical tasks, seeing to it the palace was evacuated, moving all valuables that could be moved up to the fort, sending as many of the women and children as I could

away to their families or friends well inland, and fortify-
ing the great, sprawling building itself as well as I could
against attack, with surrounding earthworks and trenches.
That, at least, kept my men occupied, though I knew well
enough that in any serious crisis the first thing we should
have to do would be abandon the place and stand siege
within the fort.

At the end of a month rumors began to come in of a
rebel army under Medraut showing itself. The trouble was
it appeared to be in a dozen different places, all of them
remote and most of them unlikely. He had set up his
standard below Yr Widdfa, and the dissidents of Wales
were flocking to him. He had made alliance with the
Irish, and was waiting for a great pirate fleet to join him
somewhere in the Severn estuary. He was leading the
Federates of Humber Side and all the Rheged had gone
over to him. He was still in Armorica, gathering an army
and a fleet which would attack Vectis first and, having
taken it, make Camelot the next objective.

Since it was obvious he could not be in all those
places, I guessed he was in none of them, and the stories
were being sent about to confuse and demoralize us. Only
a fool would have played into his hands by sending out an
army to chase will-o'-the-wisps in a bog. But the uncertainty frayed nerves and tempers and made the waiting
time even harder to bear.

It ended abruptly, when, on one and the same day,
two messengers reached me, both men whose word I
could trust.

The first had made the journey south from Dalriada
in shorter time than it had ever been made in living
memory—a great, red-haired giant of a Clansman, his
eyelids swollen with lack of sleep, and (I suspected)
weeping. He had come to fetch Gawain, and the urgent
need to find him seemed the only thought left in the
fellow's travel-dazed head.

"I mun get to him. Himself is the only one left who
can save us. The dead will rise from their bloody graves
to follow Prince Gawain. He's the only hope left us now!"
he kept repeating wildly.

I got the truth from him at last. The Picts, reinforced

by a strong host of Angles, had swept down on Dalriada like a tidal wave, outnumbering the army of the north five to one. Gaheris and Gareth were dead—the enemy ravaging the whole countryside.

"They'll be over the Wall by now. The Rheged canna hold them. Only himself, with a host behind him, can save us. I mun get to him, happen what may!"

He was reeling with exhaustion, but I knew the tough fibre of his Clan too well to try and hold him back.

"You'll get to your High Prince more quickly than you could ride alone if I send you with one my charioteers," I said. "Get yourself food and drink while I write a message for the king."

It would be hard news for Arthur. But only he could judge what must be done. If he had beaten the invaders on the beaches, he might be able to march north himself, or he might send Gawain with half his host, and call on me for reinforcements. In any case, an eyewitness account of the disaster would help both Arthur and Gawain to judge how best to counter it.

From the ramparts I watched a charioteer whip up his black Icenian team as they came out from among the marshes. He was crouching forward, urging them as though he'd been competing in the Hippodrome. I sighed with relief and turned back, to find one of the gate guards at my shoulder.

"Another messenger just in, my lord," he reported woodenly.

"From the king?" I asked. If the battle of the beaches was over . . .

"Says he's from Lyonesse, my lord."

I found the man waiting for me in the guardroom, a man I remembered—one who had served under me the year I'd been with Leonore, grizzled, hard-bitten, quiet-spoken. When he told me Medraut had landed in Lyonesse with an expeditionary force from Armorica, and was raising the west against us, I knew I could trust his word for it.

"He represents himself as regent for the Prince Constantine, my lord. He's spread a story the king has been

bewitched out of his mind, and is no longer fit to rule.
There's talk the queen and the Lord Lancelot have seized
Camelot and hold Prince Constantine hostage. Some say
the king's been murdered, others that there's been a battle
somewhere on the coast, and he's been defeated and
killed. All Lyonesse is in uproar, and the folk pouring in
to Sir Medraut's standard, believing their High Prince is
in danger, and that Sir Medraut marches to his rescue."

"Where did Medraut land?" I asked.

"Near the Land's End. But he's moving north fast.
His scouting parties were on the south bank of the Tavy
when I crossed the ford into Dumnonia three days back."

I thanked him and would have given him a reward
for his service, but he smiled and shook his head.

"The Lioness herself sent me, sir. Abbess she may
be, now, but she hasn't changed. She said to tell you she
trusts her son to your keeping and bids him stand fast to
his allegiance, as she herself will always do. With your
permission, my lord, I'd her orders to take service with
you against the rebels."

His loyalty and Leonore's message warmed my
heart. I sent him to get himself food and rest, and went to
my quarters. I needed to be alone with his news for a
time.

We were encircled on four sides. Picts to the north,
Saxons to the south and east, Medraut to the west. If
Rheged broke, could Lancelot and Bors hold the Picts
long enough to defend Arthur's rear? If I, myself, led the
host at my command against Medraut, and the battle on
the beaches went against Arthur, I should leave him
without reinforcements. Which of the Clans could I trust?
Which of them had Medraut undermined?

We needed more men—the Fire-Scathed Branch,
which signifies total mobilization of every man and boy
who can carry arms, must go out immediately. But I
could not spare heralds and horses to carry it. Someone
scratched urgently on my door, then, before I'd had time
to answer, Constantine burst it open, breathing fast, as
though he had been running.

"Sir—my lord—I've just come from the Island—the

Lady Ygern says . . ." he paused, staring. He must have seen something in my face that halted him.

"Well?" I said.

He drew a deep breath.

"She sent me to tell you not to forget the path under the fern. I don't know what she meant, sir, but she said it was urgent."

"Gods, boy, she was right!" I was on my feet, cursing myself for a fool. The Little People of the Hills—the Merlin's messengers!

I dropped back into my seat.

"Sit down. Listen to me carefully. There's bad news, Constantine. You and I have got to keep our heads, and I need you to help me."

I told him briefly exactly how matters stood. He went a little white when he heard Gaheris and Gareth had both fallen in battle. He was new to death, still, then. But he took it well, and when he'd heard me to the end he only said:

"What must we do now, sir?"

"You are a Dragon, free of the Island. Take an escort and ride back there immediately. I've a message for the Lady Ygern," I said. "Tell her what I've just told you. Say, the time has come for the Scathed Branch to go out and I've no messengers I can spare. Say, it must go by the old road under the fern. She'll understand."

He got up, saluted and turned to go. At the door he hesitated a moment.

"Well, what is it?" I growled.

He faced me, his eyes steady, but pleading.

"Sir, I was thinking—if you march against Sir Medraut and the rebels, couldn't I go with you? I'm High Prince of Lyonesse, after all, and . . ."

"You're High Prince of Britain. Your place is where the Pendragon ordered," I said sternly. "Now get on with your errand before the daylight wanes."

I liked his spirit, but one must keep discipline. Besides, I could not rest until I knew that the Merlin's magic had been set working again, and that once more small bare feet would be running through the fern, and smoke

signals spiralling from the Outland hills the length and
breadth of a threatened Britain.

Three days later, at the hour when the women left in the
fort were cooking the noon meal, Arthur himself rode in
at the north gate, with a guard of less than a century. The
horses were sweating, the men bloodstained, filthy and
hollow-eyed with fatigue.

As I myself went to the king's side to help him
dismount, I looked up into his face and thought: "So this
is it! For the first time, Arthur has met defeat. That is
why he sent no message before him."

I gave the reins to a page and moved quickly to
steady him as he got off his horse, staggering a little, stiff
from the saddle.

He smiled at me, a quick, grim smile.

"Tell the guard to sound the trumpets for victory.
We've beaten them again, Bedivere."

*"Victory?"* I said, not believing my ears.

He nodded. In a voice so low those about us did not
hear: "You could call it that. But at what a price!" he
muttered. Aloud, with a sudden impatience that reminded
me of Kay—"Get on, man! Give the order. I must make
the announcement, and then in the name of Light give us
something to eat. We've ridden without rest to get here,
and the smell of whatever's cooking reminds me of the
wolf in my stomach!"

When the cheering was over and we were alone in
my quarters, he dropped all pretense of cheerfulness,
turned and put his hands on my shoulders.

"Bedivere, we beat them but the price was too
heavy—we've lost Gawain. He should never have fought
with a shield. A seaxe caught him in the chest and he
died hard. I can't get his face out of my mind."

I put my arms round him and for a moment his head
went down on my shoulder.

"It was a bloody battle. They were all so young—so
inexperienced," he muttered thickly, and repeated, "Gawain died hard."

A shudder went through him. Then he straightened
up and pushed me roughly aside.

"Enough of this! I've heard your news already for we met your messenger by the way. It's bad, but not so bad there's not an answer to it. I've sent half the host to reinforce Lancelot's defense of the Dike. The other half is following on close behind and should be here, barring the badly wounded, by this evening. We must be on the road to the west with all your reserves and every man of mine who's fit to fight again, before cock-light. You'll have to come with me. There's no one else I'd trust to lead the cavalry. This rebellion must be smashed before we turn to and clear the north."

"And Camelot? Who will command here?" I asked.

"Constantine. It's the only answer I can give the boy why he can't ride with us. It'll be a heavy enough responsibility to satisfy his self-respect, for we can leave him only a garrison of walking wounded, and a few grey-bearded veterans. There'll be danger in it, but less than if he came with us, the gods willing. If we do our work thoroughly and quickly enough, Medraut won't get this far, and Lancelot and Bors should be able to hold the Heartland frontier until we get back. Everything depends on speed, now."

Before we could say more, Griffin scratched on the door and came in, carrying wine and followed by a page with a platter of hot stewed meat, and a trencher of bannocks, fresh-baked.

"The men—are they fed?" Arthur asked him.

"Yes, my lord. They are eating now," Griffin assured him.

"Good. When they've finished, send them to get what sleep they can. They need it, poor devils!" Arthur said, and began himself to break open a bannock; slapping meat inside it, he looked up at Griffin and smiled. "My thanks for this! See to it my fellows' weapons and equipment are checked over for them while they rest, will you? And, Griffin, warn the guards the Lady Ygern will be here soon. She's to be passed through without ceremony and brought immediately to me here."

"I'll attend to both things, my lord," Griffin said quietly.

As the door closed behind him, Arthur said:

"There's one, at least, we can trust! It's a strange feeling, Bedivere, to have to look twice at every man before one can give an order, to be sure it will be obeyed without question," he said bitterly. The treachery of Medraut and Medraut's faction had hit him hard—the harder, I thought, because his own greatness of heart left him totally unprepared for littleness in other men.

He must have read my thought, for tearing ravenously at the bread and meat, he looked up at me, and cocked an eyebrow in the old, apologetic expression with which he'd always admitted in the past that I'd proved to have the right of an argument.

"A lesser man than you, Bedivere, would remind me I was warned!" he said with his mouth full. The grooved weariness of his face made the smile he gave me almost more than I could bear without tears just then. I said gruffly:

"Forget that! We've other things to think of. You must leave the preparations to me and get some rest yourself, if you can. Why have you sent for Ygern, Bear?"

(She had never, since his illness, left Ynis Witrin to come to us. The fact he must have summoned her had startled me.)

"I've not time to go to the Island, and I must see her. There are things that need to be settled between us. Since Blaize's death and the Merlin's going, she, as Lady of the Lake, holds full responsibility for my people of the Old Faith, now. The Hallows of Britain are in her keeping, Bedivere—and something tells me this battle may be my last," he said. His voice was level, matter of fact. He added, suddenly impatiently again, "Don't stare at me like that, man. Death comes to all of us. You know as well as I do, it's not the end—only careless fools or men who fear to face it leave the settling of their affairs to chance at a moment like this!"

I never knew what passed between those two that day, though some of it I guessed from later events. I only know that riding back, in a grey, windless dusk, from the camp that evening, I came out from the shadow of the palace trees and heard the clip-clop of a pony's trot on the track down from the fort. I thought it was one of the boys with a message, and reined my horse aside to let him pass. Then I saw her and thought I had seen a ghost out of the past. She was riding alone, dressed as she used to dress, in tartan trews and tunic, the woollen cloak shawled over her head so that her hair was hidden; and her face looked out from the folds, small and pale and determined, with eyes very dark and shadowed. Swirls of mist were rising from the river, drifting about her and the shaggy, sure-footed little beast she was riding. She was my comrade, again, the comrade I had lost so long ago. All my heart cried out to her, but I sat my horse as though enchantment had fallen on me, and if she had gone past me I could not have called her name.

It was only the impression of a moment. When she pulled the pony in sharply, the cloak fell back, and I saw her hair, silvery as the mist, and her face, calm and lined, as I knew it on the Island, the face of a Priestess, apart and used to command.

We talked together for a little, briefly, without waste of words, as men talk who, sharing a command under stress of immediate danger, must know each other's plans. I did not doubt what she told me. She had always had the Sight. To question it then would have been to lose the little time that was left to us.

"Medraut will take the coast road. He still counts on reinforcements from the sea and he may get them. When you join battle it will be between the mere and the sea, and there will be treachery up to the last. Watch for it. Now listen to me, Bedivere. If Arthur is wounded, or worse still, if he is killed, we must keep it from the country as long as possible. Without him, panic could spread and paralyze resistance. I and the Merlin's people will be close at hand to help you at need. You know the cry of the waterbird that Celidon taught you? Use that at the last extremity, and we shall be there."

"Between the mere and the sea—on the coast road? There's only one place—where old Julius used to take us hunting wild duck, not far from the home Dunn. Will it be there, Ygern?" I asked.

"That is where I see it. One can never be quite sure. But that will be the place, I think."

"You always hated it, remember?" I said.

She shivered a little.

"Yes. Always," she said brusquely. Then, as though brushing aside that memory, "By water, one could get a wounded man away from there more easily than by road. The Merlin's people know the whole network of the waterways. It could be a swift and secret going. If you need us, Bedivere, we shall not fail you. It will be for you to give the sign."

I smiled at her.

"You seem very sure I shall live to give it," I said, trying to speak lightly.

She shook her head, grave and pitying.

"My dear, I am afraid—afraid for your own sake— it's in your stars you must," she said. Then, quite suddenly, she leaned across and kissed me. "The gods go with you, Bedivere," she said, and the next moment had kicked her horse forward and disappeared into the shadow of the trees.

It must have lacked less than an hour to midnight before I could persuade Arthur to lie down and rest. Everything was in order for a dawn start by then and I'd seen weariness growing on him.

He seemed oddly reluctant and said, gruffly, at last:

"Sleep comes hardly since the battle; full of bad dreams. Leave a light burning, will you, and lie down beside me? I'd sooner not have one of the pages in the room."

I understood why, when he roused from the first deep sleep of exhaustion an hour later, tossing and muttering, and then suddenly started up with a great cry:

"Gawain!"

By the light of the cresset beside the bed, I saw his face was pale, his forehead beaded with sweat.

He blinked at me, as I bent over him.

"Is that you, Bedivere? Gods—that dream! I see him again, every time I sleep. He died so hard a death; struggling to speak and no breath left to speak with. He

seems to go past me on a great, rushing wind, drowning
again in his own blood, crying a soundless warning that
only bubbles in his throat!" and he shuddered.

"It's only a dream. He's out of that pain now. Try to
rest and forget," I said. I'd never known him like this
before.

He sighed and lay back, staring at the cresset's small
flame.

"Gawain, Gaheris, Gareth—all gone. I loved them
from the first as if they were my sons. We shall never see
them again. 'Never' seems such a long word, Bedivere, at
a time like this!"

"One does not know how long until death is the
measure," I said grimly. "But those three, more than
most we've known, would find it hard to credit the Arthur
they knew would let useless grieving rob him of needed
rest before a forced march."

That stung him, as I hoped it might, to a few round
soldiers' oaths. After which, almost at once, he fell asleep
again, and slept quietly until his pages came to rouse us
and arm him for the march.

Outside it was black dark, still, though I could smell
the dawn. The cavalry were mustering by torchlight on
the exercise ground. Below, in the camp, we could hear
the stir of the infantry forming up, and the sharp, barked
orders of the centurions.

After a few brief words with the Companions who
were left, Arthur sent for Constantine, to hand over the
command of the fort to him. The boy came forward, out
of the shadows, into the ring of torches about us. He wore
half armor, and his High Prince's circlet round his leather
headguard. He looked his full age in that dress—stocky,
grave, dependable. He was holding himself very erect.

Arthur went through the ceremony of handing him
the keys and giving him the password for the day. Then
he waved the Companions back a little, and spoke to him
quietly.

"You know your orders. Camelot must be held at all
costs until we return. You've enough men for that, though
I wish we could spare you more. You have experienced
veteran commanders under you. Listen to their advice if

things go badly with us. I was not much older than you when I took over the command of all Britain. What I did then, at need, you can do again. Remember that."

Constantine said steadily:

"I will remember. We shall hold Camelot for you, my lord." Suddenly he looked young and wistful. "But I wish I was coming with you. I'd have liked to fight in a real battle."

Arthur laughed.

"You'll fight in plenty, lad. That, at least, I can promise you!" His face grew grave, his eyes kindling as he looked at the eager, pleading face. "Remember, when you do, speed, surprise and the right use of cavalry—those have been my tactics. They'll serve you. One thing more. Never admit you are beaten. If you have only three hundred men behind you, you can make a dint in a war host of three thousand. If you have only thirty, you can still make a running fight of it, and harass the enemy's flanks. If you are the one man left, take to the forest, take to the hills, but go on fighting, until, for very shame, new recruits rally to you. I say this to you, because, if I die, you will be the Pendragon, and on you Britain's survival will depend.

"Now, get down on your knees. Before we march, I must knight you and make you a Companion."

Constantine's face had gone rather white, and very solemn, while he listened. Now the color came flooding back into it, and his eyes blazed with excitement.

"Oh sir—my lord!" he stammered. "I've done nothing to deserve that. I've not proved myself yet."

Arthur's smile was warm and approving.

"I know. But you will. I trust you. If need be, I trust Britain to you," he said. "Kneel, now, to receive the accolade."

The red torchlight ran down the blade of Excalibur like the flicker of a flame, as it touched the boy's bent head and each of his square, straight shoulders. So short a ceremony, shorn of all the mysterious magic that had marked the reception of Peredur. Yet it had strength behind it, and power, and the bracing urgency of that cold, dark hour before the dawn.

On the plain below, a trumpet sounded the shrill, high note that precedes the centurion's command.

*"In order of battle, infantry advance!"*

Somewhere, in the ring of darkness beyond the torches, a charger neighed in answer to it. As the torch-bearers began to move outwards, I caught the gleam of polished flanks and rippling manes where the heavy cavalry waited.

Arthur turned from Constantine and looked out into the darkness.

"I am ready. Bring up the horses," he ordered.

A page led forward the great white stallion of the king.

# Chapter Thirty-One

The task is finished. I have kept my word to Paulinus. He has his facts; the disposition and numbers of the troops involved, the day and date and result of Arthur's last battle are all written down, now, safe between the bull's-hide covers of his big brown book.

It is to his credit that, by the end, he was snivelling. A great tear dropped on his parchment. It will have made the ink run blurred and give a later copyist trouble in deciphering his script. He thanked me very humbly, as he closed his book for the last time; and kissed my hand and went out very quietly, wiping his nose on the sleeve of his habit. I listened to the flap of his sandals, dying away into the distance, and lay back exhausted. The memories of all I had not told him passed like a procession behind my closed eyelids. The things a man concerned only with facts could never understand. The things that only Bards and the defeated know.

I smelt again the salt wind, and saw long combers crashing on a pebble ridge in the bright September morning. I saw the horned poppies, and some blue flower, with prickled leaves, bending all one way among the sparse reed grass that covers a two-mile stretch of wasteland between a dark, still mere and those flashing breakers. It is a strange shore, Camlan. As a boy I had not shared Ygern's uneasiness there. It was a place where I had been happy for days on end, wild-fowling and fishing. Only, sometimes, when the sea mist dropped suddenly, and our

dogs came back out of the tall bulrushes that fringe the
mere, their tails low, shivering, and when the fishermen
warned that the mere lay always so still because its waters
were fathomless, it struck me it might be unchancy.

"The mere has no bottom—the waters go down into
Anawn," they said. "Nothing lost there can ever be
dredged up again."

We went westward that last three days' forced marching, by the old paved legions road through Isca to Totnesia, and turned down to the coast where men had
mounded a great earth fort once, time out of mind, on the
high hill beyond.

The green native trackway brought us to the shore at
its northern end, where the river runs to the mere and
there is an opening to the sea. Two miles away, where the
coast track from Lyonesse winds round the base of tall
red cliffs, we saw the glittering spearpoints of Medraut's
army, a great green standard, with a black dragon
sprawled across it, leading the van.

Had we engaged battle immediately, the end might
have been different. But there was delay. Medraut sent
heralds, asking for a parley. I think Arthur hoped, even
then, it might mean the man he had trusted repented his
treachery

The armies were halted. The leading commanders on
both sides went forward, to meet halfway along the shore,
while the two hosts watched, suspicious and on guard.

All men know the story. It is said, and some believe
it, that a sword drawn at the parley by one of Medraut's
men was drawn in good faith because he saw an adder
close by his heel. It may be so. I only know that, as a
boy, I never saw an adder there. The wind off the sea is
cold in autumn. Adders seldom troubled us in Dumnonia,
except when midsummer heat set the pollen of the Outland heather smoking, and the rocks were warm for them
to bask upon.

The result of a weapon's flash during parley under
truce was predictable. The men of both armies smelt
treachery. There was a wild, yelling rush of warriors,
waiting no word of command. Discipline lost at the start
of a battle is discipline lost for good. All day we fought,

hemmed in between mere and sea, a mêlée of shouting men and screaming horses, milling up and down a trampled, bloody strand, friend hard to distinguish from enemy, except where Medraut's Saxon levy, in their horned helmets, fought savagely and well. The advantage changed constantly on the constricted ground, so that the struggle swayed back and forth from end to opposite end of the shoreline. Sometime in late afternoon the wind dropped, the sun clouded over, and mist—the thick white mist I remembered—swept round us suddenly like blowing wool. Out of it, to seaward, came a snarl of warhorns, and then, looming, the curved black serpent beaks of the galleys. Not many, but enough. Their crews were fresh, our men bone-weary with the long day's battle and the forced marching before.

I myself rode up and down, slashing my way through to rally the cavalry, and we charged them as they landed. I'd forgotten the pebble ridge shelves straight into deep water all its length. Horses and men drowned together as the weight of those behind carried the first rank over the verge. My charger lost his footing. I flung off my cloak and swam beside him, urging him up the beach again, hauling on the slippery reins as I clawed my own way to a footing. Shivering and snorting, the stones flying from his flailing hooves, he came out, streaming water, and I mounted and fought on, my hands bruised and numb, my clothes heavy and hampering.

Out in the mist, darkening as the day waned, Griffin came up alongside me, shouting:

"My lord, the king's down! Just now, I saw him fall!"

Before I could answer, a crowd of Saxons from the galleys were round us and we'd our work cut out to keep alive. He was separated from me; hidden. I heard the scream of a dying horse where the mist rolled between us, but could do nothing to help him. A seaxe whirled past my ear, and a spearpoint gashed my side. Then all about me, Saxon voices were yelling guttural cries of panic. I caught the name "Bretwald Medraut!" and their word for "dead."

The enemy about me broke away, disappearing into

the gathering twilight. I heard their war horns braying, and, from far up the strand, our own trumpets, sharp, short, urgent, sounding the signal I'd never heard before except on the exercise ground—the double notes, three times repeated, that sounded for *Retreat*.

I found them, the king and the man who betrayed him, just before the last light went, when I'd searched on foot the whole length of that ghastly, abandoned shore. I understood then why both armies had fled the field, leaving only the dead and the dying to bear me company.

A little wind had risen with evening and a pale gleam of light showed me a white horse, standing, its head drooping, riderless, foundered. Without that faithful, waiting shape I might never have found him—Arthur, my lord.

Medraut I knew by his clothes only. His face no man could have recognized, mashed out of human shape by the deadly downward strike of a trained battle charger. He must have been dead before that blow caught him, for the great cross-hilt of Excalibur stood up out of his heart, as once I had seen it stand above the altar beneath the hanging stones.

I spared him one glance only. Then I knelt down at the king's side.

"Arthur—Bear—it is I, Bedivere—I have come!" I whispered hoarsely.

He was breathing—but he had taken one of the Three Great Wounds, a deep, ragged gash at the base of the neck biting deep into the shoulder. Skillfully delivered, that stroke severs the vein of the neck and is fatal. But Medraut was always a bungler. Most likely his horse had shied. "He could never rule a horse," I muttered.

Thoughts, broken, disconnected, followed each other through my mind like the drift of the mist wreaths still curling thinly all about me, while my bruised hands fumbled, trying to clear the splinters of his bronze shoulder scales, and loosen the stiffened leather strap that held them. Something puzzled me and my mind groped. This wound was on the right. Medraut the left-handed swords-

man—the traitor's blow on the unguarded side. He'd
signed his work, as Excalibur signed Arthur's. They must
have gone down together, both leaders at the same moment. That would account for the panic that had swept
the field so strangely clear—so eerily deserted.

As I cut away the bull's-hide corselet, and the torn
rags of the tunic beneath it, I saw how deep the wound
had gone. There was not much bleeding. Only a slow,
relentless welling from the centre. A bad sign. Wounds
that do not bleed freely fester fast. I needed hot water
and salt, clean linen pads and astringent herbs. I had
nothing. Nothing but torn strips of my own undertunic,
filthy with sweat and battle grime. Arthur's flesh felt cold,
even to my cold hands, as I worked to draw the bandage
tight. My cloak was lost, his caught and crumpled, a
sodden mass under him. I tried to pull it clear and wrap it
round him, but he lay too heavily—heavy already as a
dead man. A terrible lethargy closed down over me; a
feeling of utter helplessness. I lifted my head to curse the
gods and felt on my face the fine mist turning to heavy,
relentless rain.

"Sir—sir—I've brought water!"

A face peered down at me, a white, scared face, very
young. Ragged and barefoot, a small boy stood shivering
beside me, holding in both hands a Saxon's horned helmet, from which water dripped.

"It's sweet, sir. From the spring by the chapel. He
was asking for water. The others are coming. They're
getting a hurdle from the sheepfold," the piping voice
went on.

"Gods be thanked, boy!" I said. "I'd thought I was
the only man left alive here!"

I took the helmet from him, and he stared down
wide-eyed at Arthur's face.

"The king isn't—*dead,* is he, sir?" he asked.

I did not answer, for I was intent just then, bathing
that still, clay-pale face, trying to trickle a few drops of
water between the cracked parted lips.

The boy babbled on, his teeth chattering.

"We were with the baggage wagons on the hill. I'd
climbed a tree to watch the battle. I saw the Dragon

standard go down, and shouted to my father. He said we must look for the king. The soldiers were looking, but *I'd* seen where he fell. Here they come, sir. They've got the hurdle."

I rose stiffly to my feet. I was doing no good and I knew it.

They staggered up out of the rain, three weary, stumbling men, one with a bandage round his head, carrying between them a hurdle of split willow stakes. They set it down clumsily and gathered round me, glad as lost dogs finding their master.

"Sir Bedivere! Thank Christ you're alive, my lord! We'd thought you were killed. Are you all right, sir?"

"Right enough. Come, let's get him on that thing and into some kind of shelter. He's badly hurt," I said.

"We could see that, sir. My nipper here saw him fall and these two chaps, they came with us, when we said whereabouts to look. He was conscious when we found him. Swooned off now, by the looks of it." The man was small, elderly, bow-legged, one of our transport drivers, I guessed.

"As well, maybe. Won't feel the jolting when we lift him," one of the soldiers said gruffly, and added, looking to me for agreement: "We'd aimed to get him into the little old chapel, yonder. It's a poor place, but the nearest," and he jerked his head to indicate direction.

The man with the bandaged head said nothing, just stood, staring down at Arthur, dumbly grieving.

We padded the hurdle with what cloaks we could find among the dead, and laid him on it. Before we lifted him, I said:

"Wait. There's something more I must do."

I turned aside and, taking Excalibur by the hilt, set my foot on Medraut's chest, and wrenched the great sword clear. As I wiped the blade clean on a tuft of reeds, I saw the boy watching me, his face bone-white, his eyes wide and intent.

"It is the king's sword. When he wakes, he will look for it. Do you carry it for him, while I help the men to lift the hurdle," I said.

He stretched out both hands, without a word, and I

laid the sword across them. He drew himself up very straight, a shaggy-headed, ragged imp of a camp follower—yet something in the pride of him at the unexpected honor of this new task brought back to me the memory of the twelve-year-old Arthur in the forge of Lob the Cunning.

I knew the chapel—no more than a hut of reeds and wattle some hermit had built, and long vacated. It stood on a little tongue of rocky land jutting into the mere. Though we did our best to carry him softly, the men were weary and the lifting had started the wound in my side bleeding again, so that I stumbled once or twice myself. When we'd laid him down before the pitiful little altar stone, and lit the clay lamp on it, I saw Arthur's eyes were open. In a whisper like the rustle of dry corn stalks, he asked again for water.

The feeble flame in the lamp was failing when I came to myself. I must have passed out into the black sleep of utter exhaustion, sitting hunched, my head on my knees. Perhaps it was a swoon from loss of blood. Shame shook me, as I jerked awake. Beside me, in the semi-darkness, Arthur's voice, very faintly, spoke my name and I knew it was the second time he had called to me.

"I am here, beside you, my dear," I said thickly, trying to fight off the weight of weariness that clogged me, body and mind.

"Bedivere—the Sign—you must give them the Sign," he whispered.

"What sign?" I thought, then, coming suddenly full awake, got stiffly on to my knees, and bent over him anxiously. Very dimly, I could see his face, the eyes wide, unfocused, searching. I groped for his hand and held it, and felt a faint, answering pressure.

"The end. This is the end—for me." He let go of my hand and fumbled restlessly in the folds of the cloak.

Memory rushed back at me, clearing my mind, as a cloudburst washes the leaves from a choked gutter.

Ygern's promise. The Merlin's cry that would bring us help, now, when we needed it most. And I had slept, forgetting!

He moved his head restlessly, groaning a little.

"Water—this thirst—so thirsty," he whispered.

I raised him a little, and he drank from the cracked horn cup one of the soldiers had lent to me, that I dipped into the helmet the boy had refilled earlier.

"Better!" he murmured, and I laid him back as gently as I could. "Now go—quickly. But Excalibur—take it."

I thought he was delirious, that wound-fever was starting. All my mind was set on, then, was to give the call that would bring us help, if help, indeed, by any miracle, was within call.

I got up on one knee.

"Rest quietly, my dear. I'll give them the Merlin's cry," I said.

His hands came up and grasped my wrist, closing over it with a strength that surprised me, and his voice for one moment held the old command.

"Take Excalibur, Bedivere. Fling it far out into the mere, where no man's hand but mine shall ever grasp the hilt again. That is—part of the—Sign."

A cold horror clutched at my heart. Excalibur—the sword he had drawn out of the stone—the sign of the Pendragonship. His King Sword.

"No!" I cried out harshly. "No, Bear! I can't do that."

His hand tightened.

"My—last—order. Don't fail me—now. No one else must—besides—it is a Sign." His hand dropped from mine. He muttered something I could not catch. Then he said, his eyes closed: "It's my last order, Bedivere."

I said:

"Are you sure?"

He moved his head once in assent.

I had never disobeyed an order of his. This one, though I did not understand it, I knew I must obey.

Stiffly, slowly, I bent, and lifting Excalibur from his side, went out into the night.

In the darkness of the chapel doorway I tripped over a soft bundle. The boy, curled up like a puppy, was so deeply asleep he only sighed and muttered as I stepped over him.

The guard outside was leaning on a tall spear, his forehead against the shaft. It was the soldier with the bandaged head and I think he was asleep on his feet. He roused as a trained man will and challenged me.

"Anything to report?" I asked, automatically.

"All quiet, sir. But I think there are looters among the dead. I saw shadows moving and heard a cry, while back. How's the king now, my lord?"

I knew it was useless to lie to a soldier.

"Bad. Very bad," I said. "We need help. I may be able to get it."

"God, sir, I hope you can! It'll be the end for all of us, and for the country, when he goes. There'll never be another like him," the man said gruffly.

"I know," I said. "Keep alert until I get back. He may call for water. Are the others sleeping?"

"Aye, but I can rouse them." He peered at me. "Best take them with you if you're going out there, sir. Types who'll rob the dead are ugly customers—and you aren't in too good shape, yourself, sir, if you'll excuse me saying so."

"Let them rest. I'll do well enough," I said curtly. "Keep your guard."

As I left him and plunged down the rocky path towards the mere, his words echoed in my mind like hammer strokes.

"It'll be the end for all of us when *he* goes."

He had been right that I was in poor shape. The wound in my side had stiffened and the pain of it caught my breathing. I moved like a drunken man, slipping and stumbling, shivering with cold.

I came out at last to a place I'd remembered, where stones shelve out between tall reeds and I knew a boat could land. Away to my right, waves beat on the pebble ridge, and the mist crept and swirled, still, low down, about me. Overhead, it was clear, and a gibbous moon, pale as the face of a drowned man, rode among thin, scudding clouds. It cast a wavering whiteness across the mist wreaths and showed the mere, black and fathomless, beneath them.

"What must be done must be done," I thought; and since I must do it, all my mind centred on the one certainty that I must not fail to carry out the order with exact care. A fear came on me I might not throw straight and far enough, for my hands were bruised and swollen, the fingers stiff. Far out, Arthur had said—far out into water that went down into Anawn.

I drew the sword and cast away the sheath; then, with all my strength, I cast Excalibur as one casts a hunting spear, point first, upwards and outwards, in a great arc. Moonlight caught the blue glitter of the steel. White mist shone for a moment whiter from the spray where it went in, far out, into the heart of the mere. When the ripples had closed over it, and widened and lapped at last in the reed bed around me with little, stealthy sucking sounds, I stepped back and gave the Merlin's cry, three times repeated; the eerie, far-carrying, unearthly bird cry that once, so long ago, had called a dark barge across dark water, to carry Britain's Chosen One to the Holy Island of his Dragon Making.

They'd painted the boat black, and the figures in it were black. The oars must have been muffled, for it slid up to the landing place silent as a ghost-ship. The People of the Hills understand such things. The rowers had even blackened their faces.

There were three women, Ygern and two others.

The boatmen had brought a litter and they helped us carry him down, so the journey was easier than it had been getting him off the field. I don't think he suffered. Ygern had dressed his wound and given him poppy juice before we moved him.

I went on board and saw him laid under an awning on a bed they'd made ready amidships. I think he knew me still, but I'm not sure. At such times one is thinking only of what must be done and how best to do it. They would have had me go with them, but my place was with the army. There would still be need of a commander to rally the remnants; to organize the retreat.

I stepped back onto the shore and stood with the three men and the boy. The boat moved out into deep water and almost at once was lost to sight.

I heard sobbing and a small, cold paw crept into my hand.

"Sir—my lord—will the king come back? Will he ever come back?" the urchin whimpered.

I straightened my shoulders.

"He'll come back, boy. He'll come back," I said.

We slept until dawn and with first light I got them moving. About a mile inland we caught up with the first bunch of stragglers, some men who'd stayed all night with their dying decurion and just finished burying him. At noon, Griffin rode out of the forest with about a score of mounted Dumnonians. He'd been collecting a force strong enough to risk coming back to look for my body, I believe. I know he blubbered like a babe at sight of me alive. After that, I remember very little, except that day after day it rained and the forest dripped, black branches above us and the leaves falling. Everywhere there was the smell of death and wounds, and the cold breath of coming winter. That—and a great, grey emptiness of loss.

I had fever, for the spear-thrust in my side inflamed, and there were times when strange dreams haunted me as I rode.

Once I thought I saw the Merlin, standing on a little hillock under three birch trees. The wind stirred the branches in small gusts, so that the last yellow leaves fluttered about him like small birds. Bent and frail, older than time he looked, his hair and beard blowing thinly, white as bog cotton, his face transparent as honesty pods in winter. He smiled and mopped and mowed at us and I knew that he had gone mad with grief. When I cried out to Griffin that someone should go to him, that he must be cared for, taken along with us, they said there was no one there. Perhaps they were right. I have never been quite sure.

It must have been after that I fell from my horse and they made a litter of branches, and Griffin told me later that was the time he vowed to his God that if I recovered he would become a monk. It seemed to me then (and still does) too great a price to have offered for a life I myself felt I should be glad to be quit of. But he was always a good, faithful fool!

I must have been a great burden to them. I don't know how long the journey lasted. At the end we came out of the forest onto a hilltop at dusk. Very far away and small in the distance, I saw the Island's shape across the plain below.

On the peak of the green mountain a beacon fire blazed.

I must have been pretty far gone by then. I thought I was a child still, and that I had been left behind with Caw and his sons, while Arthur rode without me to Ynis Witrin.

I said:

"It must have been a very great Dragon Making!"

Griffin tells me, for the first time, then, I wept.

# Chapter Thirty-Two

I was past my fiftieth year the autumn of Camlan. At that age, wounds take longer to heal than in the vigor of youth. It is my shame still that I lay, useless as a log, all the long, black winter, when I should have been leading Britain's last desperate stand against invasion and civil war.

Patiently, skillfully, Ygern nursed me, here, on this same Island of Ynis Witrin, in just such a small white hut as the one I lie in now.

Always, from a child, she had known how to keep her own counsel. I might have guessed, after the fever left me, once my mind was clear, that she was hiding from me much I should have known; that the answers she gave me were such as all women give to children and the sick, changing the conversation quickly, promising: "When you are better," "After you have slept a while," "Some other day we'll talk of it. Today I must be doing this, or this, or this."

It was Griffin I got the truth from in the end. By then the first buds were breaking on the apple trees. He came into my hut, hoisting himself along awkwardly on crutches, for he'd got himself a broken thigh when his horse had been hamstrung and, in falling, rolled on him, during fierce fighting, away on the marches of Wales.

Medraut had sowed a bitter harvest for us. All up and down the land, as a result of his intrigues, Clan had risen against Clan, reminded by him of old blood feuds, incited to jealousy or ambition, vengeful of suggested wrongs, or imagined slights.

The winter was an open one—wet and mild. The Irish and the Saxons, gathering like carrion crows, had risked the sea crossings and raided up and down the coasts as though it were summertime. The Picts, having laid Dalriada waste, had swept south in their thousands, plundering and burning as they came. They'd forced the Dike defenses and were in the Heartland. But Constantine, with what was left of our army, still held the marches of Wales.

That evening, Ygern and I sat beside the little fire in the centre of my hut, and one candle burned steadily in its iron sconce, stuck in the wall.

"Why didn't you tell me? In the name of Light, Ygern, *why* didn't you tell me?" I asked her.

"Because it was not the time," she returned calmly. "I know you. Sick or well, you'd have been in the saddle, fighting a war that can never be won, now, by the sword. You would only have wasted strength that will be needed in the future. Most likely you would have been killed. Britain could not spare you."

She leaned forward to lay a fresh log on the fire. The light from it turned her white woollen tunic rose color, and glinted on the silver of her hair.

I was very angry, feeling she had cheated me of the truth. Wanting to hurt her, I said:

"Britain could not spare Arthur. He is dead. Why be so precious of my life? I am a soldier. My place was with Arthur's heir—with the army of Constantine."

She sat back, and looked at me, unflinching, her eyes sorrowful, but her face the calm, closed face of the dedicated Priestess.

"You are more than a soldier. You are the Merlin of Britain, now, Bedivere," she said steadily.

"Gods, girl, you're mad!" I said, gripping the arms of my chair. "How can *I* ever presume to that?"

"It is in your stars. Celidon always knew that—it is the thing appointed. Before the bolt of Apollo struck him down, he gave me the Merlin jewel, the ring and the harp to keep for you. The Power comes to you with them."

"Is he dead, too? Is that something else you have not told me?" I asked, bitterly.

She shook her head. Her face quivered for a moment, and her eyes filled with tears.

"No, my dear. He is in Armorica. His body lives on, but his mind has gone. He lives helpless and blind, believing evil magic has imprisoned him in some dark cavern. Mawgan is with him, and soon I, too, must go to him. We shall do what we can to set him free. I do not think his imprisonment will last very much longer."

I was used to bad news by then, but this was worse than I'd guessed.

"A bad end for a brave man," I muttered. "I'm sorry for it, Ygern."

In face of it my anger with her, that had seemed to me righteous and well merited, faded. I saw it for what it was, graceless, ungrateful, peevish, and I was ashamed.

We sat silent for a long while. The flames flickered and snapped and the marsh wind sighed as it went by over the smokehole.

I felt the old, close bond there had always been between us pulling at my heart. I said at last:

"Tell me what I must do, Ygern."

She had been looking into the fire. She sighed, then turned to me with her old, decisive brusqueness.

"This war's lost, Bedivere. Britain will never be free again in our lifetime. I see a great darkness over the land for many, many years to come. Beyond that darkness, a light dawns slowly, but may strengthen to a brightness greater even than that Arthur brought us. On a night of storm in the hills, the rushlight glimmering in some shepherd's cot shines very far. The sight of it is precious to the lost, bewildered wayfarer. That gleam of light in the bitter darkness must be the trust of Merlin the Messenger to our people in the years that are just beginning."

She put her hand on my knee and spoke earnestly.

"You, Bedivere, were the Pendragon's Bard and

Arthur's Chief Companion. The common folk remember
it. What you tell them, they will believe, and cherish, and
their children after them. His memory, and the memory
of the truths he lived by, are the heritage and the Hallows
of Britain. They are all he had to leave. Only you, now,
my dear, can see to it his people are not robbed of that
rich heritage, for *you* are Merlin the Messenger."

My health mended fast after that. Seeing the way before
me, I'd the incentive to make the necessary effort. Finding
me fit to hear all he had to tell, Griffin filled in for me the
gaps my winter of brooding lassitude had left. I asked
news of Lancelot and Bors first. It surprised me, I think,
to find they were both still living men.

"The Lord Lancelot's sorely stricken—he took the
king's death hard, very hard. He and Sir Bors, hearing of
Medraut's advance, were on their way to bring us reinforcements. They got back to the fort the night the king's
pyre was lit on the Island. I've heard it said Sir Lancelot
laid himself down up there on the mountain top and
neither moved nor spoke for a week or more—but that
could be just a tale folk tell. In any case, when all was
over, he seemed to blame himself some way, and so, by
Abbot Iltud's advice, took the habit of religion and has
become a holy hermit. Sir Bors is with him, for he needs
someone to care for him, now. He aged in those few
weeks until, to look at him, you'd say he was seventy
years and more."

Griffin shook his head, and I guessed something of
the old madness must have fallen on Lancelot. It did not
surprise me. That winter had taught me how close grief
and despair can bring a man to the brink of reason.

"What of the queen? Have they got her away to
Armorica?" I asked.

(I'd heard how many refugees had been pouring
across to that country again.)

Griffin's face cleared, and he smiled suddenly and
widely.

"Nothing would persuade her to it!" he said. "She's
a wonderful woman, my lord. Since she's known she was
a widow, she's become a nun herself and now they've

made her abbess. What she's done with that place you'd hardly believe! In all their troubles the poor folk flock to it for help—orphans, refugees, homeless families, the wounded—not a soul is ever turned away. Her fortitude and patience are such I dare say she'll end up a saint, my lord."

"Possibly," I said, but added, grimly: "If the enemy raid these parts, she and all her nuns are more like to end as martyrs. Have they thought of that?"

He shook his head.

"She believes God will protect them. I believe that, too," he said, defiantly.

I felt it was a point I was not qualified to argue. Perhaps he was right. When the Saxons sacked the fort and burned the palace to the ground they did bypass the forest, I heard, and the convent was left undisturbed. I'd had it in mind, before I started on my wanderings, I ought to visit Guinevere and, in common courtesy, condole with her, but something Griffin told me later made me decide I'd wait for some other opportunity. He said her greatest grief had been that Arthur's body had not received what he called "Christian burial."

"She was very put out by the old pagan rites having been observed, sir. She blamed the Lady Ygern and the Merlin for that. It's the only time I ever heard her speak harshly of anyone. She was very much angered by it, poor lady," he told me accusingly.

I felt my patience strained by that and said, more harshly than I'd meant:

"Better the fire by which the Pendragons have always gone, than a grave Saxon wolves could scratch at and defile. Tell her that next time she complains!"

He blinked as if I'd struck him in the face, then said meekly:

"I'd not thought of such a possibility. I dare say neither has the queen. You may be right, sir. Better there should be no grave for the Lord Arthur."

Ashamed of my own irritability, I turned the talk to his own future plans. He was still obstinately set on keeping that vow he'd made, though I believe his God might have waited some years for payment of it if I'd have let him come with me on my new, wandering life. Next only after Palomides, he is the most faithful friend I ever had.

The Picts had been eating the harvest out of the Heartland all winter. Soon the barns would be empty and another harvest would not be sown. The chances were they would start harrying westward with the better weather.

I understood why the Island seemed so quiet. All but a very few of those who, for a thousand years, had served its sacred mysteries were gone away, now. Some into the impregnable mountains of Yr Widdfa, some overseas, to holy places hidden deep in the great forest of Broceliande. They carried with them their secret Wisdom—which is never written down, but passed on, generation by generation, from the faultless memory of one Initiate to the next. The Great Hallows remained, buried deep under the innocence of green sheep-bitten turf, where, safe hidden, the place forgotten (as it well may be, when all of us who knew that place are dust), the Power will still belong to the land. It will remain, and those who are Knowers will feel its guardian presence. I, who for twenty years have been the Merlin, speak of what I know.

On Ynis Witrin, only the white brothers, in their little wattle huts down by the marsh, where they have served God since the days of Arimathean Joseph, went quietly about their simple, harmless lives. They and the fishermen, whose folk were on the Island always, since the beginning of time.

An evening came when all that needed to be done had been done. The black Merlin's robe, the harp, the jewel and the ring lay ready for me. I had made preparation for my journey, and Ygern, too, was ready to set out. I was anxious she should. Marshland and lake country are no barrier to a Pict.

It was a quiet, overcast evening—the cloud cover soft, the color of a dove's breast, and not a breath of wind stirring.

Ygern and I walked together up the green mountain, for the last time.

Dressed for travelling in the familiar tartan, her shoulder-length hair uncovered, her step still light and sure, she wrung my heart with old, too-poignant memories. I took her hand and we climbed in silence, until we reached a little lap of grass, just below the place where the Dragon Fires are lit. A place that looks towards Camelot. There we sat down and I put my arm round her shoulders, feeling how thin she was; the little bird-bones of her.

She said, not looking at me, but staring out into the distance:

"There are still the three of us, Bedivere. He is never far away. There will always be the three of us. Remember that, when you are lonely."

I pressed her closer to me.

"Tell me how the end came for him," I said. It was something that, up to then, I had not brought myself to ask and she had never spoken of it. Now, I felt I must know. We might never see each other again.

She did not answer at once, and I said:

"Was it hard? Tell me, Ygern."

She shook her head, quickly, decisively. I saw she was fighting back tears with the old, proud impatience.

"It was—three days," she said, still looking away from me. "Three days and nights after Camlan. He did not suffer. That, at least, I knew how to prevent. By the hidden waterways we went very smoothly. All that last night he'd slept, his head resting in my lap. I think I'd begun to hope a little, though it was a selfish hope. The muscles of the shoulder were sliced through. They would never have healed. Slowly, that strong right arm would have withered and become useless. It was not kind to hope."

I said, sharply, for I could feel her gone stiff under my arm, fighting the pain of the memory:

"Leave it, my girl! I should not have asked you."

She looked up at me then, her eyes wide and dark, her mouth trying to smile a reassurance.

"I've always wanted to tell you. Let me speak of it. I have never spoken of it before. It is something that belongs to us both."

I put my lips down on her hair for a moment, feeling its softness.

"Tell me, then," I said.

"I was so very tired, Bedivere. I must have slept myself for a while. The rising sun woke me. I saw we were passing across a little, lonely lake. The level rays shone across the water and dazzled me, and there was music—such strange, unearthly music. I looked about to see where it could be coming from. I saw a white swan, sailing between the barge and a wide, flat spread of water lilies, all in bloom, and following behind the white swan, two that were black. I thought it was strange that lilies bloomed in autumn, strange that swans were black. Then I thought:

"'The singing! It must be the swan that sings, and swans sing only as they die.' Memory came back to me of where I was and why. I felt the weight of Arthur's shoulders against my knees. I touched his forehead and felt it marble-cold. I knew then that while I slept he had gone away from us. I knew what that strange singing meant. I looked out across the water. Two black swans sailed alone. There was no more singing. Only the lapping of a spreading ripple against the side of the barge, where the rowers still slept upon their oars." A little, hard sob escaped her, then she tossed her head and said urgently, as she might have done when we were children together and she'd thought I'd doubted a tale she told: "The swan did sing for him, Bedivere. I did hear its singing."

I took her hand, then, holding it up against my cheek to comfort her.

"You heard it sing, girl darling. The white swan has gone from us—only we two black ones are left, now."

She turned to me again, drawing my hand down and holding it in a close, hard grip.

"Don't weep for him, Bedivere. We must not—either of us," she said, breathless and imperative as she used to be. "*He* never looked backward. Never. Always, with him, it was the next thing that must be done—the next advance that must be planned. Remember that. Defeat and war bring death to men, but the dream they dreamed lives on as long as we remember it. You go to sow his dream. The seed of that dream will grow and flower in the minds of his people, for you are a Bard, and will sow it faithfully. It will flower, and wither, and seed again in other minds, year after year, and never quite die out, all down the long, dark centuries ahead. As long as the tides rise and fall around this island, and the gulls call and spring brings back the small green buds, men will remember Arthur. Because their dream will call to him, in time of need, he will return to them. He is still the Once and Future King.".

# IX
# CLOSING
# CHORD

I am alone, and it is night and very dark. They are singing in the choir. The singing does not sound harsh now, but sweet and faint and distant. A fading sound.

Beyond the open door I can see the blue arch of the night sky and the seven stars that hang there. They are very bright tonight. Growing brighter. Across them moves a Cup—a great, translucent Cup, that glows the color of a red rose. The light comes from that. It is growing, shining, the whole night is lit by it and its rose-flames are all about me.

"Arturus, Arthur, Bear—it is I, Bedivere. I have come!"

# AUTHOR'S NOTE

"The story of King Arthur and his knights is a myth. Like all great myths, it has deep psychological significance. Its roots reach down into the collective unconscious, and extend back into prehistoric race memory."

This statement, made to me some years ago by the late eminent psychologist Dr. L. J. Bendit, expresses a view that is still held by many people—and it is, as far as it goes, true. But it expresses only one aspect of truth.

I believe that "nothing comes from nothing, nothing ever could." Behind every great and long-remembered legend there must exist a fact, a happening. Heinrich Schliemann's excavations proved that Troy Town *did* suffer siege before blind Homer sang its story.

Modern research and recent archeological discoveries have proved beyond question that behind the Arthurian Legend there stands the Arthurian Fact. Every year fresh evidence is added to prove it. The task of sorting and assessing the evidence still presents a major exercise in historical detection, for it involves witnesses drawn from fifteen centuries, and, as in the case of the witnesses in any trial, one is required not only to consider their evidence but to make due allowance for their backgrounds, and their probable individual prejudices.

I have found the task is simplified if the case itself is considered from two separate angles—the Legend (and how it grew) being kept distinct from the Arthurian Fact.

The Legend begins with evidence from the Royal
Bards, those Celtic poet-historians who, when the Saxons
finally conquered Britain, were driven back into the remote fastnesses of Wales and Cornwell, or sailed as
refugees to Brittany. They were men of integrity, whose
task it was to preserve the history of their country, and
transmit it orally, in verse form, from generation to generation. This they were bound to do with exact truth.
(The Bard who knowingly misrepresented facts incurred
the death penalty.) But it is worth remembering that they
were fierce and passionate Celtic nationalists, and their
emotions color their evidence.

In Norman times the story was rediscovered and
popularized by the Jongleurs, those wandering minstrels,
primarily entertainers, who were bound by no obligation
to historical accuracy. Supper and a bed, for them, depended on holding an audience. Accordingly they gave
their public what it wanted, plundering the Bardic records
for plots, but adding colorful fiction to taste, some of it
drawn from imagination, some from older folk tales. *The
Matter of Britain,* as their collective versions of the Arthurian story came to be called, was popular with the
Crusading armies and carried by them right across
Europe and as far as the Holy Land.

When, in the thirteenth century, an increasingly literate society began to demand written romances, the
Trouvères of France did, in fact, "find" their material in
the Jongleurs' lays. Christian of Troyes, Robert de Borron,
Wolfram von Eschenbach, and many others, wove the
legend afresh into books of quite inordinate length, considering that every volume of their works required hand
copying and many were richly ornamented and illustrated.
These authors complicated the issue for us today by
incorporating into the text a considerable body of mystical teaching (mainly gnostic) which, as it was frowned on
by the Church, could most conveniently be disseminated
under the guise of romantic fiction. (They cannot be
blamed for their caution, since the spreading of "heresies," by then, entailed condemnation to death by burning
alive under the Inquisition.)

In the fifteenth century Edward IV saw in those

written romances a useful vehicle for political propaganda on behalf of the Plantaganet dynasty. Accordingly, he commissioned Sir Thomas Malory to write, and William Caxton to print, a new version. Sir Thomas slanted *Le Morte d'Arthur* to suit his royal patron's fancy, giving it contemporary fifteenth-century décor and costume—a form in which it has continued to be presented up to the present day.

Finally, the Victorian Romantics acclaimed it once more, in Tennyson's *Idylls of the King*—a poetic masterpiece which, though it perpetuated the fifteenth-century décor, did recapture, to a great extent, the essential spirit of original Bardic truth.

But it must be said that both Malory and Tennyson leave us with an Arthur in some ways less dynamic, less relevant to today, than the Arthur of Fact; for the original of the Legend, by reason of the very times in which he lived, is closer akin to the modern world of change and chaos than to either medieval chivalry and squalor or smug Victorian security.

Recent research, patiently building up a picture of Arthurian Fact from contemporary chronicles and archeological excavation, has come up with a definite set of dates. It gives A.D. 517 as the year of the victory of Badon, and A.D. 537 for the final defeat of Camlan. It gives ample proof that between those two crucial dates Britain, after a period of recession and near-anarchy, regained both a political stability and an economic independence unequalled anywhere else in the Europe of the time. It also names Arturus, or "Arthur the Soldier," as the commander responsible for this near-miracle, and states that he was the last serving officer to hold the military rank of *Dux Bellorum Britannicus* (War Duke of Britain) under the Imperial seal from Byzantium.

This evidence immediately lifts the story out of Malory's familiar setting of feudal castles and nebulous Iron Age geography, to give it, instead, the backdrop of a Europe where a whole long-established pattern of life was breaking up and re-forming, as the Roman Empire crashed to ruin, its foundations rotted by financial and political decay, its frontiers breached by the pressure of

vast folk movements that had begun a century earlier as
far away as China.

Against this background, the action of the story can
be seen as taking place in a Britain fallen on bad times,
indeed, but bad times that had developed only towards
the close of four hundred years of highly civilized prosperity, under an orderly and just government. For four
hundred years (a period longer than that which now
divides us from the sailing of the *Mayflower*), Britain had
been a country where a multi-racial society, economically
self-sufficient, to a great extent literate and cultured, enjoyed a standard of life, and a degree of security, higher
in many ways than would be achieved again until the late
nineteenth century.

Disintegration, when it came, came only gradually. It
began (as in this century) with the loss of two generations of young men, going overseas in expeditionary
forces (one under the general Maximus, one under Constantine III) to fight and die in wars in Europe. It was
hastened by the extensive war damage caused by Saxon
raiding, and the decision, consequent on these raids, of
many of the richest citizens to emigrate. Taking their
wealth with them, they dislocated the country's economy.
Conditions in Europe and the removal of the Imperial
government to distant Byzantium (Istanbul) caused the
gradual breakdown of communications. It was, indeed,
the "time of the Troubles" for two generations before
Arthur was born. But the great Legionary roads still
connected town with town, the Roman bureaucracy
creaked on, the judiciary functioned after a fashion, and
ordinary people, with the exception of certain militant
Celtic elements, still considered themselves Roman citizens, who expected an eventual restoration of the old
order.

Only a man of exceptional calibre, courage and
foresight could have inspired sufficient confidence to weld
so despondent and fragmented a society together at such
a crisis. Only a leader of military genius could have
conducted a war on three frontiers at once, and, having
achieved victory on all three, gone on to restore order and
a government sufficiently just and enlightened to make

Britain the one flourishing, independent state to stand on its own feet, successfully, for twenty years after it had been abandoned as dispensable by the Roman Imperial power.

Such men are rare. They are not easily forgotten. Their names become a legend; the spirit they represent does, indeed, sink deep into the collective unconscious of their people. So, in its final conclusion, the Arthurian Legend comes back to the Arthurian Fact, and the truth of the Royal Bards is vindicated.

It was they who wrote, fifteen centuries ago:

"Foolish those who seek a grave for Arthur, *the once and future King*."